The Bark of the Dogwood

A Tour of Southern Homes and Gardens

The Bark of the Dogwood

A Tour of Southern Homes and Gardens

Jackson Tippett McCrae

The Enolam Group, Inc.

This is a work of fiction. Any characters, places, events, and names used are fictitious. Any resemblance to actual events, locales, organizations, or persons, living or dead, is entirely coincidental and beyond the intent of either the author or publisher.

ISBN: 0-9715536-0-2

LCCN: 2002100011

Published by:
The Enolam Group, Inc.
P. O. Box 2008
Norwalk, CT 06852
http://www.enolam.com

Acknowledgments

Grateful acknowledgment is made to the following for permission to reprint previously published material: PELICAN PUBLISHING COMPANY, INC.: From *Romantic New Orleans* by Robert Tallant, © 1986 used by permission of the publisher, Pelican Publishing Company, Inc. DOUGLAS SCHWARTZ: Excerpt from *Small Change*, © Douglas Schwartz.

WARNER BROS. INC.: Excerpt from *Now, Voyager*, © 1942, Warner Bros. Inc. WILLIAM GIBSON: excerpt from *The Miracle Worker*, © 1956, 1957; ©1959, 1960 by Tamarack Productions, LTD. and George S. Klein and Leo Garel as trustees under three separate deeds of trust. All quotes from Helen Keller's *The Story of My Life* within public domain.

I owe a great deal of thanks to several people for their support while I worked on this book. My family, who first suggested I begin writing and who read some of the first drafts—thank you for your support and love, especially Suzanne; my cousin Trish, who is always there for me and everyone else; Ruth Davis for her critical readings of the manuscript and other forms of advice; Louise Weiss, who tirelessly copy-edited the book and so graciously followed its progress to completion. Her expert eye for detail greatly improved the quality of this endeavor. Of all of those who were instrumental in helping me, none was more so than Peter Marino, without whose patience, technical expertise and understanding, this book would not exist.

Book Design by The Enolam Group, Inc.

Introduction

As human beings we are all fallible. Circumstances, accompanied by free will and that ever-illusive attribute we call "luck," shape us into who we are. No one knows this better than the author of this book. He has created a labyrinth of human emotions and happenings that take the reader from birth to death and back to life again.

When I first encountered the character of Strekfus (loosely based on the author), I was somewhat taken aback. But as I read the stories of Southern homes—those houses great and small which made such an impression on this writer—I became aware of hidden meanings in the gestures and lives of all the characters, and how inexorably intertwined all of us are in each other's lives. It is with caution that I advise readers to look for more than one normally would in an ordinary book. The threads of human relationships run lengthy and complex, and while the author makes us work toward understanding, such an effort is not without personal gain, for it will undoubtedly cause each of us to search our own backgrounds and lives for answers to the questions we have about who we really are.

On a personal note, I would like to thank the author, who, in sometimes not the subtlest of ways, pointed out my own shortcomings and forced me to look deep within myself for the answers. If only this book had been available to me before our relationship began, we both might have been spared a great deal of grief. It is my hope that those reading it will find some part of themselves or others in the writing, and in some way begin that journey toward hope and healing.

—Edwin Sagaser
Fondon Sass Publications, New York

Memory is a snarling dog that runs
from my outstretched hand, curling
his lip in fear. I give chase, half hoping
he won't stop and turn.

—Douglas Schwartz

Prologue

I think I knew when I was naughty, for I
knew that it hurt Ella, my nurse, to kick
her, and when my fit of temper was over
I had a feeling akin to regret.

—Helen Keller, *The Story of My Life*

The blood was now flowing with regularity, streaming down her brown shins like swift-moving paths of lava. With each kick, the steel toe of his cowboy boot dug deeper into her flesh, tearing dark pieces free from the front of her calves. They stood out from her legs, flaps of skin momentarily colorless, until the blood began to fill up the vacated spaces, seep into the shreds of flesh, and ooze out onto her body. With each attack more blood splattered the stiff white maid's uniform she was wearing and flew back onto the yoke of his cowboy shirt. She neither cried out nor made an attempt to stop him.

"Nigger! Nigger! Nigger!" he yelled over and over, punctuating each word with a kick which gathered strength and momentum each time he brought his foot back and flung it forward. He thought that she would eventually start to cry, and as he went about his task he occasionally looked at her to see if her defenses were beginning to crumble. He wasn't even sure what the word meant—he had heard it used against others and he knew the pain it could inflict, especially in Alabama in the early 1960s. He thought he saw a momentary flame in her pupils, but in an instant it was gone. She only stood there during the assault, her solid and massive two hundred and thirty pounds hovering like some gigantic rock precariously perched high atop a cliff, ready to roll down the hill at any moment and crush him.

After a while he tired of the attack, dripping with sweat and exhausted from his display of anger. And the sight of blood had now made him queasy. When he had caught his breath, he looked at her with mean eyes, squinted and tight. He realized she wasn't going to fight back or say anything. At first this shocked him. He knew that in the South, in the 1960s, regardless of how African Americans were treated socially, they were given carte blanche to discipline the children of their employers. There was only one thing lower than African Americans at that time in the volatile structure of Southern society, and that was children. As he thought about this, it hit him: She had something else in mind. But what? "You're going to tell my parents, aren't you?" he said maliciously.

"No. I ain't gonna tell your mamma an' daddy," she said without emotion or hate. She was eerily unmoved and even-tempered in her reply, as if she were on the outside looking in instead of being at the center of the drama.

"Then what are you going to do?" His fists were balled up, ready to fight with force or words—whichever came first to him.

"I ain't gonna do nuthin'," she said, her hands resting on her hips, looking down at him as if he were nothing more than a curiosity.

"Why not?" he countered angrily, but it was almost as if he knew the answer before it came, as if he were on the same wavelength, as if he could read her mind and she his. If he had chosen, he could have mouthed the words along with her, for they came to him in a stinging revelation, a split second before she delivered them, and he knew that once they started there was no stopping them, and that they would forever linger in his mind and run after him like some animal he had tortured relentlessly—one that had broken free and begun to chase him.

"I ain't gonna do nuthin' to you, Mr. Strekfus. You gonna think about this moment after you is done, and your guilt is gonna be your punishment." She delivered the words without hate or malice. She delivered them simply and elegantly, as if she knew deep down the favor she was doing for him. Her voice had

2

a prophetic air about it, but not because of any ego or hatred. And in a way she was right, she was doing him a favor, for as he felt the guilt, the pain, the very anger and hate come back on his being, he resolved never again to call any person of color that name, and he would cringe from then on when he heard others do it.

He was at that moment a five-year-old boy, physically attacking the housekeeper for denying him the right to leave the house—a denial that was well within the bounds of her duties, for at this time Alabama was a hotbed of racial turmoil and anything could happen. The day before his assault on her had been May 14, 1961—a day many in the state would remember as the start of the civil rights movement.

The first of the Freedom Riders had made their way into northern Alabama to show their support for integration on that day. Not only had the tires of their bus been slashed and the riders met by an angry mob, but when the driver was able to escape from the scene and stop six miles down the road to change the tires, the vehicle was firebombed. A second bus had followed, not knowing the fate of the first. The passengers on that bus had been beaten by a mob wielding clubs and pipes. Because of the intensity of the situation, ambulance workers refused to treat the injured. Althea had known this. She had watched the news on television that morning and knew that the world she was now living in—for better or worse—was changing all around her.

And Strekfus knew that she was keeping him inside for his own good, but despite the fact that he had been labeled a special child whose intelligence and logic were far different from others his age, he sometimes lacked common sense and maturity. When his anger subsided later and they reconciled somewhat, she cleaned the blood off herself and him, the whole time listening to his sobs as she sponged him in the large tub, his head bent in shame. As she did so, she sang softly and the song comforted Strekfus. It reminded him of some far-off land where he imagined they had known each other before.

De little baby gone home,
De little baby gone home,
De little baby gone along,
    For to climb up Jacob's ladder.
And I wish I'd been dar,
I wish I'd been dar,
I wish I'd been dar, my Lord,
    For to climb up Jacob's ladder.

"That's a pretty song," he said to her, hoping to begin the healing between them, hoping to begin a conversation that would lead to other things, which would in turn bury those wrongs he had done to her.

"Umhm. I've known that song for as long as I can remember, child," she said, as her hand disappeared beneath the water in an attempt to reclaim the soap.

"I'm sorry, Althea. I'm sorry I called you those names."

"Child, it was only the one name you called me and that was enough. But don't you be worryin' about that now. I expect you feel bad enough that you don't need me remindin' you what you done." As she dipped the sponge down into the water and brought it up over his shoulders to rinse him off, it was as if she were trying to wash away his pain, for she acknowledged his anger and it was almost as if she knew that he would someday have to face its source the way she had faced hers. And each would choose to deal with this pain and anger in different ways, the results of their inner explorations leading them through different landscapes of the mind, each seeking that same open field where blue skies stretched out like the upturned palm of God and freedom took on its many-faceted meaning.

As she squeezed water from the sponge with one hand, she used the other to turn his head slightly to the side with the pretense of rinsing the soap from his ears. He allowed her this charade now, knowing full well that she had done so to keep him from seeing her tears.

It was this scene Strekfus was now remembering, and with good cause. He had received word earlier that morning that

Althea, the woman whose shins he had so angrily assaulted in 1961, had died. But before he could go any further with his reverie, he was knocked back into reality by his boss's voice. The sound of it jerked his head up and he found himself looking out the window at the Manhattan skyline, solid and vertical in the overcast morning sun.

"Beltzenschmidt!" the man bellowed, and suddenly he was no longer in rural Alabama, but back in the sleek, modern conference room used for Monday morning meetings he and the other writers had with the editors and staff of the magazine. Strekfus had left the '60s far behind, and he was now in the very center of the 1990s.

"If you think you could stop daydreaming for a second I'd like to give everyone their assignments. We might as well start with you since you seem to have the attention span of a gnat today," and with that the short, bald, portly man paused for a second or two. There was a moment of tension in the air and then Strekfus and his boss both burst out laughing at the same time. Everyone else in the room just looked confused as they usually did whenever a conversation between the two men took place. For as long as Strekfus had worked for the magazine no one could quite figure out what the exact relationship was between the two. They seemed genuinely to like one another, but there were moments when neither seemed sure what was a joke and what was real. And the two men couldn't have been more mismatched both physically and intellectually. Whereas Strekfus was tall, athletic, and well-groomed, his boss reveled in the not-so-delicate art of unkemptness and seemed to relish the pizza stains which appeared on his tie each day after lunch. Still, there was some bond between them, and as with most people, when pressed for details about the connection, neither could come up with a reasonable explanation.

The tension having dissipated, the staff waited for their next assignments from Sagaser, the man in charge of their fate and the man who was chief editor of the magazine which covered such human necessities as A-frame housing, the latest sofa designs, and hybrid tea roses. It was a home-and-garden

5

magazine that the group assembled worked for, and lately the ideas seemed to be running out. Nothing much caught Strekfus's attention as he listened to Sagaser wade through the lists of subjects that the writers of the magazine would cover—reproduction eighteenth-century creamware, a house being remodeled in Vermont using only woods native to that state, the evolution of the dining table in the past two hundred years. But when his boss reached the young writer, he paused for dramatic effect, thinking that the assignment would please his most valued staff member.

"Beltzenschmidt, you're to do a series of twelve articles on the South and various homes and gardens in that area." As Strekfus Beltzenschmidt heard the words, he had mixed emotions which ranged from elation to dread. Now that he would be traveling to the South he would no longer have to approach his boss and tell him that he was leaving later that morning for the very place he was to write about—he could feign the excuse that he wanted to get started as soon as possible on the articles. He had feared what his boss would say about his flying home on the spur of the moment to attend a funeral of someone who wasn't even a relative, but now the problem was solved. And yet Strekfus feared the trip, almost as if he were a fugitive returning to the scene of a crime. There was a morbid curiosity about seeing the South again through a pair of eyes which had so become accustomed to New York. Yet the pull of Althea's funeral, of seeing the place he had grown up in so long ago, operated like some psychic magnet on him. He had purposely stayed away from what he sometimes sarcastically called "home" for many reasons, the least of which wasn't that area's noted intolerance of certain races and cultures, and it had been nineteen years since he had made the journey to the very place of his birth and formative years.

He thought about this as everyone cleared the conference room, pillaging the last of the poppy seed muffins, stale pieces of fruit, and rancid orange juice brought in for the meeting by one of the many catering companies that buzzed and flitted around Manhattan.

"Why do you take that from him?" a young girl in a pink mohair sweater was asking as she pawed the top of a bran muffin that lay forlornly on its side, a casualty of the '90s now that the bran craze had died. He looked up at her. He had known Sharon for most of his life, having met her in the first grade, sailing through elementary school and junior high with her, and then dating her in high school. They had also gone to college together. Finally, both had made the move to New York years ago, and while they weren't as close as they once had been, he still relied heavily on her opinion and friendship. She had been nice enough to push Human Resources into hiring him four years ago when he needed a job. Personnel trusted her judgment, and based on the fact that she was one of the most valued employees at the magazine they had taken her word—along with some writing samples from Strekfus—and hired him on the spot. But mostly she was his one lifeline to his past—a past he could never completely escape and a lifeline he could never seem to sever. She was the one person who kept him grounded, and while he professed some disdain for his upbringing and the pitfalls of its culture, he nevertheless clung to Sharon for some sort of daily reminder.

"I don't know," Strekfus was saying in response to her inquiry about Sagaser, "ours is a strange relationship. I don't think we know if we're friends or enemies." He picked up a dried-out strawberry and then set it back down. "Besides, I can never really decide if I like the man or hate him, and I'm sure he feels the same about me. I mean, we go out for drinks every now and then and play racquetball together and everything seems fine. Then the next minute we're at each other's throats."

"Maybe it's your aversion to body hair," she said with a smirk. "After all, Winney has forearms like a gorilla and I know how you hate that. Some people seek out what they hate." He winced at her use of Sagaser's nickname, partly because he was the only one in the office allowed to call him that, but also because it gave the impression that she was on the same creative level. For all their links to the past and the friendship she

7

provided, Strekfus still maintained a competitive streak that could manifest itself at the oddest times.

"I'm assuming you still shave your chest hair," she continued, trying to loosen a wedge of cream cheese with a plastic fork, but her own mention of body hair seemed to cause her to abandon the idea. Strekfus pulled open two middle buttons of his shirt, exposing a muscular chest with three-day old stubble.

Sharon rolled her eyes. "Look, what you do with your body is up to you. All I'm saying is I think you should be writing more serious literary works than the things you crank out for this magazine. You're better than this place. You should be working on that novel you've always wanted to write, not puttering about some broken-down old house researching insulation blow-in techniques and plaster molding reconstruction."

"I happen to like plaster molding reconstruction and I have never done a piece on blow-in insulation, I'll have you know." Strekfus had now decided on the only remaining cheese Danish and pried it from the silver-colored plastic platter. An overly white doily stuck to it like an infant clinging to its mother. "Besides, this is a magazine on homes and gardens and blow-in insulation happens to be a part of that. And you got me this job. What are you doing criticizing it now?"

"Look, I've read some of your *real* stuff and I think it's pretty good. All I'm saying is give it a shot. Besides, with some of the things that I know you've been through, well, you certainly shouldn't be at a loss for material. That's all I'm saying. And I got you this job so you wouldn't starve to death, not because I wanted you to become complacent." She had now gone back to the wedge of cream cheese and was making several attempts to lift it off the platter by stabbing it with a plastic knife.

"And what am I supposed to do, quit my job for a year or so to write? Where do you think I'm going to find time to work on this novel—when I'm in the john? Which is about the only time old Sagaser is not on my back about something." He noticed her vain attempt to procure the cream cheese and with one quick motion stuck a fork into the helpless white wedge and held it up to her.

8

"Better on the john than never at all," she said, cutting her eyes toward the door where their boss, Edwin Sagaser, was standing. He was waiting for everyone to vacate the space so he could take the rest of the food. "Did you tell him about the funeral?" she asked, now holding the fork and suspiciously eyeing the skewered cream cheese, not sure that she wanted it after all.

"No. I thought I wouldn't mention it. Just go on the trip with the pretense that I'm down there to write about the South."

"What a lovely, lovely idea," she said, and shot him a fake smile. She set the wedge of cheese down with the fork sticking upward out of it like some modern sculpture found in front of a Manhattan office building—a usual attempt to draw one's attention away from the fact that the building's design is totally lacking in imagination.

"Sharon, would you kindly go to hell?" Strekfus asked as he adoringly glanced at her and smiled.

"Listen," she said, changing her tone from that of a friend to one of a co-worker, "I've got to get back to that upgrade. I've got some serious software to install. And why does your boss insist I attend these meetings anyway? Aren't they supposed to be strictly for writers? I think it must be some sort of power play with him, making the computer people and the accounts payable person attend. I mean, what do we have to do with the assignments you guys are given?"

"I don't know. I guess he figures you're an integral part of the process. Besides, I'd take it as a compliment. It's just one of his many quirks. Last week it was the credit department and two people in production. I think he just likes to see new faces."

"I'd just as soon not have the compliment and have the extra time to myself." Then she cut a glance over at Sagaser who was standing there, impatiently canvassing the room and looking in the direction of the leftover food. "Looks like he's spotted the pound cake," she said and started toward the door, glancing back at Strekfus with elevated eyebrows.

* * * * *

As Strekfus sat at his desk picking at the Danish, he thought about what Sharon had said, and later as he made his way down to the lobby and into the cab he kept thinking about it. Why shouldn't he start writing his novel? Wasn't it about time he decided what he really wanted to do? He was now staring out the window of the cab, watching the grays and browns of the city's huddled-together buildings fade into the grays and browns of the outer borough's assortment of factories, stadiums, and row houses. It was drizzling and the cab driver turned on the windshield wipers. Strekfus looked up at the man, who flashed a metallic smile at him in the rearview mirror. As the wipers thumped sideways, they reminded him of something he couldn't quite place. He listened intently, then decided that the sound was irritating and wished the driver would turn them off. Soon they were pulling into the low, flat terminal of LaGuardia and he felt relief spread over him as it always did whenever he left one place for another, even if he was leaving what he considered to be the emotionally safe confines of Manhattan.

He paid the fare, pulled his bag out of the car, and made his way into the terminal. Now he found himself looking up at the monitor—the one announcing flight takeoffs and arrivals. The flight from New York to Atlanta would be delayed two hours. They weren't anything new for him—airline delays and having to travel for the magazine—but the fact that he would probably miss his connecting flight in Atlanta to the smaller airport just outside his hometown added to his already present anxiety, and on this bright June day in 1996 Strekfus had more on his mind than missing a connecting flight. He had Althea to think about, and more specifically, the fact that she was now dead, for it was her funeral he was really heading to in the small Alabama town of Infanta and not his writing assignment. With a hand which wasn't preoccupied with luggage, he reached up and scratched his chest. This equivalent of five o'clock shadow was beginning to itch. He would have to shave again as soon as he got to Infanta.

"Well," he thought, rhythmically letting his fingers dig into the ridge between his pectoral muscles, "the good news is that Sagaser thinks I'm eager to get started on the assignment." As he let his mind drift toward the job he was to do, he thought how it would be to remember the South through eyes which had not seen it for so many years. He remembered how, whenever friends came to visit in New York, he would see the city through their eyes, as if he were experiencing it for the first time. Perhaps it would be like that for him on this trip back home. After all, it had been years since he had set foot on Alabama soil and years since he had seen Althea. But now she wouldn't be there with her gold-toothed grin, her open arms, her warm embrace. Now she was dead and he knew that while he hadn't yet fully come to terms with this, he would have to before long.

The news of her death had reached him early that morning accompanied by a flood of memories from his childhood—all the memories of his life up until this point, and all of the choices he had made, for Althea represented to him more than just a housekeeper who had been employed by his parents during his youth—she represented a veritable lifeline he had been able to hold onto. Her simple insight into life had afforded him comfort at times, especially in a city where so many everyday comforts were lacking.

It was this lifeline—though not a tangible one, for she had been miles away during these past years—that he had clung to, and it had enabled him to make many decisions (usually the good ones) up to this point in his life.

Now he was forced to deal with her death. He was also forced to deal with guilty feelings about the fact that he had not spoken with her in so many years. Life in New York had not allowed for family visits, and he probably wouldn't have made them anyway given the past recriminations and accusations which flew back and forth within that group of persons one attempts to call family. And Althea was in some respects, a part of his family.

They all kept at least slightly in touch with her—at least the aunts and uncles on his mother's side—and so rather than be subjected to her constant questioning about why he had not spoken to this one or why he never called that one, he had chosen to slip quietly out of her life even though he thought of her, in some form or another, almost on a daily basis. In fact, he had slipped out of his entire family's life, having had only minimal telephone contact with them these past years and no homecoming for almost two decades. While each side had made nominal attempts at maintaining communication, it was as though everyone realized the cultural differences that New York and the South represented, and besides, his family had their lives to live and so did he.

But because of Althea's death he felt on his own now— alone in the world—more alone than he normally felt, the way one feels after the passing of a parent or beloved teacher. He feared that it was now his turn to be there for others, to have others lean on him, to be responsible, to give advice, and somehow to be a source of inspiration. In short, he felt that it was time to grow up, and it scared him more than anything he had ever experienced. He knew the truth that had been kept so well from others around him: that he was, at forty, still emotionally a child, never having dealt with the fears and trials that had haunted him in his youth, and that waited, not always patiently, in the dark corners of his mind.

His emotions were mixed, as they probably are for most people who experience the death of someone close to them. There was the feeling that the dearly departed had somehow won a prize, had been relieved of the stresses of this world, given a reprieve, and in doing so had planted a seed of jealousy in others. For doesn't everyone long for peace and freedom from frustration at some point, even if it comes in the form of death? Then there was the empty, hollow sensation which often accompanies another's demise, and in a case such as this, the feeling that one somehow has to make up that vacant feeling to the world—that it's now one's duty to replace or rebuild what was lost. There's a feeling that someone needs to carry on the goodness that the deceased perpetuated during their lifetime.

As he ruminated about Althea, his past came back to him. He started to remember the South and what it had been like. It had taken the move to New York and then the news of her death to bring him full circle to the things he loved and longed for.

"Why was it," he thought, "that you could only truly appreciate a place when you no longer lived there?"

He remembered his disdain for the South, for its hatreds, its lack of understanding. He remembered his desire to get away from everything that it represented, its culture, its heritage. He remembered how he couldn't wait to be free even of the food that he had grown up with—the plethora of fried items piled up on china plates, the collard greens, dark and brooding in bowls, the pies warming in the noonday sun at picnics. How interesting he had found the New York delis, the mounds of fresh bagels, the voluminous torrents of coffee which made its way into greedy, sleepy hands before a day's work had started.

Now, after the intense years of work in the city, he found himself longing for the simpler things in life—things which didn't require an argument, a curt order, a defensive face, a meat slicer, or a cardboard coffee cup with a Greek motif on it. He was remembering the things about the South which he had tried for so many years to erase from his mind—the food, the people, the customs, the use of language.

As part of his magazine assignment, he was going to be required to see the South again, this time through a writer's eyes, and so inwardly, whether he knew it or not, he was preparing to relive his past in order to continue to live in the present, pushing toward that elusive and circumspect landscape that everyone fears, and at the same time seeks with eager anticipation—the future.

What he didn't realize yet was that this was to be a much longer journey than he realized, for it was to bring him back to the very place he had come from, a place so far removed from New York that he couldn't imagine it until his feet were firmly planted on the dusty red clay that is north Alabama soil.

* * * * *

Finally the plane was ready for takeoff and boarding was to begin. Strekfus stood on line, ticket in hand, and waited. The attendants called the last rows of the plane first, and as usual, passengers not sitting in those rows swamped the narrow roped-

13

off area to the door of the loading ramp. As he stood there waiting for his ticket to be methodically taken by the proverbially despotic and annoyed airline personnel, he became aware of the dull throbbing in his head. Maybe it was just the stress of the funeral to come or anxiety over flying. "Probably because of all these people ignoring the flight attendant's directions," he thought. That always angered him. He tried to put the sound out of his mind, but by the time he entered the door of the airplane it had become a distant, dull roar, like the far-off sound of waves on some unattainable beach. Then it retreated as quickly as it had come.

He found his seat, but before sitting down marveled at how, even though there were barely any passengers in his area yet, the overhead luggage bin was completely full. He stowed his small carry-on bag under the seat and began perusing a well-worn airline magazine—one which offered mechanical shoeshiners and gold-plated toenail clippers to travelers who presumably would marvel at the thought of such gifts for Christmas, even though it was only June and no one they knew would want such items.

Most of the trip he slept, occasionally being awakened for the usual small bag of peanuts or Coke ("No, you can't have the whole can—we only have so much to go around."), but when he was awake he took stock of his life. He couldn't help it really; there are only a limited number of things which can be performed on a fully booked airliner, and given the enclosed and confining space and where his travels were taking him, it seemed a natural progression. After all, he had moved to New York to try to get away from his roots, and here he was flying back to them with every emotion he could think of circling inside his brain. He thought about how different his life was now than when he was a child. Now he wore black most of the time, worked in a high-rise office building for a major publishing firm, had lunches at Twenty-one and Le Cirque, and drank martinis at the Plaza with friends who had summer homes in the Hamptons and Martha's Vineyard.

When he was young he wore blue jeans, played in the dirt under bee-humming forsythia bushes, ate peanut-butter-and-jelly

14

sandwiches, and had friends who vacationed in their backyards and occasionally, if they were lucky, in Florida every three or four years. "How strange," he thought, even though it had been systematically planned, step-by-step, "that I would end up so far from home." He felt the need to clarify his mission in life, to rethink options and to further break out of this "self" he had imposed so carefully on his very being. All of this he thought about as he dozed and ate peanuts and looked at pictures of flashlights that fit on key rings and plaques that said un-urbane but spiritually nurturing things such as "Creativity, Teamwork, Solutions," captioned underneath a picture of several in-shape young men sculling on some northern college campus river. And before he knew what had happened the plane had landed, the passengers had disembarked, and he was wending his way through the vast Atlanta airport in search of his next departure gate.

The connecting flight to the north Alabama airport came off without the problems he had foreseen; there was a plane leaving every hour and this assuaged his anxiety somewhat. When the one he was on finally touched down a mere thirty minutes later he was relieved to find the rental car pick-up located so close to the main section of the airport. "Something to be said for small towns," he thought.

It always amazed him how, when landing in a new location, you immediately sensed the difference in light and air and altitude—in the very karma of the place. And it was the same here. With the oppressive humidity that washed over the landscape and the slightly mildewed smell of the carpeting in the main concourse, a thousand memories came back to him, many of them as oppressive and mildewed as the air and the carpet themselves. But the dull throbbing in his head also came back, and as he reached for the door handle of his rental car it escalated to the point where he thought he might have serious heart problems. "If I can only get into the car and shut the door, I'll be fine," he thought, as his hands fumbled with the keys.

Soon he was inside and adjusting the air-conditioning. Evidently someone had just returned the car because it only took a second for the climate inside to become glacial. The throbbing had subsided somewhat—either that he had simply been distracted with all of the new and strange mechanics he had to learn inside the car—but it was still there in the background. He maneuvered the air vents directly onto his face, hoping the change in temperature would quell the pounding in his head.

He tried to listen to his mind, to the sound. It wasn't as rhythmic as he thought. It seemed to ebb and flow and there was some other noise accompanying it. Then it suddenly stopped. This was even more alarming. As he moved the car into reverse he made a mental note to see his doctor in New York just as soon as he returned. He hadn't felt dizzy or sick. Was the sound coming from inside him or from the outside? Or both? Trying to put it out of his mind, he backed out of the parking space and was soon driving out of the terminal area and toward the place of his youth—Infanta, Alabama.

"Funny," he thought, "how everything comes back to you." After all these years he could still remember where things were in the area outside Infanta. He noticed the clean brown drive down miles of highway that stretched out along the fields of cotton and beans, their fertile green rows seeming to go on forever. How did they get them so straight? Then there were the few simplistic billboards—"Eat More Beef," with its bad rendition of a cut of sirloin or prime rib, and "Moonshine Kills," with a drawing of someone's face, the eyes just two large X's. As he approached the town, landmarks seemed to rise up from the ground or lower themselves onto the earth as if some great scenic designer were arranging them for his own amusement, like giant chess pieces on a red clay board. There on the right was the low, concrete-block pumping station, raw and completely unadorned, just as it had always been. Even the kudzu, that noxious Japanese vine imported in the 1930s to stop soil erosion, refused to grow over it so ugly was the structure.

Then there was the burned-out shell of the cement factory, its huge towering elements looking like a Gothic chemistry set with beakers and tubes and distilling pots all made of rusted metal. It was a wonder to the town. How could so

16

many tornadoes come through the area demolishing hundreds of homes and never touch this decaying monster which seemed to teeter on thin metal legs high above mounds of unclaimed cement?

Further down the road, nearer the town, the ugliness of the outlying industrial areas began to give way to the green oasis which was the town square. It wasn't located in the direct center of town—not anymore—it was now on the very *edge* of town, and because of its longevity and history, many of the houses and gardens surrounding it had been preserved. Like so many town squares in the South, it contained neighborhoods of century-old boxwoods and azaleas, white-columned homes, and low cast-iron fences whose gates sometimes hadn't been opened since the last wedding or death in the family. These were homes occupied by people one never saw—homes that had been in families for generations. Homes that probably had a mystery to solve or a story to tell. But this was not the neighborhood Strekfus sought on this day in June. He would return to these homes and what they had to offer at some later point, but for now he would turn to the left and head toward the other side of town—toward the railroad tracks and even across them—to the side of town where the non-white residents lived.

This was Althea's neighborhood. It was not as pretty as the town square, but the houses were well kept (a government subsidy years before had greatly helped the area) and there were small gardens, well-watered lawns, and clean avenues. Maneuvering the rental car along the curving street, Strekfus found the house earlier than expected. It took him a moment to realize that he was in the right place. He had stopped the car directly in front of Althea's home, yet he was still looking ahead as if he thought it was much further down the street. In reality all he had to do was look to the left.

After a few moments of daydreaming, the sound of an impatient driver's horn jolted him into reality and he turned into the driveway. Pulling up to the house, it suddenly hit him: Althea was gone. All the years of having had her "there," and she was no more. He choked back his emotions as he made his way up the walk and knocked on the screen door of the red brick ranch-style house. Peeling paint surrounded the doorframe. A half-dead cedar bush by the front steps and a weatherbeaten garden hose thrown loosely into the front flowerbed greeted him. He noticed that Althea's extensive collection of roses, hostas, ferns, and snapdragons were in dire need of attention. She obviously hadn't had time to take care of them since she had become ill.

Opening the rusted screen door, he extracted a note taped to the inner door.

Mr. Beltzenschmidt,

I've left the door open. Please feel free to go in and make yourself comfortable. I'm at the funeral home and should be back shortly.

Randolph

P.S. There's another note for you on the bedroom door.

"This is strange," thought Strekfus. "Who is Randolph?" With no one there to greet him he felt odd about entering Althea's home, especially after all these years, and even more so since he had never met anyone named Randolph. He figured it was probably the landlord Althea rented the house from. She had often spoken of him as being benevolent about late rent payments.

He opened the door and entered the house. Immediately the soft carpeting cushioned his steps. The entire house had that hushed feeling that often accompanies the passing of a friend or relative. It was as if the person had not only vacated the space physically, but spiritually also. And yet the spirit of Althea *was* somehow still here. He could feel it and literally see it in her furnishings. That is, what furnishings he could make out in the dim light of the interior. And then the throbbing inside his head

18

returned. Or maybe it had never really gone away, for it seemed to loom out of the depths of his mind with the strength of something that has been hovering in the background, lying in wait, picking up energy in order to ambush its victim.

It was almost as if this crescendo of sound and emotion came together the instant he saw the note—the one pinned to the bedroom door—the note someone named Randolph had warned him about. He could see it from where he was standing, glowing and white, written on ordinary spiral notebook paper and taped three-quarters of the way up on the door. The sound in his head seemed to increase with each step toward the door and he considered stopping mid-route to see if it would cease, but it was as if something wasn't letting him cut short his predetermined goal, as if he were being pulled by some unseen force toward this ordinary piece of notebook paper, this ordinary piece of tape, this ordinary door to this ordinary bedroom.

Suddenly he became aware that the sound he was hearing was not that of his heart, his blood pressure, or anything at all related to his physical being. It was a real sound and it was of something being struck repeatedly with anger, with frustration, with a force which seemed to want to exorcise something. It was a sound he knew but couldn't place. It came into focus with the intensity of a high-powered searchlight, its beam shining directly into the eye, blinding and white-hot. He felt like someone who has just been shot, but thinking the bullet has passed by, relaxes for a moment only to realize by reaching down, seeing the wound, drawing up his hand wet with blood, that the act has indeed happened and he must now wait for the aftermath—that the events which have been put into motion cannot be reversed and must be played out.

As he pulled the note from the door, tattered shards of paper fluttered to the floor. He unfolded the message. As he read the words written in a shaky hand, the sound in his head continued to grow. "Strekfus," the note read, "I want you to have what is in here. I love you. Althea."

As he reached for the knob, everything seemed to go into slow motion. He heard no sound except the beating in his head.

19

It was unrelenting, unforgiving, otherworldly. Turning the knob, he realized there was another sound accompanying its wooden, hollow, percussive attack. He had not heard it before, but now as he listened it lent a human quality to the reverberations in his head. He became aware of a man's agonizing groans, his muffled sobs underneath the beating. The moans were animalistic, almost sexual, angry, as if the person making them were putting all his strength into them. For a brief moment he thought that he recognized who was contributing these new sounds, but his mind leapt quickly away, not letting him get near the source, but not letting go either.

Turning the knob and opening the door, he saw the room fill with an immense white light from the back window. The sun had broken through the clouds at that instant and it seemed that every beam it possessed entered through the opened window, blessing the moment and the room with its enormous intensity.

He stood transfixed, unable to move from the spot as if held by some horrible, wonderful power which was his past, his present, and his future. The beating sound in his head had reached such a level now that its echoes melted into one continuous roar, like multiple tracks of a recording machine which looped over and over until the only sound was a wash of noise. He felt himself losing his grip on reality—the light coming in from the window, what he was seeing in the room. He only had one brief moment to take in the contents of the room before things started to spin and he lost complete control. He was seeing the window fly upward, hearing the roar in his head, the combination now like some awful multimedia event held in a horrible house of mirrors at some decadent carnival with distorted loudspeakers and the noises of a thousand eager and rowdy commoners chanting for blood. Then the loud, twisted music, the lights that swirled and streaked like some slow-motion photography, the thick groping of hands which rose around his legs, pulling him under.

The room was now an out-of-control merry-go-round and his knees were made of water, but he was to endure the vertigo for only a second more before he slumped to the ground, noticing for the instant before the end the cracked ceiling, the dusty light fixture, the thin white draperies now standing almost perfectly horizontal from the window, caught in a breeze which had suddenly blown through the room out of a seemingly unearthly locale. It was only a second and then something wiped him out as clean and sure as if an eraser had wiped yesterday's homework assignment from the blackboard of life.

* * * * *

When Strekfus came to, he became aware that there was a man standing over him. As his eyes focused, he began to make out the concerned expression of an older gentleman. But there was something else—something he noticed in his deep subconscious before his mind cleared and he began to think again about the room and what it held. There was a strand of something familiar yet buried behind the glasses, the aging face, the human patina of this individual. He tried to hold onto it, to comprehend where it had come from, what it meant to him, but he was now beginning to reenter the world of the living and the thought retreated like a garter snake slithering back into an unused woodpile, soft and silent. He knew if he wanted to recapture it—this thread of consciousness—then dismantling the woodpile was his only option, and feeling drained by what had just happened, he let the thought slip from him undeterred. Before he would answer the question the man was asking—this man who knelt over him, concerned, afraid, unsure—he would turn his head first to look back into the bedroom.

"Are you all right?" the man was asking, his hand gently resting on Strekfus's arm. Strekfus had yet to regain his speech, so he simply nodded. Then sitting up and managing to slowly stand with the help of the man, he once again confronted the room.

Again the man was speaking, saying something to him, but Strekfus's mind was a blur and he was already back there, in a time long before New York and much further away—in a land of red dust and fetid swamps and burning suns. A land where gullied roads led past dead cottonwoods and solitary eagles

21

swung high over patchwork fields. It was a land that now contained something he needed. The journey back to it would be a long and arduous one, but he knew was necessary, so without hesitation he turned again in the direction of the sunlight streaming in from the bedroom window, took a deep breath, and took his first step into the room.

- 1 -

New York, 1996

As the cool stream gushed over one hand
she spelled into the other the word water,
first slowly, then rapidly. I stood still, my
whole attention fixed upon the motions
of her fingers. Suddenly I felt a misty
consciousness as of something
forgotten—a thrill of returning thought;
and somehow the mystery of language
was revealed to me.

—Helen Keller, *The Story of My Life*

S trekfus sat staring out the window. His office wasn't much, just a small room, but it was located on the thirty-ninth floor of a sleek new skyscraper and the view was spectacular. It was late now. Seven thirty at night. The magical lights of the city were beginning to show themselves, like small bulbs on strands of electrical Christmas garlands—once dormant, now suddenly illuminated as if by some invisible source. He remembered how as a child he had sat alone in the living room late at night with the family Christmas tree ablaze in decorations and light. It never failed that while he was staring at it, some bulb which had burned out or become loose would suddenly become illuminated, giving the tree an animated effect as though it were alive and had chosen to show only him some secret. And it was this effect that Manhattan was having on him now. It was as if the soft, silent flutter of lights from the adjacent office buildings

23

were turning themselves on just for him, even though he knew this to be impossible. But it was one of the things he loved so about the city—the fact that no matter how impersonal and cold it was, there were still moments of magic to be found. "Too bad my imagination isn't lighting up," he thought as he studied his half-empty computer screen.

It had been three days now since his return from Alabama and Althea's funeral—three days since he encountered the bedroom in her house and someone named Randolph, and he was supposed to have at least the outline for the first story in the series. He was not sure exactly what he would write about. Too much had happened: the funeral, the revelations. He wanted to write something new about the South, not just the same stories one heard over and over, and yet those same stories were haunting him and he hadn't been able to escape them entirely. He pulled the latest copy of what he had written off the printer and began to read.

Alabama, at the time I was born, was a mixture of bucolic pastoral and angry confrontation, and this is not to say that the pastorals were limited to landscape and confrontation to persons, for many times the two (the land and the people) seemed to mix themselves up in such a way as to defy definition.

Not much was happening in this area in 1956, the year of my birth, with the exception of some church bake sales, a few weddings and funerals, and the occasional lynching of a Negro for some minor offense such as trying to vote or refusing to step aside on the sidewalk when passing a white woman. While the bake sales, weddings, and funerals allowed the towns in this area to socialize with their typical convivial and sybaritic excesses, feasting on homemade pecan pies, two-gallon jars of iced tea, and chicken fried to perfection in cast iron skillets whose conservation and upkeep took precedence over the ravages of adultery and genetic insanity within a family, the lynching of a Negro was regarded by some as a social punctuation mark—that rarely used but always effective exclamation point which was meant to make the inhabitants of that land look up and take notice. By the 1960s it was a way of saying to both whites and blacks, "Stop. Look what we've done, we who are invisible have the power to kill and the power to make you watch." And it was this use of the exclamation point, this punctuation mark of hate, which stretched back to the period after the Civil War and helped to define the South that I knew as a child.

In the period from 1880 to 1918—the period in which most lynchings occurred—a hanging was sometimes considered a sacred event, presenting opportunities to have one's photo taken with the dangling corpse while smiling and wearing finery usually reserved for Easter and Sunday christenings.

Such patterns of softness and hate were, and in some ways still are, buried deep within the strands of DNA and recipes that call for cornmeal. It is the dichotomy of the South. It is slowly disappearing, and there are those who have lived there for centuries and despise these ways, but some attributes are passed on with or without intention, and it takes a careful gleaning to rid preconceptions which have set down roots as deep and fixed as those of a strangler vine—a vine which, if left unchecked, will cover everything in sight.

And it was sometimes the very same people, the ones with lace-gloved hands offering up sugar cakes and mint tea, who had posed to have their picture taken beside the dead man—previously hunted down like some terrified fox and strung up with no more concern than that which would have been shown a child's piñata at a birthday celebration—possibly the very same Negro who had at one time knocked at their back door offering to chop wood or do some menial chores for a few cents.

This was the state of Alabama in the late nineteenth century and early twentieth century. During the 1920s and 1930s the lynchings decreased, but before then it had been as if the majority of the population in the region had lost its ability to see or hear clearly with regard to race and conscience, and now they were being forced to learn an entirely new way of communicating. Many resisted. Many refused. Some acquiesced. Still others had been able to see and hear all along, keeping the secret among themselves and a select few who sympathized. By the 1960s, many of the old habits and frustrations had surfaced again (although in somewhat different forms) and were making themselves known daily on television, on radio, and in our own backyards.

And so it was into this era, this place, this geography, that I was born. Not only into this prismatic culture of oppression, gentility, good manners, and concern for cooking utensils (for without an iron skillet there can be no fried chicken), but into its very topography and landscape. In this area of the country, geography and landscape seem somehow to be as intertwined with and inseparable from food, history, and prejudices as two snakes during the first warm days in spring.

One could easily make the analogy between the well-trimmed century-old suburbs with their white Victorian houses and rose gardens, and the outlying areas surrounding them—wild, untamed, harsh areas covered by the red clay dust that makes up most of northern Alabama. The analogy being that the inhabitants of each were more like the landscape than they cared to admit; that deep down, the same Alabama soil that was under the sharecropper's patch of string beans was also under the finest bed of marigolds in town.

Once outside the town square, where the roads gave way to ramshackle family homes, unpainted business fronts, and tent revivals, a visitor would see things as they really were—completely unadorned. It was this wild,

26

savage land which was always present, even in its more "citified" townspeople. They could mask it with teas and garden parties and yards of lace displayed at church socials and charity functions, but the fear of being different, whether in attitude or skin color, was always present and filtered into everything. It was one thing to be eccentric; it was another entirely to be methodically different. Premeditation with intent on bucking the system was not to be tolerated and life could be made a living hell for anyone taking that road.

And it was a road sometimes as unforgiving as the landscape outside the picket fences and gardens. Once the pavement stopped, usually at the same time the custom of painting a house also stopped, the true nature of the land came through. Left to its own devices it produced huge willows, their branches bent downward to sultry streams, their long fingers testing the waters. It also produced dogwoods in the spring, their spots of white dotting the verdant land like sprays in bridesmaids' hair. Wild tiger lilies hovered together on sides of roads and ditches filled with blackish water in the spring. The tops of pine trees silhouetted themselves in autumn like tall chimney sweeps' brushes put up until morning against bright orange-streaked skies. The long wail of a distant train threw its melancholy song over darkening hills and wet green valleys in the summer. Roads twisted like serpents and disappeared into the gray-green distant mounds that are the Appalachians.

But besides this flagrant display of nature there was an underlying element of danger. Of mistrust. Of history. Of something hidden which might or might not bring harm, depending on its mood and exactly where it perceived you to be in the grand scheme of life within these boundaries.

If a traveler to the area stopped by the edge of the mighty Tennessee River, which dipped down into the region only to rise up again into the state which bore its name like some visitor who had changed his mind after sampling the environs, he might see the small frustrated waves on the river's shore cream white and foamy with a sprinkling of brown—like the rim of a cup of barely sampled cappuccino. Across the rippling waters he would see mounds of green trees infused with shafts of sunlight. All might seem peaceful and innocent until the visitor spied the reflective eyes of an enormous water moccasin curled on a rotten log only two feet away, its thick demonic body undulating like Satan's large intestine freshly ripped from his loins. It had been lying there, watching and waiting, almost laughing to itself over the fact that it had sat undiscovered for so long.

If the visitor's luck were up, the venomous reptile would quickly lengthen out its form, mouth open wide and ghost-white with fangs dripping, ready to tear into his defenseless flesh. If fortune were with him (and it rarely was, for the cottonmouth is known for its aggressive nature, some having chased hunters for great distances before being shot and killed), the snake might slink into the brown water, taking its otherworldly movements and venom with it to wait for some other unsuspecting victim.

Undoubtedly the visitor would watch the serpent, unable to take his eyes from it, a mixture of fear, fascination, and thankfulness manifesting itself until the tail slipped beneath the surface of the murky shoals. He might just as well look upon certain events and people with the same fear and fascination and the same hope that the ones he ran across—the ones who so vehemently opposed anything they didn't understand—would retreat and not choose to seek out the newcomer.

It was this underlying whiff of violence which seemed to permeate the land and the people. The river, the sunset, the thickets of dark woods scratching thin black lines against the sky, all seem beautiful and innocent. But there is always the deadly moccasin nearby, watching and waiting. And this is not to say that all danger is physical, for sometimes the most violent acts are psychological. The cottonmouth, with its languid, writhing body and deadly poison waiting to be injected into the unsuspecting veins of some small child whose natural curiosity and daring turn him into a miniature Don Quixote, is for me as much the symbol of hate and misunderstanding as it is for the pain it can inflict on one who chooses to wander through the fertile woods by the rivers of this area.

This is the land in which my family home and so much of the South sit, nurturing and carving out those personalities which were and still are the members of my family, all of whom at one time or another seemed to try their best with what circumstances they were given.

He sat back for a moment. The writing wasn't at all what he wanted. He felt that while he had been accurate in describing the South, he had missed something. And the descriptions had come out rather purple, florid, full of a soft light. The magazine, he knew, wouldn't appreciate anything even close to the subject of lynchings. Besides, this wasn't going to be a series of stories on race relations. And he had used the word, "Negro," instead of "Black," or "African-American."

He mused over the few pages. He wanted a more concise style, but one that showed the reader how he remembered the South. He wanted to write from his experiences and not what others expected. He wanted the stories to be about the places and people he remembered, and as he began to think about this he realized that what had defined the relationships and dramas for him had been the houses he had seen, shared, and lived in with those who had loved him and been a part of his life—and also those who had not loved him so much. The houses seemed to be the framework for periods in his life, and even certain events seemed to be shaped and defined by these homes, their casings proscenium arches for the dramas of his life which seemed to have been strung together as haphazardly as popcorn on a string by someone attempting to recreate an old-fashioned Christmas. And yet they somehow made sense—made him who he was.

He stared at his screen saver, bubbling and oozing a myriad of sounds and shapes. It was so easy to get lost in this ever-changing landscape before him, both the screen of his monitor and his own thoughts, and he let his mind wander back to when he was a child, to a time when he didn't know what the world was about, what it expected of him. Before he knew what was happening, he was typing furiously in an effort to recapture the fragments of memory which surfaced like free-floating pieces from a submerged shipwreck. He would write about an experience that he had as a child, one in which he was misunderstood. After all, wasn't that how he felt about his life— that he was misunderstood? And so he wrote what he could remember:

He couldn't understand it. He thought he had done everything exactly as requested, but they still weren't happy with him. They were walking around the room like somnambulists in a nightmare and he was forced to sit there while they paced back and forth, their hands on their chins, their faces frowning, their heads downturned as they strolled about.

"Explain to us again, honey," the middle-aged female teacher was saying. As she leaned toward him, her thin, bleached moustache became more visible. He leaned back to try to regain his own space. "How exactly did you come up with this analogy. I mean, I could understand if you had picked the bird and the tree, but the bird and the car? And you seemed to have this kind of irrational thinking all through the test. Please try again and let us in on what was going on inside that little brain of yours."

He was becoming frustrated by this time. Hadn't he already spent the last thirty minutes explaining this? It seemed perfectly logical to him. He had scored so low on the aptitude test that his parents and the teacher were concerned. Concerned enough to have called this conference with him as the center of attention, and so now all three of them sat in the flourescent-lit school room with its pastel-colored molded plastic chairs and its slick, cold, hard tile floors which reflected the light.

"Look," he began, "I explained to you that there was an object to be matched up with one of the other three objects and that's what I did."

"But what I don't understand is why you chose those particular objects," the teacher was saying, her arthritic fingers fumbling with the now dog-eared papers. His parents looked on, never having removed their hands from their chins. "The first object was a bird and you were to match it up with either a nest, a tree, or a car, and you picked the car. Why?"

"Well," he stated, "I thought about it, and the first thing that came to mind was that the bird would go with the nest, so I thought that was too easy, too obvious. Anyone could get that. So I tried to figure out what the person who had designed the test wanted. I then thought about the tree, and while this didn't seem as obvious as the nest, I thought it was a pretty easy guess—birds live in trees. Then I looked at the car. I thought about a couple of things. We have a car that is always parked under a tree next to our house and I know that my parents have a hard time with bird droppings. It seemed to me that it was the end of the line in the thought process: bird in the nest, which is in the tree, whose branches are overhanging the car. Any idiot could have picked the nest and anyone of average intelligence could have picked the tree, but it seemed to me that to rationalize the car was a masterstroke of genius."

She wasn't saying anything now. She was simply curling her lips upward and withdrawing while squinting her eyes, as if she had found some mutant squash in the supermarket produce isle and couldn't decide whether or not to buy it. Then she was calling his parents over to the corner of the room, whispering in tones which were full of

S's so that the result sounded like three people sanding blocks of wood in an elementary school classroom.

"But he's only five," he could hear his mother saying. "We know that the elementary schools want to administer these tests early in order to find out what the children are capable of, but maybe he could take it again?" Then the teacher—the one who had given the test to him—"I'm sorry, Mrs. Beltzenschmidt, but the tests confirm that your child is retarded. There's nothing we can do. He placed in the lowest possible percentile and my advice to you is to put him in some kind of a home or special school. Was he hit on the head when he was a baby?"

Then his parents were turning abruptly away from the teacher and toward him, pulling him by the arm, dragging him through the hallways which echoed with their footsteps, past tiled walls with gaping doorways. Then they were in the car and pulling away from the curb.

"I'm sorry," he was saying to his parents as they faced ahead in the front seat. "I thought I was doing what everyone wanted. I thought you would be proud of me for picking . . ."

"How could you think the way you do?" his mother was asking, turned halfway around in the seat. "Are you trying to embarrass us? Don't you realize what it makes us look like to have a teacher call you retarded?"

"I'm sorry," he said, trying to hold back the sobs which had started with her angry retort, " I just wanted you to be proud of me and I thought that . . ."

"That's your problem," his father was saying. His tone was somewhat kinder than that of his mother, but there was still bitter disappointment in it. "You think too much. You should try to just be like everybody else."

"But I don't know anyone else. I'm not allowed to play with the other children in the neighborhood. I don't have anything to go by. If you'd let me play with the next-door neighbors I could . . ."

32

"You're not playing with any of the neighborhood kids and that's final. You're just going to have to figure out on your own how to act because neither of us has the necessary time to spend on this problem," his mother said. "Besides, if you're as smart as you think you are, then you can take that test again and produce a better score. I'm not having any son of mine be retarded."

He was quiet now, realizing that it was no use. He had disappointed his parents when all he had wanted to do was please them. He had been trying to use his head, think about more complex things, try and guess what the person who designed the test had wanted. Why had the other kids done so well on the test? Did they have some inside information that he didn't? Why had they all picked the correct answers, including the one about the bird and the nest? Was it that the teachers wanted you to think on the level of the lowest common denominator? He would have to do better, try harder. He could already read—he had taught himself with his father's help—and he could do basic math at age five. Still, everyone around him thought he was strange and shied away from him, even his own parents.

As they drove toward their home that afternoon, he resolved to read through every book he could find, and since his father was an obstetrician at the only hospital in town and a reasonably well-educated man, he would have access to volumes of Latin and the classics and just about anything else he could sneak back to his room. It wasn't his first choice, this spending time reading rather than outside playing, but his parents had denied him playmates, thinking that no one was good enough for him or their family, and so now he would have to channel his energies into reading and learning everything he could in an effort to reach their expectations. After all, hadn't the teacher said that he was retarded? He would have to work twice as hard to be normal, to be accepted to be intelligent. And he would have to show his parents that he could do things, be creative, be resourceful. Then maybe they would love him and try to understand him.

He had read each page as it had come off the printer, fresh and warm like some flat, alien bread. He liked this one much better—this story about what he remembered one of his first experiences in the South to be like, but he had not included anything to let the reader know it was set in a specific location. He thought for a moment. Perhaps something in between, somewhere in between, some story which would combine the South and his own personal experiences.

Again he remembered the houses he had grown up in. He remembered the people, the relationships. He remembered how he always felt he had disappointed his parents, how unhappy he had been as a child. And he was now remembering where these emotions had taken place. He was remembering his recent visit to Althea's home, her funeral. Wasn't he supposed to do a series on Southern homes and gardens? Why did it have to be specifically on plantation homes and symmetrical boxwood hedges? Why couldn't it be on the South as *he* remembered it? He looked over the two beginnings he had created. Neither one was exactly right and so he started typing again with an idea which was somewhere in the middle. He had seen something in Althea's room, something she had left him, and it had set off a chain reaction which was now as unstoppable as atoms being split in a nuclear meltdown. Only he wasn't sure exactly what it all meant, and he knew that if he were to take the journey of remembering to its full extent, then he would have to start from the beginning and piece things together. It was as if someone had given him some priceless Ming vase which had been broken into a million pieces—some family heirloom, some vital part of his very history—and he was now expected to put the thing back together and make sense of it.

He thought back to the very first house he could remember. The very first garden. What had happened. What things meant. And he typed well into the night and into the early morning.

- 2 -

Ivy Green and the Joseph Wheeler Home

Tuscumbia, Alabama, 1962

> I do not remember when I first realized
> that I was different from other people;
> but I knew it before my teacher came to
> me.
>
> —Helen Keller, *The Story of My Life*

When I was six years old I became locked inside the home of Helen Keller. It wasn't until many years later that I was able to fully appreciate this event, resplendent with all its metaphors, and come to terms with exactly what it symbolized on a deeper, more metaphysical and spiritual level. Even now I find that the journey isn't entirely over, that it is a never-ending process of self-examination and learning which will probably continue even after my death for those who knew me.

Miss Keller wasn't living in the house at the time—she had long ago moved on to bigger and better accommodations—but she was still alive when the event occurred and would probably have secretly enjoyed the upset it caused everyone. It wasn't that much transpired physically—I became locked in, someone let me out—but rather it was a psychological event for me at an early age, somehow shaping my thinking and becoming a revelation years later.

* * * * *

A relatively demure house, at least physically, the Keller home or Ivy Green as inhabitants of the region know it, occupies several acres of land in Tuscumbia, Alabama. Nestled among hundred-and-fifty-year-old boxwoods, oak, and magnolia trees, it is a cool green enclave in sharp contrast to the heat-beaten furrows of farm fields that surround the small town of its location. Here in the northern part of the state at the end of the Appalachian foothills, there is a quietness and serenity pervading the area that offers up wonderful images of what it must have been like so many years ago before the peacefulness was interrupted by one who was to find her way out of the dark landscape of the mind and into the real world.

Helen Keller, the blind, deaf, and dumb girl who learned to communicate with the outside world against all odds, is for me a symbol for all of us—struggling to find out who we are and why we are here, most of us are blind, deaf, and dumb in one way or another, if not physically, then spiritually or emotionally.

Years later, even after the incident was forgotten, my mother would admonish me for my inabilities and eccentricities, claiming that it was appropriate that I had been born in Infanta, Alabama, since it was geographically located somewhere between Tallulah Bankhead's birthplace (Huntsville) and Helen Keller's (Tuscumbia).

"Strekfus," she had said, oblivious to the fact that the sex of the two aforementioned persons was not the same as mine, "mentally you're somewhere in the middle. You're incredibly flamboyant, but too handicapped to ever carry it off."

I hated it when she tried to stamp me with her own personal brand of diminution, and I hated it when she began a sentence with my name. When she was really irritated, she, as most mothers in the South are prone to do, used both the first and last names. If they were at their wit's end they used all three

37

names, vaulting them over alleyways and front yards with the expertise and sagacity of a square dance caller. Thank God we weren't Catholic.

There were days when our entire neighborhood had to endure the name Strekfus Ovid Beltzenschmidt bellowed at it for hours while my mother stood on the front porch clawing her fingernails into the soft wood of one of the columns that graced the front of our suburban faux-Greek-revival prefabricated house. Why anyone would keep the name Beltzenschmidt is beyond me, but why anyone would name a child Strekfus is totally out of my grasp. Add to this Ovid and you've completely stumped me. You just can't name a person something like this and expect him to have a normal childhood or life. Especially in the South in 1956, the year I was born. And it was a strange year to be born into. The president at that time, Dwight D. Eisenhower, summed it up best when he said, "Things are more like they are now than they ever were before."

At any rate, as if all this weren't bad enough, it wasn't long before other kids noticed that my initials spelled S.O.B., and by the third grade everyone delighted in telling each other that I was a real S.O.B. Since cursing was strictly prohibited by our teachers and parents, the initials were hurled at me almost as often as my mother's daily neighborhood vocalizations.

I asked my mother one day how they had come up with Strekfus as a name, and her explanation was that my father at one time had a playmate in the Garden District of New Orleans where he grew up who was named this. It seemed that every so often this friend would appear, and his antics would upset this quiet area of New Orleans until it was time for him to go back to Alabama from whence he came. Evidently the last time he had come to visit, there had been some mischief over a missing necklace and the playmate had been shipped off for good. But my father had become enamored of the name, and after dropping one letter (the original spelling was Streckfus) he bestowed it on me.

So S.O.B. evidently was a more enticing nickname for me than "Strek" when it came to my classmates. I didn't mind this really; think of what they could have done with my *last* name. It didn't matter that my great-grandfather was a Confederate general in the Civil War, they simply had no respect for the Beltzenschmidt name or my family's heritage. I was to find out that not only did my childhood friends lack respect for the Beltzenschmidt name, but that the tour guide at Helen Keller's home—Ivy Green—had somehow been persuaded to join my nascent peers in their debasement of what I considered, in my mind, to be the equivalent of royal Southern heritage.

The particular day of the incident—of my incarceration in Ivy Green—the sun announced itself with typical Southern severity, blue jays screeched at the tree tops, and as we were led out of the back of the house at closing time by the spinsterish tour guide, the screen door slammed shut just before I was to exit and the latch, which probably hadn't been tampered with since Helen herself first tried to escape the confines of this "fine example of Southern architecture," wedged into place with such voraciousness that only Anne Sullivan could have coaxed it out of its resting place. A plumber and ex-bus driver who lived down the road, Merle Gibson, managed to achieve proportional results to Miss Sullivan's, but not before the tour guide had reached a state of hysteria that was only equaled years later by the assistant principal finding out that Mrs. Blanche Seriate, a fourth-grade teacher at the only elementary school in the town, was a lesbian.

The teacher who caused the upset, Mrs. Seriate, was for me the zenith of all human possibilities because her daughter played the bassoon in the town's high school band, and in my opinion this automatically elevated her to celebrity status.

Infanta was a small town.

Needless to say, I was the recipient of strange looks on the playground when, after countering charges that she had excessive nose hair for a person of her age, I was quick to add, "But her daughter plays the *bassoon!*" The bassoon comment did not endear me to my fellow classmates. The question of what amount of nose hair society finds acceptable was, however, debated for the remainder of the semester.

At any rate, the pilgrimage to the Keller home that day started off innocently enough. The family, that is to say, my father, planned these excursions every so often, and they almost always stayed in a radius of a hundred miles or so. Because of his position in the town's only hospital, he was able to create his own work schedule around the anticipated labor pains of beehive-haired trailer park wives, and since my mother was a nurse in that very same institution, she came and went as she pleased, making these trips possible in the middle of the week instead of the weekend when the majority of others would have been out and about. In the event that some inconsiderate woman went into labor, my father would rush back to the offending patient, taking the necessary steps to bring a new child into the world after having torn us away from one of the numerous decaying and historic homes that north Alabama had to offer. Moreover, these trips almost always included antebellum and historic homes from the Old South, probably because my father had grown up in such a house in New Orleans, or at least was born and lived his first few years there before the Great Depression took everything the family had. It was undoubtedly my father's search for that which had once existed but was taken away that led him to probe into other people's habitats from a grander South both remembered and wished for.

General Reginald Patrick Tecumseh Pritchard Marshall, that famous Civil War hero, had died in the two-storied Greek Revival house my father started his life in. When the family moved from place to place, ending up in Alabama, the bed in which General R.P.T.P.M. had met his maker, among so many other objects, was still functional and at a later point very much in use. The family had even managed to retain the gun that R.P.T.P. Marshall had used in the Civil War, a Le Mat revolver noted for its excellent destructive capabilities, and this was now in the possession of one of my uncles—Uncle Scott. All these things—relatives, guns, beds—moved to Infanta, Alabama, sometime in the 1950s.

The present family home in Infanta, a huge three-story house built in 1887 that most of the children, even though grown and with children of their own, still lived in, was a never-ending maze of passageways and staircases lined with ancient photographs from the Civil War. It was Gothic kitsch, if there is such a thing.

The entire house was an odd mixture of priceless antiques and plebeian household artifacts that could have been purchased from a five-and-dime in Anytown, USA. Indeed, the fact that R.P.T.P.M.'s deathbed was now covered with a faded turquoise chenille bedspread (one large poodle, French cut, butterfly inches away from the nose) lent a kind of consistency to the overall household plan.

This brass monstrosity of a bed, which was for me a recurring nightmare in itself because I knew its history, was the one I was forced to take naps in whenever I stayed with my relatives while my mother and father were at work or just not in the mood to have me around the house.

Each afternoon, after being physically carried and set down in the middle of the bed, though I was quite old enough to walk by myself, my Aunt Testa would bend down and plant a Max Factor #6 Chinese Red (it was either that or a color called Midnight Fawn, as the Woolworth's in town only sold these two possibilities for the ladies of Infanta) kiss on my forehead. It would stay there sometimes for days in the creases of my forehead and no amount of the Cashmere Bouquet soap that I found in the bathroom next to my grandparents' former bedroom would wash it away. Aunt Testa was my father's older sister and she was a fixture, not only in her own home but in the small town of Infanta as well.

As she raised up after the kiss, the brooch she always wore (again, the poodle motif continues—ruby chip tongue, sapphire eyes) would catch on some article of my clothing, yanking my aunt's head back down so that as she tried to untangle herself, her perfumed hair would be sucked up into my nostrils and send a great whiff of Charlie directly at my olfactory senses.

Aunt Testa always wore a fragrance called Charlie and almost always something with polka dots. As she had a slight waddle—a direct result of her clubfoot—and wore two bright red circles of rouge on her cheeks to match the color of her hair, she resembled, whenever she left the room, an aged circus clown desolately making his way back to his trailer in order to recuperate for the next performance. (I say aged, but in reality she was probably in her forties at the time.) This, accompanied by a rather asymmetrical wheeze which was the result of years of chain smoking, gave her a melancholy air which would have defined her totally except for the fact that she had a wicked sense of humor and refused to be pitied.

After the nap preliminaries were taken care of, I would lie awake the entire time imagining old R.P.T.P.M.'s age-spotted and shaking hand creeping up the taut, insane-asylum-white, overstarched sheets as ancient wisteria clawed against the windows, and a lazy afternoon sun squeaked through the Venetian blinds just in time to form a partnership with certain intimate objects in the room and play "shadow monster" on the hearing-aid-pink plaster walls.

There was also another attribute of this house which intrigued me, an attribute other than the bed, Aunt Testa, or the nap rituals: the basement. The reason it captivated me so was that I was never allowed to see it as a child.

"Oh, it's just an old dirt-floor basement with a bunch of junk down there," my relatives would say. "You don't want to go down there. It's filthy." And that would pretty much put an end to things. Of course this only made me want to see it all the more.

I never managed to convince my aunt to let me see the basement as a child. This basement held secrets—secrets of the family and secrets of the South. In fact, the "deathbed" had been stored in this basement a few years before it was taken out and dusted off in preparation for my naps.

Suffice it to say, the Southern experience was ingrained in me at an early age, if not by the fact that all preschoolers were made to sit through *Gone With the Wind* before ever learning to read, then by osmosis through what was considered to be tangible vestiges of a movable past, the bed being the most obvious example of this.

At any rate, this particular day we had set our sights on the Wheeler home and the Keller house, two rather formidable structures—the first, in my mind, because of its size, the second because of its association with one of its previous occupants.

Once, several years before, there had been a trip to the Wheeler home ending in unmitigated disaster when my father, experiencing an unusually bad case of diarrhea, had soiled himself before our arrival and had to spend most of the tour in a small restroom just outside the gift shop.

The trip today was not much better. Once the car stopped, I decided to run ahead to maximize my time spent in the house. There was to be a detour, however, before I would reach the cool honeysuckle-covered porch to wait for my parents.

Spying a dead rattlesnake in the carriage drive of the house, I decided to venture in its direction, and this being done at the precocious age of six, caused both my parents more than their usual degree of hysteria. Being male and having lived to see what I could remember of five summers, my natural curiosity urged me to have a closer look.

My father, being the prudent (among so many adjectives) man that he was, lurched to my side to admonish me for the veneration I had shown for what you would have thought was the largest king cobra ever seen in the Western Hemisphere. ("That's right doctor, we were just standing there admiring this lovely old house when WHAM, the cobra sprang out of nowhere and now look, he's swollen up twice his normal size.")

My mother, who always enjoyed inventing a reason for the employment of histrionics—"*Please* come back here! I know it's not dead! *Please* come back here! Oh, Paris (my father's name), make him stop!"—which led directly into a sort of hymn singing with a proclivity for sliding *up* to pitch at the last possible moment and the usual below-the-Mason-Dixon-Line use of additional syllables—"Ju-ust as I a-am with ah-out one pu-lea, but tha-ut thy bu-lud was she-ead for me"—was practicing the not-so-delicate art of hand wringing and looking about to see if anyone was going to witness the untimely demise of her son.

After closer inspection, during which time I found the snake to be half on its belly and to possess the classic dead animal grin so well known to anyone who has motored about these United States, I informed my father that I begged to differ: the *Crotalus horridus* was quite dead and no longer posed a threat to any of our immediate family. I had a penchant for Latin at an early age, my father having taught me to read as soon as I was out of the womb and insistent that I browse throughout the *Britannica* whenever possible and any other books he deemed acceptable reading. At the time I had thought it was one of the nicer things he had done for me, but I was later to discover that it was a setup for bad social relationships from that point on.

His response was typically despotic.

"Are you getting smart with me?" he spewed in my direction.

"No, sir," I said. He was a learned man, but quite often saw no reason for displaying this attribute.

"*Crotalus horridus*," I insisted. "The common rattlesnake."

My father just looked puzzled. Then, proceeding to remove the head of the snake from the rest of the body with one overly dramatic strike of a handy garden hoe, and grind the poor reptile into a pulp with part of a wagon wheel the tour guide had shown us while welcoming us up the drive ("They make the lawn so homey and provide lovely borders for the day lilies"), my father obliterated any trace of the creature. He muttered over and over to himself, "Satan in earth form," and began herding us back to the 1961 Ford.

I remember it was a Ford because our other car was a Buick. For some reason, unknown to me to this day, every time I get into a Buick, I participate in the socially unacceptable act of projectile vomiting. At the time, this caused quite an upset for both my parents when, delighted with their new purchase, we all went for a ride, and I promptly retrieved a cheeseburger, french fries, and chocolate milk shake from the Dairy Queen even though we were a good ten miles away from it at the time.

I explained that it wasn't motion sickness but rather had something to do with the combination of smell and color of the vinyl that some terribly unimaginative car designer had chosen to bestow upon the dashboard. Choosing not to believe my explanation, and determined to find cause and cure, they forced me to endure countless hours of "car testing." This consisted of my mother opening the back door of a car and my father holding me as horizontal as possible while sticking my head into the backseat area.

Timing was everything here. It only took about a second, and after withdrawing me just in time, the salesman and my parents would get to view the entire contents of my stomach, much to my embarrassment.

"We had fish last night and I guess it must have been bad," my mother would interject to counter the salesman's shocked expression while my father carried me, still horizontal, into the next row of cars.

Fortunately, after several Buicks, dry heaves were the order of the day and fewer explanations were needed. At one point, they even announced that they had given up on the Buick idea and had decided to purchase another make. With unusual glee all of us flounced down the driveway to see the new purchase (à la 1950s home movie), the entire time my mother proclaiming two phrases over and over with the same unpersuasive rhythm and cadence. "This is a different car, honey. You won't have to worry about a thing."

"How convincing," I thought, and once inside proceeded to prove them wrong. I tried to aim for the floor, but I managed to get the backside of the front seat as well. It had a built-in ashtray directly in the middle and previously digested bits of candied yams were now dripping arrhythmically from the small lip in the center.

I was ecstatic. The manager of the car lot who had driven the car over that day was less so. When I had managed to collect what was left of myself, I shared my elation with them.

"This is great. It's not just Buicks that do this to me," I said. Unfortunately, my parents informed me, this was indeed a Buick and they thought that since the whole thing was in my head—and at this point I could see my father make a mental note not to pay the one-time consultation fee to Curtis Nimblad's father, the town psychologist—they would tell me it was another brand and gauge my reaction.

Deciding that they really wanted a Buick anyway, they bought a second car specifically for the purposes of my transportation needs and I never again saw the interior of that vomitorium on wheels. But being just high enough to reach the product name on the side of the car, I managed to work loose the *B* and the *U*, leaving what I felt was a more appropriate representation not only of the car, but all incidents accompanying it.

This day at the Wheeler home, heading back to the Ford was, to say the least, only slightly less dramatic than the Buick experience.

"Get in the car," ordered my father.

"But . . ."

"Get in the car, Strekfus," said my father, "Get in the car. You don't know how many more of those rattlesnakes there may be around here. GET IN THE CAR!"

"Oh, my God! Your father is right. There may be thousands of those around here! We'll all be killed, oh, dear Jesus *do* something. Strek! Strek! Get up here in the front seat. They may have crawled in the back of the car and just be waiting to strike you! Strek! Strek! Do you hear me! Oh, God, what if they've crawled up inside of the seat and they come out when I'm grocery shopping or taking you to swimming lessons? We could be sued if they strike someone riding with us! Oh, God, do something!" Then my mother's singing: "Are you washed in the bu-lud (uv the), bu-lud uv the lamb," as she rocked back and forth while clamping my head to her breasts.

Satisfied that we were mortally terrified and locked in the car, my father strode up to the Wheeler home to partake in what was to be a particularly nasty and long discourse with the tour guide about the irresponsibility of leaving rattlesnakes lying about. I know it was a long conversation because mother managed to get through all five verses of "Love Lifted Me."

Twice.

And I still have her fingernail imprints on my temples to prove it.

Needless to say we didn't get to see the Wheeler home this time. At least not the inside of it. We missed such well-known remnants of the Old South that we had seen on previous tours such as Mrs. Wheeler's sugar chest—"Shu-gah was such a precious commodity in those days"—or the kitchen which was "always separated fro-um the house—Mrs. Wheeler couldn't stand cookin' fumes smellin' up her brocade draperies."

I insisted, as I always did, that we stop off at the gift shop so that I might retrieve a souvenir to remind me of this happy outing. My father, secure in the fact that we could drive up to it and not have to walk, agreed. "Besides," he said, "I'll run over the snake on the way up the drive and we can make sure it's dead."

"It's a *Crotalus horridus*," I said and slumped back onto the seat, preoccupied with trying to extricate the synthetic whiskers off a small rabbit whose internal music box played the song "Blue Velvet."

Looking around inside the shop, I didn't see much that interested me at first. The usual type of items that you find at any tourist attraction filled the shelves: banners with "Joseph Wheeler Home" printed on them; small glass ashtrays with bad two-dimensional pictures of the Wheeler home imbedded in the glass;

salt and pepper shakers in the shape of black mammies; rubber alligators; five-year-old boxes of taffy, their colors not found in nature.

Then I spied a small wooden bucket about four inches high with the words, "Joseph Wheeler Home," etched on it in cursive writing. Inside the bucket was a small tree, a pine tree that had sprouted from one of the parent trees that were endemic to the surrounding woods on the Wheeler estate. The tag said, "Take home a LIVING souvenir!"

Inhabiting a warm climate had enabled me to collect many species of plants which ended up either in our backyard or on one of the windowsills in our house. I, of course, managed to talk my father into purchasing this for me as I did so many items in my youth. Grumbling, he handed the clerk two dollars and me the purchase.

"It's a *Pinus taeda*," I said, fondling the slick miniature leaves. "Endemic to the area."

My father just shot me one of his looks.

"It's a *Pinus taeda*," I repeated. A pine tree. It's fairly . . ."

"Shut up," my father said.

This particular trip to the Wheeler home over, it was off to the Keller place; conceivably a more docile environment with a smaller rattlesnake population.

* * * * *

Upon arriving at Ivy Green, the birthplace of Miss Keller, we were greeted by Mrs. Bunion, a rather librarian-like creature around fifty-five years of age with an odd twisted mouth, gnarled hands, and fingers on which were located several opals the size of small bird eggs. In addition to this she wore a brown wool suit, the color of which is found on the back sides of carpeting that has been pulled up after forty years, and her feet appeared to have been stuffed into her shoes with no less than a crowbar, for they bulged over the sides like a cake to which has been added an exorbitant amount of baking powder and is in danger of escaping its pan. Her nametag was slightly askew and to make matters worse, she (or someone) had clumsily written her name so that

48

the "union" portion was in slightly larger letters. This in turn caused my father to address her as "Mrs. Bu-UNION," when he greeted her for the first time.

Having that rather common habit among tour guides (and hymn singers) in the South of adding two or three extra syllables to words which only need one—"Wh-ut a-euv-uh ahm I-a gonna dew wi-uth the-us day-ud possum?"—she was to make for an even longer tour of the house than expected, but with less enjoyment because one was constantly having to translate the true meaning of her expositions. Even for Southerners, the pronunciation of certain words can be precarious. Once, after attending a church revival with my parents in the country, I lay awake in bed all night waiting for a can of "Lard" my mother kept under the stove to come into my bedroom and make its divine presence felt. It had been made quite clear to me at the various church meetings that unless you knew the "Lard" personally, you were in real trouble. Phrases such as, "Are you touched by the Lard," and, "Do you know the Lard? Come to the Lard and he will save you," still remain with me today. It was years before I was able to distinguish the difference between the divine presence of our savior Jesus Christ and coagulated pig fat, being too afraid to admit to anyone that I thought the two were somehow connected, if not one and the same.

Having set eyes upon us as we entered the yard to the Keller home, Mrs. Bunion extinguished her cigarette on the flagstone walk, flicking the butt into a nearby patch of sweet william with the toe of her unctuous foot, and at once intimated to my parents that while they were welcome (and at this point her gaze dropped a good three or four feet downward to me and her mouth twitched in that schoolmarm-like way), children did not generally come to the Keller place to visit and "Were we *sure* we really wanted to see the glorious Keller home resplendent in oh-wal of its Southern beauty and cho-ahm?" My parents said they were, and somewhat reluctantly we were led through a garden of asters, hollyhocks, sweet peas, various leguminous plants, and numerous cigarette butts, and into the cool interior of the house which had the musty odor of something akin to a cross between a thirty-year-old pair of shoes and a decomposing mouse.

Of the decor of the house or of its furnishings, there is little that I remember except for a staircase in the front of the house with a landing at the top of the stairs. The stairs at that time were covered with worn pink carpeting whose edges curled up at intervals exactly like the tour guide's lips. To the left of the top of the stairs, in one of the bedrooms there was a window with a wide ledge. The view from the window was beautiful, encompassing the yard and surrounding land, and on the ledge sat the object that I most wanted to inspect. As we had been hurried through the house, my father had stopped in front of each item shown, frowned, and then stuck his finger in his ear as if tying to dislodge some ancient relic that could be sold to the British Museum. Having decided that it was only earwax, we were permitted to move on. But because of this and Mrs. Bunion's protracted verbal pontifications, we were pressed for time.

I had wanted to stop and perform a more thorough inspection of the house, but was told that we must "not tarry . . . there are others who would like to see Miss Keller's birthplace." Strangely enough, I had not seen anyone else about the place except us. It was around five o'clock in the afternoon and the house would be closing soon. The snake incident at the Wheeler home had evidently taken longer than I realized.

So of course at the window ledge I stopped.

So of course I automatically irritated everyone.

So of course they made this painfully clear.

"What is it?" asked my mother, but before she could answer, the tour guide was right behind us like a runaway train, urging us on, fearing that I would touch something—"I all-ways hold on to these rails. You never know when you could faw-ull. My family seems to be accident-prone. You know, my sister was in a bad automobile accident recently (out of breath here) and had to hay-uv her hand and leg amputated. She also lost one of her eye-ce," she wheezed breathlessly as her patent leather shoes, three sizes too small, squashed sideways on the steps and she elevated herself up to the second story where we now were. She then headed us toward the stairs and exit in the hope of having a few moments to herself before going home. Little did she know that she was to be there much longer than anticipated.

Thanking us for coming by to see the Keller home with a well-protracted fake smile while handing my parents brochures of other historic sites in the area—"Don't fo-ah-get to visit the Cherokee Coon Dog Cemetery just five miles up the road o-rah stop bah on ah Saturday, the only day they'uh open, and see the bromeliad gaw-den of Mrs. E. Merriweather as it only costs three dow-luz and a hay-uv"—she breathed a sigh of relief that I hadn't broken anything and motioned us toward the door.

And then it happened.

As we exited the house, my mother and father went ahead of the tour guide and me. In one final farewell gesture the guide let the screen door slam in my face as she stepped out onto the porch. As if this insult wasn't bad enough, imagine my surprise to find that the door wouldn't open. I maneuvered the latch every way I could think of, just barely being able to reach it, but the rusted mechanism had somehow broken off *into* the doorframe and I was getting nowhere fast.

Seeing that I was not coming out of the house, Mrs. Bunion grabbed the handle of the ancient screen door and tried to extricate it from its hinges. Nothing happened. Things weren't too bad at this point until I realized that all three of the grownups (and I use that term loosely) were seized by panic, and because misery loves company, and because I was six years old and locked in someone's house who was deaf, dumb, and blind, I decided to join in the panic momentarily. Realizing that this was getting us nowhere, Mrs. B. collected herself and decided that fear would be a useful tool to employ in my general direction. Pressing her face as far as she could into the screen door and gritting her teeth, she snarled, "I don't know what you de-ud, but you better undo it right now, young may-un!"

Strangely enough, it was at that moment that I noticed three things about her that I had overlooked (if you can believe that). She had lipstick on her teeth, her cat-eye glasses were taped together with black electrical tape, and she had the smell of cheap rum on her breath. I couldn't resist. I walked right up to my side of the screen door and looked up at her. "You really shouldn't dye your hair that color; it makes you look much older than you are," I said, and at this point she mashed her face even further into the screen door, to the extent that I thought it was going to come completely through in little squares just like the clay I used in my Play-Doh factory at home.

"I'll get you for this," she hissed as I turned away.

Realizing that she was angry didn't help my disposition, but the moment I became aware that I held the power in this situation I was intrigued. I had a plan, but first I had to show a modicum of effort in aiding my release. I played along with the situation for the moment. I was instructed to try to disengage the lock from the inside, which I did actually try to do. The problem was this: neither the lock nor myself were going anywhere.

"You're not trying hard enough. What kind of child have you-ah raised?" Mrs. Bunion spewed at my parents who then decided to turn their anger back in *my* direction. What you can't give back, you pass on, I've always found. That was the family motto.

"Son, cut this nonsense out this minute."

"But . . ."

"Don't *but* me. Unlock the door NOW."

(For those of you who like to be the center of attention *and* get a free show that beats anything at the circus, trust me, this was the ultimate in experiences.)

"Honey, please TRY, you've got to TRY to get yourself out," my mother pleaded. "We can't do anything, oh, my God." Then the singing, "Why do I love Je-sus, Why do I love Je-e-sus, Why do I love Je-sus, be-cau-us he first loved me."

And then my father with proverbial gritted teeth and clenched fist: "How could you people be so irresponsible and have doors that lock by themselves?" he yelled at the tour guide.

After trying several instruments I found at the reception desk—pencils, scissors, a letter opener with a "See Rock City" handle on it—I decided I was safely locked in and what was once worry became elation. Through the waning light I could see them, like absurd characters in a Mozart opera—the pressed snarling face of the tour guide at the screen door clawing at the wire like some rabid animal, my mother right behind her, head thrown back, eyes closed, voice at full volume, and my father pacing back and forth, grinding his teeth and snarling—all three in perfect counterpoint.

With this image I turned and headed down the entrance hall and as I did so the tour guide's screeching of "Where are you-ah going?" repeated over and over very quickly became less and less clear until its barely audible predictability became a sort of mantra.

The first thing I determined to do was actually to inspect the house—something the evil Mrs. Bunion had forbidden. "Now, pu-lease do not tarry," I said, loudly enough for her to hear as I flounced down the hallway. Before I had fully entered the next room I looked back over my shoulder to see her splayed out against the screen door, shrieking in my general direction. I couldn't help being reminded of the time my father tried to bathe our cat. He had placed it on a large piece of screen wire before turning on the water, a move which in my opinion was brilliant. The resemblance of Mrs. Bunion to our cat was uncanny, the only difference being that the cat was slightly less anxious.

But it was after I was completely out of sight from them that something started to happen. Evidently someone had gone for help, and the noise from the porch retreated temporarily to the front yard, giving my previously assaulted senses a much needed rest. As I walked into the parlor and watched the late afternoon sun stream in from the windows and onto the floor, I found myself caught in another time. Fine particles of dust filled the air, the sunlight exposing them as they swirled through the room. The effect was like that of a giant flashlight cutting a swath through some sepia-tinted snow globe, its elongated V-beam illuminating what wouldn't ordinarily have been seen by the naked eye. I wondered if the sun had looked like this when Helen was a child; if her parents had noticed it; if its effect had been the same on the room, causing them to think of a time long before the one to which they belonged. While sparse furnishings gave me only the barest clue of how the Kellers lived years ago, it was as if some presence was there, guiding me and trying to make a connection. Not a ghost, but an energy from long ago that still inhabited the furniture, the floors, the walls, the very sunlight streaming in from the window.

I closed my eyes and began to move about the room. At first I moved slowly, being afraid that I would bump into something.

"Be-ah shu-ow two-ah see thuh cooooon-dawg cemetarrry," I said out loud as I moved over the floor, reaching out at intervals for the sturdy arms of the Edwardian furniture which stolidly occupied the room. "Chill-dwren ah-wa not generally wel-cooome auh . . ." but before I could finish, the sharp corner of a wall jumped out to meet me and I was startled back into reality. Regaining my composure I began again, this time plugging my ears with my fingers and trying not to speak as I shut my eyes and moved tentatively though the space.

At first the sensation was horrific—blackness from the four corners of the earth. No hope of ever escaping. A void which went on forever. Then the other senses began to pick up where sight, sound, and speech failed. My feet began to feel for clues. Carpeting and stretches of hardwood flooring defined my universe as did the heat from the sun which was becoming more level and intense at that time of day, pouring steadily into the room. I could smell the sun as it landed on the walls and furniture, and I could almost hear its warm, horizontal music which seemed to guide me about the room with sounds of blue jays, gentle breezes, and the floating, dream-like scent of wisteria.

Having a mental picture in my mind of where things were, I turned in the direction of the staircase. My foot searched for the first step, and with my elbows I felt along the walls and slid upward. "Don't *but* me. Unlock the door NOW," I said in my best imitation of my father. The words had an underwater quality as my fingers were still planted firmly in my ears. I managed the staircase without too much difficulty since I had estimated the number of steps and there was a recurring pattern. Finally at the top, feeling as though I had climbed Mount Everest, I became full of myself and strode aggressively into one of the upper rooms, but no sooner had I set out than something loomed up and cut my legs out from under me. I went wheeling into space and landed on my stomach atop something soft and squeaky with my nose buried in some old and musty thing.

Strangely enough, I didn't open my eyes. I had, of course, removed my fingers from my ears, but by now my senses had become alive and I wanted to experience what I could before it was time for the rescue party to arrive. "You're not trying hard enough. What kind of child have you-ah raised?" I said, imitating the aged tour guide. My words were muffled not by plugged ears, but by whatever my face had landed in.

I reasoned by touch that I was lying on some ancient bed. That much was evident from the amount of space such a soft area covered, but I couldn't figure out what my nose was pressed up against. It felt stiff and dry and smelled like the inside of an old book. I reached up and gently began to move my fingers over the object. A few inches up I noticed a change in texture and by the time I had reached the object's top I discovered it was a doll. Then it struck me, as surely as if I had been hit by lightning—I was lying on Helen Keller's bed with my nose buried in the dress of one of her dolls. But the real fear wasn't just this insight—it was the realization that I had not yet opened my eyes. I was sure that I still could, but something unseen was compelling me to keep them shut, even in fear.

Again, the terror gave way to a thing strange and new and comforting. I was actually beginning to enjoy my new world, this world of darkness in which things were not what they seemed, and upon discovering exactly what they were, they took on entire new meanings. The smell of the sun on the doll's hair, the slight sound of dirt on the floor as my feet scraped across it, the likeness in touch of old lace to the dried-out pages of a book; all of these things opened up new vistas for me. How would I ever be able to leave this land of deft imagery and return to that of my parents with their disappointments which made their way across my psyche and their hard hands which made their way across my face? Perhaps they would be appreciative of my latest discovery and want to learn the subtle nuances that these new experiences had to offer. Perhaps not. I lightly moved my hand over the doll. Something was wrong. Terribly wrong. Still holding my eyes shut tightly, I felt the head. There was hair; I had sensed that already, but there didn't seem to be any eyes. I felt further. There were no ears and no mouth.

Something happened then. Something took over me and I felt a sadness that had only been experienced once before in my life. It was as though some inner part of myself responded while my conscious mind stayed mute. I imagined Helen receiving the doll, by this time in her life deaf, dumb, and blind, and feeling with her gentle, soft hands the doll's face only to realize that the unfeeling person who had given her the gift had not bothered to procure an anatomically correct toy for her, thinking that since she couldn't see, eyes, ears, and mouths were unimportant. This person had not reasoned that, by feeling, Helen would be able to tell that the doll was missing something—just the same as she was. What must have gone through Helen's mind? I felt that I knew. I didn't know at the time how I knew, but I knew.

As I set the doll back down and lifted myself up from the bed, I marveled at this strange thing which was taking hold of me. It was as if something were growing within the center of my body, expanding outward. I stood up, and this time without plugging my ears, decided to move about the room. I don't know how I could have forgotten about it—this object I had tried to inspect the first time through the house. As I negotiated the room my hand reached out and then recoiled at something cool but alive.

I let out a small gasp, not being able to imagine what could be alive in a house such as this. Still I did not open my eyes. Finally, after summoning the courage to reach out again I made contact with the object and held a fleshy piece of something between my fingers. Then, running my hand up and down it, I realized what the object was. As I moved toward it, feeling its moist energy in this dry and dusty house, I smiled to myself at how frightened I had been of something so innocent, and I found myself transfixed before the object of my desire. I have no idea how long I stood there. All I know is that I was comforted in the knowledge that no one could reach me, that I had been cut off from the rest of the world, deaf and dumb and blind.

* * * * *

When Mr. Gibson, the gray-haired, jump-suited plumber and retired bus driver had finally been summoned via a pay phone down the road and freed me from my prison, and the grown-ups managed to reenter the house, the light from that special day was almost gone and only a hangnail of moon was to be seen twisting its way up to the top of the litmus-paper-colored sky.

They found me in one of the upstairs bedrooms where my father's square hand brought itself up swiftly under my right arm and jolted me back into reality.

"What is it? What's the matter with you?"

"*Sansevieria trifasciata*," I said, opening my eyes and looking up at him while dangling a good three inches off the floor.

"What?"

"*Sansevieria trifasciata.*"

"He's tawking gibberish. If he waz my-un I'd give him a good switchin', tha's what I'd do," said the tour guide.

"What is it? What are you staring at?" my father exploded as he stood over me. He had managed to set me back down by this point.

Turning rather coolly to him I said, "They're mother-in-law's tongues, if you prefer the plebian vernacular. *Sansevieria*

57

trifasciata. I haven't seen these anywhere lately." They were some of the best specimens I'd ever seen. The leaves shot up in a stately way out of a mauve-and-white ceramic Roseville planter. The planter alone was worth a small fortune in my estimate.

"We've got to be getting out of here," he said, and took me by the arm.

"But I want them," I said.

"WANT WHAT?" my father shouted.

"The *Sansevieria trifasciatas*," I persisted.

"We aw-ah not in habit of selling off Miz Keller's personal belongings to complete strangers," said the tour guide with as much disdain as possible while tilting her head and tapping her foot annoyingly. Her arms were crossed and she looked more than mildly irritated.

"Son," my father continued, "you can't have those. They're not for sale."

"But I want them," I persisted.

"They're not for *sale*," my father said clenching his teeth. "Now let's get going."

* * * * *

Mother's hymn singing had practically subsided to a hum, and by the fourth chorus of "Shall We Gather by the River," it was almost inaudible. Along with the mutterings of Mrs. Bunion, it gave the cicadas in the trees their cue to begin their evening songfest, and this, with the coolness that an impending rain storm brings, hung in the air like a dragonfly suspended above a magical green pond. A heavy breeze suddenly came out of nowhere and the trees seemed to bow to us like loyal subjects to royalty. Then it was gone.

My father and I began to walk toward the car in order to make our way home after another typical Sunday outing. As I strode past the plumber and ex-bus driver who had freed me, I looked up at his craggy, weathered, and sunburned face, down past the white chest hair sticking out of the top of his overalls with their sewn-on name tag (white background with red lasso stitching), and reading his name for the first time said, "Thanks, Merle."

He looked down at me and said, "You know, y'all's lucky I was off today, else you'd be stuck in the Keller home overnight," and his face broke into a wide grin, exposing a gold-capped tooth which he turned in my parents' direction, and then toward Mrs. Bunion, who was offering up her best scowl of the day.

"Since when do you think you're allowed to call total strangers by their first names?" My father's voice rang out behind me, and the sharp slap of his hand on the back of my head moved me along toward the car.

"If he wa-us mine, I'd give him a good switchin', tha's what I'd do," the tour guide called after us through the now harmless screen door, her head still tilted in its condescending manner.

Merle just shot her a kind smile and said, "That's okay, glad to be of help. That boy don't need no switchin'," and he walked painfully over to one of the large oak trees in the front yard and leaned up against it.

"You hush up," seethed the tour guide in Merle's direction. "You and your carry-in' on. You mind your place or I'll tell everyone what I know. What does Edwina mean to you?" Then she snatched her body back into the innermost confines of the house and left the man who had freed me leaning against the massive tree, looking sad and wistful.

All the way home I sat in the backseat and tried to fill the car with as much anxiety as I could. "What if we offered her a lot of money for them," I said, extracting another clump of whiskers from the rabbit while softly singing "Blue Velvet," one of the popular songs of the day, to myself. My father simply gave me a look in the rearview mirror and I knew I'd better lay off for now.

"Whow, whow, whow," I sang under my breath.

"I'm gonna whow you in about two seconds, mister," my mother snarled back at me. Then she faced forward again. The cool evening breeze felt good on my face and the few remaining whiskers on the stuffed rabbit bent gently in the breeze. "Whow, whow, whow," sang my mother under her breath and stared out the window at the passing fields of beans and cotton.

* * * * *

The next day I woke up late and made my way to the kitchen for breakfast. I had forgotten momentarily about yesterday's fiasco. It was nice being off from kindergarten for the summer with only Althea, the housekeeper, to keep me company.

Althea was an elderly black woman that my father had hired to work for us. I say elderly because she was at that time probably in her late forties and this seemed to me to be quite old. Formerly she had been employed at the local hospital my father worked at, but he had decided that since she was such a good employee, he wanted her to work for us in our home. At least that's what he said; I was to find out many years later that this wasn't the truth. And as it says in the Book of John, "The truth shall make you free." I was in dire need of freedom, but it would be many years until it came.

"Child, yo' mama's gone off to work and yo' daddy lit out of here early this morning. Said he had some business to be attendin' to! Looks like it's jus' you and me today," said Althea. Then in her typical way of changing subjects she asked, "You want me fix you some eggs?"

"I'll just eat some cereal," I said, and proceeded to fix myself a bowl of the latest pastel-colored sugar granules and look over the paper that had arrived. I turned to the Arts and Leisure section (two paragraphs) to see what cultural tidbits there were to partake of in a small Southern town of 18,000.

"Althea," I said, remembering yesterday's excursion, "did you know Helen Keller?"

"No, child, I didn't know no Helen Keller. That was that blind, deaf, and dumb lady, wad-in it? Everybody has heard of her, but no, child, I ain't never met her," she said.

"They say she once stuck her head in a lion's mouth," I went on, remembering a story I had read about Helen in a magazine.

"Child, I don't believe I'd be stickin' my head in no lion's mouf. Maybe 'cause she bein' blind and all, she didn't *know* she was stickin' her head in a lion's mouf," she said.

"Maybe she just wanted the experience," I said.

"I don't know, child. White peoples sho do some strange things if you ask me," she continued and just shook her head. "Sho do . . . sho do . . ."

I sat there absently staring at the paper. "Merle," I said out of the blue.

"What's dat?" asked Althea. She had a look that I'd never seen before on her face.

"Merle," I repeated. "It's a name."

"I knows what it is, child. I knows it's a name."

"What's the matter?" I asked.

"Nothin'. Ain't nothin' the matter," Althea went on, and walked over to the sink to get a glass of water. I hadn't ever seen this look on her face before. Something wasn't right, but I was too young to figure it out.

"Merle, Merle, Merle," I sang.

"You tryin' to irritate me, child?" She was standing now with her hands on her hips, her jaw now moving silently.

"No, why?"

"Then stop sayin' that name." This time she moved her tongue around in her cheek and I knew what was about to happen.

"What's the matter with the name?" I asked. "The man who got me out of the Keller house was named Merle. I can't help it if that was his name."

"You's in that Tuscumbia yesterday?" She was walking toward the back door now.

"Yes, ma'am."

"Hmmm," she said. "I ain't been to Tuscumbia in years." Then she opened the back door and sent an almost invisible and completely silent shot of tobacco spit directly between two stately hollyhocks which nestled under the eaves. For a moment I marveled at the fact that Althea chewed tobacco. It had been

61

years before I noticed it, so discreet was she about how she went about placing the minute pieces of dried leaves in between her teeth and cheek. And she was even more discreet about expelling the excess liquid that formed, having perfected an almost silent and undetectable vaulting method which she employed with such casualness that only a child of six would have noticed. To my knowledge, my parents didn't know of her current vice and I was certainly not going to tell them.

She seemed to have calmed down now and I tried to concentrate on reading what I could of the paper, but it stuck in my mind how odd she had acted—as if she were shaken up quite badly just by someone's name.

"Althea?" I asked, hoping to get her attention first. "How long have you chewed tobacco?"

"Since 1956, child. Why you ask?"

"Just wondering," I responded, and then as six-year-olds are apt to do, I just couldn't leave well enough alone. "Nineteen fifty-six," I said. "That was the year I was born." She looked at me oddly for a moment and then said in a tone I had never heard before, one completely different from the "Merle" incident a moment earlier, "Well, child, 1956, that was one hard year."

"Merle, Merle, the tilt-a-whirl," I said under my breath. She shot me a glance that said I was on thin ice, so I feigned extreme interest in an article about septic tanks and decided to lie low for the time being. A few minutes later we heard a car pull up in the drive and Althea looked out the window.

"Lord have mercy," she said. "Looks like yo' daddy done come home from the hospital already, but how can that be?—it's only 'leven thirty."

It *was* my father. He had not gone to work but rather had been attending to some other business. We heard the front door open and went to meet him.

"Here," he said handing me a large grocery bag. Then he handed Althea a smaller bag and began to rattle his car keys—a sign that he would be gone soon. "I'm going back to work now," he said, right on cue, and he turned around and left as abruptly as he had come.

As soon as he was out the door Althea pulled out a bottle of blue liquid from her wrinkled brown bag. "Cleanin' supplies from that hospital," she said and made a face like someone who's been forced to eat a lemon. That was pretty much the extent of my father's relationship with Althea: he brought her cleaning supplies and she took them. Since Infanta only had one small hospital, he could pretty much come and go as he pleased, taking what he wanted. Other than when exchanging supplies I don't think he and Althea ever spoke to each other. It seemed to be some sort of implicit ritual between them, as if they needed to remind each other of who they were and what their place was at that time.

I set my bag down and pulled the paper away.

"Ooooo-weeeee! Look at that!" said Althea. "You gots you some of them mother-in-law's tongues!"

Indeed I did have some. But these weren't just any mother-in-law's tongues; they were the very ones we had seen in the Keller home the day before, complete with the mauve-and-white ceramic container. Evidently my father had driven back to the Keller home early that morning and managed to pry the plants and container away from the evil tour guide. No doubt he had to pay a pretty penny for them. ("Well, I'm shu-ah we could work somethin ou-ut if you would be willing to make a substantial contribution to the Keller Foun-day-shon.")

I sat looking at them with the same feelings most people have—elation and sadness—when they eventually get what they want only to discover it doesn't have the imagined effect they thought it would. It wasn't the object I had obtained that caused me this confusion, but rather the fact that my father, a man not given to frivolity or indulgence, had actually done something so extreme to make me happy.

"Yo' daddy sure is an unusual man," said Althea as she walked back to the kitchen, and though she was no longer within earshot, I stroked the long leathery leaves, looked down at the plant, and replied with the same amazement, "You have no idea."

* * * * *

The plants sat for years on the kitchen windowsill until a prolonged Florida vacation forced them to go without water during an extremely hot spell, the result being their untimely demise. I occasionally see these plants for sale in florist shops and greenhouses, and each time I do, the Keller home comes back to me, complete with Mrs. Bunion and her multisyllabic delivery, " . . . and this ee-us the water pump that young Helen learned huh first wuh-ud. Huh first wuh-ud was . . . (and here she paused for dramatic effect, as if she were hearing the words herself for the first time, and in doing so, pronounced them with a slightly retarded twist while tilting her head back in a helpless fashion as if trying to imitate what she thought a deaf, blind, mute person must look like) . . . wa-tuh . . . wa-tuuuuuh."

- 3 -

New York, 1996

The love which had come, unseen and
unexpected, departed with tempest on his
wings, a little island of joy surrounded by
dark water.

—Helen Keller, *The Story of My Life*

"What is this?" It was his editor, Sagaser, asking the
question, and he was an uncomfortable mixture of
anger and confusion. "I ask you for a story on
Southern homes and you give me this?" he continued, holding up
that month's printing of the magazine. "At least if you were going
to do a write-up on the Keller and Wheeler homes you could've
given me some information about the furnishings, the actual
gardens. Is this your idea of a tour? Does anyone in New York
even know who these people are? Whatever happened to General
Lee's home or that Margaret person's home in Atlanta, whoever
she was, the one who wrote . . . whatever."

"Margaret Mitchell. And it was *Gone With the Wind*," said
Strekfus, standing there with his arms crossed, the sleeves of his
thin black shirt pulled tightly into his fists.

"Yeah, whatever. Listen, you can't give me things like this
to publish. What happened to Oak Alley, Natchez, Charleston? I
gave you a list." He was staring now at Strekfus with that special
look he sometimes used on those who had disappointed him—a
look of intimidation reserved for one who hasn't quite learned his

place. It was a look that Edwin Sagaser was famous for, and today, on this bright day in June, as he stood silhouetted against the vibrant backdrop of Manhattan which loomed panoramically from the thirty-ninth-story window behind him, he used the look as never before.

"I thought it would be from a different viewpoint. I was trying to write a story which had to do with a specific area and culture. You didn't say you wanted moonlight and magnolias," countered Strekfus. He knew that he hadn't given his boss exactly what the man had asked for, but he thought this contribution was more important, and besides, he wanted to get his impression of the South, the real South, *his* South across to the reader and not some repetitious article on wainscoting and lamb's tongue molding which had just been covered by *This Old House* on television last week.

"Well, I do want moonlight and magnolias," Sagaser was now saying. "This is just some precocious kid who spews out a bunch of Latin names for plants and has two nut cases for parents! What kind of story is that? And none of our readers want to read about projectile vomiting." He slammed the magazine down on his desk and began ripping through the pages, curtly flipping them in disgust until he had located the passage he sought. His blunt, stupid fingers found it as he continued chastising Strekfus. "What is this bit about Buick? They're one of our advertisers for Christ's sake! Just wait until I get my hands on Karen. You'd think that she could handle one little assignment while I'm away," he said, and sank back down into his enormous leather chair, pushing the magazine toward Strekfus who was still standing in the middle of the office. "I want something about decorating and what these historic houses look like. I want a cake recipe for God's sake! Something about a garden party or barbecue! Is that so hard? And lighten up some. Geez, talk about your purple prose. Just write the story without all of the florid twists and turns."

Sagaser's head was now cradled in his hands. Hair-covered forearms stuck out of his starched white cotton shirt, the sleeves rolled up. A large gold watch was buried near the wrist.

He spoke without looking up this time, his voice directed at the calendar blotter. "All I am saying," he continued, but more slowly and with more restraint, "is that I wanted a story about a Southern home and a Southern garden, and I wanted one of these each month for the twelve issues of our magazine." He continued, measuring out his words as a principal of an elementary school might, hoping to get through to some detention-bound youth. "I thought you could handle an assignment as simple as this, but I guess you can't. I didn't expect . . . well," and at this point he looked up at Strekfus with the face one reserves for fast-food employees who've forgotten the fries or given you Diet Coke instead of regular, "this." And then one of his sudden outbursts with even more fervor: "Jesus, Jesus, Jesus, Jesus!" he repeated as he slammed his fist down onto the desk.

"Look, Winney," Strekfus said, "I've worked for this magazine for four years now and there haven't been any complaints about my work from any of our readers. And don't blame Karen. If you didn't want her to be in charge while you were out, you should've picked somebody else. If you want the truth, I did everything but threaten her. Not a word of that story was changed and for good reason: I know what I'm doing."

The two men looked at each other for a long time. Strekfus knew what was coming. Sagaser did this to him all the time—the intimidation factor. It made his flesh crawl. And there was another thing: Sagaser looked just like his father when he did this, even though he was only ten years older than Strekfus. Sagaser had that same pompous, egotistical air that his father had possessed. Both men were heavy-set. Both men were completely paranoid and both men could be mean-spirited. Only Strekfus's father was dead—had been for many years now. That wasn't to say that he wasn't still a powerful individual, that he didn't still have his opinions and quirks. Just because he was dead didn't mean he wasn't still a part of Strekfus's life. After all, some people are much more powerful dead than alive. Finally, Strekfus couldn't stand it anymore.

"And don't try the intimidation thing on me. It's not going to work." While Strekfus waited for the steam to stop coming from Sagaser's ears, he looked out the window over his boss's shoulder. Glittering gray and blue skyscrapers crowded each other for space in midtown Manhattan. Shafts of steel and glass jockeyed for position among the older stone and brick structures, their one-time festive turn-of-the century (the previous one) airs lost among the newer, more sterile, vertical boxes. Strekfus loved Manhattan, but he was still a Southerner at heart, and this last trip back home had proven it. Sagaser was somewhat calmer now, so Strekfus sat down opposite him and started to try to reach the man. But Sagaser was speaking again.

"I don't know," he began more slowly, and Strekfus sensed that something ominous was coming, "maybe you should be working on a different magazine, for one of those other companies across town. There's *McCall's*, and *Elle Décor*."

"I need to explain something to you," Strekfus began, trying to ignore Sagaser's look of condescension and his last remark. He knew the man could be his friend one minute and his boss the next, and that it was sometimes difficult to tell what country he was in, but he had to try.

"Something happened to me when I went home. I had an experience. I took stock of my life. There's something I want to do, to write about, and I figured that I could combine the assignment with what it is I'm trying to accomplish. There are so many magazines out there dealing with homes and gardens, but they just deal with draperies or sofas or the time to plant tulip bulbs. Yes, I know that's what they're supposed to be about, but that's not really what a home or a garden is. What about the people in those homes? What about the *real* homes, the *real* gardens? Why does a garden have to be acres of cultivated peonies and marigolds? Why can't it be somebody's grandmother's rose bush or even just a cactus on a windowsill? Why do we have to limit ourselves to the same old way of thinking?"

Sagaser just stared at him. Then he lit up a cigarette and leaned back in his chair.

Strekfus knew the routine, the intimidation, the air of superiority. But this was usually reserved for others. He was rarely the object of his boss's abuse. He had seen others torn to shreds and he wanted no part of it. He knew he wasn't getting anywhere. "Look, I'll let you think about it," Strekfus said as he got up and prepared to go back to his office. "I'm not trying to get away with anything. I really feel strongly about what I'm writing."

But it was no use. Sagaser was now looking out the window at a small plane which was underlining some clouds next to the Woolworth Building, all the way downtown at the other end of the island. "And you know we're not supposed to smoke in our offices or even in the building," Strekfus added, hoping that he might lighten the mood or at least change the atmosphere somewhat.

Just before Strekfus exited the office, Sagaser turned to him with the puzzled expression of a small puppy, pausing for dramatic effect as if to turn the final knife in by questioning his choice of names for characters, and asked, "Mrs. Bunion?"

As Strekfus turned to go, he couldn't help but wonder at his boss. He was the son of a man who was head of probably the most prestigious book-publishing firm in the country. Stories had circulated for years about Sagaser and how he had landed not only his current job with the strings pulled by his father, but all the others preceding this one. Everyone knew that his older brother was the father's favorite, having made millions not only in publishing, but real estate and the stock market as well. And everyone knew that the father had set up his younger son in an attempt to keep him from being totally left out. Still, you would think this man, Edwin Sagaser, the younger brother, would have a little more intellect and compassion for writers at least by osmosis from having sat in a chair in the middle of one of the city's most prestigious home-and-garden magazines.

Strekfus tried at times to sympathize with his boss—the pain he must be experiencing at being the son who wasn't number one, the constant attempts to please his father, the feelings of inadequacy—but he could only spur his feelings so far for the man. Sagaser was constantly pushing Strekfus away in some manner and then pulling him back toward him with plummy assignments or company perks. At times he felt like a yo-yo. Deep down he really liked the man, but this moment wasn't one of those times.

A few days passed and the two men kept out of each other's way. Then just before the week ended, Sagaser called Strekfus into his office. As he again used one of his intimidation techniques (this one involved having Strekfus wait for up to ten minutes while he rummaged through piles of papers and folders looking for some incredibly important object which always turned out to be a piece of lint or paper clip), he breathed heavily through his nose and made a few small grunting noises. Finally, he found what he was looking for, and as he read it he addressed the younger writer.

"It seems," he started, firmly adjusting his glasses (another technique), "that we've had several letters and calls from readers about your story." Here he paused for dramatic effect and looked straight at Strekfus before continuing. Strekfus knew he was being played with, but he also knew that if he showed any fear, this man would eat him alive. "I'm very sorry to report," Sagaser went on, and here he started playing with a large paperweight, feigning such interest in the object that one would have thought it contained the veritable secret to the fountain of youth, "that your short story," and again he paused, knowing that the pain was excruciating to Strekfus, "was rather well received." He mumbled the last part of the sentence. It was clear to Strekfus that his boss had been told to report this—that he didn't agree with any of it. Then he held his hands up in front of his face in a prayer-like position and said through their meaty, hair-covered sides, "I have it from higher up that they want you to write another one. Just like the first." The effect of his voice trying to exit through his big, dumb paws was something like that of Darth Vader on a respirator.

Again he paused, hoping that Strekfus would disappear or the world would come to an end or anything would happen to allow him to save face in front of one of his employees. By this

70

time, Strekfus was aware that the intense pain now belonged to Sagaser and not himself. It was killing the man to admit that he'd been wrong about the story.

"It seems that certain individuals," Sagaser continued, and with this he rolled his eyes upward, indicating the higher management on floors above, "would like this to be an ongoing series, much as we discussed earlier about Southern homes, only now with this obvious twist. There will be an introductory paragraph in next month's issue explaining to the readers exactly what we're doing since I'm sure most of them will be completely confused by these ramblings and whatnot." Once again he began desperately to look through folders and papers. After a few minutes he glanced up at Strekfus with a look that said, "I can't believe you're still here." "That's all," said Sagaser, in a tone one reserves for impertinent three-year-olds, and he curtly dismissed him. But before Strekfus was all the way out the door Sagaser called him back.

"One more thing. I forgot. One of the interns quit and we need to get a story out on Jadite." Sagaser looked up at Strekfus, waiting for some sign of resistance. None came.

"That mint-green glassware from the '20s and '30s?"

"That would be the stuff. Look, I'm sorry to ask you this, but I need a write-up on it right away. You know, how it's coming back into style. All that good stuff."

"You're punishing me," said Strekfus, his arms crossed, finally coming to the realization that Sagaser was up to something. He meant what he said, but there was neither malice nor resentment in his voice. He was simply stating what he thought was a fact. He knew not to push too much as he had already achieved one victory today with the response to his first story.

"No. I'm not. Please," was all Sagaser said and looked up at him with huge puppy-dog eyes. Strekfus just smiled and walked away, nodding his head in agreement.

He sat in his office, trying to think about what Sagaser had said, but there seemed to be too many distractions: voices down the hall, the laughter of some secretary, a fight breaking out between one of the temps and someone in the credit department. He listened for a moment.

"It was sitting right there," the girl was saying, "and I know it was someone here who took it."

"No one took your stuffed animal," one of the secretaries was countering now. "Who would want the thing anyway? It looked like it was a hundred years old."

As he sat and fingered through the glossy pages of the magazine, his eye skimmed over the first published story, the one about the Keller home. He had given the reader the narrative, but there was something missing. It was as if he had been asked a question and had responded to it, but by leaving out certain facts, the impression he had given had been false. On the surface it was a story about a childhood experience. Underneath, there was a current of darkness which he knew would eventually catch up with him. He felt the need to rewrite the story, to tell how on this trip and even before he had tried so hard to gain his parents' approval and acceptance by showing them he could be creative, intelligent, inquisitive. Nothing he did seemed to please them, and so when he became locked inside the house, the thought of locking them out of his mind seemed only logical. No one seemed to know what to do with him as a child anyway, and his parents couldn't decide whether he was retarded or overly intelligent. It seemed to him that no one, including his boss, could decide where he belonged. "Eisenhower was right," he thought, "things are more like they are now than they ever were before."

His mind was a wandering mess. He decided to get out of the office, take a walk around the block, get some air. As he made his way down the hall toward the elevators, he ran into Joe, the custodian for the floor. Joe was a rather well-built Puerto Rican man, about fifty years old, with deep-set eyes and a nervous tic which jerked his head about at the most unlikely moments. When he smiled, he exposed a gleaming gold tooth which always seemed polished to perfection.

"I'd be careful of that last stall if I was you," Joe said, in the direction of the restroom door, his head jumping nervously at the word *stall*. Strekfus had decided to make a stop before leaving the building, knowing full well that Manhattan had fewer public restrooms per square foot than any other city in the United States. "That thing runs on an' on sometimes. I'm trying to get it fixed, but maintenance doesn't want to help me out."

Strekfus just nodded in his direction and continued through the squeaking metal door and into the lime-green-tiled men's room. He opted for one of the wall urinals, and as he stood there relieving himself, staring at the tiles just a few inches from his face, his thoughts wandered. A melody seemed to float into his head. He could make out a few notes of it, accompanied by the stream he was producing below. It seemed that he stood there for the longest time after having finished, trying to make out the music, but it was as though he could recognize only fragments of it. He listened for a moment longer, but then someone was putting a key in the men's room door, turning the knob, and bringing him back to the present.

"Eisenhower and Kennedy," Strekfus said to himself as he washed his hands in the sink. Then he was out the door and heading toward the elevators which would deposit him down to ground level.

- 4 -

101 Enolam Boulevard

Infanta, Alabama, 1963

> Everything that I saw people do I insisted
> on imitating.
>
> —Helen Keller, *The Story of My Life*

The house in which I spent the majority of my childhood was not what you would call typically Southern. In fact, many years later I found out that it was simply American, and this could well be another metaphor for life in the South—the fact that at this time, the 1960s—the world was already moving toward a type of globalization well before the advent of computers and the Internet. There were remnants of the Old South still to be found in 1963, and some remain, but many of these attributes and notions today are slowly being replaced by an over-sharing of information which has left little to the imagination. At least the actual land in the South is still there, even if it is now covered by sprawling strip malls and huge chain stores.

Our house was physically located in Alabama, an area which at one time had been its own country, metaphorically speaking. In the early 1960s, ideas and values which seemed to permeate America found their way into our region, mostly through television. Sometimes the ideas blended in. Sometimes they didn't. At times it was as though we were watching America through the camera lens, with coverage of presidential campaigns and bombings in Southeast Asia. Then the next minute the world was watching the South as blacks marched and whites fought them. In between all this we watched shows such as *My Favorite Martian*, *Amos and Andy*, and reruns of movies like *Mildred Pierce*.

So it was a mélange of racism, sitcom television, and old movies that I grew up with, for in 1963, TV was everything, bringing us not only Birmingham, but Julia Child, *I Love Lucy*, and Bette Davis as she puffed and twitched her way through movies like *All About Eve* and *Now, Voyager*.

But there were a few shows which I couldn't bear to watch because they seemed too close to home and didn't afford me the fantasy life I so desperately sought. One was the *The Honeymooners* with Jackie Gleason—my father's favorite. The reason for this partiality was undoubtedly because of his resemblance to the man in every aspect (weight, looks, personality) except for the fact that Jackie Gleason played a bus driver and my father played chief obstetrician in the hospital of the small town we lived in. Each night the show was on, Paris Beltzenschmidt would gleefully sit glued to the set, never realizing (or maybe he did) that he was seeing himself.

My mother, on the other hand, loved to watch *The Dick Van Dyke Show*, fancying herself to be Laura Petrie, who was played by Mary Tyler Moore. What I found most interesting about my parents' choice of television shows was that while my father virtually *was* Jackie Gleason, complete with anger and threats of physical abuse, my mother was anyone but Mary Tyler Moore. Where the character of Laura Petrie was svelte and coiffed, my mother was overweight and badly put together. My mother was fond of having her hair teased to a height of two feet (think pink bow in the center) and plucking every single eyebrow out of her head. This last chore I couldn't understand, since she would sit at her vanity table, painfully pulling each hair out, only to redraw her eyebrows again using one thin line of black which created a sinister arch above each wide green eye, the whole time her mouth stretched open like some sinister tunnel of love at a decadent amusement park. The end result was something like a Diane Arbus photograph. Where Laura Petrie had a sense of humor, my mother had none. Laura Petrie tastefully decorated her house—my mother thought lime green and puce went together. Laura Petrie loved her son, Ritchie—my mother . . . well, you get the picture.

And I blame TV partially for contributing to my problems with my parents. After the great lockup in Tuscumbia, when I retreated into a make-believe land, television became fodder for just about everything, and given the fact that we lived in the very middle of suburbia, this sixteen-inch square screen became my lifeline to the outside world. Also, because my parents either resembled too closely a television character or seemed to be the antithesis of one, I came to rely on this complex of cathode rays and celluloid as a way of dealing with boredom and anxiety.

Another reason for my escape from reality was the fact that I considered the area we lived in to be one step above a waste dump. Our house was one of those ugly concrete-slab suburban shoeboxes just right for starting a dysfunctional American family. When it was first built there were no trees or shrubs surrounding the house, as is evidently de rigueur for neighborhood designers. They feel they must pull up every living thing in order to build a house. The result is often a sterile flat landscape that does little to soften these residences, many of which look exactly the same. Seen from an airplane, these neighborhoods give the impression of orderliness and conformity—rather deceptive when you consider what really goes on in places such as this.

I've witnessed hundreds of middle-class neighbors all over America swear to a camera lens that their neighbor was a quiet, kind man who loved children and helped the elderly, while in the background a coroner pulls sixteen bodies from under that good neighbor's home. Child molesters, serial killers, and cannibals seem to love the cookie-cutter houses, well-manicured lawns, and plastic nativity scenes which spring up at Christmas time in the suburbs. Why America has never made the connection between tract housing and psychosis is beyond me, and it wasn't just the repulsive nature the outside of these houses possessed, but their interiors as well, which could also represent various forms of mental unbalance.

In a way, I guess you could say that I thought my parents were insane. They had odd ideas about money and style, the most obvious example I can think of being our living room sofa. This thing was a monstrous, dowdy piece of furniture which had been in our home for as long as I could remember. One day my parents decided that it should be recovered and sent it out for what I deemed a "sofa vacation." Four weeks later it arrived back home covered in the most hideous material known to mankind. When I questioned my parents about their choice of fabric, they told me that it was the most expensive material made, but that they had purposely picked an unattractive color so as to appear that they weren't pretentious.

While *they* knew that they had spent an exorbitant amount of money on this sofa, anyone else would look at it and think it had been just a modest expenditure. My parents never wanted to appear pretentious, yet at the same time they wanted the best and didn't want people in town to think we weren't well off. They knew that Infanta was a small town and that within a week everyone would know how much money they had spent on this behemoth that sat six.

The décor inside the houses in my neighborhood was in keeping with the grim outside environs most of the time, and while I don't know of any others in our neighborhood playing the complicated games my parents did with upholstery, I'm sure they had their own problems when it came to fabric and style. Occasionally one could find a few antiques or tastefully decorated dining alcoves, but for the most part it was strictly Sears Roebuck with a smattering of bargain basement thrown in. If it wasn't green-and-white brocade-covered French provincial with custom-made plastic see-through slipcovers, then it was Mediterranean with harvest gold or avocado green shag carpeting. Our house was a little of both, with minor color adjustments, and so it was with the aesthetics of our home that I became obsessed. I blame shows such as *The Dick Van Dyke Show* and *Hazel* for at least the first incident which was to bring me to a climactic revelation in 1963.

While *The Dick Van Dyke Show* boasted a modern house (not my taste), at least it was artistically put together, save for the ottoman that appeared each week in the middle of the floor so that Mr. Van Dyke could trip over it for comic effect. But the show *Hazel,* starring Shirley Booth, came complete with its own built-in interior decorator—Dorothy Baxter.

While this woman was a bitch on wheels, she did possess impeccable taste in furniture and textiles. The premise of the show was this: George Baxter, or "Mr. B" as the maid called him, and his lovely interior-decorating wife were supposed to be the smart ones in the house, while Hazel was the somewhat bumbling and not very bright housekeeper. The truth was that Hazel was much smarter than either of the wealthy and snobbish people who employed her. It was Hazel that I warmed to, but it was Dorothy Baxter that I emulated, and this led to one in a series of traumatic incidents which took place during those formative and tender years one calls childhood.

It was the summer of '63, June to be exact, and my parents were furious. While this was not an uncommon emotion for them, on this particular occasion they exhibited their feelings with unrestrained relish. They had come home from an evening of dining and dancing at the only country club in the small town we lived in to find the interior of our house completely rearranged. The sofa was moved out into the middle of the floor, some of the chairs were missing, and many of the shades on the lamps had either been changed or decorated with pieces of fabric from my mother's sewing box. The draperies had been tied back with two of my mother's belts which belonged to her best Sunday dresses.

"What happened?" exclaimed my father as he opened the front door. "Who's been here? Where's Nyla?"

My mother's jaw had dropped open when she entered the house and was now still in that position. Accompanying her jaw was the release of her purse and all its contents. Her compact mirror shattered and a small cloud of pink dust rose rather ominously from the parquet wood floors. She stood behind my father and let him do all the talking.

"I sent Nyla home," I explained, trying to act as casually as I could. Nyla was the baby-sitter who sat for me after our housekeeper Althea went home for the day. Her services were employed only if my parents planned an evening out. At Althea's appointed time to leave, Nyla would show up, but the changing of the guard would not be complete until Althea had pointed out where the latest bag of candy or cookies was and how many flavors of ice cream my mother had purchased on her last grocery run. Nyla gained what I estimated to be about forty pounds a day and was rarely seen without some form of frozen dairy product or pure sugar confection in her hand. Usually she preferred dairy to sugar, and if it wasn't an ice cream sandwich, it was some melting, pastel-colored, towering form precariously balanced atop a rather feebly constructed sugar cone. In the event of a real emergency, an RC Cola and a Moon Pie would do.

"You did what!" screamed my father, moving toward the closet to hang up his coat. "Did Nyla do this?" he went on, "because if she did, I'm going to call the agency and give them a piece of my mind."

"I did it," I explained. "Nyla wouldn't have the good taste to put chintz next to sisal."

"What? *You* did this? But how? Where is all the furniture? Why is the sofa in the middle of the room?"

"You can't put a sofa against the wall," I coolly explained, "it just *dies*."

"What!"

"It just *dies*," I reiterated.

By this time my father had made it to the closet and was reaching for the knob. "Where are all the chairs?" he continued. In a moment he got at least part of his answer, because when he opened the door, the side chair that usually occupied the corner of the room nearest the picture window fell out and narrowly missed his foot. I got "The Look."

"This is crazy," my mother chimed in, speaking for the first time as she was apt to do after determining the situation was safe to enter verbally. "You mean to tell us you moved all of this furniture?"

"Of course," I replied. "Nyla wouldn't agree to help me, so I sent her home."

"But you're seven years old!" my mother continued. "What's a seven-year-old doing rearranging the living room?"

"I didn't just rearrange the living room," I said rolling my eyes, "I did the whole house. And, Mother, it's called *decorating*. Really, I know what I'm doing. I've been watching *Hazel*. Dorothy Baxter is an interior decorator on the show and you should see their house. Personally, I'm not crazy about Shirley Booth's portrayal of the maid, but then . . ."

"Dorothy Baxter? Who is . . ."

"She's the wife. I think she abuses the maid." This was true. I thought the wife's performance was *terribly* abusive, but then what did I know? My father was now struggling to reinstate a side chair in the space it had occupied before he and my mother had gone out.

"You can't put that there!" I screamed, "you've got two chairs next to each other with no table in between, and besides, it's covered in velveteen. It's not even real velvet!"

"Shut up!" my father yelled. "Hattie, come help me put the sofa back and grab that lamp. Where's the coffee table?"

"The coffee table is in the den serving as a plant and TV stand," I continued. "Besides, I've never even seen anyone drink coffee from the top of it. We don't even *serve* coffee in the living room."

"You just wait, young man," my mother interjected, "you're going to be grounded for a week."

"Good," I said, thinking that I hadn't really spent enough time on my parents' bedroom and the guest bathroom. "I can stay inside and decorate."

"Just for that you're going out and play baseball with the neighbors' kids," she shot back.

"No, not that!" I screamed. "At least let me play *inside* with them so I can see what Mrs. Handershaw has done to her dining room. She's got new wallpaper and a lazy Susan!"

"I'm going to lazy your Susan in about five seconds," my father quipped, and started in my direction. Unfortunately, my mother had not yet picked up the contents of her purse and my father, being in a hurry, stepped on an enormous tube of lipstick (Midnight Fawn—we've been through this already) and went flying across the room.

Totally caught up in the fact that they were destroying my life's work, I screamed in my mother's direction as she began to pick up objects and move them about. "That lamp is Mediterranean. You can't use that in here," I shrieked, causing her to jump at least two feet off the ground.

"You go to your room," my father said, addressing the ceiling while flat on his back, "and don't come out until I say so." Then he managed to stand, and while holding his back and limping over to the side of the room where I had stored the rug, hoping no one would see it, he glanced in my direction as he addressed my mother.

"Hattie, help me get this rug back down on the floor," he continued as he once again regained his full height. "There's something wrong with that boy," I heard him say as I slouched off to my room.

A few weeks later, after the decorating incident and while Althea had the week off, I decided that I would try to emulate another character I had seen on television: Julia Child. This woman had begun airing her show on February 11, 1963, and I had occasionally watched her in the company of my mother. My mother could be said to be guilty of many things, but being a bad cook wasn't one. Cold potato salads, fresh string beans, cakes, chocolate pies, and chicken fried to perfection were just some of her talents. I have to say that the one thing I remember most about my mother was the fact that she was an excellent food provider. She was so meticulous about my father's meals that she would sometimes prepare them separately, even adding additional spices and ingredients so that he was sure to enjoy them. So it

81

shouldn't have come as a surprise to her when I tried my hand, at the tender age of seven, at cooking.

I decided to make a cake.

Now, the act of making a cake, in itself, is probably not that strange, but the way in which I decided to make it was a little unusual. Well, not for me, I suppose.

Coming to the realization that this would be my first attempt at food preparation, I decided to dress for the occasion. My mother, being extremely fond of clothes and accessories, had about four thousand pairs of shoes in her closet. Her favorite was a pair of red taffeta high heels, so I set my sights on the ruby slippers and trooped off to find them.

After about three hours of turning the house upside down, ("Strekfus? . . . Strekfus! What are you doing in there? . . . You'd better not be in my closet." "I'm not, Mother," I replied, even though I was), I found them. I knew before I even tried them on that they would be too big, so I stuffed the toes with newspaper and put Scotch tape over the tops to hold them on. Although I wasn't crazy about the Scotch tape, when you're seven you deal with life's difficulties as best you can. Besides, I didn't plan to wear them more than once. My mother never did, so why should I? Julia Child always seemed to be well put together, so I felt the more authentic I looked, the better.

The shoes fit perfectly after all the modifications were in place. It was then that I got the idea to try them out as dancing shoes. Not just any dancing shoes, but flamenco dancing shoes. I gave this some thought and decided that in order to carry this off with panache I would have to try them out on the newly refinished parquet floors of my bedroom. The sound they made didn't satisfy me, so I decided to lay several strips of gunpowder caps from my cap gun onto the floor and hammer away at them with the heels of the shoes.

Because the shoes fit loosely even with the newspaper, it was necessary for me to assault the caps with even more force than normal. As the caps exploded under my feet they burned tiny holes into the new finish of the floor and gave off the smell of burning lacquer.

"Strekfuuuuuuus!" bellowed my mother from the next room, "what are you doing in there?"

"Nothing," I responded. "I'm just hammering some nails into wood. Don't come in here, whatever you do. I'm making a gift for you."

It was at that point that I decided that the shoes just did not go with the flannel shirt and jeans I had on, so I began to flip through my mother's dresses. ("Strekfuuuuuuus! . . . Strekfuuuuuuus! What are you doing? You'd better not be in any of my things! Get in here where I can see you!")

Finally, I found it—my mother's favorite red silk dress. Of course it was a short dress on her, that being the style in the early '60s, but a very long one on me. In fact, it was perfect evening gown length. Being an Edith Head fan at an early age, I didn't really care for the current fashion trends. I much preferred the big-time musicals of the '40s and '50s, and this dress would be perfect to re-create the scenes I had witnessed featuring Fred Astaire, Ginger Rogers, and Judy Garland.

Anyone who has some fashion sense will tell you that a red dress and red shoes just cry out for an addition, and since too much of something becomes the opposite, I began to search my mother's vanity for the appropriate accessory. Something subtle, but not too plain. Something expensive. Something my mother held dear and would probably strangle me for touching.

Like a strand of real pearls.

Like the ones my father bought her for her thirtieth birthday.

The ensemble complete, I decided that I was ready to tackle baking. Ordinarily this wouldn't have been difficult, but because I had to balance on a kitchen stool wearing high heels and an evening dress, I found the task extremely arduous. I had made it past the den where my mother was watching the soaps and eating bonbons. Since she tried not to look at me any more than necessary, she made no attempt to pry herself from the recliner she had ensconced herself in.

"You'd better not be getting into anything," she screeched at me, never taking her eyes off the television and punctuating her comment with a huge expulsion of gas. Its rubbery notes vibrated the cheap springs inside the recliner. I tried to ignore her as best I could, which I found was the only way to get through the day. I was now in the kitchen and ready to begin.

Having procured all the ingredients that I needed before I climbed up on the stool, was in my opinion very industrious, and I proceeded with the utmost confidence that this would be a culinary success.

I had decided to make a red velvet cake (because it went with the outfit), so I rounded up several bottles of red food coloring from the cabinet above the stove to assure success in color coordination. My mother frequently made this cake and I was determined to outdo her at my first attempt. Filling the mixing bowl with the food coloring, the boxed cake mix, and twelve eggs, I proceeded as if I were the head chef at Delmonico's. The problems started when I turned the mixer on.

As I stood on top of the stool, delicately balancing in high heels, I tried out my best imitation of Julia Child: "And-uh here we are at the mix-ah. Now, you might choose to uuuuuuse just a (out of breath here) simple, let me see, oh dear . . . I must have . . . well, now then . . ."

Not being knowledgeable about mixer speeds (this was my first time—I couldn't know everything), I turned the machine on high. This was mistake number one. This powerful mixer, a Hamilton Beach deluxe model with a horrible green Jadite bowl—that color which always reminds me of dentists' and doctors' offices—was not my friend. Again, I lapsed into my best Julia Child impersonation.

"And-uh now we're going to . . . just . . . and we turn the mix-ah on high because you want to (pant, pant) . . ."

Mistake number two was rooted in the fact that I had not secured the bowl onto the mixer plate. When the beaters started rotating, they spun the bowl around so fast that they wedged it against the body of the kitchen appliance at the most unsightly angle, and the beaters themselves, which were spinning at a furious rate, began slinging red-colored cake mix in every direction.

Finally, mistake number three involved the fact that I was standing directly in front of the mixer when mistakes numbers one and two took place. The good news, if there can be said to be any in a story such as this, was that I was wearing matching colors.

The sound of a mixing bowl full of red velvet cake mix slinging its contents onto a newly remodeled kitchen has a very distinctive sound. Trust me, if you hear it you'll never forget it. I had tried to dislodge the mixing bowl from the mixer, but being covered with eggs, flour, and red food coloring, the process proved somewhat more difficult than expected.

Obviously my mother was more familiar with the sound than I had given her credit for, because she came flying into the kitchen, wild eyed, and showing more than a trace of chocolate smears around the corners of her now curled-up mouth.

"What the hell are you doing!" she screamed, and simultaneously passed a huge amount of gas which reverberated in the newly decorated kitchen. Both sounds were her normal mode of communicating in even the most serene of moments.

"Can you scream a little lou-der?" I asked, never breaking character. "I can't heeeear you over the mix-ah," which was now picking up speed and throwing the beaters violently against the sides of the Jadite mixing bowl (whackety-whackety-whackety). The majority of the cake mix having been slung onto the newly painted cabinets (beveled edges, stenciled ivy motif), there was little left in the bowl.

Seeing what she was wearing, I continued, "You re-ally shouldn't wear green hound's-tooth check stretch pants with white socks and black shoes, Mother. It's ve-ery unflattering," the whole time oblivious to the fact that the mixer plate was still spinning at an abnormally high rate and still slinging what was left of the red cake mix everywhere.

"What are you wearing!" she shrieked, lunging for the mixer, aiming for the "off" switch. But she missed and the entire mixer, bowl, and contents went hurtling toward the floor. Since the electrical cord was extra long, the minute the mixer and the whirling blades struck the ugly linoleum it began doing circles at such a fast rate that it resembled one of the Three Stooges.

"People who live in glass houses really shouldn't . . ." but I didn't get to finish. She jerked me off the kitchen stool before I knew what was happening.

"I'm going to wear you out!" And then the dreaded sound of her passing gas—"Brrrrrrrrapppppp!" her sphincter exclaimed. "Are those my good pearls?" she shrieked, jerking my arm upward with each word. But then she suddenly stopped when she heard an all-too-familiar sound coming from the other end of the kitchen toward the back door. Her head jerked around like Norma Desmond's in *Sunset Boulevard*.

You see, we had a washer and dryer in the utility room just off the kitchen. Normally Althea did the laundry, but she had been away visiting her sister in Texas and my mother had decided to do a load of clothes herself. The fact that she even knew how to turn the appliance on was a shock to me.

Now this particular washer had a nasty habit of vibrating at an unusually fast rate, especially when you didn't evenly distribute the clothes in it before turning it on. Really, you can't blame *me*. I didn't remember this fact when, after my mother had loaded the machine, I came in behind her and slipped the blanket from my bed into the receptacle. Our poodle had decided to throw up on it the previous night, and I knew that if I told my parents they would banish the dog to the backyard, so I stuffed the blanket into the washer (of course being careful to make sure the drum had stopped turning completely) in the hope that I could retrieve it before my mother came back to get *her* part of the laundry. Unfortunately, it didn't work out that way.

The problem with the washer was this: When it vibrated, it did so at such a violent rate that it began to "walk" away from the wall. An off-balance load would cause the appliance to tilt to one side and then the other, until it was making its way across the utility room like an eighty-year-old arthritic ballroom dancer. Once before it had done this to such an extent that it pulled the pipes out through the wall covering and insulation, and began to dump three inches of water onto the utility room floor.

This particular day was going to be no different.

Momentarily my mother forgot that I was wearing her favorite evening dress and that the kitchen was completely covered in red food coloring. She bounced (rather unevenly, stepping over the mixer which had now wrapped itself up in the cord with the beaters turned upright like the whirling legs of some beetle trying to right itself) in the general direction of the washer.

When I finally made my way to the utility room, she was in a state of panic. Having thrown herself on top of the now-bouncing machine in an attempt to keep it from walking out the door, she was splayed out in starfish position. As the washer jerked across the floor, her legs dangled helplessly over the sides and her white-sock-clad ankles and black lace-ups kicked at the machine like a bronco rider's feet.

I had been standing there staring at her for a full minute before she saw me and turned her head in my direction. I can still see her grimacing, chocolate-smeared face as she screamed at the top of her lungs while her glasses proceeded to fly off, landing behind the water heater, and her head jerked back and forth like a teenager's at a rock concert. Unfortunately, because she had become so upset, the gastric juices began to flow and she began passing enormously loud volumes of methane through her lower intestine, the sound of which was so violent that it was in direct competition with the thump, thump, thump of the washer as it walked across the floor. The sound of this aural delight was a rather rubbery "Brrraaaap!" usually delivered in sequences of twos.

"Strekfus! . . . Strekfus! Don't look at me, Strekfus! . . . Stop looking at me, Strekfus Ovid Beltzenschmiiiiiidt! I'm trying to get this thingggggg to . . . (Brrrraaap! Brrrrrraaaap!)," and then the pipes pulled themselves from the wall and a fountain of bluish rinse water covered her, the whole time the washer never missing a beat.

"Stop looking at me, Strekfus! Strekfus! (Braaaap! Brrrrrraaaap!) Don't look at me!" she continued to screech after having made a complete trip from one side of the room to the other.

But all I could think of, standing there in a red evening dress and high heels at the tender age of seven, with my arms folded and one hip thrown out for dramatic effect, was how delicious this moment felt. I said to her, after a significant dramatic pause and rather dryly, still using the Julia Child voice, realizing that she couldn't actually hear me because the washer was now slamming itself against the water heater with the beat of a good rhythm-and-blues song, "You've got to be kidding. I wouldn't miss this for the woooorld."

* * * * *

"You gots to quit makin' problems for yo' parents! They gonna go and give you to the ASPCA or somethin'!" It was Althea, admonishing me after being told by my mother about the red velvet cake incident. She had come back from visiting her sister in Texas and was now scrubbing the kitchen walls to remove the remnants of red cake batter.

"But I'm just trying to do something that will make my parents see that I'm a person, that I have feelings, that I have some value as a human being," I said.

"I know, but you gots to quit play actin' and such. You need to grow up and be a big boy."

Whenever I had done something wrong or there had been some problem, Althea was either there or was told about it the next day. She could easily have written my life's story, so the fact that my mother had relayed the incident to her in detail came as no surprise. Evidently my mother thought Althea could have an influence over my life. She was wrong, at least for the time being.

I argued with Althea, but the truth was I loved her. She and I were best friends as far as I was concerned. Every morning when I woke up she was there, hard at work. My parents would already have left and Althea would by that time have done all the

88

laundry and cleaned the entire house with the exception of my room, and would be preparing to iron, cook, or whatever else my parents had thought up for her to do. Because she and I were so close, it brings to mind an incident which occurred around this time, an incident in which she took my side.

Having not only propensities for decorating, fashion, and cooking, as a small child I loved to put words together. My two favorite words were, "I" and "want," followed by just about anything. I employed this phrase as often as possible, usually in my parents' direction and with an air of authority. Needless to say, this did not endear me to them.

My tastes, however, were not too outlandish during the formative years of my life, at least not in my opinion, and were relegated mostly to stuffed animals. What I lacked in diversity, I made up for in quantity. At one point I was the proud owner of what I estimated to be over one hundred stuffed animals. Lest the reader think me frivolous, allow me to explain that I dearly loved and cared for each and every one of these creatures. Each one had a name, a career, and a very distinct personality. In addition, they would interact with one another, sometimes to the alarm of my parents and the guests they were having for dinner at the time. But there was a good reason for this collection of personalities—my parents never really let me have any friends. Oh, I would occasionally sneak around the neighborhood and play with the other children, but as soon as that was discovered, they put a stop to it, either by forbidding me to go out and play, or by telling the other children's parents that I had a contagious disease. I would often appear at a neighbor's door to be told, "Ken can't ever play with you again. And why are your parents letting you out of the house if you have cholera, anyway?" Because of this, I would often sit in front of the television with my assortment of animals and we would watch whatever was on. Even the news was enough to fuel my imagination.

"Senate hearings on Capitol Hill today focused on organized crime in Detroit," the TV would announce to the group of thirty gathered on various sofas, chairs, and ottomans. "One hundred fifty million dollars a year is said to have been earned by that city's mafia, and sixty-three people have been named in connection with the raid." It was probably flashes of news like this one (together with a documentary on World War II in Italy) that led to yet another unfortunate incident involving my creative abilities and animal friends, which in turn led to Althea taking up for me.

One of my favorite stuffed animals was a large moose named "Benito Mussolini," so called because he was the head of a small Italian stuffed animal crime family (in my mind) which was vying for the political limelight. My chief mistake was relating this information to my father, who promptly removed the moose and placed him in the garbage can, but not before I managed to pull the eyes off him (the moose) for what I claimed at the time was a career change on his part. My father, being suspicious of my nationalistic and political tendencies, opted to replace the quadruped with a rather well-worn and mottled stuffed dog which played Brahms' "Lullaby." Since the dog didn't appear to be planning a career change any time soon and my father was totally unmusical, I guess he (my father) figured the dog was safe.

I would have forgotten about Benito Mussolini quickly enough, except for the fact that Althea had to be taken to the hospital for chest pains after opening the lid of the garbage can in the alley and having a three-foot tall moose pop up in her face.

"Child, that moose near scared me to death! I opened up that lid and *whump!* he jumps out and scares me so bad I thinks I'm gonna faint! Yo' mamma had to drive me over to the hospital! I asks your mamma, 'Why you want to throw that boy's animals away?' and she tells me to mind my own business. Sho do. Sho do."

At any rate, I managed to accumulate a large number of other stuffed animals, and while I tried not to divulge their career ambitions or personalities to the grown-ups, I did have a rich fantasy life with them. Not being allowed playmates in the neighborhood most of the time for one reason or another, I found that stuffed animals were generally more interesting and caused less problems than real animals or people. Unfortunately, I've found that this remains true even today.

All of this would have been fine if my parents had not overheard Mr. Drithers, the dog, admonish Sister Louise Fru Fru (a large purple frog) for her necrophilia fetish. What seemed like a perfectly ordinary conversation to me evidently didn't endear Mr. Drithers or Sister Fru Fru to my parents, and the next day I was given a warning that said, "No more stories and no more careers for the animals."

So that my parents wouldn't overhear the conversations, I took to having the animals send letters to each other. This was not the brightest idea, but then I was only seven years old and I couldn't be expected to think of the infinite possibilities that accompanied animal interaction. It seems that the rather, uh, how shall I say, "vibrant" letters from the camel to the rabbit concerning her moose husband (her fourth and now missing) caused the greatest upset in our household, and when I was confronted with them (the letters), I was ordered to read them out loud as part of my punishment while my mother and father towered over me in the classical hands-on-the-hips position which parents are known to assume on occasions such as these. I'll quote one of the letters for you here, so the reader can see that I really wasn't doing anything wrong. I still have these letters in my possession. How I got them is a story I will explain later. Here's a sample:

Mr. Nuclear Scientist Rabbit
Hole in the Ground Way
Strekfus's Bedroom

My dear Mr. Rabbit,

Finally I can tell you. What a terrible time this has been for me. Benito has been missing now for over two weeks and I fear the worst. It seems he was caught making a cake while wearing a red evening gown at moose mafia headquarters. I guess they also knew of his planned career change, because they attempted to blind him so that he

91

couldn't see where he was being taken. Being the small-minded animals that the moose mafia are, they tied him up, and he was made to watch soap operas while eating bonbons. In addition, the other moose found it necessary to "pass gas" around him continuously while singing some of the worst hymns known to mankind. Lastly, they tortured him by rearranging the furniture and not color coordinating everything. His mind reeling, he finally gave up all resistance and hid in a large garbage can in back of headquarters. It was his plan to be collected by the garbage men and escape to Egypt where he could be united with me and the children. I'm praying to God (and Allah) that he is delivered safely.

Yours truly,

Felicia Frasquita Imperatore Gambino Mussolini—Camel

My parents didn't say anything after I finished reading. They just snatched the letter away from me and left the room in a huff. When I awoke the next day, not only were the Nun Frog, Dog Banker, Rabbit, and Camel gone, but so were the ninety-six other animals, each one with a special place in my life that I had created for them. I sat for hours, alone now, in front of the TV trying to forget each one of those individuals I had so lovingly helped to bring to life, feeling as though someone had reached down into my throat and pulled out my heart. It was only after viewing a documentary on the Jewish Holocaust that I was able to imagine that my menagerie had been taken prisoner by the Nazis and might possibly still be alive in Dachau or Auschwitz. At least this way there was still hope. I imagined them doing work detail to avoid the gas chamber. And I couldn't help thinking that Sister Fru Fru was ministering comfort to the trainloads of Jewish refugees despite her excommunication from the church for heroin possession.

While I thought of this, I could hear Althea arguing with my mother in the garage. "Why you want to keep givin' that child's toys away? He's just a boy. He needs to be havin' things to play with. I know at some point he gots to grow up, but he's still jus' a child right now."

I found this conversation interesting since Althea had admonished me a short while earlier in my brief youth, claiming that I needed to grow up. Being curious, I crept toward the garage to see what was happening.

"I didn't have anything to play with," responded my mother curtly as she pursed her lips and gave the twist tie on the garbage bag a quick and angry wrench, "and besides, this isn't any of your business." With that she tied up one of the remaining garbage bags of animals and proceeded to take them out back to the trash-bin area. Althea just stood there shaking her head with her hands on her hips.

"Just ain't right, the way they treats that boy," Althea muttered to herself.

When my mother came back into the garage for another bag of animals, Althea pleaded with her, "At least let him keep that rabbit. He *loves* that little rabbit."

My mother acquiesced, but not without severely admonishing Althea and making it clear that the rabbit was all I would be keeping. Unbeknownst to my parents, Althea had bought me this small rabbit and given it to me as a gift— something black housekeepers weren't supposed to do for a white child living in Alabama in the 1960s. The rabbit had accompanied me that day to the Keller home when I had experienced Helen's house first hand.

I suppose with the high volume of stuffed animals I had they couldn't remember whether they had bought it for me or not. I had managed to pull its whiskers out, and its fur was worn almost completely away, but I held it in high esteem nonetheless. After all, the rabbit was a scientist working with radioactive isotopes. Who would want to throw *that* away? When Althea turned, my mother tossed the poor nuclear scientist into the last bag, looking me in the eye defiantly as I stood in the doorway as

93

if to say, "Not one word." Then she tied the bag shut. Needless to say, I wasn't too fond of my mother after this, but the relationship with my father was even worse. I'm sure they both had the best intentions in mind for me and that they showed their love in the best way they knew how. Still, I didn't understand them any better than they understood me.

Whereas my mother could be emotionally difficult, my father was a firm believer in strict discipline. He could actually be a nice person from time to time, but his performance as a nurturing parent was uneven, and given the inclination to speak my mind, we were constantly at odds with each other. Of course, there were extenuating factors at the time, unbeknownst to me, that fueled the fire, and because I only had one side of the story—mine—it wasn't until years later that I figured out exactly what went wrong. It was basically this: My father had been the late child of a controlling and extremely old-fashioned man, and a mother who evidently was never wrong. This, accompanied by the fact that my father was genetically disposed to being unhappy did not make for a very good combination. Add to this the fact that he made a mistake marrying my mother, and that when he had decided to divorce her she became pregnant with me in order to save the marriage, and you've got one mirthless person. Throw in a smart-mouthed child (uh . . . that would be me) and you have a particularly bad combination.

Of course, I wasn't born this way. I had to learn survival techniques to get by in the world, and most of the ones I learned as a child didn't work in adulthood, even though I kept putting them into practice. But when you've been working at perfecting a technique for some forty years it's hard to switch gears.

Anyway, these two mismatched people, my parents, decided to buy a small suburban house on Enolam Boulevard in Infanta, Alabama—a house, you might have already guessed, that was badly in need of redecoration. You should also know that all the houses in the neighborhood were built on an ancient Indian burial ground.

You do the math.

It was obvious to me that the place was swimming in bad karma when we moved in, but my parents had their own problems and seemed oblivious to it.

While the neighborhood where this house was located started off "tree free," after a few years most people had verdant yards and gardens, our house being no exception. I remember pressing my father with little success to install a small goldfish pond in our backyard. It seems that he had some aversion to standing water (at least that's what he said), his explanation being a fear of the mosquito population which is so abundant in the South. But goldfish pond or not, at one point cedars, oleanders, and evergreens flourished and provided hideouts for my sometime friends and me while playing army or some other game that was socially acceptable at the time. This, of course, was done under utmost secrecy as my parents didn't approve of any activities that might have allowed me to exercise my social skills. The one place we didn't hide, however, was a large thorn bush on the south side of the house—a bush which was part of the original landscaping plan.

Because of the mild winters and humid summers, the flora around our yard flourished and some of it attained gigantic proportions. The thorn bush was no exception. It was unusual in the fact that although it was huge, absolutely nothing grew from the center of it. All the branches grew outward and then upward, creating a barrel-like structure of thorns. Anything that happened to be tossed into the center of the bush was gone. For good.

Of course in order to torture me, as older kids in a neighborhood were apt to do, they would throw some of my favorite belongings into the center of this bush, knowing full well that I would never see them again. They also knew that I couldn't complain to my parents about their behavior as this might incriminate me. I appropriately named the bush "Cleopatra," having just seen the movie with Elizabeth Taylor and Richard Burton, deciding that Cleopatra had emotionally consumed everything in her path. I had originally decided to call my mother this name behind her back, but one day while placing a bogus order on the phone to the Green Frog, a take-out diner on the

95

wrong side of the tracks which specialized in soul food, I had used this name along with a lengthy description of my mother (I thought it lent an air of believability to the process), and unbeknownst to me, she was standing directly behind me for the entire conversation. So the thorn bush got the name, although at the time I thought both of them had about the same disposition.

At any rate, we had seen *Cleopatra* at the Rutline drive-in, a rather run-down necking mecca for teenagers with raging hormones, and at the moment Cleopatra made one of her entrances—unrolled out of an oriental rug—I let out a shriek that turned every head at the drive-in. Lips unlocked and panties were pulled up for five miles around.

"What the hell was that for?" my father yelled.

"I'm going as Cleopatra next Halloween," I said, "and make my entrance rolled up in a rug."

"You're only a child!" my father snarled.

"So," I said."

"Whap." His hand came into the backseat and found the back of my head instantly. "No son of mine is going as Cleopatra. What the hell are you thinking?" he went on. "We have to live in this town and so will you someday."

"Fine," I said, and proceeded to sulk. I knew I would find a way to achieve my goal, and in fact I spent the next week trying to bribe the fifteen-year-old boy who lived next door to wear a loincloth and carry me rolled inside a rug (albeit a sculpted avocado-green pile one) into the living room where my mother was having her monthly neighborhood tea. Halloween was too far away and I couldn't wait.

Needless to say, the blessed event didn't come to fruition the way I had planned. Bobby (that would be the fifteen-year-old with loincloth) made his entrance rather clumsily through the backdoor (it was to be a surprise), knocking out the glass upper portion of the door, and entered bleeding on the living room carpet.

Twelve pants-suited, newly coiffed and bejeweled ladies sat, knees together, teacups poised midair, and open-mouthed as I was unrolled into the northernmost leg of the coffee table wearing one of my mother's see-through chiffon blouses around my waist and far too much eye makeup for a child of seven. In addition, I had dyed an old mop with shoe polish, using this creation as a wig. But I had been rather unsuccessful in attempting to cut the bangs Egyptian style and the effect was something like Louise Brooks undergoing chemotherapy. My mother, who had risen up halfway as soon as she heard the glass breaking in the kitchen, was still in this position when I was unfurled. She was frozen in space with mouth and eyes wide open.

The ladies were speechless, which in the naiveté of youth I interpreted as a good thing. I soon learned otherwise. Before I knew what was happening, my mother grabbed Bobby and me by the upper arm (a popular mode of transporting children all over the world) and threw us into the backyard like the contents of a week-old chamber pot. Because most of the backdoor glass was now missing I could plainly hear her make excuses to the ladies as they resumed their tea.

"Strekfus hasn't been feeling too well lately. Ever since he got locked in the Keller home he's been acting strangely. We thought we'd never get him out, poor thing," said my mother as she resumed her position among middle society of Infanta, Alabama. After the ladies left I was once again admonished for having tried to form some sort of relationship with the neighborhood children, the whole time my mother never mentioning my attire and the fact that the rug from the guest bedroom was missing.

So in homage to this Egyptian queen I named the bush in the backyard "Cleo." Years later when my mother decided to have every tree, shrub, and flower pulled up out of the yard because my father had refused her a new waffle iron, I came home to find Cleopatra gone and the remnants of my childhood, in what had been her hollow center (the bush, not my mother), left lying sadly on the ground.

There was a G.I. Joe doll, several cans of root beer, an obscene drawing, Mardi Gras beads, a deflated miniature football, and assorted small metal cars with most of their metallic paint worn away. I shudder to think what the bush would have contained if it had made it through my high school years, having developed at the time a proclivity for condoms and *Playboy* magazines.

Once, a few years later, when returning from France on a month-long tour with our church group, my suitcase was turned upside-down at Charles De Gaulle airport in an effort to catch some would-be terrorist. While having one's well-worn underwear splayed out for all the churchgoing world to see would have been embarrassing enough, the fact that I had managed to collect over two thousand condoms, some with very good reproductions of famous works of art on them, didn't escape the pastor of our church who was directly behind me in line, and made this one of the more difficult situations to extricate myself from. I mistakenly thought I could relieve some of his stress (the face muscles give so much away) by taking one of the condoms out of its wrapper and showing him how Jane Avril, the subject of one of my favorite Toulouse-Lautrec prints, would have looked if she had been the victim of a bad thyroid condition. The effect was something like that of a funhouse mirror I explained, stretching the latex out with my fingers and then letting it relax. Pastor was not amused and I spent the next six months with a blue-haired spinster in "church counseling."

So fortunately the bush didn't contain pieces of my turbulent adolescence. The reason Cleopatra met her demise was that my mother decided the yard needed to be redone because of her deprivation in the kitchen appliances arena. I guess the apple didn't fall far from the tree there. I can still imagine her at the window with one drawn-on eyebrow arched sinisterly as the bulldozer backed away, pulling the brand-new metal chain ever tighter around what had only moments before been a firmly rooted and unsuspecting evergreen. The tug was only momentary as the roots made a gut-wrenching tear from the earth in which they had been so comfortable.

At the time this occurred, there were over thirty trees on our property, numerous flowers and vines, and a yard of winter rye. When I arrived home that day from school, the house looked as it probably had when first built. Even the grass had been removed. There was nothing left but an acre of plowed dirt clods and the ugly red brick structure that sheltered us from the harsh Alabama summers. My mother, as usual, acted as if nothing had happened.

When my father came home, he didn't take out his anger on her for having every piece of greenery pulled out of the ground. He took it out on me.

One of the techniques I learned as a child in order to cope with my father's temper and subsequent punishments was to learn to play dead. This is basically what it sounds like: playing dead. My father would lose his temper and go into a blind rage, swinging at anything in sight—which was usually me. He either had not learned to hit with the open fist, or preferred seeing knuckle marks on a small child's head. I never figured out which. But I can't fault him. Today, fathers might be occasionally prone to over-disciplining their children. In the 1960s in the South this was simply an everyday activity, like golf or fishing.

I first learned the play dead technique when, one day, having set him into a rage because I was simply existing, he picked me up and threw me into a wall. The impact created an outline, somewhat like cartoon characters create when they exit a room so quickly that a cutout of them is the only thing left. I fell, fortunately, onto the bed. Thinking this was not a good time for a verbal repartee, I lay there completely still.

This was a shock to my father, who liked to hit but certainly didn't want to kill me. At least I don't think he did. He was a relatively intelligent man who knew that if he killed his son, he wouldn't have anything to practice his frustrations on anymore. As far as I can tell, my mother was never the recipient of his physical abuse. That pleasure was reserved only for me. How special I was.

So I lay perfectly still when he came over to see if I was okay. While this was undoubtedly not one of my favorite experiences, I dealt with it by imagining myself to be one of the characters in an old movie shown on television—one of those which a few years before had been an Academy Award winner or at least had been shown at Infanta's only downtown theatre.

"Son, are you okay?" he asked, his demeanor having changed considerably since he had had a few seconds to think about incarceration and the possibility of anal sex.

I said nothing. I was Janet Leigh in Hitchcock's *Psycho*, having just been stabbed by Anthony Perkins.

"Son, speak to me."

Again, I said nothing but thought that my fascination with old movies must run in the family, so unoriginal was his last request. I lay slumped to one side, imagining I had torn the shower curtain down and blood was now running toward the great O-mouth of the drain as the camera zoomed slowly in on the swirling water mixed with blood. Then the cut-away to the large eye as the camera turned in photo-shoot-like fashion all the while accompanied by the running water sounds of the shower.

"Son, I'm sorry. I didn't mean to hit you." Now I was Lee Remick in *Days of Wine and Roses*. Still I said nothing, although I have to admit that it was all I could do to keep my mouth shut. "Didn't mean to hit me?" I thought, "Oh, I guess you were just swinging your fists around and I jumped in front of them." Nevertheless, I just lay there and let him suffer. I figured we'd be even shortly. I mean, the guy looked like he was in a lot of pain, but then, so was I.

This scene was repeated more times than I care to remember and the psychological scars are much deeper than the physical ones. Each time, in order to survive, I found myself becoming some character I had seen on TV. I was Joan Crawford in *What Ever Happened to Baby Jane?* Susan Hayward in *I Want to Live!* or Philip Alford who played Jem Finch in *To Kill A Mockingbird,* right after Mr. Ewell has attempted to tear his arm off.

And while I employed these characters in an attempt to retain my sanity, I found other characters, not necessarily abused ones, easier to relate to. Most of all, my favorite movie was *Harvey*, probably because it took me completely out of reality. So convincing were my conversations with the imaginary mammal during my father's tirades, he would stop mid-sentence, convinced that I really *did* see someone else in the room. He might have thought I was crazy, but the desired effect was achieved and he stopped, at least temporarily, taking out his frustrations on me.

Whatever I had to do in order to get through the day and deal (or rather, not deal) with life, I did, and after a while, though I still deeply wanted my parents' love, I realized that that particular fantasy wasn't going to happen and I gradually began to withdraw from their world.

I have to admit that as I've gotten older, certain realizations have come to me that make it easier to understand my father and mother. When you're a child, you have no idea what life is really like. Of course parents know this, but you don't. Narrow perception can be a terrible thing. Someone once said that we pick our parents and the situations we're born into in order to deal with problems we had in a previous life. What was *I* thinking? At any rate, I managed to avoid my father as much as possible until he died, and then I didn't have to worry about him anymore. I did, however, still have to deal with my mother after that, but for the meantime I forged on ahead in the game of life. I was still young.

* * * * *

The cake-making incident, the house-decorating debacle, and numerous other events with my parents behind me, I felt sure that my next project in life would be a success. Here was the plan: I was going to produce a full-scale Hawaiian barbecue in the backyard, complete with roast pig, paper lanterns, and full Hawaiian regalia for everyone. As my parents were not in favor of me socializing with others in the neighborhood, I knew I would have to keep my plans a secret. The idea came to me one day while watching two episodes of *I Love Lucy*. One episode dealt with a Hawaiian vacation, and the other with a Barbecue. I'm sure I mentally created a hybrid from these two shows. Bobby's services (complete with loincloth) were again called into play, as were most of the other neighborhood kids, with Bobby

101

and his brother Derk directed to carry in the roast pig, freshly skewered, while the rest of us danced in front of the great fertility god.

Actually the fertility god was a ceramic garden gnome with one leg missing due to the fact that last summer when my father was mowing the lawn, a piece of petrified poodle dung was sent flying into it at a velocity slightly less than the speed of light. My mother had wanted to throw it away, but I rescued it and hid it under some privet bushes growing on the right side of our house, thinking it might come in handy some day.

It did.

My first thought regarding the aforementioned barbecue, which seemed to me to be terribly rational and in order of importance at the time was, "How can you have a Hawaiian barbecue without grass skirts?" Then it hit me. The town we lived in had just recently cleared the field in back of our house because of a growing rodent population (how was I to know you weren't supposed to feed them?) and the Johnson grass (*Sorghum halepense*), which had grown to a height of three to four feet, had been cut and left lying in great piles. Rather a waste of a noxious if not prolific weed, in my opinion. Within a few hours I had fashioned several grass skirts by tying the strands together with kite string. The final effect wasn't quite what I had in mind, but I figured that no one would notice if we cut down on the number of paper lanterns used to light the scene, the lack of illumination hiding any defects that I might have missed.

After hanging the Chinese paper lanterns in the trees, it occurred to me that their electric cord wouldn't reach the outlet in back of the house. No problem. I would just put small candles in the lanterns. The mood would be even more exotic. I secured a box of "votives for religious purposes," from the kitchen and was off. Then it was time to dig the pit for the barbecued pig to be roasted in.

There wasn't to be an *actual* barbecue. First of all, we didn't have a pig. What we did have was a poodle, and one that was quite used to being turned into things very un-poodle-like. At one point in the dog's rather eventful life, much later than the

102

barbecue, I figured out that if you squeezed it gently on certain areas of its rib cage, it would growl at different pitches, and being musically inclined I put this into practice as often as possible, especially to the delight of guests that my parents had over at regular intervals. ("Play 'Born Free,' " my mother would exclaim, "I just love that song.") Now before I start getting letters from animal rights activists, let me say that the dog needed a career, and if you ask me, it enjoyed being the center of attention. And besides, it was one of the few things I did that my mother approved of.

It was decided that if we tied its feet together (the dog's, not my mother's) and stuffed a tennis ball into its mouth (again, the dog's), in the right light you could easily mistake it for a roast pig, especially when you hung it upside down on a broomstick.

The luau was scheduled to begin at eight o'clock and various neighborhood children began showing up to change into their grass skirts at about seven thirty. Everyone changed in the utility room at the back of the house—the one with the notorious washing machine that "walked." My parents, who at that moment didn't really care what I did as long as I stayed clear of them, would only occasionally flick the porch lights on and bellow my name to make sure I had not been kidnapped, or worse, found a playmate. Being the dexterous child that I was, I was able to yell my answer back without ever taking my eyes off the grass skirts I was putting finishing touches on.

Seven neighborhood children, now completely naked except for some loosely constructed skirts, made their way to the previously selected location—a group of pine trees (again, *Pinus tadea*, but not the one that I had bought at the Wheeler home) in the backyard out of viewing distance of our house.

"I need you guys to help me put the candles into the lanterns," I said, and handed them each a small wax cylinder. For a time all was going well. The candles were lit and Bobby and Derk were waiting for their cue.

"All right, guys," I said. "Bring in the pig."

It was at this point that something went wrong. I had foreseen possible problems with the poodle or the grass skirts,

103

but that wasn't where things got off to a bad start. The dog, used to my antics, was quietly accepting its role as porcine entrée, and the grass skirts seemed to be holding up well enough. The problem started with the Chinese lanterns. It seems they weren't made for candles, but had there been no breeze that evening this probably wouldn't have been cause for concern. Because this was late August and the wind was picking up, one of the candles overturned in the lantern, setting it on fire.

Of course, the thing quickly burned and went plummeting to the ground like a kamikaze pilot heading for Pearl Harbor, which again wouldn't have been a problem except that the ground was covered with pine needles which tend to smoke and burn at an alarmingly fast rate. Before we knew what was happening, several other lanterns had caught on fire and the whole area was engulfed in a plume of smoke worthy of Mount Vesuvius. The paper receptacles were now falling to earth like bombs from enemy aircraft.

"Those planes are Japanese! Get those U-boats *outa* here!" I yelled as everyone became hysterical. Only a few of my playmates stopped to look at me.

Evidently the fire was more noticeable than we suspected, because by the time our neighbor Mr. Birdum turned on his spotlight which he used to scare off prowlers, we were already hearing the sirens of the fire engines. "You'll never take me alive, seeee," I said, trying to do my best James Cagney impression. My parents, who had been oblivious to the entire evening's festivities, came running out of the house just in time to see seven partially naked children shrieking and running in every direction. "Atlanta is burning!" I yelled, "Prissy, go and get Dr. Mead! Melanie is going to have a baby!"

The dog, which had been untied, had run away from the scene but had not been able to dislodge the tennis ball from its mouth, and was now completing circles on the patio at a rate of about four per second. "Mr. Finch, there's a mad dog, sure as de world!" I screamed at my parents, hoping to divert their attention away from the fire trucks.

The good news about this whole incident was that I was grounded for only two weeks (prisoner of war camp, in my mind). The bad news was that my grass-skirt-making abilities had been seriously called into question, most of the children being almost completely naked by the time the police and fire department arrived. To this day I think that the neighbors' refusal to let me play with their children was irrational and ill-founded. But I couldn't worry about them right now as I had other things on my mind. After all, it was only onward and upward in my opinion—I had the first grade to attend.

-To be continued in next month's issue-

- 5 -

New York, 1996

The Bible gives me a deep, comforting
sense that things seen are temporal, and
things unseen are eternal.

—Helen Keller, *The Story of My Life*

"Necrophilia? Six-year-olds in drag?" asked Sagaser. "He's seven. He's seven years old, not six," responded Strekfus, exasperated.

"Six, seven, who cares? And you can't have the black maid talking like she's Hattie McDaniel. Some of our readers will cancel their subscriptions if they read that! Jesus Christ! Mrs. Seriate? What kind of name is that? A bassoon?"

"The bassoon was in the first story. You're getting them confused," said Strekfus. Sagaser just shot him a look which said that the point had been missed and that something had to be done differently.

Strekfus knew this would be an uphill struggle, but he had no idea Sagaser would react this violently to his writings. He knew that when Sagaser criticized him for his style changes in the last few months, when he criticized him for his colorful Southern expressions and his stereotypical characters, he was only doing his job. But some part of it hurt and he took it personally. After all, it *was* personal. He was writing from experience. He thought he had something to give to the magazine, something to say to the world. He wasn't sure exactly what, but he knew he had to take the journey through his writings to find out. And now he was having to submit his work to this man for his review. He could have chosen to write something safe, but that seemed the coward's way out, and given the fact that he was growing tired of producing the same things day after day, he felt the need to push the envelope.

"I'm not going to allow this," Sagaser was saying. "Besides, it's too long. I wanted something under a thousand words and this thing, this . . ." (and here he made a gesture as if the writing in front of him were some type of bad soufflé which he couldn't possibly digest with his ulcers) "this is unacceptable."

Strekfus was getting annoyed. Hadn't his first story been a success? Hadn't the readers liked it and the character of Strekfus? Why then not give this one a chance?

"And another thing," Sagaser was saying, "where's this going? I mean, I know you're writing a series of stories or travelogues or whatever it is you're writing—we agreed with the top guys—but are you going to use the same characters over and over?" Then there was an uncomfortable pause. "I thought I was doing you a favor by giving you this assignment—an assignment about the South. This is how I get repaid?"

"I'm not sure what I'm going to do yet," said Strekfus, conveniently ignoring the "repaid" comment. He didn't like the idea that he had to repay anything. Besides, Sagaser had given him the assignment on the South because he was the best writer for the job and the one with the most experience when it came to that subject.

"It's a work in progress" he said, hoping this would satisfy his boss. He knew Sagaser wasn't going to go for the Enolam Boulevard piece—it was just too risky for the magazine—but he felt that whoever had given the go-ahead for him to write the series after seeing the first story would probably understand what he was trying to do and give the go-ahead for this one as well.

"Whatever you decide is all right by me," said Strekfus, and made a mental note to send another copy upstairs without getting Sagaser's approval first.

"First of all, don't patronize me. I'm still your boss. And secondly, while I'm reviewing your performance, you're late to this office most of the time," said Sagaser, perceiving himself to be on a roll. "You've been late every day for two weeks. For God's sake, you're a staff writer—try and get into the office on time!"

"I'm having trouble sleeping. I get up late," Strekfus said. "Look, Winney, what's really going on here? What's the real problem?"

Sagaser seemed to relax for a moment. Since Strekfus was one of the few people he allowed to call him by his nickname, the writer's use of it seemed to change his attitude for the moment. The man made a pretense at shuffling some papers around, turning in his chair, anything to break the mood. Finally he gave in.

"I know I can be hard on you at times, it's just . . .well, I thought I knew who you were. I mean, for God's sakes Strekfus, we play racquetball together every Thursday."

"And I let you win every week."

Sagaser shot him a sideways look with a limp dagger attached. Then he took a deep breath. "I guess I'm used to you writing about things that are a little safer than this stuff and I didn't expect, well, Helen Keller's doll." He was not looking directly at Strekfus. The man seemed embarrassed by something.

"Feeling a little insecure?" asked Strekfus, now with his hands dug deep into his pockets. It was one of those comments that, if said in the wrong tone of voice, could have caused his boss to explode, but this time Strekfus was asking with genuine concern, as someone who wants to understand and help, and his attitude came across as such.

"Jesus, that's not it," his boss answered, neither annoyed nor angry, turning sideways to look out the window.

"Then what is? Look. They're stories, that's all. They're fiction. Okay, maybe there's a little truth buried in there

108

somewhere, but they're meant to entertain. And I thought that while I was writing them I'd explore some childhood incidents. What's wrong with that? All I know is I don't want to write about vintage wallpaper and reproduction lighting fixtures. I think the magazine could use something different, with a twist. It was all I could bear to do that report on those awful green glass dishes."

Sagaser was silent now, looking down at his desk as if a teacher had just handed him back his test score and it was a failing grade. Then he looked up at Strekfus. "I just don't want you or us, and by that I mean the magazine, to go into territory that's too uncharted. That's all," and he gave Strekfus a smile.

"Can we call a truce?" asked Strekfus.

"Truce."

"Well, I'm not promising anything," Strekfus was saying now as he got up to leave, and as he exited the door, he turned, and gripping the doorframe, stuck his head back into his boss's office and said with a totally serious face, "And I can still kick your rear end at racquetball any day of the week." Sagaser just waved his hand and started digging through the piles of papers on his desk.

* * * * *

Three days later the word came down that the story was to be published without a change, but that in the future he might want to tone down the black housekeeper's speech and that given the length of the story it would have to appear as parts one and two in the magazine. When Sagaser called him into his office, he was a man of few words but his demeanor was changed. He was a calmer, nicer person; more understanding. And from what Strekfus could make out, his demeanor was genuine. The only thing Strekfus couldn't figure out was, "why."

"The next story, the one after the second part of your . . . let's see, Enolam story, is to be about a 'real' Southern home, already well known, and under one thousand words. Take one from the list I gave you. And everyone agrees that the style of writing in the Enolam piece was easier to read that the one on the Keller home. Just keep going in that direction." With that,

109

Sagaser placed a copy of the latest issue onto a stack of papers next to his desk. "I just want to feel that you're working with me, not fighting me, that's all. I don't want to be so hard on you, but I've got a lot on my plate right now, management breathing down my neck, and after all, I am your boss and we have to work together." Then the man actually smiled at Strekfus. It seemed for the first time in a long while that Sagaser was actually concerned for his well-being.

Then Sagaser was getting up, coming from behind his desk, standing next to Strekfus. He put his hand on Strekfus's shoulder and looked down at the writer. "You've got to understand something," he started saying, "If you don't look good, I don't look good, and I only want what's best for the magazine. I guess the whole idea of these stories threw me for a loop."

So that was all Strekfus had to go on. Why was Sagaser being so nice all of a sudden? Could he see what he was trying to do? But even this revelation, that others might see where he was headed, didn't quell his anger toward his boss for some of the incidents in the past. He retreated to his office to recuperate and look over the list of Southern homes he could write on, the whole time resenting his boss's intrusions and anger. Maybe Sharon was right. Maybe he should be writing his novel and not working for a magazine where he was subjected to their ideas and restrictions. Maybe he was more upset at the magazine than at his boss, and maybe he enjoyed Sagaser's anger. After all, it seemed to set him off more when his boss was nice to him, as if it didn't give Strekfus anything to push against.

But as he sat there thinking about this man who had made his life miserable up to this point, and thinking that just maybe the man was in the process of changing, of seeing things his way, the other shoe dropped and it was as if the wind had been knocked out of him.

"Mr. Sagaser wants this before you go home today." The news was being delivered by a bouncy young temp with peacock-blue eye shadow and four-inch clogs. She was chewing what appeared to be an enormous wad of gum and making no attempt to hide it.

"What is this?" asked Strekfus, turning the bulging folder around so that he could see what was inside.

"By the end of the day," the temp repeated with unusual hostility and condescension, having to turn around now to deliver her last abuse as she was partially out the door already. She couldn't have been more than twenty years old. It was as if Sagaser had gotten to her and told her what he was thinking, that he didn't approve of Strekfus, that he didn't like him. Either that or his demeanor had rubbed off on her already in the three days she had been here. "How humiliating," Strekfus thought, "being told what to do by a temp, and not even a very bright one at that."

"So that must have been the plan," thought Strekfus. "Set me up with kindness and then pull the rug out from under me."

He opened the folder and read the note from his boss. "Jesus," he said, as he rested his head in his hands, "It will take six hours at least to do research on this many uses of cardboard: cardboard furniture, cardboard houses, recycled cardboard, cardboard as insulation, as art. He contemplated doing a piece on refrigerator cartons as shelter for New York's homeless, then he thought of Sagaser and decided not to press his luck. What was this about anyway? It was research that should have been done by another department, not him, and it was for someone else's story at another of the magazines which had nothing to do with homes and gardens. Sagaser was testing him, trying to get him to explode, to start a confrontation. Did he think that a writer would actually do this kind of thing and not complain? What was the guy's plan?

Strekfus sat there for the longest time. He looked up at the clock. Four thirty. The bastard had given him this toward the end of the day, knowing perfectly well that he would have to stay late. But something inside told him to play along, not to complain just yet. He was curious as to what Sagaser was up to, and by playing along he might just find out. He set to work on the research, and by seven thirty was finished.

111

As he leaned back in his chair to relax for a few minutes, he caught sight of Sharon walking among the rows of desks in the secretarial area. At first he didn't give her much thought, but after a few expletives and frustrated heavy sighs coming from her direction, he stuck his head out the door to see what the problem was. All it took were two raised eyebrows from him, pointed in the direction of the despondent female, to get a response.

"Oh. Hi. I was just trying to get into the system," she said. "I'm supposed to have this software installed by the morning or I'm dead."

"Why exactly do you need to get into their computers?" he asked, pointing to the secretarial desks.

"Well, actually, I need to get into everyone's computer, but unfortunately that's going to take some time. Say, how long are you going to be here, and how come you're here so late?"

"Sagaser gave me an assignment on cardboard," he said, leaning up against the doorframe and crossing his arms. "Are you going to need to get into my computer at some point?"

"Yup."

"Want to do it now, precious?"

"You're such a sweetie," she said sarcastically as she maneuvered her way through the cold metal desks. "One more of these infernal machines marked off my list."

As Strekfus moved out of the way Sharon squeezed into his desk chair, reaching for the computer's mouse automatically. But before she got to it she stopped. "Since when do you chew tobacco?" she questioned, turning up her nose while holding a round rusted can of chewing tobacco. "And this thing looks like it's forty years old anyway. I knew you smoked, but this?"

"I'm not chewing tobacco," he said, grabbing it from her. "It's not even mine."

"Then whose? And you really should stop smoking. It's not good for you," she said, tilting her head and pursing her lips.

"Let's just say I got it while I was at home," he said, as she reached up to take it out of his hand. "And you smoked for years, so don't lecture me," he shot back at her. Strekfus let the small can slip from his hand into hers. Grasping it between two fingers, she gave it a shake.

"What's in here, anyway?" She attempted to pry off the top with no success.

"I haven't been able to open it just yet. Figure I might not want to see what decades-old tobacco looks like anyway. Althea chewed it for years. I guess she thought that by leaving me a can of it I would always be reminded of her."

"Yeah, okay, whatever," she said, rolling her eyes.

With that, Sharon proceeded to install the software onto the computer with Strekfus standing behind her, just to be sure she didn't cause any damage to the research he had just completed. God forbid he lose his data on cardboard evening clothes.

"Look," she said, never taking her eyes off of the monitor, "let's talk. About that first story you wrote." Strekfus didn't say anything. He just waited for her to continue.

"Something's bothering me about it."

Again, Strekfus didn't say a word. He knew Sharon. He knew she was going to say what she wanted and probably wouldn't hear his interjections anyway.

"You were locked in Helen Keller's house, right? Okay." She was moving now between screens on the monitor, typing in codes, adjusting technical components which looked totally foreign to Strekfus. "One question," she continued, never looking up. "How, after all these years, did you manage to remember the name of the plumber-slash-bus driver who let you out?"

"You'll have to wait until I'm through writing the series to find that out," he said, frustrated that the only thing she had retained from the story was the name of one of his characters. "So what did you think of the first story anyway?" he asked, hoping for a different response.

"Too wordy," she responded, still not looking up. "And you want everyone to know you played with Helen Keller's doll? Isn't that giving them a bit of ammunition?"

"I guess we should be glad that I didn't write about the time I did my Gypsy Rose Lee impersonation in front of the relatives, completely naked except for a round fuzzy lavender toilet seat cover and a pair of elbow-length gloves. *Let me* (*bum-pa-bum, bum-pa-bum, bum-pa-bum*) *enter-TAIN you*," he imitated for her.

"You were six?" she asked, finally looking up.

"Actually I was twenty-five, but who's counting," he said, and sat back down rather glumly.

He was becoming irritated now. Sharon might be his best friend, but her recent forays into flippancy were categorically irksome. They had known each other since first grade, developing the innocuous squabbling of siblings along the way, but now the relationship was showing signs of a real strain. Besides, Sharon hadn't even mentioned the use of her sister Nyla in the story, choosing instead to address his word count. After a few minutes, Strekfus became bored watching her flip through disks and download programs, and went to search for the nearest source of caffeine. "Want anything from the kitchen?" he yelled over his shoulder, but she was deep within his computer and didn't respond.

When Strekfus returned with a lukewarm cup of tea in hand, Sharon was gone. He presumed she was finished and sat down to clean up a few odds and ends and prepare to leave. At first he thought it was eyestrain or age catching up with him, but then he realized that his main menu screen was different. He scrolled around, clicking on various icons. This wasn't his computer screen layout—not the one he usually had access to.

It seemed that the idea didn't take hold immediately, but once it did there was no dispute that he would go through with it. Strekfus was now staring at the screen—the very one Sharon had just been on. Evidently she had access to network pathways and technical attributes he couldn't even begin to understand. Sharon was one of his oldest friends, but she could be scatterbrained sometimes, and probably because of the lateness of the hour she had logged into the system under a global password used exclusively by the computer department, and then neglected to log out, allowing Strekfus access not only to *his* files but to those of everyone else in the company. Maybe she had done it on purpose? No, he didn't think so. Sharon was a lot of things to a lot of people, but at work she was extremely professional. Still, she had been acting strangely as of late, so he couldn't be sure.

As he sat there, intrigued with this new aspect of the system, he couldn't quite shake the resentment he had been developing lately. Deep down he loved Sharon, but she occasionally rubbed him the wrong way with her flippant comments. She hadn't even extended the courtesy of letting him know she was finished working on his computer. And for her to say that his story was "wordy" was too much for him. It was almost as if he were looking for some excuse to be angry, looking for some incident that would allow him to pull away.

Whatever the reason, whether Sharon had deliberately left him signed in on the global password or not, he was inside the system now, and given Sagaser's recent display of animosity and disrespect, whether perceived or real, he gladly scrolled downward until he found his boss's directory. A few clicks later and not much scrutiny (the man didn't exactly have a great imagination when it came to naming files) and he was inside one of the very memos his boss had written that day. He printed it out and went to the next one. Then the next and the next, gleaning out the ones which pertained to him. As he read, he realized that under ordinary circumstances he would have been furious, but because he was on a mission, he performed his printing duties like a faithful secretary, waiting until he had everything in black and white before working himself into a rage.

He couldn't believe what he was reading. At least Sagaser's recent niceness made sense—he *was* setting Strekfus up. Strekfus knew that his boss had a cruel streak, always playing practical jokes, but he also knew that the man rarely took out his frustrations directly on the younger writer. Evidently that had now changed.

When he had exhausted the file, he sat back to read the fat stack of gleaming white pages. The first memo was written to him and another writer on staff, a new person who had only been there a week—a new person ten years younger than himself with one year's worth of experience as opposed to his twelve. The memo stated that Strekfus was to be moved out of his office and into an even smaller one, and the new writer was to get his old office.

Did Sagaser feel that threatened by his stories, these stories about this young boy growing up in the South? Or was it the fact that Strekfus had won a round and Sagaser needed to get even. Strekfus gritted his teeth and read on. The next memo was written to one of the vice presidents, asking for support in what Sagaser wanted to do, which was to force "Mr. Beltzenschmidt to perform in the capacity I deem acceptable, writing his next piece strictly on a historic Southern home." Finally, there was a memo written to someone in the personnel department. Strekfus knew this person and his reputation within the company. He was extremely bigoted and known for hiring only persons with "front office" appearance, the term being an industry-wide one for "white only." In Sagaser's memo, marked confidential and not bearing his name at the bottom (the man wasn't *entirely* inept) he declared that he would be "setting up" the receptionist with several tasks which were virtually impossible to complete. Strekfus knew this was so Sagaser could fire her without the threat of a lawsuit. He ended the memo, stating, "Once you hire certain types of people, it's impossible to get rid of them," and that "I cannot not be held responsible for their bad attitudes."

As Strekfus sat there collecting his thoughts and the recently printed memos, he ruminated over when exactly he would put this newly acquired knowledge to use. He knew Sagaser was arrogant, but he couldn't believe the man would write something as careless as the phrase, "Once you hire certain types of people, it's impossible to get rid of them." He couldn't believe that anyone would commit such words to print. Then again, Strekfus had worked in corporate America for several years now, so not much surprised him. And he also knew that his boss liked to play games—sometimes games which weren't so funny.

He remembered an incident in which Sagaser had called the entire staff of writers into the conference room to announce

116

that two people would have to be laid off. Sagaser had gone on to say that rather than pick two, he would like for everyone (excluding himself) to sit in the room and decide which two would go. After three hours of angry negotiations about who had children, college educations to pay for, mortgages, and dying parents, the writers had exited the room and dispersed in opposite directions. Those who had been friends before entering the room now no longer spoke, and those who had been only civil to each other before were plotting torturous deaths for their co-workers.

Strekfus had entered Sagaser's office after the meeting to give him the bad news—that the writers hadn't come to any agreement and that Sagaser would now have to make the decision. To Strekfus's surprise, the man had broken into a broad smile and then burst out laughing.

"I was only kidding," he had said, "there *are* no layoffs!" Strekfus had sat there stunned at the man's arrogance and stupidity. He had asked himself at that point why he associated with this monster, and he was once again asking the question as he sat and stared at the memos.

It was late now—eleven-thirty—as Strekfus sat with his chin in his hand thinking about Sagaser's antics. With his other hand he gently rolled the small can of chewing tobacco across his desk. It softly bumped up against his pencil holder and fell over, wavering around in a circle like a quarter dropped on the floor. He picked it up and tried to pry the lid off again. Nothing. The thing seemed to be glued on tight. He slipped it into his pocket and put his papers in his briefcase. Whatever was inside the tin would have to wait.

He couldn't dwell on Sagaser's theatrics too much. If he did he might go mad. He still had to be friendly to the man. But if Sagaser wanted to play games, then Strekfus would show him that he could play just as well as anyone. He packed up his belongings and headed for the elevators. He would walk home, then go directly to bed, leaving the stack of memos he had procured for some later time. Besides, Sagaser had some hard days ahead of him in the next few weeks, and Strekfus wanted to be well rested so that he could enjoy them.

- 6 -

101 Enolam Boulevard, Part II

Infanta, Alabama, 1963

> After my teacher, Miss Sullivan, came to
> me, I sought an early opportunity to lock
> her in her room. I went upstairs with
> something which my mother made me
> understand I was to give Miss Sullivan;
> but no sooner had I given it to her than I
> slammed the door to, locked it, and hid
> the key under the wardrobe in the hall.
>
> —Helen Keller, *The Story of My Life*

I remember being extremely attracted to a girl named Bunny in the first grade. This was during the time my family lived in the house on Enolam Boulevard—the house whose walls were witness to my decorating schemes, my baking attempts, and numerous other escapades. The revelation that Bunny was a hick from the wrong side of town didn't faze me in the least. She was Nyla's younger sister and so by mere association she and I became friends. Nyla had briefly been employed as my sitter until the unfortunate redecorating incident at which time my parents decided that she couldn't be trusted with anyone under twelve.

Bunny was what was known by some people in the South as "le blanc garbage," and I remember finding this extremely exotic at the time. She brought with her each day strange stories. One concerned giant moths that inhabited her backyard (not that having moths in your backyard makes you a hick) and how her father would capture them and then let them go so that the insects could procreate freely amongst the oleander and crepe myrtles. I imagined humid evenings at their rural home, her father holding up canning jars to the single light bulb that graced their back porch, studying these creatures before releasing them into the night, watching the darkness swallow them up.

The moths were allegedly three to four inches wide with a wingspan of five to six inches. The fascination with the bizarre and grotesque had undoubtedly been instilled in me at an early age, a good example being my home creation of "dinosaur land" using toy dinosaurs and any recording played on the slowest speed for sound effects, so I implored Bunny to bring one (moth, not dinosaur) to class in a jar. Basically I didn't believe her. I didn't believe that these creatures existed in such abundance and in such close proximity to her backdoor.

"Blunny," I said one day in my best Japanese accent, turning to her while the teacher was busy removing lipstick from her teeth, "hava you cap-a-tued de yiant gleen moff which has-a been-a tehlalizing Tokyo?"

Bunny squinted at me as if I had suddenly sprung three heads. Evidently she didn't warm to my Japanese impression, so I was forced to repeat the phrase in clearly spoken English.

The next day, the chartreuse monster made its appearance inside a Ball canning jar formerly used to put up peach preserves. The joy I experienced at that time compares only with the devastation I experienced moments later when Bunny unscrewed the lid and the collected freak of nature took flight across the September schoolroom and out an open window. "You ret de Acitas runa get alaaaay," I admonished after having recognized its particular species. "Now it-a going to deestloy de woooord!" She just looked at me. I decided then and there that if she couldn't understand me or possess enough logic to keep a moth captive for at least twenty-four hours, we had to terminate our friendship.

So with Bunny written off my list, at least temporarily, I turned to Yuuki who sat directly in back of me. Yuuki was of Japanese descent and lived in a Japanese-style house some twelve blocks away from school. "Did your famly have to relocate here after the giant moth fought Godzilla in Tokyo?" I asked without my accent. I figured one accent was enough. He gave me the same look which Bunny had thrown in my direction, my assumption being that this particular facial expression was universal among all cultures.

Each day we would drive by Yuuki's house on the way home and I would say, "That's where Yuuki lives" (I mispronounced it "Yucky"). My mother would say, "Shut up." Later in life I heard that Yuuki had become a gangster and that he had been basically an unhappy child—not that the two go hand-in-hand. Anyway, Yuuki and I became such good friends that we had to be separated, as is usually the case, and as geography can sometimes be everything in friendship, Yuuki and I drifted apart. I imagined him sailing back to Tokyo after the giant footprints of Godzilla had been eradicated.

Being moved two rows away from Yuuki earned me the privilege of having Bunny pass my new sitting space—a perfect opportunity to forgive the moth incident and seek her friendship again. Now Bunny weighed just under 200 pounds—no mean feat for the first grade. She was also extremely fond of a large purple raincoat which she wore year-round regardless of the weather, and a small green parasol which accompanied her every time she went outside because of her allergy to the sun. She would break out in huge blisters if exposed to its rays for more than a few minutes.

Because most of Bunny's weight was distributed around her hips, and because of her unusual choice of attire, when she decided to take a stroll around the school she looked like a giant eggplant that had barely survived an unfortunate run-in with an overzealous X-ray machine. Other than this visual malady, I wouldn't have given her appearance a second thought except for the fact that she also wore a hand-knitted shawl each day (her mother had been in a car accident, but the hands still worked), and I and everyone else used spiral notebooks for our class work. These two facts—that Bunny wore a knitted shawl and that we all used a spiral notebook—while seemingly innocuous, were not a good combination.

By the time Bunny's peregrination from the back of the room to the front was complete each day, she was covered with at least three notebooks whose well-displayed pages usually depicted our first-grade teacher in an uncompromising and not too flattering position fornicating with Mr. Malone, the elderly custodian who seemingly lived in one of the janitor closets in the hallway that led to the cafeteria. Once again, I have no idea of Mr. Malone's actual age, and I reiterate that when you're seven, anyone over twenty is elderly. As one gets older, of course, this scale of determining "elderly" moves, and by the time you're in your forties, seventy-five takes on the meaning of a youthful walk in the park, in all probability because you can now see yourself moving rapidly in that direction. ("Seventy-five isn't that old. Why there are people who live to be a hundred.") So for arguments sake, let's say Mr. Malone was in his early fifties, at least from what I could determine.

It was at this point in the first grade, after establishing that Mr. Malone was old enough to have been around when the Russian Revolution took place, that I deemed him to be a spy for that country's government. The television and radio were rife with talk of Russia and its nuclear weapons. The Bay of Pigs had happened just a few years earlier and this, coupled with the tail end of McCarthyism, which had just fizzled out in the decade before, fueled my imagination. This, plus the fact that I had just seen two back-to-back episodes of *Bullwinkle and Rocky* in which they battle the infamous Boris and Natasha, added fuel to the fire.

"Bunny," I said one day as we filed down the hallway, "vee must eradicate dis Maloneivitch in order so vee don't get poisoned." I reasoned that Mr. Maloneivitch's sole purpose was to annihilate first-graders in Infanta, Alabama, by the use of uranium dust, finding them an obvious threat to national security because of their interest in decorating and cake baking. The uranium dust was actually a sawdust-like substance which the janitors spread over recent up-chuck that we first-graders hurled onto the tiled hallways of the school, a result of having eaten that day's school lunch. ("You just can't mix peach cobbler with Sloppy Joes and not expect something ugly to happen.")

"Bunnistski," I said once again, more urgency in my voice as we neared Mr. Malone's door on our way to lunch, " vee must get rid of dis spy before he clean up vomik again vit de uranium."

Bunny just looked at me sideways. I realized at that point that I would have to take on the entire country of Russia myself and began to plan accordingly. This didn't take long as Mr. Malone had provided me the perfect way to trap him, and he became an easy target for my frustrations and fantasy life.

Each day Mr. Malone would sit in his janitorial closet when not working, and watch the children parade down the hall on their way to lunch. For optimum viewing he invariably left his door slightly ajar, and each day as I passed I would nonchalantly give it a little nudge, closing it with a metallic snap. This ordinarily wouldn't have been funny except for the fact that the door locked from the outside. Those Russians. Go figure. There was no way to open the door from the inside once it was locked—a fact that seemed to escape Mr. Malone—and this little bit of drama, of me shutting his door while he sat in the closet, was repeated every single day for several weeks.

What was so amusing about this was that he never figured out that he needed to install the lock from the inside of the closet as well as the outside—a detail I found interesting since he was not only the custodian for the school, but also the electrician and locksmith for that institution.

Each day when the "event" occurred, there would be the metallic snap of the door followed by a muffled yelp and then the barely-audible curse words through the two-inch-thick poplar-wood door. Of course this was done for the amusement of my classmates and never failed to elicit a response. I might not have been able to have playmates when at home, but I was determined to have them at school.

Poor Mr. Malone would remain in the closet each day until the principal or one of the teachers walked by and heard his groans. Then Mr. Malone would slide the key under the door and would once again be set free. Bunny and I always walked to lunch together, and so she was right next to me whenever I shut the door on Mr. Malone. Because of this, Bunny and I bonded and were always sharing secrets and laughing together.

One day Bunny brought an incredibly exotic rock to class. It was nestled within an Easter basket, surrounded by half-melted chocolate eggs and a chocolate rabbit with the ears bitten off, a child's teeth marks still showing and the pastel foil haphazardly re-shaped around the torso of the animal. With Bunny it was always something exotic—a moth, a rock, or a picture of her father's naked rear end. Although Easter was still months away, in Bunny's mind it was okay to incorporate this (the rock, not her father's rear end) into her Easter basket. I always liked a free thinker. Examining the rock closely I was able to determine that it was a black onyx.

I secretly lusted for this object.

I managed to pry the rock away from Bunny one day for a few tender moments after an extended show of angst on her part. Easily distracted that day by my usual antics and by an extremely clever plot which involved kicking the green metal garbage can out of the doorway before shutting in Mr. Malone (he had thought up this ingenious ploy about three weeks into the school year), she forgot I had it. When she asked for it back I had conveniently lost it. Or at least that's what I told her.

"Bunny," I said, thinking of prisoners of war—the Korean War had ended years earlier and we were still being regaled with stories by our parents— "wouldn't you be happy just to know that your rock is safe even if you couldn't get it back?"

She tearfully acknowledged that yes, this alone would make her happy, whereupon I produced the rock from inside my desk, careful to hold it a safe distance from her, just in case she lunged for it. Her sniffling subsided, but the puzzled look on her face has yet to be reproduced by another living creature to this

124

day. I didn't really steal it, and besides, I still have it somewhere if she ever *really* wants it back.

Years later in high school, I turned to Bunny one day for the sole purpose of appropriating the answers to a geometry exam and noticed several rather large and ugly scars on her wrists. She intimated that if I ever wanted to try to commit suicide, the best way was to cut in the direction of the vein, since surgeons could repair a slashed wrist when it is cut crosswise. Being the human garbage receptacle for facts that I am, I immediately committed the information to memory, if not for my own use, then for that of some truly needy individual to whom I could be of assistance. Secretly, however, I hoped the incident with the rock years earlier didn't have anything to do with Bunny's suicidal inclinations.

Bunny was not a happy person, and this alone was probably the attraction. I knew many unhappy people and my brain twisted on a daily basis trying to imagine the source of their misery. In addition, Bunny frequently came to class sporting a black eye, and this in turn created for her immediate popularity among her classmates, equal to that of an expensive coffee table book at a tea held by the Junior League.

But another even more ominous reason for our friendship was the fact that Bunny had a brother who had died. This in itself wouldn't have been such cause for a bond, but the fact that her brother was born on the exact same day I was, and died one day later was, we felt, something to hold on to. Over time we pieced together fragments of the story, gleaned from eavesdropping on relatives at unguarded moments, and came up with the added coloring for the narrative. It seems that her brother and I had been born only one hour apart in the town's only hospital, the one where my father was chief obstetrician. The circumstances surrounding her brother's death remained mysterious to us, but after we found out that Bunny's mother had suffered three previous miscarriages, we resigned ourselves (as I'm sure the parents did at the time) to the fact that the woman just wasn't meant to have too many children, and that Bunny and her older sister should consider themselves lucky. All of this

Bunny and I put together at lunchtime, at recess, and in those few stolen moments while standing on the curb in the hot Alabama sun waiting for our parents to pick us up from school.

But as we discussed this, we decided that Bunny's mother wasn't the only one who should have given up having children. There was our first-grade teacher, Mrs. Straussgirdle.

Mrs. Straussgirdle was not bad as far as teachers go; it was her son who was the problem.

Sanford.

Sanford Straussgirdle.

Now wouldn't you have given a *little* more thought to that name? But then, I guess I can't really criticize, with one like Strekfus Ovid Beltzenschmidt. Without a doubt, this demon from hell (Sanford, not me) had, in addition to being physically repulsive (think troll living under a bridge), missed several rungs on the evolutionary ladder, and of course I was the main target of his frustrations and acting out. This was a pattern with certain people that I was later to discover. They would make me the target of their inadequacies and I was left to rationalize how the whole process had come about.

Sanford had two chief characteristics: he threw tantrums, and he was crippled. These were not attributes that endeared him to the socially aware, and I imagined him never being a part of the town Rotary Club or for that matter ever finding a suitable mate with whom to reproduce.

He wore a built-up shoe to compensate for the shortness of one leg and delighted in kicking each of us with its three-inch-thick leather sole. This usually took place only when his mother, the teacher, was out of the room, and since we were smart enough to figure out at an early age whose side she would take in a dispute, we kept our mouths shut. Trying to rationalize Sanford's existence, I imagined he had been maimed by a mad scientist who was attempting to hybridize humans with pig waste. This allowed me to feel at least some sympathy for him. It was probably some bad B-movie being shown during Science Fiction Week on TV which prompted this revelation. But any fantasies I made up about Sanford were quickly dispelled by his constant ranting that we had all better watch ourselves as he would one day work for the FBI and make our lives a living hell.

Once, while making a trip to the pencil sharpener—a much dreaded chore since Sanford sat a mere two feet away from it—he stood up and braved kicking me in the presence of his mother whose head was buried amongst the VGs and not-so VGs of the day. Mad scientist or not, and reflexes being what they are at that age, I pushed him backward and he immediately fell into the cold green metal trashcan conveniently positioned directly behind him. "The creature is alive!" I shrieked in the direction of the class. "Igor, bring me the new brain. I must operate immediately!"

With arms and legs now vertically parallel, Sanford proceeded to throw the coveted tantrum. One leg being capped off by the built-up shoe, the flailing was somewhat asymmetrical, adding to the visual appeal and delight of my fellow classmates. Of course, the moment his mother uncorked him from the place he belonged I expected a tirade of abuse, not to mention a reprimand from her, but there was nothing. And he simply looked hurt and consequently never bothered anyone again. So this was the secret to life: you push back when someone annoys you. While this may seem obvious to many people, it was an eye-opening moment for me, for I had thought that human beings were good at heart and that I had just been experiencing a run of bad luck. For the time being I was the class hero—a position that was cut short the first time I wet my pants.

It wasn't my fault, really. The problem was with the toilet in the boys' bathroom. Not that I blame others, especially inanimate objects, for my shortcomings, but I have to call this one as I see it. And it was the toilet that brought about my downfall as most popular in the class—a position I would have to relinquish until much later when the class made a field trip to Tuscaloosa, Alabama.

The cracked procelain trough, (long, narrow, and ancient, above which hovered somewhat shakily an even more ancient water receptacle), this monster of gurgling was the object of my dread. Don't ask me for a rational explanation. By this age I

127

could speak Korean and identify several hundred plants by their Latin names, but I was afraid of a receptacle for human waste. Why couldn't Mr. Malone have fixed this? Was I tormenting him because I blamed him for my fear?

Somehow this ceramic behemoth knew to flush out the trough every five minutes (another by-product of the Industrial Revolution, no doubt). The fact that I thought it had a "mind" was all I needed to feed my paranoia. It made the most horrifying sound I could think of, turning an average urinary experience into the ultimate stress test. Having watched too many science fiction movies, I determined that the clanking toilet's innermost goal was to take over the world by mentally tormenting all elementary school students to the point of uremic poisoning.

Obviously this made relieving oneself next to impossible, so I and everyone else (after hearing my extremely rational explanation) avoided the restroom. While most chose to relieve themselves outside at recess on the back wall of the music building, I declined on the basis that it would kill the *Lilium lancifolium* (okay, tiger lilies) which had been planted there by Mrs. Herman, the now totally deaf Social Studies teacher whose claim to fame was that she had a horse buried in her backyard. How do you prove that without a court order?

Once I did try to brave it alone to the restroom to relieve myself. This proved to be a mistake. After requesting to be excused, I waited outside the door until I heard the tank flush the trough. I knew I only had five minutes, so I tentatively approached, located my then many-named urinary appendage, and was just about to mark my territory when, for some unknown reason, the tank began to shake and gurgle and release another huge rush of water. This was totally off-cue and I took the attack personally.

"Be gone, prince of darkness," I shouted at the behemoth, but it refused to give way. The physical scar I bear from trying to make myself decent in record time is still visible to this day, and because I was so traumatized, I irrigated my dime-store blue jeans then and there. Unaware that I had done so because of the extreme trauma I had just experienced, I was not prepared for the horrified look on my fellow classmates' faces and the bewildered questions of Mrs. Straussgirdle as she stood open-mouthed and staring at the ever-growing puddle around me and the trail that led out into the hallway. "My waste is radioactive," I screamed, "Aliens from planet Plebian have contaminated me! Everyone must flee!" For some unknown reason, Mrs. Straussgirdle didn't buy my explanation and sent me back to my seat.

Through the whole incident, Sanford sat quietly with his eyes averted to the bulletin board which had been newly decorated with construction paper cut outs of three-dimensional daffodils, and only once in all the time that I knew him did he again meet my gaze. We were standing together at the back of the classroom watching two newly born chicks in the incubator when it became obvious that one of them had stopped breathing and died. Neither of us said anything. We just looked at each other, and no one else noticed until the next day. The dead chick was put into the garbage, but I managed to retrieve it before the garbage truck came to haul away the debris, reasoning that I could bring it back to life by praying to the Egyptian gods as Yul Brynner had done in Cecil B. DeMille's *The Ten Commandments*.

It didn't work.

When it dried out and became hard as a rock, I hid it in the bottom of my dresser drawer. My mother found it one day and instructed Althea to throw it away.

* * * * *

Without a doubt, one of the most traumatic events of the first grade occurred in early November of that year, 1963. Because these were the years directly after the Cuban Missile Crisis, the entire country was warned that a nuclear attack might occur. We were in the throes of a cold war. Living some thirty miles from an army base, we were in even more danger.

Every week we participated in drills during which we were instructed to find our way home from school as quickly as possible without the aid of our parents. The drills took place in the middle of the day, and as each of us took turns getting misplaced, neighborhood mothers who had been instructed to do so rounded up the lost sheep that never made it back to their appointed domiciles.

I, of course, *always* got lost. One of the search ladies would find me bent over some new hybrid of daisy or camellia, totally oblivious to the fact that a nuclear bomb was headed straight for the large "X" stenciled on the top of my cranium.

In addition to the drills, part of our everyday activities was to take a nap after lunch. Not a real nap. We simply had to put our heads down on our desks for fifteen minutes or so. What this had to do with the threat of nuclear annihilation no one could figure out, but since we were considerably shorter and less powerful than the grown-ups, we complied. No one actually napped, and to this day I can't figure out why children are required to take them, when as an adult I would give some valuable body part for one. I said no one ever took naps in first grade—no one, that is, except me.

One day, being extremely stressed out after having had a cactus plant (*Echinocactus texensis*) borrowed for a science experiment by the fifth grade class and brought back to me in a less than perfect state ("We just put a paper bag over it and didn't water it to see what would happen"), I fell asleep at my desk. Undoubtedly the first and only nap ever taken by a first-grader.

When I awakened, the room was completely empty, and since the clock had been disconnected earlier in the year (we were constantly running the hands forward), I had no idea what time it really was. In a panic, I thought that a nuclear attack drill had taken place, or worse, the real thing, and that I was left alone to die. Racing down the hallway past root-bound philodendrons and glass cases containing enchanted-egg collections, I headed for the front of the building to see if my mother was waiting to pick me up. What was *I* thinking? My hopes dashed, I headed back to the classroom via the slippery tiled hallway and was rounding a sharp curve when peals of childish laughter wafted in from another direction.

I followed the sound out to the recess yard and ran up to the first teacher I saw—Mrs. Seriate. I had always been afraid to

130

speak to her but secretly longed to do so. Mrs. Seriate's demeanor was such as to remind one of a physical education teacher. That is to say, she wore gray sweat pants and hung a whistle around her neck even though she taught history. She was also very friendly with the actual PE teacher, and they often shared an ice cream sandwich together in the school cafeteria, after which time Mrs. Seriate would collect the green plastic trays—always being careful to remove any trace of food from the faux basketweave imprinted in the plastic—and then she and Hilary (the PE teacher) would retreat to their classrooms. Mrs. Seriate was, above all, neat.

She immediately understood the situation and located Mrs. Straussgirdle, who explained that I had looked so peaceful that no one wanted to wake me.

"Peaceful!" I screamed. "I could have been killed or horribly burned!"

Mrs. Straussgirdle just looked down at me with bewilderment. "Killed?" she asked. "Burned?"

"Yes," I said, "don't you know what radiation burns look like? I'd never get to be a male underwear model," I went on.

Both Mrs. Straussgirdle and Mrs. Seriate just looked at each other and then down at me. It was then that we saw it, or rather smelled it.

Now the smell of a school burning is like no other smell in the world. I had been talking about radiation burns, but I guess the teachers thought I was trying to tell them about the school. Maybe it's all the papers to be graded, or the immense concentration of textbooks in a school building, but if you smell it burning, you'll know.

"The school's on fire!" screamed Bunny, who had just turned in our direction to see the flames, having abandoned her coveted role as kickball captain.

"Oh, my God," said Mrs. Straussgirdle, "and you were asleep in there." For some reason the fire had started just as I was exiting the building. It had begun in the cafeteria wing, which was not directly connected to the wing my classroom was in. Evidently because of the direction of the wind, the smoke had blown away from the playground and had gone unnoticed by everyone until now.

"Thank God everyone is at recess," added Mrs. Seriate, and then turning to the children who had abandoned their kickball game and clustered around us, she said, "Everyone stay put. You're all very lucky you weren't in the building."

By now, black smoke was billowing out of several schoolroom windows which had shattered from the heat of the fire. The whole incident happened so fast that everyone was in a state of shock. Then we heard the sirens in the distance, coming closer.

It was at that moment that I had a feeling unlike any I had ever experienced in my life—a feeling as though someone had taken a knife and slowly performed surgery on my heart. I was frozen for a second, then instinct must have kicked in, for before I knew what was happening I was running in what seemed like slow motion, in the direction of the burning building. Any thought of creating a fantasy out of this died a quick death.

My legs felt like rubber, as though I were running a race through a swimming pool. Everything was in slow motion, even the screams of the teachers as they ran after me. I could only run for the locked door in the hallway of the cafeteria building, the door behind which was trapped Mr. Malone, the door I had shut earlier before lunch just as I always had for the amusement of my classmates.

The smoke was now a thick black mass of curls hovering just above the floor. As I slid into the hallway like a ballplayer sliding into home, my body slammed hard against the door of Mr. Malone's broom closet. Then a second pain in my chest hit me: I didn't have the key. Frantically, I pounded on the door.

"Mr. Malone!" I screamed, "slide the key under the door, slide the key under the door!" But there was no answer. What if he had already been overcome by smoke? What if he was already dead?

"Oh, God, Mr. Malone, slide the key under the door. You've got to help me get you out!" I cried as the smoke began to sting my eyes and tears began to form. I could feel the black

132

soot coating the inside of my lungs. Just as I was about to pass out I felt someone lift me up and drag me down the hallway with such swift sure force that I thought, "This must be how it feels to die and be lifted up to heaven." My head was spinning and then everything faded to nothingness.

When I came to, the entire class was standing over me. Mrs. Straussgirdle was washing my face with a cold white cloth. I was lying on one of the benches at the far end of the baseball field. "Are you okay? What were you thinking, running into that burning building? What were you thinking?"

It was then that I heard the voice behind her. I will never forget the sound of it. I had never clearly heard the voice before, but I knew instantly whose it was. Sometimes after you've spoken with someone over the phone and then met them, you're shocked at how the voice doesn't match the face. I had seen this face for weeks now, but never heard the voice. Still I knew whom it belonged to, and an odd mixture of sadness, guilt, fear, and elation overtook me.

"He was running in 'nair to try and save those baby chicks in the science room," the voice said. "Damn near got us both killed. When I found him, he'd passed out next to the incubator." The person I heard saying this and I both knew this wasn't true, but at the time I was too light-headed and exhausted to care.

As I lay there choking up blackened spittle, the faces above me parted and slits of sunlight shone down on me like broken pieces of forgiveness. Faces and bodies of my schoolmates and teachers moved aside and my guardian angel was revealed for the first time.

"Mr. Malone saved you." It was Mrs. Straussgirdle speaking to me as she wiped my forehead.

"Thank you," I tried to rasp to the figure who was now only a silhouette completely surrounded by the sun—a giant leaning down over me, his great hand reaching down to brush the hair from my forehead. "Thank you, I'm sorry." He didn't say anything; he just smiled and the skin of his leathery face crinkled

133

up so that his blue eyes almost disappeared while the sun glinted off a single gold tooth.

* * * * *

Later that day, after the commotion had subsided and we were able to return to our classrooms to wait for our parents, I sat in a stupor. When my mother finally arrived, having been alerted by the school that there had been a fire and she needed to come and get me, I begged her to let me run to the restroom and managed to buy myself a few extra minutes before exiting the school grounds. Of course, I wasn't actually going to the restroom. I'm sure if she had remembered the wetting incident she would have questioned the request, but she was too consumed with her flaking toenail polish at that moment to notice.

As quickly as I could, I ran to the cafeteria wing which had by this time been soaked by several thousand gallons of water, and slipped under the yellow tape put across the doors. I gingerly side stepped puddles of black water in the hallway, and as I approached the open doorway to Mr. Malone's broom closet, I heard crying. I crept as silently as I could around the corner. There sat Mr. Malone with his head in his huge hands. After a few minutes he looked up at me, tears streaming down the sunburned crevices of his aged face.

"You know you didn't find me in the science room," I said. I hadn't felt a need to announce myself. I figured that by now this man and I had a bond, even if it was one created out of malicious mischief. "Why did you tell them that?"

He looked at me, his eyes red and swollen. It was almost as if he had been expecting me because he didn't seem shocked that I was standing in front of him. "If I had to explain how you knew I was locked in here, I would have had to explain who it was that did it all the time," he said in between sobs and heaves.

"Then you knew it was me all along locking you in here?

"Yes. Of course."

"And you continued to let me do it?"

"You're young. I was young once also. I know how kids can be. You were just playing a prank and didn't mean no harm," he went on. "I've got a son of my own, grown now. He's adopted—the missus and I never could have children so we adopted. He was a boy like you once. Besides, I had just installed the new lock on the door this morning, one that works from the inside and not out."

"I'm so sorry, Mr. Malone."

"I know you didn't mean to do nuthin' wrong."

"I'm really sorry, Mr. Malone," I said, and felt my eyes tearing as well. There was so much I wanted to say but couldn't. "I'm sorry," just kept coming out over and over, like some worn-out and emotionless record. The man was no longer Maloneivich to me. The traumatic event had knocked the wind out of me emotionally and I thought about how my fantasy world had gotten me into this mess.

With what sounded strangely like the creak his door made each day before I shut it, he looked at me, and trying to keep his lower lip steady, sobbed, his voice cracking, "I know." Then he hugged me, and as he did so, he crushed my nose into a packet of Camel cigarettes which were in his breast pocket. I breathed in the smell of his flannel shirt, tobacco, and what all the years of his life had done to his sunburned skin, and felt his tears on the back of my neck. And then the strangest thing occurred. He said something to me that I couldn't ever remember hearing before in my life. It was muffled and tear-stained, but forever burned into my memory like the smell of the tobacco and the flannel shirt. As I felt his jaw moving over my shoulder to make the words, his grasp tightened and the sounds fell out like broken pieces of beautiful glass into sunlight.

"I love all you kids, you know?" he said to the cinder-block wall, and squeezed me as tightly as I've ever been squeezed in my life. "I love all you kids. All y'all's just like the kids I never could have with my wife. Y'all's just like my own kids." I stood there with him hugging me, stunned. I had wanted for so long for my parents to say these words and yet I never seemed to be able to coax these pieces of gold from them. Now, here in a janitorial

135

closet of an elementary school they were flowing freely from a man I had relentlessly tortured. And while I should have been saddened by this revelation, I realized for the first time in my life that love really did exist—that I just had to be able to identify it.

After a few moments, he regained his composure. When we had both calmed down, he looked up at me, and then he sighed, "You know how the fire started? It was my fault."

"What do you mean?" I asked.

"These damn cigarettes. I thought I put one out when I was cleaning the restrooms earlier, but it fell into the garbage can and started the fire," and with that he took the pack of Camel cigarettes from his pocket and threw then against the door in disgust. They made a thud like the sound of a small bird hitting a window and then slid to the floor.

"You better be running along," he said, and held me at arm's length. "Is your mother here yet? Come on, I'll walk you to the car. Just let me get my jacket," and he turned to the small inner closet to remove it. As he did so I reached down and picked up the pack of cigarettes and stuffed them into my pocket. We walked out through the darkened hallway toward the parking lot where my mother was standing, arms crossed, leaning against the car.

"Where have you been?" she shrieked, straightening her body and tensing, looking as if she had just stuck a fork into a short-circuited toaster.

"Aw, he was just telling me good-bye," replied Mr. Malone, and he rested his hand on my head and looked down at me.

"Why would he want to do a thing like that?" asked my mother with her usual brand of sneer and smirk, her head jerking upward—a defiant mordent she often employed for intimidation purposes.

"Mr. Malone saved my life," I said quietly, looking up at her. "He pulled me out of the school after it caught on fire. He's a hero."

"No, now, son, I ain't no hero, and don't go telling anyone that I am," countered Mr. Malone.

"That's right," said my mother, "don't tell anyone about this. Mr. Malone is right. Now get in the car. I'm late for my pedicure," she said, as she practically jerked my arm out of its socket. With that, we got into the car and Mr. Malone watched us drive away. I waved to him and he stood there in his overalls, waving back. Once inside the car, things went from bad to worse.

"Did that man molest you?" interrogated my mother as she took her eyes off the road and tried to look directly into mine for a few seconds. "Did he?" The car swerved mercilessly about on the newly blackened street.

"No, Mother. He's just a friend."

She swerved to keep from hitting a cat which was attempting to navigate the gutter, then righted the car.

"I'll bet he tried to molest you. Did he touch you anywhere? Did he? Tell me the truth, because if he did, you'll grow up to be a queer, and being a queer is the worst thing in the world. I'd rather see you *dead* than be a queer. Trust me, you'll never get a job if someone thinks you're one of those people. Promise you'll never be one of those people, and if anyone tries to touch you, you must let me know."

"Yes, ma'am." I was recoiling from her now, trying to mash myself into the car door in an attempt to create as much space as possible between us.

"Besides," she went on, "the Bible says it's wrong and the Bible doesn't lie." At that point she started singing "Shall We Gather at the River," complete with spoken dialogue which she interjected at the ends of verses, the discourse consisting of bits of useful information about masturbation and celibacy. But all I could think about was how I had longed to hear the words "I love you," from my parents for such a long time, and that I had heard them spoken today, for the first time, as if it were some ancient secret kept locked away from me and everyone else. It seemed that nothing she said could hurt me, at least for the moment. As I sat there, I marveled at her ability to sing a hymn with such gusto and at the same time be totally oblivious to any meaning it might possess.

* * * * *

When we arrived home, Althea met us at the door. "Child, the news is all over town about how the school caught on fire! I was worried sick about it. You come in here and sit down and I'm gonna fix you somethin' to eat!"

"I'm not hungry," I said, and sulked off toward my room.

Later that day as my mother was helping her sort the laundry (a rare occurrence if ever there was one) she came across the pack of cigarettes I had picked up from Mr. Malone's room.

"Look at this, Althea," she said, holding the cigarettes, her arm outstretched like some bad actor playing Hamlet, holding Yorick's skull, "My son, my only son has been smoking. I'm going to blister him raw. Where is he?" And with that she proceeded to become hysterical and move about the room in an agitated state, looking for a cooking spoon or another implement she could use to hit me with.

"Now you just calm yourself down, Miss. Hattie. I'm sure these ain't his," said Althea, now clutching the half-empty pack of cigarettes.

"Oh, God!" continued my mother, "my son is a pothead," and with that she sank to the floor in a sobbing heap while clutching my father's urine-stained boxer shorts.

"Now, Miss Hattie, he ain't no pothead. This here's just regular cigarettes. The boy's only in the first grade. How much trouble could he get into? Ain't no need to worry your head about somethin' like this. Come on now and get up before Mr. Strek comes in here and sees you. Come on now! Get up!" She had now positioned herself behind my mother and was attempting to lift her by the armpits, muttering to herself, "Ain't nothin' wrong with that boy. You's good parents to him."

Evidently my mother wasn't cooperating, because Althea ended up dragging her across the kitchen floor a good ten feet before giving up and placing her atop a twenty-pound bag of dried dog food.

"I'm completely paralyzed," my mother sobbed, the back of her hand now firmly attached to her forehead. "I can't move

138

my legs. Oh, how could God do this to me?" And then the gas started. Evidently my mother's entire body was paralyzed with the exception of her sphincter muscle which opened and closed like the oral cavity of a largemouth bass. "Brrrrrrrrapppppp!" it exclaimed, my mother never moving from her supine position, the back of her hand over her eyes.

"Now, the good Lord ain't done nothin' to you folks. You just sit there and I'll get you a glass of water." Then Althea's mutterings to herself, probably not realizing that anyone could hear, "This jus' all my fault with me chewin' that tobacco all the time. Poor Strekfus done taken after me and that ol' devil weed."

After a good hour and a half, my mother calmed down and regained the use of her legs. I know this because she managed to kick several holes in the backdoor out of anger before my father came into the kitchen to see what the commotion was. It seems that my mother had burned the pork chops and her only recourse was to assault the backdoor. Of course, my father, now quite used to this sort of behavior, was somehow able to appease her. We had cereal that night with buttermilk and I was grounded for a week.

A few days later I was awakened at three in the morning by something in my ear. At first I thought it was just a draft in the room, but then I realized that my mother was leaning over my bed, whispering at the right side of my head. Her faded pink nightgown was stained with cold cream and she smelled like an atomic rosebush. I lay perfectly still and pretended to be asleep even though I was terrified. It seemed that she hovered near my ear forever. The smacking of her lips seemed to go on for some time with occasional puffs of air now and then. I was becoming sick to my stomach.

Then she spoke, and the words melted out of her mouth like warm bile. She caressed them slowly and sensuously as if fondling a silken purse containing pure gold: "If you grow up to be a queer," she cooed in a sickly sweet voice, "no one will have anything to do with you," and then she slowly waddled out of the room, her pink chiffon nightgown flowing behind her as her slippers snapped rhythmically with the sound of dime-store cheapness on the cold parquet floor.

* * * * *

It was a chilly November day just before Thanksgiving, almost a month after the incident of the school fire. Everything still smelled of ash and smoke near the school, and several of the cafeteria windows were boarded up. A frost seemed to hover in the air. Autumn clipped orange and red leaves from the trees like some pernicious schoolgirl with a new pair of scissors, sending them scurrying over asphalt driveways and sad lawns, and the occasional gust of wind rattled every window in sight. It was that time of year when summer is no longer and winter is yet to come. I wasn't feeling well, and so at recess I decided to remain inside. Mrs. Straussgirdle had determined that since I was to stay in sick while the others were out playing, I might as well listen to the radio.

I sat there, trying to color inside the lines of a Tyrannosaurus Rex drawing, peruse *My Weekly Reader,* and not lose my mind listening to Lawrence Welk play the song, "Calcutta."

Suddenly the music stopped.

"This is a bulletin from the Associated Press," an announcer said. "We regret to interrupt this broadcast. Here reporting from Dallas, is our correspondent . . ."

It was then they announced that President Kennedy had just been shot in Dallas, Texas. I might have only been seven years old, but I knew who the president was. Immediately I ran outside to where the others were having recess and went straight up to Mrs. Straussgirdle.

"What is it?" she asked, "Why are you outside? I thought you didn't feel well."

"The president has been shot," I said. For a moment she looked puzzled, then she became angry.

"That's not funny," she retorted. "You should be ashamed of yourself. You're always coming out here to recess with some story. Just wait until I talk to your mother. Now go on.

140

Go on back inside," and she turned me abruptly around and marched me back into the school. It seemed to be the story of my life. I was always trying to tell people something they wouldn't believe.

I returned to the classroom and shut the radio off. The silence was icy and black, and everyone must have felt it, for as soon as the class returned, Mrs. Straussgirdle switched the radio back on—something she rarely did when class was in session. I'll never forget the look on her face when the announcement came on again. For a long time we just sat there in shock.

"Strekfus, I'm sorry I didn't believe you," she said after a long silence, with tears in her eyes. Then we sat listening to the news over and over again. Parents came to pick up their children, and it seemed that the world stopped for a moment.

That evening at the supper table nothing was said. I assumed this was because of the recent bad news that had splashed itself over everything. We ate in silence and then I asked to be excused. My father eyed me suspiciously. Then he took a look at my plate.

"You've got to be more careful," he said, and I hung my head, knowing what was coming. "You've eaten almost everything on your plate. Try not to let it happen again. You know the rules —leave at least one third of the food given and then let everyone know you're through." He returned to his pork chop.

"I'm sorry," I said, "but why is it I can't eat everything on my plate? The kids next door were telling me that . . ." but I stopped, realizing my mistake. It was a sin to compare yourself to other people, and this, accompanied by the fact that I had actually *seen* the neighborhood children, put me in a bind.

"Have you been associating with the neighbors again?" my father asked. I knew this was forbidden, but I had happened on one of them playing hide-and-seek at the side of our house and had attempted a conversation while the child waited to be discovered. In the course of this small impromptu discourse, I learned that other children were required to eat everything on their plates and that my parents were paying the neighbors to

141

keep their children away from me. While the information on food removal from one's plate left me baffled, the fact that Mrs. Stewart had a brand new car was starting to make sense. Mrs. Stewart was a single mother who didn't even have a job. My parents had paid her to keep her kids away from me—and evidently a large sum at that.

"You know we've spoken about this," my mother said. "If you happen to be in a restaurant some day and eat everything on your plate, then the waiter and people around you will think you're poor and never have enough to eat. By leaving a little food on your plate you're showing them that you have enough money to eat all the time."

"But what if I'm hungry and I *want* to eat everything? And don't we have bigger problems than what percentage of mashed potatoes I eat? The President of the United States was shot today. Can we try to put things in perspective?" I made a move for three solitary peas straggling alongside a piece of pork fat.

"Aaaaant!" my father said, anger rising in his voice as my hand moved toward the green orbs. "You go to your room and stay there."

I guess I should have known better. I mean, my parents were extremely particular about food, its preparation, and its consumption. While they actually had a mathematical formula about how much food was to be left on the plate, they seemed even more obsessed with the way our food was handled *before* we ate it. At least my mother was. She was always fixing dinner and then putting my father's food aside and treating it in some special way. I guess that she really cared for him because she was always adding a little something extra to his plate.

Once, when clearing the table, I started to finish a piece of roast beef that my father had left, thinking that no one was looking. It was halfway to my mouth when I felt my mother's hand come flying through the air and slap it away. It landed with a thud beside a set of canisters on the kitchen counter. Her eyes were wild. It seemed to me that something more than etiquette was going on here, but I couldn't figure it out.

"You know not to take food off other people's plates!" she screamed, obviously shaken. Then she added, "It's just not—well, proper," and with this statement she seemed to regain her composure. I thought about this as I prepared to exit the kitchen, making a mental note of how much food had been left on my plate and its ascendance over national affairs.

The next Monday, after my latest attempt to eat, Althea came to work despite the fact that the country was still in mourning for the President. People tried as best they could to retain a sense of normality, but it was difficult given the circumstances. My parents had decided I should stay home that Monday following the assassination, probably because of the fear that something else would occur. It was a tense time and no one was sure yet exactly what group was responsible for the president's death. In the country's mind anything could happen.

To pass the time that day, Althea and I told stories to each other and I helped her with the laundry and cleaning. After lunch, we sat watching the news on television—full coverage of the assassination with non-stop commentary. My parents had forgotten to tell Althea about the ban, that I was to have no TV, and so as long as she was at home with me I watched whatever she wanted to, grateful for the diversion.

Althea commented to me that she had had about enough, and that it was getting depressing, this coverage of the President, and I agreed. We turned the sound on the TV down and I helped her fold the sheets and towels. As she was given to do, she started to hum. This in itself was not so unusual as she usually hummed a hymn or Negro spiritual, but I noticed today that she was humming something completely different. As I listened, I thought I recognized Aram Khachaturian's ballet music, *Spartacus*.

"What's that you're humming?" I asked as I folded the last bath towel.

"Huh? What you talkin' about, child?"

"You were just humming something," I said. "What was it?"

Althea thought for a minute, and then hummed a few bars again. "I don't know. Seems to me I heard it somewhere, but I can't place it."

"It's *Spartacus*," I said.

"Who?"

"*Spartacus*. The ballet."

"I must have picked it up from one of them phonograph records you always playin'. I sure would love to get me one of them phonographs so I can listen to some church choir records. Maybe it was somethin' you was playin' on that piano you practice on. You sure do spend some time at that thing. Seems like you plays day and night."

"You don't own a phonograph?" I asked. Then I added, "And I don't practice all the time. Besides, I'm not allowed to leave the house, so it gives me something to do."

"No, child. I got to get me one, though," she said, responding to my question about the phonograph. "You know, they's high. I can't afford one right now." Then she shot me a look as she draped two clean sheets over her smooth brown arm. "And sometimes I think you's gonna grow to that ol' piano bench, you sits there so much. But I do love to hear you play."

Althea got up to spit some of her tobacco juice out the backdoor and I went to my bedroom, returning a few minutes later with a portable record player, its outer square canvas covering worn by hours of use. I also brought out a recording of Khachaturian's *Spartacus*. It wasn't a great phonograph and it was a pretty scratched-up recording (my parents not having the insight to keep records clean and in their proper jacket covers), but it got the job done. When I placed the disc onto the platter and gently lowered the stylus, scratchy sounds emerged while the needle searched for the proper groove. As the "Adagio" of Spartacus and Phrygia floated out of the eighteen-by-six-inch fabric front of the box, a big smile came over Althea's face.

"That's it! That's what I was hummin'!" and she clapped her hands. I was afraid for a minute that she was going to have one of her spells, getting happy and shouting like in church, but she didn't. We sat there for a few seconds just listening, and then

144

we both turned to the television, which was still on. It was surreal in a cinematic kind of way. There were pictures of the Kennedy motorcade making its way down Elm Street in Dallas, cutting in and out of news flashes and obituary information, all happening to Khachaturian's music. We watched for a while, not wanting to break the spell.

"Kinda creepy, ain't it?" asked Althea.

"Umm."

"You said this was a . . . ballet?"

"Uh-huh."

"What's a ballet like?" asked Althea.

"Well, this particular one is about two slaves in Roman times. They become separated and their lives go in different directions. There's the usual greed, lust, revenge, and heartbreak. You know. The good stuff."

"Does it end happy or does it end sad?"

"Unfortunately," I said, "it ends sad."

Althea thought for a minute and then looked at me.

"You know, I think you should write your own ballet. You always listenin' to music and readin' them fancy names you got for plants. You smart, Strekfus. Why you not write one of them ballets and give it a happy endin'?"

"I don't think I could write music like that," I said. "Besides, it's a classic story. You wouldn't want to mess with something that's set in stone."

"Child, there might just be somethin' to be said for messin' with somethin' set in stone. And if you not write one of them ballets, then you can write a book or somethin'. You know how you're always tellin' stories and makin' up characters with those stuffed animals you used to have."

"I don't know," I said. "Maybe someday."

The music finished and I took the disc off of the turntable and closed the lid. "Althea," I said, rather timidly, not knowing how she would react to what I was about to propose, "would you like to have this record and turntable?"

"You can't be givin' that to me. Yo' parents would have a fit," she said, and let out a chuckle.

"I'll take care of it," I said.

"No, child. Don't even ask them. I appreciate the gesture, but you don't have to do that." I knew there was no use arguing with her; she was as stubborn as I was.

* * * * *

Thanksgiving came and went after the assassination. The days seemed to crawl toward Christmas as they always do for anyone under the age of fifteen. There was a pall hanging over the country and everywhere you turned there was a tribute to the fallen President. A few days before Christmas I asked my parents if Althea could stay late so that she would be there when I got home from school. I told them what it was I wanted to do and they agreed with my plan. In fact they even helped with what I had requested.

With Althea waiting for me when I arrived home, I presented her with the gifts as my parents watched. It wasn't the record and phonograph we had listened to that day, but a brand new one of each. This phonograph was even better quality and the record had no scratches on it. I had inscribed the jacket cover, "To Althea. I love you, Strekfus," in bright purple ink.

Althea cried.

It felt good to make someone else happy. I know she liked the gifts because she thanked us for them every day for almost an entire month and then at least once a year for the remainder of her employment—always on November 22, the anniversary of President Kennedy's death.

- 7 -

New York, 1996

Everything has its wonders, even
darkness and silence, and I learned,
whatever state I may be in, therein to be
content.

—Helen Keller, *The Story of My Life*

The New York sun glared in with peculiar harshness. It struck the sides of a stainless-steel water pitcher that Sagaser kept on his credenza and reflected ripples onto the ceiling, giving the appearance that somewhere in the room was a large, effervescent swimming pool. It was into this light that Strekfus walked with memo in hand. He strode in with confidence as the second part of the Enolam Boulevard story had just been published. So far he was three months into the series of twelve stories and he felt himself brimming with confidence.

"I'd like to give you this," Strekfus said, his voice pleasant and devoid of all sarcasm as he deftly placed the single white page in front of Sagaser. The man sat there looking down, not knowing what to expect. Strekfus continued innocently, explaining what the memo contained. "I've been thinking about it, and I really don't need an office the size of the one I have, so I've taken the liberty of asking Maintenance to move me into a smaller one. I think someone like our new writer on staff should have my office. I hope you don't mind. He seems like a good

147

kid—well qualified and all. I just thought it was the right thing to do."

Had Strekfus not known he was playing a part he would have gagged on his own words, but because he had undisclosed information he fell right into character. Before Sagaser could close his mouth, which had dropped open during the presentation, Strekfus continued. "I also wanted to talk to you about the stories I've been writing." He was walking around the room now, moving with ease. "I've thought a lot about what you said; that they should be about 'real' Southern homes, you know, ones like plantations, and so I've decided to do my next story on the Gorgas house in Alabama. It's on your list," and with this last remark, he turned from a print he was studying on Sagaser's wall to see the man's reaction.

Again, Sagaser appeared as if he were going to say something, but no words came from him and his Adam's apple bobbed up and down like a sexually uptight adolescent's a few seconds before he is to ask a girl on his first date. So as not to have silence that was uncomfortable for both of them, Strekfus went on, maintaining his innocence and wide-eyed optimism. "I hope you don't mind that I've done this. I just wanted to be helpful. I'm trying to give you what you want—after all, you are my boss. As you can see, all that I've been saying is right there in the memo, and I've taken the liberty of copying several of the vice presidents in on it to save you and your secretary—she's a lovely girl, what is her name, Cankeris?—the trouble of having to make copies."

Strekfus knew that his boss wasn't going to say anything and that even if he did, there was the excuse of "trying to be helpful," which always sounded good to Personnel, even if it wasn't the reality of the situation. Yet he knew the battle wasn't over—that Sagaser would find some way to regroup. The man was now silent, sitting at his desk, staring at the memo, saying nothing, and so Strekfus excused himself and slipped out of his boss's office. Surrounded by his new and smaller accommodations, Strekfus basked in his victory, but it was short-lived, because as he sat in his office, thinking about how he had just one-upped his boss, things began to get complicated.

The magazine had been printed just two days earlier—the one with part two of the Enolam Boulevard story—so Strekfus wasn't terribly surprised when he saw Sharon heading straight toward his office, plowing steadily across the secretarial area, holding the latest issue. She barged right into his space and stood there with her hands on her hips, her lips tightly glued together. Then her right hand shot out, the whole time her expression remaining unchanged. Her left hand gripped the magazine with such strength that it buckled and folded in an almost violent fashion.

"What?" asked Strekfus.

She didn't make a sound, but the fingers of her right hand fluttered toward her palm and her entire body shook with impatience. Slowly, glumly, Strekfus opened the middle drawer to his desk and produced a shiny black onyx rock about three inches long and one inch wide. Without looking directly at Sharon, he gently placed it in her hand, and with that she turned without saying a word, and walked away.

But several hours later she reappeared and sat down in front of him. Again he didn't look up, so she waited until she had his attention. She got it because of the anxiety she was producing. It filled the entire office. Finally, he gave her what she wanted.

"I'm sorry, okay? What do you want me to say?" he asked, as he made changes to the story he was working on, trying not to look at her. He knew he had gone overboard, but he didn't want to admit it to her just yet. He was still smarting from some of her comments and feeling betrayed.

"I understand that writers sometimes need to fall back on reality for inspiration, but do you mind leaving my personal life out of it next time? I was so angry with you that I had to wait several hours to come back in here and talk about the story," she said.

"You're going to read me the riot act now?" he asked, sitting back in his chair.

"You're damn right I am," she continued, leaning forward. She again produced the mauled issue and her fingers traced over the words until she found what she was looking for. "Known by some people as 'le blanc garbage,' " she verbalized and then looked blankly at Strekfus. "White trash? And the part about me being heavy, and then my skin disease?"

"Look, I know you're upset. I didn't mean to hurt your feelings. I just wanted to write out some of my childhood experiences and . . ."

"Well, how convenient for you that I was there to provide the material," she snapped. Then, realizing that no matter how angry she was, what she was about to say would need to be couched in at least civil terms, she drew a deep breath and calmed herself. After a few moments she spoke again.

"Strekfus," she began, her tone now changed, "I may have been overweight and not come from money like you, but if you sincerely wanted to write about your childhood, you certainly picked a roundabout way of doing it."

"What do you mean? I did actually . . ." he started to say.

"Strekfus, I was *there*. I've known you since the first grade. I *remember*. Who do you think you're fooling? My parents didn't abuse me. You were always jealous of them because . . ." but then she stopped to judge his reaction, knowing that she was in difficult territory. "How many days did I come to school with a black eye?" She waited for his answer, her eyebrows uplifted. No answer came, so she continued to the second part of her question. "And how many days did you?" she asked, reaching across his desk to grab his wrist in attempt to make contact.

She could tell by his demeanor that she had hit a nerve, for he immediately jerked his hand away from hers. "Don't do that. Don't ever touch my wrists like that," he said, and looked down at the blotter on his desk. For a few seconds she merely looked at him, stunned that his reaction had been so out of character, almost violent. Then he seemed to snap out of it, addressing her again.

"Hey, look," he countered, although somewhat shyly, "I did have something in there about my father and how he could be a son-of-a-bitch, I just . . ."

"You just made it sound like it was my father. All right. Fine. And you turned yourself into Susan Hayward so you didn't have to deal with it. Fine. But at some point you have to deal with it or it will deal with you. All I'm saying is that I don't think you ever really addressed the issue and I'm not comfortable being the conduit for your unresolved disputes with your parents."

He was quiet now. He was feeling a lot of things: anger, resentment, frustration, rage, anger, sadness, anger again. They both sat there for a few moments and let the air clear. "Is there anything else about the story you thought was incorrect or that I misrepresented?" He was asking sincerely now, upset that she had been offended at a simple story in a magazine, and mindful that she had been his best friend for so many years and that he had misrepresented the truth.

"No," she said without hostility, "I think everything else was pretty accurate. And at least you called me Bunny in the story. At least you didn't use my real name."

"Okay, then?"

"Okay, then," she repeated and got up to leave. But before she left, she turned to him and spoke, her tone level and warm. "You know I love you to death."

He looked up from the corrections he was making on his next story. "I know," he said, smiled, and continued to write.

"What's this horrible thing?" she asked, gesturing toward something on Strekfus's desk, hoping to change the electricity between them.

"Jadite. I had to do a report on it. You know, that green glass from the '30s."

"Better you than me, honey," she said, with tilted head. Strekfus just smiled back at her. Then she stood there for a moment, hesitating before she exited, feeling guilty that she had come down so hard on him.

"Every time I come in here there's something strange on your desk. A tobacco tin, reports on cardboard, Jadite. I can't

151

wait to see what you come up with next," and with that she waved a hand at him and walked out of the room, hoping that everything was once again copasetic between them.

As he sat there revising his manuscript, he thought about what she had said earlier. He had glossed over his father's abuse in the story and for good reason—who would want to read about that? Wasn't it enough that he had strayed this far off the beaten path by writing about the homes he remembered as a child instead of the traditional homes and gardens he had been assigned to cover? Why go into really uncharted territory? Maybe he was better off leaving that element out of his stories. Maybe he was better off creating his own world in writing—a world where the abuse didn't exist, at least not in its most violent form. He decided that the next story would be in a different location, one that the parents couldn't enter into.

His mind was wandering through a library of ideas on which he could write. How could he pull the Gorgas house—his next story—into what he had already written. As he ruminated, he began to think of Sagaser and how he had slam-dunked the man by breaking into the computer files. He knew Sagaser would find a way to get even, and in most cases this meant getting even with everyone, for Sagaser was usually not one to make it appear that he held a grudge even though he did. In many cases he would punish the entire staff for one person's indiscretions, and as Strekfus thought about this he felt uncomfortable knowing that he might be the cause of such retribution. And it came to pass in just this manner, for by the end of the day, an official memo went out. It landed on everyone's desk like a rock thrown through a plate glass window, and this is the way it read, complete with the incorrect spelling of the editor's first name:

TO:	EVERYONE
FROM:	MR. EDWN SAGASER
RE:	LATENESS

It has come to my attention that several employees of this organization are continually late. We will maintain a professional demeanor in this company at all costs. Since many of you have be unable to function within our daily schedule, I am going to insist that each of you sign in at the receptionist desk. Those who fail to do so will receive punishment up to, and including, termination.

Strekfus regarded the memo with the same distain he regarded most of Sagaser's work—as if it were a four-month-old cucumber found lying in the back of the vegetable crisper. He sat back and cracked his knuckles, thinking about his boss. The man was an editor and he couldn't even spell his own name correctly. Then there was the phrase, "many of you have *be* unable." He knew that Sagaser wrote his own memos, not trusting even his obnoxious secretary to carry out the odious deeds, but he didn't have time to dwell on his boss or the problems of the magazine. He had a story to write and, deciding that he could write more efficiently at home, he slipped into the receptionist's area (it was after five o'clock and vacant) and sandwiched a folded piece of paper between the pages of the yellowed, dog-eared memo book she used with regularity. Then he gently closed the door behind him and made his way home.

- 8 -

The Gorgas House

Tuscaloosa, Alabama, 1966

Meanwhile, the desire to express myself
grew.

—Helen Keller, *The Story of My Life*

"Y ou must sign the registry. We want aw-ul of our
illustrious guests to be recorded for time
immemorial. If Mrs. Go-wa-gas were he-ah, she
would insist upon it," the tour guide said, handing the first in line
a feather quill into which was inserted the cartridge of a regular
ballpoint pen. "Now if you-all have any questions, jus be shu-ah
to ask," she continued and turned deftly in the direction of the
front parlor.

* * * * *

The routine at the Gorgas house was always the same.
After having us sign the registry, the pre-septuagenarian tour
guide would don her spectacles (horn-rims with rhinestones, a
free-swinging chain which looped around back) and then proceed
to crane her aged neck out and over the guest book as she turned
her head upward. Then, looking down at your signature through
her bifocals, she would scour the penned images with the scrutiny
of a handwriting analyst.

"This is truly amazing," I thought to myself. "Nothing has changed since my first trip to the Gorgas house when I was in the second grade." Here I was "taking the tour" just as I had for several years in a row. On previous visits, irritated at the prospect of having to "register," and being the mischievous children that we were, we always found ways to embellish this ritual, usually by means of employing a pseudonym. Now that our fourth-grade class was here, today would be no different.

"Why, you hay-uv the same name as our belov-ed governor, George Wallace! You must be the most popular bo-ey in yow-ah class! It's so nice to see Southern traditions carried on by our youth," the tour guide had said on my first visit. She repeated this each time, each year, including today's excursion, never seeming to remember me from previous visits.

From the first visit on, whenever my fellow students and I made our annual pilgrimage through the squeaky iron gate located at the entrance to the home, absolutely nothing changed including Mrs. Castratis, the tour guide, who appeared to be about the same age as the house. As with all tour guides, she wore a name tag laminated in plastic. Its Old English lettering simply stated, "Castratis," and there was an overly ornamented flourish underneath it.

By now her routine was so familiar to me that I could recite it word for word. It was always a treat to impress a newcomer in the group by displaying my extensive knowledge of the house. I would recite verbatim the entire tour, usually under my breath and a few seconds ahead of the guide, and then watch as our latest addition marveled at my uncanny ability to predict exactly what was going to be said. It always happened the same way, followed by laughing and our attempts to keep from getting thrown out of the house.

It wasn't my first tour of the house that intrigued me so much as those that followed for this very reason. For three years in a row I was, according to the tour guide, "the most popular boy in my class," with the same name as our illustrious governor, even though at this point (today's tour) he was no longer in office. This minor detail seemed to escape her—it appeared that she had not set foot outside the door for many years and probably wouldn't until they carried her out in a box. The fact that the former governor was no longer in office didn't register with her. One got the feeling that George Wallace would always be governor to her in some way or another as he probably would be to so many Alabamians.

"George Wallace isn't the governor anymore," I said in response to her scrutiny of the register on this day. "His wife Lurleen is, but she's really just a puppet dictator so that he can maintain his stronghold on the backward thinking of a racist state."

"Yeeeeeees, I seeeeee," the tour guide said with more than her usual amount of disdain, and looked at me as if I had a small tree growing out of my head. You really can't disturb tradition in a place such as this and not get something back for it. It really was a nice house, but it was right in the middle of the University of Alabama, in the very heart of the South.

* * * * *

Surrounded by azaleas, rhododendrons, and the typical verdant foliage of the area, the Gorgas house stands in the middle of the university's campus. Great oaks and magnolias cluster about the house, creating an oasis in the midst of bustling college students hurrying to and from class, most of them oblivious to its charm and history. A low brick wall completes the house's seclusion, setting it visually and spiritually in another era.

The house was built in 1826 and was at one time the home of Josiah and Amelia Gorgas. Josiah was an army officer whose chief responsibility was to raise arms for the Confederacy during the Civil War. After the war was over he was elected president of the university, probably because of his past association with Southern efforts.

While his son, William C. Gorgas—the army surgeon who was responsible for the eradication of yellow fever in Panama when the canal was being built—never officially lived in the house as its owner, he made regular visits there, and it is he who is most often associated with the house.

156

It is doubtful that any of the Gorgases could have imagined that someday a guided tour would be given of their sleeping quarters and chamber-pot collections. Nevertheless, its cool interior is often a welcome respite from the intense Alabama sun, being a time capsule of antiques and history, and in today's case, a place for elementary school students to amuse themselves.

* * * * *

"Now you children who want to see the Gorgas house may go at two thirty. The rest of you can go to see the natural history exhibit," Miss Dearborn, the teacher in charge of the field trip had said. Fortunately, only a handful of us desired to view the Gorgas house, the more plebeian-minded of the school preferring to see what the lack of dental hygiene did for the Triceratops whose skull was located in the archaeology department.

Miss Dearborn had decided that since the tour guide at the Gorgas house was an adult and that we would be in capable hands, she would accompany the other group of children to the science building. She really should have known not to leave me in an environment with someone who didn't understand me. You see, I had already broken Miss Dearborn in, that is to say, she was used to me and knew what to expect.

Once, in class she had asked us to pick a role model and be prepared to share with the class the next day who this was and why we had picked them. I waited my turn and listened as each student told what they wanted to be and why. After six firemen, four policemen, three nurses, and five presidents, it was my turn.

"And now, Strekfus," Miss Dearborn had said, "who is *your* role model?"

I paused for dramatic effect, waiting until I had all the other children's attention and then said, "Agnes Moorehead, the woman who plays Endora on the television show *Bewitched*."

"Why Agnes Moorehead?" Miss Dearborn had asked with trepidation. (like I said, she was familiar with my style by now.)

157

"Because anyone with that many caftans and that much eye makeup, who can turn people she doesn't like into small animals, has to have something going for her," I said.

By this time most of the class was planning my demise at recess. Fourth grade would prove to be just as traumatic as the previous three had been, and I was counting the days until I could break free from this confining environment. Still, after the fire in the first grade where I had almost killed the poor janitor, Mr. Malone, I had given up most of my fantasy life for a more social one which involved entertaining my fellow classmates. In most cases this worked out well, but there were the few instances which didn't, the example of role model being one.

"Strekfus," Miss Dearborn continued, having regained her composure after the Agnes Moorehead comment, "you have to pick someone else."

I sat there for a few seconds and then it hit me. "I know," I said, "my Aunt Testa."

Miss Dearborn knew she had to ask, but I could tell she dreaded it. "And *why*, Strekfus, is your Aunt Testa your role model?"

"Because she never worked a day in her life," I said, completely satisfied with myself.

"Let's go on to the next person," Miss Dearborn said, and then moved swiftly on to Curtis Plank who sat directly behind me and proceeded to captivate the class with why he wanted to be a linoleum salesman.

* * * * *

"Now if you children will just step this way you will notice on your left the lovely sofa which Amelia Gorgas bought for two daw-las and a hay-uv and had shipped up the Warrior River. It was originally covered in horsehair but now sports a lovely silk brocade. Please do not sit upon the divan as it is extreee-mely old and an heirloom." Of course the tour guide's commentary was exactly the same as it had been for years and I had immediately committed it to memory the first time I visited the house, hoping to be able to use it for future tours. I decided to let her start first as I was feeling especially benevolent today.

On previous tours, after signing in, I would inevitably turn suddenly in the direction of the sofa and exclaim, "Isn't that the sofa that Amelia Gorgas bought for two daw-las and a hay-uv and had shipped up the Warrior River?" Looking down at me over her horn-rims, Mrs. Castratis would then force a smile and through clenched teeth mutter, "Why, yes . . . yes, it *ee-us.*"

I learned to do this with most tours because the results were inevitably better than any other form of entertainment Tuscaloosa, Alabama could provide a child of ten or eleven. From then on, having been shaken up by the fact that I had stolen her introductory line, and given the fact that she had memorized the "script" verbatim, the rest of the tour was a combination of faltering and backtracking, giving me ample opportunity to interject whatever other bits I had managed to retain from previous visits.

Moving into the first room on the left, she would focus on the silver collection of Colonel William C. Gorgas, emphasis on the *C,* and usually draw that one letter out to at least three syllables. I'm not sure if William was actually a colonel. Tour guides, along with their multi-syllabic deliveries, have the habit of adding "colonel" to any man's name they feel deserves to have a distinguished reputation. It's like those aging aunts who put "Esquire" on the outside of the nephew's birthday card. Strekfus Ovid Beltzenschmidt, Esquire. As if my name needed another word added to it.

Having been through the silver routine, I rushed over to the Plexiglas-enclosed collection before she had a chance to launch into her recitation, turned to the others and exclaimed, "Look! It's the lovely hand-hammered silver bought by Colonel C. (emphasis on the *C*) Gorgas." Feeling brave, I continued with, "You remember Colonel Gorgas. He was instrumental in the fight against yellow fever on the isthmus of Panama!" By now the tour guide's lips were stretched to the point of breaking into what some people might call a smile. I knew better, judging from the nineteenth-century daggers coming from each of her eyes.

Adjusting her bra and glasses, she straightened herself and tried to remember where she was in the tour. My classmates beamed in my direction and I basked in their silent applause.

"Pu-leeze do not get your sticky fingers on the glass and quit popping that blow gum in he-ah."

Mrs. Castratis was speaking to a small, light-skinned black girl who had wandered in with us on this tour of the house. "Is this small urchin with you-all? she asked, turning to the class. And then, "What is yo-wa name?" she asked the girl as she scowled down at her. The taciturn black child showed no emotion and continued blowing bubbles. It was the first time I noticed her. She was a definitely a Negro, but a very light-skinned one, and there was something else different about her, almost familiar, that I couldn't put my finger on. In fact her features were those of a white person, only her skin was black and not even the black I was used to seeing. She was more lightly colored—almost café au lait. As with anyone who doesn't fit into the norm, I felt an immediate rapport with her. The tour guide regarded her with disdain but kept on going.

"If you-all will now follow me into the next room you will notice an exquisite portrait of Mrs. Gorgas over the mantel." This was the high point of the tour for the guide and we all knew it. She would give dramatic pauses as she motioned toward the portrait and dreamily drew out her sentences: "Notice the eyes . . . now, move slowly from one side of the room to the other." We would follow her directions and then she would turn dramatically and deliver her favorite line of the tour with spooky reverence. "The eyes seem to follow you as you move about the roo-um." Then she would purse her lips in a little smirk, shut her eyes and tilt her head back as if she were having an orgasm and say, "Now you know what I have known all along. There are forces about which we cannot explain."

Coming out of her trance with a rather fake shaking of her head and opening of her eyes ("How long wa-us I out for this time? Did anything happen while I wa-us undah?"), she would then proceed to walk directly and slowly through the middle of the group of tourists, her eyes fixed on the next room in the house, speaking in a more reverent tone from then on as if to say, "I hope your lives have been changed; I know mine has."

Usually the easily impressed tour groups would automatically move aside for her like the Red Sea parting for Moses. They also hung on her every word. On this particular tour I attended, however, as we entered the room with the portrait, I walked in front of it and chimed in before she had a chance.

"Loooook at the eyes!" I began with a mysterious tone and my strongest Southern accent, "Now move slowly . . . slowly from side to si-ud." The other children complied and then I delivered the final line: "They seem to follow you as you move about the rooooom!" and at that point I tilted my head back and sighed as if I were experiencing the most excruciatingly pleasurable orgasm.

The small black child shrieked at this, jumping up and down and popping even bigger bubbles. Before I knew it, the tour guide was standing directly over me and I was looking up at her between two huge sagging breasts. "Some of you have hay-ud this tour before, I suspect," she scowled, "and what is that you-a holdin' in you-a hand, Mr. 'Have All The Answers,' " she drawled and stared me down.

"It's a *Nephrolepis exaltata* 'Bostoniensis,' " I said.

"A wha-ut?"

"A fern," I said.

"A fuh-wun?" What ever are you-a doin with a fuh-wun?" she said looking somewhat interested. Then she changed her demeanor, "You didn't steal it, did yeeeew? she asked in a menacing tone, turning her head sideways and squinting her eyes so that the crow's feet on each side of her face looked like river gullies in the Grand Canyon.

"No, ma'am. I bought it at the Woolworth's downtown when the bus stopped," I replied, gazing down at the few small sprigs wrapped in paper. I had forgotten I even had them in my hand, such was my desire to lead the tour. The few tattered sprigs had made the entire day's journey in my tight fist and I had completely lost all awareness of them until this minute.

She regarded me for a moment and then, thinking she could bond momentarily with a fourth-grader (she really did need to get out more often), went on, "You know, fuh-wuns are among the oldest living plants on the earth. They were around even before the dinosaurs," she said, hoping to gain my respect by offering up this bit of encyclopediatic knowledge.

I waited. Her last statement hung in the air, like some hideous insect within slapping distance of a dirty and flaccid flyswatter. "Were they around when you were growing up?" I asked. She said nothing, but turned abruptly, squeezing her lips together so tightly that they turned blue momentarily.

"Missy, if you don't put that blow-gum away I'm going to have to confiscate it," the tour guide snarled, turning her anger from me and in the direction of the small black girl. Saying nothing, the girl merely followed the rest of us, skipping at a nonchalant pace.

"And no skipping on the Victorian carpet, Missy! This is an ancient weave that does not hold up well to small children's skipping! By the way," she shot in my direction, "it seems mighty strange to me for a boy (and she put emphasis on the word *boy*) to be playing with fuh-wuns. What ever do you want with a fuh-wun anyway, Mr. Smarty Pants?"

"It's actually a *Nephrolepis exaltata* 'Bostoniensis,' " I countered.

"Ex-cuuuuse me?" the tour guide answered, her irritation becoming extremely obvious by now.

"Nothing," I said.

We proceeded to follow the guide across the center hall, careful not to touch anything while listening to her mutter to herself under her breath, "Thirty years at this job and the children just nev-uh act as they should. Little Lord Fauntleroy and Miss High Yella."

As she hobbled to the other side of the house, her high heels made deep impressions in the carpet, occasionally catching the weave in such a way that it pulled great hunks of the maroon-and-rose-colored fibers out like uprooted sprigs of grass. Evidently the ancient Victorian weave had not been loomed to

162

withstand her matronly high heels any more than the rubber soles of Negro children's sneakers.

"Now as you know, there was no air-conditioning in those days and there were insects every-whey-uh. The windows were kept open for ventilation and there were no screens as we know them today," she continued as we started to enter the kitchen area.

Knowing the routine, I remarked, "That must be why there are small bowls under the legs of the pie safe. To keep the insects from crawling up the legs and into the pies." I continued with real gusto at this point, completely taking over her duties. I thought she needed a rest and would appreciate my helping her out. After all, she looked rather harried from the portion of the tour she had already given.

"You see," I continued, and moved in front of the group with the utmost confidence, "the insects would not be able to travel over the water in the small bowls, therefore making the pies safe from infestation," and I waved the fern in the direction of the ingenious nineteenth-century invention. At that moment, the small black child popped the biggest bubble yet, coating not only her entire face and hands, but most of the red-velvet ropes directly in front of us—those worn tubular swags used to hold back the hordes of history-hungry tourists the Gorgas house had evidently expected at one time.

"That's it!" Mrs. Castratis shouted, and at this point she became quite hysterical. Grabbing the black girl by one of her pigtails and me under the arm, she barked, "You and George Wallace come with me," and she launched into a lengthy tirade about her life as she headed us toward the front door: "Lord knows I wouldn't have to work at this job if my husband hadn't been run oh-vuh by that bus," she croaked, marching us down the carpeted center hallway. "Corrugated Cardboard Industries indeed! He worked fo-ah years at that blessed factory and fo-ah what? I should have sued the bus company! Don't you fight me, young lady," she yelled at the girl, who was showing obvious signs of resentment. "Who would have thought there'd be no life insurance! I could have been something!" Her tirade seemed to pick up momentum as she moved closer to the front door. "My hand-painted china cups were the talk of Edwina, but nooooo, I have to be a tour guide to unruly street urchins in Tuscaloosa, Al-a-bam-a."

Her unintelligible ranting continued the length of the hall until she had led us out onto the front porch and slammed the door. We waited until the glass in the windows stopped rattling.

"She's just an old bitch," the small black girl said, speaking for the first time. "I wouldn't let her bother you. You know more about that old house than she does. And her going on about some old husband of hers. That old bus should have hit her, if you ask me." We both sat down on the front steps. Then she pulled something out from under her shirt. It was the feather pen that visitors used to sign the registry—the feather with the ballpoint cartridge stuck in it. She proceeded to twirl it about nonchalantly in the air.

"Where'd you get that?" I asked.

"I took it when she wasn't looking," she answered. She sat in thought a moment, and then turned to me.

"Here," she said, "this is for you," and she handed me the feather quill pen I had written the name George Wallace with.

"Why are you giving this to me?" I asked.

"I don't know. I figure you deserve something from that house. A souvenir or something. That woman, she's just jealous 'cause you know the stories about the house as well as she does. Besides, I liked your version better." She traced the outline of some imaginary object with a stick she found lying on the steps, her mind seemingly far away now. Overhead, a blue jay screeched and the muffled mutter of students on their way to class wafted over century-old azaleas.

"I don't have anything to give you," I said, but then I remembered the small fern.

"Here," I said. "I want you to have this." I held the drooping fronds out to her.

"You don't have to give me anything," said the girl, and proceeded to work a piece of Johnson grass into one of the eyeholes of her sneakers.

"No, I want you to have it," I said, handing her the three sad little fern shoots wrapped in paper. By now the paper had become soaked from the moisture of the roots and the poor little fronds were beginning to show signs of wear. Their velvety-green and delicate leaves bent gently downward.

"I'm gonna give this to my daddy," she said, taking the wilted greenery from me. "He loves to raise things. Before long he'll have this growing everywhere. He has all kinds of plants just growing around our house."

About this time, the front door opened and the others in the group began to make their way onto the porch. The tour guide stuck her head out and gave the both of us a tight-lipped frown, rolling her eyes.

"I'm going home," the girl said, touching my shoulder, waving an upturned hand, and I was left to wait for the rest of the group to file out. I watched her as she skipped off across the campus, occasionally stopping to inspect the small plant I had given her, gradually disappearing into the background of azaleas and college students.

* * * * *

Years later when I was attending the University of Alabama, I would walk by the Gorgas house several times each day to and from classes. Occasionally I would catch a glimpse of the tour guide answering the bell and welcoming the one or two adult tourists or curious passersby who had come to see the house. As she was shutting the door, I would sometimes hear, "Now if you-all will just sign the registry . . .You know I once threw George Wallace out of this house because he misbehaved, so you all mind me now, and don't be popping any blow-gum," and then she would laugh a faint little laugh, and close the door. There was something comforting knowing that they would receive the same tour I and everyone else had, and that the eyes of Mrs. Gorgas would follow them about the room.

Still, I wondered how the carpet was holding up, if the eyes ever get tired of following the tourists around, and whatever happened to the little black girl with the soft features. I kept the feather pen for years on the dresser in my room, all through high school and college, until I moved permanently away from home and lost track of it and so many other things that had been a part of my life.

- 9 -

New York, 1996

Sometimes a new word revived an image
that some earlier experience had engraved
on my brain.

—Helen Keller, *The Story of My Life*

Strekfus looked at his watch, then at his fellow subway passengers. The train had sat in the tunnel for forty-five minutes while there was "police activity." Eventually it pulled into the Thirty-fourth Street station just as panic was beginning to set in, and everyone hurriedly emptied out onto the sidewalks either to walk or try to hail one of the plentiful cabs which, on these occasions, were scarce. He was standing on the corner of Seventh Avenue and Thirty-sixth Street trying to get the attention of one of these speeding yellow modes of transportation when it happened.

At first he thought it was just a dizzy spell, but it was as if something flashed in his mind, something more than the shiny, green-tiled image. Then he noticed the woman standing next to him, holding a screaming baby. He couldn't figure out what was taking place, but he knew it wasn't good. A sick feeling seemed to come out of nowhere and wash through his entire body. The woman was saying something over and over about the baby. Something about that word—baby—some trigger. Then he was holding onto an antique light pole for support, feeling as though his legs were going to fold on him, wishing the woman would

167

quiet the infant. As he regained his connection to the outside world he became aware that a cab driver was yelling at him, asking if he was going to get in or not. Before he could answer, two other people grabbed the cab and one of them made a rude remark to him accompanied by an obscene hand gesture. But he didn't care. He was so taken aback by his dizziness that he couldn't be bothered. Then he remembered his last visit home—the dizziness, the beating sound in his head. Maybe he *should* see his doctor. He had put it off for too long, but not without reason. He acknowledged his intense fear of anything medical, and like most men, put off going to see a physician until something was dismembered or beyond repair.

He walked the rest of the way to work, traversing midtown's crowded streets, comforted this time by the number of pedestrians on the sidewalk, hopeful that if he blacked out someone would help him. Then he remembered the time he had seen someone fall to the ground while suffering a heart attack. People had actually stepped over the person and no one had stopped. After a few minutes he found himself at the front of the building he worked in. He made his way through the heavy revolving doors, pressed the elevator button, and waited for his floor while trying not to breathe on any of his fellow passengers. He exited onto the industrial gray carpet which led to the suite of offices where his work space was located.

By the time he neared the kitchen area for his morning coffee he had managed to shake off the dizziness and regain his composure. He tried to make excuses, figuring that the subway ride, the claustrophobia, the early-morning rush had all contributed to his vertiginous state. As he rounded the corner he ran into one of his co-workers, a loud, zaftig woman who was secretary to one of the vice presidents located on a higher floor. (Why was it companies always had a multitude of vice presidents?) The secretary's boss was a member of that elite group, the ones who made the real decisions around the magazine. The ones even higher than Sagaser.

"Hey, Strekfus," she said breezily, efficiently extracting a coffee bag from one of the plastic-laminated, faux-wood cabinets.

168

It would be the first coffee of the day. "Our coffeemaker is broken upstairs and my boss is screaming for some stimulation. Thought I'd get you guys started in the process while I was at it." Strekfus noticed how her ample frame was squeezed into her brown polyester suit. She had frosted hair which hung down, somewhat unkempt, and wore flesh-colored hose with heavy black shoes. She wasn't exactly a walking fashion statement, but she was nice and always supportive of his work, so he forgave her these small gaffes, realizing how much more essential it was to be a genuine and sane person, especially in New York where the vast number of people—excessive mental baggage which roamed the streets pretending personification—could be cruel and demanding.

"Did you hear about your boss, Winney?" she asked gaily as the water began to filter down through the coffee grounds, its trickle accompanied by gaseous spurts of steam from the commercial-size dispenser.

"No. Why? What's wrong with him?" Strekfus asked. "I mean, other than the obvious. And by the way, I wouldn't call him Winney, even behind his back unless you're a good friend or have something on his tax returns that he doesn't know about."

"Well, his wife thought he had died. He was just lying there when she found him, but after the paramedics got there, they discovered that he was still breathing. They say nervous exhaustion, but I think I know what it was. I think there may have been a little, how shall I say, extra stress added to his life because of a certain attitude he has. And I think I might know what put him over the edge." She was now adjusting the Pyrex receptacle under the trickling brown stream. The orange decaf pot was conspicuously empty.

"What did it? Put him over the edge?" he asked with genuine concern. After all, he had just broken this boss in and he didn't want to have to go through the process of learning a new one's habits and abnormalities. Even though Sagaser could be difficult, Strekfus somehow understood him, and his unpredictability was sometimes comfortably predictable.

"Well," she went on, drawing the word out, demurely wiping off the counter top with a mildewed red-and-white striped rag, the mopping motions more geared toward added effect rather than cleanliness as the countertop now looked worse than it had before, "let's just say, after the higher-ups get through with him, he might not be quite so, well, prejudiced," and with that she happily walked out of the kitchen area, her legs in their flesh-colored hose rubbing against each other with the sound usually reserved for two pieces of sandpaper during mating season.

"Wait a minute," he said as he ran after her. He grabbed her arm and she turned to look at him. "What about my latest story? If he's not here, then who's going to edit my work?"

"Relax," she said, patting his chest with her plump fingers, "everything is all set. They've promoted Karen to Sagaser's spot temporarily, and you know how easily she can be handled. Of course he would probably keel over on the spot if he knew, after the run-in he had with her over your first story," and with that she rolled her eyes and began to make her way toward the secretarial area.

Strekfus strolled back down the hall in the direction of his office, but before he reached his destination, he stopped to look into the space his boss normally occupied. He never would have performed such an overt act if his boss had been around, even if the man were out for just one day, but because he felt there was a safe distance now between himself and Sagaser, he allowed himself the luxury of viewing these normally forbidden surroundings with his keen eye. While he enjoyed a relative degree of civility with his boss—calling him by his nickname, having an occasional drink or game of pool with the man—he nevertheless felt the invisible boundaries that his boss set up and he at least tried at times to respect them, even if Sagaser wasn't respecting his lately. Still, he remembered the memo—the racist one which he had printed out and left on the receptionist's desk—and he felt a tinge of guilt. Had it been the memo or his last story that put Sagaser over the edge? But did it really matter? The man was a monster. The only problem was, the man was still his boss.

170

The door to Sagaser's office had been left open and there were remnants of his presence scattered about as if he had just gone out to lunch or stepped away to the men's room. Strekfus entered the room and began to look around. Whatever had hit Sagaser had hit him suddenly, for there was still half a cup of coffee on the desk and nothing had been put away. There was some story about Mexico that one of the other writers was working on. Sagaser had been halfway through editing it. Karen would have to finish the job.

As he padded about the plush carpet (totally different from what the rest of the staff had to put up with—worn, gray, utilitarian), he began to notice things about his boss which had escaped him before. There were maybe twenty, thirty pictures of Sagaser at golf tournaments holding up trophies: arms around fellow golfers, caddies with chipped-tooth smiles. There was even one of Sagaser sitting in a golf cart with several famous personalities around him. Then there was the close-up of him shaking hands with some sturdy female golfer—a *real* close-up. Did he really have that much nose hair? And did his true hair color have that much gray in it? Sagaser's hand was draped casually over the shoulder of the female golfer. It was then that he noticed how abnormally long the man's fingernails were. He could have been mistaken for Howard Hughes or Barbra Streisand. But the most shocking photograph was one in which Sagaser had posed with a newly killed deer. The man was bending over, biting the rear end of the animal just as some fellow hunter snapped the picture. Strekfus began to feel that he really didn't know this man, his boss, at all. "And Sagaser is questioning me about *my* stories?" he thought to himself. "This man feels threatened by some cake-baking seven-year-old?"

"Find anything interesting?" It was the secretary from earlier, the one at the coffee machine. She had come in to drop off a memo on Sagaser's desk and was now standing beside Strekfus, scanning the golf photos with him.

"I just realized that I've never really been in here," said Strekfus. "I mean, I've been here, just not . . . well, *in* here, if you know what I mean."

"I know exactly what you mean," she said. "I don't think I've ever met my boss, and I've worked for her for fifteen years. Funny how you think you know someone, only to find out they weren't the person you thought they were at all. Either that or they were a lot more. Of course my boss is the only female vice president and the only one of the bunch who isn't lily-white, so she's probably got a lot more baggage than most."

He turned to look at her, thinking about what she had just said, about not really knowing people. He realized that he was guilty of this sometimes—of seeing people for their outward appearances and shortcomings, imagining a plethora of scenarios about what they ate, where they lived, what kind of soap (if any) they used. She was still staring at the photos.

"You know," she started again, "I remember when his first wife died. That had to be, oh, ten years ago, I guess. You weren't here then. He was different before that, more human if you know what I mean. Almost everyone in the office went to the funeral that day, and I remember meeting someone there, a woman, who came up to me and said that I must be so-and-so from the office. You could have knocked me over. When I asked her how she knew me, she said that Sagaser often spoke about me. And I didn't even work for him. Can you imagine?" Then she was laying a hand on Strekfus's arm, feigning self-deprecation, "I was just as unattractive then, so you know it wasn't anything sexual."

Strekfus was looking at her while she remembered the funeral, the guest who knew her, the days before Sagaser had turned into the person he was now. "I sat and spoke with this woman who had come up to me," she was continuing. "She was one of those older women who are lonely and feel that if they start telling you their life's story you'll stay and listen." She was looking questioningly at him, trying to connect, and it was working.

"I'll never forget how she described him as a child. Said that his family was well-off but that his parents had been abusive, hard-driven. I guess you know who his father is—head of that major book publishing firm. She was telling me that when he was fourteen his father forced him and the brother into cruel competitions, and that Edwin always lost. Said the father beat them both to the point where they had to go to the hospital one time. You do that now and they put you in jail. Back then it was normal. Still," she went on, "it doesn't explain why he's the way he is now. I mean, we've all been through something. Some people think that his last wife's illness did it to him. I guess that might do it to anybody," and with that she walked back over to Sagaser's desk and began to write something.

"I just want to leave a note for him. I know he's not going to be back anytime soon, but I'll just let him know that Karen took care of the problem," and with that she left Strekfus with the photographs.

He was once again alone in the room. "Funny," he thought, "how you don't imagine people like Sagaser having a wife, much less having had three, and two that are dead. And who would have imagined his father as being physically abusive. What must it have been like for him to come from where he did? He tried to imagine his boss's childhood, what games he played, how he interacted with others, what he ate for breakfast. But the images wouldn't come.

He let himself linger only a few minutes longer. His next story was due and he wanted to be able to give it more attention than the last one. Bad childhood and dead wives or not, Sagaser had been ruthless, and yet Stekfus couldn't help but feel more sympathetic to the man, knowing what he had been through. There was some part of him that wanted his boss's approval, that wanted to love him and to be respected by him even if he could be cold-blooded and mean. Yet Sagaser always pushed him away, kept him at arm's length.

Strekfus had longed for a father figure (or at least what he thought a father figure should be) to replace the one he felt had abandoned him, even if the means of the abandonment had been death. Why was it that they, these older men, never mentored or fulfilled the expectations you placed on them, just as the real fathers had not fulfilled them? He wondered if somewhere in the back of his mind he had made Sagaser into this

173

idea—the father figure. Was it in order to locate that element of his life which was missing or to be able to confront it by putting in its place that which had died long ago? Weren't we all, in some way or another, recreating our past family and relationships or what we thought they should be like in our present-day ones? And wasn't this either an attempt to recreate what once was, or to go back and rectify what should have been, or both? Wasn't that what Strekfus's own father had done in a way—not with people, but with houses? Hadn't he been searching for his childhood in those great old Southern homes that he forced his family to endure on Sunday outings, looking for some clue as to why he had become the person he was, hoping that maybe something would click and he could change or at least explain the past?

Strekfus thought about this as he walked toward the door, barely noticing that his foot brushed against a golf ball—one of Sagaser's own—sending it rolling luxuriously over the deep maroon carpeting to its appointed hiding spot beneath one of the oversized sofas where it would stay until summoned forth, as if by the hand of God.

* * * * *

Later that day, as he sat absorbed in outlining his next story, he felt someone staring at him. He looked up to see Sharon in his doorway.

"Hey, look, there was nothing in that last story about you," he said, with his hands held up as if she had a gun. "Gorgas house equals no mention of you."

"No, no problem with the story," she said casually and smiled. "I just need to get a serial number off of your computer," and she walked over to where his hard drive was located and began to look around. She spoke as she worked, never looking up from her task. "You know, I believe the receptionist called me a 'cracker' as I walked past the front desk."

"Are you serious?"

"As cancer." Her head was down, searching for the numbers. "I've heard that she really has it out for anyone white.

174

Somebody said she was suing the company." Then changing the subject, she said, "Just curious about something."

"Shoot."

"Now don't take this strictly as criticism," she started in, "but I think some of your stories are a little oblique, and by that I mean you seem to be dancing around some issues—not really addressing them."

"Such as?"

"Such as your abusive parents, what your childhood was like emotionally for you. You know, small stuff like that."

Strekfus rolled his eyes and sat back. "When I need a therapist, I'll be sure and give you a call. Besides, you've already made this quite clear. Why do you keep going over the same territory? We've had this discussion already. Drop it." He waited a moment and then spoke again. "Did you hear about Sagaser? He's in the hospital. Nervous exhaustion or something."

"Nothing like changing the subject," she countered as she moved cables and wires around trying to get a better view of the portals and switches. She finally let the mass of them drop in disgust like a fishwife throwing back a handful of eels she deemed unworthy.

"All I'm saying is that you've written these droll little stories, but what's the real story? Don't you think what really happened, and by that I mean what you felt, how you dealt with things, is more interesting? Don't you think your real family history is worth investigating?" She was unscrewing some plate now, attempting to locate the numbers she so desperately sought. "I mean, we've all got things in our past and you, especially with your strange aversions to things, should want to know where they come from, what caused them."

"You can't take a hint, can you? Aversions like what?"

"Oh, come on," she said, looking up at him. "You shave your chest because of some fear of body hair or . . . I don't know, whatever. And when I touched your wrists that time you completely flipped out."

"I didn't flip out."

"And then there's your aversion to ice water."

175

"Ice water?" Strekfus was now asking defensively. He could feel the hairs on the back of his neck standing up.

"Every time we're out eating in some restaurant you make sure they don't put ice in your water or in any drink you might have. I'd call that strange."

"There's nothing strange about not liking ice and if there is some reason why I do the things I do, I really don't care to know. You seem to want to make something dark and terrifying out of my quirks and my childhood. People who live in glass houses shouldn't . . . you know."

"Go around naked?"

"I don't think anyone wants to read about the strange parts of my childhood. Besides, all we need is one more story about child abuse. That whole 'Look at me, I hurt' thing went out with the '70s."

"Whatever you say," Sharon said under her breath as she scribbled down the last series of numbers. "I just think—and this is strictly from what I've been told—that writing can be a sort of therapy for certain individuals. It's just that from what I'm reading of yours, you're still emotionally baking cakes and redecorating the living room," and with that she smiled rather sarcastically and exited the room with a cheery, "Bon appetit!"

As always, Strekfus thought about what Sharon had said. Lately she had been irritating him. And now, especially with her needling about his past, his childhood, he really started resenting her. As is usual with people who feel distraught, he sought something to take his mind off his troubles, or at least the ones he was experiencing at that moment, and as happens with some people, he found others' problems took his mind off his own. He picked up the phone and dialed Sagaser's secretary. After getting his boss's room number he headed downstairs to hail a cab with the intention of visiting this man who had lately tormented him.

"What better way to clear your head than to concentrate on someone else's misfortune," he thought as the cab hurried up Third Avenue, but in reality it was more than that. He did feel something for his boss, some sort of empathy. After all, he had found out some interesting bits about the man's past recently and

176

it helped to humanize Sagaser, if not completely, then enough for him to make the excuse to visit his boss in the hospital. Their relationship had not been good lately and some part of Strekfus felt that he wasn't quite ready to leave the magazine yet, whether it was by being fired or by quitting. He was still cognizant of the fact that Sagaser held power over him, at least while he was employed by the publication, and some part of him wanted to rectify the differences between them, at least for the moment.

Somewhere between Sixty-fifth Street and Seventy-second he decided that it was best not to show up empty-handed, and so he paid the fare and began to walk the rest of the way in the hope that a shop selling flowers would appear. As with most things in Manhattan, one only need walk a few blocks to find what one is looking for.

Two blocks from the hospital he stopped by a florist shop and began to peruse the vibrant flora crowding the store's window. Enormous leaves of tropical foliage and various exotic long-limbed flowers jockeyed for position between sprightly pots of mother-in-law's tongues and vases of calla lilies.

Strekfus ruminated over the plants. "*Sansevieria trifasciata*," he said to himself, "*Zantedeschia aethiopica*," he mused, remembering his penchant for Latin names, remembering how he had unintentionally plagued those around him with his use of them as a child.

A small fountain gurgled in the center of the window's display and the entire shop reeked of humidity and eucalyptus. After wrestling a medium-sized plant free from a group of azaleas wrapped in bright pink foil, he paid for his purchase and headed over to the hospital, all the way smarting from having to lay out forty-two dollars for a plant which would have cost him less than ten in any other store.

He was halfway down the hall to Sagaser's room when it hit him. It was a wave of nausea and light-headedness which seemed to loom out of nowhere. Maybe he had rushed too much coming from the office. He leaned up against the sterile beige walls and waited. A metallic voice from an overhead speaker pulled him back into reality as it paged some doctor to the

177

emergency room. He hadn't thought about it since this morning, this anxiety, and it had come upon him unexpectedly. He had been so preoccupied with his irritation at Sharon that he had turned his attention to his boss, and in the process had completely forgotten his phobias. Now he was standing in the middle of one of the very places he loathed.

He knew some of the reasons for this. The obvious one: his father had been a doctor and his mother a nurse. The medical profession had been crammed down his throat as a child, and he had vowed to choose any profession but one dealing with sickness, death, and pain. Then just today, Sharon had been needling him about his past, his parents. It all started to come together for him now as he tried to shake off his overwhelming feeling of anxiety. He realized that he was attempting to make amends with Sagaser because he felt himself slipping away from Sharon, and he knew that this wasn't the way to handle the situation. But Sagaser would either see the visit as a kind gesture or be thoroughly confused by it, and either way it might work to Strekfus's benefit. He thought about the times his boss had been nice to him. Sure, they were few and far between, but they did exist.

Still leaning on the wall for support, he tried to shake off his anxiety, trying for a moment to block out the sights and sounds of the hospital—anything that might remind him of his parents and his intense fear of places such as this. Perhaps Sharon was right. He did have a lot of phobias, but the logic of this particular one, of anything medical, seemed pretty obvious to him. Who wants the needles, the pain, the suffering, the occasional death that these places bring? After a few minutes he calmed himself and the fear seemed to pass through him like some alien spirit, with only a faint remnant lingering inside.

He straightened himself and began to search for the number of the room his boss was in, walking slowly in order to make sure he was fully recovered from his latest dizzy spell. It wouldn't do to show up in front of Sagaser with any flaws or weaknesses. His eyes scanned the room numbers. Two-thirty-three. This was it. The heavy brown door was only partially

178

closed. He pushed it open slowly. He was ready to offer a cheery, if not partially insincere, "How ya doing?" the minute he rounded the corner of the small alcove leading into the room, but stopped before he could manage a sound.

There, stretched out on the bed, was his boss, blanket pulled up almost to his chin. He was asleep, and he certainly didn't look well. His mouth was slightly open and Strekfus could make out the small undulations of his chest as it moved up and down. How vulnerable he looked. Almost childlike. Immediately Strekfus felt a sense of embarrassment, as though he shouldn't be there. Here was his boss, completely exposed and unprotected. If Sagaser knew this, that he were being viewed like some object in the Metropolitan Museum of Art, he would roll over and die, but only after taking the employee's head off both figuratively and literally. The man who prided himself on never showing his true emotions, never letting on to what was really going on in his mind, was now splayed out, completely helpless and asleep.

Strekfus stood motionless, the way someone does who's just been cashing a check at a bank and hears the words, "Everybody freeze, this is a stickup." He didn't know whether to slip out of the room or set the plant down first. He reasoned that of all possibilities, the worst would be if Sagaser woke up and found him there, staring at him while he slept. As quietly as he could, he set the plant down on the nearest table, and before he left, took one last look at the man who lately had made his life miserable. He looked at the large forehead which loomed moon-like on the pillow; the shallow breathing; the pallid skin color. He looked at the textured white blanket which draped itself over his boss's mute and still form. Now his nausea and dizziness were completely gone, replaced by a memory from years earlier, and this memory came up from the depths like a submarine surfacing violently from the bottom of the sea, tearing a hole in the surface water, flinging everything above it to one side.

He was thirteen-years-old again, two weeks before his father had died, and he was entering the hospital room where his father lay, lifeless and comatose. His father had been heavily sedated and his breathing was shallow. Strekfus had been taken

179

there by his Aunt Bea and Uncle Douggie, who had opted to stand outside the room while Strekfus made what would be the last visit to his father. The man would be dead in two weeks, and the long and difficult relationship that Strekfus had endured would be over. The doctors had never really been able to determine exactly what had caused his father to die. It had taken years to get to this point with his father becoming sicker and sicker each year until he reached his present state.

As Strekfus stood there taking stock of the many tubes which entered and exited his father's body, he realized that his fear of hospitals and anything medical had disappeared. For some reason, he was able to witness this gruesome medical scene with little or no emotion. Perhaps it was some sort of survival technique his body was experiencing, allowing him to visit his father so that he could have some sense of closure. Whatever it was, it permitted him to view the man in a totally different light.

His father had always been strong, violent, aggressive. The man lying here now was completely helpless and in the throes of a slow and painful death. As Strekfus stood there viewing his sick father, the man began to roll his head about from side to side. The attending nurse, who had been sitting silently in the corner, now got up to see what was happening. As she checked the man's pulse, her head bent reverently, her bony fingers gently holding the wrist of the dying man, Strekfus noticed something else. His father's eyes were open and the man was looking directly at him. But when Strekfus searched the limp, dull blue irises, he saw that whatever his father was looking at wasn't registering. For his father, Strekfus had already ceased to exist. Then the man rolled his head to the side and shut his eyes. But before Strekfus was to leave his father this last time, he took the man's hand and held it in his, noticing the withered and almost bloodless fingers, noticing the fingernails with white streaks running up and down them. Then the last meeting was over, and he was releasing the touch of the man who had made his life so difficult.

The nurse was taking Strekfus's thirteen-year-old arm in hers, leading him out the door. "I'm sorry about your daddy, son.

You know he probably won't come out of the coma this time," she was saying, but all he could think about was that he felt an absence of illness at being inside a hospital. So many times before when taken there as a child because of some business his parents had, he would become almost violently ill at the sounds, the sights, the smells.

"It's probably because I'm so distraught over his impending death that I'm able to cope now," he thought to himself. But even so, on some level he had been emotionally destroyed by the scene, knowing that his father's death was imminent and that any hope of a resolution with the man was gone. The nurse went on, "You know your mother stayed with him last night all night long. I'll tell you, that woman is the most caring individual I've ever met. Why, she wouldn't let any of us near him all night and even kept a chair up against the door, just so he wouldn't be disturbed—so that none of us could come in. She's so protective of him. They must have really loved each other, your parents."

A nurse, pushing open the heavy door to Sagaser's room, broke Strekfus's mood and his reverie. He was once again seeing Sagaser, the plant he had brought, the cold hospital room.

"I'm sorry," the pretty nurse was saying, "I didn't know he had a visitor."

"That's okay," Strekfus said in a hushed, reverent tone, taking one last moment to look back at his boss. "I was just leaving," and he slipped back into the hallway and then into the cold metal elevator.

As he walked back to the office, having decided that he needed fresh air instead of the cab ride, he thought about the latest story he was to write, and while he tried to put the thought of his father out of his mind, it kept creeping in along with thoughts of his boss, the things he had learned that day, and broken pieces of his past. By the time he reached the glass-enclosed lobby of the building he worked in, he had once again figured out how to write the truth and at the same time conveniently avoid it.

181

- 10 -

The House on Euclid Avenue

Infanta, Alabama, 1969

> I had known for a long time that the
> people about me used a method of
> communication different from mine; and
> even before I knew that a deaf child could
> be taught to speak, I was conscious of
> dissatisfaction with the means of
> communication I already possessed.
>
> —Helen Keller, *The Story of My Life*

"Why can't I just stay here by myself?" I pleaded. School had started and I didn't want to have to perform the daily commute from my Aunt Bea and Uncle Douggie's house all the way across town. My mother and I were now in a heated debate about which relative's residence I was to end up in.

"Because you're only thirteen," my mother retorted to my question.

"What's that got to do with anything?" I asked, knowing the answer, but just wanting to be difficult. Then I added, "Besides, Jesus farts constantly and I hate being in the same house with him."

"It's pronounced 'Geee-zus' " my mother countered, giving me the incorrect pronunciation for the name which the family had decided was exactly the same as the "Jesus" in the Bible. I had pronounced it as a Spanish person would: "Hey-soos."

"And frankly I don't understand why anyone would name a Chihuahua Jesus even if it *is* pronounced differently. I think that's just sacrilegious, if you ask me," I said. "I would think with all of the hymn singing you do, you wouldn't want to see the name of our Lord and Savior used on a hundred-year-old toothless bag of bones that has intestinal problems."

"It's a Mexican name, you know—Jesus, Chihuahua, tortilla," said my mother, again pronouncing it "Geeez-us."

"Yes, but you don't pronounce it 'Geee-zuz' you pronounce it '*Hey-soos.*'"

Whap! My mother's hand came across the back of my head—a favorite family mode of communicating.

"I'm well aware of Mexican names, I just don't understand why they couldn't have named him José or something like that. I didn't name the dog. And you *have* to go stay over there. You know I have things to do since your father died. His funeral today has just about taken everything out of me," she said.

I figured this was going to be just another one of those uncomfortable experiences for me, so I resigned myself to having to stay over at my Aunt Bea and Uncle Douggie's. Aunt Bea was my mother's older sister and she was frequently called upon to help out in the family. In fact, it was she who had been given the task three days earlier of telling me my father had died. Aunt Bea and Uncle Douggie I could handle. It was Jesus I was worried about.

The dog hated me ever since I could remember. Having brought him back to Alabama from Mexico after their honeymoon, my Aunt Bea and Uncle Doug had named him in honor of the Mexican lifeguard who had pulled my aunt from the riptide along the Baja peninsula, making sure they used the biblical pronunciation. The man's name was Jesus Perez and he was some sort of boxing celebrity in Mexico. My aunt and uncle had been so grateful that they had arranged for Jesus (the boxer, not the dog) to move to Texas where they felt he could earn a better living and have more opportunities made available to him, thereby elevating his status in life. He eventually became an alcoholic and was put in jail for drug smuggling, but not before impregnating his wife. It seems they should have left well enough alone (my aunt and uncle, not the Perezes).

At any rate, as I understand it, Chihuahuas, and dogs in general, live only about ten human years. This one was sixteen years old in human years and still getting around, albeit barely.

At one time black as a crow, the dog was now almost totally gray with a few wiry white, inch-long hairs thrown in around the muzzle—the equivalent of nose hair in humans. He could barely walk, and when he did choose to, which in my opinion was only to come near me so he could expel his foul-smelling intestinal gas, his toenails would click on the hardwood floors with a most irritating sound. My aunt and uncle refused to cut his toenails, so they were a good three-quarters of an inch long, giving him the appearance of a miniature Chinese mandarin walking on his hands.

Whenever we went to visit, we could hear the dog barking as soon as we rang the doorbell, followed by my aunt's admonition of "Hush, Jesus, hush!" again, with the biblical pronunciation of the name.

Upon entering their house, the creature would lunge for my ankle. This usually didn't bother me because there wasn't a tooth left in the poor animal's head. After a few minutes of gumming my lower calf, the dog, satisfied that I was covered with his foul-smelling saliva, would hobble back to his sofa cushion which was placed on the floor beside the console television in the den, and make smacking sounds with his gums while flicking his pink tongue in my general direction. Taking things personally as I did at this age, I believed him to be making a statement on the taste of my ankles.

The den in which Jesus spent most of his time was a small twelve-by-fourteen-foot room housing vestiges from my uncle's athletic past. On top of the TV sat at least twenty golfing trophies that he had won at various times in his life, and on the wall behind the sofa were five rather unhappy deer heads, each one posed at a slightly different angle, the effect being similar to mannequin heads in a department store. The end tables were adorned with photographs of my cousin Enoch's baseball team, and there were several baseballs his team had used, each on little stands next to the candy dish (molded, not cut crystal, with four-year-old peppermints which had become hopelessly stuck to their plastic wrappers).

Uncle Doug was always winning golf trophies. He didn't appear to be that fond of my aunt at times from what I could tell and spent every waking minute playing the game at surrounding courses whenever possible. Getting away from my Aunt Bea almost always entailed either *playing golf* or PLAYING GOLF, as my aunt would sometimes say with a special inflection. The latter version of this seemingly innocuous description meant, as I was later to learn, fooling around with the ladies. "Your uncle's gone to *play golf*" meant that he had taken his golf clubs and headed out to the nearest green. "Your uncle's gone to PLAY GOLF" meant he was fooling around. I guess my aunt really didn't care. She just wanted him out of the house as badly as he wanted to get away from her. Marriages as good as this one are not that hard to find, if you ask me, and it was my guess that if they gave trophies for PLAYING GOLF instead of *playing Golf*, the television wouldn't have been large enough to hold them.

When my aunt and uncle weren't trying to get away from each other, they sat in the den and watched golf on TV; that is to say, my uncle watched the game and my aunt either painted her fingernails or flipped through the latest copy of *Parents* or *Good Housekeeping*.

In this house, golf was everything, and the continuity of the tournaments on the black-and-white screen was only broken from time to time so that my uncle could indulge in his third most favorite pastime: feeding Jesus chewing gum.

Every now and then, while Arnold Palmer was setting up to putt, my uncle would reach into his pocket, take a piece of Wrigley's Spearmint gum out, unwrap it, and pinch off a small piece. Then, rolling it up, he would flick it in the general direction

185

of Jesus who was sitting peacefully on the solitary sofa cushion beside the 1950s console TV.

The dog, who was not usually known at this point in his life for his swift movements, would lunge to catch the chewing gum and quickly inhale the morsel with a nasal "Snauuuugh" sound, and then creak back down onto the sofa cushion, folding his little withered legs under him and settling his head down on one of his gray-haired paws. He would then cut his eyes around the room to make sure everyone had seen his athletic prowess, his large black pupils turning so far from side to side that a pair of small white crescent moons would flash at me from his resting place. When he wasn't doing this, his eyes were usually closed, and his breathing was so shallow that one could have easily mistaken him for dead. He also reeked to such an extent, that had he died, no one would have noticed.

"Douggie," my aunt would admonish between swipes of her emery board while never looking up, "you know that's not good for him. Why do you do that?"

"Bea," my uncle would respond, "I'm trying to watch this golf game."

The truth of the matter was that Jesus lived almost entirely on Wrigley's Spearmint. I'm sure he did manage to eat something else, but no one every saw it. This, accompanied by the fact that he hadn't defecated in a good five or six years led credence to the myth that he subsided entirely on the stuff, and though he never passed any of it out of his system, he did pass great quantities of gas which seemed to linger like an irate bellboy waiting for a tip. At least he and my mother had something in common and this could easily explain why she was the only person that the dog didn't bark at. In fact, each time we would come visit, after assaulting me and hobbling wildly about the foyer, he would spy my mother and make a beeline for the underside of the sofa. It was as if he knew something the rest of us hadn't yet figured out.

It wasn't that we visited my Aunt Bea, Uncle Douggie, Enoch, and their dog that often, but each time we did, something interesting would happen. Something about their house, the combination of people and animals, their son, and just about anything else you could think of, always made for an interesting time.

It was in this house on Euclid Avenue that I had learned about some of my mother's sordid past several years earlier. That was 1967 and I was in the fifth grade at the time—two years earlier than now—1969. And as with other houses that I either lived in, visited, or knew about, certain events and stories will forever be associated with those particular walls, gardens, bricks and mortar, and furnishings.

Because my father was sick in 1967 and evidently getting sicker each day, I would have to stay with relatives while my mother accompanied him to the hospital in Birmingham, Alabama, and this usually meant staying at my Aunt Bea and Uncle Douggie's house. Because my father was ill, this meant my mother had taken charge of what happened in our family, and as she didn't like my Aunt Testa, she insisted that I stay with the relatives on *her* side of the family. My cousin Enoch, who was Aunt Bea and Uncle Douggie's only son, and who was several years older than me, was supposed to be in charge of my well-being. In other words, he was supposed to keep me out of trouble.

The house on Euclid Avenue wasn't very large and when I did stay over it was necessary to share a bedroom with Enoch. There were two twin beds in the room, so he occupied the one he usually slept in, and I got the one piled with clothes, records, sports equipment, and boxes of shoes. When it was time for bed we both participated in the nightly ritual of removing these objects. It usually took about thirty minutes and consisted of specific instructions as to where things went. It struck me as strange that Enoch would be so picky about where his belongings went for eight hours each night, but had no qualms about piling them carelessly on top of each other during the day.

I'll never forget the night I found out about my mother from Enoch. He probably had the best intentions, just wanting me to know about her in an attempt to explain why she acted the way she did. But whatever his objective, I took the information hard.

News that my father was gravely ill in Birmingham had just been received, and I was to go to bed with this on my mind. As always, my cousin and I lay in our respective beds waiting for the sound of the television in the den to be shut off. I would read and he would smoke cigarettes. He probably wasn't more than three or four years older than I was, and his parents had forbidden him to smoke even though both of them did so.

He would lie there quietly staring at the ceiling, exhaling slowly and dramatically the way Anne Bancroft had done in *The Graduate*. The particular night he told me about my mother was no different. I could tell something was coming, but I didn't know what.

"Strekfus," he said, never taking his eyes off the ceiling.

"Yes?"

"Do you know about your mother?"

"Know what?" I asked. "I know a lot of things about her. You know we don't get along that well," I added.

"Did you know that she's a whore?" he asked. Then he took a large drag from the cigarette, held it in for a good half-minute, and exhaled it quickly with his lower lip pointing upward so that the smoke exited his mouth like the steam from a tea kettle ready to be taken off the stove. His eyes were still focused on the ceiling.

"What are you talking about?" I asked incredulously, putting down my copy of *Breakfast at Tiffany's*. I set the book down after reading the first sentence. I couldn't believe he was doing this, with my father in the hospital, sick.

"I'll tell you the story," he said.

I really didn't want to know. I knew Enoch had a stubborn streak, but I also knew there was no stopping him. I'll tell the story here as it was told to me because it's a part of everything else. There were details that he left out, details I was to learn later from people who knew my mother at that time, and I'll include some of those here for the purpose of getting the thing straight.

* * * * *

My mother's story goes back a long way. She was raised one of two children in Edwina, Georgia, during the Depression. As soon as she could walk she started making plans to get away from the life a small town had to offer and move to another small town that had, well, not much more to offer but at least it was someplace different. She was an industrious woman but her follow-through left something to be desired. I have to admit she did very well—she married my father, but not without a series of machinations which would have turned the head of Machiavelli himself.

At the time my father met my mother, they were both living in Infanta, Alabama. My father was living in the family home at 509 Latrobe Street with my Aunt Testa and her husband Scott, my Aunt Belle, and her children. My grandparents and Belle's husband had passed away, and since it was a nine-bedroom house, there was plenty of room for everyone. My father had procured a job at the local hospital and was starting to settle down. He was now in his mid-twenties.

One day, for reasons unknown to us, my mother showed up at the door of the house. It wasn't clear exactly what type of discussion took place, but the end result was that my Aunt Testa introduced her to my father, evidently begrudgingly. At some point my mother landed a job at the same hospital my father was working at. She had obvious designs on my father, and knowing a good thing when she saw it, started weaving her web.

With the only distraction being the occasional underachieving intern who twittered about, she had plenty of time to set the trap. The truth was that she had set a trap once before. This previous snare involved a man named Parnell, the local mortician, so we'll talk about him first since her technique in handling him is paramount to how she would later handle my father.

Parnell had a lot to offer a young lady in the small Southern town of Infanta, Alabama. Parnell had money. Parnell had charm. Parnell had sex appeal. The only problem was this:

189

Parnell had a wife. This last detail however, didn't seem to bother my mother. She was a high climber, and if I'd inherited half her ambition I would be one rich man today.

In late 1948, my mother was living in the boardinghouse at 509 Latrobe, a huge monstrosity built in 1887 as a home for a wealthy local merchant and his sister. This was several years before my Aunt Testa and the gang on my father's side moved to Infanta to live in the exact same house. My mother, by that time, would have found other accommodations. The house at 509 Latrobe would turn out to be more than just a home, for after having relatives from both sides of my family live there, it held several secrets.

Finding the boardinghouse not up to her standards in those years following World War II, she began what I like to call her "seductress period," trying to catch Mr. Right, or at least Mr. Almost Right in the hope that he would "Take her away from all of this" (makes sweeping gesture with right hand).

She set her sights on Parnell.

The fact that Parnell was married didn't seem to bother her much—for that matter nothing seemed to bother her much—and Parnell, well, he'd been known to sleep around quite a bit. My mother figured he was the brass ring everyone had been talking about all these years, so she grabbed hold and wouldn't let go. After realizing that Parnell wasn't interested in buying the cow when he could get the milk for free (he already had a cow at home, anyway), my mother devised a plan. She would accept the fact that he had only used her, but "Could they see each other just one last time?" she wondered out loud to him over the phone one day.

Now there's something you should know about my mother. Hollywood definitely missed the boat when it overlooked her, because she is first and foremost, in my mind, the best actress who has ever lived. There are literally thousands of bodies littered around her—those poor people who bought the goods she had to offer and then later learned there was a no-refund policy. If only they had read the small print. It wasn't that she was such a bad person—we all have problems in childhood

190

or with our parents and the way we were raised—but she chose ways to deal with her realities that might be deemed inappropriate by even decadent standards.

At any rate, she met Parnell one last time. She lured him over to the boardinghouse she was staying in—the one at 509 Latrobe—and played the perfect hostess. When Parnell was good and sloshed, as was his natural state, she lured him into bed. Being a worker at the local hospital, she had learned quite a bit about anatomy and the workings of the male and female reproductive organs, and she put this knowledge to excellent use. Within two months, her plan was well in motion. The endless days of vomiting into the clawfoot tub down the hall from her room didn't faze her a bit. She was pregnant with Parnell's baby and things were right on course.

When Parnell heard the news from her that she was carrying his child—no doubt dramatically given as a plea, (puppydog-faced, I imagined my mother, squeezing a Kleenex for all it was worth, and in her no-nonsense fashion opening the front door, and before Parnell could even say "Hello," hitting him right between the eyes with, "I'm pregnant, and it's yours")—he undoubtedly said to her, "Yeah? You and everyone else in this town."

See, Parnell got around. He got around a lot, and as is usually the case with men who have women lined up down the block, he wasn't much to look at. Evidently he had some hidden talents.

At this point, my mother realized there was a tiny hole in her plan.

"But you have to marry me now. Besides, you said you would leave your wife," my mother said.

"Think again, sister," Parnell had said. "My wife knows what I go out and do. You think she's stupid? Get yourself an abortion and don't bother me any more about this."

Realizing the tiny hole had become a big tear, my mother panicked. "Oh, well," she thought, "if this didn't work, something else will."

My mother, above all, was tenacious.

191

Immediately she called upon some resources she had stored. She contacted a doctor in Edwina, Georgia, the town she had grown up in, who owed her a favor. This being Alabama and the South in 1950, abortion was taboo, not to mention illegal. Not that it was any better in Georgia, but at least the physician in that state acquiesced to perform her abortion. And besides, it was out of town. What could be more convenient, at least gossip-wise.

"All done," the doctor had said, dropping the bloody rags and remnants of the baby into a brown paper bag lined with plastic, which was resting beside the examining table. "You'd better stay home from work for a few days and get some rest. I'm going to prescribe antibiotics for you, I want you to take three a day for one week, and I don't want to see you in here ever again."

Then the doctor made an unfortunate mistake: He answered a phone call—an emergency—and went down the hall to check some records, leaving my mother alone in the examining room with evidence of a crime. Mustering all her strength after such an invasive event, my mother seized the bags containing what was left of her firstborn and stuffed them into a medical bag that was sitting on a nearby table. Stiff, open-mouthed, and upturned like some large, hollow, taxidermied reptile, the sturdy alligator doctor's bag seemed perfect for carrying around a newly aborted fetus. The only problem was this: my mother hadn't noticed the initials imprinted in gold on the side—A.I.W, for the Atlanta Infirmary for Women. These initials wouldn't cause her any immediate problem, but years later they would prove her undoing.

My mother went home to the boardinghouse, and probably for the first time in many years genuinely cried—at least for a minute or so. She had carried her aborted fetus and the blood-soaked rags all the way home on the train, having them sit across from her on the opposite seat, safe and secure in the doctor's bag. Fear, and the thought that she could use the evidence as blackmail, kept her from disposing of the contents along the way.

The attending physician got two of the wishes he asked for that day in his office. My mother stayed home from work and got some rest, and she took three antibiotics a day for one week, but she didn't do too well with his third request to stay out of his office. You see, the doctor had indeed performed the abortion, but this was in a day and age before sonograms or any of the modern technology that allows doctors to tell the age and sex of the baby was available.

Or whether or not the mother is carrying twins.

Because he had extracted the makings of a fetus from my mother's womb, he thought the job was finished. It wasn't, for it seems Mr. Fetus had a brother.

Now you can imagine my mother's surprise, when four months after her rendezvous with the coat hanger, the swelling began, and the vomiting wouldn't stop. Not wanting to be an alarmist and thinking it was just a symptom of having had an abortion, she put off going back to the doctor until it was painfully obvious something was wrong. Maybe, she thought, missing your period for four months was a result of having had an unborn child ripped from your uterus. Who knew?

She, of course, was thrown out of the boardinghouse. Had she even wanted to hide the fact that she was pregnant she couldn't have. Everyone would have known. This was 1951. So she caught the next train to Texas, had the baby there, and left it on someone's doorstep in the town of Greensaw, hoping they would find a home for it.

At this point in my cousin's telling of the story I interjected, "But then she really wasn't a whore, she just was a master at manipulation."

"Do you want to hear this or not?" my cousin asked, and crushed out the remains of his cigarette into a large clamshell he used as an ashtray. It was a souvenir from Florida and had a small frog made out of other tiny sea shells sitting on the edge (eyes painted on and "Greetings from Florida" shakily painted around the rim).

He lit another cigarette. About that time I heard the dreaded clicking of toenails on the floor and felt a slight weight

193

lean against the foot of my bed. "Wheeeeeeee," squeaked Jesus's sphincter muscle, and Enoch let several smoke rings float up toward the ceiling.

So there was my mother, working in the hospital after having taken a "vacation" in Texas and doing well for herself. Enter my father: a young, aggressive, headstrong man of twenty-something. A rebel at that time against the family's puritanical values, he decided to date my mother against the wishes of his sister, Testa. To this day I still ask people who knew him, "What made him do this?" and none of them know. Somehow he and my mother got married in 1952. As I've said before, she was a master manipulator and a great actress. My father told Testa that he knew the marriage was a mistake the day after the honeymoon. Testa didn't want to use the cliché, "I told you so," and so she had just looked at him.

So according to my cousin, the marriage wasn't going well. Three or four years after the fateful knot was tied, my father decided (unbeknownst to my mother) that he would divorce her. Now I don't have to tell you that divorce in the '50s was not the thing to do, but for that matter, having an abortion and child out of wedlock wasn't either.

It seems that my mother found out about the planned divorce and decided that if she became pregnant, my father wouldn't leave. Well, why not? It had *almost* worked before.

So in December 1955, just a few days before Christmas, my mother gave my father a present he would never forget.

"I'm pregnant," she said to him. The irony that my father was an obstetrician wasn't lost on either of them.

As I understand it, he said nothing—he just left the house. Now because he was headstrong he decided to stay with her and try to make the marriage work. (Okay, she blackmailed him with a letter implicating he was a homosexual. He didn't actually write it, *she* did, but in the '50s you didn't mess with things such as this—even if it wasn't true.) The town was crushed because they all despised her, many having been victims of her schemes. By this time my father had risen to some degree of prominence in the medical world, and he was now considered important in the only hospital in town. My mother relished throwing this in everyone's face each chance she got, and brought the practice to new levels, creating her own art form of sorts.

"This is Mrs. Beltzenschmidt," she would crisply quip into the phone. "I'd like you to send over one of your low-life air-conditioner repairmen to look at our system, and you'd better not keep me waiting." With that she would slam down the receiver.

Somehow she had snagged a respectable man, and now she had a respectable name and was going to make sure she rubbed everyone's nose in the doggy-doo she perceived they had made of her life. She got even with everyone who had talked behind her back or spoken ill of her. People feared her. My father feared her. And he had a right to—she was crazy.

So this was the story my cousin told. Here I was with a terminally ill father and a crazy mother.

"Great," I thought, "you couldn't have waited to tell me this . . . like . . . forever?"

When my cousin finished, he exhaled a long column of cigarette smoke from his cigarette and this time extinguished it in a can of soda by his bed. The hiss the burning butt produced made me think of all the air being let out of my body. At least that's what it felt like.

I died that night.

I remember rolling over in bed and crying myself to sleep.

My cousin went away to college a few years later and I stayed in that infamous bedroom once again. I had no idea just how sick my father really was, because in our family no one talked about such things, but I knew something was wrong. One day my mother called Aunt Bea to say that they were bringing my father back to "his" hospital. When I asked my aunt why, she looked nervous, then looked away. We were in her kitchen at the time (depressing gray wallpaper from the '20s, kitchen appliances with dusty coils underneath that made too much noise) and I could see she had tears in her eyes as she averted her gaze and focused on the plastic fruit refrigerator magnets. She seemed to be in a daze as she fingered a bright yellow banana and a bunch of grapes with an all-too-obvious seam down the middle.

"He's not going to make it," she said. "They want to bring him back to his hospital so that he can die there. I've got to fix your uncle something to eat. Why don't you go out and play." And that was all that was said.

While my family had never been good at communicating, I considered this to be a major event. Not the fact that my father was going to die, but the fact that someone actually *told* me he was going to die. The usual way this would be handled in my family would be simply to ignore the situation until he passed away. Then when I noticed him missing one day I might say, "Gee, where's Dad?" and someone would say, "Could you hand me that dishrag over there? Thanks. Oh, he died. Did you want green beans or lima beans with your dinner, sweetheart? Oh, Hattie, did you hear that Mrs. Morrison has a new cat?" The goal was to avoid the truth at any cost. I'm still working on breaking this pattern.

My mother did have one momentary lapse from this time-honored family tradition. It was a few days before my father died. He had been brought back to the hospital in Infanta and I was staying with Mother at our house after having spent a week at Bea and Douggie's—the week in which Aunt Bea told me about my father's soon-to-be departure. In order to cope with my father's impending demise, my mother had been taking large quantities of Valium, Percodan, and Darvon. I didn't know this at the time. I found out later while going through the trash one day, but I did know that her moods were strange, even stranger than usual.

The evening before my father left us for good, she called me into her bedroom. It was about seven o'clock at night and she had been sleeping all day. She had done this because she planned to sit up with him all night. She sat there in bed holding my hand and through her tears told me, "Your dear daddy is going to die, but I don't want you to worry because . . ." and at this point her facial features changed and she gripped my hand harder, "because we are going to have so . . . much . . . MONEY!" She was ecstatic,

196

and now instead of crying, she was laughing hysterically. "So much money," she kept saying and rocking back and forth on the bed. Then she did the strangest thing. She stopped laughing, and digging her fingernails into my forearm, looked intensely into my eyes. Hers darted back and forth to each of mine like a sped-up Ping-Pong match.

"Now, you know how sick he is? Well," she went on, and at this point looked down and began stroking my arm in a seductive way, "since he is in such pain, you wouldn't mind terribly if something happened to him, would you? I, uh . . . mean . . . if something happened to put him out of his misery, you wouldn't mind, would you? I mean, that would be a good thing, wouldn't it?" and she looked into my eyes pleadingly while shaking her head, "Yes."

I sat there horrified. Then I said to her when she had calmed down, "I don't care about the money. I don't want him to die."

"I have to get ready to go to the hospital now," she said, turning into a completely different person. "Get out." She pushed me abruptly away, almost knocking me off the bed, and with that I left the room completely shaken.

We didn't speak to each other until after the funeral when she took me aside and whispered into my ear with sickening sweetness, "You know, your dear Daddy died such a horrible death . . ."

We were getting ready to receive condolences from the people who were attending the funeral and she was choosing *now* to tell me this? The guests were lined up ready for us to receive them. I tried to pull away from her, but her grip was too much for me.

"He died such a horrible death," she went on whispering. "The bones in his chest were completely crushed because they had hit him so hard tying to start his heart . . ." At this moment Mrs. Transford, one of the neighborhood ladies, came by.

"I'm so sorry for your loss, it was so tragic," she said, with proverbial tilted head and outstretched hands.

We thanked her and my mother continued, interjecting these comments as the mourners filed by one at a time. She would whisper them to me out of earshot of the guests. I had to stand there and listen to them and then smile at the neighbors and be pleasant.

"They cut him open," she continued, "to massage his heart. He had so many tubes in him that he looked like a piece of machinery . . ."

"Hello, Mrs. Roberts," I said, trying to put on my best non-emotional face.

"So sorry to hear about your father. He was such as good man," she volunteered, gloved hands outstretched, head tilted sideways, seeming to do her best impression of Mrs. Transford who had come before her.

"Thank you," I said.

My mother went on whispering, even before Mrs. Roberts was out of the way. "They say there was hardly any blood left in his body and he weighed only ninety pounds." And then in full voice with fake smile, completely changing her attitude, "Why, thank you for coming, Helen. Yes, it was a lovely funeral. Thank you."

As we walked back to the car, she grabbed my arm and dug her fingernails into it. She was walking so quickly that I thought we would topple over. "There's not going to be an autopsy. The body was so crushed from trying to resuscitate him that I didn't think it was right. His breastbone was completely broken from them pounding on it to try and start his heart."

I just stared at her in horror. I don't know which was worse, having my father die, or being left alone with her. Then she told me how I was going to have to stay with my aunt again because there were a few things she had to take care of. I was to go there that evening and she didn't want to hear any back-talk. With this last statement she shoved me into the front seat of the car.

Now, as we were driving to my aunt's house, I suddenly realized something: All through the ordeal of my father dying, all through his funeral and the formalities, one thing had been

198

missing—my mother's gas. She was notorious for passing volumes of it, and during this death phase she had been conspicuously silent and odorless. At the time I figured it must have been the tranquilizers she was on, but later I began to wonder.

That evening after the funeral, at my aunt's house, as I sat in the den watching an old Bette Davis movie, *Now, Voyager* ("You would think a daughter would want to repay a mother's love and kindness"), I was again wondering about my mother's lack of flatulence. The reason this came to mind again was because while Jesus, the hundred-year-old Chihuahua, was fast asleep on his bed next to the TV, his sphincter muscle was wide awake and working overtime.

"You'll be laughing out the other side of your face if I did carry out my suggestion," the TV announced.

"Breeeeeeeeeeeee," answered the dog and then he smacked his lips, probably dreaming of a nice steak which he couldn't chew and certainly couldn't digest.

And then it happened.

It really shouldn't have come as surprise that it did, I mean, it was an old house and not on that stable a foundation. So when a large branch broke off from one of the huge oak trees hovering over the structure, it shook everything like an earthquake. Everything, including the TV.

Now the TV, being a holy temple where all the golf trophies were enshrined, was not a model of stability. One French provincial leg had been broken off years ago, and it was essentially now a three-legged monster with a fourth support composed of several Lincoln Logs and a crushed Quaker Oats box. That's why, when the tree limb fell on the house and shook everything, it vibrated the TV and everything on it to such a degree that the oatmeal box was reduced considerably in size and one of the golf trophies (silver Deco design, blue reflective center, man in tacky golfing clothing—isn't that redundant?—in full swing on the top) came tumbling down and landed directly on the dog which was snoozing peacefully on top of a dirty blanket and sofa cushion. To be honest, after I thought about it,

199

everyone was better off without Jesus (including the dog himself) but at the moment it happened I was horrified.

"What happened?" chimed my aunt from the other end of the house in that three-toned inflection that said, "I know something is not quite right."

"I think a limb fell off a tree and hit the house," I said as I scrambled to lift the trophy off the dog. This was not entirely a lie as a tree limb had hit the house, but the dog was dead as a doornail and I conveniently forget to mention this when I yelled to her about the tree. Strangely enough, the animal didn't have a scratch on him as the trophy had just grazed his head, and after suffering from a concussion, he simply went to heaven where he could pass gas to his heart's content. I imagined his popularity among the other animals in the afterlife, his name being what it was.

"We'd better go see what damage it did," my aunt continued from the other room.

"Okay," I said, trying to give my voice enough of a sing-song quality to hide the fact that I was panic-stricken. "I'll be there in a minute," I continued. Before I ventured outside to see the damage, I put the trophy back and straightened the TV.

"Dora . . . we quarreled. I did it," said Bette Davis to the nurse who had been tending to her mother on the television.

I thought to myself, "I know I *didn't* do this, but I'll surely be blamed." It was then that I realized that a small golf club had broken off the trophy when it crowned Jesus. Thinking quickly, I pinched off some of the gum I had been chewing and managed to secure it back in place, just in time to hear my aunt outside.

"Oh, my God," she said from underneath the den window, "Strekfus, come and look at this. One of those limbs of that oak has fallen onto the house."

"Coming!" I answered and gave the dog one quick last look.

We surveyed the damage, and as we made our way back into the house from the backdoor, we heard my uncle coming in the front. As usual he didn't speak to my aunt and disappeared into their bedroom until supper. He had gone to play golf after

200

the funeral. As my aunt retreated to the kitchen to fix dinner, I went back into the den to see if Jesus looked any different.

During the evening meal, the falling tree limb was discussed to the point where I thought I would scream. The evening went something like this:

"I wonder how come that limb to fall off?" questioned my aunt to no one in particular while helping herself to a bowl of green beans.

"Maybe it was rotten," mumbled my uncle, trying unsuccessfully to cut an overcooked pork chop with his fork.

"How come it to be rotten?"

"Don't know (chews pork chop for a good ten minutes, then spends another ten trying to extract a small bone from the ball of fat that had been rolling around in his mouth), maybe termites."

"Termites?" asked my aunt absently. "You just said it was rotten. Pass the biscuits."

"Maybe rotten . . . maybe termites . . . maybe both," said my uncle, continuing to chew the same pork fat while wheezing through his nose.

"But you just said rotten, and then you said termites. Which one is it?"

"Don't know," said my uncle after another ten-minute pause. "Maybe was dry rot."

"Now, Douggie," said my aunt, reaching across my plate to stab the last tomato on the center platter, "I wish you'd make up your mind. One minute you said it was rotten, then the next you said it was termites and now you just said it was dry rot. Dry rot and rotten are not the same things, if you ask me. Dry rot is when . . ."

"How the hell should I know what in the name of Sam Hill caused that damn tree limb to fall! My God, woman, would you shut up!"

It was at this moment that I made a mental note to myself to learn to communicate. I knew I would have to search for role models, but I had to try. I had learned about role models from my fourth-grade teacher, Miss Dearborn. I also knew that I wouldn't even begin this journey until after my aunt had found out about Jesus on her own.

You have to keep in mind that during this conversation I was thinking about the fact that my father had just been buried earlier that day. I guess this was my aunt and uncle's way of dealing with things, and in fact this was probably the reason I was holding up so well with Jesus's death. I really didn't know which to be more upset about, the death of my aunt's favorite dog, or the fact that my father had just been buried. It just goes to show you that when you're under strain, your priorities get all switched around.

There was a silence for about a minute, and then my aunt meekly said, "All I was saying was that dry rot and your run-of-the-mill rotten are not the same thing. You don't have to get so huffy." And then of course, my aunt and uncle continued to talk about the tree limb for a good hour or more, somehow managing to use the same phrases over and over until the thing was permutated out.

After we had eaten, it was suggested that we all go into the den and watch golf. I don't know which was worse: watching golf, or waiting for them to find Jesus dead.

I think watching golf was actually worse.

After flipping on the TV, my uncle produced a piece of Wrigley's Spearmint gum out of his pocket and proceeded to talk like the proud parent of a three-year-old to Jesus, with the up-and-down inflections that one reserves for small children and animals.

"Tum on! Tum on! Tum here, Jesus! Yeeessss! Tum here!" he said, holding the gum out in the direction of the dog.

"Doug, can't you see he's asleep? Leave him alone," my aunt admonished as she dug through the magazine bin beside her chair, never looking up.

"Well, hell, I just wanted to give him some gum," he shot back at her.

"Well, don't," she said looking at him over her glasses. She picked up the latest copy of *Redbook* and began snapping through the pages, the entire time maintaining one leg crossed over the other, her foot flailing up and down, a houseslipper precariously balanced at the end of one foot.

Not happy to leave well enough alone, my uncle got up from the sofa and moved in the dog's direction. I held my breath for fear of what would happen next, but evidently the animal's bodily gasses had been building up even after death, and just as my uncle got within a foot of him a giant "Wheeeeeeeze" escaped from the dog's back end. The smell was enough to repel my uncle, who sat back down and picked up the *TV Guide* to see when the next golf tournament was on. This dog was a nuisance even after death.

"I think it probably was dry rot. You were right, Douggie. We'll go out tomorrow and look more closely at it," said my aunt.

"Whatever," said my uncle, let out a sigh, and stuck his hand down into the front of his pants.

* * * * *

The next morning at breakfast, my aunt took her usual seat at the head of the table. After the first few bites, she broke off a small piece of bacon and called Jesus. Nothing happened. Then she called him again. Nothing.

"That's odd," she said. "He always comes to the table at breakfast for some bacon. I'd better go check on him."

"Don't!" I said a little too hastily. Then regaining my composure I added, "I just saw him this morning coming down the hall and going back into the den. He looked so tired." I tilted my head several degrees to communicate sympathy. "I think he went back to sleep."

"All the same, I'd better go check," said my aunt and got up from the table, gingerly holding the piece of overcooked bacon. She came back a few second later and sat down silently. I waited for the bad news, but she just looked up casually as she helped herself to more scrambled eggs and said, "You were right. He's asleep. You know when animals get old, they sleep a lot more. His little git-a-longs are probably worn out. He looked so peaceful that I couldn't disturb him," and with that she gingerly bit into the bacon strip.

By now I figured that my aunt and uncle weren't going to buy the sleeping routine forever, and knowing that my aunt was extremely attached to Jesus, I wanted to do everything I could so that she wouldn't find out he was dead. Also, my father's death had been traumatic and I just couldn't go through something else right now. So when she announced that she was going to get ready for work, I knew I had to act fast. My uncle made his way out the backdoor and I slipped into the den and mustered every bit of courage I had to touch the dog. I placed two fingers under his head and another two under his hind legs, trying to minimize the body area I would have to touch. He was in that pose so many animals choose, their head resting on their front paws and their hind legs curled forward. As soon as I applied the slightest leverage, Jesus came off the blanket, stiff as a board. In fact, he now looked like one of those ceramic animals that people sometimes use as doorstops. I held him up by only one of his hind legs and his shape never changed. At this point, I was more intrigued than disgusted, so I took a few minutes to marvel at the characteristics of rigor mortis. Then I sat him on the sofa between two bright orange cushions and placed one of his rawhide chew toys next to him. Slipping back into the kitchen, I proceeded to clean up the breakfast dishes until my aunt came in and announced that it was time for her to take me to school.

As we started to exit the backdoor, she looked as though she had remembered something and went back into the kitchen, leaving me on the back porch.

"I just want to check on Jesus one more time before we go," she said, and disappeared down the hallway toward the den.

"All clear," she announced after returning. We headed down the back steps and got into the car. "I just wanted to make sure he was all right, but he's sleeping again on the sofa. Thank God," she said, as she started the car and looked back over her right shoulder to back out of the driveway. "I was afraid he might be dead," and then she let out a little laugh. I managed a rather forced laugh myself and stared out the window all the way to school.

When school was out, she picked me up and we headed back to her house. I knew my uncle wouldn't be home yet and I knew that she had to come directly from work to pick me up, so there was no chance either one of them had seen Jesus yet. I was trying to figure out how I could get in the door before she did and rearrange the dog before she saw him, when she handed me the keys and suggested that I go on inside while she carried some empty Coke bottles out to the garbage. I couldn't believe my good luck, but I was concentrating too hard to have time to appreciate it. I opened the door and ran to the den with my hands positioned at the dog before I realized that he wasn't there. At first I thought I was losing my faculties. I had left him on the sofa that morning and my aunt and I were the last ones to leave the house.

My mind started racing. Maybe he wasn't really dead. But that couldn't be because I had lifted him myself and he was stiff as a board. Maybe he fell off the sofa and rolled? I got down on my hands and knees and looked under the skirt of the sofa and easy chair next to it. Nothing. By this time I was beginning to get scared. All manner of thoughts raced through my mind. What if he had come back to life? I mean, his name *was* Jesus. Could someone have broken in and stolen him? What was going on? I was down on my hands and knees when my aunt came into the den and asked what I was doing.

"Nothing," I said, trying to think of some innocuous object which wouldn't interest her. "Just looking for a pencil I dropped."

"Have you seen Jesus?" she asked from down the hall as she walked away from me.

"No, ma'am," I said, with genuine sincerity.

"Oh, here he is," I heard her say as she entered their bedroom. "He's resting on the bed."

"Resting on the bed!" I thought. "What the hell was going on?"

I crept down the hallway to their bedroom and sure enough, there was the dog, sound asleep on the bed.

"What's the matter?" asked my aunt, "you look like you've never seen him sleeping" and she whisked by me out of the bedroom. She called to me from the kitchen that dinner would be ready in an hour, and as soon as I heard her rattling the pots and pans and felt her to be entrenched in preparing supper, I approached Jesus and gave him a nudge.

Stone cold and stiff as a board, he had made himself comfortable right in the middle of my aunt and uncle's bed. I wasn't sure how he got there, but I knew I had to move him before my aunt came back and discovered him dead. Also, I figured the more he moved, the more time I could buy to try and figure out what I was going to do. By now, I was so distracted by the fact that a dead and completely stiff Chihuahua had moved from one room to another, picking him up didn't even faze me. I lifted him again by his hind leg and swung him out of the room and down the hall as nonchalantly as I could, humming all the way to try to disguise my movements. Not having much time to think, I placed him in the first place I could find, which was next to my cousin's bed in the bedroom I was now sleeping in. Hindsight really is twenty-twenty, but when you're under stress you just can't think straight.

Since Enoch was away at college I figured this room was the one with the least traffic. I was just coming out of the room when my aunt came down the hall and again asked if I had seen Jesus—she had a new chew toy for him, even though he had no teeth. I thought for an instant how strange this would have sounded to anyone who didn't know what we were talking about, and indeed I remembered an incident which occurred several years earlier when my aunt and I were at the grocery store.

There had been a religious group moving about the store in an attempt to convert the local heathens who were busy buying frozen pizzas and summer squash. One of them carried a huge sign which read, "If you haven't seen Jesus, you haven't seen the Lord." My aunt was in food-buying mode and hadn't really given them much thought. She was not the religious person my mother was. When one of them approached my aunt and with zealous fervor asked, "Have you seen Jesus?" she replied, with genuine

206

concern tinged with panic, her eyes showing real fear, "Why, is he missing?" So attached to the dog was she, that she thought someone had kidnapped him and that this woman standing before her was the "go-between" in some twisted extortion plan.

"I just saw him go into Enoch's bedroom," I said, and tried to act as if nothing were wrong.

"Well, okay," she said. "He's just not been himself lately"

I thought to myself, "Boy, you're not kidding."

Now I guess I wasn't at the pinnacle of rationality, because I had put the dog into my cousin's room, and this was the same room that I slept in when my cousin was away at college. It occurred to me that I was going to have to move Jesus before I went to bed, or sleep with a dead Chihuahua next to me all night. Just as I was ruminating on what to do, I heard someone entering the kitchen and my aunt and I turned to see my uncle, looking rather disheveled, as he came in through the backdoor.

"Hi," he said rather tentatively and looked at my Aunt Bea, and then at me. "What's going on?" He looked distressed about something.

"Nothing," said my aunt. "Dinner will be ready in a few minutes, so go on and get washed up."

Because I was now sitting at the table in the kitchen, I had a direct view of my aunt at the sink. If I looked to the right I could see the hallway and into their bedroom, so I was able to see my uncle as he turned the corner and entered that room.

He stopped dead in his tracks.

The next thing he did was to shoot down the hall into the den. I could hear him opening closets and looking into everything until I heard him go into my cousin's bedroom and the noise stopped. He reentered the kitchen with the strangest look on his face. First he looked at my aunt, and then at me. I acted as if nothing was wrong.

"So . . ." he began, "where's the dog?" he asked in my aunt's direction with too much nonchalance in his voice.

As she dumped the lima beans out of the colander, she mumbled, "I don't know. Isn't he asleep on the bed?"

"I thought I saw him in Enoch's bedroom," I interjected. "He looked asleep."

"He sleeps more than any dog I've ever known," said my aunt, and proceeded to open a package of dismembered chicken in the sink.

* * * * *

Dinner was its usual non-event that evening, except for my uncle's puzzled expression, so that when it was over I was relieved to retire to the den for an evening of TV and no conversation. Satisfied that auntie and uncle were engrossed in front of the television, I decided that Jesus had to be moved before bedtime.

"Excuse me," I said, "I need to go over some homework before tomorrow," and I left the den with only the sound of my aunt's nailfile scraping away at her lavender fingernail polish.

When I got to the bedroom where I had placed Jesus, I noticed a horrible odor—even more horrible than his usual smell. It seemed that after just a day Jesus was beginning to decompose and reek. This process had probably begun several years before— even while he was alive. Something had to be done. I decided that about the only thing I could do was try to disguise the smell, so I looked around my cousin's room for something I could put on the now withering dog. About the only thing I could find was a bottle of "English Leather." I was only going to put a drop or two on the corpse when the bottle slipped out of my hand and emptied half its contents out onto Jesus. Being the old and dried-up creature that he was, he quickly absorbed whatever fell onto him, and while the bad odor was gone, I was now going to have to spend the night with a Mexican potpourri bag. I endured most of the night with my face firmly planted in the pillow. The next morning, when my aunt came in to wake me and wanted to know what the smell was, I told her that I had tried a little of my cousin's cologne and put on a modicum more than necessary.

After my morning ablutions, I straightened up the bedroom and left Jesus where he was. This moving about was getting tiring and I just wanted the truth to be out and over with.

My aunt drove me to school and all was going well that day until I began having a gnawing feeling that I needed to do something about the dog. After faking an upset stomach, I asked to go to the principal's office in order to call my aunt and have her come pick me up. You would think an assistant principal with even the slightest idea of what goes on in an adolescent's mind would know better than to let a youngster place the call himself, but she did. She probably figured that I was having a reaction to my father's death several days before, and didn't want to rock the boat.

Of course I didn't call my aunt. I'm sure the lady at the front desk of the Green Frog soul food restaurant thought I was crazy when I told her I had an upset stomach and that she should come pick me up. ("Just because you got a stomachache from eating here ain't no reason for me to play chauffeur".) While I couldn't see through the receiver, I imagined the proverbial hand on hip and wagging head.

"My aunt says she'll be by in a few minutes," I offered the totally uninterested assistant principal, and with that I went out front to wait until it was time for me to shout at the plate glass window, "Here she is!" and run around the corner to the nonexistent car.

One block from the school was a bus stop which would take me to the street directly behind my aunt's house. What I planned to do when I got there I had no idea, but this was only Tuesday and I knew I couldn't wait until the weekend to figure out what to do with Jesus. Besides, I needed time alone to plan.

The bus driver eyed me suspiciously, but I just ignored him. Getting off, I proceeded through one of the neighbors' backyards managing to break several branches off their ficus trees in the process. Since my aunt had given me a key to the backdoor (not knowing how long it was going to take my mother to recuperate from my father's death), I already had it out and poised to go into the lock. That is, until I noticed the door was already open and the kitchen light was on.

My first thought was that a burglar had broken in and I had better not surprise him. If this were indeed the case I would

209

be able to say that the burglar had caused Jesus's demise, but within a few minutes I heard familiar voices and my hopes were dashed.

It was my uncle's voice, but the other voice arguing with him wasn't that of Aunt Bea. "What do you mean it's my fault?" said the female voice. I eased open the door and slipped into the kitchen. The voices were coming from the den.

"You're the one who decided to throw the baseball at me," said my uncle.

"Well that's because you're such a prick!" shouted the girl back in his direction. "How was I supposed to know it was going to land on the damn dog's head and kill him?"

"Well what the hell am I supposed to tell my wife now? How am I supposed to explain this?"

"I don't give a damn *how* you explain it," the girl said.

"Oh, gee, honey, I'm sorry," said my uncle in mock-conciliatory tones, "I was having an affair with this girl and one day we had a fight and she threw a baseball at me but it missed and hit the dog and he's dead now and I'm sorry. Is that what you want me to say?"

"I don't give a damn what you say. As far as I'm concerned, we're through," said the girl.

It was at that point that I became so engrossed in their conversation that I didn't notice Jesus's food dish—the one he never ate from. As I was trying to squeeze closer to the refrigerator, my foot accidentally stepped on the edge of it and it went somersaulting across the floor. Clots of week-old food lodged themselves under the stove. I don't think I've ever heard two pairs of more weighty and panicked footsteps in my life as my uncle and his friend came my way in order to perform damage control on whoever was in the house.

My uncle was the first in the kitchen, his face beet-red and covered with sweat. Before he could say anything, I volunteered. "I'm sorry. I came home from school because I had a stomach ache."

"Oh . . . well . . . uh . . . is everything okay now?"

"Oh, yes," I said, "I'm much better." I was going to continue, you know, embellish just how I had been sick and wasn't able to get in touch with Aunt Bea, how I had to take the bus home, when I saw the woman my uncle had been arguing with. She had come in behind him and was holding Jesus by one hind leg just as I had done the day before.

"Who is it, Dou . . . ?" she started to ask.

"Nyla!" I said, recognizing her even after so many years of absence.

"Strekfus!" she said. "What are you doing here?" My uncle's head then turned multiple times from Nyla to me, so many times that I lost count.

"I see you've met the dog," I said, and pointed to the animal now suspended from her hand.

"Strekfus, look," my uncle began. And at this point, my mind held myriad possibilities. I thought about just what could be gained by having such valuable information as this, but then I considered it and decided that life was full enough of mayhem. I thought it was better just to—and I really hate to do this to you—but I thought it was better to "just let sleeping dogs lie."

"I never really liked the dog anyway," I said. My uncle just looked from Nyla to me and then to the dog, then back to me. There was about a full minute's pause as we all assessed the situation. Then my uncle spoke, a look of relaxation finally on his face.

"Neither did I," he said.

* * * * *

Uncle Douggie called Bea later that day to tell her it wouldn't be necessary to pick me up at school—that he had already done so because I had called him with an upset stomach. When she came home he had dinner ready for her (I had peeled the potatoes, so he didn't prepare everything himself) and had managed to straighten up the house. We still had not determined how we were going to break the news of Jesus's death to her, so in the meantime we made him comfortable back in his favorite location next to the television.

After dinner I was helping my uncle wash up while Aunt Bea started a wash of clothes on the backporch. Having set the machine in motion, she walked back toward the den to read and watch television. My uncle and I didn't think too much of it since she hadn't noticed any difference in the dog's behavior for the several days prior, and because we now shared the secret, there was a lot less tension in the air. So it came as somewhat of a surprise when Aunt Bea walked into the kitchen, opened the refrigerator door, took out some leftover deviled eggs, and announced with the same tone as she would have declared her social security number, "Jesus is dead."

My uncle and I looked at each other (he was washing, I was drying) and didn't say anything. Then very calmly, Aunt Bea walked back into the den and proceeded to watch the news, the whole time with Jesus lying there in his coveted place.

* * * * *

My aunt and uncle's relationship seemed to improve after Jesus's death, and after a week of staying with them I was allowed to return home to my mother who had sufficiently repaired her nerves. I found out later that it wasn't really her nerves—she had procured a series of dates and hadn't wanted to miss any opportunity. After that, my aunt didn't nag Uncle Douggie as much and he rarely told her to shut up. As one concession to her, he agreed to remove all the sports paraphernalia and trophies from the den. He even allowed her to get rid of them in a garage sale the neighbors were having. When I found out about this, I asked him if I could have one of his golf trophies. "Which one?" he asked.

"The one with the broken club," I said. The next time I went to visit it was waiting for me.

"You know, I never knew that club was broken," he said. "How did you know?"

"I was admiring the trophies one day and it caught my eye," I said. I guess he thought I was becoming interested in sports, and I was somewhat. He often took me playing golf (*playing golf*, not the other kind) with him after that. In fact, I *was*

212

interested. My parents had initially threatened to make me play sports as punishment, before they discovered that I might form some sort of relationship with other children. Later, I had decided that I really did want to play, to play anything—baseball, football. They had strictly forbade it, their excuse being that I would get hurt, or worse, form a bond with another human being. So now I was *playing golf* with Uncle Douggie, very much enjoying the game. It really wasn't all that bad. Playing it was okay; it was just that I still couldn't stand watching the stuff on television. It seems that Enoch had lost his appetite for sports and Uncle Doug now needed a surrogate son. Since I was freshly out of a father, the match seemed to work. It was during one of these golf games that he told me about the final days of Jesus.

"You remember how casual Bea was about Jesus dying," he said, taking a smooth swing at a ball with his newest nine iron.

"I remember," I said.

"Well," he went on, "it was the strangest thing. While she didn't seem upset, she wouldn't let me get rid of him," and with that we watched the ball miss the hole by a good three feet. "I kept trying to get her to let me take him out back and bury him, but she wouldn't do it." He set up his tee again and took his stance, feeling the weight of the club and trying mock swings before striking the ball with masculine determination. This time he whacked it with such force that it shot out from the ground and arched gracefully out over the green. "It was nearly a month before she finally agreed. I guess she just wanted to remember him for as long as she could, resting there next to the TV," he said, and we watched his shot sail across the sand traps and into the cloudless blue sky.

- 11 -

New York, 1996

Joy deserted my heart, and for a long,
long time I lived in doubt, anxiety and
fear.

—Helen Keller, *The Story of My Life*

Karen didn't stay editor for long. As a matter of fact, Sagaser came back to work two days before Christmas, as soon as he saw the latest copy of the magazine—the one with the story about Jesus the dog. And he had evidently gathered quite a bit of strength during his brief hospital stay because when he called Strekfus into his office to say that the writer of "such fine material" was fired, he reminded him that according to his contract Strekfus owed him an additional story before he went. Sagaser also reminded him that it was to be based on the original theme of Southern homes and gardens, and that it was to be under five thousand words. So Strekfus gave it to him. And it was well under five thousand words.

- 12 -

The House on Danville Road

Infanta, Alabama, 1970

> Would that I could enrich this sketch with
> the names of all those who have
> ministered to my happiness!
>
> —Helen Keller, *The Story of My Life*

When I was fourteen we moved into a house on Danville Road. The less said about my high school years, the better.

- 13 -

New York, 1997

> Children who hear acquire language
> without any particular effort; the words
> that fall from others' lips they catch on
> the wing, as it were, delightedly, while the
> little deaf child must trap them by slow
> and often painful process.
>
> —Helen Keller, *The Story of My Life*

D ear Mr. Beltzenschmidt:

We are sorry about the confusion last week over your firing. Please know that the individual who you spoke with was under no obligation to carry out such an action without our consent. We very much wish you to return to the magazine in the capacity in which you were previously employed. Please contact us as soon as possible as we are eager to correct this misunderstanding.

The letter was signed by three of the four corporate vice presidents (none of whom he had ever seen), and the publisher of the magazine—the man who had more to do with circulation and advertising than with the actual editorial content. Strekfus really didn't have to think about it for long. He had survived the Christmas holidays and New Year's. He liked his job and he was going to write the stories with or without their help. But what he had originally set out to do, to write about Southern homes, had turned into personal anecdotes about the people he knew and places he had lived. At first he thought the pieces were just that—stories about the homes, the people—but the memories had begun to grow and take on a life of their own. Now they were becoming more than just short stories and recollections, they were turning into some morbid navigation through his subconscious. He felt as if he were losing control over the people and places he remembered and loved, and maybe sometimes didn't love so well. The work was an odd mix of fiction and truth, and lately he was unable to tell where the truth left off and his imagination began. In addition to this, what had started out as separate stories were now a series of connected events. It was, he noticed, the makings of a book.

And he had begun to string these incidents together in a way that made sense to him if not to everyone else. He was beginning to see how the puzzle fit together—long ago forgotten remnants of his past which sometimes floated to the surface, feathery and bright green, like snippets of algae surfacing from the murky bottom of some pond. It wasn't just anecdotes or short stories or the memory of a place he was trying to convey, but rather the pieces of his life which had brought him to New York, to this magazine.

It was at that exact moment he decided that he really didn't want to continue. He didn't want to know what lay behind all the things he had been writing about. The stories had started out innocently enough, but then the abuse of his childhood, the death of his father, and other things had begun to make their way into the pieces, and he wasn't sure he liked where they were going. He would tell the publisher and vice presidents that the subject material had become too personal for him to deal with. He would tell them that he wanted another assignment.

Just a few minutes before, when he had received the letter, he was determined to finish this assignment no matter what, but now he was running away from it. He didn't want to open a Pandora's box. He had already tapped on the lid and that was enough.

As he stared out the window of his Fourteenth Street Chelsea apartment which overlooked Greenwich Village, he thought to himself how funny it was that he lived here, in this particular geographic location. It was so like his personality in many respects. Fourteenth Street was the dividing line between Greenwich Village, that one-time enclave of artists and homosexuals, and Chelsea, that semi-industrial landscape of rough bars and working-class individuals. But these descriptions belonged to a time long ago—thirty, forty years ago—a time when he had been a child, totally unaware that such a place as the Village or Chelsea existed.

Now the Village was too expensive for artists and the homosexuals had moved to Chelsea, filling the area with bars, restaurants, and clubs. The blue-collar workers had moved on, there being no need for them as the gay men in the area perpetuated their dress and manners—a by-product of that group's latest quest for individuality and fashion having given up the flamboyant and flashy mode that the '70s and '80s embraced. And he lived right on the dividing line, neither in the one neighborhood nor the other. It was as though he had projected his lack of commitment to things even in choosing the location he lived in, and adding to this sudden perspicacity was the knowledge that Fourteenth Street lay directly over one of Manhattan's major fault lines.

New York City was not known for its earthquakes, but the few and far between ones it did have happened every ten years or so. Usually this was not enough to worry most stouthearted New Yorkers. Even so, at times, one imagined buildings falling in the same direction as if the gods were playing dominos with skyscrapers, and it seemed that this revelation— that life was short, that something could happen at any moment, that he lived neither in Chelsea nor in the Village, that he was not committing to anything—gnawed at Strekfus as if the geography of his choosing were trying to tell him something—just as the geography of his youth had tried. So now he had gone from wanting the assignment, to loathing it, back to reaching out for it in an attempt to understand his past.

Rationally he knew everything was all right—there wouldn't be an earthquake happening anytime soon—but emotionally he felt the tremors, and he also felt the need to define himself more, understand himself, and push his life in a new direction. He knew that this growth would require pain, would require that he look at things he had chosen to forget, would require that he dig deeper into himself for some of the answers.

As he picked up the phone to dial the publishing company, it was as if some inner strength were directing him. It was as if he had given up control for the moment and had let some divine being intervene with the understanding that in the long run he would be better off for this most recent decision.

Then he was speaking with one of the secretaries, asking for one of the vice presidents who had signed the letter, negotiating his terms, committing to finish the project. He was given almost everything he asked for. The only odd request from the publishing company was that he show them the sketches for three stories in advance, and they had asked that he start back to work before January 5. Evidently Edwin Sagaser had requested this for workflow reasons and because of his Danville Road story. He really didn't mind. He could always change certain elements within the framework he gave them.

It was as if he were in some dream, for before he knew it, he was again employed and writing the stories which had brought him this far in his life and to New York. The person on the other end of the phone had been more than gracious, offering him substantially more money and benefits, and he had taken these even though they really didn't interest him. He was more concerned with finding out what was going to happen to himself and his characters in the stories than in any type of material compensation the magazine could offer.

After he hung up the phone he remembered his last conversation with Sharon. They had been at lunch several days earlier and she had chided him once again for his writings. It hadn't set well with him, like most things in that no-man's land between Christmas and New Year's. She had wanted to know

219

why he had skimmed over his father's funeral, instead, concentrating on a dead Chihuahua. And as he sat alone now, certain memories from his childhood came up to the surface again, only this time they weren't the snippets of green algae as before, but dead bodies, bloated and white, full of holes and smelling putrid, finding their way toward the light which hovered over the water.

The writing about the dead dog had been a smoke screen for him, covering up the fact that he had never really dealt with his father's death or what his real relationship had been with that man. And now an image was coming to him, one he couldn't quite figure out. It was as though the trip back home, the stories, the memories, Sharon's chiding, his approaching mid-life crisis, everything, was contributing to this resurfacing of facts long stored away in his subconscious.

He remembered the dizzy spells—the one back home in Althea's house, the one on the sidewalk—and again an image floated up, murky and dark. Then it was clear: stainless-steel pitchers of ice water lined up in a row inside the refrigerator. Why had this floated up to the surface? Before he knew what was happening, he was yanked back across the decades and into the small suburban home he had grown up in. It was almost as if he had traveled through time, so real were the images and feelings, but he couldn't believe what he was seeing, what he was experiencing.

He got up from where he was sitting, hoping to clear his head. As he made his way into the bathroom and started to run the hot water, he leaned on the basin for support, looking at himself in the mirror. Then as the steam rose from the basin, he dipped his hands under the faucet and brought the scalding water over his face in an attempt to hide from where he had just been. The hot water turned his hands and face bright red and he reveled in the physical pain of the event as it blocked out the emotional trauma he was feeling. "Maybe this is why some people are into S&M," he thought. "It blocks the emotional pain, which is worse."

220

When he had finished, he sat back down on the edge of his bed. After a few minutes he found himself staring at his bedside table. Not at anything in particular, just in that general direction. Then he noticed the small round tobacco can he had placed there some days before. He picked it up and rattled it. Then he tossed it up into the air and caught it several times. It lay coolly in the palm of his hand now, sleeping and silent. "What a thing for Althea to have left me. What could she possibly have been thinking?" He turned the small canister over and over, thinking that by searching the outside of it he would find some clue. He still had not been able to open it as the seal was rusted shut. He set it down and spread himself out on the bed, staring at the ceiling until he fell asleep.

When he awoke, lying on his side, facing his bedside table, the first thing he saw was the tin, complacent and waiting, like some passive-aggressive clue from his past, patiently marking the decades, the years, the minutes, until Strekfus was ready for what lay inside.

* * * * *

His first day back at the office felt strange, as if he had been away for several months. It always amazed him how fast things moved in New York. Take a vacation or be out sick for a week and when you returned, several people had been either fired or promoted and your office had been redecorated. There was some new electricity in the air, as if some life-changing event were about to take place, but everyone would have to wait until the appointed time, as if the cosmos was as yet undecided what the exact event would be.

This palpable electricity was evident not only to him but to everyone else as well. The absence of mail delivery by eleven o'clock gave him the opportunity to find out what at least part of the universe had in store for him. As he made his way toward the reception area, one of the secretaries walked past him muttering something about "walking on eggshells," the full impact of which wasn't clear to him until he reached the cloistered and

221

upholstered area at the front of the offices where visitors were received.

"Charneise, have you seen the mail yet? I . . ."

But before he could finish, she cut him off with a curt "No." She made no eye contact and focused on the cheap novel she was reading, the whole time ignoring the blinking lights on the switchboard.

"Well, do you know when it's going to get here? I mean is there some problem with . . ."

"No, I do not." Again, this was said without looking up.

"What's with the attitude, Charneise?" he tried to add jokingly. "All I'm asking is where the mail is."

This time there was no curt response, but simply a long sigh and a slight shaking of her head. On his way back to his office he happened by the secretary he had passed on his way to speak to Charneise. "You weren't kidding," he said, and her tilted head and raised eyebrows answered him back. He decided to stay out of the receptionist's way at least as much as he could, but it bothered him that she saw him as one of the bad guys at the magazine, and he felt guilty that he had started this whole fiasco by slipping Sagaser's memo onto her desk, the one the man had written to Personnel. He had meant to give her some ammunition to defend herself against the company and his boss, and now she had turned against him, thinking he was a part of the conspiracy.

As he realized this, he began to think of all the other times he had been misunderstood and mistreated by other races—something he never expected when he came to New York, a place that was supposed to be so tolerant, so bending toward other cultures and customs. Because of his close association with Althea growing up, he had welcomed all opportunities to be around anyone of a different background or religion, but the results had often proved disastrous with certain cultures often rejecting him before he could even begin to befriend them.

Coming from a perceived racially prejudiced area such as the South, he had bent over backward to dispel the myth that all

Southerners were bigoted, only to be met with hostile and outlandish racism because he was either white or male or Christian. "How ironic," he thought, "that I should come from the South and have little or no hate against different races or religions, and yet be so hated by so many people in the North." It had always been something, whether being called a "white devil" on the street by some passerby or the time he was mugged and told, "All white boys have money." He had tried to explain that he lived in a cold-water flat at the time and had lost his job, but the mugger (who was an wearing an Armani suit) didn't believe him and took the only valuable possession he had—a small silver cross he was wearing around his neck. It seemed almost comical that he had fought his way through knee-deep prejudice in the South to become a different person, only to find himself in a land that was now several times more vocal and hate-filled than the one he had rejected so long ago.

There had been pockets of hate in the South, and a good amount of of it was pretty bad, but some of the people who preached intolerance at Klan meetings would sooner die than speak their disgust in front of a person of color. It was one thing to dislike other races, it was another entirely to have bad manners. Not so in the North. The resentment and hatreds were verbalized on a daily basis. And the prejudices weren't restricted to color lines but encompassed religion as well.

He remembered his first few months in New York, having moved from Houston. He had managed to make numerous friends quickly, several of whom were Jewish, and he had become fascinated by this new culture to which he had never been exposed. There were people of the Jewish faith in the South in the '60s when he was growing up, but as far as he knew he had never met any of them. They, like so many other nationalities or persuasions, tried to assimilate to the point of becoming invisible, if not for survival, then for everyday comfort.

He had never even seen a bagel until he moved to New York—not that they didn't exist in Texas, but rather they weren't part of the culture he had grown up with. So he had brought with him not a prejudice against things he didn't understand, but rather a fascination. He would find, unfortunately, that his open-minded interest as an ordinary white, middle-class male, wasn't always reciprocated.

One evening at a dinner party with some friends, a guest he had never met before asked him where he had grown up and with what religion he had been raised.

"In Alabama, and Baptist," he had responded, and then had asked the man, thinking it only polite and actually being interested, the same question. The guest had replied that he was from New York and when Strekfus pressed him further, asking what religion, there was a split second of silence before the laughter began.

After the entire table of eight regained their composure, it was pointed that the guest's last name was Sapperstein, and that he was wearing a yarmulke. But just before the laughter died out completely, he had heard one of the group mutter, "Dumb cracker."

It struck him as odd how the society he had grown up in had preached intolerance, if not directly, then indirectly, and that he had done everything within his means to fight that attitude only to be rewarded by northern prejudice—openly hostile and rude behavior. So it shouldn't have come as such a shock to him when, at three thirty that day, a memo appeared on his desk from Charneise. Typos and all, Sagaser had been copied on the offending item as had Personnel.

TO: Strekfus Beltzenschmidt

FROM: Charneise Lewis

I am writing this to inform you that I found your conduct today extremely unbecoming and unprofessional. Your comment, "What's with the attitude, Charneise, all I'm asking is where the mail is?" was extremely rude and hurtful. I am not your servant or anyone else's here at this magazine. Slavery was abolished some time ago and it's

224

time you and everyone else at this magazine recognized this.

In the future I would appreciate you speaking to me in a pleasant manner. I have done everything within my means to be a curtous and professional message technician for this company.

Please know that all future abuse by you will be reported to my attorney who is currently handling the case.

He had just finished reading when Sagaser appeared in his doorway holding the memo. She had copied him and just about everyone else on it. He held it up for Strekfus to see and gave a cheery, "Welcome to the club," as he walked away. Of all things, at least Sagaser's reaction had not come as a surprise. He knew his boss wasn't one to smooth over problems; rather, the man liked to pretend that they had never happened. It probably made him more comfortable to ignore the fact that he hadn't won this latest round.

Strekfus looked down at the paper. He wanted to tell Charneise that she had misspelled *courteous* but he thought about it and after a while decided against it. Later that day, as Sharon sat in his office waiting for five o'clock to arrive, he began to discuss the problem with her, thinking that if he spoke about it to someone who understood where he was coming from, it might help him make sense out of everything.

"I don't get it," he was saying to Sharon. She sat there, sympathetic, and listened with her arms crossed. "Why does Charneise see me as one of the bad guys?"

"I don't know. Maybe it was your portrayal of the maid in your stories. You know, all that bowing and scraping." And then she imitated a phrase, or some approximation thereof, that Strekfus had written, giving it her best Southern accent, "Now, Miss Hattie, don't you go worrin' yo' head over dis." She paused. "Aren't you afraid you set back African Americans a few hundred years?"

225

"Oh, come on. It wasn't that bad. And besides, there's a reason I have her talk that way. First of all, she *did*. Secondly, what's the matter with dialect? Don't races and cultures have dialects now which set them apart? What do you think rap music is? Isn't that an attempt to create a specific cultural dialect and art form, and in twenty years from now if someone writes down the way rap artists communicated, is *that* society going to call it racist?"

She gave him no reaction, so he continued.

"Are African Americans going to look back on that particular contribution in twenty years and say it isn't representative of the way they were? And I'm not saying that the bowing and scraping, as you put it, from the first half of the twentieth century is the same thing as an art form delivered by black musicians for the purpose of self-expression, but they're both communication on some level and they both have their messages and they both exist. In fact, don't you think most of the other cultures want to be set apart? If you really want to analyze the whole thing I'll give you my theory."

"No, thanks. That's okay."

"Look. All I'm saying is that she's speaking that way for a reason and not a racist one. You have to wait until I finish the stories. And anyway, cultures evolve with different dialects and their own customs for a reason and not usually just because it was some whim."

"How so, Margaret Mead?" She was asking now with genuine curiosity and not just to patronize him, but she couldn't resist the anthropological dig. It seemed that she had not really give the idea much thought.

"You don't think that bowing and scraping as you call it, came about for a reason?

"Such as?"

"Such as survival. If your life were threatened on a daily basis, you'd probably come up with some way of communicating that said, 'I'm not a threat. I'll stay exactly where you want me to stay, in order to survive or at least until I can figure out a better way to get through life.' We all do that at some point—play the

226

game, pretend in order to survive. If that game doesn't work, you go on to something else. And African Americans played it at one time for a reason and it enabled them to survive. If you ask me, it's a part of their culture, maybe not the most flattering part, but it's there and shouldn't be ignored."

"You mean in the same way that overly flamboyant gay men in the '60s, early '70s, and even sometimes today are stereotyped?"

"Well, yeah, if you want to go there. A lot of African Americans and gays in middle of the twentieth century tried to play the game they thought middle-class white America wanted so that they could be a part of this country. You know, dressing the same way their white counterparts did, trying to adopt the attitudes and social graces of what they perceived to be the norm, trying to fit in. When they found that for all their assimilation efforts they were still being rejected by middle America, they said, 'To hell with this,' and started to create their own culture. Of course, that same middle-class America screams bloody murder about these separate cultures, but it's really their fault—they're the ones who created them by not allowing these other groups to assimilate.

"And if you had been told your entire life that you were worthless and a second-class citizen in society, you don't think you'd have drug problems, problems with intimacy, problems with communicating the same way most of the world does, and myriad other ills a lot of gay men and other minorities have? But at the same time, these misfortunes have enabled a lot of people to look deep within themselves for things the outside world couldn't offer, the way abused children do, you know, creating their own fantasy worlds, becoming artists, musicians, designers, and just about anything else. It's like the old saying, 'If God gives you lemons, make lemonade.' Same sort of thing. I'm not saying we should abuse people just to spark some creative effort, but it's curious to me that a lot of what we call art has to do with healing the planet, if not by making available some sort of escape, then by holding up a mirror to situations and how we deal with them."

"Interesting. But what's that got to do with the receptionist?"

"I didn't say I had an answer. I'm certainly not saying that she's right in getting on my case just because she feels that white people have made her life miserable. God, no. I don't believe that just because I'm white I'm guilty, but I understand somewhat why she's the way she is. Still, it's frustrating for me and many others when we don't consider ourselves to be a part of the problem, yet we're treated as such. It's like the whole world has one big twelve-step program but all the wrong people are attending."

"You're not thinking of joining the other camp, are you?"

"Of course not. But it doesn't make for warm and fuzzy feelings either, the fact that Charneise sees me as the white devil when I've been through things that she can't even imagine. At this point Charneise isn't making lemonade yet, but she's still asking us to pay for the fact that she's forced to squeeze lemons. All I'm saying is that being treated badly by the world is no excuse for not giving something good back to it."

He and Sharon sat there for a minute or so, letting this last verbose assault settle in. It was as if Strekfus wasn't sure exactly where they were going, but by verbalizing his thoughts maybe he could begin to make some sense of the thing.

"Well, look, I've got to get back to work and I'm sure you've got pages to write and theories to ponder," Sharon said as she slowly got up and stretched. She yawned as she turned toward the door. "Just let me know when you solve all the world's problems and we'll go out to lunch and celebrate."

"Sarcasm is unbecoming in such a lovely and svelte person as yourself," he shot in her direction as she exited his office. Then he turned his attention to his computer, to the next story, remembering how he and Sharon had started off on their journey together away from home, in a strange new land which afforded them more freedom than they had ever known before. They had thought college would be the promised land, releasing them from the slavery of high school and parents, but as with any type of freedom, there are costs associated with the goods, and as with all youth, when the invoice is received they look aghast at the amount they owe and wonder if it was all worth it.

- 14 -

The Apartment on Eighteenth Street

Tuscaloosa, Alabama, 1974

> I thought they desired the freedom of
> their fellow men as well as their own. I
> was keenly surprised and disappointed
> years later to learn of their acts of
> persecution that make us tingle with
> shame, even while we glory in the courage
> and energy that gave us our 'Country
> Beautiful.'
>
> —Helen Keller, *The Story of My Life*

My first year of attending the University of Alabama was occupied with trying to juggle my classes and attempt a social life. I didn't notice the Gorgas house—the place where I had verbally tormented the poor tour guide as a schoolboy. My classes kept me pretty busy, but it always seemed to be in the back of my mind and I always wanted to find time to pay it a visit. Of course, this didn't happen until many years later since I was busy with school and practicing the piano. I had chosen a major in music with hopes of someday making my living at this noble career.

While botany had been a great interest of mine, and still was, I had become enamored of the idea that an auditorium of individuals could be made to swoon when they heard Rachmaninoff's Third Piano Concerto, its pyrotechnical demands and surging emotions always able to bring an audience to its feet.

To further educate myself in music, I had taken to buying every recording I could, especially those of Wagner. While Wagner wasn't known as a composer of piano literature, he represented for me the lush romantic ideal, and I could easily get lost in his never-ending chord progressions and aural longings which floated out over the room from my small stereo. I was going through my German phase at the time, so I bought all the recordings I could find: Beethoven, Schumann, Schubert, and especially Wagner. Because I was so caught up in my music activities, my friends and I didn't have much time for television or any extracurricular activities which would have taken us away from hours of practicing. We would, however, occasionally take breaks from our grueling schedules, and when we did, we almost always managed to get into trouble.

We weren't totally immune to the outside world, as news of President Nixon's resignation on August 28 of that year was on everyone's lips. The impending investigation and possible impeachment were all anyone talked about. The Watergate hearings would soon consume the nation, its televised technicalities being just another in a string of real-life soap operas—much as the televised civil rights struggle had been—paving the way for other shows of the future in which the nation would watch, captivated, while ordinary people aired their dirty laundry in public. These future shows would give the perceived lower classes an even worse name than they already had, and many of them seemed to come from the South—an unfortunate side effect.

The South has long been branded backward, and while there is some truth to this, there are also a good many things about this area of the country which are positive, including the many beautiful homes, gardens and institutions of learning. The University of Alabama is one such place.

While some sections of the South are poverty-stricken and dilapidated, the campus of the University of Alabama has a plethora of trees and shrubs, and a center quadrangle unique in its design and execution. Across from the front of the quadrangle stands the home of the president of the university—a beautiful, well-manicured stucco Greek Revival structure. Many of the student buildings are old red brick, and the sidewalks are buckled because of the massive tree roots. The overall atmosphere is one of history and tradition, if not because of the longevity of the university, then because of other factors such as the school's famous football team and its engineering and law departments which have produced many of the country's top engineers and attorneys.

It has always amazed me how the rest of the country views the state of Alabama as bottom-rung even though it has produced some of the most dynamic individuals this country has had. Such notables as Hank Aaron, Tallulah Bankhead, Helen Keller, Nat "King" Cole, Joe Louis, Rosa Parks, and many others have been born in the state. The father of jazz, W C. Handy, was born in Florence, Alabama, and jazz great Lionel Hampton was born in Birmingham. The only reason I can come up with for this lack of dissemination of facts is that the people of the South are the last ones to draw attention to themselves, good or bad. This, however, was not an attitude I had chosen to adopt.

* * * * *

My first year at the university I rented an apartment just off campus in an older section of town. In contrast to the lovely old architecture of the school's massive buildings, this thing was a badly put together early '70s creation with shag carpeting, flimsy walls, and a water heater which sounded like a B-52 about to land at any minute. The entire complex was made to look Southern by the addition of fluted aluminum columns to the front, and it was, as most complexes were at that time, given some florid name such as "Magnolia Arms," or "Tara Way." These places were meant as temporary housing for students who, the university figured, would be spending most of their time drinking and

232

partying as opposed to appreciating any fine structural elements a building might possess. For this very reason it didn't appear that the builder had put much effort into his creation, and the problems this produced were endless. Nevertheless, it was in this badly designed complex that one of my more interesting experiences occurred—one which would cause me to look at myself in an entirely different way.

Never having lived in an apartment before, I was not prepared for the loss of privacy. You see, my next-door neighbors were extremely active in the sexual arts, usually starting around ten o'clock in the evening and finishing around four o'clock in the morning. It wasn't the sounds they made which were so annoying, but rather that of their not-so-well put together headboard hitting the wall over and over. To try drowning out the noise I took to playing my Wagner records, reasoning that I could educate myself and diminish the sound of their lovemaking at the same time. This worked well until about the second week of my stay in the apartment.

One evening, around nine thirty, just before the usual festivities were to begin, there was a knock at the door. Opening it, I found an extremely blond, somewhat overweight man who appeared to be about forty years of age.

"I'm sorry to bother you," he began, "but my girlfriend and I were wondering what that is you play every evening?"

"The music?" I asked, afraid I had disturbed them, but then I thought, "Me, disturb them?"

"Yeah, the music," he went on. "We were wondering if you could lend us the record for a while. We really like that song . . ." and here he tried to hum a few bars. He seemed somewhat shy as he shuffled from foot to foot, his hands in his pockets.

"Oh, *Die Walküre?*"

"Yeah. Yeah, I mean, I guess."

"You like Wagner?" I asked, happy to have found someone else who shared my German music fetish.

"Yeah, Wagner, sure," he replied, anxiously looking around, obviously not quite sure what I was talking about.

233

Now wanting to be friendly (when would I learn?), I tried to put him at ease, making conversation. "My name's Strekfus," I said, and stuck out my hand.

"Bob Castratis," he responded, and shook.

"Castratis?" I asked.

"I'm originally from Georgia—Edwina," he said. "My mother and I moved to Tuscaloosa years ago, so if you're thinking we may be related to any Castratises you know . . ."

"No, it's not that," I said. "I'm from Infanta. It's up near Tuscumbia."

"Yeah, I know that area. What's your major here at the university?"

"Music," I said, hoping that he would appreciate not only my choice in opera, but the fact that I probably knew what I was talking about.

"Guess I should have known that," he said sheepishly. "Look, I've got to get going. I'm planning a party for my mother since she's retiring this year and . . ."

"Oh, is she a teacher here at the university?"

"Uh . . . no. She's not a teacher," he said, and smiled. "She was a tour guide at the Gorgas house. You know, that house that stands over there next to Morgan Hall."

"Yeah, I know it quite well," I said, remembering my many trips there. "Hey, that's where . . ." I started to say with enthusiasm, but he cut me off. I would find out later that it probably was a good thing he didn't let me finish, didn't let me tell him exactly how well I remembered the Gorgas house and the name Castratis.

"I've really got to get going. About that, what did you call it?"

"Wagner."

"Yeah. Wagner. Do you think I could borrow those? It. Whatever."

"Sure," I said, "I'll be glad to let you borrow them," thinking that a night of Wagner coming from next door would be better than a night of headboard banging. Thank God I wouldn't have to listen to another evening of their rhythmic lovemaking.

Or so I thought.

At about ten o'clock the following evening the music started, and just as the strings were sweeping up and down and horn sections were hammering away at their relentless motifs, the couple next door started hammering away at their own. At my bedroom wall. Again.

"Oh, Bob. God, you're good!" the girl started. And then the headboard did time trying to keep up with the Walküres. "Yes, Bob, you are good," I thought. He certainly seemed to be working hard at it anyway with all of the grunts and squeaks that emanated from their bedroom.

"Don't tear the sheet," I heard him yell at her one time. "Aw, honey, now I've got to send this thing to the cleaners."

The next day I appeared at the apartment of my friend Bunny and her roommate, a few doors down from mine and in the same complex. Bunny and I had suffered through elementary and high school together, so the progression to college seemed natural. Besides, when you're charting new territory, you need all the moral support you can get. Bleary-eyed, I asked if I could borrow some milk for my morning coffee as I had forgotten to make my weekly run to the grocery store.

"Sure, come on in," said Bunny. "You look terrible."

"You would too if you hadn't been to sleep all night."

"Rough night, huh?"

"Yeah, the couple next door were going at it all night long and Siegfried never found the Rhine gold as far as I could tell."

"You don't mean the couple in 2A, do you?" Bunny asked, as she suddenly stopped tearing into a rather uncooperative cereal box.

"Yeah. They're the ones. Know them?"

"Well, I don't know them. I know *about* the guy, though," she said, rummaging through an assortment of other boxes, hoping to find one which wasn't going to put up a fight at this early hour. She was still wearing her nightgown and I noticed for the first time her shapely figure. All through elementary school and most of high school Bunny had been overweight, but now she had lost volumes of weight and she was becoming quite attractive.

"What about him?" I asked, referring to the guy in the apartment next to me, but before she could answer, her roommate Melinda came in.

"What about who?" Melinda asked, pouring herself some coffee from the Corningware coffeepot (white, painted flower decals, modern plastic handle).

"The guy in apartment 2A," said Bunny.

"Oh, you mean the Grand Dragon," countered Melinda nonchalantly, not yet fully awake. "Damn, I spilled the coffee grounds everywhere," she said. "Bunny, where are the paper towels?" Melinda proceeded to rummage about under the sink.

"Forget the paper towels. Grand *who*?" I asked.

"Grand Dragon," Bunny went on. "Evidently his place was firebombed last week and he's staying in apartment 2A for a while."

"Grand Dragon of the KKK?"

"That would be the one," Bunny said, sitting down and unfolding the morning paper. She now had a large bowl of cereal topped off with strawberries and was dividing her time between the sports section and fruit-laden cornflakes.

"You mean I'm living next door to the Grand Dragon of the KKK?" I asked. I knew that the Grand Dragon lived in Tuscaloosa at that time, but I had no idea where.

"Well, only for a week or so until they can determine the damage to his house. Melinda, Strekfus says that the guy and his girlfriend kept him up all night playing 'hide the banana.' "

"At least you don't have ten frat boys living above you. It sounds like they're giving tap dancing lessons to elephants up there about four o'clock every morning," countered Melinda and trudged back into her bedroom.

"Looks like nobody is getting any sleep around here," said Bunny, and scooped a mouthful of cereal into her eagerly awaiting orifice.

"Let me get this straight," I said, "we've known each other since first grade and I've been living next door to the

Grand Dragon of the KKK now for several weeks and you didn't feel you needed to tell me this until this moment?" My arms were crossed in a defiant gesture.

Bunny just stared at me blankly as she was prone to do when she wasn't quite sure what, if anything, she had done wrong. I realized that she had a lot on her mind. She was in the process of changing her major from music to art, but I didn't think the conversion from one subject to another would have riddled her brain with as many holes as it evidently had.

"Bunny, " I said, somewhat irritated, "you know how I feel about the KKK."

While I certainly don't condone the actions of some of the more infamous men's clubs, I have always tried to adopt a live-and-let live attitude.

"You know the thing that bothers me the most about the KKK is the fact that they use the Confederate flag as a symbol and their logo."

"I know," she said, a trickle of milk running down her chin.

For most of us Southerners, the Confederate flag is not a symbol of hate, it's a symbol of a past lifestyle—one which doesn't necessarily include slavery. I doubt whether any Southerner thinks that slavery should not have been abolished. Most people in the South are trying to embrace values and a lifestyle they hold dear, and one which doesn't always fit in with today's society. Quality of life issues are one of the main things the Confederate flag represents to this group of people.

"It's always a few who make the many look bad," I said to her.

"Hey, listen, Jocko, you're preaching to the converted."

"Jocko?"

"You know I feel the same way as you. My question to you now is, 'What are you going to do?' Are you going to confront him and tell him that Wagner is a no-no, or are you going to let sleeping dogs lie?"

"Jocko?"

"I don't know. I just made it up on the spot."

237

"Look, for most Southerners, the flag stands for a time when food, family, community, and honor meant something. And that something isn't the KKK."

"And it still does mean something in some places," she countered. Then to Melinda who had wandered through again, eager for more coffee, "Could you look in the closet over there, the one next to the front door, Mel? Yeah, I think we've got a soapbox for Strekfus to stand on."

"I can remember when Sunday dinner lasted five hours because of the number of guests, food to be consumed, and conversations which took place around the table," I continued. "Sunday dinners were served with the best china and crystal and your grandmother's white tablecloth. There was always more than enough food to go around, and as you were leaving, the hostess would insist that you take some of the leftovers home. That's some of the things that the Confederate flag means to me, not hate. It represents history, tradition."

"And your point would be . . ."

"My point is that the South created its own environment in a way—its own culture." I hadn't meant to preach to Bunny since she knew where I was coming from, but I guess I just needed to let off some steam.

And I believed in what I was saying about the South. Towns were smaller years ago. We didn't have access to theatre or the performing arts as our northern counterparts did. We usually made our own entertainment by telling stories or engaging in non-pernicious gossip which was more interesting than most television is now. And let's not even talk about the differences in weather—not that holding onto a fabric representation of the South determines the weather, but it is one more thing we're proud we have. Well, except for the humidity.

I sat there thinking about what I had just said. About the Grand Dragon. I sat there thinking about Bunny. Mostly I was thinking about the South and what it meant to me.

In the South, so much attention is given to quality of life issues, and this encompasses everything from the best recipe for homemade eggnog to what color azaleas looked best next to the iron hitching post. The South also represents a time when family heirlooms were lovingly passed down through generations along with stories which accompanied them, a time when neighbors helped one another, when home and hearth mattered, and when walking around the neighborhood to see the cherry trees bloom was more important than stock options or working a fourteen-hour day. Who would want to let go of that?

The South has known something for years that the North can't even imagine: that is to say, when all is said and done, a good cup of coffee is more important than what your year-end bonus will be. If you have to kill yourself all year to get ahead, how are you going to enjoy the things in life that really matter? Hell, yes, we're slower. Let the North rush ahead and be miserable; we want to spend two hours at Commander's Palace in New Orleans savoring the Shrimp Remoulade while the waiters treat us as if we had just won the lottery, even though we had to save up for six months to be able to eat there.

Understandably, many people find the Confederate flag offensive because they equate it with slavery, and that admittedly was a part of the South at one time. The irony is, I would experience more prejudice years later in the North than I knew ever existed in the South. While there may be prejudice in the South, *most* of the time people (with the exception of some tour guides), have the good manners to keep their mouths shut about it. At least they do today. Years ago, it might have been different.

"So you haven't answered the million-dollar question," Bunny was saying through the bathroom door. She had retreated to that inner sanctum in order to make herself more presentable.

"I have no idea," I said. "What am I supposed to do, go over there and tell him he has to move? Tell him I think his ideas are wrong? I can't believe he's the Grand Dragon. I mean, I let him borrow my Wagner records and he's only listened to *Die Walküre*. He's got *Siegfried* and *Götterdammerung* to go and I don't think he even *knows* about *Das Rheingold*. I'll never get them back. Do you know how long these Wagner operas are?"

239

"I wouldn't ask for them if I were you. He's a pretty intense guy. They say he likes to make love with his KKK uniform on—imagine it how you will."

"No, thanks. I'd rather not. And it's a sheet, it's not a uniform. And you just asked me what I was going to do. Now you're telling me not to go near him. Make up your mind. Besides, are you sure he's the Grand Dragon? I mean, how do you know?"

"Well, that's what they say. Okay, maybe he's not, but better safe than sorry. I'd just steer clear if I were you. Maybe you should try listening to some Scott Joplin and see how he reacts. Personally, I never cared for Wagner," and with that she emerged from the bathroom with a towel wrapped around her head.

"Oh, God," I said, suddenly putting my head in my hands.

"What?"

"I just realized something. He said his mother used to be the tour guide at the Gorgas house."

"So?"

"So. I can't tell you how may times I've been in that house. Don't you remember when we were kids and our class would make a trip there every year?

"Hey, I always went to the science building," said Bunny.

"This is great," I said, "I used to torture the mother of the Grand Dragon when I was a child."

"I really wouldn't worry about it if I were you. I seriously doubt that she remembers it, and besides, even if she did, *he* wouldn't know."

"Maybe you're right," I said, and tried to dropped the subject. It was then that I noticed a book which had been sitting just to the right of my arm. In an attempt to get off our most recent topic I turned it around so that I could read the jacket cover. "What's this?" I asked.

"*The Dogs Bark,* by Truman Capote," Bunny responded, adjusting the towel on her head.

"That's an unusual title. I haven't heard of this one," I said.

With that, Bunny took the book from my hands and flipped through the first few pages. Then she read, " 'The dogs bark, but the caravan moves on.' It's an Arab proverb. That's where he got the title. They're a collection of writings. You know, travel sketches, articles that have appeared in magazines. That sort of thing. You can borrow it if you want."

"Thanks," I said, and took the volume from her, thinking that I probably wouldn't get around to reading it for several months.

* * * * *

I decided not to ask for the Wagner records after all and stayed out of the way as much as I could. The Grand Dragon, or whoever he was, ended up staying much longer than a few weeks. Several times I ran into him since our front doors were less than a foot apart at right angles. He was always nice to me and I tried my best fake smile to let him know I didn't want any trouble. Still, I thought, "Maybe Bunny and Melinda are just playing with me."

This front door arrangement ordinarily wouldn't have been a problem because I minded my own business and he minded his, but one particular incident did put a bit of a strain on our neighborly feelings. It was during that open-ended, anything-goes-holiday which college students love, always taking it to a new level of decadence: Halloween.

It was my first Halloween away from home, and feeling bored I went to round up Bunny and Melinda. Deciding that Tuscaloosa was not exactly the happening place, and having no parties to go to, the three of us made the decision to walk around campus and see what trouble we could stir up. When the entertainment doesn't come to you in the South, you create the entertainment.

I had called it quits on practicing at the music building that evening, having practiced and studied myself into a stupor. The three of us made the rounds to several of the bars just off campus, and after spending about an hour in each one, we were sufficiently inebriated and ready for anything. As we walked around the campus we tried some of the doors to the buildings, hoping to find one open so that we could amuse ourselves by writing provocative things on the blackboards or turning all the desks backwards so that when classes resumed our fellow students would have something to break up the monotony.

Ending up in the main auditorium of the fine arts building to play the piano on Halloween night seemed innocent enough, but soon Bunny, the most industrious of our trio, became disillusioned, wandering backstage and up one of the spiral staircases in the corner. A few minutes later she appeared at the foot of the stairs just as Melinda was launching into a pig Latin version of Gershwin's "Summertime," while I accompanied her on the out-of-tune Steinway.

"You guys have to come see this," Bunny shouted. "It looks like the entire costume collection from *Gone With the Wind* up here in the loft."

Melinda and I followed the sound of Bunny's voice until we were at the top of a spiral staircase looking into one of the storage rooms at the top of the theatre. The drama department had stored costumes from a former production upstairs and had forgotten to lock the doors—a lethal combination for freshmen on Halloween night.

"What a find," Melinda added, as we made our way into the attic of the theatre. Immediately we began digging through boxes of Confederate uniforms and hoopskirts. After a few minutes Melinda and I were dressed as generals of the Confederacy and Bunny was a Southern belle in a pale blue-and-white hoopskirt. For a while we admired ourselves in the mirror and then we all seemed to have the same idea.

"I know what you guys are thinking," I started, "because I just thought the same thing. But it's not going to happen."

"Why not?" asked Bunny.

"Because," I said, "I haven't been in a dress since I was seven and I don't plan to repeat the experience. We could be arrested or beaten up. And we don't even know if Melinda could get into a hoopskirt with those hips."

My rationale fell on deaf ears, and before we knew it, Bunny was wearing the Confederate general's uniform and Melinda and I were dressed as Southern belles.

"I should have gotten the blue-and-white hoopskirt," I said, "This green taffeta makes me look fat."

"I really don't think looking fat is your biggest problem," countered Bunny.

I really didn't relish the idea of appearing before Tuscaloosa low society wearing a dress, much less one from a nineteenth-century plantation, but I thought it would be an experience, and as I hadn't yet seen what I considered to be enough of the world, I agreed with their plan. Besides, I've never been one to let well enough alone, so I figured, "Why not?" The truth was, Bunny was always pushing the envelope, trying to steer me in some direction she thought I should go. I don't think she always anticipated the consequences.

"All right," I said, "How do you think we're going to get down that staircase in these things anyway?"

"Look, the hoops just mash in. It's either that or take the thing off and have to put it back on again," said Melinda.

"No, thank you. Let's go. I can't believe I let you guys talk me into this."

So off we went, down the staircase. Fortunately we were quite drunk, so venturing outside wasn't as big a problem as I thought it would be. About halfway down the block we encountered a group of fraternity boys and I thought to myself, "Here's the test. If we're not killed it will be a miracle."

"You guys look great!" they shouted and began slapping us on the back and fingering the layers of tulle. "Where's the party?"

"I didn't think it was possible to be more drunk than we were," said Bunny under her breath as she gripped my elbow.

"There *is* no party," I started to say, but she gave me a swift kick in the shins.

"Why don't you guys come with us," they continued. "We're going over to the Pike house."

"Sounds great," said Bunny and we all looked at each other with an expression that said, "What the hell." With that the three of us linked arms, à la *Wizard of Oz*, and headed down the sidewalk.

We followed them over to the fraternity house and much to our delight they were having a costume party. As a matter of fact, we were some of the more sedately dressed guests. After several hours of intensive partying we decided to call it quits and head back to the building where the auditorium was, to reclaim our real clothes and return Scarlett, Melanie, and Ashley's attire before anyone noticed them missing.

Upon reaching the fine arts building where the auditorium was located, we tried the door but discovered it was locked.

"This can't be happening," said Bunny. "My head is killing me and this wool is scratching me to death."

"Try having a sixteen-inch-waist for three hours and see how you like it," I replied.

"What are we going to do now?" added Melinda, fear and desperation creeping into her voice. "We can't keep this stuff and our clothes are in there. Besides I've got a chemistry exam tomorrow at nine o'clock."

"Look, we'll just have to try and find a way to get into the building," I said, and we proceeded to try every door and window in the place with no luck at all.

After several minutes we decided that the best thing to do was to go home to our respective apartments, get some sleep, and come back tomorrow to return the outfits. We could always say we found them. With this in mind we headed toward our apartment building ten blocks away, each of us with a hangover in the making.

Now, since it was three o'clock in the morning I wasn't really expecting to run into anyone I knew, and besides, it was Halloween. People expected this sort of thing, didn't they? Our appearance hadn't shocked the fraternity boys, but then I thought about what I had seen going on in the houses on fraternity row just a few streets over and I thought, "No, I guess this wouldn't shock them."

As we neared our apartment building, Bunny and Melinda made a beeline for their door and I for mine. But as luck would have it, I tripped and fell over a dead boxwood bush and then promptly landed on my bicycle which was chained up to one of the columns holding up the verandah of the building. Evidently I made quite a commotion, because several lights came on in various windows and just as I picked myself up and was trying to insert the key into the lock, a loud and booming voice came from inside my neighbor's apartment, several decibels above the Wagner which was playing even at this hour. Bunny was nowhere to be found.

"Who's there?" my neighbor bellowed. "You better get the hell out of here before I blow your head off!"

I reasoned, as one is prone to do at this hour of the morning, in this attire, that he was worried that I had come to fire-bomb his apartment.

"It's just me," I responded with as much fortitude as I could. "No need for alarm. Go back to bed. It's just your neighb . . ." But before I could finish he opened the door.

By now, I had managed to drop the key and as I was retrieving it from a tangle of dead morning glory. I straightened up to see my neighbor, the Grand Dragon, holding a twenty-gauge shotgun and looking rather surprised. The two barrels were pointed directly at my nose, only inches away.

"Hi," I said, as cordially as I could, while trying to act as if nothing were the least bit out of the ordinary.

I had obviously interrupted a night of lovemaking because he was wearing his KKK robe, sans hood, and his timid girlfriend was cowering behind him, naked except for a pair of zebra-print panties (hands criss-crossed over breasts, knees together with one foot slightly behind).

"Trick or treat?" I said, hoping he would somehow find this amusing. "I see you made it to Valhalla," and I craned my neck out and to the side as if to see his apartment better, feigning interest in what décor he and his girlfriend might have.

245

"What?" he asked, lowering the shotgun.

"I'd love to stay and chat," I said, "but I've got to get ready for the barbecue at Twelve Oaks. The Yankees are coming, you know," and with that I fell into my door, pushing it open and landing facedown on the floor of my living room. When I got up to close the door, he was still standing there open-mouthed, and his girlfriend was making lunch out of her fingernails.

"Look," I started again, "I know you don't approve of this sort of thing but . . ." and then something happened to me. I just seemed to come out of myself. I thought about closing the door, hoping he wouldn't come after me, but then I changed my mind. It was as though deep down inside I knew that if I didn't go through with this—what I wanted to say—I could never live with myself. I guess it was a combination of the beer and the lateness of the evening, but I started in, and before I knew it I was so deep into it that nothing could get me out. Besides, I was standing there in a dress.

"I don't care who you are," I said forcefully, "I'm not in the least bit scared of you and your kind. In fact, I'd like to kick your WHITE-SUPREMACIST ASS RIGHT NOW." I was quite inebriated and it was showing. Standing there in an antebellum hoopskirt with my hands on my hips I continued, swaying slightly from side to side. "You people make me SICK. You should be ashamed of yourself, although I can certainly see where *you* got it from with a mother like *you* had. What a *bitch* that woman was to me when I was in elementary school." I went on like this for several moments while he stood there with the shotgun lowered and a confused look on his face. After a few minutes I ran out of steam and stood waiting for the air to clear. Sweat was streaming off me and the bodice of my outfit was soaking wet. Finally he said something.

"What the hell are you talking about?" he asked with genuine concern, looking at me sideways.

"What do you mean, 'What am I talking about?' You're the Grand Dragon of the KKK, aren't you?" I shot back, again, my hands on my hips, my neck stuck out both literally and figuratively. I wasn't backing down. Not yet.

"Huh?"

"Look, I know who you are—that your house was bombed, that . . ." But I didn't finish. Something about his face, the genuine confusion, a momentary doubt on my part, made me rethink what I had planned to say.

"So, uh, you really aren't the Grand Dragon?" I asked, now somewhat more sheepishly. It was beginning to dawn on me that Bunny and Melinda might have played a trick on me, probably to get even for all the times I had tormented Bunny. I thought about the rock in first grade and several other incidents. I would deal with Bunny later. Now I had to get out of this situation.

"No. Why? Should I be?" He was looking at me sideways again, as if he were ready to call the police.

"But the robe," I said, looking at the sheet he was wearing.

"We went trick-or-treating with the kids at Christ Church down the block. They didn't want the little ones to go alone so my girlfriend and I went along." It was then that I saw he wasn't wearing a KKK robe at all, but a regular sheet, and as I glanced inside the door of his apartment I could see orange plastic pumpkins and bowls of trick-or-treat candy. His poor girlfriend was standing there with not a single fingernail left.

"I went as a ghost, a rather large ghost," he laughed, "and the missus went as a witch. Show him, honey," and with that the girlfriend held up a pointed black hat and tried to smile, the whole time still balancing on one foot.

"I'm sorry," I said, "I was evidently given some wrong information about your social status." I tried to hold myself steady, but the beer was beginning its second round of assault on my brain and I was feeling wobbly. "I'm really sorry. I should let you guys go now and get some rest or whatever else it is that you do. I'm really very, very sorry. I really am," and with that I politely shut my door after waving a rather timid "bye-bye."

I couldn't tell what he was saying to his girlfriend after I shut the door and I really didn't care. The next day after the incident, bright and early, I made it a point to knock on Bunny's door.

"Go away," she said through the thick wooden door after taking a good twenty minutes to answer.

"No, darling, you're going to answer some questions for me." After a moment she let me in. She looked awful; her hair was a matted mess and she was still wearing part of the Confederate uniform.

"Come on in," she mumbled. The legs of the wool trousers she was wearing scratched against each other as she retreated to the sofa.

"Grand Dragon, huh?" was all I said as I sat down.

"Why, what happened? Did you confront him or something?"

"When we came home last night, I stumbled against his door and he came out with a shotgun." Bunny's eyes were wide now and she was awake. I had her attention.

"Basically, I told him off and in not the nicest way, and, I may add, while wearing a hoopskirt."

"Oh, dear," she said, fingering one of the brass buttons on her uniform. "Did you get hurt? Did he hit you?"

"No, he didn't hit me! For Christ's sake, Bunny, you knew he wasn't the Grand Dragon of the KKK and you led me on!"

"Well, you didn't know that at the time you stood up to him, did you?"

"No!"

"So you thought you were standing up to the Grand Dragon who was holding a shotgun, didn't you?"

"Yes. So?"

"So now you know what kind of a person you really are. How many people do you know would stand up to someone like that, especially while they're holding a gun?"

"You have a point," I said, thinking about what she had just said. It really shouldn't have come as such a shock to me, the fact that Bunny instigated an event such as this, complete with faux Klansman and Civil War costumes.

248

Bunny had a way of doing things like this—showing you what you were made of, testing you, always trying to get you to go beyond what you thought you were capable of doing. So I should have seen it coming. Then again, it was much more effective because I hadn't had a clue at the time. After I had a chance to think about it, I realized that I had done something rather extraordinary. I was not one to stand up to someone in such a position of power. I wasn't sure I had it in me. To poke fun at tour guides when you're in elementary school was one thing, but to take on the Grand Dragon of the KKK was something else.

At any rate I managed to avoid my neighbors for the remainder of the semester and they kept up their nightly ritual with only an evening off here and there (they had been together for some time) and while I kept my distance, neither Mr. KKK nor his girlfriend bothered me, but would wave to me if I were within twenty feet or so of them. Regardless of my display of courage, I was smarting from my outlandish display in front of a perfectly innocent person. I came home from class one day toward the end of the semester to find my Wagner records neatly placed next to my door with a note that said, "Thanks for the music." And then a P.S. "Hope you had a good time at the barbecue."

The neighbor and his girlfriend moved out, and the next person who rented that apartment was a divorced housewife who was going back to school for her degree in library science. She didn't make much noise, but every now and then I could swear I heard Wagner playing, ever so softly. I guess Wagner really is music for the masses.

I never returned the dress and I could only imagine how surprised Althea must have been when I came home from college between semesters and asked her if she would do my laundry. She did several months' worth for me and in the process came across the green taffeta hoopskirt that I had inadvertently stuffed into the bottom of my laundry bin. I had taken the wire hoops out of it in order to make it fit underneath the pile of gym shorts and blue jeans that sat waiting to be taken home each semester after finals.

I could hear her saying as she fingered the shiny green folds, "Mmmmmm. That Strekfus is one creative white child."

I didn't keep in touch with Melinda, Bunny's roommate, or any of my other fellow students at the university after that semester. I guess I knew that I would be transferring to another college at some point as I didn't feel the University of Alabama was the place for me, and so I threw myself into my studies for that period of time, waiting for the moment I could escape the confines I had unknowingly set up for myself. When you're young you make all kinds of strange decisions and then ask yourself afterward, "What was I thinking?" This had been the case with choosing my major and the school I had sought to attend. At any rate, a year later in mid-semester, Bunny and I decided to transfer to a college in Texas not only because it was farther away from Alabama, but also because it was located in a town where one of her aunts lived. I was excited about the prospect of meeting new people, being in a new environment, and learning new things. I didn't take into consideration, however, just what kind of new things there would be to learn. Still, I knew Bunny would be there to guide me, and so off we went together, right into the middle of the 1970s.

- 15 -

New York, 1997

> We walked down the path to the well-
> house, attracted by the fragrance of the
> honeysuckle with which it was covered.
> Someone was drawing water and my
> teacher placed my hand under the spout.
>
> —Helen Keller, *The Story of My Life*

It was the key in the lock that awakened Strekfus Ovid Beltzenschmidt of Fourteenth Street (neither of the Village nor Chelsea) at this early hour of the morning. His mind recognized the sound and knew that it was occurring at an unusual time; that something was wrong; that he should prepare himself, but before he could fully awaken, the intruder was already on him, cuffing a large and sweaty hand over Strekfus's mouth, tearing him from the bed. The man attacking him was enormous compared to Strekfus's stature. Strekfus could smell his breath, feel the heat from his hand. It was dark and he couldn't see the man's face, only hear his breathing, heavy and solid, sure of himself. It was as if Strekfus were a rag doll to this giant, totally subject to the intruder's every whim. Everything had happened so fast that there had not been time to cry out or to fight back, and now all Strekfus could feel was fear. Everything had happened in an instant, as if in a dream, the disjointed, quick incidents strung together like a hastily executed science project by some hormonally-questionable and attention-challenged teenager. And yet it was so real.

He felt himself being pulled through the darkness of his apartment, onto something cold and hard. He saw elements of his home fly past him—cabinets, a desk, some chair which had been overturned. He tried to cry out but fear paralyzed him, taking his voice and his strength. Then something was being tied around his wrist and ankles. He was being pulled across the cold floor again. The panting sounds continued—then the blinding light from above. For a second he could make out the wall switch, some appliance. His pupils tried to resize themselves but they were no match for the light which had come so suddenly out of the hollow square from above, illuminating him and the intruder. But before he could focus, before he could make sense of what was happening, the cold torrents of water began to pour down onto his face, into his eyes, his gaping mouth, down his chest. The freezing water paralyzed what little fight remained and he felt himself leave his body and hover, high above the room, taking in the scene. Again the fast-moving ice water, the swift kick of a hard shoe into his ribs, the soundless mouth of the intruder moving, grimacing, gritting, angry, hard. Chiseled words which tore at him in a deafening silence. Strekfus opened his mouth in an attempt to cry out, but the water poured into him. Then one of the giant steel receptacles clattered to the floor, echoing in his ear until the sound reverberated with such intensity that he felt himself falling into space, careening over and over into a void with his heart firmly planted in his throat.

He woke with a start, sitting straight up in bed. He was covered in sweat, his body tense. He looked around the room, unable for a moment to shake the bad dream, to realize exactly where he was. The sound of the steel hitting the floor hadn't yet ceased and he looked around to try to make sense of what was happening. Then seeing the phone as if for the first time, he reached for the receiver, realizing that he had not been hearing a metal object hit the floor, but rather this obnoxious, tenacious and somewhat dangerous-sounding thing meant for communication.

"I think I know where this is going." It was Sharon speaking, having called Strekfus now at eleven-thirty at night.

252

"It's eleven thirty at night," Strekfus said, turning his alarm clock so that he could better read it, still shaken from the place he had just traveled to. "Give me just a second. I just . . . I mean, hold on for a minute, I'm already in bed. Hang on." He held the phone away for a moment, trying to catch his breath, trying to shake the nightmare. But it seemed as if some great weight were on his chest, not letting him breathe, not letting him up. "I'm sorry," he said, trying to shake the grogginess from his voice. "Why are you calling, waking me up? What's wrong?"

"I read the last article you wrote, the one about the University of Alabama and the Grand Dragon. I see now this is going to be your life story, or at least how *you* see your life."

"Can we talk about this tomorrow at work? I'm really tired and need . . . you called to tell me that?"

"Listen. Wait a minute. What I want to know is, if you plan to have anything in one of the next stories about our, how shall I say, 'good times' at Greensaw University and the apartment we shared on Sul Ross?"

Strekfus realized he was going to be on the phone a while, so he reached for a cigarette and lit it. He would have needed one for this conversation alone, but given the fact that he had just suffered through another nightmare he saw even more reason to light up. He waited a moment and then exhaled a slanted column of cigarette smoke toward a nearby lamp. The smoke rose up under the black shade and came out the top. "I might have something in the next story about you. Is this a problem?" he asked in response to her question.

"Problem for me? Nooooo. Why would you say that? For Christ's sake, Strekfus, do you remember what happened back then? On second thought, let me rephrase that: I *hope* you don't remember what happened back then. Do you actually think anyone is going to want to read about that kind of thing?"

"I'll decide when I write it. Besides, I'm not using your real name. I called you Bunny in the story and I changed around some of the characters."

"Oh, so you've already written it?"

"I didn't say that. Look, I've got to get some sleep. I've got an early day tomorrow with Sagaser. The man is actually being somewhat nice to me now and I don't want to blow it. Ever since he found out I took a plant to him when he was in the hospital, he's been a little more civil. It seems that maybe my story *didn't* put him in the hospital after all. At least that's what he told me."

"You took him a plant, for Christ's sake?" She was screaming now, almost hysterical, her adrenaline level having shot up at the very mention of Sagaser. "I thought you hated the man."

"I'm not crazy about him, but I have to work with him. Listen, I've really got to go to bed."

"I just want to say one thing before you go. You be very careful writing these next few stories. I don't want anyone coming up to me at work and asking me about certain incidents. I would really appreciate it if you would let me read them first since I seem to be showing up once again in your, whatever it is you're writing." Then she turned somewhat cold. "But I really guess I shouldn't worry since you seem to have such a selective memory."

He tried to ignore the last remark.

He was unsuccessful.

"Jesus, you and everyone else are after my ass lately."

"How so?"

"Oh, Charneise, the receptionist. Sending me that memo about how I was rude to her, the whole time she was treating *me* as if I were radioactive waste."

"Maybe she'll like this last story on the KKK."

"I don't think she can read. Probably had someone else write the memo. You know, it really gets me. You try to do something for someone and it backfires on you."

"Now don't go getting the 'once-bitten, twice shy' syndrome."

"But it's true," he countered, letting his frustration out completely. "After a while you just don't want to deal with *anyone* anymore, not even your *own* race. Look, you know me. I've

254

always been extremely liberal, very accepting of everybody and everything. But when you're that way and you keep running up against others who hate you because you're . . ."

"Don't say it."

"Free, white, and twenty-one . . ."

"I told you not to say it. And besides, darling, you're hardly twenty-one any longer, and you may be white but you're certainly not free—at least not yet."

"Then you start getting really angry at everyone else's stupidity," he went on, not even hearing her last remark. He knew he would have to deal with this—his anger over everyone else's prejudices that in turn were causing him to question his universal acceptance of all cultures—but for now he allowed himself to feel frustrated. He didn't want to hate others just because they disliked him for his race or religion or any other reason they could come up with, but at the same time he felt a burning in his gut over the fact that he had fought that particular monster already while others hadn't even started.

"Look, I'm sorry. I'm just a bit stressed out lately with Sagaser, these stories hanging over my head, a whole lot of things," he said. Then he added, "Just be glad I skimmed over the high school years."

"Why? What about them?"

"Oh, come on! I could have written something about you and your first boyfriend," he said. "You know, how he serenaded you on your first date in the ninth grade."

"You wouldn't dare."

"That's why I left out high school—all the things that happened to us. You think I'd tell the world he played "Wipe Out" on his catcher's cup after the big game, *while* he was still wearing it? And at McDonald's, no less? And that you actually found this attractive behavior in an adolescent?"

"I see your point."

"Yeah. I left out the good stuff."

"That's okay. Really. No need to go into detail for the purpose of increasing magazine circulation. I just want you to be careful about how obvious it is that I'm one of the characters in

255

your stories, which by the way appears to be turning into more of a book than a series of short stories. Other than that little word of caution, I'll let you get back to sleep."

"I'll see what I can do, I mean about trying to keep you out of trouble in print," he said.

"Okay. Sorry sweetie," she said, returning to her normal self. "Good luck with Saggy-ass tomorrow." Then, changing the subject abruptly as she was apt to do: "Say, speaking of enigmas, did you ever get into that tin?"

"What ten?"

"Tin. The tobacco tin, silly. The one that you had sitting on your desk at work. Don't you remember anything?"

"No. Why are you so concerned with that, anyway?"

"Well, I mean, you brought it all the way back here from Alabama. It must have some meaning for you."

"Nosy female."

"Look, I'll let you get back to sleep. Talk to you tomorrow."

"Thanks," he said and hung up the receiver, accidentally dropping a large chunk of smoldering ash onto the nightstand. It flared up momentarily and then died, sending up a miniature smoke signal that curled about in the artificial light of the room. Outside a solitary car horn sounded-off in the distance.

As Strekfus sat on the edge of the bed, he let his mind drift back to the story he was working on—the one involving himself and Sharon when they had transferred to Greensaw University. He didn't see anything in it that would upset her. Most of what happened in that story had to do with other characters they had known. He didn't think she would mind, and besides, she came off as being more levelheaded than he did. What was there to be upset about?

He thought back to her latest dig at him—the one about selective memory. So what if he picked out certain incidents in his life and left out others? What business of hers was it? Besides, he had enough trouble dealing with the demons coming up in his dreams; he didn't need to discuss them with her or write about

256

them. At this point he decided that he was awake and reached for another cigarette and the latest revision of his story.

As he read the copy, he was remembering Sharon, or Bunny as he called her in his stories—how they had traveled from the University of Alabama and then to Greensaw, Texas. Then to New York. They had both wanted the same thing at one time, but now it seemed as if they were growing apart. He thought about his first impressions of Greensaw. Sharon had been to Texas, several times before him as she had an aunt who lived there, and because she had chosen to move her belongings to Greensaw several weeks before, she had found enough time to assemble an interesting entourage of friends before his arrival.

He was reading the story now, realizing that he had left out one of the most important elements: his mother. Their relationship had been strained up to that point, but when he moved to Texas things really heated up. He knew her shortcomings, her conniving and manipulating ways, but there was something else there, some resentment or mistrust which ran deeper than just the usual family differences. Was this just another prejudice—shunning the woman who had given birth to him because he'd never felt she was a nurturing being? No, that wasn't it. In fact, he didn't hate her. He didn't hate either of his parents—he loved them very much. The problem was that they hadn't loved *him* and nothing he could come up with, then or now, could change that.

His eyes were tired and the cigarette was dangerously close to his fingers, so he extinguished it and put down the copy. As he lay there, staring up into the white-hot glare of the lightbulb which could be seen from the underside of the lamp, his dream came back to him. And it came back easily, for it wasn't really a dream after all but rather a recurring event which had been playing itself over and over in his head ever since a few weeks ago. He had tried to block it from his mind, but it, like so many other memories, had begun to follow him like some snarling wild dog that smells blood and refuses to go away. And it had all started with his trip back home—the memories coming back to him, the crying baby, the heat and humidity, the houses,

257

Sagaser, the magazine, New York. They all piled on top of him like children on a playground at recess who run after and tackle the one with the ball.

He had come to terms with this latest revelation and dream. He knew the truth about it. He knew what had happened as a child: that his father had kept stainless-steel pitchers of ice water on hand for the sole purpose of pouring it on him after tying him up. But what he couldn't seem to remember was where his mother had been during the whole process. These incidents almost always occurred late at night, after his father had come home from the hospital, and therefore his mother would have to have been home. Why had she not done anything to stop him? Where had she been in the house at the time? It was bad enough to have recall of these events, but still to have missing pieces of the puzzle was excruciating. Why was his father this way—angry, mean? Why had he tortured him in this manner? And why was this becoming such an issue for him now, at his age, in New York?

He could make *some* sense out of it: how his parents' treatment of him had affected his life. He was forty and had never had a fulfilling relationship other than his friendship with Sharon, and that seemed to be falling apart as late. He chain-smoked and was always having problems with jobs, bosses, authority, and just daily living. He had been in therapy for seven years, trying to deal with several attempts at suicide and his self-destructive behavior. He knew that at some point he had to stop blaming others for his shortcomings, but before he could do that, he had to know why certain things had happened. After all, he didn't live in a vacuum; others had affected his life for better or worse.

Strekfus was wide awake now, rummaging through the pages of his next story, revising it, cleaning it up, trying to make sense out of it and his life. He knew that the story wasn't going to give him all the answers to why he had become the person he was, but he also knew that it would contribute to his makeup. He went into the kitchen to look for caffeine, even though he was awake, and a new pack of cigarettes.

After a while he took a break from writing. He noticed he had consumed too much tea and started thinking about the things life had subjected him to. As he sat in the chair next to his bed he became aware of a change taking place within himself. It wasn't just an emotional change, nor just a physical one, but a combination of the two. It was as if some fusion of the caffeine, the remembering, the stress lately, all had pooled to bring on a karmic morphing of his entire being. He felt as though he was on fire, as though someone had touched a low-voltage wire to him somewhere and a current was now flowing through his body—not killing him but shaking him to the point at which he must act or go mad. Then something was taking over, making him move, thinking for him. He could see and feel himself doing things, but it was as if some outside force were controlling him.

Before he knew what was happening, he was searching the room, rummaging wildly about his dresser, his night table, under the bed, everywhere he could think of. So intense was his search that he momentarily forgot what it was he was looking for. Then he saw it. It was sitting next to his keys, right in front of him the whole time. Strekfus had no idea why he wanted this thing, what it meant, but some part of him knew he needed whatever information was inside. He grasped the small tobacco tin, the very one Althea had left for him, and with all his energy tried to pry the can open. It wouldn't budge. He was tired of this thing, of wanting to know what was in it, of Sharon's wanting to know, of her wondering why he had brought it back to New York. And in fact he wasn't totally sure himself. Why had Althea left this for him? He knew that Althea wasn't given to doing something without a reason. She wouldn't have left him this as a reminder of herself without good cause. He wondered if this had something to do with his past, if he was supposed to figure something out, if it was some kind of code he needed to decipher.

Then he was becoming hysterical, hyperactive, obsessed as one can when something doesn't yield to a first attempt. It is as if by not yielding to us, the object takes on superhuman importance and the conquest of the thing becomes a matter of

259

life and death. This thing, no matter how small, becomes enormous and takes all our energy, just because it has yet to yield.

He was searching the room again for something, anything with which he could pry open the small tobacco tin. It was almost as if something unseen were compelling him to open it, to release whatever was inside. He shook the object. There was something in it, but now he knew it wasn't tobacco. He knew it was something else.

But why now? Why was he focusing on this when he had just been thinking about his father, his tortured childhood? Did his subconscious mind know of some connection that his conscious one didn't?

Finally, he grabbed a pair of scissors from his desk and stuck one blade into the seam of the can, at the same time sinking down onto the floor in kneeling position. Then wedging the tin against a table leg, he gave the handle of the scissors a heavy blow with the heel of one of his dress shoes which had been lying nearby, forlorn and solitary. One half of the can flew up into the air and the other half rolled under the bed. He scrambled under the frame, through the dust bunnies and boxes which hadn't been touched in years, and brought it out into the light of the room, expecting to see at least some identifiable item which he would throw away, secure now in the knowledge that one of the earth's great mysteries had been solved and he could continue with his life.

There were two small objects inside which at first made no sense to him, and it seemed that he stared forever at these two items, yellowed and aged, as they pressed to the sides of their home—a home they had occupied for many years.

After he took them out, he stared for an even longer time. Now he knew what they were, and as he held them up and turned them in the light, he wondered at their meaning and at the woman who had left them for him inside this small, insignificant receptacle, this miniature holy grail, this link to his past which he would follow in an effort to explain why he had become the person he was. He slid his fingers carefully over them, caressing them gently in an effort to calm himself, for he knew that before the journey was over—the journey that the contents of the tin would cause him to take—he would be mentally tearing at them like some crazed animal stalking its prey, trying to extract what secrets they possessed so that he could piece together who he had become. But before this could happen, before he could know everything, he would have to follow the path as it had been laid out for him—finish his stories in the magazine—and though he wanted to be at journey's end, he was only up to his college years. He knew that skipping a step might cause some cosmic upset. He knew that he must make the trip without haste in order to appreciate and realize fully all there was to know. And he knew the tin's contents and his stories would help lead him in the right direction.

- 16 -

I.O.O.F. Street

Greensaw, Texas, 1976

> I remember well the first time I went to
> the theatre.
>
> —Helen Keller, *The Story of My Life*

O n June 15, Roman Yapigacy entered the house on I.O.O.F. Street, poured kerosene on the walls and floors, struck a match, and promptly burned the hundred-year-old domicile to the ground. It wasn't the belongings lost in the fire that upset everyone so much as the fact that a chapter in our lives had been closed forever. And it was this place, this old Victorian ghost of a home, which held our lives and secrets and the lives and secrets of so many others in the past. So when flames consumed the physical structure, we all mourned its demise because we knew that an era was gone, as if its passing were a signpost which said to move on—that this part of the journey was over.

True, the four people who lived there at the time, including Roman, lost everything (he had to make it look like an accident, and besides, he really didn't own that much), but it wasn't the tangibles and the house that went up in smoke so much as a part of our youth—our youth and a time that would not and could not ever be recreated again. Those were irreplaceable.

Roman was never arrested after the conflagration—he would suffer a much worse fate—but the fact that he had set the fire had been common knowledge. He had admitted it to almost everyone.

"I had to," he had said to a friend of ours, "that place was evil. It was the cause of everyone's problems. I know Chandelier is mad about it, but I don't care. She'll thank me someday."

Chandelier, the girl Roman spoke of, *didn't* thank him for burning down the I.O.O.F house, but then she didn't really have it in her personality to thank anyone. The history she and I would share would be the catalyst for a breakup with my family some years later and an unlocking of secrets as to who Roman was and what place he had in my life. The history she and Roman would share, along with his own personal quirks and experiences in Greensaw, would cause him to burn down the I.O.O.F. Street house.

The first time I encountered this person who called herself "Chandelier" I was a sophomore in college. It was a few days before classes were to begin in the town of Greensaw, Texas, where the I.O.O.F. Street house was located. I had transferred there with my friend Bunny, and in doing so had changed my major. Bunny was seeking a degree in art, as she had at the University of Alabama, and I was now a drama major, both of us having abandoned the bumpy ship of music for something equally as risky and lucrative, and it was because of our association with the arts that we met Chandelier, the person who would have an eventual adverse effect on our lives.

The first attribute you noticed about Chandelier was her walk. It was something like that of a runway model carrying the transmission from a '65 Chevy while wearing high heels and maneuvering an ice-covered driveway. When I first encountered "the walk" on I.O.O.F. Street, she was wearing black lipstick, black fingernail polish, a nose ring connected to a pierced ear by a string of paper clips, army fatigues, and six-inch stiletto heels.

Her hair—bright red, thick, and teased—stood almost straight up to a height of two feet with the help of several cans of mousse. Her skin was so pigment-free that people were constantly mistaking her for an albino—a fact that usually sent her into immediate ecstasy when someone told her that a new person to our group had asked about this.

"How fabulous!" she would shriek while flouncing around the room in her six-inch stilettos. "You mean they actually asked you if I was an albino? I'm never going out in the sun again if I can help it." And she usually didn't. Whenever the group she was with went to the lake in the summer, Chandelier would wrap herself in yards of white chiffon. Sitting in a white lawn chair and holding a white umbrella while the others swam and sunned, she was guaranteed her chalk-white complexion.

Unusual characters were not unheard of in Greensaw, Texas, but they certainly weren't the norm. By today's standards, Chandelier's look might not seem strange, but in 1976, the year I transferred to Greensaw University, it was definitely considered odd. And Texas, being a little farther along than some of the other states in the Union when it came to accepting liberal attitudes, still had a long way to go before it caught up with Chandelier. True, eccentric characters have long played their roles on the Southern landscape, but Chandelier was extreme and technically we weren't really in the South—we were in Texas.

* * * * *

Most Southerners will tell you, and most Texans will tell you, that Texas is not the South. Texas is Texas. Texas is its own state. Texas is its own country. Texas could secede from the rest of the Union and be just fine. "Hell, it's big as—well, Texas," and it can take care of itself.

I've never met anyone from Texas who wasn't proud of the fact that they had been born in that state, and I'm sure they would cringe to be associated with the South. They really wouldn't want to be considered a part of anything other than their own state, and in truth, it is like no other state, rattlesnake population notwithstanding.

Now the South doesn't really consider Texas to be truly "Southern." Of course, this definition differs from territory line to territory line, but in Alabama, the place of my birth, it went something like this: The South is composed of Mississippi, Louisiana, Georgia, Alabama, and South Carolina. Tennessee is too far north and too cold in the winter; North Carolina has the word *North* in it, so that rules it out; Arkansas is too close to Texas; Virginia (even though the capital of the South was located there at one time) is too far north and it's above North Carolina—we've already covered that—and, well, Florida, that's just some piece of land stuck down there: "We're not really sure what that is and hell, there's all those retired people from up north living there." Some people actually consider Maryland and Kentucky to be a part of the South. Where I grew up, people would laugh hysterically at this.

In fact, the term South is such a movable one that I remember being at an all-state debating team function for high school students once, when the person in back of me (he was from Mobile) nudged me and asked where I lived. When I responded, "Infanta," he asked what part of the state that was in. I told him it was in north Alabama. "Yankee," was all he said, and the debating continued. It seems that because I was from "north" Alabama, I didn't qualify as a true Southerner. The bottom line is this: I'm including Texas because the action takes place in "Southern" Texas. I know it's a stretch, but it's the best I can do.

* * * * *

One day at the beginning of the semester, in the school cafeteria, I was telling Roman, that colorful individual with the match, about this exotic creature I had seen. "Oh, you must mean Chandelier Delacroix," he said.

"Of course. What was I thinking?" I said, hitting myself on the forehead with my palm. "Chandelier Delacroix. You mean you actually know this person?" I asked.

"Well, sort of," said Roman. "But Chandelier isn't her real name."

"Nooooo," I said, my eyes sarcastically wide.

"It's something like Sally Smith. I mean, who would want that? And before she changed it to Chandelier it was Argentina Teasedale. I don't know her personally, but we've all heard about her," said Roman. "She's friends with Henry. You know Henry, the guy who has dead birds lacquered to his living room wall."

Yes, I did remember Henry. I had met him at a birthday party he gave for himself (aren't other people supposed to give *you* a birthday party?) the day of which just happened to coincide with the first day of the semester.

Greensaw was a party town.

Henry's house was on Imperative Street just north of the campus. He had picked the house primarily because of the name of the street and because the landlord he rented from allowed him to laminate dead parakeets to the walls. I remember thinking at the time that those wouldn't have exactly been my priorities for being able to rent a house, but then I was nineteen going on twenty and I thought maybe I'd missed out on something, having grown up in a small town.

I had been invited to this particular birthday party because I was a member of the unusual group of musicians, artists, actors, and strange people that inhabited the liberal arts dorm known as Sedgwick Hall. This dorm, the one that Bunny and I ended up in, had a notorious reputation around campus, so much so that ordinary students crossed the street to keep from having to walk on the sidewalk next to it—especially if they saw Henry in the vicinity.

Henry, the birthday boy, liked birds in any form, and he had a small aviary located off the back porch of his home. He liked them so much in fact, that when they died, he couldn't bear to part with them, so he dipped them in formaldehyde and

266

stapled them to the walls of his house, laminating them with a plastic material he bought from the art supply store in the student union building. He positioned them in Christ-like-crucifixion style.

Liking anything with feathers, he also collected the wings of dead birds he found on his way to class, and being the creative sort he was, he made hats, vests, lampshades, and objets d'art out of our fine-feathered friends' wings. As if this wasn't enough, he had fashioned a large pair of angel wings out of satin and then covered them with white feathers. The result was a fantastic pair of wings that served as a blanket to his bed.

"How come if Henry and Chandelier are friendly, she wasn't at his birthday party?" I asked, thinking that I couldn't have missed her.

"Let's just say that she has a volatile personality," said Bunny, who had now joined us. "On and off. That sort of thing. One minute she likes you and the next . . ."

"That plus the fact that she was in rehab," shot Roman.

"Roman!" Bunny admonished and then turned her attention to her mashed potatoes.

"Henry, Chandelier, and the rest of the group, they all hang out at the I.O.O.F. Street house," said Roman. The entire table of students snickered at this.

"Yeah, the I.O.O.F. Street house," said Bunny, "appropriately named if you ask me." Roman reached over toward her tray, maneuvering dangerously close to an already melting ice cream sandwich. Bunny slapped his hand away.

"That's for sure," said Roman, abandoning the idea of procuring the item. "Everybody who hangs out there is odd."

"What do you mean?" I asked.

"Well," said Bunny, "probably more drugs traffic through that house than the rest of Texas combined. It's sort of mecca for anyone on the edge. And then there's the story about what I.O.O.F stands for—Independent Order of Odd Fellows. You know, back in eighteenth-century England before there was a

Red Cross, people used to band together to give help to their fellow man."

"Yeah, but about the only help that goes on there now is the kind that allows you to totally reject reality," chimed in Roman.

"As I was saying," continued Bunny, cutting Roman an irritated glance, "these people banded together to provide help for their fellow man, and since doing charitable work was considered odd at that time they were called 'Odd Fellows.' The whole thing was started in England and America had its first charter in 1819. Greensaw has a lot of strange street names, you know. Not just I.O.O.F. And probably a story to go along with each one."

"My, aren't you just a walking encyclopedia," said Roman.

"Roman, shut up," Bunny casually tossed in his direction.

* * * * *

Theirs was a strange relationship. Bunny knew Roman and most of the other colorful people because she had visited the town previously. She was already comfortable with Roman and some of the others as she made friends easily and hung around with these people whenever she got the chance. But I was holding back, never having been exposed to some of the new ideas and lifestyles. Still, I knew what she was saying about the street names. The founding residents of Greensaw had a penchant for strange-sounding streets, a few examples being Uncommon Street, Cenotaph Drive, Praiseworthy Lane, and Canopic Way. The name of the street this house was on, I.O.O.F., was enough to get my interest.

"Well, you guys know there's a party tomorrow night, don't you? Bunny, why don't you bring Strekfus along?" Roman asked.

"No, that's okay. I've got a run-through of lines tomorrow afternoon in the drama department and I'm going to be needing my strength and my sanity," I said. "Anyway, I remember Henry's party and that should last me for a while."

"Hey, you can come for just a little bit, you know, get exposed to some different ideas, loosen up," Roman said. "Besides, all you do is hang around with Bunny. You need to get to know some more people."

One thing I've always had a lot of is curiosity. Of course I wanted to go to the party, but I was apprehensive, not having made many friends (a consequence of my parental warnings about playmates), and as a result I stayed close to Bunny and threw myself into studying. So I opted not to go this time. During the rest of the semester there would be many other parties to attend. Bunny chided me constantly, pointing out that I had wanted to expand my repertoire of life experiences but was running in the other direction. I didn't listen to her for some time, but when I did it completely changed my outlook on things. Perhaps I was still smarting from the incident with the Grand Dragon, but for whatever reason, I concentrated on my classes and my new major in the dramatic arts.

And so, precisely because of my new major, it was toward the end of my first week that I was formally introduced to Chandelier Delacroix, this exotic life form that I had encountered on I.O.O.F. Street. But this wasn't a social introduction. Rather, she was in my drama class, and as luck would have it, assigned to a play I was to be in—*The Miracle Worker*—a production which we would "perform," for lack of a better word, toward the end of the semester.

The Miracle Worker is the story of Helen Keller and her teacher, Annie Sullivan, and what trials and tribulations the two endured while Helen learned to communicate with the outside world. Chandelier was to play the part of my mother and I was to play that of Helen's brother, James. The rehearsals were on and off for a couple of months with the usual boring back-stage jumping-through-hoops that accompanies such student productions. We had to paint sets, block scenes, build doorways, and dodge falling sandbags. Finally, a few weeks before the end of the semester we were scheduled to perform this play at a matinee in the student theatre. While no one expected a professional performance, they did expect at least a coherent one, and as a result, busloads of blue-haired ladies and their dates from the three nursing homes located in Greensaw arrived half an hour before what I will respectfully call "the curtain." But before this happened, this performance of the play, I finally accepted one of the many invitations to the I.O.O.F Street house— it was an evening not to be forgotten. What I didn't know was that the one night and the following day—the day of the performance—would change my life, or at least the way I looked at my life, forever.

The plan for the party was simple. Bunny and I would go there about seven o'clock. I had no idea what to expect, but the others had already been in the house for one reason or another and couldn't wait for me to be initiated into this strange new world.

Originally, the house where the party was to take place, the one on I.O.O.F. Street, had been the home of the president of Greensaw University many years ago. At one time the house must have been grand with its many rooms and pleasant façade. Built about 1860, it was used as the president's mansion until 1937, when it came into private ownership.

The structure was a conglomeration of gingerbread woodwork, columns, and peeling forest-green shutters which flapped in the Texas wind. There was a widow's walk sitting astride the top gable, and huge dirty windowpanes looked out over ancient hitching posts and granite curbs like fading dowager eyes which had ceased to hope for love long ago. Its O-gape of a front door was almost always open with constant traffic, and it was rare not to hear some type of music floating out from the upper-level rooms and over the daffodil-covered yard. Throughout the years it had fallen into disrepair and gone through several metamorphoses until it was finally rented out to college students who then sublet rooms in it to people they thought were creative or unusual enough to maintain its bohemian air. I would meet some of these bohemian people the night of the party.

When we arrived at the house, the celebration was in full swing with music playing about two hundred decibels louder than the human ear can stand. A thick cloud of marijuana smoke seemed to move about from room to room of its own accord. I found myself surrounded by about sixty people, all of whom were doing drugs, or so it seemed at the time. I would later find out that many of them never touched the stuff; they were just naturally strange.

"What's that?" I asked Bunny as we entered the foyer. I was pointing to a rather unusual grouping of objects which appeared to be a large tripod firmly bolted into the floor next to a ten-speed bicycle, and what looked like a papier-mâché effigy of Patsy Cline.

"It's a tripod next to a ten-speed bicycle and a papier-mâché effigy of Patsy Cline," answered Bunny with a look that said, "I can't believe you don't know what this stuff is." This wouldn't have been so strange except for the fact that she was wearing a replica of the costume Glenda the Good Witch wore in *The Wizard of Oz*, complete with wand, and this particular look of condescension just didn't fit the get-up. As with all I.O.O.F. Street parties, dressing up was encouraged. I, however, had decided not to participate. Bunny, by this time, was a pro.

"Okay," I said, "you want to elaborate?"

"On what?" asked Bunny, "The tripod, the bicycle, or Patsy Cline?"

"The tripod," I said. "I'm quite familiar with bicycles and Patsy Cline."

"Okay. Yes, the tripod," she began as she picked at some lint which had made its way onto the chiffon of her dress. "There are five or six of them all over the house. In the early '70s several Vietnam vets returned home to the good ol' U. S. of A. with some, how should I say, uh, psychological problems. I'm sure you've heard about guys like that—guys a few sandwiches short of a picnic. Anyway, they rented this house and placed these tripods in strategic areas in the house."

"Because?" I asked.

271

"For their machine guns, silly."

Okay. I thought I had experienced the zenith of weirdness with Henry's laminated birds, but I guessed there was more to come. I should have known when to stop, but I kept going.

"Why did they have machine guns, Bunny?" I asked as innocently as I could with an inflection that one uses when one is not sure one really wants the answer.

"Well," she explained, while waving to several newcomers who were arriving, "evidently they were paranoid about the Viet Cong attacking them in their sleep, so several of the guys would stand watch each night with their machine guns loaded just in case."

"Just in case of what?" I asked.

"In case the Viet Cong attacked them," she countered.

"Viet Cong in Greensaw, Texas?" I said.

"Hey, the Japanese bombed Pearl Harbor. You never know. Let's see if we can find Bebe," and with that she led me down a back hallway.

Bebe. That named sounded innocent enough. Who could have a name like Bebe and be anything but a wholesome, clean, all-American sort of . . .

"Hi, I'm Bebe," said a girl wearing glitter eye shadow and a harem outfit like Barbara Eden's in *I Dream of Jennie*. There was also an addition of about two or three hundred small silver bells. She grabbed my hand and shook it hard. With each movement she sounded like a pile-up of camels at rush hour.

"Ooooo, you have such unusual eyes. He has such unusual eyes, doesn't he, Henry?" asked Bebe. "You've got to come back here and see these fabulous vinyl pants I just picked up from Goodwill. They're lime green with the tiniest pink poodles you've ever seen on the butt," she continued. "Do you guys want any hash? There's plenty in the back bedroom," she added, turning and looking at everyone.

I gave Bunny a terrified look but she just squeezed my hand and mouthed the word *enjoy* as she drifted away from me and toward a game of strip poker being played by a midget, a man dressed in a gorilla suit, and a woman who was now totally naked and obviously not very good at the game. I wondered if Bunny was playing another of her tricks on me like the one involving the alleged Grand Dragon in Tuscaloosa. But I knew I couldn't live my life always trying to dodge her antics, so I turned my attention to Bebe in an attempt to immerse myself in the evening's festivities.

The truth was this: Bebe was one of the most charming creatures I had ever seen in my life. There was something about her that spoke of a childlike quality—albeit a childlike quality in a harem outfit smoking hash—that made me want to get to know her. She didn't have a malicious bone in her body and would give you the shirt off her back as she had proved in a rather unfortunate incident in Houston some years earlier. It was during one of those extremely hot Texas summers and Bebe was enjoying a nude sunbath in one of the city's parks. The Houston police were none too pleased and promptly picked her up for indecent exposure. When they questioned her, she explained that a woman walking two borzois had complimented her on the blouse she was wearing, so she took it off and gave it to her. She explained that she was just being sociable. "After all," she told the police, "you know the word Texas comes from the Indian word *Tejas,* meaning 'friendly.' So I was just doing my part to uphold the image of the state."

The police, after an hour of exasperating questioning, finally let her go, giving her a bright yellow policemen's rain parka to wear on her way home. Of course, she immediately added this new item to her extensive collection of eclectic apparel.

"What's your name, Mr. Unusual Eyes?" Bebe asked me.

"Strek," I told her.

"Well Strek, why don't you come back here and we'll fix you up some," she said, leading me down a hallway toward the back of the house.

I had no idea what "fix you up some" meant, but I figured tripods, machine guns, harem outfits—what the hell.

Besides, even if you don't smoke marijuana, when you're in a house with people who do, you're eventually going to be elevated to that next level.

"Now just take a seat and we'll get you something to wear," Bebe soothed in my ear as she led me into her bedroom and positioned me atop a rather lumpy ottoman. From where I was sitting I could see the room next to us through a gaping hole in the wall. The poker game Bunny had joined was positioned directly in its center, and judging from what I could see she must have been better at it than most because she was still entirely clothed. I made a mental note not to look in the direction of the naked midget again as the gorilla raked a pile of chips toward his chest.

Meanwhile, Bebe had gone into her closet (actually a sectioned-off corner of her bedroom) and had begun to pull out an amusing assortment of clothes. After several minutes of careful scrutiny, she discarded the ermine cape, chartreuse feather boa, and gold glitter 1960s miniskirt for a more sedate pair of knickers with suspenders.

"Here, try these on," she said, handing me the gray wool knee-pants attached to suspenders. Sensing my uneasiness, she also handed me an already lit joint.

"A few puffs of this and you'll be on your way," she said, beginning to unbutton my shirt. Then, "Good stuff, huh?" she asked as she untied my shoes and began to unzip my pants. By now I was down to my underwear and stepping into the knickers.

"Where did you get these clothes anyway? You look like you came right out of Sigma Chi," remarked Bebe as she held up my pants and shirt, gave them a look of disgust, and dropped them in the far corner of the room.

"It's my attempt at normality," I said, and she winced.

With Bebe's attention now focused on the closet again, and wearing my new attire, I finally had a chance to look around. The bedroom, lit only by candlelight, contained a large mattress in the middle of the floor. Several Indian print bedspreads covered the makeshift bed. The walls were masked by either exotic pieces of fabric or old posters from movies and theatre productions. In one corner of the room, a poster from the early 1900s advertising Mascagni's opera *Isabeau* looked down on the scene—the naked girl on the horse with an orgasmic look (the girl, not the horse) and bearing a striking resemblance to Bebe. Threadbare oriental carpets and pieces of earth-tone and harvest gold shag remnants covered the floors, along with well-used piles of pillows. Stained and tattered sheer lace draperies covered the windows, and the thick smell of incense hovered near the top of the high-ceilinged room like a spirit conjured up from a séance.

About this time, Roman came into the bedroom to see what was going on.

"Roman," said Bebe, "Mr. Unusual Eyes here needs some eye shadow."

"No, that's okay," I said. "No eye shadow."

"Oh, come on, darlin'," said Roman, "you need something to liven up that outfit. You look like you just came from visiting the Waltons."

"Roman, that's not nice," said Bebe. "I didn't want to give him the miniskirt. At least not just yet," and she gave a big fake smile and tilted her head to the right.

"That's okay," said Roman as he dipped the eye shadow brush into a Max Factor bright pink, "a few more parties and he'll be begging to wear it." He positioned himself at Bebe's dressing table and pushed me onto a rather ratty-looking chair beside him. Roman then proceeded to chew his lip as he threw his head back and made several practice strokes in the air with the brush.

"Not too much, Roman," I said, "and you won't get me in a dress. I haven't worn one since . . . oh, never mind."

"You know," said Bebe, turning her attention from a purple-beaded evening gown, "I just now noticed that you and Roman have the same skin coloring. Are you guys related?"

"God, no," I said. "Besides, Roman is a good four or five years older than me."

"Look down for me, darlin'," said Roman as he applied the eye shadow and assumed various poses like those of a Hollywood makeup artist, turning his head from side to side and framing my face with his hands while moving in closer and then backing away.

"You veel be beautiful," he said with the strongest Italian accent he could muster. "I am Gabayso Faggottiessemo, the great Italian director. When I'm-a through a-wid-a you, you veel be exquisite!" And then turning to Bebe with his strongest Southern accent, "Strekfus is from Alabama and I is a gen-you-ine Texan. Don't be confusing me with no Alabama redneck."

My DeMille close-up in the Turkish harem was short-lived however, being interrupted by the sound of a police bullhorn. Roman drew back suddenly, one hand to his heart and the other holding the makeup brush high up behind his head. "Vhat is-a-dis?" he shrieked Italian style at the sound of the police.

"Turn the music down and nobody move," the bullhorn-carrying officer announced. Before I knew what was happening, Bunny appeared at my side and hustled me out the front door and onto the porch.

"What are you doing?" I gasped, seeing the entire house surrounded. "I thought the idea was to get *away* from the police!" There appeared to be at least five police cars, all with their lights flashing, and a circle of policemen standing around the house (legs spread too far apart, hands hooked into gun-belt loops, perpetual scowl).

"Just follow me," she said, leading me to a banister on the front porch.

"We're in plain view," I rasped, "and I'm wearing knickers and eye shadow and you're wearing a fairy godmother outfit! Are you crazy?"

"Look, I know what I'm doing," she said, "Nobody in their right mind would come and sit right in front of the police if they had anything to hide, would they? Just be cool."

"Be cool! What are you, nuts?" I asked.

276

She didn't say anything but whacked me on the back of the head with her wand.

"Owww!"

"I reinforced it with a curtain rod. Behave. Look," she said, "you wanted to experience everything you could in order to find out who you are? Well, start experiencing."

"Sure," I thought, "Glenda the Good Witch and John-Boy from the Waltons, sitting right under the cop's noses. How's that for experiencing?" But everyone at the party was remarkably calm during the police event. Everyone seemed nonchalant. What I didn't know was that most of them were emotionally peeing in their pants; they had just mastered the outward appearance of being in control.

The police secured the area and proceeded to enter the house to look for drugs. "No problem here," I thought. "If they're not immediately overcome by the huge cloud of marijuana smoke which was now traveling from room to room and had such a distinct size and shape that some of the others had named it 'Aunt Clara,' they would undoubtedly find the hash and other goodies the crew inside had assembled in the back boudoir."

About fifteen minutes later the police emerged from the house empty-handed, and issued a warning to Henry to turn the volume down because the neighbors had been complaining. My first thought was, "You people used to live next to a bunch of Vietnam vets with machine guns mounted on tripods and you're worried about the music being too loud?"

"All right, everybody," yelled Henry, "let's par-taaaay." I thought this was a particularly brave statement since the police weren't even to their cars yet. It was an extremely amusing sight to see some twenty officers shaking their heads sideways in unison like mass-produced little animals that sit in the back window of the car and jiggle about when you run over the speed bumps at the A&P.

"That really scared the be-Jesus out of me," I said to Bunny.

"I've got news for you, that scared everybody," she said. "Let's go back in. Be-Jesus?

"Yeah, whatever," I said.

Once inside, we made our way to the front room which had been a parlor in the days when the university's president lived there. Sitting along the walls were several people I had met before and some I hadn't.

"This is Larry," said Bunny. "He lives here with Bebe and Zak."

"Hi," I said, "nice to meet you," and shook his hand.

"Yeah," said Larry, "want some acid, man? It's in the fridge. Sit down, man. Make yourself comfortable. I'll get it for you, man." Larry was about six feet three with short brown hair and a beard. He was wearing biker leather and his pupils were about fifteen times their normal size. Larry was having trouble standing up. This guy was tripping in more ways than one, because after a few minutes he literally fell onto a small antique rocking chair in the corner, smashing it to bits. It was one of the few pieces of real furniture in the house.

"Oh, bummer, man," croaked Larry, as he surveyed the damage around him, not bothering to get up. Then he appeared to be reaching for something, like a blind man looking for the light switch. "The planets, they're dumping on me, man. The planets are dumping on me, the planets, wooooaaah the planets. Man, there's dung-beetle food everywhere." This went on ebbing and flowing in volume until everyone figured out this was the extent of Larry's LSD trip, and we started looking for new ways to amuse ourselves. I was becoming a quick study.

"What's that?" I asked Bunny, trying to make out a design on the floor of the living room. We were standing around like people at an art gallery, and for a moment I thought, dress these people up and we could be anywhere. Then I thought again.

"Oh, that's a pentagram. The people who lived in the house after the Vietnam vets were practicing witches and they used to perform satanic rituals here," said Bunny.

"I'm afraid to ask this," I said, "but who lived in the house before the Vietnam vets?"

"Oh, just some hippies from the '60s who raised marijuana. They moved out after one of their commune members blew his brains out in the kitchen."

"Charming," I said.

"Before that it was the wealthy eccentric lady named Marsha Tebdo. She was quite famous at the time. It seems she didn't have any children and the story goes that unwed mothers would drop their children off on her front porch. She would then send them over to the orphanage. That way there wasn't any way to trace where they'd come from. My aunt told me the story when I was a kid. You know, when we would come to visit in the summer."

"So she was sort of a letter drop for unwanted children."

"Exactly."

"Well, would *anyone* be able to tell where the children came from?

"No, that was the whole point. Mothers allegedly came from all over the South in the '40s and early '50s just to get rid of their little bundles of joy. The widow Tebdo. That's what they called her. Sounds like a spider," she said, and took a huge draw off the joint she was holding.

By this time I figured I had pretty much been privy to all there was to be exposed to.

I was wrong.

Needing something to drink, I excused myself from Bunny's tutelage and made my way to the kitchen which was located at the back of the house. It was your basic kitchen: stamped enamel-top table, refrigerator circa 1950, puke-green walls and cabinets, a fluorescent light in the shape of a circular tube that winced on and off at irregular intervals, several thousand roaches, and a blue-and-white parakeet that had been alive at one time but was now lacquered to the wall. Evidently Henry had been here already.

"The Coke's in the fridge," I heard Bebe yell in my direction as she floated through the hall, now wearing a tight-fitting gold lamé bodysuit and Jackie-O pillbox hat which looked as though it had been shot through a fruit factory. She often made several changes in one evening, showing off her large collection of outfits.

"Isn't this hat fabulous," I heard her telling a somewhat shy and well-drugged young man as I opened the refrigerator door and stuck my head in. "I got it from the Greensaw Funeral Home," she continued, "Henry and I went there yesterday to crash someone's funeral. You know, we just showed up and pretended we actually *knew* the person. It was great. This elderly woman had died. I mean, it wasn't great that she died, but the idea of going to a funeral of someone you don't know for the fun of it and not because you have to—that's what was great. Larry went in white-tie and tails and top hat, and I had on this black miniskirt with fishnet stockings and stilettos. And of course a veil. Well, to tell the truth, I didn't actually get the hat from the *home*. More like from a *person* in the home," continued Bebe.

"We were standing around before the funeral got started," she went on, "and they were all talking about how beautiful the corpse looked, and how well they had made her up. It was then that I noticed her hat. I overheard one of the women standing near the coffin say that the deceased didn't have anything decent to wear and that they had run out to Goodwill to get her some clothes. I thought, "That's where I get my clothes," and then I remembered I had seen the hat in Goodwill last week. Obviously these people had bought it, but that was my hat. I had seen it first."

As Bebe continued her story, I listened with one ear and continued my search in the kitchen for something to drink. True, there was *some* type of coke in the fridge. There was also about seven ounces of pot, some hash, and two trays of discolored sugar cubes which looked like they had been treated with something.

"I want Coke," I yelled into the hallway over the music. "Coca-Cola, you know. To drink."

"Oh, *that*. Look in the cooler beside the back door," she yelled.

I extracted a well-chilled bottle from the bed of ice it was resting in and opened it using one of the drawer handles. Then I made my way over to Bebe and the others.

In the hallway Bebe continued, "I had Henry distract the relatives with a mock epileptic seizure while I slipped over to the casket to snatch the old girl's hat. Can you imagine being buried in a hat anyway? I mean, what bad taste," and with that she drew a long breath of smoke from the joint she was holding.

"Talk about bad taste," said Henry, "I thought it was an ugly hat with those little yellow-and-white flowers . . . and those lemons. What a hoot!"

"Don't make fun of it," Bebe said, fingering the concoction which now rested on top of her head. "So there was Henry," she continued, "this white-tie and tail-clad figure, flailing around on the floor, and me slipping over to the casket. The only problem was, when I went to grab the hat, it didn't come off. So I was standing there tugging, and then I noticed that whoever had made the old lady up had attached the hat to her scalp! Can you imagine? Like they were afraid it was going to blow off in the afterlife or something. People can sure do some weird things. Anyway, every time I pulled on the hat, her face would come up just a little because I guess it was sewn into her . . . somewhere. The first couple of times I pulled, I noticed that her lips came up in a smile, in fact her whole face did, so I stood there just pulling the hat, watching her face go up and down like a marionette or something. Not a whole lot, you understand—you could just barely see her move.

"The others were busy tending to Henry and his fake seizure, and in their hysteria, one woman pulled out a Tampax applicator to stick in between Henry's teeth so he wouldn't bite off his tongue. She kept yelling about how her nephew was epileptic and had bitten off his tongue and that Henry had to have something stuck between his teeth.

"Finally the hat came off, along with the corpse's wig, which had been attached to the scalp thank you very much, and I ran over and kicked Henry in the shins. He immediately got up and we both rushed out. Before we left, Henry turned to the whole group and said in his best Porky Pig voice, "Be-daaah, be-dah, be-dah, that's all folks!" You should have seen the look on everyone's face, including the honored guest. I'll tell you, the things I do for fashion."

"Yeah, you took your sweet time trying to pry that thing off her head," said Henry, who had reappeared at Bebe's side after having given out several joints to some of the guests. "I thought you'd never get that thing off. Do you know how hard it is to maintain a fake seizure? You're lucky I didn't have a real one, especially after that old lady stuck that tampon in my mouth."

"It wasn't a tampon," countered Bebe, "it was a tampon *applicator*."

"Yeah? Well, what I want to know is, what's a sixty-five-year-old lady doing with a tampon applicator?" asked Henry.

I eyed the hat and it seemed strangely familiar. It was obviously well-worn and the lemons were slightly dirty. I couldn't place where I had seen it.

"What did you do with the wig that came off?" I asked.

"Oh, I gave it to Roman," said Bebe. "He's always dressing up as something."

"Let me get this straight," I said, "somewhere in Greensaw there is a bald corpse and several very confused relatives standing around a coffin, wondering what just happened."

"Pretty much," replied Bebe.

At that moment a series of screams went up like flames in one of the other downstairs rooms. In truth, it was hard to tell exactly where it had come from—the first floor of the house alone probably had six or seven rooms. At that moment Roman grabbed me. "Come on," he said, "Chandelier is in the next room," and with that he pulled me in the direction of her nasal voice. Roman wasn't enamored of Chandelier—it was more that he wanted to keep tabs on her, to make sure she wasn't stealing any of his ideas.

"Roman, the last thing I want to see is that girl. She's in my drama class and we get on like oil and water," I said, but he was pulling me in her direction, completely ignoring my last comment.

Sure enough, Chandelier was in what had at one time been the dining room. The room was now a photography studio used by Zak. She was holding court like an exotic princess but speaking with an extreme Southern accent. I thought it odd that someone this hell-bent on changing her appearance and obsessed with seeming other-worldly should have chosen not to do anything about her speech patterns. She looked like something out of a Hieronymus Bosch painting but sounded like she had just come off a dinghy from the outermost bayous of Louisiana. ("Paw, now I dun tole you to GIT! So now GIT, and take that damn 'gator meat wit youuu.") Her accent was perfect for the play she and I were in—*The Miracle Worker*—but deadly for something as exotic as a party in college where everyone was pretending to be something they weren't.

At any rate, her court was gathered about her as she regaled them with stories about simply walking down the street. It seemed that pretty much anywhere Chandelier went she caused a commotion. With her dress and manner she was easily spotted fifty or sixty feet away.

"So the-un, the girl at Jack-in-the-Box stares at me the whole time I'm order'n my chocolate shake and fries and I says, 'What are you stare-in at honey, ain't you never seen no drag queen?' Well, the girl jus keeps a stare-in and even after I pays, I looks back and I kin still see her just stare-in into space. It was reeeeeal funny."

In truth, Chandelier was not a drag queen. Nor was she really that funny. She was a real girl, but she had unusual friends, many of whom *were* drag queens, and she knew the shock value this could generate.

"You know, Chandelier, you look just like Columbia in *The Rocky Horror Picture Show*. You really ought to dress up as her next time we go," chimed a girl sitting on the floor near the center of attention.

"Well, honey, you just come on over and do me up," said Chandelier.

"Oh, let Roman. He's great. You'd do Chandelier's makeup, wouldn't you?" asked Bebe, after slipping into the room while exhaling a particularly long intake of marijuana smoke.

Roman then responded in the thickest Southern accent he could manage, sarcastically mispronouncing Chandelier's name, "Why I'd be deeee-lie-ted Chan-de-lee-ear Dela-cruex."

It was a well-known fact to most people that Roman couldn't stand Chandelier. This was probably because she diverted attention away from his own make-believe kingdom. You see, Roman was also a drama major during that particular semester, and even though this speaks for itself, I'll expatiate for those of you who have never had the privilege of knowing an actor firsthand. It's information you learn in order to sidestep life's, how shall I say, more interesting moments when you really just don't have the time, much less the energy to deal with things.

It's like what they say about anyone studying voice. Never ask them what part they sing, especially tenors, because they won't tell you—they'll *show* you. Ask a tenor what part he sings and you'll instantly get some well-worn aria from *Tosca* or *I Pagliacci*. And I don't mean just an excerpt, either. Anyway, Roman had a particular dislike for Chandelier because she was always stealing the spotlight—no mean feat when it came to Roman Yapigacy. Roman took acting seriously. Too seriously. He would develop a character and then stay in it for days.

Once he created the character of "Old Aunt Emma Tour," so called because the characterization was "immature." Basically this consisted of Roman wearing an Egyptian-cut platinum blond wig, a beige woman's slip with coffee stains on it,

284

Adidas running shoes, sweat socks, and to finish off this ensemble, an alligator handbag that could easily have held all the contents of the student union store—and quite often did. Roman, you see, was a kleptomaniac. We would venture around Greensaw with him just to see how people reacted. In the process, he would take everything that wasn't nailed down.

The most memorable of these excursions occurred when he decided a trip to Gibson's, the discount store, was in order while dressed as "Emma." Because of the type of clientele that Gibson's attracted, no one noticed at first. Then word began to spread through the store among the battered housewives and unwashed retirees and a crowd began to gather.

"Darlin', can you tell me how much this lovely polyester pantsuit is?" asked Roman, holding up a sky-blue textured-weave ensemble and addressing a Mexican salesgirl who looked about nineteen years of age.

"Tha'd be nineteen ninety-five," said the salesgirl, who just happened to be wearing the same item Roman had picked out.

"Oh, darlin'," exclaimed Roman, "I'm on welfare. I can't be affordin' no nineteen ninety-five. And another thing, why can't y'all just say twenty dollars and be done with the whole thing?"

The salesgirl blushed. "Well, I'm sorry, ma'am, that's what it costs," she said, completely oblivious to the fact that not only was Roman a man, but that he was wearing a slip, a bad wig, and running shoes.

"Darlin', you gonna have to show me somthin' a little more in my price range, say, oh, about three dollars and fifty cents. See, I gots me seven chillrin to feed at home 'cause my man, he done stuck his thang in me too many times and them chillrin jess keeps a-comin'. I may look old, but honey, I kin still reproduce," said Roman. Then, taking off his spectacles and looking the salesgirl up and down, he went on, "You looks to be about childbearin' age yer-self. Thems some big hips you done got on you there. Yo' man been a-sticking his thang in you, honey? 'Cause if he ain't, I'm telling you, you better be puttin' out or he'll run off with one of them Greensaw State cheerleaders."

By this time the salesgirl had pretty much gone into shock. She just stood there staring, but not moving, like someone who's seen a bad accident on the highway but can't look away. "Let me get the manager," she finally said, backing away and not taking her eyes off of Roman. She walked off to find her boss, weaving slightly as she went and bumping into a circular rack of children's clothes. By this time, Roman had made his way to the housewares section of the store and was fingering a pair of salad tongs.

"Can I help you?" asked another salesgirl, buck-toothed and cross-eyed, who up until now was unaware of who or what Roman was, not being witness to the pantsuit incident.

"Oh, Lordy!" shouted Roman when he looked up and saw her. "Darlin', get that stuff fixed or you'll be next year's Halloween inspiration."

The salesgirl just looked confused.

"Can I help you?" she repeated, this time with her neck sticking forward, her voice adding a few extra question marks.

"I's just admiring these here salad tongs," said Roman, snapping the forceps in the girl's face, almost catching her nose. She drew her head back like a turtle. "Ain't y'all got any of them stainless-steel jobbies? I can't use this here plastic shit. I'm a using these to remove turds that is too large and has stopped up my toilet bowl. Hell, I done give that dumb-assed plumber a call, but he ain't never showed up. Ye thank this here will remove one of them big turds I got stuck in my toilet?" and he snapped the tongs all around the salesgirl's head as if he were giving her a trim.

By this time the girl, who evidently was somewhat more perceptive than the first had been, having noticed Roman's extremely hairy legs and green eye shadow, was running screaming down the aisle, looking for the manager who was already huffing and puffing in our general direction—all three hundred pounds of him. The previous salesgirl was following up the rear, occasionally peering from behind the large man to see what Roman was up to.

"I'm not working here anymore," the second salesgirl exclaimed as she met the manager head on. "You got a bunch of crazies in this town. I'm leaving!" And she threw off her badge and stormed out of the store. By then, Roman was holding up a plastic cheese grater and playing it like a washboard while singing. His head was thrown back and his voice was at full volume.

> I'm Emma, from Tex-as,
> I gots me white hair.
> My hus-band, he pokes me, on top of a chair.

"Excuse me, ma'am," said the unctuous manager, wiping away the sweat that had begun to bead on his upper lip, "you're disturbing the peace. I'm afraid I'm gonna have to ask you to leave." He was breathing heavily and huge stains had begun to form under his arms, the wetness spreading like a series of bad Rorschach tests.

Roman pretended not to hear him and kept singing.

> He pokes me all day and he pokes me all night,
> He pokes me so much that my hair done turned white.

Then he turned to the store manager and looked at him through squinting eyes.

"Leave?" exclaimed Roman in a loud, obnoxious voice. "Hell, I jus' got here fat boy! You ol' fuckin' country lard-ass. Who you askin' to leave? Hell, I'll tear up that ass of yours faster than you can slap a tick. Speakin' of which, ye got about the biggest ass I's ever seen. That thang got its own zip code? And what's with that shirt ye got on? They taper that thing or does the buttons naturally pop off?"

By this time, the manager was in shock also. He turned around, with the first salesgirl dangling along side him like a raccoon-tail key chain, and headed for the back of the store to call the police. As he was leaving, Roman yelled after him, still in the character of Emma, "Honey, if those two butt-cheeks grind together any faster, you're gonna start a fire and I'm gonna have to git me one of them new-fangled fire extinguishers jus' to keep this here place from going up in smoke. Hell, y'all got so much plastic in here the fumes would probably kill us all before the fire did!"

Hearing the sirens, we grabbed Roman's arm and dragged him out of the store. On the way out he yelled to a young Mexican girl who was being trained as a cashier, her first day on the job, "Honey, why don't you jus' git yer straw and swim on back across and under the Rio-Grand-eee, 'cause this minimum wage shit is fer the birds."

We pulled Roman out of the store through the garden supplies area. Seeing a small evergreen with its roots wrapped in burlap, he grabbed hold of a branch and dragged it all the way back to campus, never once letting go.

Once back on campus, Roman opened his "purse," and produced several items he had stolen from the store.

"Now here's one of them Pyrex measuring cups for you," he said, handing the cup to Henry, who had come along with us, "and a plastic Jesus for you, Bunny . . . and I got this here kitchen spatula fer you, Strekfus," he said, still in character and with accent. It was to be one of many incidents with Roman we were to be a part of, all of them equally sordid, unpredictable, and entertaining.

So that was Roman. And judging from his escapades, we could see why he and Chandelier were at each other's throats all the time. At any rate, Chandelier just ignored Roman's snide comment when someone suggested he do her makeup and kept right on entertaining her crew. While she did this I had a look around. The room had its windows blacked out and all the walls were covered with black tar paper. There was a bed and a couple of chairs. Most people sat on the floor.

"What kind of photography does Zak do?" I asked Bunny as we stood in the corner watching the show.

"Porno," she answered, not taking her eyes from Chandelier's stand-up routine.

"Oh," I said, "what kind?"

"You know, bestiality, animals, that kind of stuff."

"There's a market for that?"

"Sure, you're in Texas now, baby. There's a market for anything if you know where to look." Just then I began to feel a bit queasy. "I need to sit down," I said to Bunny, and proceeded to find my way back to Bebe's bedroom. I thought I would be alone, but there were now three or four people gathered back there, each in varying degrees of repose.

* * * * *

The party started breaking up about two o'clock in the morning. Guests began filing out the front door and the scene began to calm down. By three o'clock there were only a handful of people left.

"Zak and I are going into Houston," announced Bunny, entering Bebe's bedroom.

"Bunny, I can't move," I said, from an overstuffed paisley pillow. The drugs had taken full effect now and I wasn't going anywhere. I looked around the room and suddenly the décor made perfect sense. So that's why the people who lived here did drugs. "Bebe said I could crash here, if that's okay."

"Sure," said Bunny. "Call us if you need us." With that she departed, knowing full well that the I.O.O.F. Street house had minimal electricity and no phone. I watched her stuff herself into Zak's car from the bedroom window.

Later that day, I was the first to awaken. The others were still in drug rehab dreamland, strewn about the house except for Bebe who was missing. I got up to find the bathroom. In the I.O.O.F. Street house there were no facilities on the first floor, only on the second, and they were located at the top of the stairs. I padded up the well-worn oak steps to the drafty bathroom and attempted to shut the door that had become so warped from age and humidity that it now resembled a half moon in one of its more slim phases. Having found the ancient porcelain toilet, I proceeded to relieve myself.

Most of the bathroom was occupied by a monster tub. Resting on four claw feet, the relic looked extremely inviting after a night of heavy partying. I decided to take a bath in order to relieve the soreness my body was experiencing from having put it through unnatural rigors, and while the water was running, I noticed a box of Mr. Bubble above the sink. Not having used the stuff since third grade, I couldn't remember how much to put in, so I dumped in the whole box. I settled into the bath, building myself a bubble castle complete with moat and dragon.

After a while I decided to call it quits. I pulled the plug and while the tub drained I dried myself with a well-worn towel I found hanging behind the door. Feeling renewed, I opened the bathroom door and started for the stairs, determined to find food.

At first I thought, "This must be what they mean about flashbacks." I had heard that you sometimes had bad experiences with LSD and other drugs, and that hallucinations were part of the everyday drug scene, but what I was looking at seemed extraordinarily real to me. I made a mental note to myself never to touch anything stronger than aspirin.

Standing between me and the stairs, the only way out, was a full-grown Doberman pinscher, complete with spike collar, a very unhappy growl, and a mouth full of large teeth which were more than adequately displayed.

It was obvious that this mirthless being had decided that I was to be the recipient of his anger. I say, "he," but to tell the truth, I wasn't close enough to differentiate. Trying to make light of the situation, I joked, "Oh, I'm sorry. Was that your Mr. Bubble?" After a few minutes of badinage and repartee, I deduced that the dog had no sense of humor and wasn't going to step aside to make my food-searching efforts any easier.

At first I tried calling softly, "Bunny, Bebe, Henry . . . anybody?" There was no answer. Somewhere in the backyard I could hear bits and pieces of someone screaming in the distance, "My anus, my anus. This is Little Lord Fauntleroy's anus we're talking about," and I would catch glimpses of Larry through the large window over the tub, running naked back and forth across the back lot, but he was too far away and in no condition to help.

I decided to try calling a little louder. "Bebe, Bunny . . ." Again there was no answer, and each time I increased my volume, the dog's growls increased. My cries for help perfectly counterpointed Larry's occasional screams in the distance and the hound from hell's ostinato growling. Just when I thought I would be stuck there forever, I heard Bebe open the front door.

"I can't believe they were out of bananas. That's the only thing that . . ."

"Bebe," I said, with more than a trace of hysteria, "help!"

"What is it?" she asked, making her way up the steps, holding a bag of groceries, seeing me at the top of the landing, half naked. She was completely oblivious to the Doberman. "What is it, sweetie?"

"What do you mean, 'What is it?' " I asked incredulously. "It's a hundred-and-fifty-pound Doberman."

Bebe, without the slightest hesitation, grabbed the dog by the collar and led it away to a back bedroom on the second floor, the whole time admonishing the beast. "Bad dog. Adenoid is a bad dog. That's Strek you were growling at and he's a nice guy. Bad dog."

She returned to find me in the same spot, wrapped only in a towel. Normally this would have been embarrassing, but Bebe had just rescued me and I really didn't mind. Besides, I thought it an improvement over the knickers. "Adenoid?" I asked, with more than my usual degree of curiosity.

"She's one of Zak's dogs," countered Bebe. "She's really sweet, but she didn't know who you were and she's just being protective. And she snores."

291

My first thought was, "Protective of what? The tripods and the Patsy Cline dummy?"

"The others are a little more sedate," Bebe went on. "Adenoid is probably the most temperamental of the bunch."

"Bunch?" I said, "How many are there?"

"Six or seven. Zak raises them."

"What does he do, sell them?" I asked, as we walked down the stairs with Bebe ahead of me.

"Nooooo," she said sweetly. "He butt-fucks them. You know, in the porno movies he makes. Zak is really into animals."

"Oh, of course," I thought. "That would explain the dog's bad mood this morning."

"So that wasn't her Mr. Bubble after all," I said.

"What?"

"Nothing. It's a long story."

The truth was, I didn't have much time to think about Adenoid. Bebe was planning another party and the house had to be in order. It was to be a get-together for Terrence Bayard, one of Bebe's closest friends.

"I'll need some help getting everything back together," said Bebe. "Think you could lend a hand for a couple of hours?"

"Sure," I said. "I just have to be at the theatre for a performance at two o'clock."

"Theatre? What performance are you going to see?"

"Well, actually, I'm *in* the performance."

"You're kidding!" she shot back. "I didn't know you were an actor," and she steered me into the kitchen. She gathered up my clothes from last night—the normal ones—and handed them to me.

"I'm not really," I said. "I just changed my major for a semester to see how I'd like it. It's amateur really. As part of our acting class, we're required to be in several plays."

"Which play?" asked Bebe, measuring coffee into an ancient percolator.

"*The Miracle Worker,*" I said.

292

"Oh, the one about Helen Keller. I saw the movie they made of that. What part do you play?"

"I've got a small part," I said. "I'm the brother of Helen."

"Helen Keller. Isn't Chandelier in that play also?" she asked.

"Yeah. She plays my mother."

"What a trip," said Bebe, accidentally dislocating the handle of the coffee pot. Then she began to rummage through an overstuffed drawer for something to take its place.

"Well, okay," she continued, trying to attach a tea strainer to the side of the now-handleless pot. "Anyway, I'll see you sometime after the performance. It's probably better you don't help me get ready for the party. You need to concentrate on the play. I'd come see you in it, but I've got a lot to do."

"That's okay," I said. "I'm not sure how good it's going to be anyway. I think Chandelier really hates me and she doesn't know her part that well."

In truth, Chandelier didn't know her part at all. The director had been pulling his hair out over her and the rest of us were none too thrilled either. She would be late for rehearsals and when she did show up she was usually drunk or on some sort of "pain killer." In addition to this, she hated me because of my involvement with Bunny. Yes, to top it all off, Chandelier, my mother in the play, was a lesbian and extremely attracted to my best friend.

The unfortunate (or fortunate, depending on which side you butter your bread on) thing for her was that people were always misunderstanding her. She would somehow manage to incorporate the phrase, "I'm a lesbian," or some variation thereof, into almost every conversation, but because she was an actress it was always being heard as "thespian." The impact was somewhat less than desired. While no important information was lost in the translation, her maverick side was not as evident to those she wished to make an impression on, if for nothing else, the shock value of the thing was lost on them.

I made my way to the theatre that afternoon hesitantly as I wasn't sure exactly how the audience would respond to our less-than-perfect performance. As I entered the theatre lobby I spied Bunny busy at work on one of the art department's projects.

"What are you doing here?" I asked.

"Jus' 'utting ne 'inishing 'uches on ne ress exnibit. 'Eventeenh nd 'ighteenh 'enury."

"Excuse me?"

"Sorry. Mouth full of pins, you know," said Bunny after removing several forbidding-looking straight pins from between her lips. "Just putting the finishing touches on the dress exhibit. Seventeenth and eighteenth century. How do you like it?"

"It's great," I said, "but aren't you afraid to leave these out here in the open like this? I mean, in the lobby of the theatre building?"

"No," said Bunny, "the guard comes around every so often and the building is locked at night. It's part of the art department's exhibit in conjunction with the theatre department. You know, gives them an excuse to pull the art of making clothes in with the art of making characters in a play. Look," she said, as she began to gather her supplies into her backpack, "good luck with the performance. I've got to run after I finish here, but I hope to see you at Bebe's tonight."

"You're not coming either?"

"I'd love to, but I've got a seminar on ceramic glazes at two thirty. Who schedules a play for two o'clock in the afternoon, anyway? Besides, Roman said he would be there to see you and Chandelier perform."

I was running late, so I bade Bunny farewell and looked back at her putting the finishing touches on the Catherine the Great mannequin. The riding crop jutted out at just the right angle. Bunny was really gifted at her craft, but then she was an art major and had always shared my love for anything creative.

It was nearing two o'clock. Most everything was on schedule. The audience were in their seats and no one in the cast had thrown up yet. But ten minutes before curtain Chandelier was nowhere to be found. Not that this surprised anyone. We were used to this sort of behavior; we just thought that at the last minute she would pull herself together and show at least a modicum of professionalism. Optimism tends to run rampant when you're twenty. It's only after you enter the real world of work, psycho bosses, and income tax that you start to see things for what they really are or aren't.

We were just about to have someone announce that the performance was canceled (this was student theatre and there were no understudies) when Chandelier made her appearance. Instead of being made up as had been instructed in the trial run-through we had performed a few days earlier, she had applied her own makeup, completely ignoring all previous instructions. She had made herself up at the last minute with what looked like clown paint.

The result was less than flattering and at best morbid. Although she was dressed in her period costume, her hair had been teased out as far as possible and pulled to the sides in enormous ponytails which resembled two witch's brooms stuck into each side of her head. The only makeup she wore was black eyeliner, about half an inch thick, clumsily circling her now extremely wide eyes, and two perfectly round red dots, one on each cheek. To top off the costume, she was holding a mannequin arm she had wrenched from one of the fiberglass bodies in the eighteenth-century dress exhibit located in the lobby of the theatre—the same exhibit that Bunny had been working on. A paste diamond bracelet still clung to the limb and the hand was slightly askew, giving support to the fact that the appendage had not been wrested from its owner without a fight.

"I'm ready," she said with clenched teeth as she took her place in back of me, and with her free hand dug her fingernails into my side. I managed to squelch my desire to yell as the lights in the theatre dimmed and the student director shook his head and walked away.

"We're sunk," he said, and exited the backdoor of the theatre. Since we were all students and new to this, we thought

295

this was the way theatre was done in Texas and decided to put our best foot forward. But many of us had never acted before, and soon this would be more than evident to everyone in the theatre.

All in all, we didn't do *too* badly. Everyone remembered their lines and no scenery fell over, sending someone to the hospital as it had in last weekend's performance of *The Lady's Not for Burning*, by another student group at another small theatre in the arts and sciences building. The stage in that performance had, strangely enough, caught fire, and theatregoers who didn't know the play (most of the people in the theatre at the time) thought that the special effects were spectacular. That is, until the fire curtain was brought down and the announcer of that day's cast changes, who was none other than Roman, advised the crowd of blue-haired women (it was a matinee) that they should make their way to the exits in a calm and orderly fashion.

Seeing that the calm and orderly fashion was taking longer than expected, Roman yelled in the general direction of the slow-moving crowd, "Free glycerin suppositories at the exits. Giddy-up now, y'all!" before running out the side door to tend to one of the lead characters who had suffered a broken nose—an unfortunate incident since the lucky fellow was to play Cyrano in the town's opening performance at the new arts center later that week.

We made it through most of the play with no major disturbances other than the fact that Chandelier had refused to play every scene so far without the aid of the mannequin arm. The problems started when we began the scene where Chandelier and I are to have a conversation. This scene occurs during a family dinner that takes place at the end of the play. There is supposed to be a general discussion weaving itself back and forth across the table while we pass around the fake mashed potatoes and green peas. Ordinarily, in the proper version of the play, this discussion takes place between my character and my aunt—Aunt Ev. But the director had rewritten this section of the play so that the discussion would be between Chandelier and my character.

Lucky me.

It began just after Kate—my mother in the play, portrayed by Chandelier—asked me to say grace.

And Jacob was left alone, and wrestled with an angel until the breaking of the day; and the hollow of Jacob's thigh was out of joint, as he wrestled with him; and the angel said, Let me go, for the day breaketh. And Jacob said, I will not let thee go, except thou bless me. Amen.

I delivered my lines to Chandelier and waited for her reply. There was none. She only stared at me with wide eyes for what seemed like several minutes and then slowly rose from her chair at the end of the table. I repeated my lines, but before I had delivered the last few words, Chandelier lifted up the mannequin arm above her head and brought it down with such force on the table that the hand, which wasn't attached well in the first place, went flying off somewhere into the first three rows of the audience.

As soon as the dishes stopped rattling and everyone regained their places, she spewed forth a verbal tirade unlike any I had ever heard. It was directed at me and encompassed just about everything an insane person could think of, ending with the phrase "And you can keep screwing that girlfriend bitch of yours, too!"

After she finished, she turned slowly (probably because of the incredible amount of drugs she was on) and started for the wings. Just then, thanks to some brave soul in the audience (it shouldn't be too hard to guess who), the hand which had become dislocated from the mannequin arm came flying back on to the stage and hit Chandelier directly in the back of the head. Since the majority of people who attended these student performances didn't know theatre etiquette or have a good working knowledge of stage blocking, most of them thought the person hurling the severed hand was connected somehow to the performance.

Furious, Chandelier turned, and moving much faster now, lunged over the footlights for the audience member who was smart enough not to be present by the time she reached the first row. All Chandelier got was an empty seat and for a moment we thought maybe she was just going to sit and watch the rest of the performance. She didn't seem to want to move. Both audiences held their breath. Was she going to stay there? No such luck. Within a few agonizing minutes she climbed back up on stage, the heavy black eyeliner running down her cheeks and sweat pouring off her. She glared at the rest of the cast and then wandered off, stage right. You might think at this point that everyone in the play was relieved, but we still had the final scene to finish.

As if things weren't bad enough, I had several major revelations at this point: 1) Chandelier was acting far too much like my own mother; 2) Changing my major from music to theatre hadn't been such a good idea; and 3) The following scene contained most of my dialogue and a discussion between Chandelier and myself which could no longer take place with only one of us being on the stage. While I wanted to think seriously of terminating the relationship I had with my mother, and knowing that Greensaw didn't offer a degree in environmental biology, I was determined at least to finish this play.

Deciding that the drama was already ruined, but being too petrified to leave the stage, I decided to milk it for all it was worth. I sat in my chair and spoke my lines, and when it was time for Chandelier to respond, I ran around to her chair, affected a female voice as best I could, and responded. The audience, which by this time was sure we were performing some avant-garde version of the play, stayed, if nothing else, for the sheer unpredictability of the thing.

Unpredictability is the key word, for no sooner had Chandelier left the stage than she reappeared just when she is to have a confrontational scene with Annie Sullivan, Helen's teacher. And confrontational it was. Annie Sullivan and the mother (Chandelier) are supposed to argue about Helen's behavior, during which time Helen runs about the dining room, screaming and throwing herself against the furniture. While Helen performed her necessary duties, Chandelier, with one swift movement, pushed the woman playing Annie Sullivan backwards off the raised stage into a row of lights which were illuminating the background, and flat onto her back. Since teacher wasn't getting up anytime soon, Helen was forced to continue her tantrum for longer than rehearsed. Chandelier, having surveyed the damage, looked directly at me and with the biggest sneer she could manage, said, in the thickest Southern accent she could muster, "Fuck it," and walked off the stage.

By this time, Helen had worked her way over to me, kicking and screaming. She approached me, and while beating me as violently as she could, reached up and grabbed my belt loops (Helen was at most four feet tall—I later found out that she was the girlfriend of the midget I had seen playing strip poker at the I.O.O.F. Street house party) and swung me around so my back was to the audience. She looked up at my face and hissed, "Do something!" Then she swung me back around and continued her tantrum.

Annie Sullivan managed to drag herself up onto the stage again, and the entire cast, with the exception of Chandelier, managed to finish the play without additional distractions. That is, until the final moments of the play when Annie Sullivan and Helen are at the pump and Helen understands the word "water" for the first time. It was at this point that Chandelier entered—a few moments before the final tableau—and began working the pump handle with the mannequin arm and reattached hand. The woman who was playing Annie Sullivan and the girl who played Helen decided to brave the final minutes of the play and sauntered uneasily over to where Chandelier was violently pumping water. By this time, because of her furious sawing motions, the small receptacle which held the stage water had run dry and the only sound emanating from the pump was a high-pitched screech.

In the play, as Annie and Helen kneel by the pump and the word "water" is spelled into the blind, deaf, and dumb girl's hand, Helen finally understands. So Annie Sullivan gleefully exclaimed that Helen understood and Chandelier, still violently pumping the handle with the mannequin arm, delivered the final words through clenched teeth while shaking her head in an exaggerated fashion so that her two large teased ponytails shook violently up and down. "Isn't it *wonderful!*" she seethed and the curtain came down just as the mannequin hand broke off at the wrist.

After the fiasco, the student director dropped out of school and it was determined that all student performances had to be approved by the faculty before going public. We all went home and tried to put ourselves back together. Besides, I had to prepare for that night's party at the I.O.O.F. Street house.

* * * * *

While I thought the last party rated as an all-time experience, and though some of the people there had been costumed (Bunny as a fairy godmother, Bebe wearing her own creations), the next party was to be strictly a dress-up affair. No one was to show up without a costume, and if they did they were subject to being dressed in something Bebe would pick out.

I had decided to go as whoever I had been at the last party. That is to say, I had kept the knickers that Bebe had given me and decided to accessorize with odds and ends I found in a thrift shop. One of the items was a large plywood cutout of a flamingo, painted pink. It stood about four feet tall and had an outlandish grin on its beak, but it was safer than having Bebe pick out something *completely* outrageous.

The difficult part about these dress-up affairs was that I lived in a dorm at the time, and while the inhabitants of this place were very liberal, they weren't above giving me strange looks as I made my way out the front and to the I.O.O.F. Street house

300

carrying a plywood flamingo and dressed in a pair of wool knickers. But the darkened streets with their huge overgrown oaks and shrubs offered some protection from prying eyes, and as I made my way toward this house which was home to so many of Greensaw's creative elite, I felt something like a modern version of one of the Finch children on their way home through the woods after Scout has presented herself as a ham in Harper Lee's *To Kill a Mockingbird*. The only difference was that this time there would be no Mr. Ewell or Boo Radley.

Arriving safely at the front door, I was greeted by Henry, the bird guy.

"Hi, come on in," he said, extending one of his hands. Something red and wet ran down the sides of his arm and then dripped onto the floor. It was fake blood that he had painted on, the paint not quite dry. You see, Henry was dressed like Jesus Christ. His costume was ingenious, really. It consisted of a large foam rubber cross about seven inches taller and wider than he was. He had painted it brown and strung Christmas lights up and down it. The lights were powered by a battery concealed under his toga. Because the cross was foam rubber and was attached to the backs of his arms, it would bend and move with him so that he could do useful things such as serve hors d'oeuvres and mix drinks. To complete the outfit, he was wearing a long brown curly wig and a fake beard. His sandals smacked on the wooden floors as he led me into the house while the Christmas lights blinked on and off.

"Hey, guys, here's Strekfus," he said, handing me over to Bunny, who was wearing a mermaid outfit and holding an oversized martini glass, the diameter of which was no less than twelve inches. With her long, naturally blond hair she was a perfect mermaid. Topless and beautifully endowed, she was clothed only in a tight green-sequined gown which narrowed at the bottom and ended in a fishtail.

"Great costume," I said.

"Thanks," she said, and inhaled a joint she was holding in her other hand. "I worked on this thing all last weekend."

301

"You mean you actually made this?" I asked, fingering the sequins.

"You don't think you can buy this sort of thing, do you?" she answered. "How did the play go? Sorry I wasn't there. Had that seminar."

"Let's not talk about it," I said.

"Okay. Let's go see what Roman is up to. He's in the back room with Terrence."

Terrence was the guest of honor. I had seen him briefly at the last party playing strip poker. He was the midget. What I hadn't realized was that he was also in a wheelchair. As we turned the corner I ran directly into him.

"Watch where you're going," screamed Terrence as he wheeled into my shins.

I would normally have been irritated except for the fact that I was so shocked at the sight of him. He was dressed in a powder-blue and pink baby outfit complete with bonnet. Add to this the fact that he was holding a giant lollipop and had a can of beer stuck between his legs, and you can see why I was standing there open-mouthed.

"Hey, nice flamingo," he said, his tone changing upon seeing the cartoonish Audubon rendition I was holding.

"Thanks," I said, "and happy birthday."

"Yeah, I'm not crazy about birthdays, but consider the alternative."

"Is the wheelchair part of the get-up?" I asked.

"Uh . . . no," interjected Bunny, "Terrence is actually paralyzed from the waist down."

"Oh, sorry," I said.

"Whatever," said Terrence, and deftly fingered his urinal bag.

About this time, I heard something coming in our direction and noticed Roman. He was completely naked except for a large plastic garbage bag, wearing it as if it were Pucci's latest creation. He had decided to top off the outfit with a pair of high heels and he was pushing a rather ordinary grocery cart

302

which was empty except for a small tape recorder from which emanated pig noises. He had obtained the recording by visiting a nearby slaughterhouse. Sounds of pigs being slaughtered shrieked from the tiny speaker and he was furious.

"I can't believe that bitch, Chandelier," said Roman as he wheeled up next to us.

"Why?" I asked. "I mean, other than for reasons I may have at the moment."

Bunny interrupted. "Roman's pissed because Chandelier showed up in the same outfit as him. Now neither one will go home and change."

"Not only the same outfit," seethed Roman, "but she's even got the shopping cart and pig noises."

"What are the chances?" I offered.

"Look, I'm going to go in the kitchen and help Bebe," said Roman. "See you guys later," and with that he clattered off to the back of the house with the squeals of pig slaughter drifting behind him.

About this time I noticed Bebe on her way to the kitchen also. Somehow she had managed to procure a costume exactly like the dress that Barbra Streisand wore in *Hello, Dolly*—the one in the big scene where Louis Armstrong sings to her. She waved a matching parasol at Terrence who was wheeling his way through the entrance hall now.

"Get out of my way you fucking little midget," she said, and poked him directly in the chest.

Bunny rolled her eyes. "They're mad at each other," she explained. "Terrence specifically insisted on rattlesnake meat for his party and Bebe couldn't come up with it in time. You wouldn't think it would be that hard to find in Texas."

It was then that I felt something sniffing my leg. Already having had a number of experiences in the house, I have to admit I was afraid to look. When I did muster the courage, I noticed Adenoid, who was sporting a red velvet Santa dog suit and hat even though Christmas was nowhere in sight.

"Hey, Adenoid," said Bunny, and proceeded to blow a huge cloud of marijuana smoke into the dog's ear. The dog smacked her lips and shook her head from side to side in slow motion.

"Don't do that," I said, "she doesn't need any encouragement."

About this time Roman reappeared. Somewhat calmer now, he explained to us that he had moved into the I.O.O.F house that morning after having been thrown out of the dorm. Evidently, the drag show he put on one evening at dinner in the cafeteria had proven too much for the counselors and they had asked him to leave. It seems that his rendition of Lizzie Borden, complete with axe, had not gone over well, with two cafeteria tables being reduced to splinters before the performance was over.

"That bitch Bebe gave me the smallest room in the house. Can you believe that?" he snarled.

"Roman," Bunny countered, "you should be happy you have a place to stay."

"I know," said Roman. "It wouldn't be so bad except that I have to share it with three of the dogs. I guess the good news is that Bebe and I wear the same size."

About this time Adenoid went tearing across the front of the house.

"She's after Anita Bryant!" shrieked Terrence.

"I'm afraid to ask," I said.

"Anita Bryant is Terrence's ferret," said Bunny.

It was then that Terrence began wildly wheeling himself after Adenoid. He had stuck the lollipop into the beer can (firmly planted between his legs) in order to free up his hands and wheel himself about. As he plowed through guests and costumes, the only thing missing was a soundtrack from a hillbilly movie, banjos strumming and bass fiddle thumping.

"Stop him!" he was screaming. "He's going to kill Anita!"

Several of the other guests at the party managed to capture the poor ferret and subdue the dog, but not before

Terrence had entangled himself in a rosebush at the corner of the house and turned himself over. He had also wheeled himself too close to Henry (Jesus) and had pulled several strands of Christmas lights off the costume, entangling them in the spokes of his chair.

"Damn!" he said. And then, "Bunny . . . Bunny, come get me! My catheter is leaking. Bunny!"

"Here we go again," said Bunny and handed me her now empty martini glass.

"Again?" I thought, "How many times has this happened?"

The scene was cut short, however, as we were all distracted by another commotion inside the house. It seems that Roman and Chandelier had finally "had it out" and were both hotly debating which one of them should leave since they were dressed identically.

Roman, in a fit of rage, had produced a cigarette lighter and proceeded to set fire to Chandelier's plastic garbage bag. She had managed to get out of the thing without being burned, but she was furious and had taken Roman's tape recorder and smashed it above his head on the wall in back of him. Her own tape recorder had accidentally been turned up to full volume and it was now almost impossible to distinguish the vocalizations coming from the box and those coming from Chandelier and Roman. Bebe had come running out from the kitchen with a tray of hors d'oeuvres, each in the shape of male and female genitalia, and was standing there open-mouthed. This was too much even for her.

"Roman," she finally admonished, when she had managed to restore order to the scene, "you could have burned the house down! You guys have to be more careful. This house could go up in a few seconds—it's a veritable tinderbox. No more playing with fire," and with that she exited back to the kitchen.

Chandelier and Roman, each taken aback by Bebe's outburst, just looked at each other and said, both at the same time and to each other, "Tinderbox?" But Roman was mad and those of us who knew him figured that he was planning something.

The party wound down with considerably less excitement than the last one. There were no police and no hostile Dobermans this time. I guess we were all tired. I know the play had worn me out. Besides, we did actually have schoolwork to do. We were, after all, in college.

* * * * *

Several weeks later, after we had recovered from the party, I caught pneumonia and ended up in the student infirmary for several days. It was toward the end of the semester and school was winding down. The second day I was there, Roman, who had been sitting in the audience the night that Chandelier made a fiasco of *The Miracle Worker*, brought me the mannequin hand which had played such an important role in my brief theatre career.

Roman and I sat talking about the way the semester had turned out and how our grades had really suffered because of the partying we had done. For some reason he wasn't able to let go of Chandelier's rebukes. He really couldn't stand anyone else having the limelight and he was still furious with Bebe. I was worried about him, but I was more concerned about passing my finals and preparing to go home for a few weeks. With everyone exhausted we went our separate ways with minimal good-byes. Bunny had decided to stay on in Texas while I returned to Alabama to recuperate from my illness. Roman had also decided to stay on, thinking that he could no longer tolerate the stifling home environment his foster parents provided for him.

My first day back home, Althea helped me unpack. I remembered my experience at Greeensaw and asked her, "Althea, have you ever been to the theatre?"

"No, child, I ain't never had no need to go. Life's a drama enough for me." I thought then about taking her to a regional theatre in one of the neighboring towns, but I wasn't sure if she would enjoy it or not.

"What's this?" she asked as she dug through my many boxes and pulled out the mannequin hand and the head of the pink plywood flamingo.

"It's nothing," I said, and took them from her, placing them in the back of one of my dresser drawers.

"Um, ummm, ummm," was all she said, and shook her head. "You getting some kind of education out there in Texas."

"I'll explain it to you sometime," I said.

* * * * *

Most of my time home was spent fighting with my mother. To retaliate, she would cut up my gas credit cards with a large pair of pinking shears. The pieces looked like dentures made for a toy shark. My nerves were beginning to get frayed and I was thinking about returning to Texas to finish the summer there when a letter and newspaper clipping arrived from Bunny.

Opening the lilac-scented envelope with wildlife stamp, I extracted half a folded page of the Greensaw *Chronicle*. It was the front page and in large bold letters were the words KIDNAPPER KILLED IN HOSTAGE RESCUE. There was a picture of Roman on the front page, his head sticking out of the drive-through window of a Tico Taco. He was holding some sort of semi-automatic firearm and wearing the platinum Egyptian-cut wig that he had worn while doing his impersonation of Aunt Emma. Topping this off was the yellow pillbox hat—the one with the flowers and lemons—that Bebe had been so enamored of.

The gist of the story was this: Roman had entered the Tico Taco on Hewitt Drive at approximately eight thirty on the evening of Saturday, June 16. He was carrying a large alligator handbag containing a weapon. As he approached the counter to demand money for his sex-change operation, a rather portly man, who was later identified as the manager of Gibson's, recognized him. Just as Roman was pulling out the weapon, the Gibson's manager tackled him and the weapon went off, shooting wildly around the restaurant.

While no one was killed at that moment, the bullets managed to disarm the system used to call the police and fire department, so no one was aware for some time that there had been an attempted robbery.

Roman had then ordered everyone into the back room and forced the girl at the drive-through window to give the customers in cars—who were unaware what was going on, this being Texas and gunshots not being that uncommon—their food for free. Again, no one would have complained about this, but one unruly customer had not received his Tico Taco deluxe combo plate (extra guacamole on the side) and had complained, even though he wasn't paying (again, this being Texas).

Roman had appeared at the window and shown him the semi-automatic weapon. It seems that the customer was more upset about Roman's wig than the gun (once again, the Lone Star State) and immediately drove off and called the police, reporting that a transvestite was working the drive-through window, the whole time forgetting to mention that Roman was armed and dangerous.

The police arrived shortly thereafter, not having a tolerance for transvestites, and several hours and tireless negotiations later, the Greensaw SWAT team stormed the restaurant and in the process killed Roman and injured two of the previously paying (now non-paying) customers. The article finished by saying that even though Roman Yapigacy was now dead, an investigation was underway to determine if he was also responsible for several acts of arson in the area, not the least of which was a house on I.O.O.F Street known for its drug activity and "hippie" types.

It also went on to say that Roman's foster parents wanted everyone to know that their prayers were with those injured and that they felt horrible that this had happened. There was also a brief family (or lack thereof) history about Roman. It seems he had been abandoned by his mother in 1951.

308

The reporter who wrote the story had done some investigating and found that the mother had placed the baby on the front porch of the home of Mrs. Marsha Tebdo, a wealthy but eccentric woman who was known to take unwanted babies and deliver them to the orphanage outside of town. The reporter was unable to determine who the mother was as no records were kept by Miss Tebdo. The only solid fact he had been able to come up with was that the mother—the one who left Roman—was from northern Alabama. Eventually the Yapigacy family had adopted Roman, but his childhood had been turbulent. The article went on to insinuate that Roman's lack of contact with his biological mother may have been the basis for his destructive streak.

I folded the newspaper article and opened Bunny's letter. I got caught up on the latest happenings in Greensaw and who was or was not planning to attend school that fall. She didn't mention anything at all about the I.O.O.F. Street house in her letter. I guess she figured that the newspaper article said it all.

The few weeks I was at home were pretty boring. Mother and I fought about whether we would watch one of her religious shows or a rerun of some 1940s movie. Whenever one of us left the room, the other one would switch the channel.

"And Moses said . . ." some unctuous preacher on television would announce as I moved toward the box in order to change the program.

"Start gearing up now for the big Fourth of July sale at . . ." it would then blare when I switched the station, and my mother would run back into the room so that we could argue.

My bedroom had been made into a den, so we now had two of them (a necessity for any household, in my opinion), and all of my childhood possessions had been thrown out or given away. Once again, Althea had admonished her for the way she treated me, shaking her head as she walked from room to room with her loads of laundry.

Most of those few days I just stayed in my room and read. Anything that I found among the bookshelves was deemed

309

acceptable, but when I came across a copy of *The Story of My Life*, by Helen Keller, I sank so deeply into it that I didn't come out until I had finished. I had known who she was in childhood, and now I had even experienced a slice of her life through William Gibson's play about her early years. It was probably this enduring desire to know more about her that propelled me in new directions. Every word of the book seemed to infiltrate my being and even the opening sentence consumed me: "It is with a kind of fear that I begin to write the history of my life." But like so many things in life that we swear will always be with us, that we will always preserve and protect, I eventually put the book away.

After a few days of sitting around on my mother's mock colonial beige plaid furniture, I decided I was better off back in Texas and contacted Sharon to see about setting up a roommate situation with her for the remainder of the summer. She was quick to respond, adding in her letter that she needed help paying the rent, that she planned to move to Houston and, "Would I be interested in living there?"

What could I say? I wanted to get away from home for good, and what better place to start than a city the size of Houston.

- 17 -

New York, 1997

> I believe that all through these dark and
> silent years God has been using my life
> for a purpose I do not know. But one day
> I shall understand and then I will be
> satisfied.
>
> —Helen Keller, *The Story of My Life*

"Who's editing this thing?" It was Sharon's voice on the other end of the phone, calling Strekfus, and she was furious. He looked at the caller I. D. just to be sure, so altered was her tone.

"What do you mean? Why are you calling me? Why don't you just come . . ."

"Is Sagaser editing your stories?" she asked, her voice rising.

"No. Someone upstairs. They took the job away from him. He was unsympathetic and . . ."

"Because you used my name in the last story, you moron!" She was screaming now, completely livid. "You actually called me Sharon in one part of the story—not Bunny!"

"What are you talking about?"

"Look on page sixty-one of the magazine," she continued as she breathed heavily into the phone. Strekfus scrambled through the glossy pages of the latest edition. His eyes scanned the page until he was halfway down its length. Then he stopped, frozen in place.

"Oh, my God," he said, apology oozing from his voice. "How could I have done that?"

"I don't know, but you did." Sharon was seething now. "Wasn't it bad enough that you wrote down the things we did in college? Now you go and use my real name? What were you thinking? What the hell do you suppose is going to happen when everyone reads this? Don't you think they'll pick up on the fact that we went to college together and my name is Sharon?"

"I'm really sorry," he said. He tried to make his voice sound even more apologetic than he really was in order to calm her down.

"You've got me smoking pot and dressing up like a mermaid and . . ."

"You did have a mermaid costume."

"That's beside the point!" she yelled. "You have me with a twelve-inch martini glass. I look like some fruitcake addict! And you couldn't have mentioned the fact that this story was so explicit two days ago?"

"Two days ago? What does two days ago have to do with anything?"

"At your birthday party. You know, the one I threw for you and won't ever again?"

"I'm really sorry," he said, "I've just been under a great deal of pressure. I've really got to talk to you about something." He was trying to get everything out now, knowing that it would only be a second before she exploded again. "I finally opened that tobacco tin and found out what was inside. It seems that . . ."

"I don't give a *damn* what was in it! I'm so pissed I could scream. Do you know this might cost me my job? Are you insane?" She was breathing heavily again and he waited, not saying anything but fumbling for a cigarette. Then he remembered that he didn't smoke in his office, only downstairs in an attempt to curtail one of his many habits, and he set the cigarette down. Finally she seemed to regain some composure. "I'm going out now for a walk and try to calm down. This whole thing has just upset me so much. Look, I'm not angry with you,

312

really. Really. I know I'm screaming but I've got to let off some steam. I know you didn't do it on purpose, but I've worked so hard to get to where I am and just because you need to go through some process to relive where you were and what happened to you, well, I don't need to be a part of that."

He thought about what she was saying and a part of him didn't want to push, especially at this moment, but he had to tell her something and he thought that if he put it in the right terms with the right tone, maybe he could reach her. And since a part of him had decided that he wanted to tell her about what he had found, he was now thinking that he could at least begin the story in an attempt to derail her anger.

"Listen to me," he started saying, "I'm really very sorry but I've been totally stressed out. I don't think anyone is going to recognize you and besides, we may have bigger problems than my story."

"All I know is that we spoke about this story before it happened and you still went ahead and wrote it." He could see that she wasn't going to allow him to explain what he had found—that there was something in the tobacco container of paramount interest to them both.

"Look, I'm sorry. I don't know what else you want me to do, but I've really got to get back to work," he said. He knew it was no use. Sharon wasn't going to buy any explanation, no matter how justifiable, so he pretended to be busy in order to excuse himself. He didn't want to tell her that the next story involved her; that it might make her appear in an even more unflattering light, albeit in a different way.

"Let's call a truce for now, okay?" he asked, hoping to get off the phone, wondering how he could rewrite the story he had written about their sharing an apartment in Houston. At least this last story, the one about Greensaw, Texas, had been heavily edited, taking out choice words and some of the more risqué scenes. By the time the editor had finished there wasn't much left, but Strekfus had kept the original, resplendent with sex, drugs, and rock and roll.

313

"Fine. I'll get over it, I'm sure. I always do. I've got work waiting anyway after I go out and cool off. I just had to get this thing off my chest," she said, and with that they cut the lines of communication momentarily.

As Strekfus sat there, it wasn't their conversation that he thought about. It wasn't the fact that he had accidentally used Sharon's name in the last story. It was the dream he had suffered through last night—the one which had been coming back to him all morning, its images like broken pieces of music which faltered and backtracked until they were nothing more than a jumble of black-and-white collages which seemed to have been cut out of a forty-year-old magazine. This wasn't just any dream. It was one he had endured in childhood, but hadn't had again until just last night. And it was one which was even worse than the memory of the ice water and how his father had treated him.

In the past when he had experienced these dreams, they had seemed to him meaningless clutter: blurry and dark cutouts like some badly decoupage-covered lampshade which allows only a few pinpoints of illumination to escape. But now, with past, present, and future colliding on a daily basis, they became clearer, more intense. It was as if God had handed him a gift, only each time he attempted to unwrap it, to get past its packaging in order to obtain the prize, the Almighty had snatched it away. It was the same with his dreams—the one about the ice water and the one he had experienced just last evening.

The dream was always the same—brief and painful. He had never tried to figure out exactly what it meant—the darkness, the door opening, the man in green surgical scrubs standing over a crying newborn. But each time it happened he awoke in a sweat, sitting bolt upright. The previous evening he had experienced the dream again, but before daylight saved him, he visited this unearthly place with its dank, fetid meanings and knew that something was different, that something was going to happen which would change everything.

He relived the dream in his mind as he sat in his office: he was once again seeing the murky darkness, hearing some sort of medical machinery, seeing the faraway door open, the shaft of

314

ominous light, carrying with it the scent of ether on its beam, the doctor in surgeon's scrubs, his green smock open to the waist exposing a chest of thick and matted hair. Then the doctor moving to the newborn. It always seemed that the doctor was there to check on the child and it was as if he resented the doctor's caring for the newborn and not him. But why should the doctor care for him? Was he also a newborn in the room? Why was he seeing this? And why did the doctor carry a flashlight?

Then something else was happening but he couldn't remember what. Each time he awoke at exactly the same moment, before he could find out what had taken place. Each time he awoke never being able to get closer to the truth, the real event, and though nothing in particular transpired in the dream itself to upset him, he always awoke feeling physically sick. But he was used to the dream, at least he had been during his childhood. It had visited him regularly at almost the same time each year the way a cold or the flu does. Only now he was noticing something different about the dream. Why he hadn't put this together before he couldn't say, but the thought seemed to leap into his mind and it was almost as if his brain were trying to hide the results from him, not let him make the connection, hide this thought as if it were some family secret that an innocent child had blurted out in the presence of company.

Today was two days after his birthday, The dream, from what he could remember of it from childhood, had always happened on this day. This pushing and pulling of remembrances was becoming trying. One minute he was having flashbacks and the next his mind was trying to shut down in order to forget.

He sat there staring up at the ceiling of his office, trying to remember previous years as a child. He could remember being seven. He could remember being ten. He could remember having the dream two days after those birthdays. Why hadn't he put this together before? As he concentrated he could remember other birthdays, other times the dream appeared.

So this dream which had haunted him in childhood had ceased during college, probably because of the intense release college had granted him in the areas of creative freedom and experimentation. Either that or the incredible amount of drugs he had taken had overshadowed it. But now it had resurfaced at middle age when many people take stock of their lives, and this, along with his recent revelations, added to his anxiety.

He decided that work just wasn't going to happen for him today, and this ever-present feeling of anxiety, exacerbated by Sharon's latest fit of anger, made him leave a note for his boss saying that he wasn't feeling well and that he needed to go home early. But once there he only moped in front of the television, channel surfing and consuming whatever junk food he had stored in his apartment. Before he knew what was happening, the entire day was gone and darkness let down its veil like some grieving widow. He had completely forgotten about the dream by the time he went to sleep, but somewhere in the middle of the night, in that hollow portion that is neither yesterday nor today, today nor tomorrow, the dream he feared, the one involving the doctor and the newborn, returned.

He sat up in bed, the soaked sheets twisted about him, trying to figure out why it was following him like some rabid animal. His last story had been concerned with leaving home, Chandelier acting as his mother in the play about Helen Keller. He couldn't help but wonder if this had brought up the dream again, but if it had, what did it have to do with a newborn and a doctor? After a few moments he gave up trying to rationalize the dream's visitation and lit a cigarette. He looked at the clock—six thirty. He might as well stay up until time to go to work. If he went back to sleep now he'd never be able to get up.

He tried to write, but the flash of the nightmare kept coming back to him. It was as if it were some kind of omen; a black cat crossing his path in order to prepare him for some cathartic event. He felt himself drawn back to the vision like a criminal to his handiwork. Now he was remembering his visit to Sagaser in the hospital, the nausea, the discomfort at being in those surroundings. He tried to shake it off by working on the next story. The further away he could get from the dream the better. He would write about anything but childhood now. He had safely made it to college in his stories and was preparing to go beyond. He would not look back. He would bury this thing, whatever it was, and move on.

But before he knew what was happening, some other voice, some inner impulse was gnawing at him, making him move, making him think in two opposite directions at once. One said to bury the truth, and this he would attempt to do in his writings. The other said that he couldn't live without it, and at this moment the voice involving the truth, his truth, overwhelmed everything else and he found himself acting as if he were not in control. He was reaching for the phone, even at this hour of the morning, and he was dialing long-distance information, hearing the ring, waiting for what seemed like forever to have someone pick up on the other end of the line. Then he was speaking to the operator, telling her that he was going to need several numbers and that she should stay on the line with him.

"The first number," he was saying as he looked down at the lid of the rusted tobacco tin which he held in his hand, "the first number I'm going to need is for the main hospital in Infanta, Alabama." As he waited for the number he extracted the small, thin plastic strips from the tin's lid and fingered them from one end to the other as though they both were the holiest of rosary beads; beads created for him, saved for him, entrusted to him; rosary beads which by merit of their origin and history, could lead him to salvation.

- 18 -

The Apartment on Sul Ross

Houston, Texas, 1976

> Many incidents of those early years are
> fixed in my memory, isolated, but clear
> and distinct, making the sense of that
> silent, aimless, dayless life all the more
> intense.
>
> —Helen Keller, *The Story of My Life*

After a memorable semester at Greensaw University, I decided that dorm life and the I.O.O.F house had offered too much excitement for me. Not having been allowed to make friends as a child, I had gone to the extreme. My voracious appetite for human contact in any form had caused an overload on my brain cells and I began thinking about narrowing down the number of acquaintances that I had. Coming to the conclusion that home life back in Alabama was the other extreme, I made plans to move to Houston for the remainder of the summer. Some of my friends had moved there and I felt that I was ready for a taste of big-city life, but with more defined goals and fewer friends.

It was agreed that Bunny and I would look for an apartment in or near the bohemian section of the city—Montrose. At the time, Montrose was a cultural mix of galleries, gay bars, and bookshops. It was extremely liberal and getting more so every day.

Bunny and I set out one day early in July to look for a place to live. Since she wasn't working yet and I had just procured a minimum-wage job at a seafood restaurant in the neighborhood, our prospects for a place to live looked grim. This was a few days before the Bicentennial celebration and the city was abuzz planning fireworks displays and media events. Everywhere you looked there were red, white, and blue festoons, and most of the city's avenues were lined with some form of the American flag.

After scouring the neighborhood for days and finding nothing, we were ready to give up. It seemed that the entire country was in the throes of the nation's two-hundreth anniversary and little time was allotted to those of us looking for a place to live. We had parked Bunny's car several blocks away from Montrose and were walking up and down the streets looking for vacancy signs when it began to rain. With steam coming up from the asphalt, we started to run back to the car. Houston can be tropical in the summer, and the humidity on this day was excessive.

"Excuse me," a voice said to us seemingly out of nowhere. We stopped and looked around to see a huge purple Lincoln Continental with two portly men inside pull up beside us. One of the men appeared to be in his forties while the other was about our age. Both men could have been poster boys for child molesters, their clean-shaven faces seemingly hiding something. As the older man leaned out of the window to address us, billows of air-conditioning poured out in our direction.

"Yes," said Bunny as she struck a pose and exhaled after taking an unusually long drag from her foot-long cigarette holder, completely oblivious to the fact that it was now pouring. Bunny had been overweight and uncoordinated in elementary school, but by the end of our first year at college she had blossomed into a svelte and beautiful young woman. With her newfound beauty came the desire to dress and accessorize flamboyantly.

"Can you-all tell us where the Old Plantation is?" asked the driver. He had an oily leer on his face and his upper lip looked as if it could use its own windshield wiper. His jet-black hair was greased down and matted together in large strands that looked like licorice. He smelled of cheap aftershave.

"You're in the wrong neighborhood," said Bunny. "It's a good ten blocks away," and with that she pointed in the general direction with her cigarette holder while maintaining her other hand firmly planted on her hip. Giant raindrops found the burning end of the cigarette and extinguished it with a hiss. Discarding it, Bunny re-lit another and rooted it firmly into the holder, being careful to maintain its position downward this time to avoid extinguishment.

"You two looked like you might know where it was," said the man. At least he was correct on this point. The Old Plantation was a bar in Montrose frequented by gays, artists, and just about anyone who didn't fit into the mold that society said was "normal." Bunny and I would visit it often in the months ahead. I found that visiting places where there were unusual and creative people was much more tolerable than having to live with them twenty-four hours a day.

"What are you two doing out walking around in this weather anyway?" he went on.

"Looking for apartments," answered Bunny.

"Find any?"

"Not yet."

"Tell you what," said the man, "get in the back. We know of some apartments."

"Is he kidding?" I asked Bunny. "He's got to be some kind of nut."

"Don't worry," Bunny whispered to me, "I've got my switchblade."

"Your swit . . ."

"Shhhhhh! Just get in. I can handle this." And with that, we slid across the plush plum-colored velveteen upholstery and started to cool off.

320

The older man with the sweat on his upper lip turned around as best he could and began to address us.

"You're just the type of people we want to move into an apartment complex we're renovating."

"You've got your own apartment complex?" I asked before Bunny could punch me in the ribs.

"How much and where is it?" asked Bunny in a clipped and utterly professional tone. She could be the ultimate businesswoman when the situation called for it.

"Why it's just around the corner. On Sul Ross," said the man.

"Sul Ross!" I said, "But that's . . ."

"Let's go take a look at it," said Bunny, and settled back into the seat, an elbow resting on one of her arms which was placed across her mid-section. She held the cigarette holder high aloft. Its burning tip just barely missed the plum-colored felt roofing. We drove off in silence as Bunny blew clouds of smoke into the front seat and the air-conditioner blew them back at us.

When we pulled up in front of the building our spirits fell. It was a 1920s Mediterranean-style stucco edifice that had been neglected for years. A huge oak tree towered over the two-story roof which was missing about a third of its terra-cotta Spanish tiles. The sidewalk was cracked and grass was growing at intervals within it. As a matter of fact, that was the *only* place where grass was growing. The front yard, if there could be said to be one, was entirely dirt. There was a half-dead palmetto reclining next to the front doorstep, the lower leaves of which had not been trimmed for years, and its brown sunburned fans bowed over ungracefully, like an awkward teenager curtseying at some ill-conceived coming-out party.

"Rustic," said Bunny, and blew a large cloud of smoke in the direction of the younger man in the front seat—the one our age—who had remained silent throughout the proceedings. A large cloud of smoke engulfed his head but he did not cough or move out of the way. Then he turned to her and smiled, showing a mouth full of dental work which looked as though it had been done by a one-eyed Soviet orthodontic intern. The majority of the work was steel-silver, the exception being one lower front tooth which was gold.

We got out of the car and headed for the front door despite our reservations about the façade and the surrounding neighborhood. This was the first time we had gotten a good look at the two men in the front seat. They resembled Jehovah's Witnesses in that they were both attired exactly the same: blue-black pants with too much polyester in the mix and white short-sleeved shirts with pencil protectors in the pockets. Bunny shot me a look.

As we stepped into the "foyer" we were immediately transported back to the '60s. The walls were stucco like the outside of the house, but they had been painted baby-blue, and what had once been bright blue, green, and yellow carpet covered the floor. The carpet design was that of huge fake symmetrical flowers. It was in bad need of repair. Enormous torn threads stretched out over the flat garden like anemic tendrils belonging to an aged octopus. We climbed the narrow stairs and found ourselves at a single French door.

"Go on in. It's open," said the first man. The second man, the one with the mouthful of elements, had yet to say anything, and the two of them plastered themselves against the wall in the narrow stairwell so that Bunny and I could pass.

We entered an immaculate apartment that seemed to have been redone from top to bottom. The hardwood floors gleamed and the rooms still smelled of fresh paint. In all, there were five huge rooms and a kitchen. Strangely enough, the kitchen was the only room that had not been redecorated and it boasted the same blue, green, and yellow flowered carpeting that we had seen in the entrance hall of the building.

"Now this here is your living room," said the older man, stretching out his fleshy white arm in the direction of the enormous picture window which overlooked the neighborhood. It would have been a great view except for the tree whose foliage blocked all sunlight. "And over here, is a dining room, and in back," he continued, as he walked toward the rear of the

322

apartment with the younger man following him, "are the two bedrooms. There's a back stair and one bathroom."

"What's that noise?" asked Bunny wrinkling her nose, and this time it was my turn to punch her in the ribs. It was at that point that she noticed what I had already observed a few minutes before—that the younger man had a built-up shoe because one of his legs was shorter than the other. His handicap had become suddenly apparent because of the reverberation qualities of the hardwood floors, and as he followed the older man around from room to room, his asymmetrically weighted "shu-thump" echoed within the walls.

"We'll take it," said Bunny emphatically, turning to the older man.

"Well, that was quick," said the man.

"How much?" she asked.

"Well, now . . . I figure about one hundred and fifty dollars a month."

"One hundred and fifty dollars a month!" I said, knowing that this was a low price even for this neighborhood and market. "What's the catch?"

"No catch," said the man. "And you guys can move in just in time for the big Fourth of July celebration."

We exchanged pleasantries about how well the place had been redone and retreated back to the plum-colored Lincoln. Once they had dropped us back at Bunny's car we discussed going to their office the next day to leave a deposit and fill out the paperwork.

"Look," I said, "I can't imagine us being this lucky. Something's up."

"Oh, don't be such as gloomy Gus," replied Bunny. "Can't you just accept that some things really do come your way?"

"No."

"Well, they do. Just accept it."

"And what did he mean, 'We were the kind of people they were looking for?' "

"Who knows? Maybe he meant young. You know, they might not want any old fogies."

"Fogies?"

"I know. I just couldn't think of any other word."

We moved our meager possessions in and Bunny started her job as a dance instructor even though she had never officially studied that art form—it seemed to be another talent she came by naturally. On the Fourth we attended a twelve-hour-long party at the Old Plantation, culminating in a fireworks display held in one of the neighborhood parks. The Bicentennial came and went, and the flags which decorated the city were left up to wear and fade. I was working at a restaurant down the street and we were rarely in the apartment. Even when we were off work, we managed to head down to one of the many discothèques that had sprung up in the neighborhood and partake of the sordid nightlife that Montrose had to offer. The first few weeks were relatively peaceful as we fell into a rhythm of work, going out dancing, and trying to get some sleep.

One day while standing at the kitchen sink I noticed a window in the building next door. It wasn't hard to do as the apartments adjacent to ours towered above us, cutting out any possibility of light. Since there was only a short distance between its walls and ours, privacy was at a premium. The window directly opposite ours had white muslin draperies that were continuously drawn, but there seemed to be some movement behind them whenever I stood in the kitchen. We, of course, had no curtains whatsoever. The first few times this happened, when I saw movement at the window next door, I didn't think anything of it. Then it began to unnerve me. It was as though someone was looking at me, trying to catch me at something, or even worse, just curious.

"Probably the neighborhood lunatic," said Bunny one day after I mentioned it.

"That's impossible," I said. "I'm the neighborhood lunatic. You can't have two in this close proximity."

"True. Then it's probably a nosy neighbor. By the way, speaking of nosy, I know we're just starting out as roommates, but could you lay off my liquor a little and stop going through my stuff? I'm running low on the vodka and cash to *buy* the vodka."

"Excuse me?" I said. "I haven't been drinking your liquor."

"Hello? This is Bunny you're talking to. Look, I don't want to get into a fight. I don't mind you going through my stuff or even drinking the booze, but replace it if you're going to go through most of the bottle."

"I haven't been into your things!" I screamed at her. "I don't even *like* vodka!"

"I'm not going to argue. All I know is the bottle's more than a little low."

"Fine," I said.

Bunny and I argued from time to time but I didn't think much of it. We had been friends now for some time and we knew what buttons to push, but evidently she had been more upset than I about the liquor incident. Finally one day she came into my bedroom and announced that we had a new roommate, thinking that my lack of inclusion in this decision would push me over the edge. She wanted to see my reaction.

At first I couldn't believe what she was telling me, and then I spotted the "roommate." It was a large cat she had found outside the apartment building. The cat was completely black and completely enormous.

"Bunny," I said, "we can't keep a cat. Besides, it's huge!"

"I know," she said, "and I have the perfect name for it: Diva Perez."

"Oh, God," I moaned. Bunny had named the cat after a rather infamous drag queen who performed at one of the gay bars in the neighborhood. Diva Perez was an enormous dark-skinned Hispanic man who dished out outlandish routines at the the Old Plantation in Montrose. Gay magazines constantly noted her performances complete with pictures of the 400-pound artist. And to say she was dark-skinned was conservative, for while she was of Hispanic heritage, she was the color of tar at midnight in a room with no lights as seen by a blind person who's been knocked in the head.

Diva's story was known by just about everyone in the area. She was the son-slash-daughter of a well-known Mexican boxing instructor and former lifeguard, Jesus Perez, whose mother was allegedly a descendant of Pancho Villa. Because Diva (not his given name) was an overweight child, his father berated him frequently. As Diva got older, the elder Perez would practice his boxing techniques on the poor youngster. This eventually led to a life of homelessness, alcoholism, and prostitution because of an obvious lack of self-esteem. It also led to an enormous amount of involuntary head-shaking which sometimes made its way into Diva's routines. Some had actually credited the drag queen with starting the shaking of the head which so often accompanies women of color on those infamous talk shows which are now the rage—"You can't have my man, bitch! I will cut you!"—finger snap to the right, left hand on hip.

At some point in his life, after a suicide attempt, Diva decided to clean up his act (the alcoholism and prostitution—not the head-shaking), and in order to pay the rent became a female impersonator. So good was he at what he did, that there was no time for drink, drugs, or fast persons, and Diva now made enough to donate a large portion of his income to charitable causes.

"You can't name the cat that," I said. "What if he finds out?"

"She won't find out. And besides, I know her, and she would be flattered. He would be flattered. They would. Whatever."

At least part of this was true. Bunny did know Diva as she knew most of the drag queens who performed in the bars in Houston. Bunny had a knack for befriending the most colorful people in the neighborhood and this sometimes led to us having a rather strange assortment of dinner guests who dined on takeout food, sitting cross-legged on our floor since we had no table to eat on.

Once Bunny told me that a friend of hers was coming over to try on some gowns she wanted to get rid of. Because my bedroom had a double closet, Bunny kept half of her clothes in my room. On the particular day that the friend came over, she hung two of her gowns on the door to my bedroom.

When Candida appeared on the other side of the single French door that was the entrance to our apartment, I was taken aback. I had never seen such a beautiful woman in my life. I immediately recognized her from ads for some of the major cosmetic companies, and from having seen her picture on the covers of well-known magazines. To tell the truth, I was a little starstruck.

Candida explained that Bunny had given her instructions to come over and "take whatever fit." She had proceeded to undress right in front of me and I thought my mouth had fallen open as far as possible until she removed her slip and panties and then my mouth hit the floor. Candida was a he, complete with male genitalia.

This beautiful woman who had graced the covers of fashion magazines and appeared in ads stepping out of limos with a handsome man on her arm was a guy. What a wonderful joke played on the public. This ideal of American beauty was not even a real female.

I'll say this, Bunny certainly did have colorful friends and besides, who was I to deny her the right to name the cat after a female impersonator? All through my years with Bunny, she had taken me by the hand and exposed me to new and different things. From what I could tell, her knack for constantly surprising me and pushing the envelope wasn't losing any speed. She always seemed to be coming up with some colorful idea for something. Once, after visiting the real Diva in her apartment in Montrose, Bunny returned with what she thought was an innovative touch to our cat's wardrobe.

"What's that?" I asked, as Bunny fastened a thick plastic collar around Diva's neck. Bunny said nothing, so I reached over to Diva and fingered the new addition.

"I thought this would be a nice touch," Bunny stated. "I didn't have enough money to buy her a collar, so Diva gave me her identification bracelet that she had on while she was in the hospital—you know, the time she was in there for her attempted suicide? Since she's so big, they gave her an extra-large one and it fits perfectly around Diva's neck." She finished, holding the cat high up and turning her in all directions to admire her handiwork. "I had to make a minor adjustment to it. You know, make a fastener since Diva broke it when she took it off."

"What was she doing keeping her identification bracelet from the hospital? They let you keep those things?" I asked, as the cat looked down at me from its perch atop Bunny's hand.

"I guess so. It seems Diva just got tired of the whole medical, psychotherapy thing and got up and walked out of the hospital." Bunny had now set Diva down on the floor and I bent over to inspect the tag. Sure enough, it had the name "Diva Perez" in blue Courier font, along with the date of her admittance.

With the cat's name decided and her new accessory in place, we set about making our apartment comfortable for the creature. A large litter box was procured along with feeding dishes and a rather extensive assortment of catnip mice. I was constantly finding one of these in my bed in the middle of the night by turning over and feeling the saliva-soaked item with my foot. I would sit upright and moan while Diva just sauntered over to the mouse, picked it up with her mouth, and then casually began playing with Mickey while on her back. This usually occurred around six o'clock in the morning, as this was the time Diva most liked hearing the sound of the can opener. And Diva could eat, sometimes stretching our budget to the maximum.

Because we were short on funds, Bunny had the brilliant idea that, instead of completely dumping out the kitty litter, we could just scoop out the offending items left by Diva and continue to use what clean kitty litter was left. After searching for a suitable implement to perform this function, Bunny came up with a bright orange kitchen spatula which we never used.

My kitchen spatula.

It had been a gift from a friend during our college years at Greensaw University—that rather unusual character by the name of Roman Yapigacy. The spatula stayed right next to the litter box so there would be no mistake in using it even though there was no danger of this as neither of us knew how to cook. I'm not even sure the stove worked.

Having Diva Perez was like having a child. It brought Bunny and me together, and we momentarily forgot about the liquor incident. That is, until I came home from work one night and found my bedroom smelling like a French whorehouse.

That evening I noticed a bottle of my cologne out on a table in my bedroom. I confronted Bunny with this evidence but she vehemently denied using it.

"What would I want with your cologne? I don't wear men's cologne, you jerk!"

"There's no need to be vicious. I know you used it because when I came home last night the room smelled like someone had taken a bath in the stuff," I said.

"I don't know how you could have smelled anything since you were probably drunk from all the liquor you stole from me," she shot back.

"Again with the liquor!" I said. "You bitch! How dare you keep accusing me of that!"

The fight escalated until we were at fever pitch. We had followed each other around the apartment screaming and flailing our arms until we found ourselves in the kitchen. Diva was sitting on the counter calmly bathing herself as Bunny and I hurled insults at each other. She eyed us with minor disgust and then rolled over on her back.

In the middle of our argument (which had reached decibel levels that could have caused deafness several states away), the phone rang.

"Who could be calling at this hour?" I said.

"Probably your mother," said Bunny. "It's possible she heard us all the way over in Alabama. Hello," Bunny said curtly after jerking the phone practically out of the wall in order to retrieve the receiver.

"Yes . . . yes . . . well, I don't care . . . Well, you can go straight to hell," I heard her say and then slam down the phone.

"My mother?" I said.

"The neighbor," said Bunny, momentarily shaken.

"What neighbor?" I queried. We called a truce for the moment and the fight was forgotten.

"I don't know which neighbor," said Bunny, reaching for a cigarette. "They said we had to either cool it or they would call the police."

"The nerve," I said. "And right in the middle of a good fight."

It was then that it hit us. We looked at each other, and united in a common cause, put what we thought were two and two together.

"It must be that nosy neighbor next door who's constantly looking at us through the curtains," I said, as we both looked out the kitchen window toward the run-down building next door. "But how would they have gotten this number?"

"I'll fix that wacko," said Bunny. "I don't know how, but no one speaks to me like that. They were so nasty! I couldn't believe it. I mean, we might have been loud, but you don't have to call me a bitch."

"They called you a bitch," I said. "How *dare* they. Are you sure it wasn't my mother?"

It was then that Bunny had her brilliant idea. With the determination of a woman on a mission, she stormed out of the room and returned with Diva's litter box and orange spatula. Placing the items on the counter next to Diva, who was by now sound asleep, she wrenched the kitchen window open.

"What are you doing?" I asked.

"You'll see."

And indeed, I did. Bunny carefully and methodically scooped out the biggest piece of cat excrement she could find with the plastic kitchen spatula. Careful to make sure the piece she had chosen was located directly in the middle of the implement, she grasped the end of the spatula and bent it back as far as she could. Then, with perfect aim, she pointed this miniature war machine directly at the window of the nosy neighbor who had placed the call. With military expertise she sent the cat turd flying across the twelve-foot yard between our apartment house and the neighbor's, and landed the still-moist object directly onto the screen covering the window. The wet thud it made as it hit the screen and stuck will forever be etched in my mind.

"Good shot," I said.

"Thanks," she replied, and proceeded to return the spatula and litter box to their proper place. By this time Diva had awakened from her nap and was trying to figure out our fascination with her body functions, dreamily rolling over on her back and purring loudly.

This ritual was repeated as often as Diva was able to produce the desired ammunition, and by the end of the summer the neighbor's screen was a good three quarters covered with Diva's droppings. Since Bunny and I now managed to keep our voices at a minimum, the neighbor never called to complain anymore, but Bunny's wrath had not subsided and her wrist was getting a workout pulling the spatula back each day to release the odoriferous projectiles. I would often be lying in bed on a Saturday morning and hear the already identified "thwack" and know that Bunny was once again directing her anger at the neighbors.

We fell into a routine again and finally got used to the fact that items would come up missing. The toothpaste would be squeezed in the middle, the toilet seat would be left down, and Diva was getting fatter by the day. Bunny still accused me of drinking her liquor and I still accused her of retaliating by using personal articles of mine. Diva just stared at us during our spats and kept gaining weight. "I put her on a diet," said Bunny, "but she just keeps getting bigger."

One day we came home and found Diva out of sorts. She was hacking and coughing, and at first we thought it was just a fur ball, but the hacking continued, and becoming worried, Bunny and I bundled her into the car and took her to the vet.

When the vet extracted what looked like a giant splinter as Bunny and I held Diva down, we both just looked at each other.

"It's a chicken bone," the vet said. "Or at least part of a chicken bone." He turned the splintered object in the light. It was

331

firmly gripped by the pliers-like instrument he had used. Diva just looked annoyed since her naptime was being seriously cut into.

"What have you been feeding her?" shot Bunny in my direction.

"I haven't been feeding her," I said. "*You* feed her."

"Well, whoever fed her should have known not to give chicken bones to her. They can kill a dog or cat when they splinter," said the vet, and he dropped the poultry femur into a small metal dish. It made a metallic "ping" and Diva rolled over and shook her head several times, trying to convince herself that she had no idea where the bird's leg had come from.

With both Bunny and I swearing that neither of us had fed her, we got into her car and drove back to the apartment. Diva was sound asleep on the seat between us as if nothing had happened. We couldn't figure out where she could have picked up the bone. Bunny's theory was that the next door neighbor must have sneaked Diva the chicken and tried to kill her as payback for producing such a plethora of fecal matter. But Diva was a house cat and never left the apartment. It would have been impossible for the neighbor to slip Diva anything to eat.

I looked at Bunny and asked, "Are you thinking what I'm thinking?"

"Probably," said Bunny. "You know we've always been on somewhat similar wavelengths. Remember how thrilled you were to find out that I put Tabasco sauce on my tuna fish just like you?"

"And that we can both describe every single *I Love Lucy* episode in chronological order?"

"The liquor, things missing from time to time, the chicken bone. Something's definitely up," said Bunny. "Besides, we haven't ever eaten chicken in the apartment." And with that she turned a puzzled expression in my direction.

The next day we decided to try something different. We both called in sick to work, but planned to leave the apartment just as scheduled. As we always did, Bunny and I got into her car and drove away, but we didn't go to work. Instead we drove around the block and parked. Then we made our way through the alley that ran in back of the houses across the street. Trying not to look suspicious, we casually walked between the houses facing ours until we were directly across the street from our front door.

Finding a rather overgrown and fungus-laden rhododendron (*Rhododendron davidsonianum*) between two houses, we ensconced ourselves. It was our plan to watch the apartment and see who came and went, hoping to catch someone. We had discussed the liquor incidents and the fact that certain things were missing from the apartment, and now with the chicken bone found in Diva's throat, we knew something was amiss.

After several hours of waiting, there was nothing. No one came or went and I began to get hungry. Besides, it was starting to get tedious just sitting in a rhododendron bush, so we flipped a coin to decide who would backtrack to the car and go for food. Bunny lost.

No sooner had she left than a car pulled up in front of our building, and not just any car. It was the plum-colored Lincoln the two men had been driving the day we met them and they showed us the apartment. And it was not just any man who got out; it was the second one—the silent partner that day who hadn't said anything, the one with the built-up shoe and the Boris-and-Natasha dental work.

Still dressed in his mock-Jehovah's Witness outfit, he nervously looked around and then entered the building. I figured he must be entering the apartment, but decided to wait. It seemed that it was taking Bunny forever to get back and my adrenaline was pumping.

A few minutes later another car pulled up, this one pale blue. I immediately recognized it as a Buick. What was up with these color schemes? A rather shady man, completely dressed in black, got out, looked around, and then entered the apartment building. I waited a few minutes hoping Bunny would return so I wouldn't have to confront them myself, but she didn't show up. I did the old grammar-school thing of "I'll wait exactly two minutes and then I'll go in," but two minutes passed and I tried the "I'll wait exactly three more minutes and then . . ." Finally I mustered the courage to go into the apartment and confront them.

I had just extricated myself from the rhododendron and begun to cross the yard when I heard a commotion behind me. I looked over my shoulder to see a man lunge for me. He tripped on one of the rhododendron's exposed roots and landed facedown in the dirt, giving me a moment to try and figure out what was going on. For a moment I thought I was imagining the whole scenario. It was broad daylight. I was in plain view. And here was a complete stranger coming straight at me for no apparent reason. Since my adrenaline was already going at full speed, fear kicked in, and having no time to think rationally, I started to run. It's true what they say about "fight or flight" syndrome. It really does take only an instant for your body to decide what to do and everything seemed to happen in a second. Evidently his adrenaline kicked in also, for he was directly behind me in no time.

Not wanting to find out exactly who was after me, and suspecting that it had something to do with the two men who had illegally entered our apartment, I ran—no, flew—to the front door of the apartment building. I could actually hear the hot breath of my attacker and feel the gusts of air he exhaled on the back of my neck—that's how close he was.

The minute my hand touched the doorknob to the outer door of the building, everything went into slow motion. I remember thinking that because I had to slow down to open the door, my attacker would catch me. For some reason he did not, but out of the corner of my eye I saw what appeared to be ten or twelve other men dressed exactly the same as the man persuing me, coming toward me from around the sides of the building. They had something printed on their jackets as if they were in the same club.

With no time to think and my mind reeling, I flew up the steps to the inside door of the apartment, taking at least three or four steps at a time. Halfway up I felt a hand grip my ankle with such ferocity that I thought my leg would be broken. Just before my face slammed into the carpeted stairs, I looked up to see the man who had stepped out of the plum-colored Lincoln gaze down at me through the panes of the front door and mouth the words, in slow motion, "Go away." Before I lost consciousness, my only thought was, "What a strange thing to say to someone who is being tackled on the stairs of an apartment house you don't even belong in."

When I came to, I was lying flat on my back. As sights and sounds faded in and the picture slowly came into focus, I realized that I was in my kitchen on the garish flowered carpet. There were no less than twelve armed men standing around.

The first words I recall hearing were, "Here it is," as one of the men held up the orange kitchen spatula.

He continued, "Here's the damn thing they used to sling that cat mess all over the window." Then the face of one of the other men hovered over mine and asked if I was all right. I mumbled something about my ankle.

"Yeah," said the man, "sorry about that. We had to stop you before you walked into something you shouldn't. We were after the bad guys."

"Bad guys?" I said. "Who's the bad guy? Who are you? What's going on? Where's Bunny?"

"Who? Oh, your girlfriend?"

"My mother wishes," I said.

"Look," he said, straightening up and standing over me, "These guys are the FBI and these others are a division of the Houston detective department." He flipped out his badge. (This always amazes me. As if anyone who is completely freaked-out is actually going to look at the thing to make sure the person is who he says he is.) "We've been watching this place for the past several months. That's us over there," he said, jerking his thumb at the window of the house where Bunny had been slinging cat excrement for the past sixty days.

"Great," I said, managing to sit up. "We've been throwing cat shit at the FBI."

"That's correct, you have, but that wasn't the problem. It seems that while you and your friend went out every day, certain unsavory characters would use your apartment for drug deals,

335

laundering money, whatever. We've been photographing them for months through the windows. Good thing you guys never put up curtains."

"We couldn't afford them," I said, holding the cold compress one of the men had given me to my busted lip.

"It seems," the agent went on, "that the owners of your building were into all kinds of trouble with the law and you guys were the front for their operations. They would stake out the building to see when you came and went and then set up their deals here. The apartment was perfect for them because it was rented in your name and had a set of back stairs for easy escape. Plus they had keys to it since they rented it to you. The neighborhood wasn't bad for this type of thing either—no offense. We've got pictures of them making themselves quite at home," and with that he produced several large black-and-white photos of our apartment as seen through the windows on the northern side of the building.

There were pictures of the older man in the plum-colored Lincoln enjoying Bunny's vodka. Pictures of him dousing himself with my cologne, enjoying a bologna sandwich, and cleaning his fingernails with a kitchen knife. There was even one of him feeding Diva from takeout he had gotten at the Klukin' Chicken down the street.

Of course there were also pictures of the drug deals, the briefcases of money, the shady characters with sunglasses, all slightly blurry and with dates and times stamped on the lower right hand corner. As the dates of the photos came closer to today's date, the pictures took on a surreal quality. I thought maybe the film the FBI had used was bad, but then I realized that as Bunny slung more and more cat excrement onto their window, the harder it was for them to take pictures. Because their view had been almost completely blocked, they were forced to make their move.

Evidently having had someone go outside and clean the screen might have given away their position. They had actually been the ones to call and complain the time Bunny and I had the fight. It seems they were afraid that the apartment was being watched by the drug smugglers, and if someone else called the police about the noise, they might have been frightened away.

"Fascinating," I said, holding the black-and-white photos. "That would explain the chicken bone."

"Excuse me?" the agent asked.

"Nothing. Oh, where's our cat?" I said, and right then Diva made her appearance beside me, rubbing against my badly bruised side.

"Listen," I said. "There's something I don't understand. I was sitting in the bushes trying to figure out myself what was going on. How did you guys happen to be there the same time I was? I mean, if you knew this stuff was going on, why didn't you just go in and arrest them right away?"

"We'd been watching them for a while and we needed concrete proof and those pictures. We had planned a bust right after you and your friend went to work today, not realizing that you guys had the same thing in mind. When we staked out the place and took our positions, I came upon you across the street just as you came out of the bushes. Obviously I knew who you were from staking out the apartment and the photographs. We couldn't very well have told you that your apartment was being used every day for drugs and money laundering. And in addition, one of the men, the one with the clubfoot and metal mouth, decided to turn informer on his friend, helping us out. So it all came together for us in the end. Besides, we weren't sure in the beginning if you and your friend were involved or not."

"Gee, thanks," I said, and then it suddenly dawned on me that Bunny had not returned yet from her appointed food run. I was just about to say something when the other agents came into the room and said that everything was tied up and they were going to take the suspects down to the nearest police station.

"Listen," said the agent, "we're going to pay for any damage to the apartment. Any personal damage, that is. As far as damage to the actual building, well, that's another matter. You see, the people in charge of repairing it are going to jail and I don't think you want to wait until they get out to have the front door fixed."

337

"Front door?" I asked.

"Yeah, we made a pretty big mess of it when we broke it down."

The agents finished up their work and I was asked for all kinds of information and to sign things and make statements. I kept wondering, "Why are they asking me for my full name and Social Security number? They're the FBI—shouldn't they know this?" They had some medical person there who attended to my busted lip and then insisted that I go to the hospital just to be "checked out." I refused and they made me sign something saying that I had declined medical attention. I tried to point out my intense fear of hospitals, but they just looked at me blankly. At this point I just wanted to be left alone.

When they were done they picked their way out of the apartment, stepping over shards of broken glass and fragments of what had been the front door. No sooner had they left than Bunny appeared holding two greasy brown bags from Tico Taco. We had become enamored of the food while at Greensaw University and Bunny usually picked up something from the place in Houston at least once a week in order to pay a sort of homage to Roman.

They had locations all over Texas.

"What happened?" she shrieked. "Are you okay?" she asked, setting the soggy bags down on the kitchen carpet.

"I'm fine, really."

"What happened?"

"Well, I began, it's a long story, but let's just say that we won't be slinging cat poo at the house next door."

I explained what had happened and I have to say that not everything was a surprise to Bunny. I mean, we figured *something* was up but we didn't know what. We had no idea that it was this involved. We ended up fixing the front door ourselves with an extra door we found in the basement of the building, and we hung curtains on the windows. Other than that, we didn't change much.

Diva lost some weight and seemed to really miss the daily intruders and their extra treats. She pouted for a few weeks, and then one day when I was taking out the garbage, she slipped out the door and was gone. Bunny was heartbroken, but I figured she'd had enough intrigue and besides, she was named after a drag queen—maybe her career took her on tour or she just wanted a change of scenery.

The summer over, I returned home for a brief visit to Alabama. Whenever relatives asked me how the summer in Houston was, I would just say, "Oh, you know. It was hot," and leave it at that. I really didn't feel like going over the whole thing again.

But I had definitely decided some things about my life. I had transferred to a school in Texas because I was seeking adventure, and I had found it there and in the Montrose section of Houston. Experimentation with drugs, sex, and out-of-hand creativity had taken its toll, and I wanted to move on to the next phase in my life. In the meantime, I needed to get back to school and finish my studies.

In a few years, I would eventually decide to move to New York with Bunny and try my hand at the Big Apple, hoping that my New York phase would provide me with experiences that I had not already been through. I would eventually sever all contact with my mother, and as a result, lose a good amount of contact with the one person I had cared for most—Althea.

But again, this was somewhere in the future and that in itself is another story. For now I concentrated on streamlining my life and trying to move in a more positive direction. I really hadn't liked myself very much up until this point. I guess it sometimes takes large experiences to shake us out of ourselves and this is exactly what had been happening to me over the past few years, culminating with the FBI incident.

My innocence had been lost, as most things are, not all at once, but piece by piece. I didn't even notice it until one day I woke up and didn't recognize myself. I was still trying to escape from the Keller home in Tuscumbia, Alabama, but the total life experience would prove to be much harder than just opening that one door. I was still waiting for someone to call the plumber-bus driver on the pay phone.

Bunny and I didn't have too much as far as possessions go, and we split up what little there was in preparation for our return to school and impending trip to New York. She felt that Diva's remaining catnip mouse and orange spatula should go to me because she couldn't bear being reminded of her, so I took them and they became part of my section of the den at home until my mother did spring cleaning and threw the mouse away. But, being the practical woman that she was, she informed me via telephone one day, "You know, that was a perfectly good kitchen spatula that you had in with your possessions. You can really flip hash browns nicely with it. What were you doing with it anyway?"

Thinking about my relationship with my mother, remembering some of the choice things she had done to me in my life, and thinking that if you wait long enough people really do get what they deserve, I paused for a moment, then said, "Nothing . . . nothing at all."

- 19 -

New York, 1997

Before I left New York, these bright days
were darkened by the greatest sorrow I
have ever borne, except the death of my
father. In the autumn I returned to my
Southern home with a heart full of joyous
memories. As I recall that visit North I
am filled with wonder at the richness and
variety of the experiences that cluster
about it. It seems to have been the
beginning of everything.

—Helen Keller, *The Story of My Life*

The envelope appeared on his desk with the usual Monday morning mail—a direct result of having a new receptionist. At first he thought nothing of it, but holding it in his hands the few minutes before he opened it, something told him it was not good. An instant before his letter opener sliced through the thick, fibrous paper, he realized there was no return address and it signaled to him something ominous. Drawing the three sheets of paper out of their casing, he unfolded them and began to read. At first he was simply stunned. He hadn't expected it. Then he thought that it was possibly a joke, but something told him it wasn't. The first page said it all. It was an application for membership to join the Imperial Klans of America. The person applying for membership was asked to sign a statement that he was white, had never used drugs, had never been a follower of

341

the Jewish religion, and had never participated in interracial relations. There were other questions about criminal acts and the information requested ranged from driver's license numbers to national descent.

He put the pages down, not knowing exactly what he was feeling. Had someone read his stories and sent him this as a joke, or worse, because they were angry? The story about the apartment on Eighteenth Street concerned the Grand Dragon, but there wasn't anything terribly incriminating in it, at least not anything that would cause this. As he sat there and thought about who could have sent it, he remembered Charneise and her comments to him along with the memo accusing him of treating her badly. And Sharon had said something about her probably not liking some of the portrayals of the characters in his writings. Or maybe someone else from inside the company read his stories and thought it would be funny to send him this. And if it was a joke, would the person come forward and want to know if he thought it funny? He tried to put it out of his mind, thinking that it might be an isolated, one-time incident from some disgruntled reader. He didn't want to give the matter much thought anyway since he was due at one of the required Monday morning meetings.

He arrived in the conference room at exactly three minutes to nine. Everyone was standing near the heaters which hugged the massive hermetically sealed windows, out of which could be seen the forbidding jumble of buildings that is midtown.

"Shouldn't we get started?" someone was asking. And then the reply of another voice without a body from within the crowd of writers and secretaries which stood looking out the window: "We're waiting for old Saggy-ass." Everyone laughed at this, but the laughter was cut short when Sagaser walked into the room at that instant, looking his usual dull and angry self.

By ten minutes after nine the group had managed to cover only one story that the new writer was to work on, and the muffins and tepid coffee had barely been touched. But then something happened that caught everyone's attention.

At first it was just a voice in the distance, yelling something indistinguishable. It was the voice of Ricardo, the manager of the mailroom. What was it he could be yelling at this time of morning? But a few seconds later and everyone knew—there was a fire in the building. And not just in the building, but on the very floor the magazine was located on. No sooner had Ricardo pulled the alarm in the reception area, than he had rushed back to the conference area to warn the others.

A typically slow group of people, especially at this time of the day, the writers and their cronies vacated the room with a speed usually reserved for gazelles on the African plains. And it was for good reason, for by now thick gray smoke was pouring into the secretarial area. The soft plumes rose and sank with an evil undulation, covering typewriters and filing cabinets without prejudice.

Everyone made the pilgrimage down thirty-nine flights of stairs with the expertise expected of them, remembering the many fire-safety meetings they had been forced to attend over the years, presided over by retired firemen, their thick Brooklyn accents and moustaches commanding attention as they pointed out escape routes and safety procedures.

Once outside on the sidewalk, things lightened up. The air was cool and fresh, but the acrid smell of smoke still lingered in everyone's nostrils. As they milled about and talked (about anything except work), Strekfus couldn't help but feel that something was wrong—something other than the fact that the building was on fire. The group would stay downstairs on the sidewalk for another thirty minutes, but when the firemen had extinguished the flames and the workers had reentered the building, the gnawing feeling returned with a vengeance and continued right through the overheard description of where the fire had started.

Strekfus was standing behind one of the yellow-and-black-clad figures whose dirty, massive hands held an axe. The fireman was speaking with Ricardo, telling him that the fire had started in the small office just to the right of the big corner one. Evidently someone had placed a cigarette on the edge of the desk and it had rolled into the trash can where a significant portion of the wastebasket's contents had burned. The fire had started slowly, smoldering amid the papers and wet coffee lids, but it had taken hold a few minutes later and spread quickly through the overstuffed, claustrophobic office. The good news was that the fire produced more smoke than damage and that most of the manuals, papers, and hard drive of the computer in that small office had been saved.

The bad news was that the office in which the conflagration had occurred belonged to Strekfus.

He had figured out that much, but was still trying to put together how it could have happened since he didn't smoke in his office; he only smoked downstairs where he could commune with the other nicotine addicts of his building. Once again, he only had a second to run this through his mind because Sagaser was heading directly for him.

"You! In my office now!" he yelled at Strekfus without breaking his angry stride. He moved so quickly by Strekfus that the breeze from the man seemed to suck up everything in sight like a fast-moving truck on the highway. Strekfus followed, neither scared nor anxious—he knew he had done nothing wrong—but when they were behind closed doors, Sagaser started in on him, tearing at him like a hungry animal.

"What the hell were you thinking, huh?" he shouted as he walked about the room like some insane, caged, overweight leopard. "What did you want to do, burn the magazine down? Do you have any sense at all?"

"I didn't . . ." Strekfus started to say, but Sagaser had now stopped moving and was standing directly in front of him, his face frozen, his right index finger pointing upward toward the writer's face.

"I've just about had it with you, my friend," he sneered. "You are on thin ice," he continued, gritting his teeth. "First you start writing some crap about some kid who nobody cares about, then you try and trick me into letting you continue. *Then*, you have the nerve to go over my head about these stupid stories, and now you've tried to burn the place down. What kind of a maniac are you? Are you trying to get me to *fire* you again? He walked over to his desk and stood behind it. Then he looked out the window, his whole body shaking, seething with anger. After a few seconds he turned again to Strekfus, but his mood was no better. He looked over at Strekfus, who now sat, stunned from the fire, from the KKK application, from the fact that he hadn't slept well the night before, and it was as if what Sagaser did then was worse than any of the previous tirades he had hurled at him. Sagaser just looked at him and shook his head, his lips pursed in a condescending smile.

It was then that it happened to Strekfus, and it was only an instant, but it represented a portion of time larger than anything he had ever known. It was vicious and terrible—as if some giant piece of fabric had ripped away and he had been shown something which his mind had forced him to forget. There was an enormous sound and then a flash of something, but only he was aware of it, for it played out only in his mind.

Sagaser was still going on about his lack of work ethic and his irresponsibility but Strekfus didn't hear him. He had seen something in his mind and he was trying to figure out what it had been, where it had come from, and why it was appearing now. What had that scene been—the one that flashed before him? There was something green, like the tiles in the bathroom, like the slick Jadite glassware he had done the report on. There was something glinting, metal, sharp. And somewhere in there was his father. He sat frozen, trying to make sense of it, unaware how long he was motionless. It was almost as if an eerie calm had come over him while he analyzed the flash. Then suddenly, he was back to reality. He was once again hearing Sagaser's ranting, seeing him pace, seeing the smirk. But it didn't matter. He knew that there was something else happening to him and whatever it was, it was bigger than Sagaser.

After Sagaser finished, losing steam and energy finally, he dismissed Strekfus. The writer walked back to his office in a daze to collect what he could and move it to one of the vacant offices on the other side of the secretarial pool. "At least I'll be further away from the man," Strekfus thought as he settled into his new but bleak surroundings—his third office so far. While this new office had a window, it faced a wall of yellow brick and the overhead fluorescents blinked on and off continuously, occasionally staying off for minutes at a time only to burst on again with blinding intensity. After thirty minutes in this environment he had a headache and felt that he would never again be able to tolerate the color yellow, but he made it through the rest of the day with no more altercations, the numbness somehow allowing him to function at least on a relatively primitive level.

Somewhere toward the end of the day he called Sharon, hoping she would commiserate with him and lend a sympathetic ear. She had been absent from the morning meeting because of some off-site work she was doing and had missed all the excitement. As they sat together at one of the outdoor cafés in midtown he filled her in on the details of that morning. It seemed that she had forgiven him for the I.O.O.F story, and that the one involving Diva the cat and the FBI hadn't even fazed her. So now he felt it safe to try and share with her what he needed to discuss.

"Listen," he began, fingering his cup of cappuccino, looking down, not sure exactly how to broach the subject, "I've been meaning to talk to you about something." He was looking up at her now, trying to gauge her mood, her responses. She said nothing but gave him a look that told him it was safe to continue. Then she began to assault the frothy chocolate shake which the waiter had just sat down in front of her.

"You remember a few weeks ago when you were getting on my case about the I.O.O.F story?"

She took her lips off a straw which was firmly imbedded into the confectionary goo and nodded, swallowing at the same time.

"Well, I was trying to tell you something then—something about that tobacco tin that Althea left me."

"Oh, yeah. Did you ever find out what was in it?" she asked casually.

"I did. And I think you and I may have bigger problems than the fact that you didn't like the way you were portrayed in some of my stories."

"Listen, Strekfus," she said, her tone sympathetic and clear, "you've always been my best friend. You've seen me through some pretty rough times, like the one when that awful boyfriend tried to blackmail me and I was hysterical, and all those other times when I needed a shoulder to cry on. We won't even talk about, well, you know . . ." and here she paused, hoping he understood.

"Your abortion?"

"I said we wouldn't talk about it. And besides, it was that same bastard who tried the blackmailing thing. Let's not get into that. Anyway, back to the present. I was mad at you for a while about your stories, but no one seemed to make the connection, and if you want to know the truth, I may have overreacted a bit." She was now gauging his reaction, having read his face while she spoke the last sentence. It told her that he had something more to say, something more serious than just an apology.

"This is really difficult for me," he said, but before he could finish she cut him off, realizing that she had never seen this look on his face before and that something was seriously wrong.

"Oh, God. What do you mean? What's wrong?" She was listening now with genuine concern, wondering what could be worse than having her life splayed out on the pages of a best-selling magazine. "Is it the fire? The application? Strekfus, you know I didn't send that to you."

"If you'll just give me some time, I'll explain. As I told you before when you were screaming at me," and here he gave a slightly sarcastic smile in the hope of somehow lightening up the conversation, "I got into the tobacco tin—the one Althea left to me."

"You said that already. Stop stalling. Tell me. And?"

But at that instant something silently spoke to him. It was as if some inner voice told him to stop, as if some intuition told him that he shouldn't continue, even though he felt alone in the world and Sharon was his best friend, even though he wanted

347

someone to share his pain. So before the words spilled out of his mouth, unretractable and hard, he listened to the voice and altered what he was about to say, for he immediately realized that, although he had figured out what the tin's contents meant, there might possibly be more to the story. Yet he had already built up the contents inside the tin and if he lied now, if he told Sharon that all it contained was a ruined and moldy piece of tobacco, she would know he was being untruthful.

"Well," he started, as genuinely as he could, "there was an identification bracelet inside. You know those plastic ones the hospitals use in order to identify patients?"

"So?"

"Well," he started more slowly now, not sure exactly where he was going, trying to think on his feet so that he wouldn't have to say what he had initially planned, "it was my identification bracelet." He waited for a moment—a dramatic pause not for the drama, but because he needed to catch his breath. Then he continued. "When I was a baby." He paused again. "It was my identification bracelet when I was a baby in the hospital." He was now looking at her, directly into her eyes, making sure they were connecting, that they understood each other.

"I don't get it," she said, lightly running her fingers up and down the fluted soda glass. She wasn't yet on his wavelength, not having had the same amount of time or stress to process the information as he had, and besides, he had altered the story in midstream, so it was only logical that she couldn't follow what he was saying.

There was silence now from Sharon's side of the table. Her breathing had changed and she was quiet, and not just in the purely physical way, but in some sort of emotional way as well. Then she managed to speak.

"Why do you suppose Althea left you that?" she asked with genuine curiosity. There was no other element in her voice, nothing that gave away her thoughts of any mystery or ulterior motive. She seemed confused by the whole thing, not really having had enough time to try and piece together any type of scenario.

"I don't know, but I've been on the phone now for the past several weeks trying to get some information from the hospital I was born in. I have to try to figure out why a housekeeper in my parents' employ would leave me such a thing. I mean, the woman didn't do things without a reason. She was one of the most intelligent and thorough people I've ever known—in her own way. Not book smart. Not educated, but intuitive-smart. You know?"

"I understand," she was saying now, almost completely void of emotion. He could tell she was somewhat withdrawn, as if internally some part of her knew something and wasn't letting her conscious mind get near it, and while Strekfus hadn't used this information for the sole purpose of disarming her anger at him the previous week, he still thought he had better get everything out now.

"Well, what do you think it means?" she was asking again, having pushed her chocolate shake away.

"Don't know, but it's been doing a number on me. I've been having these nightmares that I haven't had since I was a kid. And all kinds of things are coming up for me. I guess this latest trip back home, Althea's house, the tin, work, you name it. It all seems to be coming down at once. Sagaser was screaming at me today and I almost flipped out. It was like I had this flashback or something. And to make matters worse, I got a call from someone on my father's side of the family that my Aunt Testa is pretty bad off. She's got Alzheimer's and evidently she's in one of the last stages. I've known for some time, but I never wanted to face reality."

"Boy, fun just follows you around."

"You're not kidding. And to top off my week, Sagaser has told me that the next story I write should have a Gothic twist."

"Gothic? Did he read the one about your father's death? How much more Gothic can you get?"

"Evidently someone above him asked me to do it, you know, to break up the string of stories somewhat. I guess they figure that I can't keep going in the vein I'm in if I have to switch to Southern Gothic. Whoever this is, this person requesting this, feels that the terms Gothic and Southern just go together."

"Go figure," she responded. "I guess in the same way that anything written by a Southern writer has to have someone named Jesus in it."

"Right. I've already covered that one."

After a few more minutes of conversation in which they both tried to lighten the mood by not speaking about hospital bracelets, sick relatives, or horror stories about the South, they slowly got up from the table and went their separate ways toward their respective apartments, neither one noticing that they had been the only ones left at the café.

As they separated, he turned and watched her as she crossed the street—Fifty-third and Madison—and made her way home. He watched her until she rounded the corner and was out of sight, for he was feeling guilt now—guilt at not having told her the truth about what was in the tobacco tin.

As he turned to head for home, he tried to absolve himself of this feeling that he done the wrong thing. Besides, hadn't that inner voice, that intuition, told him to be silent about the real facts? Surely there was some reason for this, some reason he had shut out the truth from his best friend at the last minute. Still, he wished that he could have shared with her the tin's true contents—the fact that it contained not only his identification bracelet as a child, but that of her brother as well.

* * * * *

The next Monday, one week later, Strekfus again found himself seated around the enormous oval conference table with his co-workers. It was becoming a habit, these Monday morning meetings in which his life began to fall apart, and so he wasn't totally surprised when two strange but rather well-dressed men pressed their way through the heavy double glass doors of the conference room and announced in overly confident voices that they were looking for Strekfus Beltzenschmidt, completely mispronouncing his name. He found himself raising his hand as

350

if he were in the third grade again, and while he hadn't done this intentionally, it drew laughter from the room. From everyone, that is, except the two Brooks Brothers-clad men who had come to collect him.

"Could you step outside, please," one of them asked, his right arm extended, gesturing toward the reception area. Strekfus could imagine his co-workers wondering what was going on, much in the same way he was, but in a few moments it was all made clear to him. Both men had managed to maneuver him over to a small alcove in the reception area, away from prying eyes, the ringing phone, and a rather gangly rubber tree in need of watering. They stood, one on each side of him, arms folded, their jackets thrown back, exposing a pair of compact and deadly looking pistols. Then one of the men flashed a badge and the party really began.

"FBI," the taller one began. "We'd like to ask you a few questions if you don't mind, Mr. . . . (and at this point the man looked at his miniature spiral notebook, already having forgotten the name), Beltzenschmidt."

"Well," thought Strekfus, hearing the pronunciation, "at least that time you were somewhat closer. "Sure, go ahead," he offered.

"We received a call from an anonymous source that you may have been trafficking in drugs," said the first man, leaning back slightly and eyeing Strekfus, waiting almost a full minute to gauge his reaction, if any. Then he continued, not having received the response he so coveted. "Now we sometimes get these from people who want some type of revenge or to play some sort of game. Sometimes it's nothing. Still, we have to check it out. We've been watching you for several weeks now and . . ."

"Several weeks! What do you mean, watching me?"

"Relax. We're not here to arrest you. We're actually more concerned that someone has reported a false alarm, at least with respect to you being involved in drugs. We've been following you. Watching you. We're well aware that you're not involved in any illicit activities."

351

"The only drug I'm involved with is my blood pressure medication, which I don't believe is working too well right now," said Strekfus, and gave a slight, forced laugh. Then he looked to the two men, neither of whom had even twitched.

"Have you had any run-ins with any persons recently?" The man asking the questions had his notepad out, jotting down something even though Strekfus hadn't yet responded. He looked like a new waiter on his first Saturday night at one of the city's more popular restaurants, desperately trying to keep up with the patrons.

By now, Strekfus realized that the two men weren't there to take him to jail or hassle him and he calmed down—somewhat. He put his hand to his forehead, trying to think where this accusation had come from. Sure, he had made enemies through the years (who hasn't), but nothing to warrant this. He remembered the KKK application and related to the agents how he had received it just last week—Monday, exactly a week from today. Then he remembered that the fire had consumed it, so there was no proof. Still, he was able to tell the FBI men about it and how it had unnerved him. And then there was the fire itself. He thought for a moment. Three things: the application, the fire, now this accusation. What was going on?

"I'm really sorry," he began, "but I can't think who would have done this. At first I thought that I might have offended someone in the KKK with a story I wrote about the Grand Dragon, but I don't think they would go to this extreme. Besides, I didn't make them look that bad." Again he gave a little laugh—perfect counterpoint to the two stone faces peering at him.

"Well, we hope you understand that we have to check these things out. You're not under any investigation, not any more, but we would like to ask you about any plans you might have—if you're planning to leave town anytime soon. Just precautionary, in case we find out who gave us the tip or if we need you to confirm a suspicion we might have."

"As a matter of fact, I *am* leaving town," Strekfus volunteered, "but I can tell you exactly where and why I'm going there. I can even give you the phone number in case you want to reach me." He wasn't laughing now. He wanted to appease these men, make them go away. And besides, he didn't have anything to hide.

"Shoot," said the other man, the one who up until this point hadn't spoken. He was addressing the floor, not yet having looked up at Strekfus.

"I'll be at my aunt's home in Infanta, Alabama," Strekfus began, slowly and methodically so that the other agent could write it all down in the small notebook. "The address is five-o-nine Latrobe Street."

"Business there?" the second FBI man was asking now, still not bothering to look up.

"My aunt is ill with Alzheimer's disease and I'm taking a month off to spend time with her and take care of her. I'm flying out in three days. Delta. It's a nine o'clock flight. I can get you the number if you hold on."

"Please," the man said, looking up for the first time and catching with his gaze the other FBI man's attention. And it seemed that Strekfus felt both men's eyes follow him down the corridor, through the secretarial area, past the kitchen, and around the corner into his temporary office. When he emerged a few minutes later he saw them still standing there, in exactly the same position as before. Even the taller man's pen had retained its position, poised just a few inches above the paper like some stolid, emotionless snake, ready to strike the paper with any information he might give them.

When they had finished with him they neither smiled nor frowned but simply nodded. Then they were gone, and Strekfus was left to think about what had just happened. He sat down in the corner of the reception area, not wanting to go in and face his co-workers, knowing that they would have questions, knowing that the explanation, even though it was innocuous, would take out of him what little there was left.

- 20 -

509 Latrobe Street

Infanta, Alabama, 1997

> How shall I write of my mother? She is so
> near to me that it almost seems indelicate
> to speak of her.
>
> —Helen Keller, *The Story of My Life*

At exactly eleven fifty-three, the M29 bus on its way to the corner of Twelfth Street and Main in downtown Edwina, ran over and killed Mr. Brad Castratis. It was the only news in town for weeks, but not because the forty-eight-year-old had reached his untimely demise beneath the wheels of a sixteen-ton bus. No, what shocked the small town of Edwina, Georgia, on this bright summer day in August 1935, was the news that the M29 bus had been ahead of schedule, and rumors were flying about why this had happened.

You see, the M29, or any other bus in Edwina for that matter, had never been on time, much less *ahead* of schedule. No one was too surprised to find out that Mr. Castratis had been run over by the vehicle—Mr. Castratis was stone deaf and couldn't have heard a freight train coming if it were to personally tap him on the shoulder. In the end this event would leave the town of Edwina changed very little, but the events which followed, those

354

involving blackmail, hatred, and manipulation, would change the lives of my family and everyone around us forever.

Now I should tell you how I know this story since I wasn't even born when it happened. I learned about it when I went back home for a visit; a visit after many years' absence; a visit to one of my family's residences—the home at 509 Latrobe Street in Infanta, Alabama.

* * * * *

"I've got goose bumps," said Suzanne. We were standing over my father's grave in the only cemetery in Infanta.

"I know what you mean," I said, looking down at the date on my father's headstone. "I had no idea."

Truly, it *was* strange. I had decided to come back home to Alabama on the anniversary of my father's death. If I had known I was returning on the very same day he died it was subconscious, because I certainly hadn't planned it that way.

Now living in New York, I had managed to remove myself from my family and friends in Alabama, with the occasional phone call being virtually the only link to them and my past. One exception to this had been my return several months before to the funeral of someone dear to me—someone not a family member—but that trip had been short and I had found myself back in New York before I could completely process the excursion.

I did have some connections to Infanta. There was my friend Bunny who had moved to New York with me, but she and I were so much alike, so much removed from the land of our youth, that she didn't qualify as a link that much anymore. At least that's what I thought at the time. And just as I had thought Althea and I had no real connection other than the relationship we had shared in my formative years, I would find out that Bunny and I were linked in a much closer way than could ever be imagined.

But on this day, as we stood at the grave—contemplating the flat, dull headstone, the writing in Old English lettering, the

355

freshly mowed grass—New York and Bunny were the last things on my mind.

"That *is* strange," echoed Aunt Belle as she walked up behind Suzanne and me. Her arms were crossed as she looked down at the grave, then up at us. My Aunt Belle and her daughter Suzanne had been nice enough to drive me out to the cemetery to pay homage to my father before we returned to their house, and we were now standing on the small hill he was buried on, overlooking the rest of the cemetery.

"There are fresh flowers in the vase," continued my aunt. "I wonder who's been out here?"

"Obviously it wasn't my mother," I said, confirming what she and Suzanne had been contemplating. My aunt and cousin had about as much use for my mother as I had. My mother and I hadn't spoken in years, much to the delight of some of the family members, and to the chagrin of others. ("I just think it's awful the way you treat your mother. Why, she's your *mother*. She gave *birth* to you.")

The breakup in communication had occurred several weeks after my final semester at school. After my stay in Houston and a couple of semesters at Greensaw, I had decided to return home for a brief visit before determining exactly what I wanted to do with my life. One day, I queried my mother on the status of the Social Security money I had coming to me—the money reserved for children with a deceased parent. As my father had died several years before, I was still waiting to see this money. She replied that the compensation was hers and that I wasn't entitled to any of it. Feeling rather left out of the loop, I had visited the Social Security office in town only to be told by one of their representatives that I had been signing my checks for the past several years, and with that, the clerk behind the desk produced a stack of checks with signatures on them. Looking closely at the signature of one of the checks, I returned home and confronted my mother with her forgery scheme.

"I don't owe you anything," she had said, "and besides, you're going to have to go to work now and get a job to support me. We're broke."

"But what happened to all the insurance money you told me about?" I asked.

"Don't be stupid," she said. "That money was mine to spend and you'll never see any of it."

After further investigation into things, I found out that my father, or rather someone, had signed his will the day before he died. The odd thing about this was that he had been in a coma for three days prior to his death. This, accompanied by the fact that he had left everything to my mother, made me extremely suspicious. I decided at that point that I didn't want anything from her, I just wanted her out of my life, and I severed all communication with her.

So here I was, standing at my father's grave, thinking how pleasant the years had been not speaking to my mother. But I had not come home for the purpose of visiting my father's burial place. This had been a side trip on a much longer journey, and it wasn't the physical space between New York and Alabama that encompassed the greatest distance, but rather the emotional geography, for the heart feels separation much more than the head. The reason for my return home was this: I had arrived to help take care of my Aunt Testa who had developed Alzheimer's. She was in the "middle" stage of the disease and was becoming a handful for my aunt and cousin who shared the two-story Victorian house—the family home now—with her. The house had actually been my grandparents', but when they died it was left to my Aunt Testa and Uncle Scott, and Aunt Belle and her family. It was in this house that I would find out things about my family, and it was in this house that I would discover why the M29 bus had run over Mr. Castratis in Edwina, Georgia.

I knew the house quite well, having spent many of my childhood days there under the care of Aunt Testa. The place was a conglomeration of antiques, middle-class furnishings, and remnants of my grandparents' past.

Situated on a large corner lot in the historic section of Infanta, it wasn't a pretty house. As a matter of fact, it was quite plain, but its attraction lay in the fact that it was a maze of passages and rooms which housed the family history, the family secrets, and the family memories.

The ceilings were quite high, the framing strong, and the mahogany staircases—two of them—were stately and majestic. It was surrounded by enormous oaks, and Aunt Testa had filled the front yard with azaleas and impatiens so that in the spring a burst of blooms surrounded the house, making up for the fact that it was so very ordinary in design.

It had originally been built for two families in 1887, and structured so that you could close off the dwelling completely into two separate living spaces. Since the time my Aunt Testa and Uncle Scott occupied most of the upstairs and my Aunt Belle and her family occupied the downstairs, the house had been opened up. The owners of the structure, before my family owned it, had run a boarding house because of the large number of rooms and convenient layout of doors leading to the outside. They had rented mostly to women, and mostly to nurses who worked at the town's hospital. My mother had been one of these renters.

There was no shortage of bedrooms, but whenever I visited I always occupied the downstairs one that my grandparents had slept in. It was in this room that I now found myself ensconced as I proceeded to unpack after our brief stop at the cemetery, putting my things away in the ancient armoire that had once been in the family's home in New Orleans—the home that R.P.T.P. Marshall had died in on Prytania Street.

My Aunt Testa had not come to the airport with my Belle and Suzanne, so I wasn't prepared for the shock of seeing her when she crept up behind me.

"Who are you?" I heard a voice ask, and turned around to see what was left of her. What had once been a vibrant, energetic woman was now not only someone I didn't know, but someone who didn't know me as well. A loss of weight and an asthma condition had confined her more and more to the easy chair in the den, and she had slowly run down like a favorite clock that someone had forgotten to wind.

While she had always endured a mild form of arthritis, it was now evident that she had more and more difficulty moving around, and it would sometimes take her a good minute and a half just to cross the room. Whereas she was once expertly turned out, she now wore an assortment of colors and textures that made her look like an explosion in a fabric mill. The bright orange sweater with gravy stains on it clashed dramatically with the red-and-turquoise plaid pants she had chosen to wear that day, and the whole ensemble was completed by mismatched shoes and pink socks.

The crowning touch was her new hairstyle, which was punk-rock short, having replaced the elegant French twist she had worn for years. The only familiar thing about her was a poodle brooch which she always wore, and two almost perfect red circles of rouge on her cheeks.

As I stood there staring into her face, her eyes searched mine, darting back and forth with incredible intensity as if trying to see what lay behind the pupils.

"Who are you?" she repeated, squinting, trying to pull the fragments of memory up from the depths of her mind.

"It's me, Strekfus," I said. "Strekfus, Aunt Testa."

It was probably a good thing that she didn't know me at first. That way she wouldn't have been disturbed by the look of shock and hurt on my face.

"Who?"

"Strekfus," I answered, much louder this time. It always amazes me how everyone (myself included) will talk louder than usual in an effort to communicate to foreigners and elderly people who haven't understood what you've said. If they don't speak your language, no amount of decibel increase is going to help, and Alzheimer's can definitely be considered its own language.

"Strekfus? Strekfus?" she attempted. And then the light went on. Her face changed. I could see into her soul. She became the old Aunt Testa again. Tears filled her eyes and she lunged at me, grabbing me with such ferocity that I had bruises on my arms from her grip for days afterwards.

"Oh, Strek, I've missed you so much," she sobbed as she gripped me. "How are you?" she asked, and held me at arm's length again, her eyes searching mine.

"I'm fine, Aunt Testa," I said, brushing away a large tear that hung precariously onto her lower eyelash. As she attempted to wipe her face she knocked my hand out of the way accidentally, and in the process smeared one of the rouge circles on her cheeks.

"You've gotten so big," she went on, still gripping my arms. "You've gotten so big!"

We hugged some more and then she abruptly turned away and hobbled down the hall toward the kitchen as if I were some sort of impudent servant who had just insulted her. I turned to see my Aunt Belle standing in the doorway.

"She comes and goes," she said, making her way over to the bed to help me unpack. "One minute she knows who everyone is and the next minute she can't remember anything. But what's really strange is that she will seem completely lucid for hours and able to remember what she wore for a birthday party when she was ten,"—she held up one of my polo shirts and proceeded to fold it for me—"then you'll leave the room," she continued, "and when you come back she's crying hysterically and can't even remember her own name. The other strange thing is her arthritis. You know she can't get around too well most of the time, but every now and then—and I don't know if it's an adrenaline rush or what—but she has incredible strength and could run a marathon."

"Strange," I said.

"Very," said my aunt cutting her eyes in my direction while folding the sleeves of a pastel-colored shirt.

I stood there for a few moments while Aunt Belle finished matching up some socks that had become entangled in the unpacking.

"You know," she went on, "you don't have to do this. I mean, Testa helped take care of your father when he was dying, but she doesn't expect you to do the same for her. And nobody in the family does either."

I thought about this for a minute. The last years living in New York had been hard on me. I had seen well over forty friends, co-workers, and acquaintances die of AIDS—brilliant, gifted, giving people who had made the earth a better place for the short time they inhabited it. I knew the pain of having to deal with terminal illness, but I also knew that I couldn't stand by without offering help.

When the first people I knew began to get sick, I stayed away, unable to deal with the prospect of suffering and death. Perhaps it had been my own father's long-term decline that I was remembering, and not wanting to experience that again I had found excuses when it came to visiting friends. While the pain of dealing with death was great for me, the pain of *not* dealing with it was even greater. I couldn't pay that price again, especially not for someone who had loved me so much. I had to help Testa, if in no other way than by visiting her and showing her that I loved her.

"But I want to," I said. "She was so good to my father all those years, especially since my mother was so unsympathetic."

"And you know how much she and your mother disliked each other."

"Yes, I remember," I said returning her a gaze.

"You know it's going to be difficult," my aunt went on. "It wasn't really too bad until recently, but she's going downhill fast. Just yesterday we couldn't find her anywhere in the house and we were getting ready to call the police when the Robinsons next door called to say she was in their garden wearing nothing but her bra and panties. We found her holding onto a magnolia branch, bent over a headless, plastic flamingo."

"I guess she has the same penchant for nature as Uncle Scott had," I tried to joke.

My Uncle Scott hadn't had Alzheimer's before he died three years earlier, but he was given to incredible eccentricities. He had been known to disappear in the middle of the night for several hours and the family couldn't figure out what he was doing until they put together a strange story that appeared in the paper with his nocturnal excursions.

It seems that several people in town had reported finding new trees planted in their yards when they got up in the morning. At first it was just one or two houses in the neighborhood, but when over a hundred people called to say that they now had a magnolia or spruce in their front yard, and that the tree had been nonexistent the day before, the police got involved and sat up for several nights waiting to catch the tree-planting culprit. It turned out to be Uncle Scott, who couldn't sleep and had decided to "beautify" the area at his own expense.

While no one removed the trees, it was nevertheless disturbing to the town and they worried about what else the tree-planter was capable of. In fact, one night, Uncle Scott hit a water main while planting a chinaberry tree on the south side of town, the result of which was a minor flood that had taken days to remedy.

So Uncle Scott had his driver's license suspended. He had also had his extensive gun collection taken away, having lost his permits, and as a result signed the assortment of firearms over to my Aunt Belle who kept them under lock and key. This was probably a good thing, since Uncle Scott kept most of the guns loaded, his paranoia about break-ins being another excessive side of his nature.

In this collection he had several prize firearms, the most coveted of which was a Le Mat revolver—probably the most famous firearm associated with the Civil War. The Le Mat was unusual in that it had two barrels: one which could hold nine .40 caliber rounds of ammunition, and the other which held buckshot. The shooter could simply move his thumb after firing the first barrel and unload the second. It was extremely deadly and had been carried by some of the most famous generals of the war. Indeed, General R.P.T.P. Marshall had carried one and it was this exact gun that my Uncle Scott had in his collection. With his gun set taken from him and no driver's license, he became depressed and eventually suffered a mild stroke. He died shortly thereafter. Now it was Testa's turn to cause excitement in the family.

"What a pair," said Aunt Belle, and proceeded to the kitchen to check on the pot roast she had put into the oven before she and Suzanne came to pick me up at the airport.

That evening at dinner, we all sat around the ornate carved dining table which had been in the family for three generations. Everything seemed to be going fine throughout the meal until my Aunt Belle suggested it was time we clear the table because Testa needed to take her bath and get ready for bed.

Now my Aunt Belle usually gave Testa her bath as the woman was incapable of completing the task herself and would sometimes eat the soap. The moment my aunt mentioned "bath" that evening, Aunt Testa started crying in her cream of potato soup which she hadn't touched during dinner.

"I want Strekfus to give me my bath," she sobbed, and turned in my direction.

My Aunt Belle looked horrified and stared at me with her mouth open.

"Strekfus can't give you your bath, Testa," my aunt finally said. "He's a grown man."

"I want Strekfus to give me my bath," said Testa, and proceeded to hurl a dinner roll at Belle's head. She dodged it, and the projectile landed perfectly inside a piece of seventeenth-century Chinese porcelain on the sideboard. Belle just stared from me to Testa, then back to me.

"Well, at least she remembers my name," I said, trying to bring some levity into the situation.

"We'll talk about this later, Testa," said my aunt, and proceeded to clear the table of everything except the bowl of now-cold potato soup on which Testa had placed a death grip.

In the kitchen Belle addressed me as she rinsed the plates, preparing them for the dishwasher. "Would you mind, Strekfus?" she asked.

"No. That's what I came here for. To help," I said.

"It shouldn't be a problem," she said, scraping the remains of a pile of green beans Testa had mashed into a pulp into the garbage disposal. "She insists on wearing a nightgown the whole time anyone bathes her anyway."

"I don't mind, really."

"Well, if you think it's okay," she said, and finished placing the silverware into the dishwasher.

Just then, a sound from the dining room broke into my thoughts and I turned to see what it was. "Come on, Tessie," I said, seeing her beyond the doorway, "time for a bath." Testa emerged from the dining room still gripping the bowl of soup, and followed me to the upstairs bedroom without spilling a drop.

"That Belle is so mean," she said. "She's just hateful to me sometimes."

"Now, Tess, you know Aunt Belle loves you very much. She just has a lot on her mind right now with you not feeling well."

Upstairs in her bedroom I managed to get her to release her grip on the potato soup and got her to change into her nightgown for her bath. Testa had lost considerable weight and this now became evident when I saw her with fewer clothes on. Her bones practically stuck out through her skin and she seemed extremely sensitive to anyone's touch, but she was still strong and could put her fingernails right through you if she latched on as she now did while I guided her down the hallway.

Opening the door to the bathroom, a flood of memories came back to me. This was the same bathtub that Aunt Testa had bathed me in when I was a child. Nothing had changed. There was still the same claw-foot tub and soap dish, both showing signs of wear. Streaks of rust ran down from the dish onto the hairline-cracked glaze of the enormous tub, and down toward the drain. The wallpaper was still faded and pink, and a series of cracks in the ceiling, which had been there since I was a child and had a shape resembling a miniature Mississippi Delta, still loomed overhead. The only thing that was different was a fuzzy pink cover which had been added to the wooden toilet seat. It seemed at that moment that I was five years old again.

I remembered that once Aunt Testa had bribed me into taking a bath by promising to give me a small wind-up donkey that my grandmother had brought back from Mexico. I had cried and cried for it until she gave it up just to keep me quiet. It was a gray plastic rendition of the animal with real horsehair for a mane. When you wound it up, it would vibrate until it fell over on its side and continue to tremble, turning in circles. It wasn't supposed to do this, but I thought the effect both magical and ominous, like an animal having some sort of seizure. I played with the donkey until it virtually fell apart and then relegated it to my toy box with all the other playthings my mother would eventually throw out. It seemed strange for this particular incident to come back to me. I began to run Testa's bath and the water came out slow and tepid as I thought about the donkey. After a few minutes there was enough water for her to sit in.

"That tub is hard," said Testa. "I can't sit in that hard tub."

I looked around and found a small hand towel. "Here," I said, "you can sit on this," and I proceeded to fold it in a small square. As I held it beneath the water a series of bubbles escaped, and I felt as if I were drowning a small animal. A great sadness overcame me, as if my DNA molecules were remembering something that had happened a long time ago—something that had happened to someone in my family. Testa regarded the hand towel now—a strange look coming over her face. Then she gingerly stepped into the porcelain receptacle.

Having now positioned Testa in the tub, I began the bathing ritual. I had just turned around to retrieve the soap when she started crying hysterically.

"What's the matter, Tessie?" I asked.

She just shook her head and continued to cry.

"What is it? Can I do anything?" I felt completely helpless. Testa didn't speak for several minutes, but when the crying had stopped, she looked up at me somberly with lucid eyes, and said in a monotone as if remembering something far away, "She did it."

"Did what?" I asked, accidentally losing the soap so that I had to fish around in the water to find it. My face was now right below hers.

"Killed him," she whispered hoarsely into my right ear.

"Killed who? What are you talking about?" I asked, getting up and wiping my hands.

"She killed your father," she said, looking up at me with a matter-of-fact expression on her face. "Your mother killed your father." Then she nonchalantly retrieved the Cashmere Bouquet soap and returned it to the holder on the side of the tub.

"Oh, Tessie," I said, "everyone always says that." For years people had said that she drove him to his death. I had even said I thought she killed him. I meant that she had driven him so crazy he would rather have died than spend one more minute with her.

"You don't understand," she went on, and with this she reached up and put one of her grips on my arm, almost pulling me into the tub. Her eyes intensified and she pulled me closer to her as if desperate to tell me what happened before the Alzheimer's set in again and she couldn't remember anything. "Your mother killed your father," she said, tugging on my arm with each word. "She physically killed him." Then she just stared ahead and started crying again.

"Tessie," I said. "What do you mean?"

Nothing. She just continued to cry. I slowly managed to wash her and the crying subsided, but inside I was numb. I began thinking about how my mother had acted around the time of my father's death. I had always chalked it up to the stress of the situation, but pieces began to come back to me and I didn't like the way the puzzle was coming together.

"Now, you know how sick he is?" I heard a voice repeat in my head—my mother's voice. "Well, since he is in such pain, you wouldn't mind terribly if something happened to him, would you? I, uh . . . mean . . . if something happened to put him out of his misery, you wouldn't mind, would you? I mean, that would be a good thing, wouldn't it?"

"What time is it?" asked Aunt Testa.

"What?" I said, breaking out of the past for a moment. "Oh, it's eight thirty, why?"

"Where's Belle? Why are you here?" asked Tessie, and with that she grabbed her nightgown closer to herself. "I want Belle."

"But Tessie, you said you wanted me to bathe you."

"What time is it?" she asked again, her voice rising hysterically.

"It's eight thirty," I said, momentarily experiencing denial for her disease, thinking that she might have somewhere to go and the fact that it wasn't yet ten o'clock would be a comfort to her.

"What time is it?" she repeated, and began to look terrified. "Where am I? What am I doing here?"

I tried to reassure her that everything was all right and that no one was going to hurt her. After a few minutes she calmed down again and we finished her bath. I managed to convince her to dry herself off by promising to leave the room for a few minutes. As soon as I had closed the door and left her alone I heard a "click" and realized that she had locked the door. I had just accepted my mistake when I heard Belle coming up the stairs. Evidently she read the panic-stricken look on my face, and seeing the bathroom door closed with me on the other side, knew what had happened.

"She's locked herself in, hasn't she?" she asked, and tried the doorknob.

"I convinced her to dry herself off," I said, hoping this would be a good enough reason for not thinking ahead.

"Don't worry about it," Belle continued, "she did it to me the first time. There are just so many things to fret about, you just can't think of them all." And then she addressed Aunt Tessie: "Testa? This is Belle. Open the door," she said, as she rattled the glass knob. "Open up now."

"I'm not coming out!" shouted Testa, "Ever!"

"Testa, you come out this minute. Nobody is going to hurt you," said Belle.

"What do we do now?" I asked.

"Wait. That's all we can do. She'll eventually come out," said Belle, and sat down on a Duncan Phyfe chair next to the

367

bathroom door. I slid down the wall onto the hallway carpeting to wait until Testa opened the door. By now Tessie had begun to sing to herself.

Oh, I wish I was in the land of cotton,
Old times there are not forgotten,
Look away, look away,
Look away, Dixieland.

"How long does this take?" I asked Belle.

"Who knows? Could be a few minutes, could be hours," she said.

We waited for about ten minutes and then my knees started to get cramped. I grabbed one of the other chairs in the hall and positioned it across from my aunt.

"Turn on that light," she said pointing to an Art Deco Chinaman lamp with a silk shade. "It's getting dark and I don't want her running out of the bathroom and falling down those stairs."

I turned on the lamp and sat back down. While I was worried about Testa being locked in the bathroom, I was more worried about what she had said to me earlier. Evidently Testa wasn't worried about anything, because she kept singing to herself.

"Away, away, away down South in Dixie," she sang.

"She can't hear us, can she?" I asked.

"I don't think so," said my aunt. "Why?"

"Well, she said something to me while I was bathing her that I found a little disturbing," I said.

"Most of what she says is disturbing," replied Belle.

"Yeah, but this was *really* disturbing," I said.

"Like what?"

"She said that my mother killed my father," I said, running my fingers over the well-worn upholstery of the chair.

"Well, everybody says that," she said.

"I know, but Testa said that my mother had killed him. I mean *really* killed him. Not just driven him to his death like we all thought," I said.

"What do you mean, *really* killed him?" asked Belle, punctuating each word with a slight pause.

"I mean Testa thinks that my mother did away with him," I went on.

"*Old times there are not forgotten,*" sang Testa, now having repeated the song at least three times.

"Well, your father was extremely sick for years and it was only a matter of time before he died, but none of us ever thought that your mother did anything specific to cause him to die. I mean, other than nag him to death," said Belle. "Besides, Testa has Alzheimer's disease. You can't go by anything she says."

"I know," I said, "but you yourself said she has moments of lucidity where she can remember things that happened years before and then can't remember something that happened just a few minutes ago."

"*Look away, look away, look away . . .*" sang Testa now at full volume. She was repeating the song again as fast as she could so that the words ran together like watercolors left out in a thunderstorm.

"Well, she sure remembers the words to that song," I said. "Anyway, what if she's telling the truth?"

"That was years ago. I wouldn't pay her any mind. And besides, you can't go on the word of a deranged person in her condition. Who would believe her?" asked Belle.

"I believe her," I said. "I know what my mother was like. That woman was capable of just about anything."

"Well, I don't believe it," said my aunt. "Besides, why wouldn't Testa have said anything about this when she was in her right mind? She never mentioned a word of it to me."

By this time, Testa had tired of "Dixie" and was now sobbing again. Aunt Belle got up and decided to rattle the doorknob, but as soon as she put her hand on it, Testa jerked the bathroom door open and emerged stark naked. As we stood there in shock, she headed for the stairs and gingerly negotiated her way down to the first landing, steadying herself by grabbing one of the wings of a large bronze angel which rested comfortably in an alcove.

By the time Testa was at the bottom step, my Aunt Belle had managed to shout over the banister to Suzanne that Tessie was on her way to the kitchen, and that she'd better have a towel ready.

We found her sitting at the kitchen table wrapped in a faded yellow towel my cousin had rescued from the dryer before the cycle was complete. When she had calmed down sufficiently from the bath incident, we convinced her it was time for bed. Belle managed to get her dressed in another nightgown and off to sleep in one of the upstairs bedrooms. I headed off to my bedroom. I was exhaused from the combination of travel and Testa's bath.

The tarnished brass bed looked the same as it had when I was a child. I sat down on it and the squeak of the springs under the mattress immediately brought back afternoon naps and childhood fears. As I got undressed and slipped between the over-starched sheets, I remembered for a moment my trepidation as a child that General R.P.T.P.Marshall's ghost would visit me because he had died in the bed. But being exhausted, I quickly fell asleep, putting the fear out of my mind.

I'm not sure whether it was the chiming of the grandfather clock in the entrance hall or the creak of the bedsprings that awakened me, but I came to the realization at some point in the night that I was not alone in the room. As I was facing the wall, I couldn't see who or what was next to me, but knowing the stories told of a ghost who occupied the house, I was slightly less than petrified.

Now while we all thought that the ghost was General R.P.T.P.M., he was nevertheless known as "Fred." Every member of the family who had spent more than a few seconds in the house swore to Fred's existence. More than once I had been sure that someone was standing behind me only to turn around and find myself alone. This would have been bad enough in itself, but years earlier, when a cousin visiting from Mississippi, who

370

was a devout disbeliever in the supernatural, came down to breakfast and related the story of how a man had sat on the edge of her bed during the night and carried on a conversation, any family member who doubted the existence of Fred was now thoroughly convinced. At the time there had been no other men in the house—Uncle Scott had been away at a convention, and Belle's husband had been deceased for several years.

My Aunt Belle, who was the last to be convinced of Fred's existence, decided that he was more than just legend when certain items began disappearing.

"Suzanne," she had asked her daughter one day, "have you seen my silver earrings, the ones shaped like starfish?"

"No, I haven't borrowed them," said Suzanne.

"I'm also missing two pairs of shoes and my favorite silk dress," Belle had said.

My cousin and aunt had just looked at each other with the same thought in mind. This was before Aunt Testa had become unstable, and they knew that she didn't wear earrings or the same dress size as my Aunt Belle. When the dress, shoes, and earrings were found in an empty closet in one of the bedrooms which hadn't been used for years, the family suspicion was confirmed: Fred was a cross-dressing ghost.

Testa did later adopt the habit of hiding things, but they were usually hers. She would often take what she perceived to be valuables and bury them in the yard or stuff them under some ancient piece of furniture in the house. My aunt and cousin were always finding her eyeglasses or a half-eaten box of Cracker Jack in some unusual place. Once, Belle was repotting some impatiens on the back porch and noticed a silver brooch in the shape of a poodle, belonging to Testa, in the bottom of the pot. Testa walked up behind her and snatched it away with a look that accused my aunt of stealing it. She had even buried a pair of scissors in the front yard, thinking at the time that someone was trying to stab her with them.

At any rate, we knew that things started missing before her illness and the escapades were attributed to Fred and not Testa.

So it wasn't total relief that I felt when I finally managed the courage to roll over in bed and see who was sitting there. The room was almost totally dark except for the outline of a person wearing a nightgown. I say person because I thought it was Fred.

"Fred?" I rasped, in a tentative voice.

"It's Tess," whispered the figure, "Aunt Tessie."

I sat up and pulled the sheet around me. "What's the matter, Tess?" I asked, relieved but only moderately so.

"She killed him. You have to believe me. Your mother killed your father," she said.

"Not again, Tessie. How do you know this?" I asked, reaching for the light on the bedside table.

"Don't turn on the light," said Testa, and gripped my wrist with one of her strong holds. "Fred told me." I felt a moment of sickness as she squeezed my wrist, a desire to jerk suddenly away from her, but then she released it and I regained my composure.

"Oh, great," I thought, "a cross-dressing ghost has told my aunt with Alzheimer's disease that my mother killed my father. This should hold up well in a court of law."

"Listen," I said, "I know you mean well, Tessie, but you can't just go around telling people this when you don't have any proof."

"But I nursed your father when he was sick," she answered. "I know he was scared of your mother and he often told me that he was afraid she would do something to him. He thought that she had poisoned him. Once when we were talking about it she came in and heard us. She later told me that if I ever said anything to anyone about it, she would . . ."

"She would what?" I asked, my curiosity piqued.

"She said she would blackmail me again," said Tessie, who was now looking down and crying.

"Blackmail? What for? And what do you mean, *again*? What did you do, Tessie?"

But Testa just shook her head and sobbed. Finally she said, "I can't tell you that right now. But your mother was evil and I really believe she killed your father. Besides," she went on,

372

"Fred said that he knew your father in the afterlife and that your father told him that while he was in a coma, your mother came into the room and injected something into the intravenous tubes in his arms. He was semi-conscious but he knew what was going on even though he couldn't speak. Then she disconnected the tubes and put them into his nose and down into his lungs so that fluid would get into his lungs and cause pneumonia."

"Tessie, this is really too much. You're not well. You shouldn't be saying things like this," I said as gently as I could. I was trying to be patient, but her morbid descriptions were making me slightly queasy. "Let me help you get back into bed," I said, and I took her by the arm, leading her back upstairs. She was sobbing quietly now and holding on to me for dear life. I could tell that she was exhausted from telling me this story, and so when I put her back into bed, I said, "Now Tessie, get some sleep. You've got an overactive imagination. Just try to relax. All that was a long time ago. There's nothing we can do about it now."

I left her sobbing into her pillow after a few minutes of trying to calm her down. I hated to, but the entire incident had drained me and I was exhausted. I needed to get some sleep. I decided to return to my room downstairs and try to put Tessie's ramblings out of my mind.

Getting back into bed, I slid between the sheets and stared at the ceiling, but after a few moments of lying awake, I decided that I would get up and lock the door. It wasn't that I didn't want Testa coming into my bedroom again, it was that I knew if she really needed me, she would make a racket and I'd get up and let her in. I just couldn't bear the thought of being awakened suddenly by her at my side. I guess that was why it was such a shock when I *was* awakened again sometime after I had gone back to bed. I don't remember what it was that woke me. It was really just a feeling that someone else was in the room and it wasn't Aunt Testa.

I didn't see anyone. I looked around the room with its peeling paint on the ceiling, its yellowed lace curtains underneath the heavy velvet draperies, and saw and heard nothing except for the soft ticking of the mantel clock.

It was the ticking sound that drew my attention to the timepiece and led me to notice a particular reflection in its face. Still somewhat groggy, I sat halfway up and pulled the quilt around me, squinting at the mantelpiece. It was then that it appeared.

At first, I thought it was just a reflection of light on the glass face of the clock, but the illumination began to get brighter by degrees, and I realized that I was looking at what appeared to be a single flickering candle flame. No candle—just a flame. Thinking I was imagining things, I lay back down and tried to clear my head. The street light was just outside the window on Latrobe Street. That was it. It was the light playing tricks.

All this talk of my father, family ghosts, Aunt Testa's problems, and the long trip had probably taken its toll on me. When I looked up again it wasn't just a flame, but a candle that had materialized out of thin air, suspended in front of the mantel.

Like a highway traveler unable to look away from a bad roadside accident, I stared at the candle until it grew by degrees to form the vague figure of a woman. The image became stronger until I noticed that it wasn't a woman, but a man in women's clothing holding a candle. The image was completely still and in profile, and the moment it turned to face me directly, it fell to the floor as if it had been a sheet of glass which had soundlessly shattered. Only the candle remained for an instant and then vanished.

Not sure of what had just happened and still half asleep, I wasn't panicking at this point. I wasn't sure if I was dreaming or not, and since the image had gone away, strangely enough, I lay back down and just looked at the ceiling, raising up every so often to see if anything was there.

Now while I believe in the likelihood of an afterlife and even in the possibility that some sort of energy inhabited the family home and was named Fred, I didn't really think I would be privy to a manifestation of the spirit. Being a somewhat rational person I figured, once again, that I was under a considerable amount of strain from having to take care of Aunt Testa, and the power of suggestion being such a powerful thing, I probably imagined or dreamed the incident.

Just lying there thinking of this exhausted me, and before I knew what was happening, I fell back asleep, having convinced myself that I had just been hallucinating.

When I was awakened the next morning by the screech of blue jays and the sun streaming in through the lace sheers, it wasn't the apparition that I first thought of, but of all the times I had slept in this bed as a child and the fact that my *father* had slept in this bed as a child, and that General R.P.T.P. Marshall had actually died in this bed.

As I lay there enjoying the crisply starched sheets and trying to shake off the grogginess, I heard noises outside the door. The rest of the household was already awake.

The doorknob rattled and I recognized my Aunt Belle's voice. "Strekfus, time to get up. Open the door."

"Just a minute," I yelled, and got up to unlock the door. "Sorry," I said, as I peeked around the solid cherry partition. "Testa came and paid me a visit last night and I didn't want any more surprises."

"That's okay," said Belle, "just get ready and come on to breakfast."

It was at that instant that I remembered the dream and was about to mention this to her, but she had already begun to make her way in the direction of bacon and coffee smells which were wafting through the house.

I really didn't give the vision much thought as I got dressed and made my way to the dining room where breakfast was always served. When I entered the room, Testa was already at the table, dressed in a blue chiffon blouse and trying to stuff an entire square of toast into her mouth. She looked up at me and then quickly looked down again.

"Hi, Testa," I said. She didn't say a word and just kept chewing.

"How did you sleep?" asked my Aunt Belle.

"Okay," I said. "I had a weird dream, though."

375

"Do y'all want your eggs scrambled or over easy?" asked my cousin from the kitchen as she peeked around the corner, her hand gripping the doorframe with an oversized oven mitt in the shape of a lobster claw.

"Scrambled," I said.

"What was the dream?" asked Aunt Belle from the kitchen while wrestling with a package of bacon. She was trying to put the uncooked remains back into a storage bag.

"Well, it wasn't actually a dream," I said. "It was more like a vision."

"Here's some more toast," said Suzanne, casually slipping the plate under Testa's right arm as the woman tried to extract a glob of raspberry jelly out of a jar in the middle of the table. Each time she had the jelly positioned onto the spoon, hovering above the opening of the jar, it would slip back into its receptacle with a sickly "plop."

"His testicles didn't drop," said Testa quite unexpectedly, having momentarily given up on the jelly, but nevertheless being reminded of something by the sound the coagulated fruit made when it plunged back into the jar.

"Excuse me?" asked Suzanne, now with the other lobster mitt on.

"General Marshall," said Testa. "His testicles didn't drop."

Belle and I just looked at each other and tried to continue our conversation. "So what was this dream?" asked Aunt Belle again as she maneuvered the uncooked bacon back into the refrigerator.

"Like I said, it was more of a vision. It seemed to be a man in women's clothing."

"Fwed," said Testa, with a mouth full of toast. "It was Fwed. His testicles didn't dwop when he was a child. Evidently this twaumatized him and to make mattews worse, his mothew dwessed him up in giwl's cwothes."

Belle and I just looked at each other again. "Well, the vision did appear to be some old guy in women's clothing, but I don't know for a fact that it was the general," I said.

"What time is it now?" asked Testa. Belle and Suzanne just ignored her.

"At any rate," I went on, "this vision didn't say anything. It just stood there and disappeared."

"You know your cousin Ethyl claimed to have seen Fred once," added Suzanne as she scraped several spoonfuls of scrambled eggs onto each plate. "She claimed he came to her during the night and wanted to borrow the taffeta bridesmaid dress she had worn to her girlfriend Eunice's wedding just two weeks before. Claimed he had found a pair of shoes to match. Go figure, a ghost being so picky."

"Well, I've never actually seen Fred," said my Aunt Belle, "but I'm sure he's got one hell of a wardrobe. Suzanne, put that skillet in the sink to soak. We've got to get ready to go downtown, so hurry up and finish eating," and with that we proceeded to finish breakfast.

We did have to go downtown that afternoon. Testa had an appointment with her doctor and we were going to take her after Belle straightened up the house. While Suzanne and I sat there and talked, Belle got up to finish with the dishes. Testa just sat watching us with toast-stuffed cheeks, rocking back and forth, gently humming to herself. After a while, Belle headed toward the back bedrooms. She returned a short time later, throwing me an unusual glance as she made her way into the kitchen, her high heels amicably tapping on the linoleum. She came back through the dining room carrying a dull butter knife and disappeared again toward the back of the house.

"You don't have to go with us to take Testa," said Suzanne. "We've managed all these times before, so if you want to just hang around the house, you can."

"No, I want to go, really," I said. "Besides, I'd like to run some other errands if we can. At some point I need to stop by the hospital for some research I'm doing. Story for the magazine. You know. That kind of thing. Anyway, Testa is what I came back here for."

After a few more minutes, Belle reappeared and headed to the kitchen again. "Strekfus, what did you have in your room last night?" she asked, never breaking her stride.

"What are you talking about?" I asked.

"I was back there straightening up and I noticed something all over the mantel and hearth," she said, holding out her hand to show what she had scraped up with the butter knife.

"Looks like wax," said Suzanne, peering into her mother's hand.

"Were you burning something in there?" asked my aunt.

"No," I said. "It's probably just some wax from some candles you had in there."

"Well, that's impossible," said Suzanne, "we don't have any candles in the house."

"That's right," said Belle, "we haven't had any candles in this house since . . . well . . . ever. Your grandparents wouldn't allow it because they were so scared of having a fire. Flashlights. That's all we've ever used. You didn't burn a candle in there last night?" asked my aunt.

"No, I . . ." And then I remembered the apparition.

"Well, I don't know where it came from," said my aunt, "There's not been a candle in this house since 1958."

"Fwed," said Testa. She was standing in the doorway and had heard the last piece of our conversation. She still had one cheek stuffed with toast.

"Fred," said my cousin Suzanne. "Testa is saying it was Fred."

"He often carries a candle," said Testa after swallowing her last mouthful and then shuffling over to a kitchen cabinet to take down a box of toothpicks. "His testicles never dropped properly, you know," she said as she cast a glance to us. She was now inserting the toothpicks, one by one, into an avocado she had found on the counter.

"Testa," said Suzanne, somewhat exasperated, "what on earth does Fred's un-dropped testicles have to do with anything?"

"They never dropped properly and . . . and," and then Testa began to cry.

378

"What's the matter, Tessie?" asked Suzanne, putting her arm around Testa.

"Phuuu, phuuuu, pu . . ." sputtered Testa as she held up the avocado with toothpicks sticking out of it. "It's a porcupine. It's a porcupine. It's . . . it's . . . a porcupine and it's so sad."

"What's the matter? Didn't its testicles drop?" asked Belle under her breath as she placed a remaining glass in the dishwasher. The strain of dealing with Testa's Alzheimer's was beginning to show and occasionally these little digs would come out. I think Belle felt guilty afterwards, but no one had really noticed. It was just her way of dealing with Testa's illness.

"Tess," said my aunt, her tone changed now as she had a moment to think about her last remark, "we need to get ready to go to the doctor's office. Now you go upstairs and get changed." Suzanne herded Tessie off to her bedroom to change her for the appointment. My aunt and I were left alone in the kitchen.

"I don't know what we're going to do," said my aunt. "She seems to be getting worse every day. You just pray for those times when she's lucid, and she does have a few."

After several minutes and the last of the coffee, Belle called up the stairs to Suzanne. "What's taking so long? You know her appointment is for twelve o'clock." And then to me, "It's such a shame, you know, Scott was a doctor and if he were still around maybe he would know what to do."

"Yeah," I said, "I really do miss Uncle Scott."

"Suzanne, you-all come down now. We've got to get going," my aunt called, concern rising in her voice.

"We're coming in just a minute," said Suzanne. "Testa says she has to get something for Strekfus and she can't find it."

"Well, hurry up. I've got to run over to the pharmacy and get those prescriptions refilled for her."

Soon we all headed out to the car, my aunt and Suzanne in the front seat and Testa and me in the back. Throughout the entire ride none of us said a word as we made our way through vintage neighborhoods and into the area of town which accommodated office parks and doctors' offices near the hospital. Finally we reached the office. We all knew how Testa hated these visits, but felt we had to do everything we could to ease her pain. We thought that maybe by all going together she wouldn't feel so lonely, but all through the ride, none of us seemed to be able to think of anything to say. Here we now were, in the cold, sterile, clean, and overly bright reception area. I felt a wave of nausea flow over me as it always did in places such as this. Most of my family had been in the medical profession, but I had been unable to stomach it. Still, I knew that Testa needed care and so I momentarily swallowed my anxiety.

"Now Testa, you sit here with Strekfus and the doctor will be out shortly," said my aunt after registering Testa's name at the front desk. "Suzanne and I have to go over to the pharmacy and get your prescriptions."

"As soon as you guys get back I need to go over to the hospital for a while and look something up," I said, hoping that they wouldn't want to come with me, that they would take Testa for a walk or something. I watched them head out the door. There was only one other person in the waiting room with Testa and me, and as soon as their name was called, Testa, who had been perfectly still, turned to me with purpose in her eyes.

"Strekfus," she said, and touched my arm. I knew something was different because she had said my name and was gently making contact with me—not her normal mode of communicating lately. I looked into her eyes and it seemed that I was seeing the old Testa.

While she had long ago given up chain-smoking and no longer wore perfume, she looked remarkably like the Testa I had known in my childhood. Foot surgery had long ago corrected her clubfoot, and even though she had Alzheimer's, she could get around well enough. When her face lit up, as it was doing at this moment, I felt as though I were a child again.

"Tess," I said, "what is it?" Then she unsnapped her well-worn camel-colored pocketbook and produced a rather dog-eared envelope with my name scrawled on the front in china marker. She handed it to me and snapped her purse shut.

"I haven't got much time," she said, still touching my arm, and tears began to form in her eyes. "There is a letter in this envelope for you, a letter I wrote you about a year ago when I found out I had this awful disease. I was in my right mind when I wrote it and every word of it is true. There are things I thought you should know about your life, your mother, and myself. I never meant to hurt . . ." and then she stopped and just stared past me at a copy of *Sports Illustrated* which was lying on the table in front of us.

"Testa," I said, "what is it?"

"I . . . just . . ."

"Are you all right?"

Then she turned to me and with what appeared to be all the strength she could muster continued. "Please put this away," she said, and touched the envelope. "Read it by yourself when no one else is around." With that she clutched her pocketbook to her chest and bowed her head.

I folded the letter neatly and put it in my jacket pocket for reading when no one else was around. A few minutes later my aunt and cousin came back, having had no luck in procuring the prescriptions. Just then, Testa was called in, and we sat and waited until she was finished. When she returned, carrying a lollipop that the doctor had given her, we headed out to the car.

"Don't you still need to go over to the hospital?" my cousin asked in my direction as we tried the door handles on the car.

"Later," I said, thinking that I could go some other time before I made my way back to New York. Besides, I wanted to see what was in the envelope.

After eating lunch and running errands, we returned home with Testa. She seemed to revert to her now-usual pattern of being on and off almost as soon as we entered the door. That night after dinner, I made the excuse that I needed to visit an old friend from high school, and after borrowing my aunt's car, I drove to one of the gas stations on the edge of the neighborhood. I figured that since it was well lighted I could pull over to the side and read Testa's letter. Not knowing what it contained, I didn't want to be in her presence or theirs when I did this. I parked the car near the restroom doors at the side of the gas station and opened Testa's letter. It was dated a year and a half earlier.

Dear Strekfus,

I have been diagnosed with what the doctors believe to be Alzheimer's disease. I'm telling you this because I'm in the early stages and I still have moments when my mind is clear and I remember everything. At present, I'm having one of those moments, so I want to put down on paper some things you should know.

None of this is meant to hurt you or anyone else—I just thought the story should be told. I've lived with this for so long and it has been so painful. Please don't hate me for the things I've done. I tried to do my best in this world and hurt as few people as possible, but I'm afraid I've failed at times.

I need to tell you about your mother and father and some things that happened in the past, but in order to do that, I need to start at a time before you were born.

In 1935 I was living in the town of Edwina, Georgia, where Scott and I had moved after living in New Orleans. The rest of the family had already moved to Infanta at that time. As you know, Scott was a doctor and attended to everyone in the town.

One day a man showed up at the door with a Negro woman in labor. This wouldn't have been so unusual, except the man arrived by bus which was empty—except for the pregnant woman. Evidently there was some complication with the birth and the midwife couldn't attend to the needs of the woman. When Scott delivered the baby, it was a white child. Now I don't have to tell you that in Georgia in 1935 this was not acceptable to anyone. Scott had suspected that the Negro woman had been raped, but there was no way of proving it. When he pressed the woman for details, she was hesitant to tell

382

exactly what had happened. Scott wanted to know why the woman had been brought in on the bus and how the bus driver had known to pick her up in the first place.

Realizing that the whole story would come out, the bus driver told Scott and me everything, or almost everything: how he had accidentally run over a man in order to get this black woman to a doctor.

All of us realized that if the truth came out—that a white man had run over *another* white man in order to get a black woman to a doctor—the town would probably have lynched the black woman, killed the child, and then sent the bus driver to the electric chair. Everyone in town knew the man who had been run over. He was not liked by most, and Scott and I didn't think that three other people needed to be hurt. That is why we all decided to fabricate a story that the bus driver had suffered chest pains while moving his bus that morning and thought that he could drive himself to our place. We conveniently ignored the Negro woman when telling the story, pretending that she didn't exist. The bus driver's chest pains were to be his reason for speeding and the reason the bus was ahead of schedule. There was a trial and the bus driver was found not guilty, mainly because of Scott's and my testimony.

As we were leaving the courthouse, a girl of about ten years of age approached Scott and me and asked to speak with us privately. She then proceeded to inform us that she had been playing in the woods the day of the accident, become lost, and had come upon our home.

Hearing voices, she had stood under the window and listened for quite some time. In short, she knew the truth and knew that Scott and I had lied to the jury. She then related the entire scene for us with uncanny accuracy. She would have to have been there listening in order to know some of the details.

When Scott asked her what she wanted, she told him, "Nothing. For now." She simply wanted us to know that she held our fate in her hands. I'm telling you this for a reason. This ten-year-old girl was your mother.

What happened next was even more strange. After years of not hearing from the girl, we decided that she had either forgotten about the incident or had decided not to do anything about it. Then one day, Scott received a visit from her. She had moved out of town, out of state—she wouldn't tell Scott where—and was now pregnant. This was about 1950. She wanted Scott to give her an abortion and he did, telling her, "We're even now." "Not quite," she had said, leaving Scott with an uneasy feeling. But then several years passed and we went on with our lives.

About 1957, Scott and I decided to move to Infanta, Alabama, to be with the rest of the family in this house at 509 Latrobe. The first couple of months were fine, until one day when I went to answer the door, and that's when I saw her again.

She looked just as shocked as I did at first, claiming that she had lived at this address when it was a boarding house and was just curious to see the interior again.

Then she noticed your father, who was about her age, working in the front yard. She asked to meet him and I refused. She then reminded me that there was no statute of limitations on perjury. She also told me that she "had the goods" on my husband and the bus driver.

Strekfus, I did introduce her to your father, but warned him about her. I suppose I thought that she was just enjoying the power she had and that she never would really do anything with it. I also warned her that blackmail or not, she wasn't going to hurt another member of my family. At one point, I even told your father the story of her blackmailing Scott and me, but he didn't believe it; she had so charmed him that he didn't want to see the truth. As with so many people, when you tell them that something is bad for them, they seem go after it even harder, and your father and I weren't getting along too well at that point. I guess your father thought we were trying to wreck his happiness when in fact we were only trying to save him. Of course, after he married her he found out the truth, but by then it was too late.

As you probably have heard, your father was planning to divorce her and she became pregnant with you. I'm not telling you this to make you feel bad, I just thought you should know. I thought it might explain some of the things in your life—the anger your parents had, the abuse. Scott and I tried to save innocent individuals from what we felt was wrong-headedness and I'm afraid in the process, many people got hurt along the way.

The disease which I have will not only take away these bad memories, but the good ones also. I hope you can forgive Scott and me for what we did. I helped take care of your father when he got sick because I loved him, but also out of guilt for introducing him to your mother. I hope I've done some good in this world. Just remember that I love you with all my heart,

Tessie

In addition to the letter was the newspaper clipping from the *Edwina Times*. It told how Brad Castratis had been struck down, what time, and where. What it didn't tell was the story of my mother—that, I had just gotten from Testa.

It was the sound of the gas-station attendant that brought me back to reality. "Are you all right?" he asked to the closed window on my side of the car, his face bent down to my level.

"Yes. Yes, I'm sorry," I said, rolling down the window and letting several night insects in. I folded the letter and put it back in its envelope.

"Well, y'all need to be either getting some gas or moving along, now, ye hear? We can't have people just sitting here."

"I know," I said, "I'm sorry, I was just looking at a map. Just temporarily lost."

"Well, if you need any help," he said, "just let me know. That's what we're here for," and he patted the door of the car and then hobbled back inside the station to his stool where he proceeded to read that day's paper, probably for the second or third time.

"All right. Fine. Thank you. Yes, I will," I said to myself, as he was already inside, and with that I started Belle's car and pulled out of the station.

When I arrived back at 509 Latrobe, Testa was upstairs asleep and my aunt and cousin were in the den. Belle was watching television and Suzanne was rummaging through the bookshelves, having pulled out at least twelve volumes of books on the Civil War and its aftermath. I told them that I hadn't gone to see a friend, that I had been reading Testa's letter, and then I showed it to both of them. For a long time none of us said anything. My aunt turned down the sound on the TV and Suzanne casually flipped through one of the coffee table books on Reconstruction.

"What do you plan to do?" my aunt asked.

"Well, for starters, I'd like to confront my mother with this."

"Do you think it would do any good?"

"I'm not sure," I said. "I've got to sleep on it. It's pretty heavy stuff."

"Here it is," said Suzanne, having now found the coveted bit of information she was looking for. "It's a whole paragraph devoted to the capture of General R.P.T.P Marshall after Lee surrendered."

Belle and I just looked at each other, not quite understanding what the general had to do with my mother. Suzanne explained, seeing our puzzled expressions.

"Well, we were talking about him earlier today and I think I've figured it out." She began to read from the leather-bound volume while Belle and I just looked at each other. Suzanne, evidently was not quite as concerned with my mother's story as Belle and I were.

The capture of General Marshall should be noted as it is of some important historic significance. Around two thirty on the afternoon of the fifth, Union soldiers stopped two ladies on a rarely traveled road just outside of Ripley, Mississippi. After questioning both ladies, a commanding officer became suspicious of what appeared to be day-old beard growth on one of the Confederate females. Removing the woman's bonnet, the officer made the discovery that the suspect was indeed General Marshall, completely outfitted with hoopskirt, corset, and pantaloons. It was suspected that General Marshall was attempting to flee the area in order to evade authorities who were in the process of securing him for his arrest. The other female was identified as his wife.

"Well it makes sense, doesn't it?" she continued, looking from Belle and to me. "General Marshall was in drag. He was a Civil War drag queen. Fred is a cross-dressing ghost. Fred is General Marshall. When the family moved from the Prytania Street house, Fred, who is really General Marshall, followed us. He's just updated his wardrobe now."

Belle and I just looked at one another. I opened my mouth, but just as I did something happened.

It was then that we heard it—a sound like nothing we had ever heard before—a scream that seemed to come from the very bowels of the earth. My aunt and cousin jumped up—the fastest I'd ever seen them move—and started in the direction of the hallway leading to the kitchen, the same direction I was already headed in. When we reached the door to the kitchen we found it locked. Testa had locked it and it was her scream that had pierced the evening, but it wasn't coming from the kitchen. The screams continued at full volume, so loud that they sounded as if they were happening in the same room even though the walls of the house were almost two feet thick in places. Testa howled as though someone were tearing her internal organs out, one at a time. With each scream, the pain in her voice increased until the primal sound wove itself into an almost continuous unwavering pitch.

Fueled by her hysteria, I ran around to the other end of the house where another hallway connecting the living room to the dining room allowed me access to the kitchen.

As I entered the kitchen, I saw the door to the basement open, and as I started down the stairs I realized that Belle and Suzanne had caught up with me. None of us hesitated to descend the stairs. Suddenly, at the bottom of the steps I stopped, causing Belle and Suzanne to run into me like some bad comedy routine. Testa, at that exact moment, ceased her vocalizations as quickly as she had begun them. She had been this way all right, and she had managed to smash the one light bulb hanging above the foot of the stairs—the light which would have illuminated the basement. The only reason we had been able to make it as far down the stairs was because of the light from the kitchen.

"Have you got any candles?" I asked, turning quickly to Belle.

"We've been through this."

"What about a flashlight?"

Before I even had the words out of my mouth Suzanne bounded back up the stairs and returned with an enormous twelve-inch, yellow-cased light, its beam already on and dancing around the basement walls. She handed it to me and we stepped carefully onto the damp dirt floor.

"Testa?" I called, and aimed the beam of the light into corners and through decades-old cobwebs. The light cruelly illuminated broken chairs, boxes overflowing with papers and magazines, and remnants from my grandparents' past. The effect was like that of a *National Geographic* special with underwater divers shining their invasive lights on the interior of a shipwreck which had not been seen by human eyes for a hundred years. I felt a tinge of guilt for disturbing such a place, but it was mixed with anticipation at what else I might find.

After scouring the main part of the basement with my searchlight and finding nothing, my hand instinctively jerked in the direction of some whimpering which seemed to come from a far alcove where the coal chute was located.

"Testa," I said, as the beam caught in her hair and pulled her slowly around. When she had made a full revolution, all three of us sucked in the damp basement air at the same time.

Her face was like that of a wild animal. It was contorted beyond belief. She was also covered with dirt and her hands were bleeding. Her nightgown was torn and she seemed to be shaking so violently that we thought she was going to have a heart attack. She brought her hands to her anguished face, and as she moved them down, blood and dirt streaked her cheeks.

Before we knew what was happening she lunged past us, past the beam of light, and up the stairs. It seemed that she had gathered strength from someplace yet unknown to us. She slammed the basement door and we heard the sickening sound of the hundred-year-old latch snap into place. We were left with only the warm beam of light shining up after her.

"What are we going to do now?" asked my aunt with disgust in her voice.

"Forget about that," said my cousin, "did you see the way she looked? And what was she doing down here anyway?"

"Look, I'll climb out the coal chute and go around and open the door," I said, and began picking my way across the uneven dirt floor as quickly as I could. Just as I was about to reach the chute, I tripped and fell over something.

Shining the light at my side I could see a shovel in the exact location where Testa had been. Obviously she had been down here trying to bury some object she thought valuable. She had managed to dig up a good portion of the soft earth which covered the floor. It was then that the light scraped across something else—something old and worn, and something which glinted in the half-light—gold and dusty.

On my knees now and holding the flashlight as far away as I could, I discovered what had upset Testa so much. There, beneath the dust-swirling beam was what appeared to be an aging and cracked alligator bag, inside of which was another bag and some plastic. The entire ensemble was quite old and decomposing. Testa had pulled the decaying remnants of the bag open and exposed what looked like some ancient dirty rags. She may not have been able to tell what was in the bag, but she had recognized the receptacle itself and knew the story behind it. There on the decomposing bag were the peeling gold, broken letters, A.I.W., for the Atlanta Infirmary for Women.

We all stared at it for an instant and then, either because we knew we had to get out of the basement or because we wanted momentary denial, none of us said anything. It was as though we weren't sure what we had seen and didn't want to confirm it until we were at least out of the basement and in more familiar territory. There would be plenty of time later to discuss what we had found. For now, we had to get into the air above us where we could see things as they really were.

We worked together in silence, quickly moving bits of coal and furniture to make a platform high enough for me to climb onto and reach the coal-chute door.

I don't remember hoisting myself out of the basement through the opening. I don't remember unlocking the door to the basement and letting my aunt and cousin out. I don't remember much of anything that is, until we were in the car and driving. My mind was reeling, going through all the possibilities. I had been given too much information today and I felt sick.

We hadn't even bothered to look for Testa in the house—we knew she wouldn't be there. None of us had spoken a word. It was as if we knew what was going to happen, as if we had all come to the same conclusion and had set about the task without question. It was as if it were already written in some great book, heavy and covered with dust, and as if all we could do now was follow the sentences, one by one, to the conclusion some unseen and morose author had written—his sick, moribund fantasy finally played out.

We piled into my aunt's car, and after running two red lights we sped toward the neighborhood located nearest the river, finally turning onto an unlit street. We were headed to the apartment where my mother lived, a short distance from my aunt's house. The night air was thick with the sounds of insects and a full moon shone its obscene, female light onto the tops of the trees lining the street. Everything seemed to be magnified as it always is after some cathartic event.

We were less than three blocks from our destination when we heard the gunshot. It was at that point that my aunt slowed the car, knowing we were too late, knowing that we were only one sentence away from the end of this pathetic chapter in our lives.

Missing the driveway of the small apartment complex where my mother now lived, the car jerked over the low curb and came to rest facing the front door of my mother's apartment. The headlights shone onto the scene with the intensity of a Hollywood premiere. An occasional moth flitted into the light and then disappeared, and as our eyes adjusted we took in the scene.

My mother lay sprawled on the small front porch, a bullet wound to her chest, with Testa standing over her, gun hanging at her side. Somehow Testa had found the key to her husband's sequestered guns, the ones Belle had thought were safely put away, had taken one either before or while we were locked in the basement. She now stood there holding the prize of the litter. She stood holding the Le Mat revolver that had once belonged to General Marshall.

With the car lights illuminating the scene and distant sounds of police sirens approaching, Testa slowly turned toward us. Feeling like passive viewers at a bad drive-in horror movie, we watched as her eyes took on an accepting and serene quality, probably for the first time since the day her husband had delivered a baby in Edwina, Georgia, back in 1935.

She looked directly at us as we sat frozen in the car, and with the calm, slow determination of a performer in a kabuki play, lifted the gun to her head, placed the barrel into her mouth, moved her thumb to the alternate chamber containing the buckshot, and pulled the trigger.

- 21 -

New York, 1997

> But the angel of forgetfulness has
> gathered and carried away much of the
> misery and all the bitterness of those sad
> days.
>
> —Helen Keller, *The Story of My Life*

I t was as if someone were watching out for him, as if some
invisible force had said that his time was not yet up, that
death was to be postponed a while, for no sooner had
Strekfus reached the curb than an enormous pair of hands dug
into his shoulders and pulled him back, well beyond the hard
metal bearing-down front of the bus. He couldn't understand
why he hadn't seen it, this monster of steel and speed, as it raced
toward him, and why the bus driver hadn't seen *him*. He had only
a second to reflect. It seemed that his mind was spinning out of
control. It was early morning and Strekfus felt obscene having to
get out of bed, get dressed, and pull himself through another day.
And it was cold. A gray mist hung over everything and seemed to
dull the sharp edges and sounds of Manhattan. Was that why he
hadn't heard the bus coming? Had he been so preoccupied with
the events of the last month that his mind was now nothing more
than a tired, worn-out thing, barely able to hold onto reality? He
felt as if his defenses were worn away, as if he were coming down
with a cold.

Strekfus turned now to the yet-unseen person who had saved him. It seemed at first that the individual blended in with everyone else on Fifth Avenue at that hour—thousands of fast-moving, determined people, all of whom seemed to be wearing black or gray and heading to some job they hated in some decaying building on some dirty street in some cold section of the city. Then he realized what made this person, this angel, this savior, this rare individual whose hands had just pulled him out of the path of a speeding bus, different from the others: the man was smiling.

He remembered how he had once seen a clown standing in front of Macy's years earlier. The clown was making balloon animals, happily twisting them into shapes which resembled dachshunds, mosquitoes, DNA molecules. As pedestrians walked by, the entertainer would throw some amusing comment their way, begging them to smile. As Strekfus passed, the clown announced that the first person to smile would receive a balloon. He moved on, hearing the clown repeat the phrase over and over until the voice faded into the traffic noise. Several hours later, after some job interview or errand he had run, he walked back to that same street. The clown was still there, and so were no less than fifty balloon animals. It seemed that this technician of smiles had not been able to give them away—facial dispositions of New Yorkers being what they usually are.

So now Strekfus connected for a moment with this man who had pulled him from the path of the bus—this smiling man with no balloons—this man who separated himself from the crowd which pressed on to early morning jobs—and as they stood there facing each other Strekfus took stock of the man's features.

A grin made deep creases in his handsome face which, though it was freshly shaved, appeared already to have a five o'clock shadow. The individual seemed to be of Arabic or Mediterranean descent. When the stranger spoke, a glint of gold appeared. A long blue-black overcoat covered most of him, the collar upturned around his face.

"You should be more careful," he said in a thick, strong accent from some land Strekfus couldn't place. "You could have been killed."

"Yes, thank you," Strekfus managed, as the determined workers brushed past, jostling him every three seconds or so. "You saved me. My life. You pulled me to . . ." but no matter what words he tried to find, they all seemed inadequate, false. A hundred ramifications ran through Strekfus's mind. Was this person going to expect something? Should he be happy that the man had pulled him out from the path of the bus? Should he be glad to be alive? And he was glad to be alive, it was just that he had so much on his mind that he wasn't sure what he was feeling or why.

"It's not your time," the man was saying, as Strekfus mentally returned to the scene.

"Look. Thank you. I really feel stupid about this. Thank you, really," he heard himself saying as he touched the sleeve of the man's coat in appreciation. His guardian angel seemed satisfied, not by the appreciativeness but rather by the fact that Strekfus now seemed to have recovered from his traumatic experience. The stranger began to leave, raising a prosaic upturned hand which seemed to signal that nothing more was needed, and he pivoted and joined the crowd moving up the avenue.

"Is there anything I can do to . . ." Strekfus started to say, but the man was gone, blending into the crowd from which he came. Then it hit him, what the man had said—that it wasn't his time yet.

"What's the matter with me?" thought Strekfus as he headed toward the subway entrance and down into the dark, oily subterranean caves which housed the city's major mode of transportation. He tried to shake off this feeling he had—a feeling that he needed to do something, that it was time for action—but it wouldn't leave him. It was like some small, lost child who, finding your hand, refuses to let go until you locate its parent, clinging to you helpless and at the same time persistent as a bad case of head lice. Sure, he was under some stress. After all,

394

he had just returned from home where his Aunt Testa had killed his mother and then herself. Who wouldn't be stressed? And if that weren't enough, he had endured not one, but two funerals. Then there was the cleaning out of his mother's apartment with its boxes of papers and income tax statements and the will. There was the storage of her belongings until it could be decided what to do with them, the final locking of the front door, the remembering, the pain. All of this was on his mind as the number 6 train rattled and bounced through the bowels of New York, hurtling him toward Times Square, the shuttle, Grand Central, and then his job just a few blocks away.

Aware that he was moving through the revolving doors to the lobby of his building, he couldn't remember how he had gotten there. He remembered nothing of the walk between Grand Central and the building he worked in, but the touch of the cold metal bar, the sound of the heavy glass doors as they scraped over the rubber entranceway, the difference of air and light and humidity as he was deposited into the lobby, all seemed momentarily to awaken him.

He made his way over to the small newsstand in the lobby. It boasted those items which, while seemingly frivolous, could at times become necessities in the city: mints and gums of every conceivable description, shape, and size; cigarette lighters; aspirin; Hostess Twinkies; assorted bagels and fruit; and a medium-sized cooler, lighted and clean, which displayed rows of soft drinks and bottled waters. He sleepily asked for a tea with milk and waited for the usual curled lips and crinkled nose of someone standing nearby. It always happened: Someone would say, "Tea with milk?" as if he had asked for a colonic. Had these people never been to England or at least watched a Merchant-Ivory film? He was feeling cynical, confused, judgmental. What was so unusual in New York about tea with milk? Sure, most New Yorkers drank coffee, but wasn't this supposed to be a tolerant city?

After paying for his purchase with exact change, he sauntered past the security guards and toward the bank of elevators which would take him to his new office—the one without the burned smell and melted file folders.

The elevator ride today was fortunately a non-event. Lately the cars had been getting stuck. The week before he left for Alabama five passengers had enjoyed one another's company for two hours while workmen tried to free them. Finally the doors opened and he was released onto the gray industrial carpeting. He made his way past the new receptionist. Her head was buried in a book while several lines of the switchboard blinked and lights accompanied the odd sounds which had so long ago replaced ringing.

It seemed that he had just removed his coat and sat down, his hand on the plastic lid of his tea, when Sagaser's secretary appeared at his door, looking rather like the bearer of bad news which she would prove to be.

"Mr. Sagaser would like to see you," she announced with a grimacing face that said, "I'm sorry. Don't blame me. I had nothing to do with it."

Shuffling toward Sagaser's office, he tried to brace himself for what might come. It had not been a good morning so far. He had nearly been run over by a bus and his body was feeling the effects of travel, stress, and being back at a job which neither fulfilled him nor paid him that much money. He had been suffering through a repertoire of nightmares lately that would rival anything on the silver screen, and in addition he hadn't told anyone about the death of his aunt or mother. As was usual in this office, no one would ask about his trip and he couldn't help but feel grateful, knowing that the less information he gave his co-workers, the better off he was. He had not even seen Sharon since his return—he was too tired to explain everything that had happened. He stopped at the narrow door to his boss's office and waited, completely drained, completely soft, completely ready to give up.

"Come in. Sit down," Sagaser said curtly while writing something, never looking up. It was clear that the man was already seething and it was barely nine o'clock. He had not been happy with Strekfus for some time now. There had been the fire and the month off that the writer had taken in order to care for sick relatives.

"The intimidation continues, or a least the condescension," said Strekfus under his breath as he entered and took a seat, unconsciously feeling the rough black burlap-like material which covered the chair. He thought he saw his boss flinch. Had Sagaser heard him?

"I need you to start on this next project as soon as possible," Sagaser said. He was now handing Strekfus some sort of documentation. It had something to do with an article he was to write on Palissy wear, those ominous-looking plates and pitchers covered in ceramic lichens, lizards, and snakes. It was the farthest thing from Strekfus's mind at that moment, and after the instructions were given and he got up to leave, the writer let out an enormous sigh which was anything but intentional.

The instant he did so, Strekfus realized his mistake, for there was enough electricity in the air to power a small Alaskan town. He felt Sagaser's eyes staring at him. But it was only an instant that the stare lasted. In a split second Sagaser was standing, moving, coming from behind his desk and straight for Strekfus. A blind person in the room could have seen Sagaser's anger such was its force. The man had obviously been keeping his resentment bottled up while Strekfus was away and had now decided to let it completely out.

Strekfus knew what was happening. He knew his sigh had set Sagaser off and there was no turning back. It was as if the man needed just one small incident for all of his frustrations to come out, and once opened, the valve which had held them in for so long refused to close. It was as if Sagaser had been waiting for this moment, breaking Strekfus down, tearing away at him, hoping to find something to admonish him with, and it happened with the speed of a striking snake. Strekfus had been able to tell that his boss was in a mood, but he never expected this and certainly not for something as innocuous as a sigh. Certainly not on his first day back after two funerals and all the other things his mind was forcing him to endure.

"I've had it with you," Sagaser was saying, charging forward with the energy of a freight train, a finger pointing directly at Strekfus's nose. "You've been nothing but trouble for me, embarrassing me, showing me up in front of the others. I'm through. Do you hear me?" Sagaser was now standing directly in front of Strekfus, and as the writer got up, their noses were practically touching.

While the outburst had shocked Strekfus, he found he wasn't responding, wasn't reacting other than by simply standing up. It was as though he were seeing the scene from high above, protected and unafraid. He felt an enormous calm taking over his body, probably because of his extreme tiredness which now protected him by not allowing him to have the normal adrenaline rush that would have accompanied a scene such as this. It was as if he were in a concrete bunker, completely safe and warm while outside the storm raged and destroyed everything in its path. He could hear Sagaser's rantings but his mind was on something else at the moment. He felt as though he couldn't shake his morning mood. It was the same feeling he had experienced after almost being run over. He was glad he was alive, but all reaction was gone from him. It was as if he were overdrawn from his emotional bank account and there was no Checking Plus to cover it. Testa, his mother, the letter about his father, Sagaser's rantings the weeks before his trip, all had taken their toll and he was now dead inside, feeling nothing, completely vacant. He thought of himself as one of those cavernous New York apartments (the ones no one can afford) after the owners have moved out— vacant and yawning, waiting for something or someone to fill them up again with energy and memories and life.

And for this very reason, because of Strekfus's extreme tiredness and emotional drain during the past few weeks, he was able to remain somewhat detached, at least for the time being. He didn't have the energy to fight—not yet. The moment Sagaser reached his space and stood in front of him, Strekfus looked away, to the right top of Sagaser's desk, and he marveled at the human brain and how it could piece something together in an instance such as this.

Had his mind been sharp as it usually was, constantly taking in everything in sight, the obvious would have escaped him. But not now. Now his relaxed stance aided him, allowed him to see things he had never seen before—the way death and love changes the color of leaves on the trees and how food tastes. It had been there all along. He had just been too caught up in life to notice.

There on Sagaser's desk was a pack of cigarettes, and something about the angle at which they precariously rested on the edge reminded him of what the fireman had said: "Evidently someone had placed a cigarette on the edge of the desk and it had rolled into the trash can." It all made sense now. The fire in his office, started by a cigarette, one he hadn't been smoking; the KKK application; the FBI. He suddenly realized that Sagaser had been behind all the incidents. So that was why he had insisted to upper management that he wanted three stories in advance. He had turned the tables on Strekfus, taking elements from his stories and torturing him with them.

The fire set by Roman Yapigacy was now the fire set by Edwin Sagaser. The Grand Dragon in the story hadn't sent the application to Strekfus—Sagaser had. And it had been Sagaser who had anonymously contacted the FBI to inform them of alleged drug trafficking, which corresponded perfectly with his college stories about drugs and the FBI incident in the Sul Ross story. Sagaser was even slinging metaphysical feces in Strekfus's direction, just as Bunny had done toward the windows of the neighbors in Houston. The only thing missing in Sagaser's case was the orange kitchen spatula.

But before Strekfus could respond to this newly realized information, something else was happening—making itself known. It flashed for an instant in his mind, this picture of something tiled and green, something hard and abusive. He heard a tear, like some great canvas pulling apart and revealing what lay underneath as his eyes took in Sagaser's grimacing face. It was like a bad cartoon, this face of his boss. It undulated and writhed like the face of some dark reptile from another era. Strekfus could see the man's bridgework, his yellow teeth with their spaces and dark openings. He could see the very pores of the man's skin, so close was he to his boss.

Strekfus couldn't remember how or when he got back into the chair. He had been standing just a moment before in an attempt to flee the scene, but it didn't matter now. Sagaser was over him, screaming, his eyes bulging, his breath fetid and thick, and Strekfus could no longer hear the words—he could only see the violent lips move and the veins bulge from his boss's forehead. And in that instant he became aware that Sagaser was holding his wrists down onto the arms of the chair. He felt himself losing his grip on reality as if there were another dimension which people couldn't see but which one could slip into by finding the narrow opening and timing things just right.

Then the tearing sound again. Now the image, staying in his mind for a moment longer. He was on some sort of horrific journey, unable to stop, and he knew that it must be ridden out, fought with, wrestled to the ground like some angel of death which wanted to take him ahead of his time, like some runaway bus which had his name on it. The tear happened once more and there was an instant when he saw not the face of his boss standing over him, but that of his father. Both men were one and both had the same ugly, pouting, twisted mouth now spewing hatred and disgust.

The canvas was now completely torn away and he was once again eleven years old, a frightened, crying little boy, completely helpless as his father pulled him into a hospital emergency room, past staring nurses, elderly women, and someone holding a bandage on some bleeding wound. He remembered his father's rage over his fear of hospitals and doctors, but he also remembered what he thought was his father's love for him as the man pulled Strekfus into the operating room, wanting him to lose his fear. His father was proud of this hospital which mended and fixed and smoothed the lives of the people in town. How could Strekfus not feel the same way as his father? How dare he cause his father pain. How dare he be such a bad son, such a bad employee, such a bad person.

His father was now saying how there was nothing to be afraid of, how there was nothing that could hurt him and how did he ever expect to become a doctor if he didn't learn to curtail his fear of the medical profession. He was trying to explain to his father that he didn't want to be a doctor, but the words were falling on deaf ears, being sucked into some third-dimension vacuum toward the future and then back again into the past. His father was becoming more and more angry, pulling Strekfus farther and farther into the operating room. Strekfus remembered seeing a nurse as she bravely inserted her face into the echoing arena, then his father ordering her out of "his" operating room. He remembered how everyone in the town feared his father, how his father was best friends with the police and other law enforcement officials in the town, how no one crossed his father, how people stayed out of his way. Strekfus knew that even if he cried for help, no one would come.

Sagaser's rage had almost peaked now. He was walking about the room, throwing his hands into the air, using expletives. His anger moved from his face to his body and it was as if a downed power line were flailing about the room, just missing Strekfus with its energy and death, snapping about his head like some electric viper intent on torturing its victim before moving in for the kill.

Then his father was showing him the medical instruments and his fear was becoming more and more intense. His father was becoming enraged and finally, exploding, the man grasped the handle of one of the drawers which lined the mint-green tiled walls and flung its contents into the center of the room. Shiny scalpels, bright needles, cotton gauzes, and flexible yellow tubing suspended themselves in mid-air for a moment like some twisted Salvador Dali painting. It seemed that Strekfus held them there with his mind for as long as he could, knowing that when they hit the floor another wave of anger from his father would begin.

And it did. His father was now pulling him over to the drawers, his large hand gripping Strekfus's wrist, cutting off the circulation. He was tearing the drawers from their resting places with one arm, hurling the contents into the air and onto the floor,

401

saying over and over, "See, there's nothing to be afraid of. Why are you afraid? Why are you afraid?" Strekfus was now more terrified than ever and his eyes gave him away. He knew that the moment his father looked at him and saw his fear that it would be all over. He knew that his father would destroy him as he sought to destroy all those around him whom he considered weak and unworthy of life.

Sagaser was now out of control. He was moving his thick forearm, raking the entire contents on the top of his desk onto the floor, kicking the papers, the binders, with such force that they flew up against the wall and landed on the sofa and chairs. Another swift kick and a paperweight flew under the sofa, dislodging a solitary golf ball which was now rolling in Strekfus's direction. For some reason, the writer's eyes focused on the ball, and as it rolled toward him he seemed to bend in its direction. The ball seemed to grow with such strength that it now became enormous—a boulder rolling in Strekfus's direction in order to crush him.

He felt himself being lifted up into the air and suspended just as the surgical instruments had been, only he seemed to hover there longer. Was his father holding him there, like some offering to the gods or was this just his imagination? But then the reality of the situation came back and he was slammed down onto the operating table with such force that his breath was knocked out of him. There was no time to be sick, no time to panic. There was only time for survival of the body and mind. His psyche shut down for a minute—blackness—then he was once again aware of his surroundings.

"What are you afraid of?" his father was screaming, holding him down, looking directly into his face with gritted teeth and wild eyes. As his father's feet kicked the fallen instruments away they rang out against the tiled walls. "Why are you so stupid?" he asked over and over, and with each question he picked Strekfus up and slammed him down onto the table as if he were a rag doll, over and over and over, until Strekfus began to count the times in his mind, thinking that the very act of keeping track of the blows would take him to another place.

402

"You think I'm going to hurt you? Is that what you want? Is that what you want?" his father was screaming. "Is that what you want? Is that what you want?" And then the room began to turn slowly. He could see what was happening, but now there was no sound, only the beating of his heart and the blood rushing to his ears. He seemed to rise up from the table and view his body from above. He seemed to float high in the ether-and-antiseptic air, far above the operating lights, the hoses, the medical instruments normally reserved for saving lives.

He could see his father pulling up the heavy rubber straps which hung down from the sides of the operating table, see them stretch as his father pulled them high over him, tying them together and letting them snap back down onto his body, hitting him with a sharp pain, like some giant rubber band. He felt the sting of them as they crashed into his body, the first strap breaking one of his ribs. The muffled snap of bone seemed to vibrate through his entire body. He couldn't allow his mind to dwell on that. There was too much else to think about. His father was tying his chest down, then his legs, then moving on to his wrists, tying them now with hate, frustration, anger, tying the straps tighter and tighter. In his mind Strekfus was crying, "No, I love you, I love you, please stop," hoping that if he thought it strongly enough his father would hear, that some God would hear, that anything in the world would hear and make the torture cease.

And then, "I'm sorry I was afraid, I'm sorry, I'm sorry, I'm sorry." Surely if he loved his father enough right now, at this moment, if he could get past the pain and the suffering, then he could mentally get through to his father—speak to him with his mind. He strained with all his energy but it was no use—the nightmare wouldn't end. And it seemed that his body was now vibrating continuously, as if the tremor from his broken rib was gaining energy, shaking him as a bolt of electricity shakes its victim before releasing him to death.

Sagaser was livid, his entire body contorting. As he screamed at Strekfus, completely out of control, saliva flew from his mouth and his hands flew from his body with violent intent, accompanied by violent words. With one singular, animalistic movement he grasped the back of his chair and hurled it against a small table, sending a lamp crashing to the floor.

Strekfus knew his father's mouth was moving and that there were sounds emerging as the medical instruments were flung about the room, but he could hear nothing as the entire scene was now accompanied only by the beating sound in his head. He saw his father pull the heavy fibrous silver tape off the roll, tear it, and place it over his mouth, winding the excess around the back of his head. He saw the man reach for something—a switch—and turn on huge glaring lights over the table. He saw the tray of instruments his father jerked over, some of the scalpels and forceps flying off the tray and hitting the floor, but he could not hear their metallic song several feet below as the room now seemed to spin quickly and become distorted. He tried to concentrate on the textured weave of the sterile cloth that the remaining instruments rested on. He tried to make his mind go into the neat squares which made up the design— anything to escape. He could see Sagaser now, ripping the cord which held the blinds, pulling them from the window, exposing the brilliant sun which screamed at them both like some howling animal.

He could see his father positioning the operating room lamp into his eyes. He could see his father's mouth moving angrily now, hysterically, as the man picked up a scalpel and held it over him; his father tearing Strekfus's shirt open, then moving to his son's waist. He felt the heavy denim fabric of his pants being torn downward until the rubber bindings stopped their progression, then his underwear being stripped away and his pants being ripped with the scalpel, expertly stripped away from his thin legs. He was completely naked now, vulnerable. And now the bright, shiny scalpel, moving in slow motion toward him, held by a man who seemed to have trouble breathing.

There was laughter from somewhere. Carnival sounds. Death. Women in tight suits. A stack of papers strewn on the floor. Someone had a scalpel and was bringing it down slowly toward him. He was standing in some modern office, reaching

404

for a doorframe, trying to escape from someone. He was seeing the hallway, the open area, the square, impersonal fluorescent lights, the secretaries in their tight suits—their breasts stretching the material. Their laughter at something. A typewriter. Sounds. Something cold. A metallic taste in his mouth. His father. Sagaser. A light.

Then as if saved by some large, silent bird from another land which swung down from the vermilion sky and lifted him up, darkness overtook him. It was closing about him, sheltering him, protecting him. For before the scalpel touched him he was in a land of blankness and peace, in a land where the smooth, warm waters washed over his body and he was safe.

- 22 -

The House on Prytania Street

New Orleans, Louisiana, 1997

> Consequently my work was painfully
> slow, and I had to read the examples over
> and over before I could form any idea of
> what I was required to do. Indeed, I am
> not sure now that I read all the signs
> correctly. I found it very hard to keep my
> wits about me.
>
> —Helen Keller, *The Story of My Life*

My Dear Mr. Beltzenschmidt,

This is in response to your letter about your family having once lived in my home. Many people have claimed to have lived in this house. Your disillusionment is a mystery to me, and why you would want to make such a claim is beyond my grasp. Before 1935, this was a tenement house, no electricity, no plumbing, a family lived in each room, dead cow in the backyard, etc. It took a year to restore the house. You may see the interior if I am here but I am going to Maine next week.

Sincerely,

Ima Chitbill-Tallymen

The letter made me uneasy. I kept trying to reason that Mrs. Chitbill-Tallymen hadn't meant the tone to be so harsh, but it bothered me nonetheless. A dead cow? My grandparents had a dead cow? Or even one that was alive at one time? What was the cow's name for Christ's sake? And the hand this note was written in looked aged and crooked, like some great un-pruned wisteria vine whose gnarled and looping curves were attempting to send a message out, one other than the written and obvious communication. I picked up the phone and called information.

"Mrs. Ima Chitbill-Tallymen in New Orleans," I said.

Immediately I dialed. Normally I would allow myself a cooling-off period, but I was curious and angry she had written such a negative letter.

"Mrs. Chitbill-Tallymen?" I asked, when a voice answered the phone.

"Yes."

"This is Strekfus Beltzenschmidt. I wrote you a letter about . . ."

"No, I've already subscribed."

"I'm sorry, I'm not selling anything, I . . ."

"Hello? Hello? Just a . . . I have to turn up my hearing aid . . . there . . . go ahead," she mumbled.

"This is Strekfus Beltzenschmidt. I wrote . . ."

"Oh, yes. You wrote me that nice letter. Yes, I remember you."

"I want to apologize to you," I said, backing down somewhat, thinking that I might get more information with kindness rather than antagonism, the whole time trying not to choke. "I didn't mean to imply that my family lived in that house at the same time yours did. I had the wrong dates. They lived there from 1922 to 1935."

"No, we've not had much rain," she said. I realized at this point that she was stone-deaf and the hearing aid wasn't helping much. If I yelled into the phone she could hear me. I started again.

407

"I had the wrong dates. My family lived in the house from 1922 to 1935," I screamed.

"Well, you know, I find that very interesting, because it was a tenement house. There was no running water, no electricity, a dead cow in the backyard."

"Yes, ma'am," I screamed.

"It took a year to restore," she went on.

"Yes, ma'am. Well, my family lived there in the '20s."

"It was a tenement house then. My friend was over here the day your letter arrived and she said, Ima, that was a tenement house, no electricity, no plumbing, a dead cow in the backyard."

"Yes, ma'am," I shrieked. My voice was getting hoarse.

"This was not a nice neighborhood then. It took a year for us to restore this house."

"Yes, ma'am."

"So if your family lived here, they lived in a tenement house."

"Well, I guess they did, then," I said, hoping that agreeing with her would put an end to her rambling.

"Well, I certainly wouldn't want anyone to know my family had lived in a tenement house."

"If that's the truth, then there's nothing I can do to change that," I screamed. "I would still like to see the inside of the house if you would allow me." The reality was that I wanted to wring her neck, but I knew that if I argued she'd never let me see the place.

"Well, I'm going to Maine next week, but I will be back in the spring."

"That's fine," I said. "May I give you a call then?"

"What?"

"MAY I GIVE YOU A CALL THEN?" My vocal chords were beginning to show signs of strain.

"Yes, that's fine."

I hung up, feeling better at least about the prospect of seeing the inside of the house, and called my Aunt Belle.

Aunt Belle is my father's sister. The two of them, along with my Aunt Testa and another brother, Sebastian, grew up in the house on Prytania Street. Sadly, three of the siblings were now dead, leaving only my Aunt Belle. Testa had died just a short time ago, but before her death she was known by the family as a vast repository of information. She remembered everything before her Alzheimer's set in, often having regaled me with stories about the Prytania Street house, sans mention of plumbing and electrical problems. Testa's death had triggered in me a desire to know more about my family and where we had come from. It was because of her death and other recent revelations that I was now prying into the tightly shuttered confines of the Prytania Street house, hoping to experience what it had been like to live there; hoping to find some answer as to why my family had become, well . . . my family. I was still living in New York, but I found myself drawn more and more to the South and where I had come from. I needed to know what my father's life had been like, what had made him the way he was, what had caused his anger, his frustrations, his sense of right and wrong (if any), and my only hope now was whatever light my Aunt Belle might shed on the family—that and a visit to this historic home in New Orleans.

I couldn't help but feel that by visiting the physical surroundings that my father had grown up in, that perhaps I could better understand him and, in the long run, better understand myself and the relationship we had endured. But that would have to wait. For now, all I had was my aunt. I picked up the phone and called her.

"Well, I got a letter back from Mrs. Chitbill-Tallymen."

"What did she say?"

"It wasn't quite what I thought it would be."

"Was she nasty?"

"How did you know?"

"Oh, honey, the Garden District is very snooty. I'm surprised she gave you the time of day. What did she say?"

I read her the letter.

"That's a lie," she said, when I told her about the electricity and plumbing. "All of the light fixtures were made for gas and electricity and there were three bathrooms in the house in 1922."

"I'm just reading you what she wrote," I said. "Don't shoot the messenger."

"And there never was a dead cow in the backyard. Now let me think. I do know that Testa said that at one time Daddy kept a cow, but you know that house had lots of property and there was even a barn way in the back. That property went way back and those people sold off a lot of it to pay for the renovations they did. I mean in those days you didn't have grocery stores like you do now. New Orleans wasn't as up-to-date as the rest of the world. If you wanted chicken for dinner, well, you went down to the French Market and bought a live chicken, brought it home, and took it out back and wrung its neck. Things were very different back then."

"My grandmother used to wring chicken's necks?"

"No, no, not your grandmother. The cook would do it. You know, we had a cook and a gardener. We didn't keep any chickens in the yard, but you sure had to have a live one if you wanted dinner."

"Well, I know my father said at one time he had a pet duck he used to walk around on a leash."

"Yeah, your daddy was a little strange, but you know, *his* daddy wouldn't let him have a dog. And I don't remember him being crazy about the duck either. And that Chitbill-Tallymen woman's statement about different families living there is just a lie. Our daddy padlocked the front gate every night so no one could get in or out. That doesn't sound like a convenient way to run a tenement house." Okay, I thought. They lived in a tenement house with a cook and a gardener. Not a bad set-up.

I knew what Aunt Belle was saying was true. Knowing what I did about our family and especially my grandfather, the family was a very closed organization. Visitors were rarely allowed, and he was an extremely private person. He wouldn't have dreamed of having boarders in the house. None of his children were allowed to play with anyone in the neighborhood— at least they weren't allowed to admit it to my grandfather. This time-honored family tradition was carried down to my father and I had carried it down one step further: I didn't have, and didn't plan to ever have children, so there was no possibility of my repeating the same mistakes my relatives had participated in. It was almost as if God had ordained for me not to have a family, as if he were saying, "Enough—you people just can't seem to get it right."

This aversion to playmates was only one aspect of my grandfather's controlling personality. As I understand it, when he wanted to go to bed, my grandmother had to go to bed also, and some part of his body had to touch hers at all times. In the event that she tried to get up, he would know she was moving and would then immediately question her about where she was off to. Of course, my grandmother found ways around her husband's eccentricities, occasionally sneaking a hot water bottle into bed so that she could press it against her husband's thigh after he had fallen asleep, thereby escaping downstairs to the library for a game of solitaire while wearing her kimono and smoking perfumed cigarettes. But other than these stolen moments in the night, life for her could not have been easy.

She had courted my grandfather in order to get away from home. At the time they were married my grandmother was sixteen and my grandfather was thirty-seven. He had been married once before, but his first wife had died (probably of stress), and as just about any thirty-seven-year-old man would be, he was overjoyed to have a sixteen-year-old wife.

My grandfather was an inspector of imported goods when they met (bananas being his specialty), and the happy couple moved to Mexico City where they lived in marital bliss until Pancho Villa started a revolution and Mr. and Mrs. Isaac Beltzenschmidt had to escape in an armored railway car with only the clothes on their backs. After that, they moved to New Orleans, at first living on Camp Street and then at the Prytania Street house. It seems that grandfather had convinced the company he worked for to let him inspect bananas at the port of entry rather than the country of origin.

411

"You know how those New Orleans families can be," my aunt went on, "they want everyone to think they're the only ones who have lived in a certain house. She's just trying to get you to drop it—this idea that our family lived there."

"Yeah, I kinda got that feeling. I know some of the books about houses in the Garden District say 'only one family has ever owned the house . . .' It doesn't say who actually lived there though."

This had always been a problem for me. New Orleanians have a strange way of naming houses. For instance, the P. G. T. Beauregard house in the French Quarter was named for the general who fired the first shot on Fort Sumter. It didn't matter that he stayed in the house only a few weeks and never really owned it. No, the people of New Orleans wanted to name it the P. G. T. Beauregard house even though someone else built it and several others actually owned and lived in it for years.

If this formula holds true, the Prytania house, which my relatives had lived in for over a decade, should be named the Beltzenschmidt house simply by the fact that I wrote a letter to someone who now lived there.

I had seen pictures and descriptions of the Prytania Street house in coffee table books on New Orleans' finer homes. They were usually resplendent with visuals of lush interiors and commentaries on the families who had lived there and what part they played in the history of the city. One particular book's description of the Prytania Street house read as follows:

Only twelve families have ever owned the house on Prytania Street. The present owner is Mrs. Ima Chitbill-Tallymen. Mrs. Chitbill-Tallymen's mother was Eura Salohens and she married John Chitbill. Ima Chitbill, Eura's daughter married Scott Tallymen. Eura Salohen's father was John Salohens, a prominent attorney and one-time slave trader. The house was occupied during the Civil War by Union soldiers who used the grand piano as a feeding trough for their horses and confiscated the family silver. It has been lovingly restored and is cared for to this day by Mrs. Chitbill-Tallymen.

At the top of the page, which contained a full front view of the domicile, was the name of the house: The Barbatine—Wilks—Randolph—Woodsborough—Smith—Clancy—Wilks (no relation to the first one)—Guterier—Malahoney—Salohens—Chitbill-Tallymen House of Prytania Street.

Now don't get me wrong—New Orleans is my favorite city in the world. It's just that I think a few of their customs are a little odd, one of these being the naming of houses. Still, there are things about this below-sea-level-place that haunt me, and it is these things, these eccentricities and past memories, that force me to return time and time again.

I remember encountering the city for the first time when I was very young, having been taken there by my parents for the purpose of seeing where my father had grown up. I was overwhelmed by the mixture of cultures, sights, smells, colors, and traditions.

At one time, huge bales of cotton rested near the docks and open bags of coffee slouched on the sidewalks of the French Market. The thick walls of that building were surrounded by azaleas and fresh-cut flowers for sale. There used to be a shop near the Market which sold real stuffed alligators in numerous sizes. They were attired in every fashion statement imaginable, from Supreme Court judge to housewife, and my favorite was a Rhett and Scarlett duo—him with top hat and her complete with hoopskirt, looking slyly demure while holding a bouquet of flowers in her delicate little alligator claws.

I also remember tamales sold on the street corners, still wrapped in cornhusks. The red juice would run down on everything in sight, but it was worth experiencing the satisfaction that these homemade treats offered. And the whole time the Mississippi River rolling by overhead (New Orleans is six feet below sea level in most places) and wafting its delta air into the French Quarter, that subtropical, European transplant of

413

buildings awash in hanging baskets of ferns, dank carriageways leading to courtyards with trickling fountains, and history so thick that its taste is second only to the overpowering experience of a Southern praline.

The attractions that I loved (the bales of cotton, the open coffee bags, and the alligator store), are sadly no longer there, but the French Market is, and even the tables and chairs are from another time—if not a century ago, at least from the 1930s. I personally don't like coffee, but for some reason whenever I'm in New Orleans I can't get enough of it. The Market truly has the world's best coffee. New Orleans seemed, and still does seem, to be the most magical place on earth.

For those who prefer quieter neighborhoods, there is the Garden District which has, in my opinion, some of the most beautiful homes in the country. Greek Revival to ornate Italianate style and everything in between, it is home to some of the South's oldest and wealthiest, if not most eccentric families. I have yet to see a more beautiful oasis of live oaks, azaleas, and oleanders coupled with historic residences anywhere in the country. Whenever I need a rest from the bustle of the French Quarter I hop the streetcar, descend in the middle of St. Charles, and take a walk through this faubourg which is still happily lost in time.

By contrast with other places, New Orleans leaves them far behind. When I moved to New York after college I had been sorely disappointed: New Orleans was much livelier, more liberal, and lascivious than even Greenwich Village. Visiting Paris years later, I found that city to be a wealth of architecture and art, but without the incredible debauchery and decadence of New Orleans. New Orleans seems to have it all. Where else can you dine in some of the world's best restaurants, stroll down Royal Street and see more chandeliers for sale that you will ever encounter in your lifetime, and then head over to bawdy Bourbon Street where the bars and striptease palaces spill patrons onto the sidewalk like overturned baskets of Mardi Gras beads? There's nothing like that in New York. But in some ways New Orleans is a lot like New York: Both cities have very little to do with the rest of the country and in their minds that's just fine.

They're their own person, completely self-generated and unconcerned with what others may think.

"Now I'll tell you, your granddaddy was well off until 1929. Of course he lost everything in the Great Depression. Had a heart attack the day it happened and didn't work another day in his life," my aunt was saying.

"Well, what exactly did he and grandmother do?"

"Oh, they were into all sorts of things. Your grandmother had her own company at one point, selling high fashions to the New Orleans elite. Your granddaddy financed towns in Mississippi. You know, he would go into those areas where people wanted to start a town and he'd put up the money for it. Of course, when the depression hit, no one could pay him and the banks failed. Things really changed after that.

"But that's a historic house, that Prytania Street house," she said, returning to the ancient family home. "Everything in it was oversized—the columns, the grounds, even the doorways—all of it was huge. *Is* huge. There are enormous steps in the back and, well, one time your daddy fell down them and broke his arm. And of course, there's the story about the famous general who died there."

I knew some of the history of the house. It was previously owned by the Malahoney family, who had been friends with General R.P.T.P. Marshall. On one of his visits to New Orleans, General Marshall had become ill while staying with the Malahoney family and had died in one of their bedrooms. But while this was the version I was given as a child, I found out years later from my Aunt Testa that the truth was slightly different.

It seems that the good general was visiting the Malahoneys sometime in late October 1898 and, unbeknownst to anyone, the youngest child of the Malahoney family had coerced others in the neighborhood into hauling a forty-pound pumpkin up to the widow's walk where it would be carved. The plan was to light the pumpkin so that it could be seen all over the Garden District, but as soon as the children pushed the orange orb onto

415

the flat part of the roof, it began to roll of its own accord and broke through the spindly wooden railings.

Its plummet toward earth was interrupted only briefly by General Marshall, who unfortunately happened to be taking a stroll in the side garden directly in the line of fire. He was only grazed by the large vegetable, but nevertheless rendered unconscious, and after being put to bed for three days, died quite peacefully in his sleep.

My aunt and I were discussing this when she said, "Can you imagine? I mean, how rude. You go to visit someone and then just die in one of their bedrooms. If you knew you were going to die, wouldn't you just stay at home?"

"I don't think he planned on being the victim of a flying pumpkin," I said meekly, trying to take up for the general.

Years after the vegetable incident in 1898, when the Malahoneys no longer wanted to live in the house, they rented it to my grandfather, complete with all the original furniture. My father ended up sleeping in the same bed that the general died in. Mrs. Malahoney wanted to give the house to my grandfather because he had paid rent for so many years, but her daughter, being evidently of a somewhat more financially aware generation, wanted to sell it.

My Aunt Testa remembered when the Chitbills came to look at the house. It probably wasn't in very good condition at that time with the Depression having hit several years earlier. That, accompanied by the fact that New Orleans heat and humidity can wreak havoc with any building not made of steel, probably didn't make for the best impression. I've always envisioned Mrs. Chitbill's lips curled back slightly, clutching her pocketbook and trying not to touch anything as she crept about the antebellum home with its towering ceilings and paint-peeling crown moldings.

The house is essentially the same structure today as it was then—a two-story building with columns stretching from the ground floor to the roof of the second floor—and occupies one of the largest lots in the District. It is brick covered in stucco and surrounded, as it was years ago, by the extensive foliage the

Garden District is noted for. Originally built in 1860 for a wealthy banker, it was part of a former plantation that had been cut up to make homes for wealthy New Orleanians who wanted to live in the suburbs.

At the time my father's family lived there, two huge crepe myrtles occupied the corners of the front yard, and an ancient wisteria vine climbed up to the second story verandah and back down to the front gate. An enormous date palm stood on the northern side of the house. My Aunt Belle remembers standing on the verandah during a terrific thunderstorm—the kind New Orleans is noted for, where the sky turns green-black like a bad bruise—when a bolt of lightning struck the date palm, bringing it down.

Unfortunately, before the tree hit the ground it hit the side of the house and took out every single window. There was also a row of banana trees across the back of the house, perpendicular to the servant's quarters which were added some time after General Marshall's death.

As magnificent as the house is today, I couldn't imagine it was ever as bad as Mrs. Chitbill-Tallymen had led me to believe. There were too many stories. One was about how my Aunt Testa had left the upstairs verandah door open one day, and another famous New Orleans thunderstorm rained for hours onto an upstairs bedroom floor. The water soaked through to the dining room below and the plaster walls had become saturated. A large series of shelves containing my grandmother's collection of antique crystal had come crashing to the floor.

Then there was the time my father slid down the banister in the entrance hall and knocked over a marble statue. According to my Aunt Testa, my father was constantly teasing her and getting into trouble, being quite a handful in his early years. One example of this involved a fern garden in the rear of the house.

Aunt Testa had planted the large fern garden sometime around 1931, and my father was constantly confiscating a few fronds each day. He had a large ceramic duck that was given to him by his mother—an appeasement to make up for the fact that his real pet duck had died, evidently in one of those legendary

417

New Orleans thunderstorms. The ceramic duck was sitting on a stump which had holes in it so that you could fill it with water and put flowers or fern fronds into them. This duck sat on my father's dresser all his life until he went into the military service. My grandmother had kept it and then given it back to him when he married my mother. Later he would give this to me and I would accidentally break it into a million pieces, its loss taking a terrible toll on my father at the time.

These were hardly tenement-house stories that my aunt told. There were many others also, including the one about my grandmother refusing to eat in any restaurant that did not have white tablecloths. Toward the end of her life she dined out less and less, given the fact that tablecloths had gone out of fashion. This, along with the fact that much of the furniture that had come from the Prytania Street house (ornately carved rosewood chairs, chifferobes, mahogany living room sets) was now in the 509 Latrobe home which my aunt lived in, I was sure something was up. I decided to wait until my visit with the Chitbill-Tallymen family to further pry into the house's secrets.

That spring, after arriving in the Crescent City, I called the house.

"May I speak with Mrs. Chitbill-Tallymen?"

"She's in a business meeting. Can I help you?" asked a young woman's voice.

"Yes, uh, I had written her about possibly seeing the inside of the house."

"Sure, come on over."

"Well . . . shouldn't you ask her?"

"No. It's okay. What time would you like to come?" She seemed quite nonchalant about the whole affair.

"Uh, I'd really feel better if you would just check with her." I wasn't sure how happy Mrs. Chitbill-Tallymen would be to see me. Her letter had led me to believe that when she said I could see the interior of the house, she was probably just being polite and that was her Southern way of saying, "Don't even think about calling again."

"Okay," said the girl, "let me check."

418

I waited, knowing she'd probably have to run downstairs.

"Why don't you come at four." she said when she had returned to the phone.

"Four today?" (It was two o'clock already.) "Sure, four is good," I said, thinking four o'clock couldn't be a more inconvenient time for me.

"Okay, see you then," she said, and hung up.

* * * * *

Having been raised in the South, I know there are certain things you do not do. One of them is show up at someone's house empty-handed. Immediately I went to the front desk of the hotel where I was staying.

While the particular hotel that I had chosen was one of the loveliest small hotels in the French Quarter and generally the staff is first rate, today I had to deal with Charnise. Charnise was the girl sitting at the front desk. Approaching her gingerly (she was doing her nails), I asked if there was some place nearby where I could buy two-dozen roses. Charnise regarded me as if, even though I was a three-headed monster, she had seen it all before and was bored. After a search through the greater New Orleans Yellow Pages, Charnise (who took a good minute and a half to turn each page because of her attempt not to do damage to her newly painted nails), gave up. I decided then that I would just drive up and down St. Charles and see what I could find. Politely thanking her, I told her of my plan. Charnise seemed offended at this, though I don't know why, and proceeded not to speak to me for the duration of my stay at this particular hotel.

Procuring roses turned out to be more difficult than I had planned. The only place I could find open on St. Charles *had* no roses. "How can this be?" I asked the dark-skinned girl behind the counter. "You're a florist! It's not like I'm asking for an arrangement of *Solanum nigrum*."

She just shot me a blank look.

"Deadly nightshade," I said, clarifying my last-named plant, hoping she hadn't read anything into the last part of the name.

419

"Let me check in the back," she said, after more verbal prodding on my part. She came back about twenty minutes later and asked me to follow her to the rear of the store. We then went into a refrigerated room where dozens of flowers were clearly on their last legs. She pointed out two or three containers of peach-colored roses that looked as if they had been used in someone's wedding the day before.

"These were used in someone's wedding yesterday, but they're still good," she said rather dryly.

Well, at least my keen sense of perception was intact. I surveyed their droopy little heads and my watch, which said three thirty, and asked how much.

"Sixty-five dollars a dozen."

Holding back a cough, I asked for two dozen. She rang the roses up, gave me the MasterCard bill to sign, and then proceeded to go into the back. "Maybe it's just me," I thought. "Surely she's going to come back out and wrap these up."

She didn't.

Spying a woman of about fifty, with the proverbial nametag (Hello! My Name is Eunice!), and purple-tinted hair, I asked if she could wrap up the roses for me. I might as well have asked her to give me a kidney. After a while I was on my way. As I pulled up to the next stoplight I looked into the backseat at the roses and immediately thought, "I better look around for something else."

Driving back across the District, through avenues overhanging with century-old live oak branches, I made my way to Magazine Street, finally spotting a small business, its windows filled with Christmas arrangements even though Christmas was nowhere in sight. This bounty of poinsettias, ornaments, and over-flocked items was also home to a mechanical Santa Claus which moved his body from side to side, completing each movement with a machine-like jerk and stop. Because the legs were stationary the entire time, one had the perception that he was trying to perform the '60s dance craze, the Twist, in slow motion, and this, accompanied by a well-worn recording of "Alvin and the Chipmunks" lent a '60s charm to the shop even though this was 1997. Someone once said that New Orleans is behind the times, but this place hadn't even gotten the season right.

The woman behind the counter was chain-smoking and talking on the phone when I entered. Ten minutes later she was still chain-smoking and talking on the phone. Finally, she accidentally dropped some of her cigarette ash onto a pile of receipts and they started smoldering. Throwing them onto the floor, she stamped them out, and because her phone concentration had been broken, she turned her attention to me while the receiver was still firmly attached to her ear. Seeing a medium-sized white poinsettia (I never buy red for other people—how many do you know who have a living room that matches *that?*), I asked her to wrap it up, courageously bringing it over myself to the checkout counter, figuring that since it was a leftover from the previous holidays it would probably be on sale.

"Thirty-six ninety-five," said the woman, taking my card. Several minutes later she returned it, complete with a cigarette burn on the lower left-hand corner, the whole time holding the phone between her right shoulder and her ear.

All I could think of was that the Garden District hadn't gotten its name because the rich alluvial soil had produced acres of abundant flora, but rather because this was the most expensive place in the world to buy anything garden-related. Then I thought about it. Why would you want to buy roses if you lived in the Garden District? You could just as well grow your own.

With only five minutes to spare, I managed to park the car and chain-smoke three cigarettes. Then, taking a deep breath, I walked around to the front of the house and rang the bell on the massive iron gate. The entrance was part of a larger iron fence which guarded the stately home from intruders, its thick spikes and fleur-de-lis motif frozen in time. Enormous hemlocks pushed through the vertical openings as if trying to escape.

"Just reach on up and turn the knob." It was the gardener who was pruning a rather overzealous bougainvillea vine to the left of the entranceway, and his delivery of the line included a sun-glinting gold tooth. As I did what he had instructed, the front door of the house opened, and a young woman stood there looking down the walk in my direction. As naturally as if I had lived there my entire life, I sauntered up the front walk of the house and proceeded to step up onto the lower verandah, the first person in my family to do so in over sixty years. Armed with two dozen roses and a rather large, plebeian poinsettia, I announced, "Hi, I'm Strekfus. I called . . ."

"Oh, what beautiful flowers!" said the girl, cutting me off. The door was open and as I handed them to her I stuck my head inside a few inches to see into the house. But my attention was suddenly diverted to the long staircase which stretched itself out towards the door, starting almost from the back of the dwelling. A dull, thudding sound caught my attention, and I searched the dimly lit foyer, trying to make sense of it. Then I saw it. Something round and hard was bouncing its way down the thinly carpeted stairs. The girl who had answered the door turned, and together we watched the object make its long, methodical journey over the multitude of steps, careening over the velvety edges like an escaped baby beach-ball over a series of waterfalls at an amusement park. Finally it reached the bottom step. When it had finished that part of its actions, it continued on its way, traversing the remaining length of the center hall, rolling along the hard plank floor, sounding now like a miniature bowling ball making its way toward a set of imaginary pins. As its momentum slowed, it came to rest, stopping only inches from my right foot.

I looked down and tried to focus. At first I couldn't believe what I was seeing. I appeared to be looking into the clear blue center of an eyeball. As I bent over to get a better look, the girl reached down and scooped the object up, turning toward the staircase with an exasperated look on her face.

I followed her gaze to the top of the stair landing. There, hovering like some arthritic, outcast, undernourished animal, was a woman who appeared to be in her late seventies or early eighties. She was attired in a jogging suit and her left hand held onto a wobbly, crooked cane. Her right hand was now busy fluttering about her face, resembling from this distance a bird attacking her in slow motion.

422

I looked at the glass eye which the girl was now holding. She turned it over in her hand, studying the object as if it were a golf ball hit out of range and through her living room window.

After what was probably only a minute or so, but seemed like hours, the girl spoke using a loud voice. "Mother, we've discussed this. You have to use the new eye the doctor gave you. This one is too small. Why don't you take the elevator and come down? Mr. Beltzenschmidt is here." Then she looked at the woman, then at me, and smiled a little Cheshire cat smile as if to say, "She's old, but I live here too and possession is nine points of the law."

"Look, mother, what beautiful flowers," yelled the girl in the old woman's direction after the octogenarian had managed to remove herself from the small elevator located in back of the stairs.

"Mother? But I thought . . . I thought you were her secretary," I said, turning to the girl.

"Why would you think that?" she asked, sticking her nose into one of the peach-colored blooms amidst the baby's breath and fern fronds. The poinsettia had been relegated to a table located in the very center of the hall and was now looking forlorn.

"Well, when I called, you said Mrs. Chitbill-Tallymen was in a business meeting and I thought . . ."

"No, I'm her daughter," she completed matter-of-factly. "My name is Beth. Beth Chitbill-Tallymen. I'm sorry, I should have introduced myself."

I had imagined that being inside this house was going to be a religious experience with ghosts coming out of the walls and my DNA molecules remembering something I hadn't been aware of. Instead, everything happened so fast that I found myself sitting on the sofa across from Mrs. Chitbill-Tallymen, who had now managed to ensconce herself into a chair across from me, and I was somewhat unaware for a moment that my family had actually lived here, so distracted was I by this last series of events.

I started to look around at the furnishings, the thick carpets, the huge moldings, the damask draperies. We were in the library—the first room just off to the left of the front door. The sun filtered through the wavy-glass panes of the enormous windows which reached upward, clear and cathedral-like, allowing the afternoon to flood the room. Shadows and images of leaves flowed over the furnishings—the oriental carpets, the heavily carved credenzas, the damask-covered sofas.

The daughter, Beth, had gone to the kitchen to procure a vase for the roses and Mrs. C-T and I were alone as my head swiveled from side to side, taking in the room.

"YOU HAVE A LOVELY HOME," I yelled in her direction, noticing that she was now in possession of both eyes, obviously having fitted the correct one in before coming downstairs.

"Yes, thank you," said Mrs. Chitbill-Tallymen. Thereupon followed a long silence. I'm usually a rational person, but I swear it had to be a good hour and a half until Beth came back with the roses in hand.

"Where should we put these, Mother?" screamed Beth in the direction of the sofa. I reasoned that the old woman's deafness probably accounted for the uncomfortable silences.

"Oh, let's put them in the general's room. You know, he hardly ever gets flowers," said Mrs. C-T.

Judging from the mother's present state and this comment, I wasn't sure if she knew General Marshall had died. We all followed Beth to the bedroom and it was then that I noticed a limp the older woman had. One of her legs seemed incredibly stiff, almost as if it were artificial.

"Look, the color is a perfect match for the bedroom. I just love this color," said Mrs. Chitbill-Tallymen, hobbling into the room. "You know, we were at a wedding yesterday and all the arrangements were roses this color."

"Is that right?"

"Yes, and I kept saying to Beth, what an unusual color it was for roses," she continued, reaching into the flowers and arranging their prickly stems.

"Well, I was going to get a red poinsettia, but you know, red just wouldn't work in your living room."

"No, red would just not do," and then turning to me abruptly with concern in her voice: "Would you like a drink?"

"There's nothing like a good train of thought," I said to myself. This woman gave new meaning to the phrase Non sequitur.

"No," I said, "red would not have done, and yes, I would love a drink."

We now moved into the front parlor where the extensive liquor tray was kept. "Would you like me to fix you one?" I yelled after seeing Madame C-T struggle with what appeared to be a two-gallon bottle of Dewar's. She nodded a "Yes." I hadn't noticed it previously, but something seemed to be wrong with one of her hands—the one which was gripping the cane. As I maneuvered the bottles around on the tray, I tried to get a better look.

"We need some glasses," she said, craning her neck over the tray.

"No, look, here are some," I said, seeing about fourteen large tumblers right in front of us. Obviously Mrs. Chitbill-Tallymen's one good eye wasn't working so well. I poured her a Dewar's and soda and handed it to her. With what appeared to be her normal hand she took it.

"My, that's too much Dewar's. Are you trying to kill me?" she asked, holding up the glass to the light. I thought about her letter, inwardly smiled, then composed myself and said, "Oh, I'm sorry, let me add some more soda to that."

"Oh, goodness, we need some ice," she said, looking around.

"I'll get some if you'd like. For you. I don't need any. I don't take ice in my drinks."

"All right, yes, the kitchen is just . . ."

"I know," I said, and proceeded on my way through the house toward the kitchen. It occurred to me how strange it was that I knew my way around so well. Then I realized why: I had been in this house before. Well, not *this* house. I had been in an exact replica of the structure.

425

My uncle Sebastian (Testa, Belle, and my father's brother) had lived in the Prytania Street house as a young man and had become so smitten with it that he built a replica in a small town in Mississippi. He had lived in that facsimile until just a few years ago when an unfortunate incident involving urination and an electric fence took his life. Having visited there, I knew the floor plan inside and out, so naturally I understood where the kitchen was.

Opening the door to the butler's pantry—the small room in between the dining room and the kitchen—was something like Dorothy in *The Wizard of Oz* opening the front door of her house after the tornado has set it down.

Only in reverse.

The rooms I had seen so far were opulent in décor, but the butler's pantry and kitchen probably hadn't been changed since my grandfather lived there. Soon Mrs. Chitbill-Tallymen appeared behind me.

"You know, the children like this ice dispenser, but I don't," she said, waving her hand in the direction of the only new appliance in the kitchen—a refrigerator. "We need a spoon for the ice," she continued, and proceeded to dig through an ancient silverware drawer. Pulling out the largest tablespoon I had ever seen, she smiled triumphantly and turned to go back into the dining room, the whole time with the spoon quivering violently.

I noticed at this point just how frail she was. I had heard she was not in the best of health, and after spending some time with her it was now even more evident. She explained that she had been in a bad car accident back in 1961 and injured her left hand and right leg, and that she had never fully recovered. She had also had one of her eyes put out.

"You know," she went on, seeing that I had observed her frailness and wanting to explain, "I called my sister to come out here and stay with me, but she said she was too busy. I told her, 'I thought you would want to get out of Tuscumbia,' but she said she didn't have the time."

"Your sister lives in Tuscumbia, Alabama?" I questioned loudly.

"Yes, she *did*," said Mrs. Chitbill-Tallymen. "She lived there with her husband. She's dead now, of course."

"Like the cow in the backyard," I said in a normal voice.

"Yes, and *how* is right!" answered Mrs. C-T. "You know, she was a Bunion," she added.

"Excuse me?"

"A Bunion. She was a Bunion. Of course her maiden name was Chitbill, but when she married she became a Bunion. It's a very old family she married into, you know."

"Is that right?"

I managed to fill the ice bucket and we made our way back to the front room and then to the library where we sat and attempted to talk. I looked around the room again. I wanted to say something like, "Nice place you've got," but I thought better of it. Communication was touch-and-go here, so I didn't want to interject anything that might be taken as snide. At least not at full volume. A few drinks later and I would change my mind. After several minutes, Beth entered again and I was thankful for the extra company.

"So where do you work?" asked Beth, settling in beside me on the sofa.

"I work for Fondon Sass Publications in New York," I said. "You know, fashion magazines, shelter books, that sort of thing."

"Oh, we love those house-and-garden types of magazines. I really loved the last issue of one of your magazines with an article on Claudette Colbert's old house. And that house Israel designed. It was so . . . well so . . . what is the word I'm looking for?"

"Brave?"

"Well, yes, brave. You know, one of the magazines you work for came here once to photograph mother's gardens, but it's so hard to catch them in bloom, and besides, this house isn't really decorated in the proper sense. I mean, they always want stories about who decorated this and which Scalamandré fabric was used for that. This is really more a historic house." She took a drink and then turned to me. "What exactly do you do at Fondon Sass?"

"I'm a staff writer for one of the magazines," I said.

"Beth, fix Mr. Beltzenschmidt another drink. He's getting kind of low there."

"No, thank you. I'm fine," I said, feeling a little woozy already. "I'm still working on this one."

"Well I'll have another. Beth, will you fix me one?" Beth went to procure another Dewar's and soda for Mrs. Chitbill-Tallymen and appeared shortly with the refreshed libation. Then she excused herself to make a phone call and Mrs. Chitbill-Tallymen and I were left alone. Once again we lapsed into an uncomfortable silence and I couldn't tell if she wanted me to leave or was just napping.

"Well, I guess I'd better be leaving now," I said, hoping she would agree. I didn't think that she really wanted me to stay and I was beginning to wonder if asking to see the house had been such a good idea.

"What?" she asked. "Did you see the house yet?"

"No, ma'am, but I thought . . ."

"Nonsense. You've got to see the garden too. You can't go yet. Did you notice the portrait over the mantle?" She seemed to come alive again and was now giving me the grand tour. She even managed to get out of the chair without too much difficulty. We were standing in front of the ornate marble fireplace, looking up at a portrait of a rather beautiful young woman.

"Of course if your family lived here there weren't any portraits like these. It was a tenement house back then with no electricity," she reiterated.

"Who's that?" I asked, seeing another portrait between the two front windows. I was hoping to get her off this subject of tenement houses. The whole experience was starting to irritate me—her constant references to how bad the house had been, along with her deafness.

"Yes, we do get rain from time to time . . ."

I remembered that I had to yell for her to understand me, but since Beth was out of the room, I decided to have a little fun.

"Why not," I thought? "She wasn't exactly the most likable woman." And the scotch I was drinking wasn't helping my disposition any either.

"That's Mr. Tallymen's father," she said, moving to the next portrait. "Personally, I like the style much better."

"Oh, no. I think this portrait of your husband looks as though a three-month-old baboon with muscular control problems painted it. I hope you didn't pay a lot to have that done. And how many bottles of Grecian Formula did he have to use to get his hair that color?"

"Yes. Yes, he was. You know, his family owned more slaves in the state of Louisiana than anyone else."

"Not even close that time," I thought, and I realized at this point that she couldn't make out *anything* I was saying, so I decided just to let it rip. Besides, I was getting inebriated and I really didn't care. She deserved to be told off, even if she couldn't hear it.

"Is that so?" I said, trying not to choke. Then I put on my best smiling face. "You know, I'd rather have a hot anal probe from PMS-prone aliens than stand here and talk to you, but I need to see this house for my own sake and therefore I'll tolerate your nauseating behavior." And then straightening myself somewhat, "And besides, the dead cow in the backyard was probably killed when the tornado set the house down on *it* instead of on *you*." Of course, just to be sure she didn't hear me, I turned slightly to the side. The thought crossed my mind that given her deafness she might have picked up lip-reading.

"Why, yes, they owned hundreds and hundreds of slaves. Now I don't think any livestock was ever taken into town," she continued. Speaking with her was like communicating with some of my mother's relatives: we each had our own conversations going, not really caring what the other party said.

"Did they have any dead cows?" I screamed.

"What?" She was leaning forward now, almost falling over.

"Nothing."

She just looked confused and then turned vacantly away.

429

"Will you excuse me just a minute?" she said, turning back to me politely, and with that she left and Beth came back into the room holding a drink.

"Your mother was just showing me the portraits," I said. Beth made a face at this. "What's the matter?" I asked, hoping she hadn't overheard my tirade.

"My mother. She's old, you know. I mean, she's walking around like she's half dead. And stone deaf. We never know what she's going to do next, and just between you and me, we've been trying to get a look at the will. Well, she can't find it and none of us know what's in it. Still, she has some presence of mind. She just sold off the lots next to the house on the side street. She was so afraid blacks would move in, she made sure she sold them to white people."

"I don't know, she seems to have her moments," I said, lying through my teeth. "Besides, she probably would have made them into slaves if they had moved in," I said, trying to get some reaction from her.

"That's because you don't have to live with her. That's why you think she has her moments. Did she go on about the slaves again?" she asked, but at that instant Mrs. Chitbill-Tallymen came back into the library.

"You have to see the garden," Mrs. C-T said, and we started for the back of the house. Soon we were on the back porch and heading down the steps. I noticed the worn edges of the concrete rectangles and was immediately reminded of a story I had been told.

As a child I had noticed a small scar on the bottom of my father's chin and inquired where he had gotten it. "I fell down the back steps of the Prytania Street house," was his response. It was strange now to be walking down the same steps. We went first to the rose garden, and as I stood looking around, I couldn't help but wonder where the dead cow had been. I wanted to ask but thought better of it.

". . . and this is the greenhouse where we keep the orchids. The winters are just too cold in New Orleans for them, you know."

"That's ginger, isn't it?" I yelled, pointing to thick green foliage against a brick wall. "*Alpinia zerumbet*," I added.

"Yes, that's ginger, and over here we have the impatiens and some monkey grass," she said, waving a crooked finger at the low-growing foliage, leaning on the cane with her other waxy hand. The plants crowded each other in a tropical profusion, each one seemingly elbowing the other for more room. In New Orleans's sub-tropical climate plants sometimes grew too fast for their own good, spilling over onto everything. A house left alone or a vacant lot could easily become consumed within a year.

We walked back toward the house while she showed me her assortment of ferns, ginger, and elephant ears, then on toward the side patio garden.

"Was this section of the garden always here?" I asked, as we approached a secluded area, the center of which was a goldfish pond—its cement edges caked with moss and lichens from decades of use. Several slender koi swam leisurely about the tropical water lilies, and ripples came from a small fountain in the pond's center, sending ridges outward to the edges like slow-moving radio waves.

"Yes, this section is original to the plan, though I don't know if anyone actually had flowers planted here," she said.

"Ferns," I said. "There were probably ferns planted back here, according to my aunt."

Suddenly I was brought back to what it must have been like for my family to live here—the profusion of greenery, the excessive heat and humidity. The backyard must have looked like a jungle. I imagined my Aunt Testa on her hands and knees, gardening, being surprised by a gentle cow poking its head through a thicket of bamboo and fig trees.

"The reason I know it was probably a fern garden is because my father used to come back here to pluck a few of them so that he could put them in his ceramic duck," I said in a normal voice, more to myself than her.

Mrs. Chitbill-Tallymen looked confused. "His duck?" she asked.

"Oh, yeah," I thought, "she heard *that!*"

I laughed, realizing she didn't have a clue as to what I meant, and without wanting to go into the whole story, but realizing she needed an explanation, I went on, yelling as loudly as I could.

"Yes, he had a green porcelain duck that had holes in it so that you could fill it with water and put flowers or leaves in the holes. It was an antique. He was always stealing my Aunt Testa's ferns to put in the holes." It was then that I noticed the woman who lived next door. She had risen up from weeding around her caladiums, a good twenty feet away, and was now standing there with a puzzled look on her face.

"What was your father doing playing with ferns?" asked Mrs. Chitbill-Tallymen.

"Don't know," I yelled. "I guess it runs in the family."

She still looked confused, so I dropped it. She continued to show me her roses, gingers, and boxwoods, and then we walked up the steps, through the sunroom and back porch until we were finally in the library again. Beth came back from whatever she had been doing and joined us.

"Beth, fix Mr. Beltzenschmidt another drink," Mrs. C-T ordered as she settled into a wing-backed chair. Before I could say anything Beth went to freshen up my glass.

"And see if you can find something to eat," she added. At this point I wasn't sure or not if this was my cue to leave.

In old New Orleans there used to be a tradition of "passing." This was something started by the Creoles who lived in this area and involved offering something to eat or drink to the guests. In Robert Tallant's book, *The Romantic New Orleanians*, he describes it this way:

> It is traditional with all Creoles to "pass" something to every caller in his home. It does not matter much what it is. One gentleman remembered that when his family were so poor they had little else, they had always passed bananas. Out would come a silver platter, a treasured family heirloom, filled with big yellow bananas,

which used to be about the cheapest thing a New Orleanian could buy. Another family would simply set up a silver platter and some goblets on a table and at the proper moment would become most insistent that the guest enjoy a nice glass of water.

The formal call was popular with Creoles of another era. The visitor went at a specified time and if he were not an intimate or relative of the family he was entertained in the best parlor. There he would sit and converse with his host and the family, sitting usually in a not too comfortable or relaxed position upon a chair pushed against a wall—for some reason Creoles always sat around in a kind of square, with the chairs against the wall, often with the width of the room between them. If it were warm palmetto fans were distributed and everyone fanned and chatted, often gaily for Creoles loved their kind of subtle wit and laughter. After a while, perhaps thirty minutes, something was always "passed," usually not bananas, of course, but a little wine and fruit cake, or something of the sort. This ritual over, the guest talked only a few minutes longer, then made his departure.

Beth made her way to the kitchen and then reappeared some time later with something on a silver tray for each of us.

"Beth, unwrap Mr. Beltzenschmidt's banana for him," Mrs. Chitbill-Tallymen said, as her daughter neared me with the yellow fruit.

"No, that's okay, I can handle it, but thank you," I said, trying to break the stem so that I could peel away the outer layer. After several unsuccessful attempts I realized that the piece of fruit was still green and tried to dig my fingernails into the fleshy stem in order to start the peeling process. Evidently, Mrs. Chitbill's banana was quite ripe, because she was halfway through with hers and I hadn't even started. She mouthed a piece of fruit and then swallowed. I imagined the lump of soft banana sticking in her throat and producing a bulge equal to the size of her head, much like a boa constrictor which has swallowed its prey whole, but the sustenance slid down unhindered and she was speaking again.

"You know, I find it real strange," began Mrs. Chitbill-Tallymen after taking another bite, "that your (*smack, smack, smack*) family lived in this house." She was holding the banana high in her right hand like a precious scepter, a good six inches of exposed fruit-flesh sticking out from the peel which drooped over her hands and caught in between her fingers like giant wax drippings from some surrealistic candle. The whole area around her was taking on a Cocteau-like air.

"This was a tenement house at one time," she continued with haughty dignity, and at this point the ripe fruit broke off from its high perch, totally unbeknownst to her, and landed squarely in front of her. "And when I say tenement house, I mean that it was really quite bad," she continued moving her arthritic right foot accidentally onto the now-prostrate cylinder of soft fruit.

"Uh, Mother," Beth interjected, seeing the now-inedible banana being ground into a pulp, but she was cut off by Mrs. Chitbill-Tallymen.

"No running water, no electricity," Mrs. C-T continued as she unknowingly mashed the banana into what I estimated was an oriental carpet worth well over two hundred thousand dollars.

Beth, immediately sensing my uneasiness, interjected loudly, "Well, Mother, you know people lived very differently back then," and tried to draw my attention away from the fact that the mashed remnants of banana now covered the entire side of Mrs. Chitbill's velveteen-slippered foot.

"I know," countered Mrs. Chitbill-Tallymen, "but I remember once an FBI man came to the door and said he was going to have to investigate the house. He said it was a noted house of ill-repute. Well, there I was standing with a three-month-old baby in my arms, and I thought, what's he talking about? I said, 'No, you must be mistaken,' but he insisted, 'No, ma'am, this here was a house of ill-repute at one time.'"

Mrs. Chitbill then evidently had an itch on her left leg, because at this point she reached up with the toe of her right foot to scratch it, coating her left calf with a thick layer of pale yellow goo. Her right hand was still holding the now-useless banana peel in its original position.

"Great," I thought, "we've gone from having a dead cow in the backyard to a house of ill-repute. What's next, bootlegging during Prohibition?"

Beth evidently had heard all this before. She went to the kitchen to check on something—probably to get some paper towels. I figured since I was alone with the old woman again and she was really starting to irritate me, I'd have a little more fun.

"And they say," continued Mrs. Chitbill-Tallymen, "that bootlegging went on here during Prohibition."

"Right on cue," I thought.

"Are you sure your family lived here, because you know, this was a tenement house and a house of ill-repute and bootlegging went on here," she said, sticking her neck out toward me.

"Yes, ma'am, I'm sure. I've got a picture of my family standing on the front porch. It was made in 1922. But you realize," I continued, knowing she couldn't hear and smiling as big and friendly a smile as I could manage, "that your incredible insecurity is overwhelming and the fact that you protest to the extent you do about my family only reflects badly on yourself," and I shook my head up and down and raised my eyebrows in order to show that I was bowing and scraping.

"Yes, you're absolutely correct. We paid cash for this house and I realize it is quite big," she answered, and smiled.

"My family LIVED here in the '20s," I shouted.

"Well," countered Mrs. Chitbill-Tallymen, "there are lots of houses that look like this one. You've probably got the wrong house." I didn't want to tell her (I was a guest in her house and I also didn't want to get into an argument) that I had the original lease from the law firm and canceled checks for water, gas, and electricity from 1922 written on Hibernia Bank checks. This tenement story was beginning to get on my last nerve. In addition, I had letters from Mrs. Roseanne Malahoney, the woman who had rented the house to my grandfather.

Sure, if you look at the picture I have from 1922, you can see the house doesn't look the way it does now, but what does? I had kept this photograph, sepia-colored, with a tear in the lower right-hand corner, ever since I found it in my aunt's basement on Latrobe Street. You can see the family standing there next to the towering columns.

By now I figured Mrs. Chitbill-Tallymen was going to hang on to her version of the story no matter what, so I decided to leave.

"I guess I should be going now," I said. "I don't want to wear out my welcome." Beth had reentered the picture and we were all standing. We walked into the main hall, Mrs. C-T following behind us with a "step, *shuulp*, step, *shuulp*" rhythm, and Beth looking over her shoulder to make sure the old woman didn't fall. As we passed the door to the front parlor, I stuck my head in to look one last time.

I noticed that the original mirrors which were present in General Marshall's day were still being used over the fireplaces in the front parlor and dining room, but that the original light fixtures were gone. These two elements had been described to me in detail by my Uncle Sebastian who had grown up in the house, and indeed, when showing me a picture of the interior of the house at a later date, he had remarked how the mirrors were original to the design.

"What happened to the original chandeliers that were in this room?" I yelled, leaning over slightly into Mrs. C-T's ear. "They were cast metal with figures holding palm trees on them," I added. I had pictures of these light fixtures—old family photos which showed them in their original form. They were probably one of a kind, as I have never seen any that resembled them since.

"Oh, those," said Mrs. Chitbill-Tallymen. "I couldn't stand those things—gave them to the junk man. He was some old Negro who used to come around and ask if anybody had

436

anything they wanted to get rid of. I gave them to him. They're probably worth a fortune now."

How odd, I thought, that you would have moved into a tenement house but kept the original light fixtures and mirrors over the mantels, at least for a while. But then she had later done away with the chandeliers and replaced them with more modern ones.

"Well, the house certainly looks like it's in good shape now," I said loudly. "You've done a wonderful job of preserving it."

"Of course it is," hissed Mrs. Chitbill-Tallymen. "It took over a year to remodel this house. There was no electricity, no plumbing, there was a dead cow in the backyard . . ."

I moved toward the door, and as I did so, Mrs. Chitbill-Tallymen grasped the doorknob and opened it for me.

"Joe," she said, speaking to the gardener once we were all standing on the porch, "you make sure to cut that vine way back now. I don't want it growing all over that hedge."

"Yes 'um," he responded, and gingerly snipped a purple bloom from the vine growth.

"Beth, go unlock the gate for Mr. Beltzenschmidt," said Mrs. Chitbill-Tallymen. It seemed this gate was always locked, no matter who lived here. When my father's family lived there it had been locked to keep everyone in. Now it was locked to keep people out.

"Thank you so much for allowing me to see your house," I screamed descending the front steps. "It really has been one of the highlights of my stay in New Orleans."

"Well, you're more than welcome," countered Mrs. Chitbill-Tallymen. "You wrote me a very nice letter, and we're glad you came."

When I reached the gate, Mrs. C-T called from the porch, "Be sure and notice the bushes by the gate. They're called *Philadelphus coronarius*, and they were planted at entranceways and at front gates of houses in the South because of their fragrance. They welcome visitors with their scent as you enter the yard. They really are quite lovely."

437

Beth had evidently forgotten to let me out, so the gardener was on hand to open the gate. Now with a safe distance of at least twenty feet between me and Mrs. Chitbill-Tallymen, and with no one around except the gardener, I smiled as widely as I could and said to her in a normal, cheery voice, "Thanks so much for treating me like radioactive waste," and with that I gave a friendly wave to her and she waved back. Joe, the gardener, just cut his eyes in my direction and said, "I do that all the time," and we smiled at each other.

The *Philadelphus coronarius* really were quite lovely. I leaned over to better enjoy them before walking toward my transportation. As I slid into the front seat of my rental car, I turned the air vents in my direction, lit a cigarette, and thought, "I wonder what the cow's name was?"

I had only partially gotten what I had come for. I had wanted to see the house my father grew up in, but I had also come searching for clues to why he had ended up being the man he was. I wasn't expecting the house to look as it had in the days when my grandparents lived there. Still, I was able to imagine my father, my aunts, and my uncle moving about the twenty-two-foot-ceiling rooms, and get a feel for what it must have been like living in this historic district. No wonder my Uncle Sebastian had built a replica of this house. He too, like all of us, had been searching for something in his life, and I suppose he felt that if he recreated his childhood environment, he could go back and set things right, or at least the way he had wanted them to be.

- 23 -

New York, 1997

Before me I saw a new world opening in beauty and light, and I felt within me the capacity to know all things.

—Helen Keller, *The Story of My Life*

Strekfus read the story again—the one about the house his father had lived in—the one about Prytania Street. Something bothered him and he now knew exactly what it was. He had written the story word-for-word as it had happened, and by doing so he was now able to see that he was no closer to finding out what his father's life had been like than before. He had taken the New Orleans assignment after his unfortunate episode in Sagaser's office—the one which had earned him a good deal of time off from the magazine—to write about yet another Southern home, this one at least somewhat historic. And as with the first assignment, he thought that he could combine a fact-finding mission for himself with another story he had to write.

He thought things would turn around for him after he blacked out in Sagaser's office. It seems that he scared his boss and everyone on the floor with his display of unintentional theatrics. His co-workers thought he had suffered a heart attack and had called an ambulance—probably the worst thing they could have done considering that a flashback to his youth in which his father had tortured him in a hospital was the very thing

439

that had caused him momentarily to check out. He had tried to explain that he didn't need to go to the hospital and that it would even be harmful at this point for him to go. With what energy he had left, he had managed to convince the paramedics of this. But the irony wasn't lost on him—the fact that those who sought so desperately to help him were only going make his situation worse by placing him physically in the location of his psychological flashback—the very flashback which had brought him to their attention in the first place. And it was this seed, this irony, which was planted in his mind at the time of the ambulance's arrival, that was now growing inside him, nurtured by other pieces of his past he had come to recognize and catalogue.

He thought about this and the flashback for several days after it happened and decided that he needed to know why his father had felt the need to control everything and had harbored such anger. And since his father, his mother, Althea, and Aunt Testa were dead, he felt that he would have to try to piece together some history himself in order to make sense of his father's life. He had decided to start by visiting the house his father had grown up in, the very house that his father's family had been forced to leave shortly after the Great Depression, the very house which had influenced his father to make all those weekend road trips to the Keller and Wheeler homes and to so many other houses in the area in order to try to recapture something that was lost.

He had thought that if he could see the house, the very floorboards, the plaster walls, the gardens, the rooms in which his father and the family had lived, there would be some clue as to what had happened in the past. But the visit had proved fruitless in this area. Oh, he had been able to imagine his grandparents and their children in the house, but any remnants of what had caused his father to be the way he was had been removed or lost.

And it was at that moment that he realized another aspect of his visit that bothered him. He had been forced to acquiesce when it came to arguing about the quality of life his father's family had experienced there. He had feared that by telling the Chitbill-Tallymen woman off he would lose the privilege of seeing the house. Had he known that the visit was going to produce nothing in the way of information, he would gladly have spoken his mind and made sure she actually heard it. He also realized that what she had said about the house being a tenement at one time was true, only not in the way she thought. While the Beltzenschmidt family had plenty of money, they had been virtually poverty-stricken when it came to love and understanding.

He realized that it was too late to go back and try to set the old woman straight, but it wasn't too late for his boss. Something about the visit, the lack of information, the absence of closure, the mental torture he had been going through lately, fueled a fire inside him.

The incident in his boss's office had sent shock waves through his physical and mental being. He had determined on his way back from New Orleans, after his black out and his experience on Prytania Street, that he was no longer going to stand by and take whatever life gave him. He was going to make his own way in the world and carve out a life for himself—one which involved writing the kind of book he wanted to write and not something commercially successful or literary or accessible or whatever other terms agents and editors and publishing houses could come up with. It was as though there were some invisible wall in front of him that he needed to punch through, and only by taking a stand could he break into the clean air of the other side and begin to breathe. He also thought that by writing of these Southern homes in the present, the way he had done with the Latrobe chapter and the Prytania Street home, by presenting them as they were now, he would be able to exorcise his demons and get closer to the truth, or at least find the right road to that promised land.

As he thought about this, he began to write a letter to Sagaser. Not only would his boss receive it, but Strekfus would read it to him before handing over the written article. He was glad he had waited a month before putting the words onto paper. He had waited until he could see more clearly, until he wasn't so angry that he would spew out some emotional tirade which would only be seen as hate and not as information that his boss needed. And the waiting had enabled him to access additional clues—information which would help the case he was going to make. Others had come forth after his last meeting with Sagaser, the cataclysmic one involving his black out, and had offered additional facts that helped him fit the puzzle together. Strekfus had spent the better part of two weeks making sense of these new data, and he had pieced together quite a damaging scenario with the energy he had left. He put the finishing touches on his last story—Prytania Street—and organized his ammunition for tomorrow's meeting. He wasn't happy with this last story because he felt it to be incomplete, but he also realized that it wasn't just a story anymore, but rather a chapter in a book about his life.

It was late now, well past five o'clock, when he finished the assignment he had given himself. He headed for home where he would go over in his mind exactly what he needed to say, and where, for the first time in several months, he hoped to get a good night's sleep.

* * * * *

The next morning, he dialed Sagaser's secretary and made an appointment to meet with his boss that afternoon at exactly three o'clock. Strekfus could just as easily have strolled down the hall and made an appearance, but his boss could have feigned the pretext of being busy, and when things started to heat up, the man could have used the excuse of an impending meeting and extricated himself from any scenario Strekfus had in mind. After confirming the time and the fact that Sagaser had no more meetings after three o'clock, he went to work on what would be the last story in the series, and since it would be the end of the stories, he felt the need to tie things up for his readers and bring them back to the place where it had all started—where the remembering had begun. He was halfway through when he glanced up at the clock and started to prepare for his meeting. Then, with letter in hand, he took a deep breath and headed toward his boss's office. As he neared the door, he looked at his watch—exactly three o'clock—the very time he was to meet with the man, and yet his boss was on the phone, having some innocuous conversation about what his wife was to fix for dinner.

"Does he know about my appointment?" Strekfus asked, turning to the secretary who had penciled in his time. She was sitting directly across from Sagaser's office, directly in his line of view. Strekfus said it loud enough and with enough force that Sagaser looked up from his conversation and held the phone slightly away from his ear for a moment. Then he furrowed his brow and continued speaking into the receiver.

"He knows," the girl said, tilting her head and pursing her lips.

So Strekfus turned and looked straight at his boss. It was just the extra irritation, this hold-up of the meeting, that Strekfus needed and it worked, setting him off just as his sigh had set Sagaser off on the day the man abused him and he experienced the flashback. Strekfus walked directly into the office, stood before his boss, pointed to his watch and mouthed the words, "Get off the phone. I have an appointment with you."

It was probably Sagaser's initial shock that allowed him to tell his wife that he had to go. Or maybe it was his memory of the fiasco which had taken place in his office the last time he had a conference with Strekfus. Whatever the reason, Sagaser hung up the phone. But he wasn't going to make it easy for Strekfus—he would see to that. The man, his boss, had seen a weakness in an employee, and like a pack of wild dogs that senses frailty, was ready to take Strekfus down for everything he imagined the writer had done to him.

"So, Mr. Beltzenschmidt, what can I do for you?" the older man began in a condescending, guarded tone. His voice was unctuous and fake, the way a child molester might talk to his next victim. Strekfus had walked over to the door and shut it during this sad excuse for an inquiry into his needs, and he was once again standing before Sagaser who was seated behind his massive desk.

"I'll be glad to tell you what you're going to do for me," Strekfus began, and with these very words, Sagaser's phony optimism drained out of his face and puddled onto the blotter in front of him. "I have here a letter stating everything that I'm about to say to you. After I say it, I will give you and your boss a copy. As a matter of fact, the copy to your boss is already on his desk in a sealed envelope, just in case you feel you need to make a call upstairs after our conference and warn him about anything."

"That's all fine and well," Sagaser countered, trying to regain his composure, "but please be brief. I've got a meeting at three fifteen," and he smiled his best fake smile while leaning back in his chair and crossing his arms.

"Actually, you don't, Mr. Sagaser. I took the liberty of checking your schedule with your secretary and you have no meetings until four thirty, so we have plenty of time."

By now, Sagaser realized that he was up against something new and he began to get defensive. "You might want to adjust your attitude or I'll have to write you up for insubordination, Beltzenschmidt," and then the man began to search through some manila folders on his desk, pretending to look for the proverbial invisible object. After a second or two, still not looking up, he added, "We wouldn't want you to pass out like you did last time, now would we?"

It was at that moment that something welled up inside Strekfus, something not unlike the last time when he blacked out in front of his boss. Before he knew what was happening, his body was taking over and he was observing someone he didn't even know. His physical being wasn't responding by shutting down as it had last time. Instead, it was gathering energy to prepare to defend itself. It was as if years of cowering, compromising, and backing down in situations he hated had come to a head and he could no longer continue in that vein. He knew that he either would back down and die, or fight. He knew that everything he had been through in his life had prepared him for this moment and all other moments to come, and that he must not deny his birthright—this birthright which had been so twisted and torn, abused and ransacked to the point where he felt all the years pile up now like a bad freeway accident. Strekfus felt as though someone had touched him with a live wire for the purpose of destroying him, only the energy and voltage had fortified him, made him stronger so that he could now turn on his abuser with the very tools previously used to try to destroy his being, and fight this demon in front of him.

With one large, smooth, swift motion, Strekfus reached his right forearm across the top of the desk belonging to his boss, and raked every item off. Computer monitor, blotter, stapler, lamp, stacks of papers, and telephone piled up against each other and rushed toward the edge like barrels heading over Niagara Falls. They crashed to the floor with an enormous noise and the desk now looked like some vast blank teakwood canvas. Sagaser sat back in his chair, completely stunned, looking like someone who had just been spared by a falling steel beam.

"Do I have your attention now?" Strekfus asked, leaning over the desk, looking his boss directly in the eye. "Do I?"

"Yes," Sagaser stammered. Then Strekfus saw another look in his boss's eye. The man was afraid and had made a furtive glance to where the phone had just been.

"And don't even think of calling security, at least not until after I've finished, because you're going to sit there and listen to everything I have to say." Strekfus was still looking him in the eye. "Do you understand me?"

Sagaser nodded and tried to pick up what pieces of his composure he could.

"Good," Strekfus went on. "Now, the first thing is this: You have treated me badly ever since I came to this magazine. While you may have been superficially nice to me from time to time, you have failed to acknowledge the contributions I have made and you have insulted me in front of my peers and colleagues. The few times you feigned niceness were only to get some information out of me or to satisfy some superficial faux-male-bonding. This is going to stop immediately. Do you understand?"

Sagaser nodded. It wasn't a nod of defeat, but rather one hopeful that whatever rage Strekfus was experiencing would disolve and Sagaser could get the upper hand. "I'd like an answer," Strekfus was now saying with more intensity, leaning closer over the desk. It was at that point that something snapped for his boss. Possibly it was an animal instinct that told him to fight, but whatever the reason was, the man seemed to regain his footing emotionally as well as physically and he was now standing.

"You listen to me you little piece of shit," Sagaser was saying, trying to fake anger and force. "Who the hell do you think you are coming in here and trying to intimidate *me*?" And with this, he leaned over the desk and pointed a fat finger at Strekfus's face.

But all it took was one look from Strekfus and Sagaser knew he wasn't going to win this one. Strekfus wasn't faking, and the intense focus and anger that shot out through his eyes said it all. Strekfus stretched his head out even closer to the standing man. But just in case Sagaser hadn't gotten the message, he reinforced what his eyes were saying. "You're going to sit down and listen, or I'm going to throw you through that window," Strekfus said with complete calm and control, jerking his head toward the sheet of glass which separated the two men from a thirty-nine-story drop. "Do you understand me?"

Sagaser staggered back into his chair, determining it to be safer than standing in front of plate-glass windows on the thirty-ninth floor with an irate employee opposite him. Something about Strekfus's calm was even more disturbing than his anger, so Sagaser stayed quiet.

"As I was saying before you so boorishly interrupted me, you have been nothing but rude and obnoxious to me. It is going to stop now. I'm *telling* you. I know it was you who set the fire in my office. I know it was you who sent me the KKK application. I know it was you who contacted the FBI and had them investigate me."

Sagaser was now looking intently at Strekfus, trying to project a stone face. The man leaned forward over his naked desk and looked Strekfus in the eye. "You're paranoid," he said, hoping to knock something out from under his employee, hoping to hit a nerve, anything to find a crack in Strekfus's façade so that he could work a finger in and begin to tear the writer apart. Then, pretending to be at ease, as if he had figured out every fiber of his employee's being, he looked nastily up at Strekfus and said, "Jesus Christ, you are one fucked-up individual."

"Not any more!" retorted Strekfus. "And I'm not only *not* paranoid, I'm actually a rather nice, patient, well-adjusted person, considering all I've been through, who is about to metaphysically kick your ass." Sagaser looked shocked and leaned back in his chair again. The intimidation against Strekfus wasn't working for him anymore. Strekfus was on to him as no one else had been. Sagaser had usually been able to destroy his opponents, his employees, his enemies, with one or two words, with the fact that he was a powerful man, that his father was a powerful man, that he had connections, but this time it wasn't working and he was running out of ideas.

"I'll produce exhibit 'A,' " Strekfus continued with calm intensity, and pulled out a photograph which had been enlarged several times. In addition, there were several shots making up a series which showed his overweight boss entering Strekfus's office and then leaving. Another series of shots, all with date and time stamps, showing the smoke coming from his office, filling the space, covering the lens.

"What is this, some kind of a joke?" Sagaser asked as he stared at the photos.

"No joke. It seems that unbeknownst to this magazine, there is a video surveillance camera in the ceiling just above the secretarial area. Evidently these "higher ups" as you call them, don't trust the employees *or* the bosses around here. It seems that they didn't feel the need to tell anyone, not even the editors and others on this floor, that there was a camera located within our vicinity. And it never occurred to anyone to look at the footage because the fire had been an accident caused by me, or so they thought, thanks to you. After I spoke with the custodian on this floor, he let me in on the secret about the camera. It seems that he had to let the electricians in last year to install it. Because he likes me and is well connected with the other, how is it you call them, "low-lifes" in the building, he got the security guards to let me look at the footage and make a copy. How convenient for me.

447

How inconvenient for you. See, Edwin, it sometimes pays to be nice to people you perceive to be lower than yourself. And I stress the word *perceive*. You never know. They sometimes hold very valuable keys to things."

"What are you going to do, blackmail me?" Sagaser had now shrunk back into his chair and was barely moving.

"I'm not done yet, so if you'd please shut up until I'm through, I would greatly appreciate it. Now, as for the KKK application, I again can prove that you had that sent to me."

"You have no proof . . ." Sagaser started to say, sitting up with a disgusted look on his face, but he was cut short by Strekfus's raised hand indicating that he should stop.

"You actually requested this application via the Internet," Strekfus said. "There's something called 'computer history.' I'll explain to you what this is, since you obviously haven't familiarized yourself with it. Each time you go into a site and request information, a history of what you've looked at is stored and recorded. Here is a printout of the sites you've looked at for the past several months." He was now pressing the sheets in Sagaser's direction. Sagaser's face was falling.

"As you can see, sandwiched somewhere in between Kinky Kelly Does Kyoto, and Krauts of the Twentieth Century, is the site for the KKK and the Imperial Wizards. Coincidence? I think not."

Strekfus paused for a minute to let the information sink in. Sagaser stared at him with a blank expression which was neither hate nor disgust. Strekfus stared back. It was as though the writer was looking at something not human, something with no feelings, but this didn't matter. It didn't matter whether Sagaser processed the information. What was important was that Strekfus said it—for himself more than for his boss.

Continuing, Strekfus pulled out a rather badly photocopied list. Then looking it over, he began to speak without looking up. "The phone booth on the corner of Seventy-second Street and Broadway. The phone booth on the corner of Ninety-sixth Street and Broadway, the phone booth next to the Plaza Hotel." He paused now, looking up at Sagaser.

"And your point would be?" Sagaser queried, trying to remain calm, his meaty paws covering his mouth and the side of his face like some badly reproduced mask in a high school version of *Phantom of the Opera*.

"That your apartment is near Seventy-second Street and Broadway, your doctor is located at Ninety-sixth Street and Broadway, and the trysting place for you and that temp secretary of yours is the Plaza. The FBI was happy enough to give me these phone records. It seems that they are just as upset with whoever it was placing false reports as they would have been had they actually caught someone who was dealing in drugs. You made the calls to the FBI—the ones implicating me in drug sales. You made them from these pay phones."

"You can't prove any of this," Sagaser said. He was standing again, his anger returning. He was in survival mode, but guarded. "What do you want from me? What's the reason behind this?"

"I only want you to know that you're not ever going to do this to me again. I want you to know that I'm on to you. You have committed several crimes: harassment, fraud—oh, and I'm sure the FBI will think up something for you."

Sagaser was now pacing back and forth between his desk and the window, like some caged animal. "You're insane," he spewed in Strekfus's direction. "You're completely paranoid."

"I think not, Edwin," Strekfus said with complete calm.

And it was then that Edwin Sagaser lost it. His eyes became wild. His face turned beet red. Veins bulged from his forehead. His fists clenched and he began to shake. Strekfus was sure that the man was ready to explode. Then he did: "What are you going to do to me? What are you going to do to me?" Sagaser yelled, now completely hysterical, his voice rasping, his vocal cords strained as though they were being fed through a paper shredder.

Strekfus paused, looked down at the papers, the photos, the phone lists. He looked out the window at the darkening gray sky of late afternoon. He focused on a small turret of some ancient office building in midtown, one that had not yet been devoured by all the other vertical excuses for structures. Then he looked at Sagaser, who was still waiting for his answer. Strekfus smiled. He cleared his mind of all hate, all revenge, all disgust. He felt an inner calm, as if Sagaser were some curiosity to him, some trifle. He paused, not for dramatic effect, but because his mind was moving at a leisurely pace now. And then he spoke.

"What am I going to do to you?" Again a pause while Sagaser shook and fumed. "You really want to know?" He could tell his boss was already in hell, turning on the spit. He again felt all hatred draining, all negative energy leave his body as it was sucked up by Edwin Sagaser, the very man who had projected so much of it onto the world. It was as if his boss were some human conduit for everything evil at that moment and Strekfus felt a mixture of emotions for the man, knowing full well what he would be going through and wondering if he would be strong enough to handle it.

Strekfus remembered back to 1961 and thought about how he had assaulted Althea, kicking her shins to the point where she bled horribly. He thought about the name he had called her. He thought about how he had felt after he had finished. He thought about how she had handled it.

Then he spoke without emotion or hate.

"I'm not going to do anything to you, Mr. Sagaser."

Strekfus waited, looking over the man as if he were some rabid animal in a cage, some animal whose death was imminent, but who—as a human, if he chose correctly, if he began to work, to seek the truth, to try and uncover himself—could redeem himself and seek forgiveness. And then he continued, pausing again so that he could be sure his boss heard him. So that he could be sure the message was received.

"I'm not going to do a thing. Not a solitary thing," and with that he turned, opened the door, and stepped from the room, leaving his boss standing there in the corner, in the fading light which was that day's Manhattan late afternoon.

* * * * *

The next day his boss didn't arrive at work and Strekfus neither cared nor wondered why. He had said what he had to say and he was finished with the man. Besides, he had only one more story to give the magazine and when he finished his assignment he could begin writing his book. The day at work was remarkably calm with no news. Everyone seemed to stay out of his way, and he couldn't help but wonder if they had seen the mess he'd made of Sagaser's desk the day before, and thought that he might be dangerous. And he was dangerous, but not in the way they feared. He was a new person after his talk with Sagaser and he felt a new sense of pride and well-being spreading over him. If feeling good could be compared to a beach, then he was on some secluded white strip of sand in St. Bart's with a drink in one hand and a good book in the other. His writing seemed to flow from him now, and he found himself closing in on the last few pages of his story, like a racehorse in the final stretch.

So it was with some surprise after this perfect day, that Strekfus arrived back at his apartment to find a package waiting for him—a package that contained something which would be his undoing and his salvation, jogging his memory as so many other things had done lately. And it wasn't as if this thing waiting for him acted alone, for all the past experiences of his life, coupled with the especially strenuous previous year, had combined now as if his mind were piecing some great jigsaw puzzle together.

He tried to read the return address as he juggled keys, overcoat, and briefcase while ringing for the elevator. As the square metal box hoisted him up to his fifth-floor apartment, he tried to place the name. Then it came to him, partially—the box was from Beth Chitbill-Tallymen in New Orleans. He knew who Ima Chitbill was, but it took him a minute to place Beth.

He tore into the box as soon as he reached the kitchen table, his keys still in his hand, his briefcase still beside him. Inside the package there was a note accompanied by a rather well-worn and faded blue-velvet-covered book. The book seemed to have a clasp of sorts which appeared rusted and fragile. He opened the envelope and started to read:

Dear Mr. Beltzenschmidt,

I hope you will remember me—you came to visit us a while ago at our home on Prytania Street. I'm afraid we weren't very good company at the time, with mother's illness and all. I was the girl who answered the door— Beth—Mrs. Chitbill's daughter.

I'm sorry to tell you that my mother has passed away, leaving no will. The children have been forced to divide up her belongings (many of which have gone to the state) and sell the house, which brings me to the enclosed diary.

It seems that there were boxes of every conceivable book, magazine, newspapers, and whatnot in our attic. When this house was restored in 1935 they must have missed a few things. At any rate, the enclosed diary seems to have belonged to your grandmother. I hope you don't mind—I read part of it thinking it was Mother's and when I realized it wasn't, I read even more to try and find out who it belonged to.

Based on things you said during your visit, and a badly scrawled signature in the front of the diary, I was able to make out the name Beltzenschmidt. Had you not visited us, I would have never put together the fact that this diary was linked to you.

I hope you will accept this as a sort of peace offering for the way you were treated when you visited us.

Also enclosed, taped to the back of this letter, is the key to the diary. I hope this finds you in good health and spirits.

Sincerely,

Beth Chitbill-Tallymen

Strekfus pried the simple key from the back of the letter, trying not to tear the paper, without much luck. Inserting it into the rusted lock, he released the mechanism with a dusty click and broke open the book. Its pages were beyond yellow—they were brown—and water stains covered most of the writings, but he was able to read whole passages and glean vast amounts of information from the diary. As the musty air rose up from its pages and wafted into his nostrils, he read of his grandmother's loveless marriage; her husband's efforts to keep her away from friends; his efforts to keep his children from having any sort of normal childhood; and the abuse, both psychological and physical, that the family had suffered.

He moved to the sofa, still dressed for work, never taking his eyes off the ancient pages.

He read about his grandfather's attempt to drown his son, Paris, in a goldfish pond in back of the house one hot New Orleans summer. He read of his grandmother's struggle to pull her husband's hands from her son's throat as she watched the life drain out of the boy under the rippling, koi-filled water of the pond; of her husband's hand coming back across her face; of her breathing life back into the body of her six-year-old child when the man she loved tired of his effort to kill the boy; of her anger and rage and hurt and frustration.

Strekfus read about his grandfather beating his son, of his mentally tormenting him, of his locking him away for days at a time in closets and the attic. He read of his grandmother's heartbreak at the fact that she couldn't stop this man she had married because of fears both social and physical.

He read of stories told by relatives, of how his father's father had been, of where the family had come from and whom they had known. He read for hours, carefully translating the blurry-inked hand as it traced years of dysfunction and heartbreak. He read well past dinnertime, well past the hour he would normally have gone to sleep, and well into the night until he fell asleep with the diary at his side.

- 24 -

Somewhere in Between

> I must have read parts of many books (in
> those early days I think I never read any
> one book through) and a great deal of
> poetry in this uncomprehending way,
> until I discovered "Little Lord
> Fauntleroy," which was the first book of
> any consequence I read understandingly.
>
> —Helen Keller, *The Story of My Life*

The thunderstorm bumped and bruised overhead. Thick raindrops landed on the wavy-glass panes of the enormous windows. The transparent openings reached upward, clear and cathedral-like, allowing the afternoon tumult to flood the room. Shadows—wavy images of leaves and rain—flowed over the furnishings: the oriental carpets, the heavily carved credenzas, the damask-covered sofas. It seemed that despite the outdoor theatrics, all was calm and serene in the room.

Paris Beltzenschmidt sat in the far corner of the room, gently holding a string which was carefully knotted about the duck's neck. He prayed that it would remain quiet so that no one would suspect he had brought it inside, out of the thunderstorm. The duck sat peacefully, unmoving for the most part, hidden by an antique jardinière in the corner, just to the right of an enormous bookcase.

"Hello, Lord Fauntleroy," Paris said, resting his head on his elbow as he lay sideways on the plush carpet. There was no response from the duck, but its head turned to regard him. Then its beak gently nipped at the young boy's forearm—a sign of affection.

Paris had raised this duck after its mother had been killed accidentally by a motorcar—a rattling Model T which had swerved into the side yard. While there had been other animals to pick from (a cow and two goats), the abandoned duckling seemed so innocent, so helpless, that he had taken it in and cared for it in a pen at the back of his parent's property—their Prytania Street home—far enough away so that his father not would not notice.

His father refused to allow him to have a dog, as most boys had at the age of six or seven, and Paris, along with his brothers and sisters, wasn't allowed playmates from the neighborhood. So he had become attached to the duck, feeding it daily, making sure that none of the neighborhood cats took advantage of it, and now here it sat, sheltered from the rainstorm in his father's library.

While the thunder echoed overhead, rattling china on the shelves in the dining room, the duck silently preened itself, burying its beak deep within the down of its breast. As it pulled its head away, a single white feather was launched upward. The tiny plume hung there for a moment and then gently floated downward. Paris watched it as it made its journey, somersaulting over and over, its downy edges gently bending in the humid summer air. It seemed to lose momentum and float even more gently as it neared the plush carpet.

At first Paris wasn't sure what he was seeing. The feather had landed on something other than the carpet, something hard and black. He viewed the scene as one whose eyes have not yet adjusted to the light, trying to make out shapes and colors. After a few seconds he realized that the feather had not landed on the carpeting or the hardwood floor which boarded the perimeter of the room, but rather on a large, black wing tip shoe. He followed the shoe to the crisply creased pants leg and upward, like a tourist

455

looking up at some New York skyscraper, until he viewed his father's face, solemn and stern, looking down at him.

His father said something—Paris knew because he could see the lips move—but he could not hear it, for the thunderstorm overhead had intensified, and just as the man spoke, the enormous rumblings which seemed to come from below the earth as much as from above, blotted out his father's words. It was as though when the man opened his mouth to speak, the enormous energy and noise emanated from the opening in his face and not from nature. Then a blinding blot of lightning lit up the room. It seemed brighter than any electric light and lasted for a full two seconds before breaking into pieces. It seemed to alter time and space also, for before it finished, Paris Beltzenschmidt found himself in the side yard, in the pouring rain with his father and the duck beside him.

His father wasn't saying anything now—there was no need. Paris knew his father. He knew the man's thoughts on things such as this, things such as keeping a pet. He knew that he was going to be punished and he could accept that. But when his father grasped him by the forearm and began to drag him toward the barn, he froze, his eyes wide with terror. Paris had seen what happened in the barn. He had seen his mother selecting chickens for dinner—the ones she had ordered from the French Market. He had seen what fate they had succumbed to.

But now Paris and his father were in the barn and the man was tearing through gear and tackle, bringing out the object the boy feared most. Under one arm his father now had an axe, while with his other he held firmly to his son, who in turn had not relinquished his hold on the duck.

At some point the young boy's body refused to cooperate, sensing what was to come, and Paris found himself being pulled through the mud—his father totally unaware that he was no longer in an upright position. Another flash of lightning and his father was standing over him holding the axe. It all seemed dreamlike and surreal. The rain began to fall harder, and in a corner by the barn a small grove of banana trees whipped and twisted in the wind like some sick crowd at a bullfighting match. The rain stung Paris's face as he looked up at his father with pleading eyes. Then something happened. Something came from deep inside the boy and he managed to pull it out even further until it was a word. And the word was directed upward into the rain-filled air.

"No!" he shouted up at his father. "No!"

He had never dared to speak back to this man. He had endured years of punishment and abuse for virtually nothing, so he knew what rebellion could cost. But it didn't matter—the word had come out and it had done so with force and anger.

His father didn't respond. There was a moment of silence with no movement. Then, grasping the frightened, rain-soaked duck by the neck, the man angrily carried it over to the barn and threw it inside, shutting the door. Returning to his last position, without saying a word, he reached down and wrenched his son's arm upward with incredible violence. There was a crack of bone and a scream of pain as the limb snapped. The howling that Paris emitted echoed throughout the yard and into the lush foliage. It was only briefly drowned out by the enormous thunder which shook everything. It was at that moment that Paris Beltzenschmidt sealed his fate, for before he knew what was happening he was at war with his father.

Father and son were now a tangle of anger and confused flesh, but the struggle lasted only minutes as Paris was small and weak compared to this giant of a man. Then the boy felt himself being pulled through the mud again, but this time in the direction of the side yard, toward the rose garden and the goldfish pond. There was almost no pain now in his arm (the very one his father had broken and had chosen to drag him by), and as shock set in and Paris's mind veered toward the abyss of insanity—as though something were overtaking him in an effort to assure his survival—he felt a part of himself leave his body.

It was at that moment that he saw his mother as she began to run toward him, her white muslin dress clinging to her ample white body as the rain beat down upon her. It seemed as if she were running in slow motion, for by the time she got to father and son, Paris was already seeing the ripples of the pond close up. He was already under water, and his father's hand was placed firmly around the back of his neck, shoving him deeper into the pool. Large koi slapped the sides of his head in an attempt to retreat from the commotion. The father's hand gripped harder now and shoved his son's face into the concrete bottom of the pond, cutting open the boy's chin so that plumes of bright blood floated upward and then darkened the water. The boy could make out sounds now as his breath began to escape from him: sounds of his mother's pleading, of the thunder. Sounds which seemed to be filtered as through a dream or some drugged hallucination. Then a sharp noise and his father's hand released him. He came up for air and as he spun around he caught the motion of a large hand striking his mother's face. Then the red trickle of blood from her mouth. Then her body falling to the ground.

Out of the corner of his eye he caught sight of his older sister, Testa, but she seemed to be standing there frozen in space, not moving or speaking. She seemed almost catatonic. In another second he caught sight of his other sister as she gripped the upper railing of the balcony. She was framed by the outline of an enormous date palm, its huge leaves forming a halo about her like some dark sun. Paris knew she could not help him—that she was too far away and too young. He tried to reach her with his thoughts but something took hold of him and he lost his resolve.

His father was on him again, this time flinging him down, holding him more firmly under the water. Paris felt his will giving in and allowed all the air to leave his body, thinking that if he gave his attacker what he so desired the man would leave him alone. The bubbles burst upward around his face and just before he lost consciousness he saw the lightning flash above him. He secretly hoped it would strike him now and take the pain away, but as if tormented by some hateful God, nothing happened and he slowly gave in to death. He felt all resistance leave his body. He felt himself being lifted up. He felt calm. He felt peace. What a joy it was now to be free. To be free from fear and torture. To be free from pain and life.

And it was almost as if at the moment the freedom was most exquisite, that it was taken away, for at the height of his pleasure he began to see flashes of light. Then he began to hear the rain again. Now he was seeing something marbled. A sky? But why was this? Hadn't he died? Why was his mother's face over him and the taste of blood in his mouth? Why was she crying, bent over him, out of breath?

It seemed that he could only momentarily make sense of the scene before he saw his father shove her to the side. The man was standing over him again. Then his mother's pleading, the thunder, the lightning. Paris was once again being pulled across the yard. Wasn't it enough that he had died and been brought back to life? Wasn't it enough that he had suffered? Why was his father doing this? All through it the man had not said a word. And for all the pain, the cruelty, the degradation, that was the worst part—his father's silence.

Paris was once again being confronted with the axe—his father standing over him, the rain pelting them both. He knew what the man wanted him to do. He knew that if he didn't perform the task, his father would kill him. And he was tired. He loved his pet but he needed to survive and he felt so drained that he didn't even have the strength to die. It didn't matter now anyway. He was numb. He knew what it felt like not to be loved. He knew that his life would never be the same and an anger rose up in him, blinding him, making him invisible to himself.

Paris stayed down, kneeling in the mud as his father brought him the duck and picked up the axe. He knew that if he faltered this time that death would be certain. The sky above had turned a greenish-black like some ugly bruise that refused to heal. The rain was coming down harder now. Paris looked to his left briefly to see his mother, kneeling in the rose garden, praying. His elder sister still stood there, motionless, witnessing everything but saying nothing. He looked farther to the left, to the verandah at the front of the house which was visible from the side yard. He could see his other sister still standing on the upper level. She was also motionless, white and frail.

459

His father was now holding the duck, its neck stretched out over the fetid and damp stump. Rain pelted the animal's frightened open eyes. Its beak opened but nothing came out.

The axe was in Paris's hand now. He was holding it with his good arm, the one not broken by his father. Pain was now familiar to him, so much so in fact that it was a comfort. The physical pain which racked his body was his friend, taking away energy from the mental torment he was enduring. He knew better than to miss and hit his father with the axe, but for a brief second the thought entered his mind. But he knew that he would only injure his father and the man would see to it that he died after that.

Then Paris thought about striking his father in the head. If he brought the axe down hard enough, the blow would surely kill the man. But one look at his father's ice-cold expression told him to be quick—that there was no time for thought, only survival. Paris also knew that he barely had the energy left to kill the duck, much less bring the blade crashing down through his father's skull, and even if he did so, he feared his father so much that he knew the man would find a way to get even with him, even after death.

Paris raised the axe as high as he could. He wanted to be sure that the death was as quick as possible. He thought that if he could be done with the incident he would wake up from this nightmare. The earth seemed to go into slow motion as the axe fell and he thought he could once again see himself from above, watching the scene. Slowly the axe came down, weighted, floating through the atmosphere as if through water.

At the moment it made contact, severing the duck's head from its body, an enormous strike of lightning plummeted from the sky, hitting the giant date palm on the other side of the house. It seemed that the crash it made as it brushed against the mansion, taking out every window on one side, was an amplification of his pain. He watched now as the body of his pet twitched even after being separated from its head. The blood continued to flow onto the ground, running in a smooth stream, carried by the hard rain which bore it away from Paris.

But it seemed to carry away much more, for he found himself in a place he had never been before, unable to justify what had happened and thinking of a way to avenge it. And yet he knew that the revenge he now so desperately sought wouldn't be doled out directly to his father. He knew that it might take other forms, that it might be years in the making, that it might consume him before he was through. But he knew that it would happen someday, and yet he also knew that he wouldn't experience freedom when the act was done, for on this day in 1933, during this thunderstorm in New Orleans, Paris Beltzenschmidt had become someone other than the person God had meant for him to be.

Now there was no turning back.

- 25 -

New York, 1997

The beautiful truth burst upon my
mind—I felt that there were invisible
lines stretched between my spirit and the
spirits of others.

—Helen Keller, *The Story of My Life*

"I did it," he said into the receiver before Sharon could respond. Strekfus had called her not realizing what time it was. "I've started it. I've started the book."

"Do you have any idea what time it is?" she asked, groggy with sleep.

"It doesn't matter. I've started it. God, so much has happened. I've got so much to tell you." He was becoming more excited by the minute, spewing out everything so that she could be a part of it. "Remember when I went back to New Orleans to visit those people who lived in the house my father grew up in? Well, the daughter sent me a diary that belonged to my grandmother. I didn't want to say anything until I finished it, but now I've got this whole new outlook on what it was like for my father and his family."

"It's six thirty in the morning. Have you been up all night long doing this stuff?"

"Listen, you know how I was told he had a pet duck?"

"Does anyone use the phone during the day? Is this something that only happens when other people are asleep?"

"You've called *me* at all hours. Now it's your turn. I'm trying to tell you something. Will you listen, please?"

"Okay, okay, go ahead. I'm listening. Something about a duck and a diary." She was groggy but sympathetic now. "What's this got to do with your stories, the ones in the magazine?"

"Nothing. Everything. That's just it. I've decided to finally start on that book we spoke about. And I've already got a title for it. I'm going to call it, *Somewhere in Between.*"

"Somewhere in between what?"

"That's the title. I've lived half my life in the South and the rest in New York, and there's a whole part of me that is neither here nor there. I don't even know where I belong anymore. I'm always 'somewhere in between,' like I'm living in a no-man's land." His voice had taken on a desperate air, as happens when the message being sent is not the same as that being received. "Are you awake? I need you to hear this."

"Why, am I in the stories again?"

"No, not this time. I've already written one about my father. The next one is going to be about *his* father." He was hurrying now in an attempt to transfer all the information to her, hoping she would understand, be sympathetic, supportive. "I've got to be able to trace the line from generation to generation, to show what made me the way I am, what made my father the way he was, and back even further."

"And this will prove . . ."

"I don't know it will prove anything. It's just something I have to do."

"Not a bad idea, this writing a book. Perhaps you could sell it," she said, now apparently awake and feeling resentful for having been disturbed. "After all, you probably don't have a job anymore since your little tantrum in Sagaser's office." She knew she had hit a nerve and she waited for his response, expecting at least a modicum of silence before he jumped on her, but there was neither the pause nor the attack.

"Who cares? Besides it will probably be the best thing for me if he does fire me. And I don't think he's going to with all the evidence I have against him. And he raked everything off his desk once before. What's he going to do now? Complain?"

"Have you even spoken with him since you went off?" she asked, stifling a yawn.

"We've been dancing around each other. He's not said anything and neither have I, and since it's been a week I figured that if he were going to fire me or take some action, he'd have already done it. Whenever we pass each other he either nods or pretends that I'm not there."

"Poor son-of-a-bitch is probably scared stiff," she said, intending no sympathy, just an observation.

"He should be, that bastard. After all he did to me."

"Don't you think just maybe you're being a little hard on him? Just maybe you're projecting a little?" she asked, trying to make her voice sound more prodding than intrusive.

"Projecting? What do you mean?" He reached toward the nightstand for his cigarettes, then remembered that he had decided to quit. He had not told anyone of this decision, indeed he had not even verbalized it out loud to himself. He drew his hand back and began to mutilate a paperclip in an attempt to soothe his nerves.

"I think you see Sagaser as this person, this father figure, whatever you want to call it, that is supposed to pay for all the things ever done to you," Sharon continued. "Your father is dead, your mother is dead, your Aunt Testa, Althea—all of them dead. You never got a chance to confront them, to make things right, and I think now you're transferring all your anger onto Sagaser."

"How could I possibly see Edwin Sagaser as my father?" he asked, completely indignant, but silently mindful that she was correct in her observation.

"A lot of people seek out others to act as their parents or reenact something in the hopes of getting what they never had as a child. Sometimes it's an attempt to set the record straight. All I'm saying is that despite the fact that Sagaser is a bastard and has made your life miserable, just make sure you're not crucifying him for all the ills done to you in your life by those who professed to love you or were family."

"I can't believe what I'm hearing," he said, not even bothering to couch the words in a velvety covering. "You can't stand the man and now you're lecturing me on how to treat him."

"Obviously I hit a nerve."

"Obviously."

"Don't get all bent out of shape. I'm not the enemy, remember?"

"I know. It's just that I'm really onto something. And I don't need any lectures or additional baggage."

"Am I going to get to read this beginning of a book anytime soon?"

"Tomorrow. I'll show it to you tomorrow. I'm working on the second story right now—the one about my grandfather. I'll let you see the first two stories so you can get an idea of where I'm going."

"Okay. Fine. Can I get back to bed now? On second thought, I might as well stay up as I'm sure you're going to do, writing until the last minute before you have to be at work. Besides, you might call me back, and even though you're my best friend, there *are* certain limits to our relationship."

They hung up and Strekfus turned his attention back to the narrative he was working on. He had finished the last story for the magazine and set it aside, and now he wanted to work on this second idea for his book—the chronicle about his father's family, and most specifically, his grandfather. What a gift the diary had been, giving him glimpses into his grandparents' lives and answering at least some of the questions he had about the way they lived and what they thought—even if it was gruesome and depressing.

What questions weren't answered were easily figured out by reading between the lines, so he set to work on the story of one of the journeys his grandfather had taken. And he did this in an attempt to explain the even longer journey the generations of Beltzenschmidts had endured—the one which wasn't over yet.

- 26 -

Somewhere in Between

Still there is much in the Bible against
which every instinct of my being rebels,
so much that I regret the necessity which
has compelled me to read it through from
beginning to end.

—Helen Keller, *The Story of My Life*

H e was used to the blindfold now. They had been traveling
for at least two hours—the sun's intensity told him
this—so Isaac acclimated himself to the rough piece of
cloth that his father had tied around his head. The sweat, which
poured off him, had soaked through the entire circumference of
the blindfold. He now resigned himself to the fact that it would
be at least another two hours before he would be given
permission to remove it.

They both sat silently—Isaac and his father—as the
wagon bumped along the dusty road. Occasionally a horsefly
flitted about the boy's face or a raven cawed high in one of the
dead trees lining the path, but other than this there was only
silence. His father had not told him of the plan. Indeed, if Isaac
hadn't overheard it being discussed with his uncle the evening
before, then he would not have known what was to happen.

He wondered if his father thought it strange that he had
not asked where they were going, or why he had been

blindfolded. His father was not a man of many words. Still, this event seemed to be such a unique experience that Isaac couldn't help but wonder why the man made no reference to the planned activities. If what was to take place would indeed happen, he thought that the least this man he called "father" could do would be to show some hint of mercy, some explanation, some justification. But then that would have been out of character for his father—a man who himself had been at the mercy of those before him.

Had Isaac's father meant for him to overhear the conversation? Was he supposed to know what lay in store? Isaac had listened to his father and uncle speak of what was to take place as they sat by the fire the evening before—speaking of that day's hunting and of the harvesting of crops—all the while thinking that he was asleep. For a time, the two men discussed their past stories about the War Between the States: how many Yankee soldiers each had killed, the burning and looting, and the rape of their land by those they considered to be foreigners—the soldiers from the North.

After a while, Isaac's father had told his brother that it was time for his son to become a man, and that in order to achieve this he would take the boy, now twelve years old, blindfolded into the wilderness, miles away from civilization. He would leave him there to find his way out. If he did so and came home, then he was a man. If he didn't, and died, then it was the Lord's will and the boy wasn't meant to survive.

When Isaac had heard this, lying under the coarse, heavy blankets, it had come as no surprise. His father was a stern man, not given to frivolity or sentimentality, especially since the death of his wife two years earlier. Isaac missed her—this gentle woman, his mother—even though he had known her only briefly. He remembered that both his parents had been extremely religious. That had been the chief bond between them. And his father still was. In fact, Hezekiah Beltzenschmidt read the Bible constantly, his favorite story being that of Abraham and Isaac. Isaac Beltzenschmidt had heard the story so many times now that he had lost count: the way God had commanded Abraham to

467

bind Isaac, his son, and sacrifice him as a burnt offering. The way God had stopped the sacrifice just before it was to happen.

So this, accompanied by the fact that his father, this man who was about to take him into the wilderness possibly to die, had named him Isaac, was no coincidence. How many times had the boy endured the embarrassment of his father calling after him, the man's voice ringing out over the harsh Mississippi land, and how many times had he cringed at the name Isaac, wishing that he could change it to something else.

He thought of all the books in his father's library, the ones with pictures and stories about far-away lands. Why couldn't he have some name like those in the exotic manuscripts? He decided that if he ever had a son of his own, that his name would have nothing to do with the Bible. And he vowed not to be the tyrannical man that his father was. He felt that by being named Isaac, he had been cursed, almost as if he were required by the universe to play out some role dealt to him. Perhaps if he lived to be old enough to have a son he would name him after some city associated with beauty or ideals—anything but a name associated with the Bible. That way his son wouldn't be expected to fall into some role predetermined merely by association to a name. Rome Beltzenschmidt—he liked the sound of that. Or Constantinople Beltzenschmidt. No, that was too long. Still, it was an improvement over Isaac or anything even remotely related to shepherds or sacrifices or commandments or unbending and archaic laws. But this fantasy about growing old and having a son would have to wait. Now he had to concentrate on his own survival.

Isaac knew his father was playing out his own biblical fantasy, offering his son as a sacrifice. And even though his father had never said that he loved him, Isaac knew, or thought he knew, that this man who was his parent wanted only the best for him. But his father's obsession with the Bible and desire to make his son strong sometimes undermined the intended outcome. Isaac had rebelled against all religion, at least in his early years.

So strictly did Hezekiah Beltzenschmidt interpret the Bible that he thought all snakes should be destroyed—the reptiles being the incarnation of the devil himself as represented in the Garden of Eden. And the section about "an eye for an eye," had taken on a new meaning years earlier when Isaac's father had become unintentionally involved in a brawl at the county jail, accidentally putting out the eye of a convicted felon about to be hanged. So determined was Hezekiah Beltzenschmidt to keep the laws of the Bible literally, that he never cried out in pain nor showed emotion as he plunged the hot poker into his own eye socket, thereby achieving retribution for the now-deceased horse thief who had refused to take part in the task shortly before his death.

So now Isaac sat stoically in the front of the wagon with his father beside him, thinking of these incidents. His father had not explained anything, and Isaac had not asked. He knew better. His father was not a man you crossed or questioned. The man had fought in the Civil War (he had both eyes at the time), and had been a highly decorated general. People respected and feared him. People stayed out of his way. And now, somewhere deep in Tishomingo County, Mississippi, in this hungry and tired year of 1875, Hezekiah Beltzenschmidt was going to leave his son as far away from civilization as possible in order to test him—to see if he could become a man.

After several hours the wagon stopped and Isaac heard his father climb down. He waited a few moments and then did the same, feeling his way to the ground. His father put his hand on his shoulder and then removed it. It was the most anger-free physical contact the two had ever shared.

It was getting late in the day now—again, Isaac could tell from the way the heat of the sun fell on him. His father led him over rocky terrain, over a brook, through several open fields, and then over another stream. Was it the same brook as the first? Had they crossed it twice or was this another? Then after traveling still farther, Isaac felt his father lead him onto something unstable. It was a raft. Soon they were moving. But Isaac knew his father and he wondered if this was a trick. Was his father actually ferrying him across a river or was he merely paddling around in circles, trying to confuse him? Soon they were on dry land again and Isaac was unable to tell if this was some new shore or the site they had set off from. His father led him a short distance away. When the man was secure in the knowledge that his son was completely lost, he once again placed his hand on the boy's shoulder as a signal.

Isaac could feel the intense sun burning down on him as he heard his father's footsteps move away. In fact, the sound they made was incredibly clear due to the fact that his sense of sight had been cut off for such a time. But the fact that neither he nor his father ever communicated made him feel as though he were dumb, without a voice, and in some way this also heightened his other senses. It was as though by not speaking, by not letting out what it was he wanted to say, that Isaac was forced to communicate in some other form, to retreat within himself, to find a way to deal with his life and what he had been given, and to do it on his own terms.

Isaac knew not to remove the blindfold. His father had not told him to—it was unspoken. He waited until the sound of human movement was well out of range before loosening its frayed and damp ends. The sun was directly in his eyes, almost blinding him. He had been in the darkness for so long now that the bright ball of fire seemed to scream through him, burning its arcane message into his retinas. He wanted to look at the light, but the darkness had been with him now for so long that he shielded his eyes, afraid of the intensity the large object displayed.

Calmly he assessed the situation. Isaac reasoned that he had heard his father move away on land after the river journey and now he saw the raft, tied in some rushes along the river's edge. That would have to mean that his father had only circled in the water and not actually crossed the river because he still had to return to his cart and horse in order to travel home. But again, he wondered if this were some trick, some device to throw him off the trail of returning home. What if his father had actually taken him across the river and then moved away on foot to another raft or small boat that the man had previously hidden upstream or downstream? His father could have then recrossed the river and made his way back to the horse and cart on the other side.

Isaac knew how his father's mind worked. He knew the man was capable of something such as this. To make matters worse, Isaac wasn't even sure which river he was now looking at. And he knew that rivers didn't necessarily run from north to south. Some of them, like the Tennessee River, looped sideways and then back up, so there was no way of telling where he would end up if he followed the body of water. He knew he could vacillate about whether or not his father had actually crossed the river, and so he decided to make a decision and stick with it. Isaac reasoned that his father's journey across the river had taken too long and that if his father had actually ferried him to the other side, the trip would have been much shorter. Perhaps this was the key. His father had tried to throw him off by doing this. Secure in this knowledge, Isaac headed away from the riverbank and toward what he thought was innermost Tishomingo County, Mississippi.

Isaac knew not to panic as he made his way into the wilderness. He knew that he had no food, no water, no protection. He knew that his father had done this to make him strong. He knew he must survive at all costs and that he only had a few hours to head in the direction of some small town before night fell. Still, something inside of him burned with anger. It burned with hatred for his father. It burned at the thought of being tested in a time when life was already difficult.

It burned with anger at the fact that he was only twelve years old.

And yet, at the same time, he felt sympathy for his father. He had been told stories about his father's father. How strict that man had been, how demanding. He knew that being left in the wilderness was harsh, but he remembered what his father had told him about his own childhood and he was silently thankful, at least for the moment, that this was all he had to endure.

Isaac stood alone now, trying to calculate the position of the sun and which direction it had traveled from. When he had determined what he thought was his position in the universe, he began to walk slowly, ever mindful of the difficult terrain, trying to keep near the stream and avoid the dark, confusing woods. But

471

after the first hour, his mind began to wonder, and it did so to such an extent that he never noticed the deadly rattlesnake which lay just a few feet away—its thick, scaled body undulating and coiled. Isaac's foot came down on it with such force that the snake's body seemed to leap straight up, then arch outward and toward his calf with lightning speed.

It was at that moment that instinct took over, releasing him from all fear and anxiety, for as soon as he assessed the situation—the second the snake suspended itself in the air—he reached down in the direction of the tail. It was as though some part of his mind had seen the reptile previously, and while he was stepping on it and the snake was preparing to strike, he was already planning to fling it away.

For some reason the serpent's fangs missed his leg and were now snagged into the thick material of his trousers. The reptile's head thrashed wildly about for only a moment before Isaac's hand grasped the snake's tail and flung it away, tearing one of the serpent's fangs free in the process.

As the injured creature slithered off into the underbrush Isaac tried to slow his breathing. Had this really just happened or was it some sort of dream? In the moment of crisis he had acted with conviction and without fear. But now that he was free of the danger, his mind reviewed all the possibilities that could have happened. He wanted to sit down because his legs were shaking, but he knew he had far to travel and he feared other dangers in this untamed land. He continued to walk, wondering why he had been so careless as to miss the snake and why he had not heard the reptile's rattle. He didn't even bother to remove the solitary fang which had broken off from the snake's powerful jaws and now hung precariously from the thick material of his pants leg.

As he walked, Isaac remembered a story his father used to tell him when he was younger. Isaac's grandfather, Hezekiah Beltzenschmidt's father, had been determined to make *his* son grow up strong and unafraid—a Beltzenschmidt custom that had been passed down through the generations. Each day the father would find some new way to test his son. At one point, Hezekiah's father held live snakes up to his son's face when the boy was only six or seven, telling him that if he showed fear he would release the snake's head and allow it to bite the boy. Hezekiah also told his son of waking up in the morning and finding several dead snakes in his bed. *His* father had placed them there overnight.

Isaac knew these types of incidents had made his father strong, but he wasn't sure they were doing the same for him. He also knew these episodes had made his father slightly crazy. But he knew not to show fear, even out here alone in the wilderness. It was as though his father could see him, read his mind, even though the man was nowhere in sight. There was only one thing which his father found acceptable to be afraid of, and that was God.

Now, Isaac kept his wits about him. He would watch more carefully for other dangers. He traveled for hours over rocks, shallow streams, vast fields, and edges of forest. At one time he thought he heard the sound of a hunter's gun, but as he stood completely still, trying to will the sounds of nature to stop long enough for him to assess the situation, he lost the hollow, echoing note and found himself once again traversing the uneven terrain of this harsh land.

For three days, he traveled the desolate landscape, eating what he could off the land, sleeping next to the enormous trunks of pine trees which spread a soft and sweet-smelling bed of needles for him. He lay awake at night, terrified of the sounds of animals he knew and even more of those he didn't, until exhaustion took him over and he rested.

But it wasn't the physical hardships which took their toll on him as much as it was the emotional and mental ones. It was as if he were some victim of mental illness or weakness. He felt himself becoming someone other than who he wished to be, and while he traveled through the actual wilderness of the South, he also traveled through the lands of denial, anger, depression, and fear, and these landscapes was more terrifying than anything the physical world could show him. It was as if he had to explore every one of the possibilities before he could come to the conclusion that he reached, and the final verdict was this: No matter how much his father professed to love him, no matter how much this act was being performed for his own good, no matter how in keeping it might be with God's law or divine doctrine or biblical stories or honoring his parents, he hated his father at this moment and he would continue to despise him for the rest of his life.

Isaac would come out of the experience alive but not whole, like one of the men his father spoke of so often—those who had survived the war but were forced to live without an arm or a leg. But for now he continued to search, to walk the land, to hope for survival, putting this hatred toward the back of his mind where it would remain until called up for use some time later.

* * * * *

Isaac Beltzenschmidt was found sometime late on the third day of his wanderings. He stumbled onto a remote farm in northern Alabama, not far from the Mississippi line, having chosen the wrong direction to travel in. As the farm's dogs ran barking and snarling at him, not realizing he was completely helpless, he collapsed near a water pump. It would take him several months to recover physically, and after doing so he never again trusted his father or anyone else other than one man. And as soon as he could, at the age of fourteen, he left home, remembering forever the experience he had endured at twelve and the fact that when his father came to retrieve him from the farmhouse, not a word was spoken.

But something fascinated him about the experience. It was the fact that his father had been so obsessed with the Bible and the story of Abraham and Isaac. And it was other stories in the book as well. One would have thought that Isaac Beltzenschmidt would have developed an aversion to the Bible or anything related to it, but rather he had become overtaken by every aspect of the book in an attempt to try and understand what kind of God would allow this to happen to him and what kind of God it was that asked Abraham to kill his own son. It was as if the thing that repelled him the most simultaneously attracted him.

474

In addition to this love for the Bible, Isaac would have one other enthrallment, and that was with the man who had found him on that third day in northern Alabama—the one person he would trust. Isaac would maintain contact with this man for years afterward, completely taken by this individual who had showed him kindness, offering a drink of water from the pump in back of the house, laying him on the patchwork quilt on one of the beds. And he had been intrigued to find that this loving man had known his father—had served with him in the Confederate army—for it was this very man who sent word to his father in Tishomingo County, Mississippi, that his son was safe from harm and that God should be praised. It was this very man who sat with him and cared for him until his father arrived and took him home.

For years Isaac kept in touch with this gentle man, this savior, until the former Confederate soldier's life became too complicated and the correspondence ceased. Years later he would come to understand why, as the man who had showed him kindness—Captain Arthur Keller of Tuscumbia, Alabama—was known throughout the South and much of the world not for his gentle nature, but rather for his daughter, Helen, who at the age of nineteen months, became deaf, dumb, and blind.

As with so many things in a family's past—old photographs, memories, and mementoes—stories are apt to get lost, and as this was just one of many for the son of Hezekiah Beltzenschmidt, its telling became less and less until there was only the barest of threads left, like the covering of some well-worn doll which has been played with relentlessly and now lies broken and covered with dust, waiting for some member of the next generation to find it.

- 27 -

New York, 1997

All the sun's warmth left the air. I knew
the sky was black, because all the heat,
which meant light to me, had died out of
the atmosphere. A strange odour came up
from the earth. I knew it, it was the odour
that always precedes a thunderstorm, and
a nameless fear clutched at my heart. I felt
absolutely alone, cut off from my friends
and the firm earth. The immense, the
unknown, enfolded me.

—Helen Keller, *The Story of My Life*

S haron sat at the outdoor café in midtown, reading the limp
and soggy pages that Strekfus had handed her. The rain was
pouring now with the intensity of a hurricane and the
patrons who sat nearest the awning's edge got up to move nearer
the wall of the restaurant or to disperse inside the spacious deli's
interior.

"Intense," she said, as she laid the sheets on the marble
top. "Should we move, do you think?" and with that she looked
up at the awning whipping furiously in the wind.

"We're not getting wet. What's the harm? As a matter of
fact, I rather like sitting this close to a storm." No sooner had
Strekfus finished this statement than a middle-aged woman came
whirling up to the canopy, pushing a plastic-covered stroller with
a screaming infant inside, while dragging a six-year-old boy along

with her. The woman bent attentively over the baby and attempted to comfort it, but as she did so, the wind picked up and caught the plastic covering which protected the stroller, almost sending it reeling onto the sidewalk where sheets of violent rain pelted the slick gray pavement. She caught it with a gasp and moved it toward the doorway of the restaurant, next to one of the large, square garbage cans now overflowing with napkins and debris. As soon as she noticed the half-open mouth of the receptacle with its partially eaten sandwiches and food-smeared wrappers—blood-red from sauces, dirty and used—she made an attempt to move the baby away, somewhere nearer the middle of the outside portion of the café, somewhere in between the doorway and one of the outer walls of the building, somewhere safe from the raging storm. The small child whom she held by the hand seemed to take the scene in stride.

The entire incident with the baby, with the stroller, the garbage can, had taken only a minute, but something registered for Strekfus, confusing him, pulling him down mentally until he knew he had to get away.

"If this rain doesn't let up we may be here a while," said Sharon, craning her neck around to see outside the covered space.

Strekfus looked at her, then nervously at the inside of the fluorescent-lit deli which could be seen clearly now because of the impending darkness. The crying baby had unnerved him, but suddenly it, the mother, and the other child were gone. It was as if they had disappeared into thin air.

"Listen, I've got to go to the little girl's room," Sharon said as she extricated herself from the table and straightened out her skirt. "Won't be but a sec."

"I'll wait for you. I don't feel like heading back to the office and besides, this rain isn't getting any better," he said, feeling somewhat calmer now that the family trio had disappeared. But no sooner had Sharon gone than he felt an eerie presence near him, as though someone were watching him. He looked up and to his right. There was the small child, the boy who had come into the café with his mother and the screaming infant. The boy's head was almost even with the top of the table and all Strekfus could see were his eyes and a shock of blond hair. For a moment or two the child simply regarded Strekfus, making no sound. Finally, Strekfus, hoping to relieve the tension of being stared at, and thinking how he had to start dealing with children at some point in his life, leaned slightly forward, and as good-naturedly as he could, spoke to the boy. "Hey there, little guy," he said in a friendly tone, but no sooner were the words out of his mouth than the boy began to cry hysterically.

At first, Strekfus just sat back, shocked at the child's reaction. Then he noticed that the few other patrons left outside were staring, and he looked around to try to locate the mother. He remembered what she was wearing, and so he stood up and scanned not only the outside, but also the inside of the deli through the large plate-glass windows, in the hope of seeing her.

She was nowhere to be found.

By now, the child's crying had increased to virtual screams, and the boy stood motionless, directly in front of Strekfus, wailing as if he had been struck by a fist. Strekfus was so shocked and upset by this that he moved around the table and over to the child—something he normally never would have done—in an attempt to comfort the boy. He gently touched the small child's arm in an effort to placate him, but the child only continued to scream. As Strekfus stood up, the boy threw himself at Strekfus's legs and held on tight, screaming into the material of his dress pants. A type of panic—one which says to run—overtook Strekfus, but another emotion was coming to him now, telling him not to make a mistake, not to take flight.

Now he felt something deep inside him take over, as if some primal urge had oozed to the surface and nothing he could do would stop it. He felt the overwhelming need to comfort this poor individual who was in pain, and before he knew what was happening, he reached down and scooped the boy up. The small child threw his arms around Strekfus's neck and sobbed, tears streaming down his face. Strekfus noticed that he too was crying, but before he could make sense of the situation he heard a voice in back of him, and as he turned he was confronted by the angry mother. Her twisted mouth moved, but Strekfus couldn't hear anything, for the rain had increased to such an extent that it produced a roaring in his ears.

She was pointing to her son, calling for help, gesturing to the other individuals in the café now in an attempt to get them on her side. A few words seemed to make their way through the throbbing in his head: pedophile, child molester, kidnapper, but these were distorted, and as the rain had now increased and a flood of images seemed to take over his brain, he found himself turning over the limp body of the child to his mother. He felt himself moving away from the woman. He felt himself going almost limp.

Everything seemed to fall away from him: his present worries about his job, the general anxiety New York produces for those living and working in such an environment, the petty cares of other office workers, his worries about his health, his desire to write stories about his past. It all seemed infinitesimally small now as panic set in and shot though his body like some bullet which he had dodged unsuccessfully.

The woman had now managed to put the child behind her, but Strekfus had already seen the boy, seen the infant, seen the debris spilling out onto the concrete floor of the canopy-covered sidewalk, heard the words from the mother's mouth. He had also heard the child's cry of pain and he had felt the storm raging all around him, but as if regressing to some time before, long ago, he suddenly became deaf, unable to hear Sharon as she called out after him. He bolted into the rain, unable to see the cab heading for him as he crossed the street, unable to cry out as the fender of the automobile came toward him, seemingly in slow motion, knocking him into the air and over the hood of the car. It seemed that he hovered there for an instant before landing on the windshield with a tremendous thud which shattered the glass into a million pieces and created a fantastic labyrinth of spider-web-like designs, like some avant-garde crystal sculpture created out of something ugly and violent and at the same time beautiful.

And as he lay there waiting for the ambulance, hearing the milling voices around him, seeing Sharon at his side take his pulse, breathing hard, telling him everything would be all right, he thought to himself what a fascinating design the web made, and noticed quite calmly, how intricately connected all of the fractures in the glass seemed to be. It was as if at this moment everything in the universe made sense, for the sinewy, glinting lines in what had previously been a sheet of glass cut into his mind like a thousand beautiful surgeons opening the way to freedom and liberty, to peace of mind and health.

- 28 -

Somewhere in Between

It seems to me that there is in each of us
a capacity to comprehend the impressions
and emotions which have been
experienced by mankind from the
beginning. Each individual has a
subconscious memory of the green earth
and murmuring waters, and blindness and
deafness cannot rob him of this gift from
past generations. This inherited capacity is
a sort of sixth sense—a soul-sense which
sees, hears, feels, all in one.

—Helen Keller, *The Story of My Life*

The way it came to him was strange, for memory is a delicate, unstable thing—wild and savage at times, docile and meek at others—depending on circumstances and place. So it wasn't with total shock that Strekfus knew he was on the edge of experiencing something unusual. It was almost as if his body were preparing him for the vision, having conferred with his mind sometime during the night, finding just the right moment and location to present its gift. And in a way it was a gift, for it washed up so innocently on the shores of his mind that at first he hardly noticed. It was as if while strolling along the soft sands of memory he had bent down to pick up some luminescent and pearly shell, intent on taking it home and placing it on a shelf.

481

Instead, the moment he lifted the shell from its foamy edge of beach, something began to stir within, and he was now left to contend with this living creature in his hand.

So it was that this memory, this vision came to him as he lay perfectly still on his back on this gray day in New York. At first he simply noted how strange it was that he had awakened on his back. He never slept on his back—never—yet here he was awakening in that very position. He remembered only once coming out of a deep sleep in this position. It had been when he was still quite young, and the hysteria he had felt was so intense that he made sure it never happened again.

Now he had no choice.

As he slowly came to, he realized that he was in a hospital room. He tried to lift himself from the fog, but something held him down, some mental weight, and as he moved his eyes around the room he realized that he was on his back for a reason—this was the way they put you in the hospital while they hooked you up to intravenous tubes and monitoring devices, not to mention traction equipment.

The amount of painkillers he had been given prevented him from turning even slightly, and it was as though he were neither asleep nor awake, but in a half-dream state. He could see the room and hear the traffic outside his window, but he was not totally aware yet of the real world around him. So when the dream he had endured since childhood floated up in his mind, he lay perfectly still, watching it like some long-forgotten movie.

He knew this part of the dream, the apparition, the vision: the darkness, the door opening, the doctor standing at the base of the child's incubator. But what happened next frightened him more than anything he had ever experienced in his life. He tried to attribute the fear to his surroundings—his phobia about hospitals—but this was somehow different, somehow more intense, as though being trapped inside one of the very institutions he feared had set off this recurring nightmare.

Usually at this point, after he had experienced one or two seemingly unrelated incidents, the vision ended and he was left to feel nauseated and groggy. But today was different, and the moment he realized that the dream or vision or whatever this was, was going to continue, was going to play itself out fully, he became paralyzed with fear. Literally, he was unable to move an inch of his body, and it was as though his eyes were forced open and made to watch. Equally horrifying was the fact that, while he could "see" the film before him, his conscious mind was still working on some rational level, allowing him to experience and think as he normally would, naming people, defining places, searching for some rationale, but above all allowing him almost to see inside the individuals in this nightmare.

It was as though he had connected to some sixth sense and he could hear the thoughts and pain of others, as though at that moment he knew that everyone on the earth was connected, that everyone who had ever lived in every country in every time, had a thread that ran through them and then onto the next person, and that we were all a part of one big plan whose twists and turns we couldn't even begin to imagine. It was as though for one brief second in this one brief life, in this small New York hospital room, he knew that there was a reason for everything in life and that he was but a small cog in some unseen and great plan for mankind.

He knew that there would be days when he failed to see the beauty of a sunset, when he hurt friends, when he couldn't rationalize others' thinking, when he cursed life, when he took for granted love and beauty and pain, but at the same time he had been given a glimpse into that other side—somewhere in between—to a land that made sense only for a second before moving and changing in its three-dimensional or four-dimensional or five-or-six-dimensional way. As he lay still now, thinking of these things, his rational waking mind and his dream mind placed their bets, like two poker players whose game would never end, even with the demise of the universe and matter itself.

He began to reason that the stress of visiting home, writing the stories, fighting with his boss, with Sharon, with life, had taken its toll, but this, this vision was too much. Then he became confused. Hadn't he experienced the worst flashback in his boss's office? Wasn't that the key to his pain? Wasn't that

483

everything? There couldn't be more. There couldn't be anything worse. There couldn't be anything more to experience. He had walked right up to his fear. He had conquered it. He had taken control of his life, and now he was having to relive something else.

While his mind refused to accept this, another part of him was made to stay and watch. But again he was trying to rationalize. He had confronted his boss. He had taken the prize. He had regained his sense of self, so now nothing could hurt him. Was that it? Was it because he had taken control of his life that some God, some being, some energy felt he could handle what he had been avoiding all his life? Wasn't the experience with his father in the operating room the secret?

Then he remembered the café. The baby crying. The rain. The cab. The blackness that followed. This was the reason he was here. The day of the small child crying, of the thunderstorm, of the infant and mother all came back to him. But now it was all turning into the nightmare he had endured as a child—the one with the doctor and the baby.

As he once again relived the darkness, the doctor, the shapes, and sounds, he came to realize what he was seeing. His eye once again traveled over the doctor, whose green surgical scrubs were open to the waist, exposing the man's hairy chest. The doctor was doing something—something small, seemingly inconsequential. He was examining the baby, picking up the infant's wrist, turning it, looking at the plastic identification tag, reading it carefully over and over. Then picking up something soft and white, turning it over, setting it down.

A pillow.

Strekfus was fully into the vision now. He had let go of the present world, this present hospital room, and was back in a time long ago. The baby was crying loudly. The doctor fingered the white square of foam ominously, squeezing it with some inner, brooding anger. The man was hesitating. He put the pillow over the child, then removed it suddenly. The infant began to scream uncontrollably. The man stood there like some caught animal, holding the pillow, appearing to be unsteady as if he were drunk. He looked around nervously.

Then the doctor was picking up something else. Something smaller than the first white object—long pieces of almost transparent material. Dirty gauze or tape. There were bloodstains, dark images on the material. It appeared used and old, as if it should have been thrown away. The man was doing something that Strekfus couldn't see, moving something, unfastening something. The doctor seemed to adjust himself higher, then he was reaching for the baby, digging his broad, square fingers into the newly created flesh.

Strekfus could now see the infant's head, completely swathed in the dirty blood-soaked gauze, with the largest portion stuffed in the baby's mouth. The muffled screams of the infant bounced around the tiled room, soft and muted now, like a ball in some uneven tennis game played by ghosts and heard only by the mentally ill.

Then Strekfus became aware that the man was moving in some strange fashion, some rhythmic manner that appeared inexplicable. It seemed almost amusing to Strekfus as he watched this, trying to figure out what was happening. Then things started to make sense. His conscious, rational mind traded places with his remembering and he could now identify some of the scene. Some higher part of his mind was allowing him to define the time, the place, the event, and it was this: he was only one or two days old. He was just an infant, reliving some episode while still in the hospital. He could turn his head slightly or maybe it was just his eyes, and now as an adult watching this, he could make out his surroundings and explain some of the visuals. Probably he had known this scenario always in his subconscious, but now it was making sense to him, having been once again pulled from the depths and paired with his current psyche.

Again his eyes followed the doctor, the exposed chest, the rhythmic movements, as though Strekfus had hit some mental rewind button and replayed the tape over from the beginning. As his eyes moved downward to the man's stomach he began to feel sick. Then he found himself trying to stop the film—the memory—in order not to continue, but something was making him watch, making him re-live this event, saying it was time, that the world had been patient enough and that now he should know the truth.

Again, the mental tape seemed to be jerked back and he was having to experience the event from the very beginning, each time being allowed to see a little more of the room, the man, the other baby. It was as though he would have to watch from beginning to end without trying to control his thoughts, or keep reliving the scene and over again for all eternity. Perhaps that was what had been happening to him all his life: he had been reliving this pain over and over until he was ready to move on.

He mentally steeled himself, realizing that he didn't have much of a choice with his body completely immobile. He felt physically weak, drained already, the way someone does who has been pursued for years by some nemesis seeking death. Tired of running, he felt himself stop and welcome whatever he was to have in the hope that the torture would stop. It was as if he welcomed death, anything, that would relieve this suffering.

Again he watched the doctor—the man's chest—and this time he allowed his eyes to follow the path down toward what the man was holding in his hands. He forced himself to look, to follow through. He hoped that by confronting it, by walking into it, that it would either stop or play itself out and leave him.

At first he couldn't quite determine what was happening. The man appeared to be holding the baby in both hands firmly in front of his waist. Then the man appeared to be bouncing the baby. Strekfus thought this was possibly to keep the baby from crying, but as his eyes moved again to the baby's head, he was visually reminded that the man had stuffed something into the infant's mouth. Strekfus's intellect tried to rationalize this, thinking there must be a medical reason, but also remembering that the material seemed dirty, like used cotton gauze, and that the baby's cheeks seemed to be bulging. Then he noticed the baby was a strange shade of blue and covered in blood.

As he stared at the scene before him, it was as if a camera were panning back, showing him more of the vision, showing

486

him the full horror of the event, for he now became aware that the man dressed in surgical scrubs had his pants open and he appeared to be thrusting something into the baby, over and over again with such anger and force that it seemed he would tear the infant in two. Blood now covered the front of the man's surgical scrubs and he seemed to be in agony, grimacing and sweating.

The doctor was gripping the baby so tightly now that its soft flesh squeezed between the man's immense fingers like the soft insides of an overripe banana. The small head jerked back and forth, lolling from side to side as its neck had been broken, and blood covered most of the surrounding area. The baby was dead, but the man kept rhythmically assaulting it with unrestrained relish. Strekfus smelled something harsh and hot. Alcohol. The man had been drinking. The man was drunk.

Strekfus's first reaction was one of horror, lying there helpless, watching the innocent baby be raped by this monster. Then the anger he felt melted into pity and he began to weep internally for this poor being who was suffering so. He wanted to help but couldn't. He wanted to make the man stop but couldn't. He wanted so badly to stop the baby's pain, to stop the pain of the world, to stop the pain of this man who must have known such anger and mistrust in his own life that he would commit such a horrific act. He tried with his mind to reach the man, to make him understand, to try and explain to him that what he was doing was wrong. Something in Strekfus's soul tried mentally to cry out to this person, this one-time child himself, to say, "No, this isn't right," but it was as if his mind's words vanished into some dark and bottomless pit, some hellish tunnel with streaking lights and harsh metal sounds, as if he were now pursued by a runaway train with its tons of steel and metal and violence, all bearing down on him.

Then the man stopped. There was quiet. Strekfus felt no fear that such an act would be committed against himself. Somehow, instinctively, he knew the man had gotten what he had come after, and that he need not fear anything. Then there was the opening of the door—a woman's voice. It was a black woman and she was looking at him and then at the doctor.

Strekfus could hear the man saying something about walking in and finding the baby dead, about how something must be done, about how the doctor needed a maid to come work for him, about how no one must know what had happened, about how he had just come from the operating room and that was why he was covered in blood.

But then the voices stopped, or he could no longer hear them, for something else was happening to Strekfus—something much worse than what had just happened to the baby next to him, only it wasn't a physical sensation—it was an emotional one. It was unexplainable, but it was torture just the same and as his mind made what could be called "sense" out of what had just happened, he felt himself slipping into a dark abyss and falling, faster, and faster into the void, and it was a void which contained no love, no hate, no remorse, and no retribution. It was simply a blank, and he would stay there for quite a while before he emerged into the light of knowing, the intensity of hearing, the duality of seeing, for he had recognized the man in the surgical scrubs and it had taken years, emotions, pain, and the writing of many words to jar his memory to the point where he could follow the dream through from beginning to end.

Strekfus knew now why he shaved his chest. He knew why the sound of a baby crying sent him into panic. He knew why he had a fear of hospitals, and he knew, although he tried to fight the thought with all his strength, that the man in his vision, the one assaulting the baby, had been his father, and that the man had taken his revenge out on this child, this helpless being that had only moments before slept so peacefully in the security of the institution created for its well-being and health.

And now something else was coming to Strekfus, for the vision, the revelation hadn't presented itself in linear order, but in bits and fragments like some long-lost cut-up movie. He was remembering something even earlier now, something moments before the door opened and the doctor came into view. He was remembering the black woman—the one standing now in maid's uniform—coming in before the assault and switching his name tag with the other infant's, prying the plastic sheath off his small, pudgy hand, nervously breathing, frantic, replacing it with another plastic sheath which would determine his future, and he knew at that moment the answer to everything which had ever happened to him.

It was as though he could sense the black woman's pain at this early age of his—as though he was not yet tainted by the earth and all its emotional debris—and could somehow experience what the woman was thinking, feeling, being almost psychically connected to her. He could experience her pain up until that point in her life: her frustration, her knowledge, and most of all, her instinct. And it was an instinct that had told her something was going to happen, that she had to act on a yet undefined impulse or regret the decision for the rest of her life. It was an instinct which had said that, even though she didn't know exactly the why, what, or when of things, that she must do what some inner voice was telling her, and do it without question. As the fragment solidified, Strekfus let himself go once more into the land of remembering, somewhere in between this dream and the world as he would later know it.

The woman had begun to sing. A Negro spiritual fell softly from her lips, the blue-green notes cascading downward and enveloping him as he reached up with his small fist to grasp one of her fingers. She allowed the baby this contact, not pulling away as Strekfus played Adam to her God, floating high above on a Sistine Chapel ceiling.

De little baby gone home,
De little baby gone home,
De little baby gone along,
    For to climb up Jacob's ladder.
And I wish I'd been dar,
I wish I'd been dar,
I wish I'd been dar, my Lord,
    For to climb up Jacob's ladder.

She watched as Strekfus silently stared up at her with wide eyes, calm and unafraid. But before she could physically switch the two babies, a sharp sound of something falling jolted her entire body. Someone was coming. Someone had clumsily fallen in the next room or knocked over something, so she slipped out of the room and into an adjacent one, finding the door to the hallway.

With this latest revelation, Strekfus knew even more of the puzzle than he cared to, for he had now seen the key to his survival. He felt as if some avalanche of ice and snow had covered his body and his very soul, cutting off his emotions now, no longer allowing rage or fear. It was as if the darkness he had experienced had become so black that it had turned to a blinding light. He knew hate and he knew love at that moment as if they were two snakes on a summer day. He knew cunning and joy. He knew lust and power.

But mostly he knew that the horrific act of retribution he had just witnessed—this rape, this murder committed by his very father in an attempt to reclaim his own life, this unspeakable act which must eventually be spoken of—had been meant not for the unsuspecting infant who was in reality Sharon's brother, but for him.

- 29 -

New York, 1997

On the third day after the beginning of
the storm the snow ceased. The sun
broke through the clouds and shone upon
a vast, undulating white plain. High
mounds, pyramids heaped in fantastic
shapes, and impenetrable drifts lay
scattered in every direction.

—Helen Keller, *The Story of My Life*

"Hey, you weenie." It was Sharon, peeking around the massive door to Strekfus's hospital room. "Thank God you're awake. I couldn't bear to come to this place every two hours like I did yesterday and the day before when they had you knocked out. Feeling better, I hope," she said cheerily as she wrestled in a large vase of gladiolus. Their showy blooms caught on the door and then freed themselves.

"I hate gladiolus," he said, trying to inject some humor into the day while peering over the mounds of white sheets and blankets covering him. He watched as Sharon set the flowers down on the heating and air-conditioning unit, their artificial-looking colors jubilantly trumpeting upward. A series of unopened buds reached higher above the wide-open mouths of the already fecund lower stalks.

"It is freezing in here. Mind if I turn this thing down?" she asked, referring to the blast of cold air which seemed to come from deep inside the hospital walls. Before he could answer, she

491

was searching for the knob which would alter that arctic atmosphere.

"Guess not," he said.

She made her way over to the bed and sat down, careful not to sit on his badly bruised leg. "Well, at least the sense of humor is intact," she continued and began to rummage through the large macramé handbag she had brought.

"Actually, just about everything is intact," he said, suspiciously eyeing her as she dug into the bottom of the oversized purse. He was still reeling from his last revelation—a numbness covering his whole body—but he put on a strong face for Sharon. He hadn't yet determined what to make out of this last bit of information that the cosmos had decided to bestow on his person.

"I know," she said, not looking at him, "I asked the doctor and he said it was a miracle that nothing was broken. Just some bruised ribs and shinbone. But boy, the windshield of that cab was a mess."

"Thank God for the pain killers they gave me," he added. "I've at least had some rest, that is, when I'm not having nightmares."

"Here it is," she said, pulling out the latest issue of the magazine—the one containing his last story. "Page fifteen."

"Page fifteen? Gee, I'm moving up in the world," he said, as he thumbed through the glossy pages of the issue. He held up the cover and made a face.

"I know, honey. Everyone is upset about that, but I didn't have anything to do with putting a picture of that Guggenheim addition on the cover. If you ask me it makes the whole thing look like a toilet bowl."

"That addition was done years ago. Why are they just now putting it on the cover? Whose idea was that anyway?"

"Some new person they've hired on one of the upper management floors. They're starting to make all kinds of changes now," she continued, producing a bag of potato chips and pulling it open. "Want one?" she asked, before putting several into her mouth.

492

"I'm only out for a few days and all of this stuff happens," he said, taking one of the chips. Then he saw something else, some other publication sticking out of her handbag. He pulled it out and stared at its cover.

"Aliens meet with the President?" he asked, as he thumbed through the cheap tabloid. "I can't believe you read this stuff. And here's an interesting article," he went on, folding the pages together. "It seems that people all over the world are claiming that they've woken up with gold teeth in their mouths. It's some kind of religious thing, like they're chosen or ordained by God." He read further, "Guardian angles ordained by inclusion of gold teeth."

"Give me that," Sharon said, taking the paper out of his hands and stuffing it back into her bag. "I'm putting these chips away if you're not going to eat any," she said to no one in particular.

As they sat there, he began to look around the room. His eye rested on a large seashell which sat complacently on the windowsill. Sharon's eyes followed his to the object. Then she spoke, knowing that he was wondering where it had come from.

"I brought that the first day you were in here, completely knocked out. You remember that souvenir shop we went to that summer we stayed in Provincetown? I picked it up then and for some reason it just reminded me of you and I thought you'd like to have it. You know, to get your mind out of here and on some sandy beach. Just a thought."

"Thanks," he said. "Sort of an odd thing to bring to somebody in the hospital, don't you think?"

"I'm sorry, I'll take it back."

"No, don't. I was just kidding. It was really nice of you. I guess it makes sense, somehow, when you think about it." He continued to scan the room, this being the first day he was not completely drugged to the point where he couldn't sit up. A large plant huddled in the corner as if it were afraid of being seen. "What's that?" he asked gesturing to the sturdy flora obviously intended for him. "I don't remember that being here yesterday.

As a matter of fact, I'm not even sure I remember yesterday. It must have come while I was asleep."

Sharon pried herself from the bed with her usual alacrity and made her way over to the thing, picking it up with some effort. She maneuvered it over to one of the tables near the window and opened the card.

"Well, that's something," she said, and the look of shock on her face piqued Strekfus's curiosity. "Sagaser," she said, and handed him the note. "That bastard is scared stiff of what you've got on him. You'll probably get one of these every day for the rest of your life."

Strekfus eyed the plant. "*Sansevieria trifasciata*," he said. "A fairest Caesarian visit. Satanic safari varities."

Sharon turned to him, one hand on her hip. "No speak-a En-glaise," she said, and then turned to the long, leathery leaves, running her fingers up and down them.

"They're *Sansevieria trifasciata*. You know, in my first story, the one about Helen Keller's home? When I'm standing there at the top of the stairs and there's this plant that I want? That was a *Sansevieria trifasciata*—mother-in-law's tongues." They both just looked at each other.

"Okay. But what's all that hocus-pocus about Satanic safaris?"

"That's an anagram. 'A fairest Caesarian visit' and 'satanic safari varities,' are sentences made out of the plant's name."

"You don't actually think Sagaser sent these on purpose, do you?" she asked, turning the vibrant, upright plant around, searching for its best side. "It was probably just a coincidence." Then she paused, looked over at Strekfus, and then back at the plant. "That is one strange man," she finally said, and Strekfus, while lost in thought, not totally aware of what he was saying or who he was saying it to, more to the air in the room than to her or any one person in particular, and while thumbing through the pages of the magazine she had brought him in an attempt to locate his last story, replied, "You have no idea."

- 30 -

705 St. Christopher Circle

Infanta, Alabama, 1996

> Again it was the growth of a plant that
> furnished the text for a lesson.
>
> —Helen Keller, *The Story of My Life*

The phone rang at two thirty-three on a Thursday morning in New York. There are some things that are universal in all cultures: life, death, suffering, hope—and a phone ringing at two thirty-three on a Thursday morning.

No matter what country you live in, or what religious or economic background you come from, a phone ringing in the early hours can only mean one thing—bad news.

I picked up the receiver, extremely groggy from not having slept well for the last several nights. The previous week I had been experiencing a feeling of foreboding, as if some cataclysmic event were going to take place in my life, setting me on some wild journey or internal expedition deep within myself. This was the first night I had been able to get to sleep and now it was being interrupted by a nagging ring which emanated from a small black object with lighted push buttons. I reached over to the nightstand and brought the receiver under the covers and up to my ear.

"This better be good," I said.

"Strek?" the voice asked over the receiver.

"Oh, God, I hope so," I said, "because if you've dialed a wrong number you've just really pissed off some poor New Yorker."

"This is your Aunt Bea," said the voice. By now I realized there *was* something wrong. Not only was my aunt calling me in the wee hours, but there was definitely something strange about the sound of her voice.

"What is it? What's the matter?" I asked, sitting up and reaching for a cigarette.

"I thought you'd want me to call. I know it's early, but I knew how important this would be to you," she said, and then there was a pause. A pause I'd heard only once before in my life.

"Althea died this morning," she said, choking back her emotions."

"How, why? What happened?" I pleaded, sitting up straight and moving to the edge of the bed.

"She just died in her sleep," Aunt Bea went on. "She had been sick for some time, and she was old."

"Sick," I said, "how come no one told me?"

"Well, she had some problems with her back, her arthritis was bad, and then her diabetes. After a while she just got worse and worse," she continued. "We just didn't think she would die though. Evidently she knew she was ill because she had asked her son to come home to help her out."

"Her son!" I said, being almost in as much shock over the fact that she had a son as I was that she was dead.

"Yes, she had a son. He's the one who called all of us. Althea had evidently left instructions for him to do so, though I don't know why he couldn't have waited until a little later in the day. I guess when something like that happens you just don't think too clearly. He told me that he was going to call you in New York but I asked if I could do it. I knew you wouldn't know who he was."

"But she never said anything about this, about a son," I said. "I knew her for years and she never mentioned it. How could that be?" I was awake now and the truth was, I was glad Bea had called me. Althea and I had been close and I would have been upset with my aunt if I thought she had waited to tell me the news.

"Well, I knew her too, you know," she went on, "and she didn't want to bother anyone with her problems or her family. She came from a different generation and time, and, well, African Americans have always been treated differently in the South, or really everywhere for that matter, so I guess she had her own ideas about what was right and wrong and what you talked about and what you didn't."

This was true. During the time I had known Althea I had learned many strange attributes that she possessed. They were strange to me, but to her they were merely survival techniques. We had come from two different planets, but somehow managed to communicate. How odd, I thought, that the one person I had been closest to as a child and young adult, the one person that I could talk to and who understood me, was a black woman from Georgia who, when I met her, could neither read nor write. I had experienced things with Althea that, as a young white male growing up in semi-rural Alabama, I might not otherwise have had the chance to experience.

One of my earliest forays into Althea's life was with an event that among some people in the South is called "getting happy." This happens when someone starts thinking about how the Lord has blessed them, even though in other people's eyes they may not seem so lucky. The person is filled with such a sense of joy and happiness that inevitably they start shouting, singing, dancing, and just generally having a good time. Occasionally, people have been known to throw themselves on the floor and foam at the mouth, but this level of "happiness" is only seldom attained, it being reserved for church revivals, major world events, or the healing of some crippled or blind person.

The first time I saw Althea "get happy" it scared me to death. I had just awakened one summer morning and was climbing out of bed when I heard shouting and screaming

497

coming from the kitchen. My mother had not yet gone to work and Althea had already arrived at seven thirty that morning to get a start on the laundry which she did each day. In addition to this, Althea cleaned the entire house, *every day*, including the kitchen and bathrooms, and cooked most of the meals. Despite this, she found time to listen to my problems and take care of me in a way that no one in my family ever had. So it was with great concern that I approached the kitchen to see what was the matter on that summer day.

I ran down the hall in the direction of the commotion, only to find myself in a head-on collision with my mother, who, knowing that I would be on my way to see what the problem was, had decided she'd better do some explaining.

"Don't go in the kitchen," my mother said, ushering me back into the bedroom.

"Why?" I asked, "what's the matter? I heard Althea screaming and crying."

"Nothing's wrong," answered my mother. "She's just happy."

"Well, she's sure got a funny way of showing it," I said.

"Now listen to me," my mother said, "there's something you need to know. Black people are different from white people."

My first thought was, "Thank you, Captain Obvious," but I didn't say what was on my mind, thinking that the day was off to an unusual start already and I had better not tempt fate.

"They have a certain way they deal with problems and religion, and when they're emotionally overcome they 'get happy.' They scream and cry and carry on because they start thinking about certain things and they get carried away. It's not a bad thing, it's just what they do. You must never make fun of her for this, and I'm serious. This is sacred to them." She was bending down now to my level, almost on her haunches in order to look me straight in the eye. "Their religion is sacred to them. You know we take our religion seriously too, but this is different." It was one of the few times I saw my mother as an understanding person, and because of this I took what she said seriously.

Later that day, I crept near Althea as she was doing the ironing.

"Child, I'm sorry if I scared you this mornin'. I just got the happiness of the Lord in me and I couldn't keep back. You know, sometimes old Althea just starts thinkin' about all that the good Lord done for her, and she just can't help it," she said, shaking her head back and forth.

"That's okay, Althea," I said. "I understand."

"No, child, you don't understand, 'cause you ain't grown up a Negro, but I thank you just the same for tryin'. Y'all go on now and run along and play with those little friends you got next door and I won't tell your mamma and daddy." As she wiped a tear from her eye I made my way out the back of the house, thinking about what differences lay between us.

*****

The African American culture in the South has incredibly strong roots in the Christian religion. I don't mean the Christian religion as most people know it, with everyone sitting properly in church pews while some hypocritical multisyllabic preacher's tongue lashes the congregation about how drinking, gambling, and promiscuity are sins, the whole time thinking about how he can't wait to get out of church, go home, and get drunk while he places bets and tries to get the local male hustler on the phone. No, I don't mean white folks' religion. I mean the religion of Southern African Americans. The *real* religion. I was fortunate once to go with Althea and attend one of her church services when I was a child, so I know the difference.

"You want to go with me?" she asked me one day. "Sometime when I go to church, if you wants to, then we can go together. I'll ask your mamma if it's all right."

My mother had acquiesced, and one Sunday Althea picked me up in her 1953 turquoise Oldsmobile. The car was already several years old—older than me—and had an unusually bad muffler. It was slung low to the ground and had the appearance of a battleship as it maneuvered around the curvaceous streets and avenues of our town. Before this particular car, she had driven an even more ancient make, but after several wrecks, a prominent citizen had bestowed the 1953 turquoise Olds on her in the hope that the other townspeople would be able to identify her better and sooner, thereby avoiding the almost certain accidents she caused. As she pulled up in front of our house I keenly eyed the rumbling monster. At least this car wasn't a Buick.

Once inside the car, Althea would crouch down and peer *through* the steering wheel as she wove from one side of the road to the other. She was not a consummate driver, and everyone in the town knew her and knew to stay out of her way.

I sat in the front seat that Sunday she picked me up, with a copy of the King James version of the Bible, a pair of three-D glasses that I had gotten at the movies two nights before, and a small stuffed rabbit that Althea had bought and given to me on my last birthday.

"What you gonna to do with those glasses, child?" asked Althea as she made a right turn, first swinging out so far to the left that an unsuspecting visitor in a Chrysler from two towns away was run up on the curb and onto a neighbor's lawn, completely flattening a butterfly bush that was getting ready to bloom.

"I don't know," I said, "use them as a bookmark, I guess. Do you want to look through them?"

"No, child," she said, and then laughed her high-pitched, extended laugh. "I see just fine if you ask me."

About this time Althea pulled up to a red light, did a complete stop, and then proceeded right through it, oblivious to the fact that there was a line of cars at each of the other three sides. I watched through the rear window as the motorists lurched from side to side, trying to keep from hitting one another, all the drivers completely confused as to what had just taken place.

"Child, don't you be tellin' yo' mamma that I bought that stuffed rabbit for you," said Althea. "Black folks ain't supposed to be buyin' white chilren no presents. If your mamma found out, ain't no tellin' what she'd do. But you sho do love them stuffed animals!"

"I'll always keep this rabbit, Althea," I said. "Even after I'm grown."

"No, child, you got to give that up at sometime in your life. Can't no grown man be playin' with stuffed animals," she said, as she passed from one lane to another even though it was only a narrow two-way street with one lane for each direction.

At the next corner, she made a left-hand turn, barely missing a bicyclist and forcing him into a large privet shrub. The bicycle remained stuck in the bush, but the cyclist landed a good six feet away, shaken up but unharmed. I looked back at him through the rear window.

"Althea," I said, "do you think God thinks I'm different from everybody?"

"Everybody different from everybody else," she said. "You just growin' up and that's hard for anyone. Yes, sir, growin' up is hard on a person. And don't you be worryin' none about it. Child, old Althea's here now to take care of you. Ever since you was a baby I made me a vow to do right by you, no matter what."

Pulling into the church parking lot, she maneuvered too close to another already stationary vehicle. A long screech ensued, but she just kept going, totally oblivious to this fact. Her car settled itself comfortably into a flowerbed of marigolds some three feet from the marked parking place.

"Now you behave in this here church," she said. "These people know you as Mr. Bellensmid's son and you got to make a good impression on them."

The church was filled with about seventy people, all of them Negroes except me. They were dressed to the nines—the women all in hats, the men in suit and tie. Althea herself wore a yellow chintz suit with a small round hat. The hat had a veil and little yellow and white flowers on the top. There were also miniature lemons around its edge and a small yellow-and-white butterfly.

"That's a pretty hat," I said, admiring the yellow concoction.

"You know, I buy my clothes from the Goodwill store," she said, taking the hat off for a moment, gently fingering the small lemons and flowers which were glued around the rim. "They got lots of different styles and when I get tired of wearin' somethin', I take it back and gets me somethin' else. I got me a sister, she be livin' in Texas, and she says she does the same thing. Every now and then, we send each other hats, and gloves, and shoes, and things just to trade off. I've about worn this outfit plum out! Soon I'll send this to my sister in Texas." By now she had secured the hat firmly atop her head once again, and after a cursory glance in the rear view mirror we exited the car and made our way into the church.

The service consisted of almost continuous shouting and singing, clapping and praying. When it was over, everyone was exhausted, but I was elated. It would be hard to return to my Baptist church with its sober organ music, perfect flower arrangements, and slick moral lessons.

Being with Althea was always an experience, whether it was going to church with her or listening to her tell me about her life. She was always trying to lead me down the straight-and-narrow path, and she had a deep sense of right and wrong. That's why it came as such a shock to me when I learned she had been in jail. It happened one day when I was eight or nine.

"Child, you got to watch what you say and do, and stay out of trouble, 'cause if they get to you, they can make you miserable," she said.

"What do you mean?" I asked. "You were never in trouble."

"Yes, I was, child. I was in jail for six years," she acknowledged.

"What?" I asked, my eyes getting bigger and bigger. "Do my mother and father know?"

"Yo' mamma and daddy? Yes, child, they know," she said. "They probably told you that I was such a good employee at yo' daddy's hospital that he hired me. The truth is, yo' daddy knew that I was in prison and he didn't hold it against me. He gave me a second chance."

"What happened?" I wanted to know. I couldn't image this woman being in jail. "What did you do? Did you kill somebody? Did you rob a bank?"

"No. It wasn't anythin' like that," she replied. "It was about in nineteen hundred and twenty . . . nineteen hundred and, let's see, twenty-nine. Somewhere thereabouts. I was about seventeen years old and workin' in a box factory down 'bouts round Edwina, Georgia. You knows where Edwina is? Down near around 'Lanta. Well, one day the boss man—he was this mean old man—he says to me, 'Girl, you come on over here in my office, I got to talk to you.' So naturally I got on over there, and when I got in his office he locked the door. Then he starts tearin' my clothes off and tells me, 'I'm gonna rape you, you dirty nigger. Y'all ain't good for nothin' else.' I broke free and I told him straight to his face, 'You kiss my ass, you ol' piece of white trash.' Well, for that they put me in the jail for six years."

"They put you in jail because you told someone to kiss your ass even though he tried to rape you? That's all you did? And they didn't do anything to him?" I asked.

"No, child. This was nineteen hundred and twenty-nine. Black folks didn't tell white folks to kiss their ass. I was lucky I got out alive."

"But that's not fair," I said.

"Life ain't fair. We've just got to make the best of what the good Lord gives us. Someday you might look back on your life and think how unfair things is, but you just got to remember to make somethin' out of all the things given to you. You got to bloom like some flower or tree. Trees don't always have it easy with peoples tryin' to cut them down. They freezes. They gets a disease. But every spring they bloom and you gots to do the same some day."

I thought about this conversation from my childhood as I bought my airline ticket for my trip back to Alabama. Even the

503

pounding in my head that had developed in the cab on the way to the airport couldn't pull my thoughts always from Althea. It had been years since I had seen her, having spoken only briefly on the phone to her. I had almost visited her once or twice on my few trips back home, but I always seemed to miss her. Once when I called, she had gone to visit a brother she had living in Louisiana, and another time she was out running errands for one of her neighbors. I remember asking my Aunt Bea at the time where she could have gone.

"Why, she gets out and about," my aunt had said. "She gets in the car and just goes."

"But she's eighty-one years old. Don't they have some law about people driving at that age?" I asked.

"Honey," my aunt replied, "she couldn't possibly drive any worse at eighty-one than she did at forty."

This was true, and I had to acknowledge that Althea was a wonder. For all she had been through, she always made the best of things and never once felt sorry for herself. She just kept on going and doing no matter what hand life dealt her. Once, when I called her from New York after not being able to see her on a trip home, I said, "Althea, what do you do with yourself now that you don't work anymore?"

"Oh, I takes care of old people. I help them get dressed and cook their food, go to the shoppin' center for them," she said.

"But Althea," I said, "you're eighty-one years old!"

"Well, child, some of them's ninety," she shot back.

"What else have you been up to?" I asked, thinking there couldn't possibly be anything else.

"Well, I've been tryin' to learn to read better. You know I never learned to read as well as I would have liked. I know you spent hours tryin' to teach me. I'll never forget you did that for me. I want to be able to read my Bible more than I do now."

I *had* spent a good deal of time trying to teach her to read. When I was young, she came to me once and asked me to look at something for her. It was an order for a dress design.

504

I said, "Why, Althea, you can read that, it's just asking you to fill out your name and address and what order number you want."

She looked embarrassed and then said, "I never learned how to read or write. Never was no time when I was growin' up, and I've been meanin' to learn, but I just ain't had the time."

I can't tell you how low I felt. Here was a grown woman asking a child to read to her. It was the beginning of my realization of just how lucky I had been in my life. I filled out the form for her and then I said, "Now, Althea, all you have to do is sign your name."

Her hand shook as she made a large wobbly *X* at the place I pointed to. Having finished my task, I went into my room, locked the door, and cried for over an hour into a pillow.

From then on, Althea and I would spend hours going over letters and sounds and how they related to the printed words. One day she asked me, "What's them big words you use all the time?"

"What words?" I asked.

"You know, them words you use for plants and things."

"You mean the Latin names for plants?"

"Yeah, them words." I could tell she had something up her sleeve—some plan.

"Althea, you don't need to know those," I said.

"I'll make you a deal," she said. "You teach me some of them big words and I'll teach you what the 'real' name is for plants and flowers. That way people won't make fun of you like they do sometimes when you say the, what you call it? Latin names?"

"I don't need to know what the real name is," I countered, "I know the Latin name."

"You is one stubborn white child, Strekfus. Seems like sometimes you want to know everythin' and then you turn around again and only want to pick and choose. You need to learn to embrace life more, learn everythin' there is to know, not block youself off from things."

"All right," I finally agreed, "but you're not going to like it."

We spent most of the time on the alphabet and simple sentences and then I would take a few minutes to teach her the names of some of her favorite plants. We went over honeysuckle (*Lonicera nitida*), day lilies (*Hemerocallis*), and meadowsweet (*Filipendula palmata*). She mastered these three after several weeks by sound, not spelling (I think it may have taken me much longer when I first learned them), and I tentatively agreed that when we saw these in the yard, she would name them in Latin and I would call them by their common name. I know she used the Latin names a few times at her church socials, because she told me about the congregation's surprised reactions to this.

One day while in the backyard, she leaned over the fence that separated our plot of land from that of our neighbors.

"What are these flowers here?" she asked, pointing her smooth brown finger toward something that I could not yet see.

"Which ones?" I asked, peering through the fence. "Oh, those." I kept quiet for a moment, thinking how funny it was that she was inquiring about these particular flowers and knowing that she wouldn't believe what I was about to tell her.

"Those are called Rose of Sharon, or sometimes they're called Althea," I said, looking up to her to gauge her reaction.

"Althea!" she said. "There's a flower called Althea?"

" 'Fraid so," I said, smiling up at her.

"How 'bout that!" she said, settling her hands on her hips. "I've got me my own flower."

"Perhaps I should call you *Hypericum calycinum* or *Hibiscus syriacus*," I said, still looking up to her.

"Better not," she said, tilting her head down at me, "you and me got problems enough of our own without addin' to things."

I remembered these incidents now as I was preparing to return home and wondered how many other names of plants I could have taught her had it not been for time, a culture difference, and my rabid desire to grow up so quickly.

On the plane back to Alabama, I sat and thought about how much Althea had taught me—the difference between right and wrong, how to respect people, and how to try and understand things and make something out of my life. I didn't always live up to these expectations, but I tried. I can't ever remember her saying anything bad about anyone in all of the years she worked for my parents, and even after my mother called her one day, after twenty years of service, and told her not to show up for work on Monday, that she wouldn't be needed anymore, she only had good things to say about her.

One incident involving Althea sticks in my mind most of all, though. It was when I was maybe eight or nine years old. I was awakened one morning by a sound which emanated from outside. I got up to see what was happening and noticed my father in the backyard. He was angrily assaulting a dogwood tree with a broom handle, and the trunk was becoming quite damaged. As he struck the body of the tree over and over he seemed to be attempting to kill it, such was his frustration and anger. His eyes seemed to be on fire. His entire body was shaking. He seemed to be trying to drive some demon from the tree or rather from himself and into the tree, I couldn't tell which.

"What are you doing?" I screamed at the window, and ran down the hallway toward the backdoor wearing only my pajamas, determined to stop him before he killed the poor unsuspecting sapling.

"Where you-a goin?" asked Althea as she caught me with her big brown hands.

"Daddy's beating the *Cornus florida* tree in the backyard! What's he doing that for?" I cried.

"The what?" asked Althea.

"The *Cornus florida* trees," I said. I was becoming hysterical now, not realizing why, just knowing that I must somehow stop what was going on. It was as if I had seen this sort of thing before and had not been unable to stop it, and now every fiber of my being was straining to keep this man, my father, from killing something so innocent and helpless.

507

She looked out the window and said, "Child, that's a dogwood tree, that ain't no . . . whatever you called it."

"But why's he doing that?" I cried. I felt myself becoming sick to my stomach. I felt as if I had to do something, not just watch.

"Now you just sit down and calm youself," said Althea, picking me up and depositing me into one of the kitchen chairs. "He ain't hurtin' that tree none," and with that, she dusted off her apron and pulled up another chair directly across from me. I heard her words, but as her mouth said them, her face gave away an entirely different meaning. I could see she was trying to get me to understand something, but the inner conflict she felt was evident to me.

"But the *Cornus florida* . . ."

"Look, lets me explain something to you," said Althea, settling her ample frame further into the mock-colonial chair, "some peoples do that to dogwood trees—they believe it makes 'em bloom better in the spring. It's a, how you say, *myth* in the South. Beat dat tree and he be givin' you more blooms than you ever seen!" she said. I noticed that her speech seemed to change. It was almost as if she were imitating someone in a minstrel show the way she seemed to lapse into a subservient patois. It was as if she were remembering something also, regressing into another land entirely—one which wasn't necessarily safe but whose geography she knew and could maneuver in.

"By beating it half to death? That's going to make it bloom?" I asked, the tears running down my face.

"Child, I can't explain everythin'. Lord knows some things in life is strange, but dats de way it happens. You beat the bark on dat old tree and in the spring he be full up of blooms!" Her voice was trying to comfort me now, but tears were also streaming down her face. I noticed her lower lip as it began to quiver. "And why you keeps callin' it a . . . whatchamacallet? You knows we agreed that you would try to learn the names that ordinary peoples call things. We agreed you'd teach me to read and say some of dem fancy Latin names, and I's teaches you to say de names that real peoples uses," she continued, trying to pull herself up emotionally so that I wouldn't see she was just as upset as I was.

She was standing now, moving toward the screen door, speaking to me but the whole time looking at my father. "Now you listens to me," she said, trying to get a grip on her emotions as well as mine. It was as if we were seeing the same thing, my father beating a tree in the backyard, only she was aware of something I wasn't.

"That old tree ain't bein' done no harm. You promises me somethin' . . . you hear?" and with that she leaned down to where I was standing, next to her by this time, and looked me in the eye. "You say *dogwood* and not that fancy name," and with that her eyes searched mine and she wiped a slow-moving tear from one of my cheeks. "Someday you gonna have to face up to facts, to things that have happened in your life, to the way life is, and it jus might not be too nice. I want you to try and understand me, at least dis once." Then she took my hand, and as I was standing beside her now, we both looked through the screen door out into the yard. Neither of us looked at each other now but we continued to speak.

"That a true story?" I said as much as asked. "The one about beating the tree and it blooming? The part about it being a myth in the South?"

She didn't answer.

"*Cornus florida*," I said stubbornly, looking straight ahead, trying to find the inner strength I knew she wanted me to have. There was something inside me fighting to get out, fighting her, fighting myself.

"Nuuhuuu. Yo' daddy's beatin' the bark of dat dogwood," she tried again. "Dogwood. Say it now." Her hand gripped mine as she stared out the top portion of the screen door in the direction of my father who was leaning on the broom handle now, exhausted from his tirade.

"Strekfus," she said, "I ain't gonna believe you have respect for me and my ways until you call it by its proper name.

509

It's the principle of the thing, child," she said, trying to convince me of something I knew she herself didn't totally believe—that it was strictly out of respect for her ways that she wanted me to acquiesce. "I's glad you know the name of everythin', but you gots to learn to speak normal too. When you do dat for me, I'm gonna knows you loves me. Lord knows you is thickheaded, but some day you's gonna come around." While she seemed to have regained some composure, silent tears streamed down her cheeks. "Someday you'll understand all of this, and you may not like what it is or what you see, but you're gonna have to call it by its real name and not some name that other folks can't understand."

"I'll think about it," I said, and reached out with my other hand, the one not holding hers, to touch the fine mesh of the screen door. As I pressed my forehead into the mesh, I noticed how it made everything appear slightly fuzzy.

"You thinks hard, now, 'cause some day I won't be here. Don't you wait until somebody is dead and in de ground to do the right thing. You and I's been through too much together, now. Come on, you think about it."

I did think about it. But I wasn't going to let her have her way. At least not yet. After a while we both calmed down and my father retired the now-broken broom handle to the garbage can in the alley. We didn't speak about the incident for a long time.

That spring, the trees in the backyard bloomed profusely. Althea came to work one day and asked me as I walked through the kitchen if I'd seen the trees. I just kept my head down and pretended I didn't hear her. Gradually we called a truce, but I was approaching puberty and she was getting older, and regardless of how much two people had once cared for each other, some chemistry now kept us apart.

But now that I was an adult, I had come full circle: from loving her, to resenting her intrusions into my life, and back to loving her again. Only now it was too late to tell her. So here I was, readying myself for the final visit—the visitation which, after all was said and done, would ferry her away to a land free from the hatred and injustices of the world.

The flight from New York to the small north Alabama airport had been uneventful. I wasn't able to determine whether my blood pressure was unusually high or I was simply feeling the stress of returning home. There was a throbbing in my head which was almost continuous by the time I reached Infanta, and as I proceeded through town it only increased. I headed in the direction of Althea's house, not even bothering to stop by the hotel or to visit my relatives.

I had decided to pay Althea's son a visit before the funeral to offer my condolences. The neighborhood in which Althea lived was at the far end of town—she had moved there sometime in the '70s after the house she lived in had been bulldozed by the government to make way for a new interstate. This was a safer neighborhood, but it was lacking the character that the old one had and resembled too closely every other suburban district in America.

All the streets were named after either saints or birds, this canon never once being broken. One wished for a breath of fresh air—an "Elm" or a "Main." Whippoorwill Lane, Bobwhite Road, St. Ignatius Place, and St. Zita Avenue were just some of the examples. Althea's house was at 705 St. Christopher Circle, a cul-de-sac located at the end of Mockingbird Lane. Never having been in her home before, I didn't know what to expect, but it would turn out to be one of the most important houses in my life up to this point, setting off far-away memories and drawing me toward that ever elusive horizon known as truth.

Pulling up to her house, it suddenly hit me: Althea was gone. After all the years of having had her "there," she was no more. I choked back my emotions as I made my way up the walk and knocked on the screen door of the red brick ranch-style home. Peeling paint surrounded the doorframe. A half-dead cedar bush by the front steps and a weatherbeaten garden hose thrown loosely into the front flowerbed greeted me. I noticed that Althea's extensive collection of roses, hostas, ferns, and snapdragons were in dire need of attention. She obviously hadn't had time to take care of them since she had become ill.

Opening the rusted screen door, I extracted a note taped to the inner door.

Mr. Beltzenschmidt,

I've left the door open. Please feel free to go in and make yourself comfortable. I'm at the funeral home and should be back shortly.

Randolph.

P.S. There's another note for you on the bedroom door.

"This is strange," I thought. "Who is Randolph?" With no one to greet me I felt odd about entering Althea's home, especially after all these years, and even more so since I had never met anyone named Randolph. I figured it was probably the landlord Althea rented the house from. She had often spoken of him as being benevolent about late rent payments. Then I remembered Althea's son and the fact that Aunt Bea had not even mentioned his name. Randolph must be Althea's son, I reasoned.

I opened the door and entered the home. Immediately the soft carpeting cushioned my steps. The entire house had that hushed feeling that often accompanies the passing of a friend or relative. It was if the person had not only vacated the space physically, but spiritually also. And yet the spirit of Althea *was* somehow still here. I could feel it and literally see it in her furnishings. That is, what furnishing I could make out in the dim light of the interior. But my head was throbbing—had been now, on and off, even before my plane landed. I tried to write it off as tension or my blood pressure, but it kept returning and now as I made my way through the interior of the house it seemed to escalate. Or maybe it had never really gone away, for it seemed to loom out of the depths of my mind with a strength of something that has been hovering in the background, lying in wait, picking up energy in order to ambush its victim.

It was almost as if this crescendo of sound and emotion happened the instant I saw the note—the one pinned to the bedroom door—the note someone named Randolph had warned me about. I could see it from where I was standing, glowing and white, written on ordinary spiral-notebook paper and taped three-quarters of the way up on the door. The sound in my head seemed to increase with each step toward the door and I considered stopping mid-route to see if it would cease, but it was as if something wasn't letting me cut short this predetermined goal, as if I were being pulled by some unseen force toward this ordinary piece of notebook paper, this ordinary piece of tape, this ordinary door to this ordinary bedroom.

Suddenly I became aware that the sound I was hearing was not that of my heart, my blood pressure, or anything at all related to my physical being. It was a real sound and it was of something being struck repeatedly with anger, with frustration, with a force which seemed to want to exorcise something. It was a sound I knew but couldn't place. It came into focus with the intensity of a high-powered searchlight, its beam shining directly into the eye, blinding and white-hot. I felt like someone who has just been shot, but thinking the bullet has passed by, relaxes for a moment only to realize by reaching down, seeing the wound, drawing up his hand wet with blood, that the act has indeed happened and he must now wait for the aftermath—that the events which have been put into motion cannot be reversed and must be played out.

As I pulled the note from the door, the tattered shards of paper fluttered to the floor. I unfolded the message. As I read the words written in a shaky hand, the sound in my head continued to grow. "Strekfus," the note read, "I want you to have what is in here. I love you. Althea."

513

As I reached for the knob, everything seemed to go into slow motion. There was no other sound except the beating in my head. It was unrelenting, unforgiving, otherworldly. Turning the knob, I realized there was another sound accompanying its wooden, hollow, percussive attack. I had not heard it before, but now as I listened it lent a human quality to the reverberations in my head. I became aware of a man's agonizing groans, his muffled sobs, underneath the beating. The moans were animalistic, almost sexual, angry, as if the person making them were putting all of his strength into them. For a brief moment I thought that I recognized the person who was contributing these new sounds, but my mind leapt away, not letting me get near the source but not letting go either.

Turning the knob and opening the door, I saw the room fill with an immense white light from the back window. The sun had broken through the clouds that instant and it seemed that every beam it possessed entered through the opened window, blessing the moment and the room with its enormous intensity.

I stood there transfixed, unable to move from the spot as if held by some horrible, wonderful power which was my past, my present, and my future. The beating sound in my head had reached such a level now that its echoes melted into one continuous roar, like multiple tracks of a recording machine which looped over and over until the only sound was a wash of noise. I felt myself losing my grip on reality—the light coming in from the window, what I was seeing in the room. I had only one brief moment to take in the contents of the room before things started to spin and I lost complete control. I was seeing the window fly upward, hearing the roar in my head, the combination now like some awful multimedia event held in a horrible house of mirrors at some decadent carnival with distorted loudspeakers and the noises of a thousand eager and rowdy commoners chanting for blood. Then the loud, twisted music, the lights that swirled and streaked like some slow-motion photography, the thick groping of hands which rose around my legs, pulling me under.

The room was now an out-of-control merry-go-round and my knees were made of water, but I was to endure the vertigo for only a second more before I slumped to the ground, noticing for the instant before the end, the cracked ceiling, the dusty light fixture, the thin white draperies now standing almost perfectly horizontal from the window, caught in a breeze which had suddenly blown through the room out of a seemingly unearthly locale. It was only a second and then something wiped me out as clean and sure as if an eraser had wiped yesterday's homework assignment from the blackboard of life.

* * * * *

When I came to, I became aware that there was a man standing over me. As my eyes focused, I began to make out the concerned expression of an older gentleman. But there was something else—something I noticed in my deep subconscious before my mind cleared and I began to think about the room again and what it held. There was a strand of something familiar yet buried behind the glasses, the aging face, the human patina of this individual. I tried to hold onto it, to comprehend where it had come from, what it meant to me, but I was now beginning to reenter the world of the living and the thought retreated like a garter snake slithering back into an unused woodpile, soft and silent. I knew if I wanted to recapture it—this thread of consciousness—then dismantling the woodpile was my only option, and feeling drained by what had just happened, I let the thought slip from myself undeterred. Before I would answer the question the man was asking—this man who knelt over me, concerned, afraid, unsure—I would turn my head first to look back into the bedroom.

"Are you all right?" the man was asking, his hand gently resting on my arm. I had yet to regain my speech, so I simply nodded. Then sitting up and managing to slowly stand with his help, I was once again confronting the room.

Again the man was speaking, saying something to me, but my mind was a blur and I was already back there, in a time long before New York and much further away—in a land of red dust and fetid swamps and burning suns. A land where gullied roads led past dead cottonwoods and solitary eagles swung high over patchwork fields. It was a land which now contained something I needed. The journey back to it would be a long and arduous one, but one which I knew was necessary, so without hesitation I turned again in the direction of the sunlight streaming in from the bedroom window, took a deep breath, and took my first step into the room.

"What? Yes," I was saying now, trying to shake what had just happened to me. Then it was as if the dust were blown away from everything, for my head cleared and I realized that I was standing directly in the middle of Althea's room.

"I was asking if you are all right, if you want a drink of water or anything," the man said. Then he extended his hand. "I'm Randolph," he said, and I reached out to him. "Why don't we go in here and sit down?" he continued and motioned me back into the living room. I followed him, my ears still ringing.

"My name is Strekfus Beltzenschmidt," I said. "I just thought I would come by and offer my condolences for Althea." I added her name since I was embarrassed by my actions and realized that the man might not know exactly who I was. You can always find some excuse for everything and I figured that he was probably the person Althea rented her house from or someone who was there to take over the sale of the property. I knew it wasn't her son—after all, this man was white. He was elegantly dressed and well spoken, wearing a conservative brown suit, tie, and bifocals, and he had the air of a professor. He carried himself upright, but I noticed now as he moved about the room that he had a slight limp.

"Yes. Yes," he said gracefully, "I was hoping you might come. I'm Althea's son, Randolph. Randolph Malone."

"Excuse me?" I said, thinking I hadn't heard correctly, but not wanting to be rude. "Her son?" I had stopped just short of a Victorian settee and found myself looking at him in disbelief.

"Yes. You know, that's most people's reaction."

516

"But you're . . ."

"White. Yes, I'm white."

(I wasn't actually going to say "white." He said it. Maybe I was thinking it, but I wasn't actually going to say it. Okay . . . maybe I was.)

"My father was white," he went on. "It's a long story. And don't worry—yours is the same response I get from most people." He hobbled through the room, artfully dodging the clutter and disarray. The space was a mass of chairs and ornaments of every shape and size. The furniture ranged from expensive antiques to aluminum lawn chairs with frayed green-and-white plastic webbing. In the center of the room stood a kerosene heater and on one wall was a monstrous china cabinet filled with every kind of doll, cup, vase, and dime-store item you could imagine.

"I'm sorry," I continued, still embarrassed from my shock at finding out that Althea's son was white. "You see, I was surprised to find out she even had a son. She never spoke of a son, or of any relative for that matter, other than a sister in Texas and I think maybe a brother in Louisiana."

"That's quite all right. In Alabama, it's not one of those things you talk about. I quite understand."

"It's just that the shock of her death, and, well, I'm realizing that I really didn't know that much about her. I mean, I was close to her—at least I thought I was—and I grew up with her, or rather she raised me . . . I don't know what I mean," I said.

"Please don't worry. She cared for you very much. She really didn't get to know me until I was much older, and so I think she always felt you were hers in a way—as though you were the son that had been taken away."

"Where did Althea meet your father?" I asked out of genuine curiosity, albeit a somewhat morbid one. I guess suddenly realizing that I knew little or nothing about the person who had been closer to me than my own mother had created a thirst for knowledge about Althea's past and I was eager to catch

517

up. Part of me felt that if I could establish any relationships the woman had been involved in, then I could better make sense out of this son who had so recently appeared on the scene.

"Mother met him after she got out of prison. She did tell you she was in prison?" he asked somewhat concerned that he had shocked me again. He motioned me further into the room and we both navigated our way around a now-dead kentia palm.

"Yes," I said, "I believe she did mention that. What an awful experience it must have been for her."

"Well," he continued, "that was when she met my father. Right out of prison. But I'm so sorry, where are my manners? Would you like some refreshments?"

"No. Thank you," I said.

"Please have a seat, Mr. Beltzenschmidt," and he motioned me toward the Victorian settee covered in cut-brown velvet. "You see, as I said, my mother had just been released from prison and Mr. Gibson was driving his normal route . . ."

"I'm sorry," I interrupted, "but who is Mr. Gibson?"

"Let me start over at the beginning, or somewhere thereabout," he said, settling himself into an overstuffed armchair opposite me.

"Okay," I said, and leaned forward.

"Mr. Gibson was my father. I call him that because, well, you see, I never met him—he died before I found out who my real parents were. Chapelwaite was Mother's maiden name, or rather the name that she kept and used. See, Mr. Gibson—Dad, if you will"—and with that he leaned forward to give it emphasis, "and Mother weren't married, and in fact, my mother was never married to anyone after my birth. How could my parents have been in that day and age? That was back in, oh, nineteen hundred and, let's see, thirty-four or so. A white bus driver and a black housekeeper? I don't think the community would have been too happy about that now, do you?" he asked. "It's an interesting story really," he said, "if you have the time."

"Sure," I said. "I'd love to hear it. And I think I might actually take something to drink now—if you don't mind," I added sheepishly.

"Not at all," he said, and began to make his way to the kitchen, sidestepping a large collection of plastic dolls huddled on the floor around an eighteenth-century Chinese box.

"What would you like?" he asked, as he disappeared into the kitchen. "We've got Coke, water, lemonade . . ." His voice echoed as his head was now in the icebox, in the other room.

"Well, to tell the truth, I, uh . . . was thinking . . ." but I didn't finish the sentence.

He appeared at the kitchen door with a sly look on his face. "You don't have to go on. I think we're on the same wavelength today," and with that he once again retreated to the back of the house. A short time later he appeared with two ruby-colored, cut-crystal wineglasses and handed me one. Each glass was filled with Althea's own homemade wine and we both raised a glass in each other's direction.

As we sat and drank, we discovered that neither of us knew what Althea made it out of. I was privy to it while growing up and had developed a taste for it. Randolph also had enjoyed it in the short time he had known his mother.

"I'm hoping to find the recipe for this," he said, holding the glass up so that it reflected shards of red-and-white light about the room. "Lord knows I've found just about everything else in here," and with that he motioned around the room. "Mother never would give me the recipe, but I'm hoping just maybe she wrote it down toward the end of her life.

"Well," he began, as I settled back into the antique velvet-covered settee, "Mother had been in prison, like I said. Now she told me the story just a few years ago when we got back together after all these years, about how I was born. She had worked in a box factory near Edwina, Georgia, when she was a teenager. One day her boss, let's see, what was his name? Castratis, I believe. Yes, it's been so many years ago that I have trouble remembering, but I believe his name was Castratis. At any rate, he tried to rape my mother and she promptly told him to 'Kiss her ass.' Now, I don't have to tell you that Negroes didn't tell whites to 'Kiss their ass,' back in 1929. My mother was lucky that all she got was a prison sentence, attempted rape or not.

"Well, she was sent to prison, like I said, and when she got out several years later she was standing on the corner with only a paper sack holding her belongings, waiting for the bus to make its way down the street." Then Randolph stopped and looked at me carefully. "Are you sure you don't want me to get you a doctor or something? I mean, it isn't every day that I come in and find someone sprawled out on the floor."

"No. I'm fine. Really," I said taking a sip of the wine. "I'm fine. Go on, please."

"As I was saying," he continued, settling back, "she was going to take the bus to her mother's house and try to get her life back together. When she got on the bus she moved to the back like all Negroes did at that time and took her seat. Now her stop wasn't until the end of the line, so as the bus gets near her mother's house, she gets up to stand near the door. Since there's no one else on the bus, the driver asks her where she's going, and even though my mother was nervous because she had just gotten out of prison and here was a white man speaking to her, she answered him and struck up a conversation. By the time the bus had come to her stop, that bus driver had given my mother twenty dollars cash. At first she didn't want to take it, but to tell the truth, she was flat broke. She promised she would pay him back, but he said she didn't have to.

"One day she was waiting for the bus, in order to give the bus driver back the money he had lent her. When the driver pulled up, instead of paying just the fare, my mother gave him fare plus the twenty dollars. I'm not too clear on the story after that—how things really progressed—but they came to know each other and actually became friends. They would see each other every day, as Mother was now working for a family in town.

"Anyway, the long and the short of the story is that they came to know each other and discovered they really enjoyed each

520

other's company. Over a period of time, the bus driver fell in love with my mother and she fell in love with him. You can't always tell where your heart is going to lead you, and sometimes, I guess, it leads you down quite an unexpected path.

"Now I don't have to tell you that a white man and a black woman falling in love today is cause for some people to get upset, but in 1935? There would have been some fireworks going on in that town if anybody had known. To make matters worse, my mother came up pregnant with me while living at *her* mother's house and managed to keep it a secret for as long as she could, leastwise from the people in the town. It wasn't that she and Mr. Gibson just wanted to fool around—no, they wanted to get married, but it was illegal. And *yes* the baby was Mr. Gibson's. Can't say that my mother never made a mistake in her life, but I guess if you love someone you'll do just about anything.

"She quit working for the family in town and stayed at home mostly. My father gave her what money he could, but the day came when the baby needed, I mean I *needed,* to be delivered. Now no one was concerned because a midwife lived down the road and was called when the labor pains started. As soon as the midwife arrived she took one look at my mother's condition and knew something was wrong.

"What was the matter?" I asked, completely caught up in the story by now, for my fingers had dug into the velvet upholstery. As soon as I noticed, I relaxed my hand.

"The midwife knew I wasn't going to come out easily, if at all, and she told my mother's mother that they would have to go to the doctor who lived on the other side of town.

"Now since hardly anyone had a car in those days, least of all Negroes, my mother thought of my father, Mr. Gibson, and told *her* mother to tell one of the boys who was playing in the yard to run next door and call him. There were very few people who knew about this, and all but one of them was black."

He stopped again, scrutinizing me, looking me up and down.

"What? Do I still look that bad?" I asked.

"Just checking," he said.

"Please, go on. I'm really interested and I feel all right now. Go on, please."

"Where was I? Oh, yes. Evidently my mother picked the only day Mr. Gibson's car wasn't running to give birth. What's it they call that?" and he looked around the room.

"Murphy's law?" I interjected, thinking how many times I could have applied this maxim to my own life.

"That's it. Murphy's law—if anything can go wrong, it will. Now, the only way my father could get to my mother was by using the bus he drove on his route. So within a few minutes, the old M29 bus comes rumbling down the dirt road and screeches to a halt in front of the house.

"My father runs in and gathers up my mother in his arms and puts her in the bus wedged on the floor under some seats. There wasn't anyone else on the bus because it wasn't time yet for his run. He was supposed to go on duty in a half an hour or so, but he knew he had to get my mother to the doctor. He ran every red light in the town and was approaching the corner of Twelfth Street and Main when the accident happened.

"What accident?" I asked, bending forward.

"Well, he ran right over Mr. Castratis and killed him. Now the thing was, he felt bad about it, but he couldn't stop because he had a pregnant black woman about to give birth to his child on the floor of his bus. I don't think I have to tell you what that would mean. And this is the strange part: he didn't know who the man he ran over was until later—he just knew it was a white man."

"The unfortunate thing was that Mr. Castratis was blind as a result of an accident he had while working at the box factory. I think they say he was deaf too, and he never saw or heard the bus coming and just stepped right out in front of it. There were those in the town who said it was suicide, that he wanted to get away from his wife who was a nag. But that was just hearsay. And to make matters worse, he and his wife had had a child of their own just one year before. I don't have to tell you that this was a pretty complicated scenario, especially for a town as small as Edwina."

"No," I said, "I can pretty much imagine."

"So my father manages to get my mother to the doctor, and he delivers me and everything is fine. Everything, that is, except the fact that my father had just run over and killed the man who had put my mother in jail for six years. That's right, he had run over and killed the very man who had tried to rape my mother. Fortunately, the only people who knew the truth were my mother, Mr. Gibson, and the doctor's wife who was there to assist in the delivery."

Randolph stopped and drank from his glass. While he did so I thought about the story my Aunt Testa had told me—the one about Uncle Scott delivering a black woman's baby. I wanted to tell Randolph that there had actually been four people present at his birth who knew the truth, but then I thought better of it. But before I could give it much consideration, he was continuing with the story.

"The trial was short and tense but Mr. Gibson was freed because the doctor and his wife vouched that he was having chest pains and was trying to drive himself to their place because it was the closest for medical attention. They never let on that they knew the truth. See, it would have been bad for my father, but he didn't care about that—he just didn't want my mother to suffer any.

"Years later, he became a plumber and lived in Tuscumbia, Alabama, doing odd jobs and such. He occasionally drove a bus after that, but he was never the same. He and my mother only saw each other sporadically for years, the cultural climate not being conducive to an interracial relationship, and he sent her money as often as he could."

"I'm sorry to interrupt you again," I interjected, "but you said your last name was Malone, not Gibson."

"That's correct. I was put up for adoption and eventually given to a family named Malone, right here in Infanta. Funny thing, you know, growing up in the same town my mother moved to. Both she and I had no idea until a few years ago. My adopted father was good to me and the other children he and his wife took in. He was a hard-working man. He worked as a janitor at one of the elementary schools right here in town. Toward the end of his career he had an unfortunate incident involving a fire—a fire they discovered he accidentally set, and he retired soon afterwards. He's dead now too, I'm sorry to say. He really was a very loving man. When I got older I attended the University of Alabama. I lived in Tuscaloosa where I studied and then married. That's where I live now." He paused for a moment and took a drink. "So that's me. That's the story of my mother—and me."

I sat there taking in everything he had said, thinking about how little I knew of Althea's life, yet how much she had known about mine. Randolph and I sat quietly for a moment, and then I began to look around the room for more clues to Althea's life.

Then I saw it. On a sturdy table that looked as though it had been handmade, there rested an enormous metal washtub in which resided the largest fern I had ever seen.

"This thing is enormous," I said, in the direction of the plant as I got up and made my way over to it. It reached upward toward the lace-covered windows and ran down the sides of the table, almost covering the rustic stand on which it rested. New shoots were still coming off from the plant and it looked vital and thriving.

"*Nephrolepis exaltata* 'Bostoniansis,' " Randolph said, more to the room than to me personally.

"Yes, I know," I said, somewhat shocked at having heard these words come out of his mouth. "I've always had sort of a green thumb, and especially when I was younger I had all sorts of plants. But I'm curious," I said, turning to him, "how did you know the Latin name for it? Not that you shouldn't," I went on, afraid I had somehow insulted him. "Not too many people would know that." And then seeing his reaction, I added, "black or white," and smiled, letting him know that I meant no offense.

He laughed and then said, "Yes, you're right, not too many people would know that." I wasn't sure if the silence which followed was because of my last comment or the fact that he was now remembering something and was in deep thought, but whatever the reason, after a few moments his reverie lifted and he began to speak again.

"Like I said," he continued, reaching back into the past for the rest of his life, "I attended the University of Alabama shortly after they let African Americans in. While I don't look like a Negro, my birth certificate said I was at least half black, and my attendance had been questioned years earlier. I was admitted shortly after George Wallace tried unsuccessfully to bar all Negroes from the university. I had been living in Tuscaloosa since 1959 and trying to educate myself. I already had an interest in plants and I was growing just about everything you could imagine. It was there, at the university, that I studied botany among other things. I too have a green thumb and I guess I got it from my mother," and with that he gently fingered one of the fronds which nuzzled him like an overly affectionate cat.

"Where did Althea get this fern?" I asked, walking around the plant as if it were a part of some sideshow in a circus. "It looks like it's a hundred years old."

"Well, it's not quite that old. That plant is only about thirty years old or so. Actually that's another unusual story," he continued, obviously being a gifted storyteller who enjoyed relating past memories. "See, I was living in Tuscaloosa, trying to get into school. My daughter at the time was about six or so. One day, she skipped school and when I found out, I really laid down the law, grounding her for a week."

He went on. "Well, after I got through lecturing her, she says, 'I was going to give you something I got today, but now you've made me mad.' She eventually made up to me, and it was then that she gave me these three sad-looking little fern shoots wrapped in paper. When I saw that this wasn't a plant she had picked up from out in the woods, that it was wrapped in paper like something you'd get from a store, I said, 'Girl, where did you get this? I know you didn't have any money, so you must have stolen it.' I was getting mad by this time. She says, 'No, sir. I didn't steal it. It was given to me.'

"Of course, I said to her, 'Don't you lie to me now, because you know I'll tear up that behind,' and she said, 'Honest, that day I skipped school, I met George Wallace down at the Gorgas house and he gave it to me. He did give it to me, honest.' "

" 'George Wallace?' " I said to her, 'girl, you better hope George Wallace didn't give that to you,' and we both laughed.

"Well, I couldn't be mad at her for long, so I took the plant. The thing just kept growing and growing. When I did finally find my mother a few years ago I still had it, and as you know, Mother loved plants, so I brought it to her. Personally my daughter never did confess as to where she really got it, but I guess after all these years it doesn't matter."

"Where is your daughter now?" I asked innocently.

His mood changed and he seemed distraught. "We don't speak anymore," he said and looked up briefly at me, then down again. "She lives pretty far away."

"I'm sorry, I didn't know."

"Of course, you didn't," he offered. "It's all right, really. It was a long time ago and we stopped speaking over something very insignificant. I know she's just got some things to work out by herself, and when and if the time is right she'll come around. She won't be coming to the funeral."

"What about Althea's brother and sister?" I asked, thinking I might get to meet her siblings.

"Both have passed away," he said. "Long time ago. I never knew them but Mother showed me pictures." We both sat in silence for a moment.

"Mr. Malone," I asked somewhat tenuously, "when I came to the door, you had left me a note. How did you know I would come?"

"I wasn't totally sure, but I hoped you would. I hoped your aunt would tell you. My mother spoke about you and your family the last couple of years of her life. Of course, we had a lot of catching up to do and she couldn't cover everything. She said your people were so good to her and that she thanked God for letting her work there, but the real reason I was glad you came, is because before my mother died, she asked me to help her with something. I figured that if you didn't show up for the funeral I would still find some way to get in touch with you. That's why I called one of your aunts and asked her to let you know Mother had died."

"I'm sorry. I don't follow you," I said

"Well, I knew my mother was sick, so I came back a few days before she passed to stay with her. About two days before she left us I was sitting by her bed reading to her and she asked for a pencil and notepad. I didn't know she could write."

"I know," I said. "I taught her a little. You know, how to sign her name—simple things like one-line questions and answers for forms she had to fill out from time to time. Actually I taught her a few Latin names for plants too. Did she tell you that?"

"No, she didn't mention that."

"Oh," I said, hoping I didn't show my disappointment.

"Anyway, about two days before she passed, like I said, she asked me for a pencil and notepad because she wanted to write you a note. And like I was saying before, I'm hoping to find that recipe around here, because if you taught her how to write, maybe she wrote it down," and with that he took a long sip of the wine.

"A note to me? About what?" I asked.

He walked over to the short hallway off the front room and I followed him. "Here it is," he said, picking the envelope up off the floor. "The one you already read. To tell you the truth, Mr. Beltzenschmidt, I'm a little embarrassed by this. Embarrassed, to say the least."

"Why," I asked, "what's the matter?" though I was also feeling embarrassed now as we were standing in the doorway to Althea's bedroom—the very room which had been the cause for my concern earlier.

"Well," he went on, "this was my mother's bedroom and she wanted you to have what's in it. I know this seems like a strange request, but what makes it even more odd is the fact that the room's filled with nothing but strange odds and ends, much like the rest of the house. You can see my mother had a knack for collecting things," he said, looking around, "but what I can't understand is why she kept some of the things she did, especially in her bedroom. She never would tell me, but she said you'd understand. You're certainly welcome to have what's in there. I just hope you know what it means. I know you've already been in here. I just hope that wasn't what upset you—caused you to black out like that. You really might want to have a doctor look into that."

We both stood at the threshold of the room now, side by side, and I once again had the opportunity to peruse its contents. I moved forward. Now I found myself in the center of the room, somehow strangely comforted and at the same time anxious. I considered these emotions an improvement from when I had first been confronted with the possessions Althea had left for me. My mind had gone back to a faraway place the first time and something in me had shut down.

So now I took in the tableau once again, this time with a calmer mind and clearer heart, and it was with this attitude that I revisited the room's contents.

The entire room read like a book, with objects from every period of my life. Almost everything I had ever touched or been given occupied the small twelve by fourteen foot room. Objects were piled high—one on top of another. The walls were hung with rather naïve drawings that I had done in elementary school and there was a one-legged garden gnome standing in the corner next to a pink flamingo head. The garden gnome had played an integral part in my Hawaiian barbecue when I was a child, and the flamingo head was from my college days.

On the bed was every stuffed animal I had been given as a child, the assorted animals including Benito Moose with his button eyes, a camel, and a stuffed frog. Althea had retrieved the moose from the garbage without my knowing it, and he was now sporting what looked like a green taffeta dress. On closer inspection I realized it was the very hoopskirt in which I had greeted the alleged Grand Dragon during my freshman year at the University of Alabama. The hoops were removed and the sleeves had been pushed up around his arms. The green fabric pooled about him like a beautiful algae-covered pond.

There were several other assorted animals I recognized, including the small rabbit, sans whiskers, which Althea had given me as a child, the rabbit I had carried to church on the Sunday she took me with her, the one my mother had so defiantly dropped into a garbage bag.

On Althea's dresser was a green ceramic duck which had been broken into several hundred pieces and then glued back together. The duck had replaced my father's real one after that horrific incident in New Orleans, and I had accidentally broken it, not knowing its significance when I was young. Now it took on a whole new meaning.

Next to the duck rested a small wooden bucket with the inscription, "The Joseph Wheeler Home,"—a souvenir from that infamous Helen Keller-Wheeler journey that my family had taken in 1962. And next to that was a three-legged wind-up donkey— the tuft of hair now only a wisp. I stroked the poor excuse for a mane on the small animal, remembering the time Aunt Testa bribed me with it at the Latrobe Street house. Setting it down, I moved over to a pair of faded red taffeta high heels, size six. The only things missing were the mixer, the red evening dress, and my mother's pearl necklace from my cake-baking attempt at age seven.

The nightstand was home to a mauve-and-white ceramic planter—the very one from the Keller home which had held those plants I had become so fascinated with, the *sansevieria trifasciatas*. The planter was now filled with old photographs, Mardi-Gras beads, and a shiny black onyx rock—the one I had managed to take from Bunny in the first grade. In addition, there were several metal cars, a pack of Camel cigarettes, and a dried-up baby chick that I had rescued from the garbage that day in the first grade. I was amazed that Althea would have kept these things for me, especially the cigarettes which had belonged to the kind elementary school janitor who had pulled me from the fire during that first year of school.

Standing in back of all of this was an Art Deco golf trophy, the club broken. It was the very trophy which had landed on Jesus at my Aunt Bea and Uncle Douggie's house. I remembered back to that time when Enoch told me of my mother's sordid past, in that house on Euclid Avenue.

In another corner of the room sat an antique metal light fixture, exactly like the one that had hung in the house my father had grown up in. It was still in relatively good shape except for one of the candelabra's arms which was broken and leaned out as if to greet me.

I caressed the fixture, noticing the frayed wires as they shot out of the top like frozen fireworks. Althea had placed candles into the open light sockets and wax dripped down the sides and onto the table it sat on. Then I noticed a dog-eared book, wedged slightly under the fixture. It was Helen Keller's *The Story of my Life*. I picked it up and thumbed through its aged, brittle pages. There were quotes that I had underlined on virtually every leaf.

Joy deserted my heart, and for a long, long time I lived in doubt, anxiety and fear.

I do not remember when I first realized that I was different from other people; but I knew it before my teacher came to me.

I believe that all through these dark and silent years God has been using my life for a purpose I do not know. But one day I shall understand and then I will be satisfied.

I set the book down and moved on.

Opening the first drawer of Althea's dresser I saw an orange kitchen spatula and a feather pen resting on what appeared to be some type of gray material. I lifted the spatula and the pen out and set them on the dresser. Then I took out a pair of knickers from the 1920s, the very ones Bebe had dressed me in that infamous night I first encountered the I.O.O.F. House. Their faded gray material brought back a plethora of emotions and sensory recall, parading before me all the characters I had known in those fresh young years at college.

But the pen, which had been resting so comfortably for years, now begged for my attention. It was a simple feather with the plebian cartridge of a more modern cousin stuck inside. Twirling the writing implement in my fingers, I was reminded of the small black girl who had befriended me that day at the Gorgas house, so many years ago. I was reminded of what Randolph had said, about he and his daughter no longer speaking, and I thought about how similar people are, especially when it came to family disputes. Then I thought of my own mother and the difficult years we had shared. From there it was only a natural progression to the mannequin hand, the one Roman had retrieved for me after the performance of *The Miracle Worker*. Between the broken and paint-chipped fingers were what appeared to be a letter of some sort. I gingerly extracted it and began to read. It was the letter which had gotten me into so much trouble—the one from the stuffed camel to the rabbit about her missing moose husband.

"Finally I can tell you. What a terrible time this has been for me," the first line of the letter read.

I looked up. Mr. Malone stood in the doorway, shaking his head, "Like I said, I'm embarrassed that she wanted you to have this, but she said you'd know what it meant."

I picked up the orange spatula and pulled it backward to test its slingshot-like capability, remembering the many times Sharon had used it against the neighbors in Houston—the neighbors who were in fact the F.B.I.

531

Spying the antique light fixture, the one with the frayed wires shooting from it, Randolph continued, "Mother did tell me about one thing. My uncle was a junk collector in New Orleans back in the '30s. He gave that light fixture to her years ago. She said he got it out of one of those big ol' Garden District homes. Seems this lady that had taken over the house thought it was junk. Mother said she knew you had an appreciation for unusual objects and thought you might like to have it."

I just smiled at him, saying nothing. Still standing at the dresser, my hands moved as if under some incantation and I found myself reaching for an old phonograph recording of *Spartacus*, the Khachaturian ballet music, which was propped up on the bureau. I turned it over and read the inscription that I had written so many years ago. "To Althea. I love you, Strekfus." It was faded beyond most people's recognition and I could barely make out the words, but I recognized the outline of my own hand, the purple ink I had used, the awkward youthful letters that leaned to the right like tulips reaching for the sun. Reading the inscription brought back those days of my youth when Althea and I had shared so much, and I remembered how deeply she had been moved by President Kennedy's death.

Standing within the confines of the room was like experiencing the totality of my life in one instant. It was as if all my years I had been on the outside looking in, as if life were a painting being viewed in a museum where you could see yourself either stepping into the thing or stepping out, but never actually being inside—never able to stand in the center and be a part of the trees, the sky, the landscape. Now I was in the middle—being shown who I was and where I had come from.

In the room were all the things that had been thrown away or lost track of. Althea knew what they would mean to me someday and understood the importance of each treasure. She had always been there for me when I was a child, and now, in a strange way, she still was.

I had often seen similar objects like the ones from my childhood on my journeys through the flea markets of New

York. Some color or shape was always catching my eye and pulling me toward it. It might be a set of mixing bowls like the ones my mother had, or a toy metal car with the paint almost entirely gone. It seemed I was always searching through these flea markets in an attempt to reclaim some of my past, and now here it was, laid out before me.

"You know the *Spartacus* ballet?" Randolph asked, seeing the faded record jacket.

"Yes," I said. "It used to be a favorite of mine."

"My mother told me it was hers too," he replied. "You know, she must have played that record over and over for years because it's almost worn out. My mother wasn't much for classical music from what I could tell these last few years. It's strange where she would have gotten it."

I gingerly extracted the record from its cardboard sleeve and placed it on the now old and worn portable record player. As I lowered the needle, the first scratch of notes came through the material covering the speaker and filled the room with their blue-green notes. Then the soaring melody flooded the room and settled on the many memories now lining the floor and walls.

I couldn't help but laugh to myself at what Althea used to say to me when I was a child: "Always try to make somethin' outa yo' life, 'cause God don't always give us what we wants and there's a reason, but child, you just got to do the best you can and give somethin' back to the world." I still hear her saying, as if it were yesterday, "Now you listen to me 'cause I done seen it happen over and over again. You be good and live yo' life just the best you can with what the good Lord done give you, 'cause, you know, like I done told you so many times . . . everythin' you does in life comes back to you."

I had tried hard to escape my past throughout the first four decades of my life, and now I knew that I would probably spend the next four, if I was lucky, trying to get back to the place I had come from. I was always wanting more, never being happy with where I was at the moment. My journey seemed to have begun on that summer day in Tuscumbia, many years ago, when a retired bus driver set me free from the Keller home.

Out of that house I had ventured into the cool Alabama evening, freed by the very same man who had loved Althea and saved her life—the very same man who had, unbeknownst at the time, run over and killed the person responsible for putting her in prison. But in a way I suppose my journey began even before that—it had began in 1929, the year a box factory worker attempted to rape the woman who would become my guide through the first half of my life, and in reality it probably began even before that, for we are all a part of our past and the pasts of those around us.

I was a product of my family and my environment, just as my father had been and his father before him. And now I was left to pick up the pieces of my life and of those around me. I thought about what the Bible says about the sins of the fathers being visited upon their sons, and realized that it was up to me to try and make sense out of what had happened, somehow come to terms with it, and put it right. It was up to me now, but I had the knowledge that I was not alone, that there had been others along the way to help.

Again, I found myself looking at the objects Althea had kept. As my hands moved over the small broken toys, the remnants from my childhood and youth, they stopped on a small round can. I picked it up and turned it over. It was a container, at least as old as I was, of chewing tobacco. I tried to pry off the lid, but it appeared to be rusted shut. As I held it up and shook it, something rattled inside. I remembered how discreet Althea had been about chewing the stuff. So discreet, in fact, that she had worked for us for years before I discovered her secret. I sat the small can down and turned my attention back to an object I had already examined.

I picked up the feather pen again which was now lying next to the record jacket cover—the very pen that Althea's granddaughter had given me that day at the Gorgas house in Tuscaloosa. Rolling it gently again between my fingers, the now-tattered edges of the feather caught the air as it moved back and forth, driven by my thumb and forefinger.

I was beginning to feel a new appreciation for my life, and for the South which had given me such a remarkable set of circumstances to experience, allowing me to find my way out of the darkness with the help of a few individuals who themselves were searching for their place in the world. I was beginning finally to see what light there was in this unique universe.

The ability to hear and speak, a lengthy and painful process for me, was falling more into place each day. I was still a part of the South and it was very much a part of me, but now I was becoming aware of just how complex and intertwined we all were as human beings, not only in that geographic area of the country, but all over the world. For even though we may forsake people or places in one area for those in another, we carry with us a type of internal programming that seeks out individuals and circumstances—circumstances and situations which, although unknown to us, lead us in the direction of self-discovery. I had made my way through this extraordinary, never-ending labyrinth of life so far—a maze of human emotions and situations—and I now realized that I couldn't know the complexity or longevity that my actions had produced or what they would contribute in the future to this unique plan.

Some of the attributes of the South—the multifaceted social relationships, racial problems, my turbulent youth, the strange customs and dialects—had seemed to me at the time to be one roadblock after another in my travels, when in reality they were only a part of the tapestry of life, giving me insight into myself and those around me.

As I stood there and thought about my life, I became aware of Randolph's presence near me. He had been moving about the room examining the menagerie of objects that had been my life, and I could tell he was now hoping I would provide some explanation for the unusual collection of items which seemingly had no connection.

"What's that?" inquired Randolph, now standing beside me. "A pen, a writing pen?" he asked, leaning toward the object.

"Yes," I said, now stroking the well-worn implement while never taking my eyes from it. "Someone gave me this many years ago and I lost track of it. I traded them something for it." He looked at me for a moment questioningly, and then straightening his posture he spoke.

"Oh," he said, brightening somewhat, "then it was a gift of sorts."

I thought for a minute about what he had just said. I thought about all the possible permutations my life could have taken without the help of certain individuals. I thought about where I had come from and the people I had known, and when I was ready to speak, I did.

"Mr. Malone," I said, and turned to him, smiling as I felt a new chapter in my life beginning, "my whole life has been a gift."

- 31 -

New York, 1997

I remember especially the walks we all
took together every day in Central Park,
the only part of the city that was
congenial to me.

—Helen Keller, *The Story of My Life*

The sun was shining now, almost directly overhead Central Park. Strekfus lengthened his stride as he veered off the sidewalk opposite the corner of Fifty-ninth Street and Seventh Avenue and entered that vast green enclave which is the city's lungs, its soul, its very reason for surviving when the aggression, the competition, the pettiness get too overwhelming for its inhabitants.

Almost immediately a change of air, cooled and perfumed by decaying leaves and the moist soil, greeted him, and sunlight filtered through the wind-swayed trees as he followed the curving path that led toward the West Side of Manhattan. The park always had a magical effect on him, stripping away the stress, the office politics, the traffic sounds, all by simply showing him nature and open space. He tried as best he could to ignore the slight twinge in his right leg—a direct result of his run-in with the cab almost a month ago. His body had healed now, miraculously, as if touched by some angel or voodoo priestess.

After a while he stopped, somewhere near Seventy-second Street, and settled himself onto a bench. It would be another hour before Sharon appeared at their prearranged meeting place and they would make their way to the company softball game and then on to a picnic in the Sheep Meadow. He set his backpack down and removed his laptop computer. After the initial waiting period of warm-up and questions ("Do you want to update virus check?"), he began to accustom himself to the feel of the keyboard. He wasn't normally given to typing in the park, but lately he felt the need for a change, and the rigid, vertical office spaces of the city weren't working for him now, somehow blocking his creativity.

As he looked around, it was as if he were noticing the park for the first time. It was as though he had just moved to New York and was seeing the city through an entirely different set of eyes, experiencing all it had to offer without the years of cynicism and anger he had come to know. It was as though, because of his recent revelations—his attempts to make sense of his life, his letting go of things he couldn't control, his acceptance of the truth—he was beginning to feel free.

He had finally decided to write his novel and to give notice to the magazine that he would be leaving in two weeks. Two or three stories were already written—the ones about his father, his grandfather, and himself.

He wanted to jump in with both feet—no waiting for a more financially feasible time, no easing into it—and so, on this bright spring day as he sat and watched life go by, he decided to start immediately, or at least make some sketches with words.

At first he thought the stories about his father and grandfather would be the book. Then he decided to combine the stories about Southern homes with those of his relatives. Now he felt the need somehow to pull New York into the whole thing. He was, after all, a New Yorker in some respects, so he decided he would incorporate the city into his book. But where would he start? With midtown? With the magazine? He looked around at the park, the people, the everyday little human dramas, and suddenly it was clear to him.

Looking at the park was like going to the Metropolitan Museum of Art and finding one of those quasi-abstract paintings—one in which the artist has used distorted shapes and colors. You stand there in front of it for as long as you can, trying to see the artist's vision, trying to get into that person's head, trying to imagine that some simple scene of a village in Provence could actually be blue and pink and full of lopsided rectangles. He was seeing Central Park this way—not the everyday way he saw it with its dust-covered trees, its potential muggings, its dangerous skateboarders and bicyclists.

It was as if something clicked in his brain and he could now understand the blues and the pinks, the rectangles leaning in different directions. He took in what his eyes could hold and then was typing in an effort to capture this most recent gift—what he could remember, how he felt about the city, and how he felt about himself with those inadequate tools writers use when trying to paint their own pictures: words.

As he began to type, it was as though the entire piece was coming out as a poem, for its fragmented imagery and faceted moods blended together, not as a work of fiction but as some huge description of the life he saw before him.

Central Park: Stick figures of ordinary women in their fifties who perceive themselves to be a part of the art scene—their black quilted jackets setting off luminescent white hair, punk and short, they sit near the West Side, one leg (like a coat hanger) bent over the other as they lounge on the wooden rain-sooted benches while reading Kafka. They become oblivious even to themselves amidst joggers and boom boxes.

Thick-legged brokers wearing gray gym shorts with sweat stains run and wheeze past sandstone-carved banisters sprouting algae and memories of movie shoots, while great gnarled tree trunks pass judgment silently, and octogenarian parents, long ago cast off by children busy with market buys and pre-schoolers, move like dreams of T'ai Chi on bocci ball courts, framed lovingly by a thicket of ferns.

Deeper in the woods, young men court and dance an almost sex-minuet with each other, interrupted by continuous strollers unaware of their findings, and flocks of birdwatchers are carefully eyed from above by their borne-aloft friends.

Bovine tourists squeal and point, their Midwest fashions leaving an impression stale with catch-phrases and souvenir T-shirts long after their physical appearances have departed on airplanes.

Black-coated rabbis with cell phones; Juilliard piano teachers, their hair in buns, their oversized minks nearly touching the new spring ground; ballet students spilling out of Lincoln Center, their feet splayed apart, their sweater sleeves too long; the constant beggar with his newspaper feet; pigeons that coo and strut their iridescent inflated breasts toward you, pleading for food—they pile up like an accident on the highway until one strong foot sends them reeling into the air like some bad magician's act.

The lone jogger again, face grimacing.

The blind boy being led across the street, head cocked and smiling, his eyes squinting as if to block his imaginary sun.

Poodles of every shape and size.

A downtrodden carriage horse reeking, his hoof-music pulling sounds from the pavement a hundred years old; crooked inlays of cobblestones, worn by a thousand feet not conscious of their plights, huddled together as if there were truly safety in numbers.

The once bright, now dusty colors of an aging woman's afghan, out of which emerges her dirt-caked wheelchair—too poor to be clean, but not poor enough to give up the stoic African American companion who waits on her, eager for the day to end.

An old woman's neck straining against her scarf, inching its way toward Icarus as she leans on her silver-tipped cane.

And everyone taking their own inventory, unaware that they themselves are being counted so that the whole merry-go-round colors and changes itself into a faceted, ever-moving circus of whirling, sped-by, got-to-go images.

One thousand running shoes
Three hundred bicycles
One rape (unreported)
One murder (undetected)
Two fistfights
Seventeen fallen ice cream cones (there are actually government grants for this sort of thing)

A puppet-maker, his cast suspended from his hand, with heads down turned, bounding to invisible music that only he can hear.

On both sides of the park, buildings line up at attention, their solid façades protecting wealth and fame within.

And a wash of people, moving, ebbing and flowing, striding up and down the tree-lined boulevards and walkways, taking in the green sounds of life beginning over again as it does each spring.

The city's backyard—resplendent with humanity and awe, christened with the sweat of runners in soft blues and grays—stretching endlessly into Harlem, unafraid, sitting sternly on its haunches, keeping the rest of Manhattan at bay with its Dakota—now clean (New Yorkers liked it better when it was dirty—their equivalent of the Sistine Chapel) and its multitude of glass boxes and balconies which crowd each other like parade bystanders straining for a better view.

And all of this underlined in the park, signed as a painting would be, by enormous wisteria vines which loop and splay themselves against the trees, thick as a child's arm, sinewy and frank, like the handwriting of some ancient dowager whose last will and testament leaves nothing to those who crave it so, and everything to the most unsuspecting.

New York. Central Park. The city at recess, at play, while the schoolyard bully sits in his office, working weekends to pay for his middle-aged mortgage and ungrateful children.

And at night, when the park is quiet, when all have gone home, those handful who are brave enough to venture there will see the magic of the starry sky and hear the hum of a thousand insects which mimic their suburban counterparts.

And each morning, the far-off buzz of lawnmowers will float over the soft treetops and into the edges of Manhattan where cow-eyed Monday-morning workers head off to cold office buildings, beginning their wait until the next Saturday when they can be free.

He sat back and read over what he had written. The writing wasn't at all what he wanted. He felt that while he had been accurate in describing the park, he had missed something. And the descriptions had come out rather purple, florid, full of a soft light. Publishers, he knew, wouldn't appreciate anything even close to this style of writing. Besides, this wasn't going to be a novel about New York, it was going to be a novel about the South, or maybe somewhere in between.

He mused over the few pages. He wanted a more concise style. One that showed the reader how he saw the city. He wanted to write from his experiences and not what others expected. He wanted the book to be about the places and people he remembered, and as he began to think about this, he realized that what had defined the relationships and dramas for him had been his friends, his co-workers, his memories, the city itself, and mostly, home.

He stared at his screen saver which bubbled and oozed sounds and shapes. It was so easy to get lost in this ever-changing landscape before him, both the screen of his laptop and the park, and he let his thoughts wander back to when he first came to New York, to a time when he didn't know what the city was made up of, what it expected of him. Before he knew what was happening he was typing furiously in an effort to recapture the fragments of memory which surfaced like free-floating pieces from a submerged shipwreck. He would write about an experience that he had once; one in which he misunderstood the meaning of things. After all, wasn't that how he felt about his life—that he had been misunderstood? And so he wrote what he could remember about how he saw himself years earlier. He would somehow fit that in with what he wanted to say about his life.

The most realistic view of oneself, he decided, was not that which appeared in mirrors while shaving or critiquing that day's choice of clothing, but rather those times when one glimpses one's own image in those dark storefront windows unexpectedly, like a ghost among the Zeniths, Motorolas, and Panasonics. At first one doesn't recognize the image, and for a split second an honest assessment occurs, taking in the shape, the size, the personality, and the soul. Then the realization sets in that the vision is yourself, and after the initial shock (which is always like realizing you are dead and viewing yourself from some other dimension) wears off, you take stock of your weight, your imperfections, and your good points— all in a second before anyone notices.

How strange, but entirely reasonable, that we should trust this split-second surprise rather than that of a well-lighted mirror with no passersby or wavering sitcom to distract us. Strange in that, from what we are told, this isn't the most logical choice. But reasonable if you consider that the surprise image is more accurate, for in that split second we are looking not at ourselves, but at some other being with all its prejudices and worries, all its years of pain and suffering, all its joys and hopes, and whatever we choose to call the truth. It's almost as if God has given us a gift, one which isn't necessarily the most beautiful, one which isn't tied up neat and presentable, one which isn't exactly what we asked for, and though we may recoil from the image at first, we later become fascinated with it for all time, constantly trying to change it, understand it, call it by some other name.

No, that wasn't right either. Too intellectual. Too introspective. He needed something else. Again he let his mind wander, and as it floated through the trees, hovering high overhead like some wavering kite, taut on its string, a voice broke into his reverie—this reverie in which he was neither at home nor in New York, but in this special place he had created for himself.

"Boy, are you lost in thought," Sharon began, and proceeded to set down several shopping bags and her backpack. "I could have hit you over the head and you wouldn't have known it."

"I was thinking about what you said, you know, about writing that book."

"Well, *you're* quick. Wasn't that a year ago? You're just now getting started?" she asked, while settling in on his bench. She opened one of the shopping bags and brought out a pair of cleats. "Snazzy, huh?" she asked, holding up the shoes for his inspection.

"I didn't know you were going to play in the softball game today. As a matter of fact I'm not even sure I knew you *could* play softball." He was fingering the leather uppers of the shoes now, having taken them from her. "How much did you pay for these anyway?"

"They were free. You know, one of those promotional give-aways that the new sports magazine has. So what's this book going to be like?" she asked, looking over the shoes, having retrieved them from his grasp.

"Well, for one thing, I've decided to change the title. It's not going to be called *Somewhere in Between* any longer.

"And?"

"And I'm not totally sure what it's going to be called."

"You'll come up with something," she said, and began trying to squeeze her everyday shoes into the box the cleats had come out of. "I think I should have gotten a size bigger," she said, working her foot around inside one of the shoes, gripping the asphalt with the nubby bottoms. "At least I'll be able to get better traction now." She tied on the other shoe, giving it the same treatment as the first. Then she was reaching into another one of the bags, pulling out something wrapped in tissue paper.

"Here," she said handing him some flat, disk-shaped object. He took it from her and began to unwrap it, peeling away the layers of paper as if they were years of bad memories. Then he held up the object.

"It's a *C*," said Sharon, seeing his puzzled expression. "You know?" Then seeing he still didn't understand she continued. "In your first story, the one about Ivy Green, you mentioned that your father had named you Strekfus and had left out the *C*. You know, *S-T-R-E-C-K-F-U-S*. I got you the *C*." She regarded him for a moment more and then added, "I found it in a secondhand store."

"Thanks," he said, turning the letter over in his hand, only partially comprehending the reason for the gift. Then he slipped it into his backpack. "I shall cherish it always."

"Question," she stated emphatically.

"Shoot," he said, while trying to move some files around inside his computer.

"Did the cow have a name or not?"

"Cow?"

"Cow."

He thought for a moment. It was comical, Sharon referring to his Prytania Street story and he laughed inwardly at her ability to pull out the smallest things in life. "Gamaliel," he said, rather smugly. Sharon just looked at him blankly.

"The cow was named after President Warren G. Harding because he was in office when my family took possession of the house. The *G* in Harding's name stands for Gamaliel."

"Harding, huh? You know, some have speculated that he was poisoned by his wife. I don't think they ever proved anything."

Streckfus listened now. It was nice, this casual talk about anything besides work or his past or his nightmares, and he was supremely grateful for the fact that Sharon hadn't pressed him for information about the plastic identification bracelet which he had found in the tobacco tin left by Althea. And even more grateful that she didn't know there were two of them.

"So listen," Sharon was saying, working one of her fingers into the back of her right shoe, "we never resolved that whole issue with the identification bracelet that Althea left you. I'm dying to know. Did you get switched at birth with my brother or something?" She wasn't looking at him, and her fingers were concentrating on the cleats, totally unaware how jarring her last question had been.

"Is that what you thought? That we were switched at birth? That I'm really your brother?"

"Well, isn't that what happened? I mean, you did all that research on the thing—even went back to Infanta to the hospital. You got the files and death certificate and whatever else." She was admiring her new sports shoes now, holding her legs straight out in front of her, turning her feet in and out like some little kid. "I mean, think about it. Why would a woman who didn't know you at that time keep the identification bracelet you were born with? How would she know to do that?"

He thought about it for a moment. Approaching this subject was a little like getting into a freezing cold swimming pool when you really wanted a dip. You either inched in as slowly as possible, hoping your body would acclimate to the temperature, or you jumped in all at once and hoped you didn't die of a heart attack, and as usual, Streckfus hadn't really done either one—he had waited until Sharon had splashed him, partially covering him with freezing droplets. What could he tell her? That he knew the truth—that his father had killed her brother, mistaking that child for himself? How well would that go over and could she ever forgive him and his family? Would she ever be able to look at

546

him the same again? Even if she could, it might be years from now.

No, he knew in his heart what most psychiatrists don't know—that the finding out, the uncovering of the truth may set you free, but it doesn't mean you are healed and in some cases it's better not to know—the knowing doesn't always heal, and only after years of facing the truth can a person get past the hurt, the anger, the deceit, and even then it's questionable.

So he knew that he would lie to her, his best friend, not only because he wanted to protect her, but because they were in some ways already brother and sister, and because if she really needed to know then she would do her own research to find out. He could only hope that it never came to that—that she could be spared the knowing. He started out as casually as he could, aware that Sharon could spot a lie at thirty paces.

"Yes, I did find out what the bracelet meant," he said, turning to her, feigning the ultimate seriousness. "It seems that I was a clone from the Nazi Empire and that my DNA is like no other on the planet."

"Well, honey, *that* we knew," she said casually, standing up, grabbing her shopping bags. "Come on, let's get over to the Sheep Meadow and stake out a place before the picnic. I wonder if Winney is there? You can tell me all about the bracelet on the way over."

"I just did. And don't call him Winney. Seriously," he continued, getting up, taking his place beside her, "I never told you about that trip home—the one after Althea died."

"I read the story, remember," she said, looking at him while they moved through the in-line skaters and joggers. "And what's this with Sagaser? Have you two made up?"

"It's not complicated, really," he said, ignoring the latest Sagaser reference, hoping that she was so distracted by the eclectic group of people who had chosen to inhabit the park this day she wouldn't pick up on the lie he was about to tell her.

"Althea worked for my father's hospital at the time I was born and he thought she was such a good worker that he offered her a job in our home. The day he offered the job to her just happened to be the day I was born. She had been so thrilled by the prospect, because it paid so much more, that she asked for my identification bracelet as a reminder. She always said how good my father had been as a boss both in the hospital and at home."

"That's a sweet story," Sharon said. She had stopped now, completely taken in by the fantasy, and Streckfus was amazed at how easily the whole thing came off. "You really were close to Althea, weren't you?"

He looked at her, directly in the eye, without any emotion other than his matter-of-factness and said, "If you only knew." As they began to walk toward the meadow, Sharon spoke about her new boyfriend, what dresses she had bought on sale, and how Sagaser would react to Streckfus, seeing him in a semi-social situation for the first time in a week since the incident when the writer told him off. But Streckfus was lost deep in thought, wrestling with the knowledge that he hoped Sharon would never be privy to. He had found out so much about that day he was born. The revelation, the vision had been one thing, exposing all kinds of awful truths and past secrets, but after experiencing it, he had done even more research by phone and fax and pieced together more of the story.

After Althea had switched the identification bracelets, and after the assault on the other infant, his father had offered her the job as housekeeper. There had been one more problem though in the equation. Thinking that his only son was now dead, his father had instigated a full investigation into the infant's death for the purpose of generating a cover-up, knowing that he would be able to control any damaging information that might emerge. In order to make the investigation look authentic, he instructed some of the interns on his staff to look at several things, careful to avoid areas of interest he knew might lead in his direction. But one particularly over-eager intern had gone to the trouble of looking at the birth certificate and footprints of the surviving infant, matching them against the one who had died. It was determined at that point that the survivor was indeed the obstetrician's son (in spite of the identification bracelets) and before much else could happen, the deceased newborn was cremated. The family, Sharon's family, had been told of the horrible mix-up and a settlement had been offered. The sum had been enough for Sharon's father to semi-retire, choosing to work instead in the breeding and care of butterflies and moths—a job that paid little in wages but was convenient, as his backyard was now his office.

The good news had been that Althea hadn't had to disclose the fact that she had tampered with the identities of the babies, an action which might have cost her dearly in 1956. So she had become Streckfus's guardian over the years, having snatched him from the yawning jaws of death, knowing and worrying what he might remember. And she knew that even if he never put the pieces of the puzzle together, even if he never consciously remembered, that deep down he would know the truth, and until he could see things as they really were and come to terms with them, he would never be whole as a person.

Someone once said that our mind records everything that has ever happened to us in our lifetime and that if we could find some way to tap into that record, we could go back and view the pieces of our life just like a movie. In some way that was what had happened to Streckfus. He had seen some of these pieces—lost footage that had been discarded on the cutting-room floor of life. It was as though he were a janitor assigned to clean up after hours, and out of curiosity he had found the celluloid strips lying forlorn, discarded on the cold concrete floor. Holding them up to the light he had glimpsed himself and others, and the snippets had now brought him to a new place in his life—a place where he no longer felt the need to hold the world at arm's length and a place where he could finally be comfortable with who he was, regardless of the fact that the circumstances which had molded him were less than admirable.

"And I've decided that I want to have your baby and that we should live together in France for the next three years," Sharon was saying.

"What? What are you talking about? What do you mean have my baby?" Streckfus was genuinely confused as they neared the meadow, and as reality reared its head once again he was almost run over by someone on a skateboard.

"Relax. I was just seeing if you were paying attention," Sharon said, gently pulling him to the side so that the half-naked teenager with no less than thirty-two body piercings only brushed by Streckfus. "You seemed to be lost in thought again. Oh well, such is the life of Sharon and Strekfus. You be Goofus and I'll be Gallant."

"*Highlights?*"

"Hmm."

They were at the Sheep Meadow now, standing in front of the chain-link fence, watching countless Frisbee throwers and sunbathers. He squinted at her, unable to see her face clearly because of the intense light, and was just shading his eyes when some big, meaty arm threw itself around his shoulder and forced him into a headlock.

"Submit, you little weenie," a voice said, and as he gazed down at the gray asphalt pavement he realized it was Sagaser's voice. After a second he was released and as he stood up trying to regain his composure, his boss's hand reached out and gripped his shoulder.

"That's my line," Sharon said, looking slightly dazed at Sagaser, "I call him a weenie, you can't."

"You don't mind if I borrow him for a minute, do you Sharon?" Sagaser asked.

"It's all right with me," she said, "as long as you don't kill him."

"I'm not going to kill him. I just want to talk to him." Streckfus wasn't sure whether to be glad his boss was speaking with him or not and he wasn't sure where the conversation was headed, but Sagaser now wheeled him around and pointed him in the direction of the bocci ball courts.

"I'm not sure I want to hear this," Streckfus said, remembering the last time he had addressed his boss and knowing Sagaser's penchant for pretending that nothing had happened, the entire time plotting against whomever had made him angry. "By the way, thanks for the plant."

"I wouldn't worry if I were you," Sagaser said, squinting up into the sun, "you seem to be able to take care of yourself all right. And you're welcome. And yes, I know it's the plant from your first story and yes, I did it intentionally." He paused a moment, looking around the park. "I know you were wondering about that," he said, nodding at Streckfus. Both men seemed relaxed around each other now, so much so in fact, that anyone seeing them from a distance might have mistaken one for a lawnmower salesman and the other for a customer. The only thing missing was Sears itself.

"Listen, to tell you the truth, some part of me wants to apologize, but then I have to tell you that I meant every word," Streckfus said, decidedly pointing the conversation in the direction of their last encounter. Then he added, hoping to diffuse any animosity, "But it was good of you to remember the first story."

"I want to tell you something," Sagaser said, as a skater artfully dodged both men and made his way around them. "You really pissed me off." They waited now, one for the drama of the thing and the other because he had to. "But I have to tell you that you were right. I mean, I'd like to fire you, and I actually considered it, but I thought about what you said and did, and I have to say that I didn't think you had it in you."

Strekfus said nothing.

"Well, I want to tell you something and this isn't going to be easy," Sagaser continued.

"Easy for you or for me?"

"Easy for me," Sagaser said, stopping under some trees, looking at Streckfus. "I'm really sorry for the way I treated you. I've been under some strain lately. Personal stuff. The magazine. The new direction they're taking the publication. A lot of things. Regardless of how well upper-management likes you, I could have still fired you for the way you acted." Sagaser paused, taking in the trees, the sun, the sky. "You're a really good writer, you know, but a real pain in the ass at times." He waited, probably hoping Streckfus would jump in and say something.

"You're not going to say anything are you? You're just going to stand there and let me go on," Sagaser added.

"I'm rather enjoying it, if you must know," Streckfus said, a smirk forming on his lips.

"You bastard."

"Look," said Streckfus, smiling, "I've been through a bit myself lately, and I'm not sorry for what I said, but I'm sorry for the *way* I said it. I could have been a little more professional, but given the circumstances I just lost it. You know, you really are the biggest A-hole that has ever walked the earth. And you wouldn't be apologizing now just because you know I have the goods on you, would you? I mean, I'm not personally into destroying another human being, but I do have evidence that you tried to annihilate *me*."

"But you said you weren't going to do anything," Sagaser answered.

"And I meant it. See, Edwin, I know that deep down, below all of those layers of excrement that life has dumped on you, that you have a conscience and that your guilt is going to seek its own punishment. You're right—I'm not going to do anything. But I feel genuinely sorry for you, because you have to pay for what you did. Oh, not by me. I'm not the one going to make you pay, but life is, and that's what's really sad—for you. At least you could reason with me. But life, Edwin? Life is a strange thing. I have yet to learn how to reason with life."

Both men walked together now, not saying anything. It was as though they had to absorb what had just taken place, to try and fit it into how they were going to treat each other from now on.

Finally Streckfus spoke again, trying to lighten the mood. "So you're not going to fire me." He didn't really care, it just seemed something to say to keep the lines of communication going.

"If I were going to fire you, I'd have already done it. Besides, you're valuable to me now."

"How do you mean?"

"Didn't you wonder why a magazine that deals with homes and gardens let you get away with writing what amounted to be virtual short stories?"

"I guess I was too busy writing the stuff after the first one to really consider it." They had stopped now in front of a park bench, and almost as if it were choreographed, they both sat down. Streckfus felt an ease spread over him, the way it does after having had a fight with someone—a fight which is then resolved. One of two things usually happens in these situations: either you completely remove the person from your life, or it strengthens the bond between the two of you. As with most things in Streckfus's life, it was neither, but somewhere in the middle. Both men were without pretense now, having dropped any false jocularity or pretended bruised egos.

"Well," Sagaser went on, casually throwing a handful of small pebbles, one at a time, at the pavement in front of him, "the magazine has actually been bought by another company and this 'other company' wants to turn it into a more culturally aware publication. You know, have articles on politics, trends, some fashion, and even fiction. Some of the higher-ups, vice presidents and the like, decided that your series might be just the right transition. Test the waters. See how the readers responded. That sort of thing."

"So your making up to me isn't strictly personal," Streckfus said with raised eyebrows.

"Now don't go there. Listen, you of all people ought to know that life isn't black and white, no pun intended, and that nothing is cut and dried."

"You are truly amazing," Streckfus said, turning to his boss, looking him straight in the eye. He wasn't mad at the man, he just marveled at his boss's ability to combine so many elements into one package.

"Oh, come on now," Sagaser said as Streckfus got up, "don't be that way. I'm trying to say I'm sorry. I'm asking you if there's anything I can do." Streckfus was now turning, getting ready to head toward the ball field.

"I'm not mad, Winney, I just have to get to the game. I'm the third baseman. I'm not sore at you, really."

"Well, is there anything I can do? I mean, to make it up to you, the way I've been?" Sagaser was now asking. "Are you sure you should be playing, I mean, so soon after your accident?" A slight desperation was creeping into the man's voice, but not because of any legal implications the conversation had contained. Some part of him seemed genuinely concerned for Streckfus and wanted him as a friend or at least some facsimile of that word.

As Streckfus walked away he thought about his boss and what that man was trying to accomplish. He knew that his boss wanted to ride along on his already-approved coattails, but he also knew that some part of the man (some very small part) was sincere in his apology. He had known Sagaser for over four years now and had learned that no one person is totally bad or totally good. He stopped and turned in his boss's direction, seeing the man stand there, squinting in the sun which was now behind Streckfus.

"Anything you can do? Anything you can do for me, Edwin?" Streckfus asked. His boss just stood there, silent and composed, his hand held up above his eyes, guarding them from the intense sun. Streckfus fantasized that his boss was saluting him.

"Yeah. There is one thing you can do," Strekfus continued, and paused to make sure he had his boss's attention. The man said nothing but waited patiently. Streckfus thought about the book he wanted to write. He thought about Althea and the story of her life and how intertwined it had become with his. He thought about how difficult it was to get ahead in New York, how you had to know someone even to get a foot in the door, how he had something he wanted to say to the world. But mostly he thought about missed opportunities and how he was now in charge of his life. And he thought about the fact that Sagaser, for all his shortcomings, was a respected man in the publishing community—how this man's father was head of a major book-publishing firm. Then he spoke.

"You can write the introduction to my book. And you can help me get it published."

"What book is that?" Sagaser was asking now as Streckfus made his way to the baseball field. The writer turned around but kept walking backwards, occasionally looking over his shoulder.

"The one I'm writing about you and me. The one about the South. The one about my childhood. The one I've already written part of, in the magazine. The one that I hope is going to set some things straight."

Streckfus was now turning, waving his hand high above his head as he traveled away from his boss, and just before he turned, he glimpsed his boss doing the same. He couldn't tell if any reply had come—he was too far away now, and besides, he half meant it as a joke—but whether his boss acquiesced in the request or not, at least an attempt had been made at mending the relationship. Whether or not Sagaser was genuine in his apology or not was yet to be determined, but it really didn't matter to Streckfus anymore. His boss was responsible for his own life now. Edwin Sagaser would have to find his own way out of the darkness.

Just before Streckfus moved out of sight, in the direction of the ball field, he turned and shot one more comment in Sagaser's direction, hitting the words like some tight new tennis ball perfectly vaulted over a finely hung net. "And another thing," Streckfus said, trying to add levity to what remained of the situation, "I wouldn't worry about my playing so soon after the accident. I'm sturdy, you know. Very sturdy," and with that he disappeared out of sight and into the trees which separated the street from the ball field.

Epilogue

I have many far-off friends whom I have never seen.

—Helen Keller, *The Story of My Life*

The meeting began as usual—on Monday morning. Only today there was a charge in the air. New management would be coming in to explain what changes were to be made in the structure of the magazine and how it affected the employees. As usual with these types of conferences, everyone was nervous, fearing for their jobs and the possible change of pecking order. Meetings like these were something like being chosen for sides in gym class when you were young—you hoped you were picked for the "good" team even though you weren't totally sure what sport was being played or how well you could play it. This choosing sides—the ultimate litmus test of where you stood in the elementary school society—was surprisingly unchanged in today's corporate world. The only difference was that the players had gotten taller.

As the entire staff of writers, accountants, and circulation and marketing departments crowded into the conference room, the buzz reached deafening proportions. It occurred to Streckfus that the term "worker bees" wasn't totally out of character. Just at that moment, the entire room became quiet, so suddenly that the second after it happened, a ripple of laughter broke out. It was as though everyone were plugged into the same electrical outlet and someone had tripped over the cord, severing the current. It had happened for no visible reason. Then someone spoke. At first it was a voiceless body, but as everyone focused their attention and scanned the room, the source became obvious.

"If I can have everyone's attention," a svelte young woman was saying, "we'll get started. For those of you who don't know me, my name is Bernice Hollis and I'm one of the vice presidents of Fondon Sass Publications."

Streckfus eyed her with more than the usual amount of curiosity. There was something about this woman which was familiar, some thread of history about her which tugged at him. She was strangely colored, as if she were a very light-skinned African American or someone of Caribbean descent. Her features were soft, yet there was an ethnicity about her. He remembered a conversation he had once with a secretary to one of the vice presidents. The secretary had said that she worked for the only woman in upper management. Was this the woman? He found himself looking at the speaker once again, trying to remember if he had seen her before.

There was a recognizable mannerism in the way she moved her hands, something about the way she pronounced certain words. He was completely lost now in thought, trying to place her, and something about her stance was taking him back to another time and place. So it was with complete surprise that he heard his name being mentioned and awoke from his daydream to see everyone starring at him. He had caught only the portion of the sentence that contained the words, "Mr. Beltzenschmidt," and it had been said by the woman speaking at the front of the room. He felt as though he was nine years old again in school, caught daydreaming by the teacher, and now he would have to ask her to repeat the question. Everyone would laugh. She would admonish him for not paying attention.

All eyes were turned toward him.

But before he could complete his panic-filled projection of the future, the woman was speaking again. She had not asked him a question, but rather had been commenting on the series of twelve short stories he had written and how they had fit in with the magazine's attempt to restructure that publication. She was saying something about his style, his Southern roots, his imagination. From what he could make out she was praising him.

Now the conversation was turning to more mundane matters: insurance, a new CEO, package deals for early retirement, a new game of musical offices. Clearly some of the staff were distressed. There were huge swaths of writers and marketing people who would be out of jobs because the publication was now gearing itself toward a culture broader than fabric samples and the latest designers of celebrity homes. But Streckfus was safe. They had praised him for his stories and it seemed that they wanted him to keep doing exactly what he had been doing all along. At the end of the meeting, Sharon waded through the dejected and the jubilant over to where Streckfus sat, partially in shock, partially in relief.

"Well, we're lucky. They like you and they need me. One thing companies don't like to do is change computer personnel midstream. At least not right off. Let's go downstairs and get some air," she said.

"How much of your job could change anyway? The only real adjustment is the cosmetic look of the magazine and some of its content. I don't even think much of the advertising will get bumped," he said, as they headed out of the office and into an elevator which had just made its appearance. They rode in silence down to the lobby. Soon the building's front doors were spilling them onto the sidewalk which was already flooded with office workers and tourists. A large red double-decker bus roared by, sending out a plume of noxious fumes in their direction.

"Boy, you don't even have to light up now, you can just inhale the fumes from the bus," Sharon said, as she waved a hand in front of her face.

"I quit anyway," Streckfus said, moving toward one of the shiny granite walls of the skyscraper that housed their workplace.

"Excuse me? Since when?" she asked, turning to him in shock.

"Since the day I told Sagaser off."

"Before or after?"

"I know what you're thinking. No, I wasn't going berserk from lack of nicotine. I quit after."

"Have you decided what to do? About your resignation? Or are you going to wait and see what happens with the new management?" Sharon asked, but no sooner had she finished than both she and Streckfus noticed the vice president, the one who had spoken in the meeting, heading toward them, making her way through the revolving doors. The woman's mouth was moving, saying some silent "hello," or other greeting through the thick moving glass, letting them know she was coming to speak with them.

"I'll let you take this one by yourself. Besides, if she wants me she can find me at the salad bar," Sharon said, slipping away from Streckfus and into a deli located next to the building they worked in. As Sharon moved away, the well-spoken woman who had headed the meeting came toward him with an outstretched hand.

"Mr. Beltzenschmidt, I'm Bernice Hollis," she said, and gripped his hand firmly, introducing herself again. "I hope you didn't mind my praising you like that in the meeting. You looked a little embarrassed." They both stood there for a moment in silence and then she spoke again, glancing over her shoulder to make sure no one else from the conference room was nearby.

"You still have no idea who I am, do you?" she asked, clutching her binder of notes to her chest like some high-school teenager. Her demeanor was genuine and she seemed amazed at his inability to put the pieces of the puzzle together.

"I'm sorry, but you look familiar. I can't place you though. I'm really embarrassed by this. Am I supposed to know? I mean, I know you're one of the vice presidents."

"It has been a long time. I'll let you in on a little secret. I was the one in upper management who made it possible for you to write those stories in the magazine. I guess it was my way of going back and dealing with some of my own childhood traumas. You know, I grew up in Alabama, just like you did." She had his interest now and he seemed to awake out of some deep sleep he had been in.

"Oh, what part?" he asked, genuinely interested.

"Tuscaloosa. At least that's where I lived most of my life. With my father." She paused and looked around. "Listen, would you like to go have coffee someplace where we can sit and talk?"

"Sure," he said, and they began to stroll across Forty-second Street in the direction of the Library. They seemed to fall in beside each other with little or no hesitation, as if they had been friends long ago and some unforeseen events had caused their separation, so as the woman began to speak, it didn't seem odd to Streckfus that she would choose to tell him about her personal life.

"I've been out of touch with my father now for many years—we didn't always see eye-to-eye," she said as they moved in between the tourists and office workers.

His mind was working now, trying to place where he had seen her. "You know, maybe we knew each other or at least ran across each other at one time. I lived in Tuscaloosa for a while," he said, hoping to connect with her. They had now reached Fifth Avenue, that great dividing line in Manhattan which is not only a point of reference, but a social and intellectual separation as well. As they turned and walked up the avenue, she took his arm in hers casually. Again, he noticed how strange it was that he didn't feel uncomfortable, almost as if she were an old friend.

"Oh, I think we may have crossed paths at some point," she said, smiling to herself. "I'll tell you a little about myself. It's only fair since I know so much about you from the stories you wrote." The crowds were beginning to thicken on the street, and as they walked arm-in-arm, the people seemed to rush around them like water over stones in a shallow creek bed.

"You see, my grandparents were never married. My grandfather was a bus driver in Georgia in the '30s and my grandmother was a housekeeper, but even so I never really met them—that is, not until recently."

As they neared the corner of Forty-fifth and Fifth, it was as though something seized up within him, for he was immediately transported across time and geography to some other place in his life. It was as though something clicked for

560

him. He felt his knees become weak, accompanied by a dizzy sensation, but in an instant it was gone.

"Are you all right?" she asked, gently touching his arm, smiling at him.

But all Streckfus could do was stare at her in wonder—at her face, her stance. And it was now that he was remembering where he had seen her before. As he made the connection, he realized that she had known who he was all along and had been there, waiting for him to find out. She gave his arm a squeeze and they continued their journey up the avenue, ignoring the throngs of Manhattanites who buzzed around them.

She continued, her tone even and strong, and to Streckfus's ears it was a safe harbor of memory and connection. "As I was saying before, my father and I lived in Tuscaloosa for a while during the 1960s. It was there that I met someone. That was a long time ago. Long before I grew up and got married." She stopped now, not looking at him, but gazing up the street, to the green haven of Central Park which was but a blurry oasis in the distance, like some dreamy mirage.

"And this someone gave me something. Nothing large or expensive in the normal sense, you understand." Then she looked at Streckfus, realizing that he had figured out who she was, and continued. "But it was a gift, and I felt that I needed to return the favor."

He could no longer tell if she was speaking or not. His mind was racing at the thought, the possibilities. It was racing back to the Gorgas home in Tuscaloosa, Alabama, and that hot day when he had befriended, ever so briefly, the strange girl who had given him the feather pen. He had heard what he needed to hear from her now. He had communicated what he had wanted to in his stories and with the beginnings of his book. And now he could see things as they really were. He could see the connection between his life and those around him, and as he walked with her, arm-in-arm toward the verdant, waving trees of the park, the two of them blended into the crowds milling below the vast vertical landscape of Manhattan. Seen from above they were barely visible, lost among so many others just like themselves—

others who had woven their threads of existence into the fabric of life, unconscious of the many crossings and re-crossings until the day when it would all be made clear and the design would be complete.

Jackson Tippet McCrae has worked for various magazines and publishing companies in New York. He now lives in Connecticut, writing fiction full time, and has just completed a collection of short stories titled *The Children's Corner*. Mr. McCrae is currently finishing his second novel.